The Gnole

Alan Aldridge: *The Gnole* is his first novel and tenth book. His other titles include *The Penguin Book of Comics*, *The Beatles Illustrated Lyrics*, *Butterfly Ball* and *Phantasia*, an autobiography. He has lived in Los Angeles since 1980 but still says 'tom*ar*to'.

Steve Boyett is the author of *Ariel*, a fantasy coming-of-age novel that has garnered a cult following over the years; *The Architect of Sleep*; the forthcoming environmental fantasy *Green*; and numerous shorter works in various magazines and anthologies. He lives in Los Angeles, where he has learned not to trust any air he cannot see.

Maxine Miller is a native of Los Angeles. She has had a varied career illustrating greeting cards, fashion layouts, rock and roll album covers and tour merchandise for the likes of LA Guns, Bon Jovi and Cher. She is developing a book of her own romantic and somewhat nightmarish visions.

Alan Aldridge

Written with   STEVE BOYETT

Illustrated with   *MAXINE MILLER*
and HARRY WILLOCK

Mandarin

Dummy cover of *Life Magazine* containing registered trademark LIFE used with kind permission of *Life Magazine*, a division of The Time Inc. Magazine Company.

TIME and the red border design are registered trademarks of The Time Inc. Magazine Company. Used with permission.

Sports Illustrated logo used with the permission of The Time Inc. Magazine Company. All rights reserved.

Fictitious cover of *US Magazine* reproduced with kind permission of *US Magazine*.

Fictitious *Rolling Stone* cover with the *Rolling Stone* logo reproduced with kind permission of *Rolling Stone*.

Fictitious cover of *Thrasher Magazine* reprinted courtesy of *Thrasher Magazine*.

Fictitious covers of *Tick Tock*, *E*, *Gorilla*, *Business Week* and *Spiritus* all reproduced with kind permission.

A Mandarin Paperback
THE GNOLE

First published in Great Britain 1991
by William Heinemann Ltd and Mandarin Paperbacks
Michelin House, 81 Fulham Road, London SW3 6RB

William Heinemann and Mandarin are imprints of the Octopus
Publishing Group, a division of Reed International Books Limited

Text, story, all characters and
illustrations © Alan Aldridge 1991

The author has asserted his moral rights

A CIP catalogue record for this book
is held by the British Library
ISBN 0 7493 0990 3

Phototypeset by Falcon Typographic Art Ltd,
Edinburgh & London
Printed and bound in Great Britain by
BPCC Hazell Books, Aylesbury, Bucks

GNOLE Mod. *gnomus* or gnome ('earth-dweller') and *talpidae* (mole). Dwarf-like, herbivorous mammal. Bipedal and standing approx. thirty inches erect, the classification of gnoles among true *Hominidae* is presently disputed among anthropologists and zoologists. Gnoles are covered with soft, black, iridescent fur, with the exception of the face, snout, and palms, which have soft, pinkish skin. The head is large and well-rounded to accommodate a highly developed cerebrum. The physiognomic musculature is similar to that of human beings, but with no recognisable chin. Neck and shoulders are heavily muscled; the snout is pointed and covered with tiny, raised papillae, which have a high density of nerve endings. The precise importance of the snout and the stimuli it detects has yet to be thoroughly documented. Possibly it acts as a teletactile receptor, detecting changes in air pressure and minute air currents by which the gnole may locate moving objects at some distance. The face and snout also have various vibrissae for detection of objects and compression in air waves denoting movement within a 20-metre radius. The small, black eyes are forward-facing, heavily-lidded, and purblind – yet, in collaboration with stimuli from the snout, the gnole has keen perception of its surroundings. The external ear, or *pinna*, is large, fleshy, and slightly pointed at the top. The strong fossier forearms are heavily muscled. The hands are extremely large and maturely developed, with fully opposable thumbs giving the gnole full digital articulation. The feet have evolved for upright posture instead of prehension (the non-opposable *hallux*, or big toe, is a vestigial grasping digit, as with human beings). The short legs are heavily muscled, particularly the calf, which (along with the *gluteus maximus*) holds the body erect.

The average life-span of the creature is unknown, and the source of much speculation. However, it is known that gnoles are hibernatory, spending from early October through to the end of January each year beneath ground in their 'sets'. During this period the body temperature drops to 378°F and heartbeat reduces to approximately 10 beats per minute. Hibernation may be a contributory factor to the remarkable longevity of gnoles. 'Fungle', the only gnole ever in captivity, is considered middle-aged at one hundred twenty years.

Encyclopaedia Britannica

Gnolidae Erectus Americanus

gnole \nôl\ *n* [fr. Greek *gnomus* earthdweller and *talpidae*, mole] **1** herbivorous mammal, disputed whether of the order *Hominidae, Talpidae* (mole), or Old World order now extinct. Short, furry, thickset, bipedal creature, tail-less, with strong forearms and crouched gait. Hibernatory with deep layer of subcutaneous fat **2** *adj* unique, one of a kind **3** *v* to walk with a waddling gait <*gnoled* happily along the sidewalk>

Webster's New Collegiate Dictionary

Part One

This is the book of thy descent . . .
Here begin the terrors
Here begin the miracles.

Perlesvaus

Walker Between Two Worlds

There are places on the earth no human foot has ever trod. Not many places, and they grow fewer by the hour, but some remain, scattered in isolated pockets across the globe: sealed caverns and floating islands, jungle floors overgrown and ripe valleys hidden by ringing mountains, they bask in unsuspected solitude, alone but not lonely.

Around the earth whirl downward-looking satellites, silently mapping and photographing every square inch of cloud and land and even ocean floor. Godly peeping toms, the cold unsleeping eyes snap millions of photographs day after day.

They see the forests, but not the trees.

On the south-east face of North America is a kindly age-wrinkle known on human maps as the Appalachian Mountains. In the far south of that range, Fungle the gnole slipped silently through the lush undergrowth by the gentle bank of a clear valley lake. Today was the autumn Equinox, the only day of the year shared by summer and fall, and Fungle was out among the riot of pink and purple rhododendron and azalea to collect special herbs and mushrooms for the dinner he would prepare tonight for his few friends who remained in the Valley of Smiling Water.

The day was unnaturally hot – most unreasonably unseasonal, Fungle felt. The seasons seemed all a-kilter these years, summers hotter and thicker each time 'round, winters more long and deep. The green world's struggle from the white seemed more difficult each thaw. Every winter his long and dreamless hibernation seemed to last a few days longer, and he awakened with thick pelt dulled and ever more sagging from the slow dissolution of fat that sustained him through a sleep that lasted three full moons.

This bright afternoon, however, Fungle's sleek dark pelt felt imprisoned within his homespun outfit from the day's leaden heat as he moved silently through thick green mountain laurel and choking kudzu along the riverbank. The silent blending with which he moved had become habit long ago. Like chanting protective 'wards' when he left his home or went to bed, moving quietly had become a daily part of life in a world that, lately, was changing faster than Fungle did himself.

What's on with the world, Fungle often wondered, when the seasons're all codswalloped up, swingin' further one from t'other every year?

Well, he reflected as he continued along the bank toward a particular plant he knew grew nearby, *arguin' with the weather only gets ya wetter*. He stopped at a fat-tipped cattail bowed before him and knelt to examine it. His hand, thick-fingered with nails dark and hard enough to seem like claws, brushed the cattail's fur. Fungle set his wire-whiskered snout against the cattail to feel its tickle, and thought how he might cook its tender stalks: cut in rings and sautéed in a smidgen of walnut oil or stewed with crab apples – something special-like to please each of his few friends.

Fungle closed his eyes and felt the spirit within the cattail against his snout. His mind filled with the warmth of its life spent growing out here in the sun, a life of pushing root into cool earth to drink of breathing out pure air for animals to breathe in, a life of simple *being*. 'Spirit o' cattail,' he intoned, 'give me yer presence and grant me yer help that thee and I may join.'

The air above the cattail began to shimmer.

Dear mage. The kind-toned words formed in Fungle's mind. *What may I provide for you?*

'If it please,' replied Fungle, 'a fan o' yer stalks to brighten up me carrot soup, fer tonight I'm entertainin' friends near and dear.'

The shimmering air formed the suggestion of a gently smiling face. *Then add to your feast, dear gnole, and to my pleasure as well.*

'Spirit o' cattail, I'm thankin' ya fer granting yer abundance unto me, and me blessings go to you and yours.' Fungle's hands traced an ancient design in the air. Quickly he harvested a dozen cattail stalks and continued his culinary quest.

Rubbing his snout with a furry cattail stalk as he moved quickly and quietly through dense thickets of rhododendron, Fungle reflected on the appetites of his remaining guesties-to-be. Ka, when he arrived for dinner in his loud and rowdy way – now Ka would want raw earthy things to eat: mushrooms still dirted and earthworms wriggling. Moving to and fro in the earth as he did – being, after all, a gnome – his tastes ran a bit below the crust. But who could fault him that?

Fungle stopped before a cluster of dog-roses, late-blooming and fragrant.

And Neema, he thought. What would Neema want? It was hard to say, for Neema Cleverbread was all rough-hewn woods and liable to leave splinters if handled improperly. She was the last of the Cleverbreads left in the valley, as Fungle was the last of the Foxwits, and so long as the generations-old feud between the Cleverbreads and the Foxwits over custodianship of these parts remained an issue, neither of them would leave if the other remained. Though Neema had been dinner guest at Fungle's home before, and brought along her own incomparable acorn breads, she had done so mostly because of her fondness for Fungle's father, Wisp, and his bottomless trove of stories from ancient times before the 'You're-a-peons' had begun to settle in Americka.

Fungle imagined Neema eating delicate and dainty, with bites small and savouring, wanting leafy things and sauces and crystal-

line sweets that dissolved on the tongue to make her wonder if she
had even eaten them at all.

Fungle smiled as he drank the velvet perfume of the dog-roses.
Now, there was an absurd image: Neema Cleverbread, dainty!

He pulled back from the roses, already fading toward winter, and
looked at them sternly. 'Whadjer laughin' at, then?' he demanded.
'It's a meal I'm plannin', and plannin' it takes, and I'll thank ya
to tend yer field and leave me to mine!'

But he smiled and blessed the roses, then stood to move his
shadow so that they could drink what light remained in the waning
hot day.

Keeping to the thick ribbon of gloom beneath the fronding willows
ever raining over the lake's edge, Fungle pushed deeper into the
thick plumage of the wood. Hot and bright though the day might
be, there were places in the forest the sun never shined. Canopied
by the arching vault of intertwined branches of chestnut and oak,
laurel and spruce, the dark wet ground of the deep wood was host
to life that had no home outside of shadow, life that needed slime
and wet to root. The air here in this dark rich place was its own
perfume, a licentious incense of honeysuckle and foxgrape sootied
with a tincture of leaf mould black and damp. It was here that
Fungle came to look for special things: potent herbs for palate
and potion, medicinal barks and roots for healing wounds of body
and spirit, dew collected from the petalled bells of flowers at dusk
following a full moon, called in the ancient language of gnoles 'tears
of the stars'.

But most special of all were what spread before him like a city
of parasols in a miniature valley between the boles of trees –
mushrooms, stolid in rings like models of the monuments erected
by Fungle's ancestors drowned continents ago. Some had caps like
large brown saucers over fleshy gills, others red-spotted and most
artificial-looking with skins luminous as deepsea jellyfish.

'Blessums!' he murmured with pleasure.

Fungle knelt among the mushrooms and removed his pack. To
him this hidden garden of potents emerging from rot was a holy
place. The mushrooms glowed faintly in the dimness underscored
by the ratchet of crickets and creak of frogs. If he had not already
known, Fungle could not have guessed if it were day or night, so
dense was the roof of twined branches above his tall green conical
cap (which, like most gnoles, Fungle wore from a belief that it
funnelled his consciousness nearer the cosmos).

On his knees with back straight, thick hands on squat thighs, knapsack beside him, Fungle felt the living and growing around him, mirror to the life and growth within. His whiskers felt curiously brittle with the power that charged the air of this claustral, dank cathedral, rank with the sour odour of rot and roots. After ten deep slow breaths he touched the wishing feather atop his cap, then said, 'Spirit o' mushroom, give me yer presence an' grant me a boon.'

In the centre of the ring of mushrooms a column of air thickened and undulated. Mushrooms are strange creatures, unique in nature and alien in design and spirit, and the soft presence he registered in the dark clearing triggered odd associations: moonlight, a smell of starch, a delight in decay. The spirit said nothing, which Fungle was accustomed to, but he felt its acknowledgement as he began to harvest the mushrooms he wanted, blessing each one before removing it from the earth. The poisonous ones he left for the turtles, who liked them.

Breaking out of the forest's cover on the way home, Fungle saw the sun about to touch the sawtoothed mountains, and he set down his bulging knapsack to watch his favourite time, when the eye of dusk closes to loose the spirits of twilight that dwell in the ephemeral world conjoining night and day.

All around him Fungle felt the changing of the light, the sun's gentle alchemy that transformed the land. Spreading shafts splintered at the mountain's edge to shatter gold against shivering leaves, bake dough-grey rock golden brown, glint quicksilver on a kingfisher splashing in the river.

He closed his eyes and still could see the setting sun, felt it burning out there immeasurably far away; felt the land on which he stood swinging 'round it, felt the turning of the earth beneath his booted feet. *Seasons an' cycles*, he thought, *'t all depends on rotation. Stars and planets, birth and life and death.* He smiled. *Even the stirring spoon that makes me gravies.*

In the air he sensed a bristling disturbance, small but sharp, like a ripple on a lake of winds. He felt a prickling in his thumbs, noted gnats scribbling frenzies above the ebony sheen of the lake. *Most pekuliar*, he thought. *Rain tonight, or I'm no judge. Best beez on me ways.*

High in the sky was something like a cloud, but ruler-straight and gilded by the setting sun. It lengthened as Fungle watched with senses more subtle than sight. Fungle felt the hurtling metal thing that drew the line in the sky. He also felt the silent whirling things looking down from far above the sky. But they were part of another world that had only recently begun to concern him, and he felt their presence the way he knew the motion of crickets' legs and noodling of worms through dirt, knew the trees' light drinking and patient growth.

The sun touched the mountains.

Fungle felt an odd flutter inside, the wingbeat of something satisfied yet trepidant at the same time. *Change afoot*, he thought. *Many roads are meetin' an' partin' here today.*

Which was why he was out here, after all.

The sun lowered behind the mountains. Fungle opened his eyes.

On this day when seasons met he watched the day bleed into night and thought, *Well met.* Above him the clouds changed colour; gold to yellow to orange to cinnamon, a hundred deepening shades between each. The changing colour seemed to roughen their texture as they darkened.

Was this something else that had changed? Fungle could not be sure, but it seemed sunsets had not appeared so bloody forty or fifty years ago: not so much murky sienna and brooding brick-red.

He sighed. *But it's all so gradjial and yer noggin' plays a passel a' tricks.*

The clouds edged toward grey.

Fungle blessed the departed sun and lifted up his knapsack, bulging with mushrooms, grasses, pennyroyal, dill, and camomile.

He threaded furry arms through the sturdy willowbark straps, bent beneath the knapsack's weight, and descended into the valley. The mountain shadows lengthened toward him like fangs in a closing mouth.

After a dozen paces he stopped. By his boots something glinted in the grass. Fungle bent and picked it up. A cylinder of thin-wrought metal, white with a red and blue design, a teardrop-shaped hole in one end. Fungle set his nose against it and sniffed. Whee-oosh! Some kind of ale, but nasty with chemicals.

A human thing, this. No human had yet set foot in Fungle's valley – he'd have felt it instantly if one had – so this must have been discarded by some thieving goblin. Yet another encroachment.

Fungle's preference would have been to crush the container and bury it with apologies and blessings to the earth that would surround it and, over the course of centuries, recycle it, but his friend Ka, he knew, collected such things – though why, Fungle could not imagine. So he emptied it to be sure the awful ale would not taint his carefully gathered ingredients, then placed it in his pack and continued his descent into the valley.

It was on the way back to his home, his head blanketed by bittersweet thoughts, that Fungle encountered what he later came to think of as the Parliament of Personages. Travelling together toward Fungle's home, they were a delegation of forest folk: woodland elves, a three-point buck, an imp, several rabbits, hob-goblins, foxes, and brownies, a fastidious raccoon, a sextet of surly dwarves, a well-mannered skunk, a couple of trolls, and an ogre. The latter, huge and imposing, was a reformed carnivore, and Fungle had glimpsed him a time or two petting rabbits with only the slightest hint of chagrin. A bluejay perched on his burly shoulder.

Even as he hailed the group, Fungle felt a sense of the impor-tance of their mission. Forest creatures dwell together in tacit communion, understanding their role in the great dance of life and death around them, but they rarely step out together. They halted on the path as Fungle approached them, and it did not escape the gnole that each face was as serious as a human being's prayer book.

'Me blessins to ya one and all on this fine evenin',' said Fungle. 'And what sends yer grave selves slouchin' toward me door?'

They glanced nervously among themselves. Fungle waited patiently, understanding that they had some favour to ask him, and that the asking of favours from a shaman came difficult for most creatures.

After a bit of glancing about and some prodding expressions, it became obvious that one of the dwarves had been elected their spokesperson. *Uniroyal*, thought Fungle, remembering the dwarf's name. *Odd name for a forest creature.* Then he remembered that the dwarf was a cobbler who had made an occupation of night-time sorties into the fringes of the Land of No in order to purloin rubber tyres, which he cut up in his workshop and used to re-sole boots.

He did a roaring trade.

In fact, Fungle recollected, about the only boot-wearing creatures who did not deal with Uniroyal the cobbler were gnoles. Traditionalists one and all, they still preferred waxed hemp to protect their feet from nettles and briars, and sniffed at such a notion as 'material progress'.

Of course, the dwarf could have named himself Michelin or Goodyear, which were fine names, and for a while Firestone had held a certain allure. But *Uniroyal*! What a ring, what grandeur! *Uni*: one, plus *royal*. 'Royal one' – who could resist?

'Ahem ahem,' said the dwarf, raising a gnarled fist to his mouth to clear his throat politely. 'G'devenin', Mister Fungle, sir.'

'A fine good evenin' to yerself, Master Cobbler.'

Uniroyal seemed pleasantly surprised at the honorific. 'Er, we all – that is, us here plus the creatures hereabouts which we represent, feel that we's bein' subjected to increasin'ly unendurable conditions from the continuous expansion of the empire of the human beans.'

'What he's sayin',' interjected an elf, 'is that the Land of No is steppin' on our toes.'

Uniroyal nodded. 'There ain't a day goes by,' he continued, gathering courage, 'when one of our brethren ain't uprooted from his home without a warning or a care. An' fer what?' he demanded.

'Mills,' said the ogre.

'Malls,' corrected a troll.

The skunk looked down sadly.

'More acres than I got hairs, turned into flat hard stuff ya can't dig or plant,' said Uniroyal. 'Streams not ten clobhops*

---

* 1 digit	= 1"	10 mozzies	= 1 wamble
10 digits	= 1 strider	7 wambles	= 1 clobhop
10 striders	= 1 mozzy	10 clobhops	= 1 grolethon

from here've become nothin' more'n muddy piddles swimmin' more with rubbish than with fish. Ya'd sooner gargle bees than drink from it.'

The three-point buck hung his majestic head.

'They's creepin' up on ya, Fungle,' said Uniroyal. 'Just wait. Spells or no spells, one day yer gonna wake up an' find one o' them mall mills plunk in the middle o' yer valley, with big noisy roads up on pillars everywhere you can shake a stick.'

The foxes solemnly shook their heads.

'It's too much,' said a troll.

The other animals agreed, and vented their anger and frustration. Fungle let it go on a moment, because part of the reason they had come was to reveal their anger and its source, but when such words as 'resistance' and 'revolution' and 'retribution' began to surface, he held up his hands for silence.

'Me own family,' he said, 'has lit'rally took flight from just such doings as yer describin'. They's headed west to deeper, darker forests.'

'Well,' growled the ogre, 'we not so lucky to have Lunabirds like you gnoles.' His sneer betrayed his salad days as a carnivore. 'We stuck here. Room and time all gone.' For an ogre this was nearly a speech of state, for most ogre conversations are as direct and eloquent as a bash on the head with a club.

Fungle frowned. 'The protection o' this valley has long been my charge, and I've always gladly done my duty to them that live in it.'

'But what about the *world*, Fungle?' asked an elf.

'That's a bit beyond me abilities,' he said. 'Me warding spells've fouled their diggin' machines and confused their directions and bent their blades for some time now to help keep us hidden.' He gestured helplessly. 'But Wily Barktea, me old master, taught me that there ain't a spell in all the world that'll stop the tide. An' what yer talkin' about *is* a tide, a human tide. I stayed here while me own family left because this land is me passion and me life's work. But beyond what I've already done an' what I already know, I have no solutions. Have ya not prayed to Molom an' told him yer grievances?'

The creatures glanced among themselves. 'We have, of course,' said the dwarf. 'But either Molom is unheeding, or we cannot reach him.'

'Molom unheeding?' Fungle was surprised. 'I've never heard tell of him ignoring the plight of woodfolk.'

The dwarf shrugged. 'Be that as it may, we've been forced to derive our own solutions.'

'I would be glad to hear them,' said Fungle.

'You are our solution,' said the dwarf.

Fungle was puzzled. 'But I've just told you –'

Uniroyal pointed at him. '*You*, Fungle Foxwit, well-read gnole of letters, mage and shaman o'er this valley, are as eloquent with words as the frog is in layin' her eggs. *You*, dear sir, must be our ambassador.'

'Ambassador?' Fungle was not sure he liked the taste of the word.

But Uniroyal was nodding eagerly. 'For our sake, you must undertake a diplomanic mission to the Land of No to meet with the King of the Humans hisself. Tell him –'

'King . . . of the Humans?' Fungle was looking a bit green around the gills. 'Meet with the King of the –'

'Meet with him,' continued Uniroyal, 'and tell him to tend to his fishin', and we'll tend to ours.'

Fungle looked from one sombre face to the next. 'But, but . . . we gnoles gave up contact with them long ago. The dark ones, the Cherokees, were our friends in these mountains – we traded tokens of peace – until the moon-coloured humans drove them west, and we elected to stay behind an' hidden. They don't know we's still here, and that's the way I likes it.'

'Them was good times,' mooned a brownie. 'They'd leave milk in a saucer on their porches at night, an' we'd do a coupla odd jobs 'round their cabins.'

'I got dinner,' reminisced a hobgoblin. 'On a big plate, too, by the fire. Ah, it were tasty! An' all fer a coupla mended boots and washed dishes. It were a good deal fer both parties, I reckon.'

'Fact is, they don't believe in us no more,' reasoned an elf. 'I can't remember the last time a human bean called up an elf to help with plantin' by moonlight, or a fairy to make a wish.' He shook his head wistfully. 'We useta trade babes, you know, changelings. Take 'em right from the cradle, leave one of ours. Kind of an exchange programme, y'might say. 'Cept the ones we take now're useless, fit fer nothin' but makin' gadgets and talking 'bout "TV" and "nine-ten-toe" and I don't know what-all. Now we just gives 'em back real quick, with no memory of their visit. We're about to just give up fer good.'

'But considerin' what events've brought ya to me,' said Fungle, 'I'd think ya'd be happy not to be believed in. Iffin I pop me head out into the Land of No askin' please-an'-than'-ya, wouldja mind leavin' us alone, it'll only lead 'em right to us.'

Fungle saw their glum faces as hope faded, and felt their disappointment in him. 'I'm agreein' with the problem,' he said, wanting to regain their confidence in him. 'But yer solution makes me uncomfortable. Not for me own sake,' he hastily amended, 'but fer the sake of the valley as well. Seems to me it'd be best if I gave it me best prayers an' meditations, and came up with some new an' better ways an' means to keep us safe. Next full moon I'll contact Molom meself an' ask his aid on yer behalf. Come to me in two full moons, an' I'll present 'em to yer. Iffin ya likes one, or iffin ya still prefer I head out fer the Land of No – well, we'll get our noggins together on it, and whatever we decide then is what we'll do fer sure. Meantime,' he concluded, 'ya have me solemn word I'll put all the trainin' an' thought at me command to unravellin' this knot.'

Uniroyal looked down at his big feet. 'Well, lads,' he said to the others. 'It'll have to do.'

They nodded, accepting Fungle's reason, but just as clearly they were disappointed that their solution was not to be immediately implemented.

As the delegation turned away, the ogre picked up a bunny rabbit and held it close, stroking its silky pelt with big, warty fingers. 'One day,' he said, 'won't be no woods to run to.'

And they were gone, the tyre-tread soles of Uniroyal's boots slapping the earth in dissatisfaction.

The rest of the way home Fungle's head swarmed with impractical schemes of giant airy-plane arks to fly the forest creatures west, or powerful spells of invisibility around the entire valley, or treaties with the human beans acknowledging the valley as sacred ground –

(*But what about the* world, *Fungle?* asked an elf's voice in memory.)

– but overriding all such grandiose notions were those haunting last words of the ogre, words that made Fungle angry and frustrated and sad. He was their mage, and they had come to him for help. He could not let them down.

Fungle swept up a handful of prickly nuts scattered beneath an ancient beech tree. Prising free their sweet kernels to nibble on occupied his hands while he pondered the day's events the rest of the way home.

*

Home.

Home for a gnole can be many things. Scattered across the world when their ancestral land was destroyed eons ago, gnoles learned to call many places home. Caverns and forests and desert sands; tunnels and grass huts and trees. Wherever they have planted their homes, legends of the Little People have taken root, be they the elves of Germany or the leprechauns of Ireland. In Hindustan they are the *Buamanus*; in Japan they wear the name *Ainu*, the little men of Hokkaido. India knows them as *Silvestras*; to Ceylon they are *Nittawo*, the 'little lost people'.

But they're gnoles all the same.

At a clearing by the edge of a circular lake, Fungle's hands formed ancient patterns as he spoke:

'Winklum, Blinklum, Blindyouzbee,
Release me spell of invisibility!'

Suddenly there was Fungle's little coracle boat, waterproofed fabric stretched over wicker hoops shaped like a giant walnut shell. The boat had not been invisible before Fungle released his spell, nor had it simply not been there. The ward he had placed around it was much like the one set to protect his house – indeed, like the wards that protected the entire valley. It worked by leading the eye away from the object it protected. The little boat was there; you just wouldn't *look* at it so long as the ward was in place. Fungle had learned the hard way that, where magick is concerned, simplest is bestest.

Fungle unburdened himself of the heavy knapsack and stepped gingerly into the centre of the coracle. He sat facing the shore and began to paddle towards the island dense with trees in the centre of the circular lake.

If the lake was an eye and the island its iris, Fungle's home was its pupil, and from within the simple comfort of its confines he watched over the valley.

At the island's bank he pulled the coracle half out the water and hefted his knapsack. His hands inscribed the air and he chanted to set the ward of invisibility again.

Following a path no untrained eye could trace to the heart of the island's wood, Fungle approached the weathered stump of an oak tree long gone. He passed his hand above the stump and muttered until he felt the warding spells relax beneath his hands. He grasped an edge of the stump and lifted, and there revealed was a doorway opening onto a passage that led down into darkness. For Fungle's house was cunning with invisibility, a stone igloo set in the earth beneath the hollow stump. It would be hard to discover even if there had been no wards to protect it, for not only is the oak itself a tree of protection and strength, but each granite block of Fungle's home had been quarried from the high Smokies by his ancestors a thousand years ago, and fitted so tightly against its neighbour that the thinnest blade could not be pushed between them. One thousand and eighty blocks (a venerated number of protective power for reasons it would take Fungle months of dogged teaching from crusty old books on arithmetic, astronomy, geometry and stereometry for us to understand), thick with moss and piebald lichen. On its nether side the secret door was carved with suns and intricate whorls to further protect the dwelling beneath.

Fungle stood a moment beside the door and gave a last look around before going inside.

Overhead the sooty clouds were all a torment now. Fungle felt satisfaction that his prediction of rain would be borne out. He loved the rain; loved to sleep to its patter and awaken to its cleansing – but his satisfaction quickly turned to puzzlement. The clouds weren't just amassing for a downpour, they were *boiling* like a thickening sauce. And they looked to be *searching*. Fungle's face, happy even at rest, grew wary. He sensed a feeling in the clouds' grey gravity, an intent.

The storm, he realised, was coming in not from the north, south, east, or west, but from all four directions at once. The roiling clouds edged towards a common centre as if a maelstrom were draining the sky, yet for all their churning they looked solid as floating boulders.

From four directions at once!

Fungle liked this not at all. Still – *arguin' with the weather only makes yer wetter.* What's to do? Best go in and batten down. Got guesties comin' and comefeastibles to fix.

Across the liquid sky of lake, bats flew among the willows like demented scraps of black rag.

Fungle shut the door. Above him came the first shudder of thunder.

Smells! Vapours! Pungent potpourri adrift on the air! If not for the rain driving down the drifting mélange aroma of Fungle's cooking, that night you'd've found his home with your nose alone, protective wards or no.

In the kitchen you'da thought thè King o' the Gnoles hisself was coming fer grub, the way Fungle carried on. Combining all the best qualities of gourmet chef and circus juggler he scurried about gathering up utensils, pots, and bowls, slicing and dicing, chopping and hopping, a master of impromptu inspiration.

Lessee, what'll be, walnut soup 'r tansy pudding wi' chestnut jelly, o why not both sez me? An' howta fix them cattails? Steamed or fried, boiled or poached, sautéed with dandelion greens? I know: I'll just set to 'em and let me hands make up me mind!

Fungle's hands fluttered like birds orbiting 'round his roly-poly body. He chopped wild onions and kneaded dough (remember to heat the quince honey for that when it's teacakes!), one hand spooning juices into sauces while the other stirred and brought the wooden spoon to fussy lips that blew and tasted. His brow furrowed for all the world as if vexed by theorems of the universe. *No, no; more horseradish to fire up the gravy!* His arms windmilled into action again.

His bulge-bellied clay stove became pregnant with newbaked odours and a sweet reek of pine ash. The air grew steamy above Fungle's head, as if thunderclouds erupted from his frenzied brain.

And, throughout, Fungle's guesties were foremost in his mind. They were the mesh through which he strained every ingredient of his meal. Their loves and hates, the thought of flavours that would bring a reluctant smile to Neema's face or puzzle Ka with a new-found taste – these guided his frantic hands as he beat and kneaded and whipped and pulped and stirred the fixings of his Equinox feast, celebrating the harvest and gathering of foodstuffs in preparation for the long cold sleep of winter.

But Fungle had also decided that this was to be a feast of going-away.

Going away?

Yes, and a sad leave-taking it was, too, for Fungle loved his home in the lake that was the eye watching over the land that mirrored his soul. He had lived here since he was a littl'un with big brother Froog and Ma and Pa and so many other gnole families and clans that it seemed impossible now that he and Neema, equally stubborn, were the last two gnoles left in the entire valley. This land was Fungle's book of days: that rock where he'd knocked his noggin bloody and run home to his mum, remembered dimly now as soothing hands and a mirthful voice; that clearing where the clans had gathered every Mayday to trade victuals and handmades, the same clearing where a newly voted clan shaman named Fungle Foxwit had nervously performed the marriage ceremony uniting an equally nervous brother Froog with a blushing Bedina Bramblebush – poor, doomed Bedina; this Old Man Willow grown wise and stronghearted above the grave of Wily Barktea, Fungle's master and the last true mage of the Foxwits, gone suddenly of food poisoning long before his fledgling apprentice had been ready to assume the mantle.

Old Man Willow had grown because a seed is planted in every

gnole grave, and throughout this protected island valley Fungle knew each and every one by name and rustle and root and creak, living markers of lives once led. And scattered through the valley were other leaves from Fungle's book of days: the spreading chestnut tree under which Fungle used to study scrounged, borrowed, and begged books to recover some of the lost gnoledge of the ancients; a scorched patch of land where many years ago his first attempt to perform a Summoning had gone awry.

So Fungle loved this living diary of all his life, but he loved his friends and family even more, and when it had become plain to him that the creeping tendrils of the ever-growing Land of No had not only touched the fringes of their precious valley, but would inevitably suffuse and ultimately choke it, his thoughts had turned toward abandoning the land that gnoles had called their home for untold generations. In recent years other, more cautious gnoles had pulled up roots and headed west, including his closest relatives. Fungle was the last of the Foxwit family left in the valley. His father, Wisp; his brother, Froog; his niece and nephew, Quince and Peapod – all gone to join with other gnoles fled before them. Fungle had blessed them on their way to Mount Shasta and hoped their fears would prove unfounded.

But Fungle had spent many decades attaining his hard-earned awareness of the land and its tastes and smells, motion and light and sound. The skitterings of field mice and contentment of tree spirits had become as much a part of him as the ridged whorls in his blunt fingertips, and every crumpled wrapper and spent rifle cartridge and cigarette butt he found attested to the fact that he would someday have to leave as well.

And now he could not even watch a sunset without such garbage tempering his joy!

Perhaps his brother had been right after all.

The night of his kin's departure had been a sad and joyful occasion, fraught with tears and laughter, vibrant music and a chorus of farewells. Fungle had prepared a leave-taking feast not unlike the one that busied him tonight, and he'd even invited Neema Cleverbread to lend a hand with puttin' away proper such a large amount of food, and also to help with raising the joyful noise that would linger in his family's mind when they set out west next night in their silent Lunabirds.

Neema was Fungle's closest neighbour – 'close' being a term of geography, not familiarity. She lived in a right spotless and cleverly compact home a couple of clobhops away that betrayed

not one whit its former life as a barren, damp cave. The rest of the Cleverbread clan had abandoned the ancient rivalry with the Foxwits over stewardship of the valley and headed west. What had finally caused them to give up the dispute was a terrible loss: the youngest of the Cleverbreads, Neema's little brother Scrapper, had ventured past the protective wards that secluded the valley. Many gnole children attempted this; the temptation was too sweet to resist. But Scrapper had gone out alone, and beyond the sanctuary of the wards he had stepped on a rusted nail. Within a day his foot had turned a bad colour, and two days later he had died. The Cleverbreads held a clan meeting where it was decided that enough was enough: leave the valley to the Foxwits and find a safer place to live. But Neema, prideful and stubborn, had refused to go.

In spite of all this uneasy history, Neema loved Fungle's father dearly, and for many years had baked him sweetcakes and acorn bread in exchange for one of Wisp's famous 'Howzit' stories. 'Howzit the Toad Got Spots' was Neema's favourite, though 'Howzit Snails Carry Their Houses' ran a close second.

That dinner'd been a feast and a fattening-up of Foxwit folk, and afterward in his spic-and-span living-room before the homey and subdued glow of a flickering fire, Fungle had played many a mandolute ditty to liven their sluggish blood and aid their digestion on its way.

Sitting in a padded armchair thick with polish like buttery syrup in the fire's light, sapling cane hooked round his elbow and his lone foot tapping time, Froog played spoons held back-to-back with stems clamped between his fingers. Neema clapped counterpoint but kept a critical eye on Fungle's playing. Fungle felt very aware of her attention, and he kept his melody intricate and boisterous – a jig, really. Had he not been so intent in its creation he surely would have danced to it. The fingers of Fungle's left hand flew along the fretboard like squabbling orioles, while those on his right raced on the strings like men in a running contest on a floating log. It was a miracle the weathered old mandolute didn't just up and fly apart with the sounds bursting from it.

Cavorting before the grown-up gnoles were Quince and Peapod, Fungle's niece and nephew. They whirled and bowed and do-si-do'd, swaddled in the tapestry of notes emerging from Fungle's hands upon the mandolute. Peapod wore a ridiculous human cap, always drooping ludicrous large atop his head like it'd melted there, all blue cloth and crescent-moon bill and hard button on top. The young gnole had seen Musrum the Mossman drop the cap from a box one night as Musrum had staggered out the doorway of Tobacco Inn – a place the littl'uns were strictly forbidden to go anywhere near. Peapod was convinced the mysterious Mossman had retrieved it from the Land of No during one of his legendary, dangerous, and clandestine forays into the Land of a Thousand Smokes, and what gnole'd tell him otherways? 'It's some human mage's hat, I'm sworn,' Peapod would say, pointing out the runic hex affixed to the front. Peapod found the cap such a dangerously human thing that wearing it seemed an act of defiance. Naturally defiant himself, Peapod was rarely seen without the cap, though he took a terrible teasing about it. Fungle remembered offering once to prepare his nephew a potion of lavender and rosemary for the restorin' of fur, bein' as he always wore that cap and Fungle could only reckon it were 'cause Peapod were getting all baldy-egged on top before his time.

For his part, Fungle soon forgot Neema's eyes upon him. Dreamy lost in his playing, Fungle considered himself engaged in a conversational concertina between himself and the spirits of the trees whose wood had gone into the making of his fine mandolute. Spruce and oak were inlaid and curved and carefully fitted, selected from the trees themselves by Fungle and blessed by him before their use. Often when he played he felt the essence of those trees, collaborators in a music of down-growing root and up-turned leaf, and therefore a music of earth and of sky.

Soon he felt the music carrying his hands along – for sometimes it was this way and not the opposite – toward an ending, and rocking with the lusty tempo he finally clenched the neck in his left hand, and with his right windmilled four crashing crescendos that left the others still and gaping at the very passion the spilled notes contained – all the others, that is, but Peapod. He had got a pot from off an S-shaped hook on the iron bar over Fungle's hearth and danced round beating it like a bodhran. When the last notes of Fungle's final chord had shattered upon the walls and died in the fire's crackle, Peapod in his silly human cap still cavorted, banging about in metre wholly removed from the tempo of Fungle's piece. Eyes closed he drummed and swayed.

'Peapod,' Froog said mildly from his chair.

Boom boom-boom bang! from Peapod's hands.

'Under the spell of me playin',' observed Fungle, smiling.

''E's under spells, a'right, brother,' said Froog, 'but the playin' ain't yours. – PEAPOD!'

Peapod opened his eyes. A hand stopped in mid-descent above the pot he clenched. He looked about the room and seemed to shrink with sudden self-consciousness. Neema hid her smile behind a hand, but her bright eyes showed it anyhow. Wisp shook his head and clucked knowingly.

'Let's 'ave it over,' said Froog.

'Have it over, Pa?' Peapod asked innocently. 'Have what over?'

'Peapod.' Froog's face, usually so ready to smile despite a life of much calamity and hardship, had grown stern.

Fungle hugged his mandolute.

Peapod lowered his head until nothing could be seen of his face below the halfmoon bill and embroidered hex of his human cap. Slowly he lowered Fungle's pot to the floor and raised a hand to his ear. From it he pulled out a curious object, a sort of thimble the colour of flesh, with a cord leading down into his tunic.

Beside her brother, Quince hung her head, clenched fingers playing nervously.

Peapod drew on the cord until a box emerged. It was of no material that occurred in their valley, a dull black hard-edged thing all corners and knobs. Peapod held it a moment, reluctant to part with the thing, then handed it over to his father's outstretched hand.

The fire seemed to cackle at Peapod's embarrassment.

As he held the object in his knuckly hand, Froog's features grew sad. For the first time Fungle was aware of his brother's weariness and the years that hung heavy about his face. Froog was younger than Fungle but looked older by far. 'I suppose ya got this from that no-good gnome,' said Froog.

'Ka's not no-good,' objected Peapod mildly.

'Not entire, no,' agreed his father. 'But he's a gnome and not a gnole, and what's good fer him ain't always best for young'uns whose parents want 'em growin' up all proper with the ways of their people, and not –' he held up the box with its thimble dangling on the cord '– all tinctured an' tainted by the ways an' means of human beans.' He patted his left thigh, which ended abruptly above the knee. 'Or 'ave yer forgotten how yer pa parted company with the leg he'd got accustomed to o'er the years?'

Peapod shook his head and looked ashamed.

Neither had Fungle forgot the night Bedina, Froog's well-loved wife, had pounded at Fungle's ceiling door with Froog propped half-dead against her. His leg had been completely severed, and the stump bound with a bandage turned all red. Though he knew many cures and remedies, Fungle was no physick. But the finest healer among the gnoles, Chicory Longpelt, had flown west years before with the rest of the Longpelts after a single low-flying plane had buzz-sawed overhead, even though Fungle had assured them that the wards protected from above as well. So because Fungle was the valley's only shaman, albeit an imperfect one, the gravely sick and seriously injured were brought to him straight away. In fearful haste Fungle had prepared potions and healing pastes for Froog, and he would not sleep or even rest until he was sure his brother would see the morn. When finally he had done all he could do and Froog slept deeply in Fungle's bed, Fungle afforded himself the luxury of asking what had happened.

'Standin' on a metal road, he was, Fungle,' Bedina'd said, her breath dispelling the steam of a calming tea Fungle had brewed for her. 'It runs at the foot of the mountains, two metal lines stitched by planks beneath.'

'I know the one,' Fungle had said. 'There's an iron demon screams along it every other night.'

'Well this night it's got yer poor brother's leg.' Bedina's eyes had misted with the telling. 'He was down there all curious an' lookin' about,' she related. 'Y'know how he is.'

Fungle knew. At that time Froog had been all taken with human things. He'd collect their tools and boxes, and fix 'em up to working (though what they actually *did* often stayed a mystery), or use their hard tools to fix up gnole things for others. He'd become quite the handyman – an odd'n ender, as gnoles called such folk – and the train tracks were a sore temptation to him, for beside them could be found many human things ferried by the shrieking metal ship on rails across the Lands of No. Fungle had long ago given up begging Froog not to venture down there. And now this.

'His foot got caught betwixt the planks,' Bedina continued, 'an' he struggled an' I pulled, but there was no gettin' free. Oh, Fungle, it were like as if it wanted him itself, that road did! The iron began to sing beneath his feet and we could hear it comin' far away. His ankle was all turned an' he was kickin' like a trapped rabbit, and the thing was bearin' down all hot-breathed like it'd been conjured with foul words, an' . . . an' –'

Fungle had hugged her and stroked her fur. 'It's all right,' he'd reassured her. 'Froog'll be all right.'

Bedina had been dead these seven years now, struck down by a hunter's bullet after bear. Looking at the healed stump of his brother's leg, as the saddened gnole sat in his overstuffed easy chair holding the confiscated human music-thing in his hand, Fungle remembered that night as the beginning of a change in his brother's obsessions. Fungle saw the secret fear in Froog's eyes each time his daughter Quince, all bright and curious, asked her grandfather Wisp to tell the story 'Howzit Humans Lost Their Fur,' or 'Howzit Humans Left the Woods'. So much sadness and a pang of old wounds reawakened every time Peapod found sparkling allure in human objects.

But Froog was goodhearted and unable to grow angry at those he truly loved. Rather than chide Peapod about the human-bean-made box, his voice stayed gentle as he said, 'It's this sort of thing sends us out o' here fer good.' He shook the box and glanced about the room, a knowing look for the other adults. 'What's left of us,' he added. 'Y'understand that, don't yer, son?'

'It's only music, Pa,' Peapod said, his voice bare above a whisper.

Froog looked at Fungle for help.

'It's not the music, lad,' said Fungle from behind his mandolute, 'but the thing that makes it. It's best not to get attached to worldly

things.' He strummed a chord. '*Be* in the world; don't let the world
be in you.' He smiled kindly and winked.

'Ere, now, that's the very thing,' agreed Froog, relieved. 'Livin'
on the garbage of others is right enough for gnomes like Karbolic
Earthcreep.' He straightened in his chair and hooked a thumb
toward his chest. 'But we're gnoles, Peapod. Of the ancient race
o' gnoles. Y'unnerstand?'

'Yes, Pa.'

'Right enough, then. Ye'll give Ka back his human-bean box an'
we'll say no more about it, eh?'

At Fungle's suggestion the children climbed out his ceiling door
to find Old Man Willow and ask the tree for wisdom. Whether or
not they really asked the old willow tree on the island's far edge,
Fungle knew that his nephew, at least, would be glad of the opportunity to be alone, for all children of a certain age need the chance
to mutter to themselves about adults who just don't understand.

When they were gone and the protective oak door closed behind
them, Fungle heated a poker in the fireplace and carried it into
his kitchen to make them all another ale. As he poured dun liquid
into mugs, each shaped like a swan with head tucked under wing
for a handle, Fungle heard his father's voice from the living-room.
'An' whose 'at with the 'uman-bean 'ammer I see 'anging from 'is
pant-loop, eh?' Wisp slapped his knee and cackled.

''Tain't the same, Pa,' said Froog. In the kitchen Fungle smiled
as the hot poker hissed into the ale. *It's a special alchemy of families*,
he reflected, *that turns a worried father into a defensive son*. He
gathered up mugs.

'I tell ya true,' continued Froog. 'His generation's different from
the ones before. All abuzz with human words and arty-facts.' He
accepted a mug of ale from Fungle. 'Ah, blessums, brother mine,
an' long may yer chimney smoke.' He drank thirstily.

'An' who was the little tyke of a gnole,' asked Wisp, face all
wrinkled amusement regarding his son, 'what cried when 'e broke
'is wind-up music box with the 'uman beans on top that danced?'

Froog fidgeted uncomfortably on his chair. His fingers played
on the handle of his cane. 'Don't remember,' he said.

'Don't remember!' Wisp hooted. 'Yer eyes was leakin' like April
maples fer two days!'

Fungle hid his smile behind a sip of burnt ale, remembering his
little brother dancing along with the tiny mechanical figures.

'Aww,' said Froog, and sealed the issue with a long draught of
ale. Done, he wiped his snout with the back of an arm. 'Ey there,

Neema lass!' he called to change the subject. 'When're you comin' to yer senses and lightin' out west with the rest of us all?'

There was a brief, awkward silence. Froog'd meant well, of course, but given the past conflicts between Cleverbread and Foxwit, and between Neema and her own clan, old feuds were suddenly made all too palpable.

But Neema understood the good feeling behind the comment and did not choose to take it wrong. 'When I've no more choice to make, I reckon,' she said. 'Right now I've berries to jell and rows to hoe, and I see no reason to leave *my* fields fallow.'

'Ah, poor Neema!' Froog replied. 'That's all because you 'aven't seen what's finally sent me out of here. Fungle didn't tell ya what I seen?'

Neema glanced at Fungle. 'What Fungle Foxwit tells or don't's his own affair.'

'Well, I'll do the tellin', then,' said Froog, 'since it's the thing's made me mind up that our fair valley's blighted fer good, and what's fetched you good folk out this eve to see us Foxwits warm an' on our way. All Foxwits but Fungle, faith.'

Fungle's only reply to the barb was to raise his mug in wry salute.

'Well, Neema Cleverbread, I'll tell yer true,' continued Froog, 'it's with me own two eyes I seen a kinda awful miracle, I did one day, fer I seen a whole wood turned into the surface of the Moon! Only 'tweren't no magic did the turnin', an' weren't no fire, neither. Leastways no fire that ever *burned*.' Froog made a disgusted sound. 'It hacked, an' it buzzed, an' it chopped and sawed and dragged and split. But it didn't burn, oh no!'

Fungle kept his silence, staring at the crackling fire. He'd heard the tale before, but somehow now with his brother's telling it rose in flame before his eyes.

'Humans?' Neema asked in a voice gone small.

'Whadjer think?' Froog shook his head. He hefted his mug to Fungle. 'Cheers,' he said with heavy irony. Fungle said nothing, knowing that his brother's bitterness was his only way of showing the pain he felt at Fungle's not accompanying him on the journey west.

'Ah, Neema lass,' Froog continued sadly, 'ya shoulda heard the trees. They prayed and pleaded and screamed, and they even shook and waved and bowed, but all those maraudin' blunderboots could hear was their own machines, *nnn! nnn! nnn!* Like some coward's victory cry.'

In the yellow flame Fungle conjured his brother's memory of
an iron demon's howl across the land, across the rails, across
his leg.

'All the trees?' whispered Neema, horrified. 'Surely there's some
purpose to such, such . . .' She was unable to find a word to match
such deeds.

'Oh, it were for a purpose, a'right,' said Froog. 'Few days later,
an' the stubbled valley's all aswarm with human beans. Hundreds
of 'em, like ants after honey, an' each one holdin' or ridin' in some
noise-makin' machine. *Nnn! Rrr! Blam-blam-blam!* Jellied me in
sound, it fairly did. Went on fer days and chased out ever' fox and
frog and cricket and bird, and when it was over there's wooden
boxes poppin' out the earth like boils on me bum, you'll pardon.'

Neema blushed but nodded her pardon.

'One minute there's a forest; next –' Froog shrugged as if all were
hopeless – 'a town. And fulla people to boot.'

'Humans,' Neema muttered resignedly.

'Not fifteen clobhops away as I'm sittin' here,' finished Froog.
'Though to hear me brother count it, they may's well all be
crowded one against another on t'other side o' the world, and us
all happy-wappy in our little homes. Fah!'

'I've never said that, brother mine,' said Fungle gently, remembering his little brother's resentment when Fungle had been picked
to be the new shaman of the clan, and aware that a tinge of the
old jealousy could still colour his tone. 'And no one here thinks
ya anything but sensical fer leavin'. But you've a family, Froog.'

Neema bowed down her head.

'You'll sing a different tune about fairness when those devils pop
up on yer own front porch,' Froog said bitterly. 'And they won't
knock afore bargin' in!' He laughed mirthlessly. 'Like as not they'll
catch ya with yer snout in a book! It's all well an' good to deal with
yer potions an' pomes an' puffs of purple smoke and vapour, but
everyday doings're a different matter, Fungle.'

'That's be as may,' said Fungle. 'But 'til then it's me own front
porch and this valley's me wife an' child both.'

Froog looked stricken. He struggled from his chair and leaned
heavily on his cane, free hand fidgeting about his patched and
threadbare coveralls. 'Fungle, Fungle,' he said, and Fungle's eyes
misted at the note of shame in his brother's tone. 'Before our pa
and on our mother's memory, I'm sorry's can be fer what I just
said. Wrong it was, an' wrong I am, and I'll say now that on
that day when yer hearth falls sooty from the trod o' strangers

o'erhead, you'll have a place beside our own. That's a promise from yer brother, and none could make better.'

Fungle hugged his brother warmly. For a while they stood embraced before the fire, and this, then, was the true moment of their leave-taking: happy with each other's love and sad at their parting, as all good leave-takings are.

Not long after, Wisp rose to his tired old feet and said they'd best be on their way. So Fungle accompanied the rest of the Foxwits one last time to the shore of his little island. Again he embraced his brother. He gave his blessings to Quince and Peapod and bade them mind their father on their perilous journey west.

Wisp merely looked at his son for a long moment. His wise old eyes danced with years and tales and lore, and so much passed between them in that gaze that parting words would only have diminished its meaning.

Neema had already cleaned up the remnants of the going-away feast when Fungle returned. Fungle thanked her sincerely, knowing that her true kindness had been to quickly allow him solitude. She refused an evening tea, saying she had things to do at home an' nuts to put out for the squirrels always a-begging at her door in the mornings. Head all full of his family's leaving, Fungle failed to notice Neema's sadness as well. Soon he sat before the fire, alone with his thoughts in his comfortabode home of one thousand and eighty blocks and a hundred times as many gentle memories.

The next morning Fungle found the remnants of Peapod's cap among the ashes in the hearth.

Now, as sauces simmered and breads baked and puddings plumped in his kitchen, readied for the Equinox feast, Fungle set green logs for slow, aromatic burning on his fireplace (which, he realised, probably still contained the ashes of Peapod's cap), and while the firelight blushed his cheeks the colour of crabapples he remembered the love and worry of that bittersweet day.

And now it's come to this, he thought forlornly, *to Fungle fixin' a farewell feast fer what few friends're left. An' what's tipped the scale's an empty metal canister, lighter than an egg an' glowin' in the grass, baneful as a wolf's eye.*

So the what of it had been decided, if not the when. For there remained the problem presented to him by the delegation of forest creatures that had come today, the Parliament of Personages. Fungle was warden of this land, and not for the span of a gnat's wingbeat would he consider abandoning it, moving an inch beyond it, until each and every creature left behind was assured of safety to the limits of his ability. Besides, leaving the valley would also mean leaving it to Neema's sole custody. The last claimant to the valley, a *Cleverbread*? After all that'd passed between the clans over the generations? No, thankee! Fungle wouldn't budge until the march of human progress uprooted him.

And what then? Let's have the truth of it, Fungle: even exiled in yer own land – trapped, in a way, inside yer very soul – are you a-certain you can leave here? This is *home*.

'Ah, enough of these thoughts,' he said out loud. 'Guesties soon this beastly night, and they're comin' fer a feastin', not a funeral! 'T'won't do atall to taint such a meal with these dark thoughts. Not on Equinox night!'

He set to cleaning his already immaculate living-room, a whirlwind sweeping of carpets and dusting the mantel, lifting every animal-shaped bowl and vase to wipe beneath. He lit long beeswax candles and set them in lobster-shaped candlestick holders, then carried those to light incense sticks in burners shaped like tiny mice hunched in spotless corners. He dusted the old varnished box that held on velvet a flintheaded Cherokee arrow, peace token from a time long past. He microscopically straightened his ancient framed map on the wall above where his musical instruments were hung – wooden pipes, dulcimers, bagpipes, theorbos, and a sackbut. (The map, it bears mentioning, showed a continent in the Atlantic Ocean between Europe and North America, and had been drawn before pyramid bricks had set to baking in the Egyptian sun.)

Out of habit Fungle ran his fingers along the door that led down to his library and felt the ward he'd set there gently deflect his hand.

Thunder shook the house.

In the dining-room Fungle practised his 'willwalking' ability: setting the table without touching any of the dining implements, but instead guiding them into place with the power of his mind. It actually required more effort than it would have to merely set the table by hand, but no ability stays sharp unless it is kept in constant use. He did drop a fork, but with everything on his mind this wasn't anything to be ashamed of. Anyway, it was a far cry from when he had first attempted it, years ago: he'd decided to go ahead and have dinner on the floor, since that was where everything had ended up anyway.

By hand he adjusted the needlepoint tablecloth an invisible fraction and readjusted the ornamental plates. Finally satisfied, he stepped back from the table and looked up to the ceiling. Even through the thick stone he heard the drum of rain. Fungle closed his eyes and breathed deep, and his mind filled with the image of the valley lidded with thick stormclouds drenching it like sponges squeezed over a bowl. The odd feeling brought by the storm remained, the searching intent behind the motion of the clouds.

Fungle opened his eyes and glanced about. Dinner warm and the kitchen rosy with stoveheat; living-room spotless and waiting to warm wet travellers this dark and stormy night; worn slippers looking much like beached flat fish inviting near the fireplace. All dry and homefortable and needing only the presence of Neema and Ka to make it complete.

They should've been here by now.

Well, the storm would surely slow them down.

No reason to worry just yet.

But with time heavy on his hands, he worried anyhow. Could he, Fungle, a mage and shaman of the Foxwits, somehow have got the date wrong? Could today not be the Equinox? Oh, don't be ridiculous.

Still . . .

He checked the circular papyrus calendar on the wall to reassure himself, eyes rummaging the chaos of glyphs and numerals crabbily written in an ancient hand. Yes, it was the Equinox.

Might the others have forgotten the date, then? Surely not; autumn Equinox was too important a marker in the year. And besides: Cleverbread or not, what gnole in history ever turned down a free feastin'?

After a while Fungle went up to check on the progress of the storm. When he pushed up the heavy oak lid of the tree stump, he was nearly snatched out of his house by the force of the wind. It flung the door from his grasp and fetched it up against the stump with a loud crack as the wind screamed in.

Fungle was drenched in an instant. The moment the drops touched him he felt the menace of the storm. The rain was warm as blood, and the drops hammered his flesh like nails. Where his soaked-through fur began to wet his skin burned like scraping a scab across a rock.

When the hot rain touched Fungle there came a pause, a lull in which the windscream barging through the trees lowered to a sigh of contentment and the downpour lessened to a mist. It happened in seconds. To Fungle it seemed as if the raindrops that had found him were scouts, each and every one of them reporting back to some titanic force behind the storm. A force that, receiving a hundred thousand wet messages of contact with Fungle, was considering what to do next. Most pekuliar!

Stepping out from the safe harbour of his doorway, Fungle peered out beyond the lake. The lull in the storm allowed him to see a good piece of the valley, and what he saw was most unsettling. All the sky was dark, swirling like a twister turned inside-out. The centre of the vortex was black as space and twice as empty. Grey clouds stalked its perimeter like wolves at prey. As Fungle watched, the vortex puckered like an obscene wound in the sky, and lowered to nearly touch the valley floor a few miles away.

Neema lives near there, Fungle realised with alarm.

As quickly as it formed and lowered, the seething centre of the maelstrom raised back to the sky and moved north.

Searching.

The whistling wind resumed its banshee keen. The rain thickened: from mist to drizzle to gusting torrent.

Fungle shut the door and saw the crack the wind had caused. Nothing that couldn't be fixed handily enough on another, drier day. Having no bolt or lock because such things were unknown in his world, Fungle repeated his strongest protective ward and scurried back down to the warm dry pocket of his home. He shed garments as he rushed for the linen shelf of his bedroom and snatched up a towel to swab away the searing rainwater. The hot rain cooled against his skin. Fungle changed into fresh dry clothes and hung the wet ones in the larder doorway.

He turned to see something struggling beneath the rug in front of his fireplace.

'Blessums!' he exclaimed, and set a hand to his mouth.

The rug began punching up and down as if being beat by a broom from the bottom side up. Beneath it came a voice deep and guttural, gasping and hoarse: 'Curse ya fer an upreat mole,

Fungle Foxwit, ya've moved yer chairs back on yer fleabit carpet! Move 'em, I say, or I'll eat my way through and yer'll hafta get a nice new one ta make yer dingy place look even worse!' And what followed after, if language it was, was lost amid munching crunching gobbling sounds.

Fungle hurried to the honey-coloured rug and slid aside a willow chair. The rug was trembling now like the pelt of a nervous doe. Fungle folded back a corner to reveal two cone-fingered hands seeking purchase at the ends of thrashing arms that looked more like mummified roots than limbs.

A dirty, mottled head appeared. Its huge mouth blew out dirt to say, 'Whatcher standin' fer, ya ignoble gnole? Lend yer diggits!'

Fungle grabbed hold of the lichen- and moss-encrusted arms and pulled. From out the land of worm and root the earth gave birth slowly to a gnome, one Karbolic Earthcreep by name. He was a heavy, barrel-shaped creature huffing and puffing for all the world like an asthmatic kettle. He shook his inverted turnip-shaped head and opened his immense slit of lipless, toothless mouth. 'Thankee kindly,' he said in a voice like rolling boulders. Fungle waited patiently as Ka stamped and shook the loose dirt covering his body. That done, the gnome stepped onto Fungle's rug – which, by the way, was not fleabitten at all but always clean and well tended.

Ka surveyed the room with tiny black eyes set into a glum face whose features were sort of chewed-looking. The nostrils widened in his vast slab of a nose. One cone-fingered hand brushed absently at an earthworm wriggling on his large paunch. It was not clear if the gnome were clothed or naked, so mottled and cracked was his lichen-ridden, moss-pelted, clay-coloured skin – which is why gnoles in fun often referred to gnomes as 'the baked ones'.

Fungle kicked back the rug and moved the chair to its former position. He turned to the gnome with a severe look. 'Y'ever think ta knock on a body's door, Ka?' he asked.

Ka laid a thick finger against a cheek as he considered this. Finally he looked back to Fungle. 'Be stumped if I did!' he exclaimed, and with that the two hurried to exchange a backslapping handshaking embrace, elaborate and near to violent among the frail ropes of pale blue woodsmoke. Their wavering shadows wrestled on the wall. You'd always think it had been ages and not a week since Ka and Fungle had seen one another, and you'd always be right, too, because for fast friends near and dear, a week's as good as an age apart.

Fungle hurried to his comfortable kitchen to fix a brew for Ka:

a generous measure of wine mixed with a heaping spoonful of ash from the hearth until it resembled river mud. Fungle handed the `concoction (which he had privately dubbed a 'Muddle-Minder') to Ka, then hoisted his own mug – free of ashes, it should hastily be made clear.

'Ash the spirit!' Ka joked. He tossed back his head and upended the mug like a baby bird begging a dangling worm.

'Cheers,' Fungle muttered wryly, a little late but not unkindly.

'Ahh, thankee muchly,' said Ka, and wiped his enormous mouth with the back of a dirty arm, leaving a smear very like a drawn-on moustache. 'Long may yer chimney smoke, dear Fungle,' he blessed.

'Another?' offered Fungle.

Ka stared at his empty mug in surprise. 'Bless me – gone already!'

Fungle accepted the empty mug with a warm and knowing smile.

While Fungle prepared another mixture, the gnome looked around the spotless living-room. 'Ah, now it's the nice thing about havin' good friends as guesties that ya don't hafta be cleanin' and scrubbin' to make 'em feel t'home,' Ka observed.

In the kitchen, pouring, Fungle blushed and kept a smile to himself.

'I'm givin' apologies for being late,' continued Ka, ''specially after yer kindly invite. An' bless yer boots fer draggin' a body in.' Fungle glided into the living-room and handed Ka another fish-shaped mug of ash wine, which Ka accepted with a nod and a thirsty widening of his small black eyes. 'But on the way under here I ran into the fossilbones of an old beastie, y'see, and ya know how much I loves 'em. I tunnelled 'round it and got its shape and size, and turn me inside out if t'weren't bigger'n yer own house! Fish, I think it were. Now how d'ya suppose a beasty-fish got up in these here mountains long-ago times, Fungle?'

'These here mountains was under the sea long-ago times,' Fungle answered. 'Just like the mountains of me people's homeland're a home to the fishes nowatimes.'

'That's how it is?' Ka was plainly impressed. 'Well, cheers to ya, then' he said, and with that drained his ash wine in his usual single gulp. He wiped his mouth dirty with a smudged arm. 'Well, I brought along a bone in case yer stuck fer victuals.' Ka patted the mesh bag near his enormous paunch. 'Lessee now . . . Eh, where's me wits tonight?' He looked up in chagrin at Fungle watching in amusement. 'Musta dropped it knockin' about. Shame; they make a lishious soup.'

'No matter,' said Fungle, 'there's plenty here to keep ya from missin' a bone from a beastly dead beasty-fish. An' there's no need for apologisin' neither, bein's how Neema seems tardied by the storm.'

Ka belched. 'It's a storm afoot up topside, is it? Wondered what all that rumblin' was. Must be a great goodun.' He shook his head. 'How ya topsiders stand it I dunno. Storms and hails and snows and wind? Twistees and freezies and flashin' floods? Sunburns and frostbites and all manner of what-alls? No, thankee. Give me th' deep dark earth around my head, sez I. A body knows where he stands in the earth, Fungle, and that's a true-known fact.'

'In or on or over,' Fungle replied sagely, 'whatever be yer druther.'

'Said like a true sayer,' agreed Ka, 'So I'll talk no more about . . .' The sentence hung unfinished as Ka's huge nose sniffed the air.

Fungle could almost see the vap'rous filaments of stewed fruits, the fumy breath of broths and sumptuous smells and spicy steams twining to form a fragrant rope that entered the intimidating cavern of the gnome's nose.

'. . . grub?' finished Ka, his voice all small and childlike, filled with a comical kind of hope.

'Grub enough to feed a clan,' Fungle agreed, 'or maybe even yerself, bless the day. But you and me'll be goodlike gents and take our wine waitin' properfectly by the fire 'til the arrival of me other guest. That's bestest, I thinks.'

'Ah, Fungle, yer a villainous taunt to a hungry gnomebody,' Ka grumbled, 'but I could find room in me heart to forgive ya if yer victuals taste half so good as they smell.'

'It's yer heart that'll hafta find the room,' said Fungle, 'because after my victuals find yer vitals there'll be no room nowheres else.'

Ka threw back his head to laugh and was interrupted by a rumbling detonation that rattled every brick down the chimney. 'Blast, but that be close!' Ka exclaimed. 'Sounds like the devil's havin' at skittles up there.' His tone grew wheedling. 'Don't yer think me hole might be a better place fer us to –'

But Fungle laid a hand on his friend's arm. 'It's all right, Ka.'

Ka nodded doubtfully. Tiny mountain ranges formed where his brow furrowed. They were quiet a moment, listening to the fire's crackle warring with the storm outside.

When it had become evident to Ka that Fungle was plainly worried about his remaining guest, the gnome piped up, 'Owzabout a riddle then? I got me a coupla gooduns from the ol' chinwaggers over at Tobacco Inn.'

'Tobacco Inn!' Fungle grew stern. 'Have you nothin' better to do with yer time in the earth than squander it with such scoundrels as accumulate there? Like rot on old wet logs, they are, worse by far than . . . than . . .' He sputtered, unable to think of what Tobacco Inn's patrons might be worse than.

But Ka paid no attention, staring ceilingward. 'Now, give us a moment . . .' he said. A hard hand pensively stroked the crusted layers of his numerous chins. 'No, won't do,' he muttered. 'That one? Ah, no; not to a friend. Aha!' He slapped his thigh. 'Got it: what patch has no stitches?'

Fungle could hardly believe his ears, for this riddle was older than the fossil fish his friend had found earlier. But he appreciated the gnome's effort to ease his worries, so he pretended to ponder. 'A patch with no stitches?' he muttered.

'Give up?' snapped Ka, and before Fungle even had a chance to respond Ka bellowed the answer: 'A *cabbage patch*! Get it? Hooo!' And slapped his thigh again to acknowledge his own wit.

'Not fair,' Fungle sulked.

'Not fair?' asked Ka, blundering into Fungle's baited verbiage. 'What's not fair?'

'A bear's behind!' Fungle riposted, closing the net on Ka, and went into a fit of high-pitched, self-satisfied giggles.

'A bear's . . . be . . .?' The joke bloomed in him then, and he started to laugh – to *really* laugh, an awe-fulsome tremor that occupied his whole gnomebody, starting with a trembling in his great paunch that built like a volcano about to blow until it shot out his enormous mouth in gleeful gales to match the downdrenching torrent outside Fungle's house.

When he could speak again Ka said, 'A'right, here be a riddle that'll logger yer noggin'. What colours would yer paint the sun and the wind?'

Fungle frowned, serious, for all the world as if asked to remedy the crying of wind or calculate the angle of the seven stars of Pleiades using only his head and no paper. He stared into the fire and ventured, slowly, 'Well, the sun would be gold. But what colour to paint the wind?'

Ka could not hide a smirk, and Fungle knew that gold for the sun was wrong.

'The wind, mm, yes,' Fungle mused.

'Give up?' Ka asked hopefully. In truth he was a bit unnerved by the gnole's sudden deep concentration.

Fungle waved his hands for silence.

'Thinkin' cap ain't gonna help yer!' stated Ka.

The wind, the sun, the wind. He knew these things the way he knew his own name, the true one and the secret one. He of all creatures should know what colours to paint the sun and wind! Fungle felt flustered.

Finally he sighed. 'You win,' he said.

Ka chuckled his victory. 'The sun *rose* and the wind *blue*!'

Fungle groaned as Ka rocked in his seat like a giant, gleeful baby, and without standing the gnome performed a little jig for joy with his chubby little legs.

Still shaking his head, Fungle went to the kitchen to put the kettle on. The gnome's chortling followed him.

While putting tea-fixin's on a tray he wondered what to do about Neema. Try and fetch her, start without her? Putting away the food for another day was unthinkable; allowing an Equinox feast to go awasting went against Fungle's nature – in fact, it went against nature itself. This day marked the harvest season and the beginning of the gnoles' great squirrelling away to prepare for the long sleep of winter. The feast acknowledged this transition from fall's bounty to winter's lean, and gave thanks for the blessings of the earth's rich yield. Not to partake of that yield on the very day ya should be honouring it would be a slap in the face to fall and a cold omen to open winter. Though Fungle and Neema were not the best of friends, over the years her fondness for his father, Wisp, had at least caused them to make an effort to be gracious neighbours. She might not dream anxiously of the next time she would be at Fungle's, but neither would she snub him.

Weighing choices while waiting for the kettle's blather to become a scream, Fungle became aware that music – or something very like it, anyway – was drifting in from the living-room. Ka had fetched Fungle's dusty dulcimer from off the wall and was strumming it. The gnome was humming with each abrasive chord, trying with his gravel voice to harmonise with dissonance. Whether accidentally or by design, the moment the kettle began to wail, Ka's voice blended with it. The wail rose in pitch to an even cry, and Ka's voice went right along:

Ohhhhh-wooooo!

Fungle laughing lifted Ka's accompaniment off the stove. From the living-room crashed a chord.

> *Fungle, Fungle, all a-bungle,*
> *How's yer garden grow?*
> *It grows 'cause it's cravin' to,*
> *And that's all ya needs ta know!*

Fungle's laughter blew steam from off the water he poured into fine-wrought cups, one an owl, t'other a cat. He lowered rosehip teaballs to bleed into the water and carried tray and all into the living-room where Ka grinned smugly.

'Oh, bravo, really,' Fungle said dryly.

''Nother verse?' asked Ka.

Fungle handed Ka the handled cat, which gave steamy thoughts from off its kiln-fired head. 'Oh, I thinks another verse'd spoil how *special* the firstun was,' he said.

Ka beamed, then stopped abruptly. His expression slid toward the floor. 'Why, yer a curbludgeonly wit and only half a gnole, Fungle Foxwit, which ain't too much to start with!'

'That's may as be,' Fungle agreed, playing his teaball like a fishing bob in a clay-owl lake, 'but nothin's bungled up me ears.'

Not offended, Ka stretched up to put the dulcimer back in place. 'I'll have ya know that, put asides yer playin', I makes better music after beany meals!' He cracked his knuckles happily. 'Er, speakin' o' which, Fungle . . .'

'Say no more, m'friend,' said Fungle, for he had already made up his mind. 'Let's put ourselves 'round an Equinox feast!'

'Let's have at 'er, then,' Ka replied – from the dinner table where he sat a'ready, knife and fork in hand.

Ka's fingers fidgeted near his fat belly while Fungle offered a simple prayer for the food and the nature's plenty it represented. To Ka it went on longer than the seasons it was meant to thank, because the mage thanked the seasons, the seasonings, and the spirits of every ingredient – including those of the trees whose wood had become bowls and forks and even the dining table itself. But finally Fungle moved his hands in ancient patterns of blessing – and for the next hour all further conversation was held between knives and forks.

They gossiped among puddings and laughed among pies, barbed the oyster mushrooms and outwitted rhubarb rissoles. Vying among themselves they critiqued the steaming heaps of greens and smoky beanpots, talked up the turnip mash in tandem and conspired with the sweetcorn. On one side of the table parsleyed potatoes parleyed with persimmon pickles, while on the other fritters filibustered fiery brandied fruits.

At last the joyful chorus of tableware slowed to silence. Fungle and Ka regarded one another across the table – and suddenly began to laugh! It hurt, oh, how it hurt! – to belly laugh with stomachs stuffed tight as favourite fireside chairs, and neither could've said why, exactly, he was laughing. Perhaps because they had performed a bit of a miracle: between them they had taken a table full of food and shovelled it all inside themselves.

Ka looked down at his polished clean plate where a lone vegedible rested. He pointed at it sitting there like a tiny island, and he hooted while his other hand strayed to his straining belly. Slowly he lifted his fork to finish off the final bean.

'Don't, oh don't!' said Fungle, laughing still. 'It's the final drop that starts the flood!'

The fork paused in mid-descent. Fungle saw Ka envision all sorts of dambursting gastrognomic catastrophics, and mournfully the gnome lowered the fork. 'Shame to let it go to waste,' he said. This sparked off a fresh round of guffaws from Fungle.

When they had calmed they eased their plumpened personages from the table and staggered to the living-room, where they fell

heavily into armchairs to slump before the fire, belly to belly, like two dormice fat as butter. Ka didn't look like a gnome as much as he looked like a stomach with a gnome attached, and for his own part Fungle felt sure his chair fitted tighter than before. They sat in utter contented quiet for a while, letting their stomachs' growls debate the merits of the meal, while firefly sparks darted among columns of woodsmoke in the hearth. Normally gnomes are mortally frightened of fire, but Ka knew Fungle's hearth was perfectly safe.

Only when the edifice of logs had collapsed to embers did the two companions shake from their reverie. Fungle took advantage of the moment to refill their mugs with ale and set between them a plate of dried pumpkin seasoned with maple syrup. Silently he toasted Ka, then, kneeling, blew into the fire. Warmth rekindled, he sat again alongside the gnome, who staring into the fire had grown glum.

Ka's hand reached absently out to pilfer a piece of mapled pumpkin which he neatly tossed into the wrinkled cavern of his mouth. 'Ah, Fungle, I'll trade my tunnels for treehouses if ya've not outdone yourself a hundredfold. The taste o' that meal be a sight fer sore ears is all I'll say an' say no more.'

But Fungle saw the change that had come over his friend's face. His enormous mouth no longer creased in smile but hangdog drooped; his face now sullen and gone all pouchy below the small dark eyes seemed serious as a bear's nose at honey.

Fungle's brow beetled with concern. He was accustomed to Ka's changes in mood, for gnomes are gone all moody at a shift in the wind, and their hearts grow cloudy from a weather more of spirit than of sky. 'Tell us what's bogglin' yer noggin, old friend,' he asked gently.

Ka fidgeted a good deal, and occupied a fair amount of time rearranging more comfortably his augmented belly. But finally he spoke, and his tone was sharp. 'Fungle, I've bin bitin' me tongue all night – when I haven't been pushing victuals past it – but now me throat's well oiled and me pipes're all het up with yer good muddy ale, and yes I'll allow as somethin's botheratin' me. Somethin' of what you'd call yer personal nature, I'd add.'

From Ka this was unusual directness, and as Fungle studied the old gnome's face his black-jewel eyes flashed with momentary suspicion, for he wondered whether he wasn't being primed for some artful verbal riposte that would leave him pie-faced and spluttering. But his good guestie's brooding countenance betrayed no deviousness, and abandoning his wariness Fungle replied, 'Me ears be all pecurious, Ka, so git vocable about it.'

'You intendin' on leavin' the valley?' Ka asked bluntly. 'Packin' up home an' hearth and abandoning yer friends?' He spat the words like poison festered long within his heart.

The question pierced Fungle like a needle, and for a moment he could only grope through a rubble of confused thoughts. This, then, had been lurking here all night like a rat in a corner waiting for the household to put to bed. 'I'll be havin' to soon or late, Ka,' Fungle finally said. 'Me family's away going on two full moons now, and I've heard nothing from 'em since. An' then there's the likes o' this.' From a shelf he took down the metal container he'd found in the grass at sunset. 'I know you hanker fer such things, Ka, but finding 'em on my lawn puts hornets in me head.' He held the object out to Ka.

'Got a hundred or two a'ready,' the gnome muttered without much enthusiasm as he accepted the can from Fungle. 'Make nice cups if ya tear the tops off. Thankee.' He looked from the can to Fungle. 'It don't excuse yer takin' yer leave, though.'

Fungle sighed. 'We been over it a time or two a'ready, Ka.'

'And I don't like it better every time or two,' replied Ka. 'First it's Mugworts, then it's Tansys, then Moldywarps, all up an' gone, *poof!* like smoke. Then the Lightbornes light out, the Sneezleberrys sneak away, the Mugworts muddle off – even ol' Puddlefoot the hermit! 'Til all the gnole folks is gone, flappin' west in their rickety loonybirds.'

'Lunabirds,' Fungle corrected for the how many-eth time.

'Whatever,' said Ka; 'they's still off like so many geese fer the season. Only, geese come back.' He swung his head sadly. 'An' now yer gonna up and go all goosy on me, too, *poof!* I see it in yer eyes, and sad it is, too. You an' that witch over at Rumblelow Holler.'

'Witch?' asked Fungle, perplexed. 'What witch?'

'What witch! Why, yer absent guest is what witch. Neema Cleverbread – her what lives alone and consorts with spirits!'

Fungle considered this. Neema Cleverbread, a witch? The idea had a certain appropriateness, he had to admit. Still, this was Karbolic Earthcreep making these claims, so Fungle asked, 'Who says so?'

'Gossips at Tobacco Inn!' the gnome said emphatically.

'Oh, *oh*. Well, then, it's graved in stone, innit? Gossips at Tobacco Inn say Neema Cleverbread's a witch!' Fungle made a rude noise. 'I'd'a been set to believe ya, if ya hadn't told me where ya'd heard it.'

Ka squirmed like a worm revealed under a stone. He'd known bringing up Tobacco Inn would be a mistake; Fungle had volunteered his opinion of the smoke-filled beerocracy often enough. 'Certain troll,' Ka ventured, 'rests upon his oath he's seen yer Miss Cleverbread makin' devil signs up at the full moon's face.' He folded his arms in satisfaction.

'She ain't *my* Miss Cleverbread,' said Fungle, annoyed. 'An' if ever'one waved the moon hullo was on the devil's side, we'd all be–'

'Goblin I know,' Ka pressed on, 'says he's seen her gather up the mist o'er the meadows an' spin it into spirits with green lips.'

'So now ya pick flowers at the dawn and yer a conjurer!'

But Ka had momentum now and continued undaunted: 'She can harm folks by stickin' pins into a likeness made from beeswax.'

'Ha! Now I know yer all codswollop fer certain. If she be stickin' pins into likenesses fer mischief, you'd've felt a prick or six, I'm sure!'

Ka grinned slyly and his tone became all wily oil. 'Funny ya should mention that, 'cause of late me arthriticals been playin' up a bit. So there.' His tone honeyed. 'Anyoldhow,' he crooned, 'methinks you be sweet on her, Fungle.'

Fungle laughed. 'Sweet on her! Get bathed, ya sullied earth-creeper! I've had you here in my home fer dinner more times than I can count, and sure as eggs is eggs I'm not sweet on *you*!'

'Faith, an' I'm sure yer right, Fungle. We'll say no more about it.' But still the grin stayed plastered across his ugly mug.

Fungle gave a disgruntled grunt and collected Ka's mug to show he thought the matter closed. 'One last tincture to temper yer blood an' I'll send ya on yer way,' he said, and headed for the kitchen.

'Ale's for what ails me,' Ka called after him, his voice gone syrupy. 'But sugar's fer what ails you.' He shook his head and *tsk*ed. 'Shame ya don't get on better, considerin' she's the only female gnole fer three thousand miles or so . . .'

Fungle made no reply, but Ka saw the arrow find its mark. He felt a little badly now, irriteasing his friend so, and after the finest mealioreating feast of his life, too. Wanting to restore the good humour of earlier in the evening, Ka called out as his friend made mulled wine: 'Mandrake the ole mystick were by t'other night to tell me a rare an' jokular tale regardin' human beans.'

In the kitchen Fungle busied himself heating wine.

'"Oh, didee now?"' Ka replied to his own self, raising his voice and heightening its pitch to imitate Fungle. '"Then pray don't keep us waitin' fer a goodun, Ka!"'

The gnome craned to see if Fungle were paying attention.

'A'right then, sure I'll tell it!' Ka answered himself. 'Seems there's this human bean name of Enoch, y'see, an' he's just moved houses, so his pal Eli asks him 'ow he likes it. "Oh, the house's a treat," says Enoch, "but the fella next-door keeps chickens, lot of 'em – cocks an' 'ens in his back yard, y'know. 'Bout four in the mornin' every morn they starts a-crowin' and a-cacklin' to wake the dead, and I can't get to sleepin' after that racket starts."

'"Well," says 'is friend Eli, "that do be a problem, 'cause he's entitled to keep fowl."'

Ka peered to see if Fungle were deliberately ignoring him, or preoccupied with his own thoughts, or if the gnole simply couldn't hear him. 'Sometime later!' he continued, near shouting now, 'Eli asks Enoch if 'e's solved his problem yet! "That I have," says Enoch. "I bought 'em off 'im! Now I've got 'em in *my* garden, and they can keep *'im* awake!"'

Silence.

Ka slapped his knee. 'They can keep *'im* awake!' he repeated, and laughed most strenuously.

Fungle was staring up at the ceiling. 'Hark at that wind,' he said. 'Storm's getting even worse.' He turned to look at Ka, and the gnome felt foolish indeed, because what was on Fungle's mind wasn't chidings about sweeties or simple petulance. The gnole was deeply worried about Neema. For a gnole to miss an Equinox feast was a serious matter indeed, and no mere storm however strong would keep one away.

But Fungle felt certain this was no mere storm.

Ka stood up from his chair, feeling awkward. 'Tell ya what, then, Fungle,' he said, more brightly than he felt, 'I'll out an' have a look for 'er. She's probly fetched up under a tree to wait it out.'

'An' have you out there too?' asked Fungle. He shook his head. 'No need fer that.'

'Won't be out there at all,' insisted the gnome. 'Be *under* it, I will! Slidin' through soil easy as a fish through water, an' poppin' me head up from time to time an' findin' out what's what. Be back with 'er right as rain.' He frowned at Fungle's sharp look. 'Er, right as somethin', anyways.'

Fungle considered. Obviously he did not want another of his friends out wandering under strange weather.

'Look,' Ka pressed, 'I'll soon be up an' gone anyways, and you off to bed. May as well have a knock around when'm on me way, eh?'

Fungle nodded slowly, finding no fault with Ka's reasoning. He embraced Ka and blessed him warmly, and the gravity with which he did so awakened the first pinprick of alarm inside the gnome. But a promise is a deed, is what Ka'd been taught, and having said as much he was as good as on his way.

When they disengaged, old Ka without any further *adieu* flipped back the rug and crawled headfirst down the hole by which he'd arrived, leaving Fungle to tidy up after.

Fungle pinched out the candles and shuffled tired feet across the room. Anxious for bed he promised himself he'd wash dishes and close up Ka's hole tomorrow first thing.

What a day it had been. *A day of cusps*, he realised. *Today was a day between things. At one and the same time I stood between summer and fall, between day and night, between fair weather and brewing storm, between a time of growing and a time of storing away, between home and leaving. And, finally, the reason for that leave-taking: because at that very moment I also stood at the shrinking edge of my land and the growing edge of another: the land of humans, the Land of No.*

With a poker he scattered embers in the fireplace to die them off.

A noise up the chimney stopped his hand.

An eerie, lamenting moan prickled hair up his arm and across his back.

Something trapped up there, he thought. He remembered his brother's words: 'On that day when yer hearth falls sooty from the trod o' strangers o'erhead . . .'

Again the throat of the fireplace let out another mournful bay, and Fungle began to feel relieved because it was obviously the wind muttering in the flue, only that an' nothing –

Soot sprinkled down the chimney brick.

Fungle snatched back the poker and went tight as a rubber ball.

Scrabbling claws and a soft rustle.

Fungle realised he was gripping tight the poker and lowered it. He knew words more potent than any cold iron could ever be – if there was time to say them.

Without warning the hearth filled with a flapping black mass. Fungle drew a breath to chant, but the shrieking phantom leapt, smothering him in its sooty cloak. He staggered back and fell with a yell that let hot rough claws thrust into his mouth. Fungle tossed his head wildly. Around him blackness fluttered in shrieking confusion. He struggled with the claws that were digging at the soft flesh inside his mouth.

Fungle looked into its eyes. They loomed sun-bright and demonic above a snapping beak. Another talon gripped his tunic.

Enough! thought Fungle, and firmly gripped the beast and yanked. The claws pulled free. Fungle sat up and opened his mouth to utter a powerful spell, but hampered by soot the words that would burst the blackfeathered thing to pillowstuffing hitched in his throat.

In his hands he held a frightened owl.

'Blessums!' Relieved almost to tears he stroked and patted the soot-blackened bird there on his living-room floor, cooing and wooing until the panicked creature ceased its struggling and Fungle felt calmness and peace loosed throughout its limbs.

When he was sure the bird was unharmed, Fungle began to chuckle. Poor owl! It had sought shelter in the bole of a hollow old oak on the island, and found itself instead in a black sooty hell! For, like the entrance to his home, Fungle's chimney stack was artfully concealed. Poor, sooty owl! Claws unable to gain purchase on the soot-furred stack, it had sunk flapping into what, fortunately, were no more than hot ashes dying.

When he felt that the owl's fright had bled away, Fungle wiped soot from its singed feathers and bathed its scorched flesh clean. 'Yer not from aroun' here, I'll venture,' said Fungle. 'I'll wager I know ev'ry owl hereabouts. What's got ya far from home this wild night, eh?' He fed the owl a mush of cornbread and water and set the heavy bird on a shelf. 'Now, young un',' he said gently, filling his tone with sleepy urgings, 'you'll be doin' no more huntin' tonight.' With the back of a finger he stroked the owl's neckfeathers. 'Doze away the night, and come mornin' light I'll send you on yer way.'

By the time he stopped speaking, the owl's lids had drooped like shutters over its baleful eyes.

Fungle left the owl to slumber and surveyed the mess in his living-room. Now on top of plates and Ka's hole there was soot, as if black-flour bags had been snipped open and waved everywhichway.

Fungle sighed. Tomorrow, he thought. Tonight me mind's all full with other things than cleaning.

Fungle hastily washed and brushed for bed. In his bedroom he knelt and chanted a prayer in strange and complex grammar, the tongue of a land drowned long ago. He summoned forth a 'spell wall', a powerful fortification against perils of the night, material dangers and spiritual ones too. Long ago he had learned the spell from one of the rare and cherished books he had scavenged: *Proteckshuns and Wyrd Wards*. He traced ornate signs in the air as he chanted, and gradually the darkness in his room grew watery with light. A pale, shimmering mist seemed to emanate from within Fungle until he was enveloped in pale blue brightness pulsing outward in rings like those left by a leaping fish on a mirrored sheen of water. The blue glowing mist flowed up the walls of Fungle's room in rippling waves until it occupied the whole chamber.

Just before he sank into the uncharted territory of sleep, Fungle heard a distant scream. It razored the night from somewhere far beyond the valley, agonised and full of horror.

Fungle listened, quickening inside. He knew that night was a time of hunting and killing and eating, a time for ravenous fangs to snuff out tiny lives with nothing but a whimper or an abbreviated squeal followed by the splintering of bones.

Fungle also knew his land by night: every flutter of batwing and digging of mole and vole, every maul and screech-owl call, all the pants and pads and howls of the wild wood – but in all his days he'd never heard anything so fully savage as this unearthly terrified howl.

It was then that he remembered the sight of the soot falling down his chimney and thought of the old gnome saying:

> *If yer chimney falls with soot,*
> *Sure as hell old Nick's afoot.*

And this had been followed by the owl, to many an unlucky omen and death's own messenger. And in his very living-room!

But he'd set the wards to guard him safe through the geography of dreams, and with their light glowing softly about him Fungle's head finally eased on his pillow. His limbs wound into a fetal ball and he fell asleep. With him went a remnant of that awful scream.

Z Journey Without Distance

Darkness there was, by darkness hidden.

Fungle fell.

Shrouded in silence he plunged within a starless void. He could not tell if his eyes were open or shut. For all the void gave him he may have had no eyes. No limbs, no heart, no lungs. Only *Fungle*, and not even a container to hold him.

It seemed he heard voices, like screeching notes from a tortured violin, but without an anchor for his senses he could not be sure if the voices came from without or within. Yet he felt a sense of *Presence*, as if the entire void were merely a bottle of ink in the talon of some shadowy intelligence.

From beneath the foundation of the void, an impression of laughter.

Pale light resolved below him, brightening until two yellow orbs shone like growing suns. Fungle felt a giddy sense of acceleration.

Slit pupils pierced the suns to make them feral eyes.

Fungle willed his own eyes to close, but they would not. He fought to cover them, but his hands would not obey. He tried to turn his head away, but a soft voice spoke with quiet menace in his mind: 'You *will* see this.'

Behind the void, an impression of parasol wings unfolding.

Fungle felt frail and naked in a bubble universe that barely withheld a surrounding chaos that sought its collapse.

Around the slit-eyed suns the darkness thickened. It seethed with dull red light. It formed a face. A horrible looming mask dredged from the oldest primal fears of what dread beast might lie beyond a fire's life, beyond life's fire.

It *looked* at him, and the gaze was like a rasp across his heart.

Its left eye turned crystalline, crimson, with cunning facets that drank as much light as they reflected.

The right eye swirled and became a world, gauzed with air above sky-blue ocean and dun of land. Flecked with clouds spinning toward night, it was achingly beautiful and frighteningly delicate within the socket of the face of the void. Yearning tears brimmed in Fungle's eyes at the sight.

The crystal eye glowed.

The right eye smeared with ashen grey that shrouded the globe until it spun empty, cold, and dead. A wasteland.

Leather wings settled across the universe.

Glittering crystal and dead world gave way to yellow goat-slit eyes.

Below them the leering mouth opened to reveal fangs in mountainous array.

Fungle fell into the cavernous maw.

Sulphur breath blew hot across him.

Baphomet, whispered in his mind.

The mountains met as the mouth closed to swallow him.

The void returned.

Fungle fell –

– to land with a thump on his bedroom floor. He awoke with a harsh gasp. His heart hammered like an echo of the impact of his fall. He looked about in confusion, taking in the pulsing blue light of the protective ward saturating his room.

Directly overhead he saw a faint ripple in the pale-blue light. It lessened to nothing even as he watched.

Fungle held his hands before him. *Blez me, I'm shakin' like a yearling's first walk!* His hands went to his cheeks and came away damp. *What's this, then? Why, I'm leakin' like a goose, to boot!*

He looked about the quiet room. Stone jars stood as cool grey sentinels in the room's protective light, holding within them coffee ground from roast acorns, barberry lemonade, gingerspice. A rack above the bed held medicines: emerald-coloured vials containing tinctures and tonics enough to ease the pains of an entire town.

Shows me t'believe old gnomish superstitions, Fungle thought. *'Medicines above yer head'll draw the vapours while ya sleep abed' – heh! Me dreamin'-vapours tonight beez about as pleasant as a waspy up me nose.*

He shivered on the cool wood floor. *Night frights've turned me colder'n a tear in a toad's eyeball. Now match that!*

He gained his feet and rubbed a furry knot above his tailbone. *Fell out abed!* he thought in vague amazement. *Like a fuzzy li'l kit, out abed an' thump! – with nothin' inbetween.*

From off a hook shaped like a heron's beak he lifted his manifold robe and gathered it rustling about him. He wound the sash about his belly, still swelled with feasting, and left the breached sanctuary of his bedroom for the kitchen to brew a cuppa camomile tea to ease him back to sleep. *Fight vapours wi' vapours,* Wisp had taught him true.

Ah, me pa, he thought forlornly. *Where could ya be this beastly night?*

The visiting owl was asleep on its perch and fidgeting nervously. Absently Fungle blessed the nightflyer as he went by, and the agitated owl calmed and returned to sleep.

The kettle was shaped like a fat cat upon its back. With it filled and protesting on the lighted stove, Fungle patted his prominent belly and said, ''Ere's yer nightmares, y'ole gnole.' He chuckled softly.

The kettle began to mewl and Fungle lifted it off the flame. A sharp pang shot along his arm and he quickly set the kettle down. He wrung his arm to ease the cramps and spoke a charm to loosen muscles. His arms – in fact, his entire body, now that he took stock of the larder of his Self – felt worn as a one-year boot on its thousandth day. He was sore abused for certain, which was only to be expected, given all the strainin' an' strugglin' –

No, hold on; that's amiss. I did no more exercisin' tonight than cookin' and eatin'. It was in me dream *I couldn't move me arms and legs, or even shut me eyes.*

Yes, that's right. In the dream he'd been a kind of puppet, a soft shell called Fungle worn by a leathery fist. And Fungle had strained against the inner steel grip of the puppetmaster that had held him fast, but his exertions were all for nought . . .

And shave me with a rusty razor if me muscles aren't all cramped an' crimped a-cause of it! Which was all a-kilter, because even held fast in a dream he should have thrashed in bed! How could something that held him in a dream grip him in his bed as well? Even in the throes of a simple nightmare, the spell-ward he erected every night should have held him deep in the heart of safety. Like his simple chant around the little coracle boat, like the ward that fortified his oak door, the protective tapestry Fungle wove about himself at night worked by directing attention away from him. It was the strongest spell Fungle dared use without defeating the spell's purpose by calling attention to himself (for those there be who can locate spells like lighthouse beacons, if they've proper knowledge), and though the ward was effective, it was not infallible. Any body or thing determined enough to find him . . .

. . . would.

Fur prickled down Fungle's neck.

He remembered that ripple in the ward near the ceiling above his bed. Like the last trace of something splashing into water. Splashing in . . .

Or dropping out?

Fungle waved his hands as if to banish smoke. *Aw, this be nonsensical!* he thought. *A hunk o' mouldy cheese gives ya nighty-frights, and here yer findin' omenous portentions. Didn't yer own pa tell ya that shadows o' leaves at night ne'er form friendly faces a'cause yer mind ain't lookin' fer friendly faces at night? It's the same with yer sleepin'-vapours, Fungle. There's a storm afoot and friends adrift, and there's no point in making a dream-Saying out o' mouldy cheese!*

He nodded agreement with himself as he poured steaming water from his cat-shaped kettle into his fish-shaped mug. *There's all the vapours ya need, mate. Next ye'll be lookin' fer omens in the livin'-room mess!*

He smiled, sheltered by his surroundings, and thought how familiarity breeds content. Reassured, he carried his tea from the kitchen through the cold living-room on the way to the bedroom.

On the rug by the fireplace the soot where he'd wrestled with the frightened owl was spread in a rough five-pointed star.

Fungle frowned. *Now, that be most pekuliar!* Absently his finger bobbled the teaball like a lure in the fishmouth of his mug.

He looked to the owl on its perch. Cool blue light from Fungle's bedroom etched the bird's feathery features in deep relief. *Asleepin' now,* Fungle observed. *But Ol' Mr Owl sure were stark unsteady when ye came out yer bedroom all ashakin' and bestirred, now, weren't he?*

As if something had awakened it.

Before going back to his bedroom, Fungle took a last look around. Living-room dark and quiet, stone-grey ruin of logs in the fireplace a monument to the cheer it had given earlier.

For the first time in memory, a sliver of insecurity about his home edged into Fungle's mind. Never before had he searched the corners for skittering things, or caught himself listening for foreign sounds.

Fungle felt invaded.

This's me home! he thought angrily. *It looks out o'er all me valley, an' now a something's barged into me home and looked out through me!*

Fungle turned suddenly and looked at the owl. 'Something's

barged into me home . . .' he wondered aloud. He cocked his head speculatively, looking a bit owlish himself. 'Night-time's yer nest, Mr Owl,' he mused, 'and them eyes don't miss much. Have *you* been sendin' me bad dreams then?'

He approached the owl. Extended a finger. Lowered it. 'What've I let into me house?' he wondered.

The owl slept on.

Ah, well – can't rightly boot ya out on such a night just 'cause I fell out a' bed. But tomorra yer on yer way back to whatever tree ya call yer home, and leave me to my own, thankee kindly.

Bathed in the blue light of his bedroom once more he chanted to strengthen the wards. Sitting up in bed he drank his calming tea, gaze straying to the spot on the ceiling that had rippled.

The spot was directly above where he'd landed beside his bed.

'Well, Fungle ol' gnole,' he said out loud, 'yer no proper mage what ignores portents that beez plain as posted signs. Methinks first light'll see us crackin' books and holdin' a Sayin' fer Mister Dream.'

He looked up at the ceiling. 'An' anything what makes itself a guestie in me own home'll wipe its feet first on me mat – I'll make meself assured o' that!'

But his bravado rang hollow in his ears. It had, after all, been aimed at something that had penetrated his most secure defences and played him like a puppet.

After a tossing and turning while the strong tea began to have its soothing effect and Fungle went to sleep – though not so eagerly as before.

Brawlligerence

Karbolic Earthcreep tunnelled urgently under the lake toward Fungle's house, cursing every earthy inch of the way: *Oh, it's a foxy poxy Foxwit gnole what closes up me own fine holes after'm gone! Livin' in the middle o' the lake like he's an island all hisself – an' the only door in the whole place standin' smack out in daylight, too! All that roasty sunlight burnin' down fit to fry such a poor old gnome as me 'til'm gone all crispy 'round me edges. Ah, but it's a trial sometimes, keepin' friends!* And so forth, on and on as his mole-like claws scooped out earth at an impressive rate.

Like Fungle, Ka had learned to lay low in his underearthly wanderings, for in recent years those rumblings that attracted him were more likely to be the massive digging and pounding involved in laying the foundation for a new human building than they were the joyful tunnelling of fellow gnomes. Ka had not encountered another of his kind in many years, and whenever he felt deep rambunctious rumblings in the earth, he used to hurry to find their source. But every time he located them, the old gnome broke into a huge pit crawling with machines that dug, scooped, hauled, or pounded the earth – and Ka, looking out from his hasty tunnel, would feel the splinter of loneliness drive a little deeper within his heart.

The damp earth yielding before his scooping hands grew dryer as he progressed, meaning that he was now under the island and not the lake. His hard, conical fingers scraped rock and he detoured slightly. Surface dwellers find their way by landmarks – left at this old tree, right at the light, stop at the blue house. It's the same for gnomes, except their landmarks are the earth itself. Ka recognised tastes and smells and kinds of soil, roots and rocks and earthquake fractures. So when his hands encountered the taproot tip of a certain oak tree, he began to dig straight up. Soon he was cursing loudly in his gravel voice, for serve him up 'tween sandwichbread if that fleabit carpet weren't right back where it'd been last night!

Ka struggled his way into the living-room, and no Fungle there to help him this time. 'Fungle!' he called, looking about. The living-room was spotless – except where he'd come in, of course. You could eat off the floor if you'd a mind; Ka himself weren't partikuler. 'Fungle! Why, yer just a short an' hairy human bean, is what you are, an' stooped ta boot, iffin I come all this way to find you out an' about. *Fungle!*'

Ka jerked toward a sound: the door to Fungle's downstairs room swung inward. From below, a blue glow lit the doorway and the first few downleading steps. Ka frowned.

'So are ya comin' down?' rang from below. 'Or are ya a piece o' sculpture in me livin'-room?'

Ka glanced around. 'Heh! It'd lend an' air o' class about the place iffin I was,' he muttered as he headed toward the door. It shut behind him of its own accord and Ka stepped down a long and twisty flight of wooden steps. The blue glow of Fungle's protective ward brightened as Ka descended, and the loose dirt still dusting his gnomebody fair to crackled in the energy field. Fungle's magic made him uncomfortable and uneasy and all kinds of other un- words.

Round one last bend Ka came upon Fungle at his study, and he stopped.

The room was bathed in cool blue light. Thick roots twisted down from the ceiling like living stalactites, and wormed down the walls like veins. Books were everywhere abundant: staid in leather bindings on sturdy shelves, stacked in arching cantilevers on desk and table and floor, concertina-folded like literary fans, tightly rolled in silk-bowed scrolls like rare wines in diamond-shaped racks. Books on parchment bound with brittle leather, woodbacked books with hinges and tiny locks – even (Ka was delighted to observe) a curling paperback book of human manufacture. Long ago Ka had found the paperback when he bumped into it in a knot of buried trash (trash and treasure's one and the same to a gnome), and he'd promptly made a present of it to Fungle, knowing his old friend's love of books however obscure. Over the years Fungle had painstakingly collected the largest library any gnole had known since ancient times – nearly a hundred books. In addition to those priceless books he had inherited from Wily Barktea, he had begged, borrowed, and

bartered books from gnole clans scattered throughout the valley.
Those who would not part with their books he persuaded to allow
him to copy them in their own homes, lovingly lettering parchment
for hours on end.

Fungle hunched before an enormous carved desk supported by
a base of thick roots protruding from the wall like muscular folded
arms. The desk was made from willow, wisest of woods. Its edge was
carved with animal heads and gnole faces, intricate patterns and
symbols, and ancient angular runes. Fungle on a high stool peered
through wire-framed spectacles at an illuminated book upon the
desk. Opened, the book was half the gnole's size.

An owl perched on a root beside the desk. Ka eyed it warily.

'Karbolic Earthcreep,' said Fungle, not looking up from the
enormous ancient tome before him. 'Welcome to me Room of
Roots.'

'Thankee, Fungle,' began Ka, 'an' well met we are, fer I needs
to tell ya –'

But Fungle gestured him to silence, and Ka had to stand there
shifting from foot to foot, itching with news and watching as the
gnole looked upward as though trying very hard to remember
something. Fungle's brow furrowed and his lips moved silently.

Rememberisin' a spell, he is, thought Ka, and felt a bit intimidated.
It's one thing to know your dearest friend's a mage and a shaman –
spells and remedies light and white, mind you! – but it's something
again to see him in his secret chamber poring over books older than
the memory of Americka. Fungle? The roly-poly gnoly what heats
the most libatious ash wine this side o' the soil; Fungle Foxwit, a
sage an' a shaman?

Never good at being silent or still, Ka moved quietly about the
room, making clucking noises at the back of his throat, aware of the
intensity of Fungle's concentration at the desk. He stole a glance
at the book on the desk: the letters made no sense to him, and
the drawings – a flaming sword, a devilish face with a jewel set
in its forehead – gave him no great cheer. Of the dozen or so
books stacked along the desk, the titles Ka could read were *On
the Origine of Americkan Evil, The Mage's Booke of Gnolish Dreems,
Summonings and Banyshments*, and *Origine and Destrukshun of the
Atlantean Realm, with an Afterword on the Propertees of Certain
Kristals*.

Hmph. Heady stuff, that. Titles alone'd keep the covers closed,
in my book.

While Fungle was occupied, Ka approached the rack of scrolls.

Ka had an instinct for old things, and a love of them as well, and he knew upon seeing the stacked scrolls holding wound wisdom in their racks that these were among the oldest handmade items he'd ever encountered. Delighted, he reached to snatch one up.

He stopped. He frowned. He held his hand up before him and wandered away from the rack. Near the entrance to the Room of Roots he found himself scratching his head. *Here, now, what was I about . . .? Why, there's Fungle a-readin' at his desk! Busy, looks like. Well, I'll jess knock about the room 'til he's time enough fer me, then . . . Hello, what's this? Scrolls! Lovely ol' scrolls, old rolled scrolls, an' pluck me guts fer fiddlestrings if the rack itself ain't least as old as they are! Like to have me a look at one of 'em, I would. Sure Fungle wouldn't mind iffin I just . . .*

Near the entrance to the Room of Roots he found himself scratching his head. *Here, now, what was I about . . .? Why, there's Fungle at his desk, a-grinnin' away like I just let out with a goodun! Why, mebbe I did. Seems like I'd remember something like a goodun, though . . .*

Fungle's smile was gentle. When he spoke, his tired voice was amused, but not chiding. 'No use rummagin' among me scrolls,' he told the befuddled gnome. 'Ye'll only end up back on me steps scratchin' yer noggin' like y'are now.'

Ka snapped his fingers. '*That's* what I'm about!' he said triumphantly. 'Havin' a look at yer scrolls!' He frowned. 'Only . . . weren't I just . . .?'

Fungle grinned wearily and took pity on the poor, confused gnome. 'There's a spell about 'em, Ka,' he said. 'A spell o' forgetfulness. Whoe'er tries to touch 'em gets all brainscumbled an' forgets what he's after. Haven't y'ever gone to yer larder fer a bite and found yerself standin' there, scratchin' yer brains and wonderin' what in Creation you'd come in there for?'

'Got no larder,' confessed Ka.

'Well, trust me, it's the same feelin', all bound up to protect me bound-up books.'

Ka accepted this, though Fungle saw he did not quite understand it. The gnome stood nodding, and in a moment his attention began to wander and he was staring about the room again.

Fungle sighed. The bad side to his protective spell was that it made a body forget what he was on about in general, and not just as regards pokin' about a person's libr'y.

Fungle shut the enormous book and turned to face the baffled gnome. 'Any news, Ka?' he prodded gently.

'News ... ?'

'You went lookin' fer Neema, remember?'

'Gadzooks, Fungle; so I did!' And he fell to addlement once more.

'And?' Fungle was tired from many hours of concentrated studies, and felt exasperated with his friend, even though he knew it was his own fault for not setting his spells more precisely.

'An' what, Fungle?' asked Ka.

'An' what *news* of *Neema*!' Fungle fair to bellowed.

'Oh!' said Ka, remembering. 'Ah! Right! I remember now!' He snapped his fingers – then froze with a finger pointed ceilingward and mouth opened. Suddenly his expression grew alarmed. 'Giblins! That's what I came to tell ya! Giblins!'

'Oh, I smells 'em a'right,' said Fungle.

Gnole and gnome gnelt behind a bramble bush. Ahead of them was an outcropping of rock, half covered with ivy and lichen and vines.

Ka laid a crusty finger alongside his great proboscis. 'Tole ya! This nose is never steerin' me wrong afore. I could smell 'em 'thout havin' to step a foot inside!'

'If it's giblins been in Neema's house, a body could near smell 'em with his eyes,' said Fungle.

'I hear tell even skunkies run afrighted when they smells a giblin,' said Ka.

'I'd not argue it.' Fungle stood and hoisted his pack. 'Well, let's have a look, then,' he said.

Ka tugged at him, tiny eyes wide. 'You gone loony? Them's *giblins* in there!' He sniffed pointedly.

'So there's no point sneakin' up on 'em, is there?' asked Fungle. 'Stealthy or stompin', them lads'll come at ya full-tilt crazy no matter how you go about. May as well expect a fact to stay a fact and say a charm to help us act, eh?' And he strode toward the outcropping bold as a frog at a fly parade.

Ka gritted his jagged teeth. Showin' his dainty hide to the sun and risking bein' turned to stone were sacrifice enough without invitin' giblins to tie his guts in a bow around a rock and drop him in a lake just to hear the splash, thank you very much! Ka'd once seen an enraged giblin run full-out head-first against an apple tree, just because an apple had fallen on the creature's ugly head. *Probly hurt poor ol' Mister Tree more'n it did the giblin, too*, he reflected as he rose reluctantly to follow Fungle toward the hidden entrance to

Neema's cave. *An' I'd lay odds the tree beaned that bugger's noggin' on purpose, just to get him out o' there so its leaves could breathe!*

He held his hands above his head in a futile attempt to ward off the sun and hurried after Fungle. *Yer own fault it is, Karbolic Earthcreep,* he berated himself. *Yer dadder allus tole ya not ta dig in others' tunnels!*

Fungle stood before the vine-covered rock. Somewhere beneath the carpet of growth, he knew, lay the entrance to Neema's house. But it wouldn't do to go poking and prodding at it, not if – as Ka insisted – giblins waited inside.

He sniffed the air. Yes, there was a definite air of rot – like week-old tomatoes decaying in curdled milk left in the sun. If no giblins were about, they certainly had been. Fungle concentrated on the door, looking for tell-tale signs of entrance. A particularly bright red blossom caught his attention, and he found himself studying it in fascination, noting the delicate contour of its powdered petals, the soft segue of colours one into the other.

'Waitin' on an invite?' asked Ka beside him.

Fungle shook his head. What *was* he waiting on? His fingers drummed at his thigh. Hmmm . . . He stared at the grown-over outcropping again. Once more the bright blossom caught his eye. So pretty, so unlikely here among the lichen and vines . . .

'Fungle!' Ka's tight whisper brought him round.

'What?' Fungle replied dully.

'Ya been standin' there full-on five minutes!' the gnome groused. 'I coulda dug us in an' outta there by now, with time out fer lunch an' a game o' darts. Are we goin' in or admirin' the scenery?'

Fungle frowned. Admiring the scenery?

He turned to the outcropping. 'Well, skin me fer a coat!' he exclaimed. 'This entrance be spellbound! Whoe'er looks fer a way in finds hisself starin' at flowers like a bee in bloomin' love!'

Ka looked smug. 'Tole ya she's a witch,' he said.

Fungle nodded. 'Could be,' he said. 'But there's a way around a spellbound door for them that knows – as' easy as countin' flippers on a oliphaunt, too.'

Ka grinned. 'Knew I could count on yer, Fungle,' he said. He frowned. 'Only, what's an oily-phant?'

Fungle beckoned him to silence, thumbing mental pages for the appropriate spell. Ah, got it!

He found a fresh-dropped pine-cone on the ground and waved it slowly in a circle before the outcropping as he whispered:

'Friendly pine,
Friend o' mine,
Show an entrance
To a friend o' thine!'

A slight rustle came from the vines as they shifted, parting like curtains to reveal a bay door.

Fungle thanked the spirit of the pine-cone and laid it gently on rich soil under the sun where it could grow. And grow it did, over the course of many years, into an enormous father pine, solitary and strong, that would drop its cones upon a huge manicured lawn as all around men with iron rods whacked small white balls out over the crowded hills.

But that day was many years away. Right now, Fungle touched the door. The moment his fingers made contact, the stench of giblin sharpened like a razor slicing the inside of his nose. The stone yielded to Fungle's shaman hand a memory of having been forced open despite the protection of Neema's spell, for anything forced retains a trace of the offence.

Fungle prepared for the worst as he pushed on the edge of the patch of vines outlining the door. A section swung inward easy as you please. It was a stone doorway, cleverly fitted and balanced so that, though it weighed a ton or more, a child could push it open with one hand – if she knew the right place to push.

An almost tangible reek exuded from the small cave within. It smelled like a slaughterhouse filled with unwashed diapers, with a background hint of rotten eggs mixed with onion pulped right under yer nose. Delightful – to another giblin.

Without a backward glance Fungle stepped inside.

Behind him Ka hesitated – uncertain which was the more frightening prospect: confronting giblins or breathing their effluvium. *But Fungle's a'ready in there, and it's no good bein' at yer friend's back iffin his back's someplace else, and the nearsighted gnole'll probably need protectin' iffin there's brawlligerence a-brewin'.*

Ka took three deep breaths, held the last, and followed Fungle into the cave.

It was not at all dark inside the cave. In fact, it was surprisingly light and airy; windows in the rock were covered on the outside by cleverly arranged vines that functioned like blinds. The rich sunlight was tinted by the filtering greenery, but all the more homey for it.

Fungle and Ka stood tense and wary as they glanced around. There was no evidence of giblins present, but proof plenty that there had been – for not only did their stench hang in the air, but Neema Cleverbread's home was a shambles. Willow chairs were overturned, and a sofa lay on its side with stuffing spilled out like lifeblood (which stuffing is to a sofa, you know). Jars and vases from Neema's larder had been smashed open, and their contents lay strewn everywhere. Painstakingly embroidered curtains had been torn from the walls and shredded.

Fungle felt alarmed and angered.

'Here, 'ave a look at this,' Ka whispered tightly, trying not to breathe. From the wreckage on the floor he pulled the remains of a corn doll, a little figure made from straw and ears of dried corn.

Fungle shut his eyes and rested his fingers lightly against the doll. Instantly he felt the taut grammar of the spell around it. A simple, artful spell to help a garden grow. Fungle admired the artistry of the spell's simplicity, the way one writer might admire the elegance of another's prose.

Obviously there was more to Neema Cleverbread than met the eye.

'Ye've the keener snoot, Fungle,' said Ka. 'Can ya tell how long away they be?'

Fungle shut his eyes and breathed deep. The odour that assailed his nostrils was overwhelming, conjuring an image of writhing maggots in green meat. He fought the urge that gagged him and focused on the strength and concentrations of the reek. 'Half-twelve hours, I'd venture,' he said. 'Much less than that and we'd not be able to breathe in here so long as we have.'

'So who's breathin'?' Ka sputtered, peering around the violated home. 'What's to do, Fungle? Go after'm?'

Fungle nodded. 'Easy enough to track a giblin,' he said. 'What I can't figure's why they took 'er at all. You ever hear tell of giblins abductin' folks, Ka?'

The gnome shook his mottled head. 'They skins 'em and eats 'em then an' there, and tosses out what they don't eat,' he said. 'Which ain't much. Why, I once seen one o' them brigands take after a poor little –'

'That'll do, I think,' said Fungle. He narrowed his black eyes and glanced around. The deplorable mess hinted at what a well-kept and homey place this had been, and how much time and effort Neema Cleverbread had invested to turn a cold cave into a warm home.

''Ello!' said Ka. 'Here's 'at music-box I give li'l Peapod!' He held up a palm-sized box from which a flesh-coloured, thimble-shaped plug dangled on a cord.

'Froog didn't want 'im havin' it,' said Fungle. 'He musta give it to Neema afore they all lit out.' He touched the music-box, but all it gave him was a memory of a haunting, willowy music. Fungle had his own memories of the human-made box, longing memories of his nephew and his brother.

A clay jar lay broken among torn-backed books. Silver needles spilled across stamped titles: *Wycce Ways; The Book of Shadows; Growings, Exhortations and Charmes; Healings, Mendings and Restorations.*

Wycce, thought Fungle. *Wise-woman.* Well, some people thought it meant *witch* . . .

Ka's muttering brought him from his sudden funk. 'Daresay she useta ride this aroun' on Hallow's Eve,' the gnome was saying, holding up a broken-handled broom.

Fungle touched the wood and straw, and let loose a memory of the broom's blunt end poking toward a giblin's eye, of being snatched from friendly hands and broken across a bony knee.

Touching flayed curtains conjured images of being yanked from vine-covered windows and torn to strips wound tight around arms and legs.

'They tied her up,' Fungle finally said. 'Broke in an' tied her up an' carted her off.' He shook his head, baffled.

'Never hearda no giblins takin' prisoners,' said Ka, looking more anxious than ever to get back to the relative safety of his tunnels.

'Wouldn't bother lessen they wants somethin' from her,' said Fungle. 'Which means she's likely still alive.'

Ka brightened, 'Say, that's a goodly bit o' deducin', Fungle!' Then darkened again: 'Wonder what they wants with 'er,' he brooded.

Fungle shouldered his pack. 'Best we beez off to find out fer ourselves,' he said.

'Off?' The ugly face grew hopeful again. 'Now, that's a right good idear, Fungle. I'll pop in over to Tobacco Inn an' rouse up a good lot o' lads to lend us a –'

But Fungle was already opening the door. 'No time fer that,' he said. 'We got a piece o' work ahead of us.'

Ka hung back a moment, watching Fungle's silhouetted form hurrying away in the late afternoon light. '*We?*' he muttered despondently.

But he followed his friend out, leaving the word to hang in the rancid air.

*

When Ka caught up with Fungle, the gnole was sniffing the air. 'There goes our course,' said Fungle, pointing east.

In reply Ka pointed behind them at the sun, no more than its own diameter above the hills. 'There goes our light,' he said.

'*Our* light!' Fungle exclaimed. 'An' since when did *you* become a sun worshipper, Mr Gnome?'

'Since me former friend lost his former wits an' set out to let giblins turn him into giblets,' replied Ka.

'Piffle,' said Fungle.

They argued some more, heading east all the while.

Following the awful smell like a trail of crumbs, Fungle and Ka found the giblins' camp sometime near midnight. They crept among the shrubs and trees until they saw firelight, then circled until they were directly downwind of the giblins' camp (tactically smart but olfactorally smarting). Slowly they edged closer until they had a clear view.

Four giblins sat on their bedrolls round a small fire. They were ugly even for giblins, which is about as ugly as a thing can get without having been dead for a long while. One giblin had a wide warty head with bulging eyes and looked like a toad. Across his knees was a well-made club of light wood with human letters engraved into the shaft. The second was a hunched-over sort, with a leering face and spines along his back like a porcupine. On a thong around his neck he wore a disk that refracted the firelight in rainbow colours. The third lifted a shiny coffee-pot of human manufacture with a ragged-gloved hand and poured thick black coffee into a metal cup which he lifted toward his long, narrow, ratlike snout. He passed the coffee-pot to the fourth giblin, whose crow-like face split with a greedy grin as he manoeuvred the coffee-pot beneath his beakish nose to pour directly down his gullet.

'Ahh! 'At'll poach me eggs, it will, it will,' said Crow, setting the pot back on the fire.

'Not hot 'r strong enough, y'ask me,' grumbled Porcupine.

'Didn't,' replied Crow, and grinned as Frog and Rat chortled.

Toad reached behind himself and produced a colourfully labelled bottle. He bit off the cap and spat it beside the fire, where it rolled against the white-picked bones of small forest animals. The bottle-cap had not stopped moving before Toad had drained the bottle and swabbed its frothy insides dry with his long thin tongue.

'Hey-hey-hey,' said Crow, half rising off his bedroll. 'You been 'oldin' out on us!'

''Ave not,' Toad replied. 'Y'drank yer share a'ready.' He belched loudly.

'Goodun,' observed Rat. He pulled off his gloves to warm his hands by the fire.

'Thankee,' said Toad. He bit the neck off the empty bottle and began crunching contentedly.

'Iffin I drank me share a'ready,' Crow demanded suspiciously, 'how's come I don' remember doin' it?'

Toad swallowed. 'Fact you don't remember,' he said philosophically, 'is proof 'ow much y'drank.'

Porcupine and Rat giggled behind their hands while Crow gave this serious consideration.

'M starvin',' said Toad, changing the subject.

'Ya just et!' said Porcupine.

Toad gestured at the tiny bones by the fire. 'That ain't eatin'.' He held up the remains of his beer bottle. 'Neither's this.' His look grew sly. He glanced left and right as if checking for eavesdroppers, and leaned closer to the others. 'Don't see why we can't divvy up that plump little gnolie now,' he said conspiratorially. 'I hear they's good eatin'.'

'They is,' said Rat. He began unlacing his crêpe-soled hiking boots. 'But we's s'posed to bring 'em back to Vixen so's she can call up the Old Codger, an' bring 'em live an' whole.' He pulled off the boots and set them near the fire. You could almost see waves of odour emanating from his feet; even the flames seemed to lean away as he wriggled his toes.

'He only wants one of 'em,' argued Toad. 'We could find another.'

'What if he wants this one?' countered Porcupine. 'You saw all them magick books an' spellers at her place. She could be what the Old Codger's lookin' fer.' He toyed with the refractive disk depending from his neck. It glinted firelight like a peculiar signal mirror sending rainbow patterns.

'I'll tell you true,' said Crow. 'I'd not lose me hide over me belly's rumblins.'

Toad frowned, pondering. Suddenly he perked up. 'How 'bout just a leg then?' he asked hopefully. 'A piece fer the li'l giblets back home, eh?'

Beneath Toad the bedroll wriggled like a giant inchworm. Toad casually picked up his club and slapped it against the bedroll. 'You best stop yer muckin' about,' he warned, 'or I'll raise a knot on yer noggin so big, yer head'll look like a knot beside it!'

The bedroll grew still.

Fungle and Ka looked at each other, aghast. Neema was wound up in the bedroll!

Fungle gestured a retreat from the giblins' camp, and they crept away.

'It's you an' me, Ka,' whispered Fungle. 'We've got to get her outta there.'

'Four o' them an' two of us,' the gnome complained. 'Don't much like the odds.'

'Nothing to be done about it,' said Fungle, 'since four's all they got!'

The gnome threw back his head to hoot at Fungle's foxy wit, but the gnole clamped a hand around his friend's mouth. Ka nodded and the hand came away.

Fungle shrugged off his pack and began rummaging inside. 'Here now,' complained Ka, 'if ye've a boojum fer every occasion in yer sack, why dontcha just pull out a big ol' hole and set it fer yon giblins to fall in?'

'Because if I carried a big enough hole in me pack,' Fungle replied reasonably, 'me pack an' meself'd fall into it first.'

Ka was not sure if Fungle were having him on. He narrowed his tiny eyes. 'If ye've a plan, Fungle Foxwit,' he said, 'you be tellin' it to me now, y'hear? A friend's more inclined to fight at yer back if he don't trip over no surprises.'

Fungle nodded. 'True as water's wet,' he said. 'But ya've backed me into a corner, Ka, fer I confess I've no plan at all. A bloke finds solutions with the things he's got.' He grew thoughtful. 'An' with what his adversary's got, come t'think of it.' This cheered him somewhat, and he leaned toward Ka to whisper, 'An' here's what they've got . . .'

Crow kept trying to trade one of his human-made cigarettes for one of Toad's beers, but Toad would have none of it. He bit off another bottle-cap and spat it to ring beside several others. 'Nails in yer coffin, them things are,' Toad said self-righteously. 'I'll have nuffin' to do with 'em.' He drained his beer and bit off the neck.

'I'll take one,' said Rat.

Crow bared his long teeth. 'You do an' you'll be scratchin' yer tail with hooks instead o' hands.'

'Oh I will, will I?' Rat stood and brandished a rusted machete.

Crow stood across from him. 'Yes, ya will!' He pulled a black handle from his belt and shook it, and suddenly it was a switchblade.

'Gents, gents!' hollered Toad, struggling stark unsteady to his feet. 'Let's settle this jabberment right and square!' He grinned, bulging eyes bright in the firelight, and rubbed his hands greedily. 'What say we resolve our differences like civilised folk over a delicious leg o' gnole?'

Just then an eerie cry arose from the woods.

The giblins whirled as one, all business now and bickering forgotten. Say what you may against giblins, they are nothing if not professional.

'Whassat?' whispered Porcupine, whose hearing was the worst of the four. In his hands was a Wham-O Wrist Rocket slingshot with a half-inch steel ball already fitted into the leather cup attached to rubber surgical tubing.

'Sounded like spooks to me,' said Rat.

'Pffh!' Crow sneered. 'Never met a spook I didn't make meself,' he boasted.

The unearthly wail rose again.

Behind them, around the campfire, objects began to move. The coffee-pot lifted itself head-high and turned its stem like a nose toward the giblins. Two bottle-caps floated in front of it like eyes. The ragged groundsheet lifted to wrap cowl-like below the coffee-pot. The gloves and boots Rat had removed glided into place as hands and feet for the eerie figure.

As the ghostly wails from the woods held the attention of the four giblins, the disjointed figure began to move toward them.

'*Oooog! Ah-wooooo!*' In the woods, Ka hooted and cried a frightful caterwaul. From the clearing he could hear the giblins' voices:
  '*Whassat?*'
  '*Sounded like spooks to me.*'
  '*Pffh! Never met a spook I didn't make meself.*'
Ka grinned at his own performance. He peeked out from behind a bush to see if all were going according to plan. Sure enough, there was Fungle, sneaking toward the campfire behind the distracted giblins. His face was tight with concentration as he maintained the 'willwalking' spell that animated the hodgepodge figure even now approaching the giblins.

Ka threw back his head to howl again. '*Ah-wooooh! Ah-wo – glk!*' His throat rasped and he began to cough.

From the clearing came the giblins' voices:
  '*Iffat's a spook, it's got a cold!*'
  '*'At's no spook, ya lummox! Whatcha think, Buford?*'
  '*Sounds like a gnome ta me!*'
'Yipe,' said Ka, and he began to dig.

Rat, Porcupine, Toad, and Crow confronted the darkness beyond the clearing's edge. Behind them Fungle untied the bedroll that held Neema, while unnoticed beside the giblins stood the hodgepodge figure, steam rising from its inquisitive nose as it regarded them blankly with bottle-cap eyes.

Crow hefted his shake-knife. 'I think I'll go an' have a look,' he said. He glanced to his right at the figure beside him. 'You mind the camp while I – *gaaah!*'

For the hodgepodge was in their midst.

The gibbering giblins scattered. Porcupine aimed his slingshot at the invader, stretched back, and let fly. The steel ball punched through the groundsheet and hissed into the forehead of Porcupine's friend Toad.

Toad looked mildly vexed. He lowered his baseball bat and brought a hand to his head. 'Well,' he said matter-of-factly, then crumpled like a sling-shot giblin – which in fact he was.

Rat confronted the hodgepodge spectre with his machete held high. The figure came toward him and Rat swung. The machete sliced the pot below the spout and hot coffee bled on him. 'Got him!' hollered Rat. 'Got him, got him!'

'You idjit!' snarled Crow. He stepped past Rat and snatched up the sheet. 'It's a coffee-pot!' He saw motion out of the corner of his eye and turned to see Fungle helping Neema out of the bedroll. '*Gnoles!*' he bellowed. '*Gnoles!*'

But the others had run away.

The hodgepodge collapsed into a heap as Fungle's concentration was broken. Fungle and Neema ran – but Neema had been bound in a bedroll the entire day and moved with great difficulty. Fungle glanced back.

Crow ran toward them, waving a thirty-two-inch Louisville Slugger bat appropriated from the recumbent Toad. His fur was up and his black eyes were wide. He was mad, bad, and as dangerous to know as a bee in a broiler.

Fungle urged Neema along. If they could make the wood they could hide. Gnoles are particularly good at hiding. Only twenty or thirty paces and they'd be among the thick growth.

From the pounding footfalls nearing behind them, they weren't going to make it.

A spell, a word, a charm, a rock to throw – anything! But the effort of the willwalking and the distraction of running and helping Neema muddled his concentration.

Fungle glanced back.

Three paces behind them, Crow swung the bat.

Then he dropped.

And kept dropping.

Fungle halted, and he and Neema hurried toward the hole the giblin had fallen into. Below them, experimentally hefting the bat, reclined Ka. 'Right good noggin-knocker, this is,' the gnome observed.

There was no sign of the giblin.

There was a moment of quiet – then Fungle and Neema began to laugh. They laughed until they had to sit down, and laughed some more upon the ground. When finally Fungle could speak again, he gave a hand up to his friend Ka. 'It appears,' said Fungle, 'ya brought yer own holes with yer!'

Ka grinned. 'A hole's where me heart is,' he said, which only set the gnoles to laughing harder.

 ## *Laden Vessels*

The good cheer of Neema and Ka at their belated feast in the dining-room high above was cold comfort to Fungle as he brooded down in his Room of Roots. Certainly he was happy at Neema's safe return. But after they had all trudged back to Fungle's home by the greying of dawn, then slept the whole day through, Fungle had awakened with many niggling questions nibbling at him.

This evening Neema performed culinary saucery over the leftovers of last night's feast, and she and Ka had sat to stuff themselves. 'I ate fer ya last night,' Ka explained, 'so it ain't like ya missed yer feast.'

'An' I suppose tonight yer eatin' fer *you*?' Neema wanted to know.

Ka had looked puzzled. 'Well . . . yer here now!' he'd replied.

Fungle had not joined them. Pleading pressing duties and apologising profusely, he insisted that they make his home their own.

So here he sat at his wise-willow desk, oblivious to the slender threads of music reaching down from his guests in the living-room above, pondering the events of the last twenty-four hours:

An unnatural storm.

An invading nightmare.

An omenous owl.

Giblins abducting Neema.

Any one of these happenings would have been remarkable by itself. But all four, occurring within hours of each other, spoke to Fungle of design.

But if design it was, it was too large or obscure for him to perceive. He needed to step away in order to observe the big picture.

He needed advice – sage advice. And who better to provide it than a sage?

He needed Molom.

Not one to deliberate after a decision is made, Fungle began to act. First he dimmed the mage-light throughout the room, reducing it to a single halo illuminating his desk to make it an island of concentration. Next he retrieved an ancient leather book from the shelf that had vexed Ka yesterday. The ward Fungle had set to protect the invaluable books had no effect on Fungle as he carefully slid the book from its place and brought it with great dignity to his carved desk.

Fungle placed his palms against the cover. He shut his eyes and concentrated on his breathing to clear his mind of stray thoughts and distractions. Not until he felt as if his attention were a clean canvas upon which to paint did Fungle reverently opened the book.

This was a *grimoire*, a book of spells. Its language and its lore were long lost to the world, drowned beneath Atlantic waves millennia before the Romans had begun to conjugate their verbs-to-be. Its archaic runes had been lettered by a hand now dust, upon vellum from an animal vanished from the earth, prepared with special rites and acts of devotion.

There were spells for protecting possessions and divining the length of a person's life; spells for finding objects lost in childhood and for losing objects that persisted through adulthood; and spells so volatile that to even describe them would be to effect them, so we must regretfully refrain.

Among the many kinds of spells were Summonings.

Among the Summonings was one that called forth Molom from the vasty deep. Not only was Molom the entity most likely to be helpful to him, but Fungle had a clue or two that the Elemental spirit had had a hand in at least some of the goings-on of late. The forest creatures revered Molom, who as Lord of Trees and Spirit of the Wood was their protector. Molom was said to have owls as his messengers and could read the travellers' tales spun by the roaming wind.

Before he studied the words of the Summoning itself, Fungle scrutinised the precise instructions. Tonight was the harvest moon, and that was good. Yes . . . Unsullied water was easy enough (though not as easy as it once had been!). Twelve acorns with ash from a fire burned in good-will, mixed with lime and bound in a bag of wholecloth. Well, acorns was easy enough, and Fungle's hearth burned with nothing but good-will. Lime? Seemed there was a sack of lime in his gardening closet where he kept seed and loam . . .

He turned his attention to the Summoning itself. More than merely the words had to be recited properly. Every inflection of every syllable, and even the length of silences between phrases, had to be performed perfectly, lest Fungle accidentally open the door of the earth upon a savage world – literally – of chaos and horror. Not only that, but his performance of the Summoning had to be utterly sincere, for to invoke the spirit of an Elemental with the emotional depth of a bored schoolchild reciting a monotonous poem would be to invite the wrath of the Elemental upon him. The passion behind the words was every bit as important as the words themselves – which is true of all things in the slippery world of words.

Fungle closed the *grimoire*, and resting one palm on it and the other upon the willow desk he thanked it for its wisdom before returning it gently to its place on the spell-protected shelf.

'Fungle!' Ka exclaimed. ''Bout time ya came up from yer gnole hole! Yer gonna turn into a gnome down there if y'ain't careful!' He slapped his knee and hooted. 'Now 'ow 'bout let's you an' me have a go at a jig, eh?' Ka jumped up and grabbed Fungle's arms as he appeared rubbing his eyes at the top of the stairwell.

Fungle stood still as the gnome began to jump and kick and dance before him. 'C'mon!' called Ka, looking around the room. 'Where's music, now?'

There was no music and Fungle would not dance.

The jollies fell from Ka's face. His final jump left his feet nailed to the floor and his sharp-fingered hands on his wide hips. His broad, lipless mouth formed a tight line. He let a long, exasperated breath out his nose. 'What's on with yer, Fungle? All serious-like an' melancholeric ever' day now, seems to me. Useta be a body got all merry an' inspired just bein' in yer company.' He stared at his sharp-nailed feet. 'Bloody depressin', it is.'

'Ka.' Neema's calm voice came from the kitchen.

The gnome looked at her, a bit chagrined, like a child caught with a hand in the sweetbin. 'Well, 'm speakin' fer us all, or so's I thought,' he said defensively.

'Leave him be, Ka,' said Neema, looking not at Ka but at Fungle. Ever since arriving at Fungle's house Neema had been a bit reticent – not ungrateful, Fungle thought, but perhaps a bit embarrassed at having needed to be rescued.

She held out a gunnysack. 'I put this together fer ya,' she said.

He accepted it from her and peered inside. A flask of water and a drawstring bag holding a dozen acorns, ash, and lime.

Fungle looked at Neema in gratitude and surprise.

She held out another cloth bundle tied with a red ribbon. 'Bit o' acorn bread,' she explained. 'Nothin' special, really.'

Fungle took the warm bundle and placed it in his pack. His look told her it was special indeed. 'Neema,' he began, 'how'd ya know what . . .? That is to say . . .' Except he didn't say, for sometimes around Neema his tongue got all fumble-fingered and his fingers got all tongue-tied.

'Don't have to know a body's business,' Neema said. 'Just got to know their needs.' Something in her tone told Fungle that this was all the explanation he'd receive.

'Be back late in the night,' Fungle told them. 'So no use waitin' up. Time bein', I beg you all keep inside until I know more of what's afoot in our valley. An' me larder an' bath an' linen's no good lessens they're used, so don't have a thought about 'em.' He headed for the ladder that led to the tree-stump door.

With a foot upon the first rung he paused. 'Neema, Ka,' he said, making a sign as he spoke each name. 'Me blessin's on ya both, an' keep ya safe here in me heart an' home.' And before they could respond he scurried up the ladder and emerged onto the dungeon-dark forest of his island.

Harvest moon was one of Fungle's favourite times. He knew that moonlight was reflected sunlight, but this kind of knowledge did not diminish its power to him. Indeed, it added to it, for the sun's gold healed and smoothed, while the moon's silver sharpened and transformed. So far away, the moon performed a special alchemy: transmuting gold into silver. As the sun drew the plants from out the earth, so the moon swelled the waves of the seas.

The full moon's light turned the valley into an underwater kingdom. Waving branches became undulating sea-fronds, bushes huge anemones. Shadows sharpened and quicksilvered animals slipped like mercurial fish among tiger stripes of light and dark.

Fungle set out through the monochromatic landscape of his island. In patches of sky between arching trees he glimpsed the grinning face of the Gnole in the Moon, always a cheering sight. In fact, it would be difficult to say whose face mirrored whose as Fungle smiled up at the harvest moon beaming down.

The wood was a patchwork of indigo and molten silver.

Guided not by trails or even senses so much as by a deep and instinctive knowledge of the island, Fungle soon emerged into a clearing.

Against the riot of shadows stood Old Man Tree – the stark skeleton of a withered oak, bereft of bark or even fungi. Tortured limbs spindleshanked from its ruined bole to divide and divide again into disfigured fingers of branches vainly clawing at the distant stars as if making a last desperate clutch at light and life. From topmost twig to shank of root the tree was scarred and marred from a lightning bolt – stroke of death for a tree, and a signature of magical potency shunned by bird and bat, wasp and caterpillar. Nothing would settle upon its deadened wood.

Old Man Tree stood unique in the lush and vital forest, and Fungle loved him dearly. Any tree was a bridge connecting earth and sky, but in Old Man Tree all four elements converged. Solid in the earth his branches grabbed the air, while his trunk devastated by lightning anchored far-spreading roots that probed the lake that ringed the island. Earth, air, fire and water: all were met in this ancient being.

Fungle set his pack near the twisted roots of the old oak. He cleared dead leaves and branches from the ground around the tree, then sat crosslegged upon the bare earth with his back against the crumbling flesh of Old Man Tree and made a simple supper of Neema's acorn bread. To all appearances he was a lone picnicker, enjoying the modest pleasure of a plain meal in the out-of-doors. And that he was, yet – as with many things concerning Fungle – there was more than met the eye. As he ate contentedly he emptied his mind of distractions and let the earth around him saturate the smoothed-over spaces. It was very much like the clear state he attained when studying the *grimoire* in his Room of Roots. Soon there was nothing but the night and Fungle, moonlight and Old Man Tree.

He finished the delicious acorn bread and sent a silent blessing to Neema. Carefully he folded the cloth that had contained it and placed it in his bag. Before attending to his preparations, Fungle allowed himself a moment to simply be aware of himself alive against the wondrous ruin of this old, old tree.

The world is so beautiful, he thought *and time so slow.*

It was a moment he never forgot, and never shared. It was his.

Then it was time to begin.

Karbolic Earthcreep surfaced among nettles, scattering spiders from their filament wheels. He pulled cobwebs and fly husks from his face, shook dirt from his head, and glanced around. He was near the top of a moonlit knoll. In the near distance was that creepy ol' tree, and in front of it stood a moonlit gnole. Ka kept low and made sure he was downwind. Wouldn't do at all to set Fungle's gnose a-twitchin'. Ka could see a good deal farther than that myopic gnole, but Fungle could smell morning breath on a mosquito.

What he saw was Fungle sowing acorns around the base of the dead oak, intoning words Ka couldn't hear. When the seeds were gone Fungle opened a bag and began to scatter birdlime with his bare hands, and when that was gone he sprinkled water from a flask, murmuring all the while.

Ka were perplexed a-plenty. Fretiful and worried 'bout Fungle, he was. Plantin' by the full moon's sensical enough, but leavin' behind good cheer and what few friends remain to ya in order to do it – not even askin' 'em to lend a hand an' their good feeling to speed the seeds on their way – that simply addled Ka. Fungle's too much alone nowatimes, Ka thought, to take friends so lightly. I should know, bein' alone so much myself. Ya'd not catch me gardenin' dead trees 'neath the moon when there's friendly fingers pickin' lovely music in me livin'-room!

Now Fungle was drawing on the damp soil with a dead stick fallen from the oak tree like a fingerbone from a skeleton.

Ka shook his head. *Right sad it is*, he thought.

Fungle stands before the tree. Barefoot, his toes like roots taste clean wet upon the ground. Curled, his fingers like branches reach toward the moon. Smooth, his fur like bark is caressed by nourishing air. His roots are in earth fed by water; his skin against wind drinks air. Tree and Fungle, Fungle and tree, flesh with leaf and time transfixed. Sap of blood flows sluggish in the veins of wood in his body.

He raises outstretched twigs of hands and chants:

> *'Molom, Molom, Father of Trees,*
> *Watchman of the Wind,*
> *Mouth of the Wind,*
> *Mind of the Wind,*
> *Open thee mine eyes*
> *That I may see thee, Molom,*
> *Proceed here from thy hidden retreat.*

'Rise up, BAALEMOLOM
BAALEMOLOM, rise up!
Thee I invoke: Spirit of Sunset,
Angel of Wind, Ancient One,
Thee I invoke.'

The full moon haloes Old Man Tree.

The breeze dies.

The pounding surf in Fungle's ears is slow sap blood coursing in his veins.

The beats of his heart grow further apart.

He tastes the metal fear that tempers the moment before a sweet descent. At the edge of knowledge tremble titanic forces that with the slightest quiver of reality's foundations will consume him. To erect this slender rampart into that other plane he must contain the seed of panic planted deep within him.

He is wood and stone.

Before him hangs a luna moth, lazy wings oaring the air, slowing until the moth hangs high and still like an ancient insect caught in amber. Sluggishly the dustwings lower like drowsy lids to push the moth another inch through thickened air.

Fungle's heart beats once.

Around him moonlight brightens nova-white to bleach the scenery bone pale. In this harsh exposure the landscape evaporates as time decays: leaves suck into twigs suck into branches suck into trees thin to saplings shrink to acorns, cones, seeds. Candlefly hides in cocoon to escape as incognito worm. Vibrant blossoms shrivel, collapse, shut tight, and retreat into diminishing stems.

His heart beats once again.

The stars are black holes in the glowing air. The constellations regress to patterns never named, starlight more ancient than eyes of man or gnole. Comets arc backward round the sun with tails preceding. Thickening galaxies rush together in the universe's implosive contraction.

The brightening moon descends. Its pockmarked face grows smooth and silver as it spreads to fill the sky until every crevice of Fungle's brain is ablaze with brilliant light.

His heartbeat pauses.

The universe is a void of white moonlight.

Black lightning cracks the sky. All around him shreds and rains away to reveal an unadorned landscape upon which Fungle sits – a green grass clearing that simply . . . ends. The horizon is a hundred feet off in every direction, where the earth sheers away to endless white void. There is no wind. No song of bird, no cry of animal or insect hum. Only this small stage of grass like a featureless terrarium lidded shut by the swollen face of the moon.

Fungle waits.

Ka didn't quite know what to do. Fungle was talkin' to a bloody tree! The little gnole stood in the clearing below him, hands outstretched, chanting rhythmically.

Ka began to pace fretfully, back and forth upon the small hill, no longer caring whether or not Fungle saw him. What to do, what to do? Fungle's lost all the nuts from his noggin'!

Ka and Fungle went back quite a ways together. Gnole and gnome were about as different as two creatures could be, but between them they had forged a friendship no amount of difference could breach. They accepted one another's quirks without question – for Ka were fair certain he had near as many quirks as Fungle did. Ka knew Fungle communed with the spirits of trees – with spirits of every other thing in the valley, for that matter. He'd seen Fungle at his spells and potions – even been helped by a few, come to think of it. But this drawin' in the dirt by full moon's light an' lettin' off old poetry to dead trees were a bit much! It be the kinda murky malarky the juggins mouth off down at Tobacco Inn, the kind that – when it concerns a friend, leastways – makes a body laugh fair to screamin'. Yet here be Fungle, before Ka's very own two eyes . . .

Only, Fungle wasn't.

Ka stopped in his pacing-tracks. Where the clearing had been below him was now a perfect sphere perfectly black. Like a hole punched in the world where Fungle had been. No tree, no clearing – and no Fungle, neither.

Ka sat down and hugged his horny knees.

Well, he thought. *This changes things, it do.*

In this moment within a moment, Fungle dwells inside a bubble pinched off from space and time. Without howl protean furies and bound potentials. Within, the frail gnole prepares to enact his small drama upon a stage that joins two worlds.

Soon waving tendrils of silver light hang before him as if dangling from the moon. They begin to coalesce like thickening mist, entwining to grow more solid by their joining. They form a twisted trunk with frayed ends like roots at bottom and branches at top, until in front of Fungle, skeletal and spindleshanked against

the infinite sky of moon, is a tree-like being. It looks as if a living
thing has taken on the shape of Old Man Tree, gnarled and knotted
from head to toe. Its fissured face is webbed and gaunt, eyeless
and deep-seeking with an expression not possible on a face of
mortal years. It is an infinitely patient face, wise and sad with the
slow-garnered knowledge that layers the thought of trees like the
rings that count their years. Framing this face older than earthly
memory is a beard of roots and crowning mass of twigged hair.

Molom.

Face to face in this timeless place, Elemental and gnole squat
close as rabbits. At the same time the little gnole feels awed and
intimidated in the presence of the mighty Elemental, he also feels
an immense wave of relief at having gotten the invocation correct.
Intimidating as Molom appears, a slip of Fungle's tongue could
have summoned creatures far more malevolent.

Fungle looks into Molom's empty sockets and finds recognition
there. Recognition, but remoteness. Molom is approachable but
unknowable, thoughtful but not discernible. He is *other*.

Molom turns his deep and hollow gaze upon the infinite plain of the moon that is their sky. His voice when he speaks is the sad creak of ancient ships upon a gentle sea. 'Dear gnole,' he says. 'Poor gnole.' One twigged hand raises to point at the silver lid of sky.

The enormous shadow of an owl glides across the moon.

'Know,' says Molom, 'that Molom listens to your world by hearing the voice of the wind. The mouths of rivers carry its taste. The owl looks out upon the land and is my eyes upon it. Alone of birds he sleeps within my eyes and tells me his simple hungry dreams.' The skeletal hand lowers and Molom's gaunt gaze turns to Fungle. 'Like you, mage, the owl flies with a wing in your world and a wing in mine. This owl I have sent as my messenger to you, but –' he sighs deeply '– he is a capricious vessel at best, and easily muddled. Yet we are friends,' he says with faint melancholia.

'You sent a message to me, great Molom?' Fungle asks meekly.

'I have tried through my envoy the owl. I know of your attempts to summon me, good mage, just as I am aware of the plight of my forest and its children as they confront the terrible onslaught of those naked monkeys whose hands have grown more clever than their brains. But there is brewing war among the shadow realms and it has been perilous to reveal myself.'

'War?' Fungle feels a chill.

Molom nods slowly. His great arms sweep wide. 'I have made this frail place beyond *place* that we may meet for a brief time outside of time. It is dangerous and I cannot maintain it long, but it is crucial that we unite, and without possibility of discovery. Our worlds are at crossroads, Fungle, and the path you choose here can affect the destiny of both.'

'Me!' Fungle is alarmed.

'The echoes of this impending conflict are being felt in your world, Fungle, for as above, so below. The wind, the river, the owl – I listen and taste and see the land, and know it is besieged by demons. And because within your heart lies the land, little gnole, I know that you are besieged by demonic dreams. Foremost in your mind is a word that is the key to what ails and disturbs you enough to accept the danger of invoking me. Yes?'

Fungle nods.

'And the word, brave gnole?'

'Baphomet,' whispers Fungle.

'*Baphomet*,' echoes Molom. 'An old word.' He pauses, and in that lull Fungle senses entire histories of memory unplaying in the incomprehensible mind of Molom.

'You have summoned me and are a mage,' continues Molom. 'You are learn'd in the lore of that sunken land from whence your people are dispersed.'

Unsure whether he has just been asked a question, Fungle says, 'I have some small knowledge of them.'

'Know you the story of the dark stone Baphomet, the stone with a soul?'

Fungle bows his head and recites: 'Only this legend, great Molom: there was once a war in the astral planes above the earth. A great battle for dominion raged between the armies of light and darkness. The dark Adversary and his rebellious minions were defeated and cast out from the astral plane. During the conflict, an angel with a flaming sword struck the crown of the Beast, wherein was set the *lapis exilis* – the crown jewel "Baphomet", blacker than the heart of the Beast who wore it. Torn from its clasps by the blow, the stone fell through the seven celestial rings beyond the immeasurable abyss, even as did the dark Adversary clutching after it, until the shadowy crystal landed upon the earth, embedded like a hungry blade in the doomed land of my forefathers.'

Fungle hesitates. So much lore, so many conflicting scrolls and histories that branch out beyond this point! 'After that, much is uncertain. I know that the stone was found by the race of people there and put to use, but the histories are partial and vague, as if some great effort was made to erase the memory of that time.' Fungle looks up to Molom. 'What more I know is from histories kept precious, but conflicting and confused, so that a whole and clear picture does not form.'

'That is a legend from before the time of my kind,' replies Molom. 'And no one can now avow its truth. But it is no matter. You have knowledge. Now you will have truth – for the two are not always one and the same.' And with that he extends the gnarled twig of a finger and slowly inscribes a circle in the air between himself and Fungle. With the circle's completion a disk of air turns wholly dark. Soon images begin to form within it, and Fungle watches a forgotten history of a drowned land unfold before him.

Ka slipped trepidantly down the hill. Of all the ridiculosity he could imagine, running headfirst into a giant hole full o' nothing that useta be a loony friend a-talkin' to a tree had 'em all beat by quite a sight.

He stopped behind a bush and peered out from behind it.

Where the clearing was now stood a circle black as a lake of ink.

It's 'at creepy ol' tree, methinks, Ka felt certain. Past times in his tunnelling he'd dug down by that tree, for, despite its ancient withered rot, Old Man Tree's roots were firm and deep and solid. Curious, Ka had once dug down to see how far they reached. He'd never learned, because all day he had dug straight down, and still the roots continued, until finally he'd had to give up, exhausted.

An' trap me fer a gopher if that selfsame creepy ol' owl what Fungle took in t'other night ain't the very one what likes to roost in that selfsame tree! Oh, it's a bad sign, that is.

Cursing Fungle's foolishness Ka edged out from behind the tree. His heart became a lump of ice caught in his throat as he approached the edge of the black circle.

There was nothing there at all. Ka looked out upon the face of absolute Nothing, as if Death embodied had claimed the clearing for its own. At Ka's feet the grass sheered off neat as you please, as if it had been cut from the world with a pair of scissors.

Ka squatted at the edge like an ancient man wondering what's beyond the rim of the world. Now he wrestled demons of his own: did he go in there after Fungle, or not?

The black disk in the air between Fungle and Molom fills with an image of crystal facets poking from the earth. A man out walking trips over it, brushes dirt from it, then begins digging with his hands. He wears the gold-trimmed robes of a white mage.

'Theverat,' comes Molom's whispered voice from behind the disk in the air. 'Advisor to kings and mage of the Great Court.'

The stone is finally revealed as a coffin-shaped crystal, red and glinting and cold. Its facets spark reflections in the eyes of the white mage Theverat as he examines it. He hides the crystal in the folds of his robe and hurries on.

The image wavers like the surface of a lake, then smooths to show the palace of the mage Theverat. Within is a dark room locked by spells and bolts, and inside the room is Baphomet, glittering upon a pedestal inscribed with runes and protective patterns. Day after day the mage Theverat studies ancient books before the crystal. He lights braziers and moves in ceremonial patterns as he performs incantations before the stone.

The scene ripples again, then clears to show an enormous temple of marble. The tenebrous crystal pulses at the heart of this temple. Around it the city is an immense centre of commerce and scholarship, a thriving hub of light and power in which great affairs are enacted beneath a sky filled with flitting conveyances. Huge ships glide like swift dolphins to and from the ports, where massive cargoes unload themselves upon the docks.

Fuelling all of this is the great jewel Baphomet.

Deep in his chambers Theverat conjures and studies and invokes. His heart is grown faceted, sharp and cold and hungry like the stone that has tainted it.

Before the Great Court of kings and advisors Theverat rants about his schemes to tap the most hidden energies of the stone, and is ejected. By night Theverat appears before the powerful stone in the marble court, and with his followers performs shadowy rituals. The stone's heart pulses with black light, and the lines of force that radiate from it grow dark and charged with malevolent power.

The circle ripples, and Fungle looks in despair upon the antediluvian city.

Taken from the forest, their intelligence enhanced by genetic surgery, chained gnoles toil under the lash of man to build a temple to house the stone. The littered streets are fraught with disease and starvation. Now the majestic flying ships bear the sigil of the Priests of the Black Crystal and take to the air only to spy on the fearful populace below.

On his obsidian throne the new King Theverat broods and schemes the stone's increase – and with it his own. He is a pale shadow of the good shaman he once was, and though he still wears the robes of the white mage, his heart wears darker garb. Alone in his great chamber he toys with a globe of the earth, greedy fingers brushing the great lands. His own island continent is too small to contain his ambitions and the stone Baphomet. He must have more.

A final time Theverat approaches the stone in its temple. In his grim ceremonies he attempts to unleash the full energies of Baphomet as a great and terrible weapon with which to yield dominion over all the globe. But Theverat is too frail a vessel to channel such power, and he is destroyed in the cataclysm of his own unleashing.

A fireball splits the land.

The ocean itself recoils.

Fungle looks in horror at the destruction of his ancestral home.

With but hours before the deluge consumes the land, the white magicians, the prophets and their initiates the gnoles, flee aboard large reed boats powered by wind and not by the terrible energies that have suddenly reshaped the world. To all coasts they scatter, blown east and west to Ægypt and the Americkas.

Atlantic waves lap at the shattered Temple of Baphomet – but the temple is empty, the stone gone from its pedestal.

The disk turns black once more before Fungle's eyes. Molom's finger traces its outline, and the disk disappears.

Molom regards Fungle in silence as the gnole absorbs what he has seen.

'And now you have truth,' the Elemental finally says.

Fungle feels a trembling fear deep inside. This is an enormous and ominous business, larger and more portentous by far than any unnatural storm or invading nightmare or abducting giblin, reaching far beyond any advocacy for the Parliament of Personages. By invoking Molom he has opened the lid on a great and terrible burden of knowledge.

A part of him resists: *No, oh no, I am too small to contain this!*

But the wise mage long trained in him knows an even greater and more terrible truth: opened lids that let forth knowledge cannot be shut again. As a more carefree gnole of but a few days ago had uttered, *Arguin' with the weather only gets yer wetter.*

So Fungle invites the remainder of the burden by asking Molom, 'What became of the stone Baphomet?'

'It was taken,' replies Molom, 'during the great panicked flight from the sundered land and innocently brought, with many other artifacts of wisdom and power, to Americka.'

'Americka!' Fungle exclaims. 'The stone is here?'

'Your histories tell you of the great library deep within a mountain cavern containing all the knowledge and artifacts rescued from the drowned land.'

Fungle nods. Discovering the location of the legendary Library is one of Fungle's greatest desires. All the original books, all the lost knowledge of ancient scrolls, are said to be contained there, a million keys waiting to unlock a million secret doors. The dream of a lifetime – of a thousand lifetimes!

'The Library is but a fragment of the great treasure stored there by the dying mages,' Molom continues. 'The stone was placed there by their servants the gnoles, who had absorbed much of the knowledge of their masters.'

Fungle looks glum.

'They set great spells to guard the cavern,' continues Molom, 'and remained behind in these lands while the mages, depleted by disease and weakened from journeying, travelled south in search of more hospitable climes in which to settle. But the faithful gnoles they left behind – your first ancestors in Americka – never received word from the mages, whose fate is uncertain, though their stone relics remain throughout the southern Americkas.'

'And Baphomet?' Fungle asks.

'The stone remained sealed in the cavern with the books and relics. Because the great mages-in-exile never returned, over the generations your people's abilities waned, Fungle, for as a race of mages they were merely apprentices to those whose relics they had remained behind to guard. The gnoles spread throughout the mountain lands and handed down among their generations many stories of the drowned land and the great exile. Unfortunately through the years those stories were diluted, and there arose some confusion as to what was knowledge and what legend, and the hidden cavern became numbered among the latter. Its location is written on no map, carried down by no rune or word of lore. The only marker in all the world that hints at its location is a stone cairn hidden near the forgotten Mound of the Dead. On the cairn are runes, but only the proper spell unlocks their tongue.'

The light dims and brightens again as the shadow of the owl slides across the moon.

'This is the story,' says Molom, 'unchanged for ages – until now.'

'What is changed?' asks Fungle, not sure he wants to know.

'An unnatural storm, an invading nightmare, abducting giblins,' chants Molom. 'The spirit of the mage Theverat is loose in your land.'

'Theverat! But I saw him destroyed in the very cataclysm he created!'

'In flesh and blood,' agrees Molom. 'But his spirit, warped and strengthened by the distorting powers of Baphomet, entered the Land of the Undead. Now he is become a demon, risen from that heinous place, obsessed with recovering the stone and unleashing its power.'

'But why now?' Fungle wonders. 'He has had ten thousand years in which to search the world. Why does he come into my valley now?'

In answer, Molom reaches deep into a fissure within his ancient body and withdraws a wooden object which he gives to Fungle.

Fungle turns its curved carved shape in his hands. It feels very old and looks vaguely familiar.

'While Baphomet was locked from memory and view within the heart of the mountain cavern, there was no finding the stone,' continues Molom. 'But something has changed. The very world is altered. The naked monkeys own the earth now. Throughout their history they have changed it to suit themselves, with little thought of consequences or effects. They have forgotten the world as a shared thing. They no longer understand the earth as an intricate web with strands so tightly intertwined that to disturb one strand disturbs others. It is as if amongst themselves they have made a pact against Arkadia, the Garden-that-was. They have betrayed us, Fungle; they are at war with us. How I hate them.' The caverns of his eyes narrow. 'The humans are relentless and indiscriminate in their decimation, and their campaign sends resonances along the web of being. And Theverat, sensing that the humans are blindly performing his work for him, has awakened to take matters into his own hands.'

Molom holds a withered hand up high. 'But I feel those resonances, too. I know that the stone is near to being brought to light. I know that Theverat searches desperately.' The hand lowers. 'He seeks out gnoles because they were the guardians of the stone and may give him some clue to find it. But twisted as he has become, he can no longer see and hear and move through the life upon the sunlit earth, and by day sends his instruments to do his work. Giblins, goblins, familiars from the shadow realms. Yet the night is Theverat's own, and if he is Summoned, or gains entry through the magick of another, he travels in it freely.'

Molom clenches both hands into wooden fists. 'The very traits that have caused the humans to wage their war against the Garden-that-was have also brought them near to bringing Baphomet into the world again.' He points to the carved wooden shape in Fungle's hand. 'That is a leg of the pedestal that used to hold the crystal Baphomet.'

Fungle suddenly feels he has picked up a branch only to find it is a viper.

'The emergence of this object from the earth,' continues Molom, 'has alerted Theverat that Baphomet's time is nigh. It was unearthed by human digging machines – weapons of their war – and found by a forest spirit named Conker, fortunately an ally of mine. He found it near the foot of a mountain not three days' travel from your valley.'

Ka paused in his careful circling around the perimeter of the blackness. Had he heard something? A cracking twig, a crunching leaf – a footfall?

He stilled his breath and closed his eyes to listen. Nothing. Pity Fungle ain't here; his vision may be worse'n a turtle's, but he could sniff a candle burning on the sun!

When no sound was forthcoming Ka continued around the edge of the blackness, looking for a way into the circle short of merely stepping on in like a fox into a hole. That smelled too much like jumpin' off a cliff fer no good reason. He'd already poked in a cautious hand, and while his fingers had encountered nothing, the

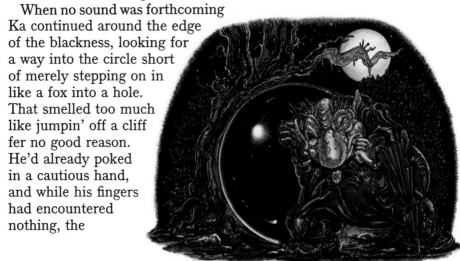

border where the blackness began was freezing cold down to the
marrow of his bones, and he'd yanked his arm back after only a
few seconds and slapped it against his side to get the feeling back.
No, thankee.

He stopped again. Weren't no sound this time, but a smell –
one he'd recognise if his nose were stuffed with rags and sealed
with wax.

Giblins!

Close by and all around, from the growing stench of 'em. An'
me here tippy-toein' round a big ball o' nothin' without so much
as a rock in me idjit hand! Oh, Fungle! Iffin we survives this I may
kill ya meself!

He glanced around. Where's to go? Me hole's 'way up yonder hill,
oh, dandy. Bushes're too far away and hardly comfortin'. Noplace
down to dig because of –

– the black Nothing before him. Oh, he didn't at all like the
thought that unfolded its desperate petals in his mind. *Devil's
in front o' me, an devils behind,* Ka thought. *May's well take the
plunge.*

He took a deep breath and got ready to jump into the blackness.

The moonlight flickers.

Fungle looks up to see black cracks spread across the face of
the sky.

'Little gnole,' says Molom, 'as your will grows tired that sustains
this fragile place wherein we meet, I can give you only knowledge
to aid you in your mission before we must return to our own
realms.'

'My mission?' asks Fungle.

An ancient gnarled finger points at him. 'You must seek out the
hidden cairn near the Mound of the Dead, and unlock its spells
to find the lost Library of your people. You must find the stone
Baphomet before the humans uncover it, and certainly before
Theverat does.'

'But . . . but –'

'Baphomet would be the ultimate and final weapon in the
humans' arsenal, Fungle, for it is the history of the naked monkeys
that they destroy with their hands before they understand with
their brains. If the humans find the stone they will destroy the
earth, by intent or incompetence.' Molom sighs. 'If they would
only wipe themselves out without harming anything else I would

count it a victory. The forest would dance on their grave and no scarce animal would mourn up at the moon at their passing.' He looks mournfully at the sky. 'The work of countless centuries in rain forests would not vanish in hours; the age-long unfurling of the stone waves of mountain ranges would no longer be gouged and blasted level to provide their homes with a better view of the land below that has been ploughed away and poured with stone to make way for houses that look *nothing –*' knotty fists clench – 'like the world around them, as if to announce, *Here we are! The naked monkeys! And the rest of you keep away, if you know what's good for you! Behave, and lie low, and perhaps you will find a niche in our world, living on our garbage.*'

Fungle is startled by Molom's vehemence.

'Yet if Theverat finds the stone it shall be worse by far,' Molom continues. 'For he was Baphomet's past master, and he will wield it with a malevolent precision no human could equal. He will own and subjugate the world and all others he can conquer. Human and gnole alike will cower and toil beneath his lash. Your nightmare was a vision, little gnole – a vision of the world under Theverat. You must find the stone, Fungle.'

Fungle stares in astonishment. 'But, but, I do not *want* it!' he blurts.

'And you will not possess it,' replies Molom, 'for you are not strong enough to wield or destroy it. But the stone is hidden from me, and from these realms I am unable to search for it. Theverat rages throughout the planes invisible, and my efforts to find Baphomet would only alert him. No, *you* must find it, little mage. Like the wind, like the river, like the owl, you will be my eyes and ears in the world while I use my powers to thwart Theverat in mine. Find the stone, Fungle, then summon me forth, and I will destroy it. By so doing we shall halt the humans' plunder of the Garden and defeat the demon Theverat in my world and in yours.'

Molom's spread branches and roots grow misty and glowing, slowly unravelling the way they had formed. 'In this mission none in my world may help you, clever mage.'

The glowing filaments of Molom's branches and roots begin to unravel his trunk like a skein of yarn turned the colour of the flickering moon above.

Little remains of Molom now. His voice comes from dispersing mist drawing upward. 'Good mage, ready your knowledge and your pure-in-heart, for they are your only true armour now.'

The grass at Fungle's feet turns brown and withered.

'My blessings on you and your quest,' comes the last faint thread of Molom's voice. 'For the price of a deed is often a companion to the deed itself.

'Dear gnole. Poor gnole.'

And gone.

A quiet interlude upon this stage between worlds.

Fungle's heart resumes its beat.

Everything around him shreds: sky of moon and floor of grass are tattered as the forces held back by Fungle's draining energy collapse the fragile bubble his will has maintained. The moon receded and grew pockmarked once more, until it was returned to its orbit in the sky. Old Man Tree stood silhouetted against it, Fungle's pack leaning against the trunk.

He felt exhausted. The Summoning had taken from him every last scrap of energy he had carefully built up in preparation. *Home,* he thought, *an' a warm bed to collapse in, and no thought of stones and demons 'til I'm awake again!*

But before he could even think of leaving, he had to collect his energy and his thoughts. His physical return to the world was only part of the process; he had to complete the mental voyage as well. So he remained in meditation posture and breathed deeply to let shine through him the deep-core radiant self that was *Fungle* and nothing else.

Deep in meditation, he was entirely unaware of the fury about to descend upon him – for clobhopping ungainly toward him across the clearing was Karbolic Earthcreep, and close at his heels was a motley crew of giblins.

Some Hasty Retreats

What in the name of all that's utterable is Fungle doing? Ka wondered as he stumbled madly toward his friend. For Fungle sat still as a twin of Old Man Tree, staring vacantly at Ka and the giblins blunderbooting behind him.

The breath of giblins was hot on Ka's heels. His feet flopped like flounders, for a gnome out of earth is a fish out of water indeed.

Fungle didn't so much as blink. Just squatted there, grasping something like a chair leg in his hands. Ka felt sudden reassurance born inside himself, confident that his friend the great mage Fungle was concocturating some intricate crafty spell to rid the world of this pesky giblin blight once and fer all. *An' good riddance to bad rubbish, sez I.*

'Give it to 'em, Fungle!' croaked Ka as he neared. He grinned. 'Let 'em 'ave it!'

Fungle's eyelids fluttered open to reveal only the whites of his eyes, and Ka realised that the gnole was still emerging from the Wherever it was he had gone. Fungle had no idea his friend was loping toward him, or that a slavering pack of giblins whooped close behind.

From on high there came a screech.

Fungle was shaking his head and blinking furiously. Ka readied himself to pick up Fungle, even though he knew that the delay would put the giblins on them like wet on a fish.

A hurled beer-bottle hissed past his ear, spraying froth from its bitten-off mouth. It was immediately followed by an assortment of heavy bones from various animals, and a saucepan lid.

'Urk,' Ka urked.

Fungle roused himself and tried to stand. His body was back in this world, but his mind had not quite caught up, and his limbs all rubbery wobbled like a newborn lamb's. Altogether he was a sorry sight, face all tuckered and puckered and pasty white. Even sorrier was Ka, who after all would have to try to scoop up Fungle and outrun a pack of giblins mad as full-moon mongrels. But friendship is friendship to the bitter end, and Ka bent to his task. Just as he did he felt a fluttering in the air above his head, and he glanced up as a taloned shape, like a piece of night itself, scythed straight into the howling mass of giblins.

An owl.

No time to question: Ka bent and grabbed Fungle. *Hnnh!* May not be a big feller, but a scale wouldn't know better.

Now, you and I are descended from apes that used to dwell in trees, and when we panic there's an old monkey in our head that wants to climb something to feel safe. But gnomes aren't like that; they have as much kinship to apes as a rutabaga has to a cuckoo clock. And, like a rutabaga, when a gnome is panicked, he goes to ground.

Literally.

With Fungle slung over his shoulder Ka stamped out of the clearing, and not one step farther. Fungle's island was honeycombed from Ka's various comings and goings, and all Ka had to do was tap into one of those routes.

He began to dig.

It was really quite an amazing sight: to watch him, you'd realise that few things on this earth are quite so perfectly suited to the task of scooping out earth as such a prodigious rate as a gnome.

From the clearing came owl screeches and giblin shouts.

Ka yanked Fungle into the deepening hole after him and dug so fast that the earth closed over their heads like liquid rushing in. In less time than it takes to tell it Ka had connected to one of his previous tunnels and was spiriting Fungle along it, heading for the once-safe harbour of Fungle's home.

Ka flung back the carpet and emerged into Fungle's living-room.

Neema set down the giblin-doll she was making and lent Ka a hand up, then helped him hoist Fungle from the tunnel. Awkwardly they hurried the dazed and confused gnole into his bed, and Ka watched concernedly as Neema administered a potion of camomile and crabapple cider from the medicine rack above Fungle's headboard. 'Now, there's a wise mage,' observed Ka, indicating the vials of tinctures and tonics. '"Medicines above yer bed'll draw the vapours from yer sleepy head."'

Neema made a pass above Fungle's head with a smoking vial of her heated potion. 'Pah,' she said, not looking at Ka. 'Superstition. Gnomes're a superstitious lot.'

Neema's bluntness always put Ka off a bit – perhaps because he was so blunt himself – but he recognised that it was simply her way and tried not to let it dim his view of her. After all, if your view of someone grows dim enough, you can't see the person for all the murk.

Ka looked at Fungle, unconscious and clutching the curled wooden shape he'd held when the ball-o'-nothin' had been replaced by the clearing again. Neema had tried to remove it from Fungle's grip, but on touching it her hand jumped back as if bitten. 'Well,' she'd huffed, 'that be most pekuliar.' Anyhow, even unconscious, Fungle would not let it go.

'Well, what's wrong wi' Fungle then?' Ka wanted to know. 'Here I'm poundin' toward 'im wi' them dogs o' war as close on me behind as a pair o' britches, and him havin' his own li'l picnic!'

Neema held the vaporous vial before Fungle's pale face. The thick white steam streamed into the sleeping gnole's nostrils as he inhaled. 'Oh, he'll be a'right,' Neema replied. Fungle coughed and croaked, the kind of dangerous deep rumble that puts the grin on a death's head.

'So's I see,' Ka observed.

But in a moment Fungle's colour began to improve. 'It's the Summoning,' said Neema. 'It'll drain a body like an upended hourglass.'

Ka smirked, remembering the gossip from Tobacco Inn concerning Neema, and began to ask her just how she might be in the way a knowin' what a Summoning'll do to a body – but Neema straightened from the bed and tamped a stopper into the vial.

Perched on her shoulder was a bedraggled owl.

'Gllk!' Ka exclaimed, sounding strangled.

'Why, an' what's the matter wi' you, then?' Neema demanded.

'Whuh, whuh, where'd that come from?' he managed, and pointed at the owl.

Neema glanced at the owl as if it were the most natural thing in the world there on her shoulder, then looked back at Ka with a bemused expression, as if Ka had just pointed at her own head and said, *What's this, then?*

'Came from an egg, I should imagine,' she replied.

'Owls,' said Ka, pronouncing the word like a sentence. 'Creepy ole owls.'

'I'll have you know that this creepy ole owl is the reason yer standin' in fronta me this evenin', an' not decoratin' a dinner table fer Mr an' Mrs Giblin an' their little giblets!' She stroked the owl's neckfeathers with a finger.

Ka eyed the owl uncertainly. 'Well . . . why's he look so roughled an' scruffy-like? He all mangy?'

Neema grew even sterner. 'Seems he had a bit o' dispute wi' some giblins,' she said. 'Unlike certain other parties what run off an' hid like a rabbit.'

'I didn't run off! I was rescuin' Fungle from the giblins!' Ka squinted his eyes at the owl in suspicion. 'Say, who told ya that, anyways?' he demanded.

Neema only glanced at the owl, then assumed a tolerant expression that Ka knew meant she wasn't going to tell him any more than she already had. 'Best we leave Fungle to sleep,' she said, 'an' see what we can fix up fer you.'

Ka allowed himself to be led from Fungle's bedroom and fed from Fungle's kitchen.

Kept things close in, ole Neema did.

Clutched by the sleeping hand of a mage gnole: ancient cells of dead grey wood. Carved by hand of mage now dead in body but in roving spirit raving. Artisan and artifact: robbed of life, infected by allegiance to a dark power beyond the capacity of mind or material.

Ancient cells of dead grey wood.
Relic.
Lightning rod.
Beacon.

Ragtag and raw beneath the full moon's fury, five searching giblins stopped as one. They stood like nightmare statues in the monochrome forest, snouts high and nostrils wide.

Sssomethinnng . . .

Rat moved his black eyes a fraction to glance at Porcupine.

Hunched, spiked, pop-eyed, Porcupine leered. Moonlight glittered coldly from his insane eyes.

Their leader, who looked a bit like a famished vixen, sniffed the air. The tip of her snout quivered. She closed her eyes.

. . . Sssomethinnng.

She opened her mouth. 'Down,' she breathed.

Smooth and silent as flowing oil, the remaining giblins dropped to all fours. Their snouts lowered to a worm's height above the ground and they snuffled like frantic dogs.

Vixen firmed her grip on her hatchet. *Oh, the hunt, the hunt, I love the hunt! Track 'em, chase 'em, stuff 'em in a bag! Tickle 'em with yer teethies so they squeal* weee! weee! weee! *all the way home. But more than this I love –*

The four giblins went rigid as trained pointers, all facing the same direction.

– finding them.

'Hunt,' she said, and raised a bent calloused ragged-nailed finger toward an island set in the middle of a moonlit lake like a pupil in a glittering eye.

The giblins raised their heads toward the moon and howled a blissful cacophony, a triumphant discord shattering enough to stop a timid heart.

Fungle's pulse quickened.

He gasped and sat upright in bed.

His mind was vague and numb from a fading dream of screams.

Something writhed in his grip.

Startled, he looked down and saw that what he held was only a piece of wood. Just a carved leg . . .

. . . from the pedestal that had supported Baphomet in Theverat's lair, eons ago, in a continent now mud-caked on the ocean bed.

Memory flooded in: Summoning Molom; the history of the crystal Baphomet and its inextricable link to the fate of Atlantis; Theverat seeking out gnoles to find the stone in its ancient, hidden cavern hold; the nightmare vision of a world endarkened if the crystal were brought to light.

And a mission:

'You must seek out the hidden cairn near the Mound of the Dead, and unlock its spells to find the lost library of your people. You must find the stone Baphomet before the humans uncover it, and certainly before Theverat does. Find the stone, Fungle, then summon me forth, and I will destroy it. By so doing we shall halt the humans' plunder of the Garden and defeat the demon Theverat in my world and in yours.'

'If he can be defeated,' muttered Fungle in bed.

Only one way to find out, Fungle lad, and it ain't by sittin' home abed.

He threw back the covers and stood. Was it only two nights ago he'd fallen from a dream in this selfsame bed? Oh, how the years of a life can change in but a few capricious seconds!

He stopped. *Fallen from a dream* . . . What if this whole thing –
Molom, giblins, an ancient, evil crystal – had been nothing more
than an accumulation of bad dreams, the result of too much food?
Certainly since the Equinox feast his noggin had felt knocked and
knackered. Could it all have happened in his head last night?

The carved leg writhed in his hand.

Neema and Ka were in the living-room. Ka was sweeping the floor
and muttering to himself while Neema looked on. Her posture was
stern, but Ka's head was hung low and he couldn't see Neema's
fond smile.

The smile vanished when she saw Fungle watching them from
the hallway. 'Fungle Foxwit, you get yerself back abed this instant!'
She headed toward him.

'No time, Neema,' said Fungle. 'I must head north, an' sooner's
better.'

Neema put her hands on her hips. 'Are ya tryin' ta make it easy
fer me to be the unchallenged warden o' this land, then?'

It was the first time the old clan feud had ever been mentioned
by either of them out in the open, and Fungle felt awkward. His
face got hot.

'Ya've not recovered!' Neema insisted. 'Ye'll get three clobhops
distance an' ye'll keel over like a poleaxed gnole.'

'Or a gnoleaxed pole,' quipped Ka.

Fungle ignored him. 'No time fer walking, neither,' he said.

'Gonna fly, I s'pose?' inquired Ka, leaning on the broom.

Fungle nodded seriously, and Ka and Neema exchanged a
glance.

'Well,' remarked Ka, 'this's turned into quite a day.'

'Molom has given me a mission,' Fungle continued. He held the
carved piece of wood before them. 'And this tells me there's dark
things lootin' the night to find me. To find *us*.'

The remnant of Baphomet's pedestal twisted slowly before their
eyes like a shed lizard's tail.

In Fungle's Room of Roots, while preparing Fungle's Lunabird for
flight, Neema insisted on accompanying him on his journey north
to find the Mound of the Dead and the stone cairn that held the
secret of Baphomet's location. Though arguing with Neema about
the danger of a journey could prove as dangerous as the journey
itself, Fungle insisted that his mission was such a risky undertaking
he would have to go it alone. He told Neema he would take her

to Ka's, where the gnome could look out for her until his return, and he would hear no more about it. Plainly Neema was unhappy with this, but arguing with Fungle was like trying to outstubborn gravity.

There was nothing to do but help Fungle collect books and scrolls and delicate ancient maps. Ka finished sweeping upstairs and came down to help. He and Neema scurried about the cramped room, searching out items called out by Fungle as the determined gnole assembled his Lunabird.

Carrying found items to Fungle's willow desk, Ka glanced anxiously over his shoulder at the delicate arches and fronds and straps of the Lunabird. 'Yer not really takin' t'the air in that thing, are ya, Fungle?'

'Mmm,' said Fungle, tightening the rickety craft's beak strap.

'I mean, that is, well . . . ya know it ain't my way ta butt in where I ain't wanted, y'unnerstand, but . . .' Ka scratched his head uncomfortably. 'Truth be, Fungle, I seen billion-year-old bird bones more airworthy than that thing.'

'Mmm,' said Fungle as he reverently removed the silk wrapping from around a rare variety of magnetite crystal, then delicately slipped it into place in the wooden beak of the Lunabird.

'Why, a good wind'd turn 'er into kindlin'!' Ka was on a roll now. 'Rain'd waterlog 'er heavier'n a pregnant cow, and just as flyable! An' if ya altercated with anything thicker than a dragonfly's wing an' more solid than dandelion fur, why, it'd just be Fungle all over, now wouldn't it? And a shame it'd be, too! One moment flyin' along like a bumbly-bee, an' the next –' he brought his hands together '– *poof!* The best cook in all the valley, fallin' outta the sky an' leaving his only friends alone to grow all sickly an' underfedded.'

'Mmm,' said Fungle, grasping the magnetite and closing his eyes to feel the magnetic patterns embedded within. He adjusted the stone within its housing to align it with the magnetic currents of the earth itself. For the earth is an enormous magnet, and most creatures are attuned to its lines of force: migrating birds read its map, insects swarm to its mysterious music, whales swim magnetic currents, and without disturbing or repleting the earth at all, Fungle's ancestors and their masters had tapped into this flowing energy as readily as the hawk glides mountain thermals. With it they powered ships of sea and air, lighted cities, predicted weather. Their knowledge and instincts, diluted though Molom might claim they were, had been handed down to Fungle, and in his mind these lines of force resonated like the hum of a hornet in a bottle.

'An' what's to become o' yer bestest friend Ka, eh?' pressed Ka. He leaned closer and whispered. 'An' leavin' a *Cleaverbled* to look after the valley!'

Fungle hesitated. How could he explain that it was more important to keep Neema safe because, even if he succeeded in his mission, he might not come back, and someone would have to oversee the valley's safety. If not him, who better than a Cleverbread?

But before he could say any of this, Neema set a bundle of scrolls on Fungle's desk and blithely said, 'Didn't he tell ya, Ka? We's flyin' with him!'

Ka said *no* exactly one hundred and thirty-seven times.

The Lunabird was ready by the time he stopped, and Neema and Fungle had loaded it up with books and scrolls and maps, then wheeled it to the hidden chamber beneath the earth some distance away from (and just as cleverly camouflaged as) the entrance to Fungle's home.

Everything was ready.

Everything but Ka.

Fungle went back for him. The gnome huddled against Fungle's desk in the Room of Roots, shaking like a puppy in a thunderstorm. Fungle hesitated at the pitiful sight. A hand strayed to the ancient pedestal leg at his side. It writhed like a snake now. *Close, they's so close by!* When his flesh touched the tainted wood, Fungle could sense the giblins' snuffling, their hunger, their greedy need to find him.

'Ka,' Fungle said gently. 'We're ready.'

The gnome looked up. '*We?*' Slowly he stood. '*We!* Have you ever seen me so much as *hop*, Fungle Foxwit gnole?' The great mottled head swung from side to side. A thick-nailed foot stamped the earthen floor. ''At's where I belong! A body don't fall an' break like an egg when he's cosy in Mother Earth!'

'Ka, giblins are on their way,' Fungle explained. 'Giblins – an' worse. I have to get you and Neema safely to your place, then go on my way from there. They'll smell you out if you stay.'

'So who's stayin'? I'm off, too, believe you me. I just ain't intendin' to flap aroun' the sky like some tossed-up twig what thinks it's a bird until the ground sets it straight.'

'They'll follow you down yer tunnels, Ka,' Fungle insisted.

'They's followin' a gnome, Fungle,' Ka said proudly. 'An' just like them that's got the sky in their hearts, this gnome's got soil in his head!'

Fungle smiled, and shook his head in wonder. 'Ka, me friend, there ain't another like you in all the world, an' that's a true-known fact.'

Ka grinned in return. 'In *or* out of it,' he amended.

Fungle nodded. They agreed to rendezvous at Ka's, and once it was decided, they said no more about who's flyin' and who's diggin', and the look that passed between them was all they needed to wish each other well.

Ka looked down. Brave he was, but grace under pressure was not his strong suit. 'Y'know I been known to say, well . . . *unflatterin'* things about Neema, Fungle . . .' He fidgeted. 'What I meant to say is, that is, it'd be a shame an' all if she were to get all strawberry jellified across the countryside –'

Fungle grinned and put a hand on Ka's lumpy shoulder. 'I'll take care of her, Ka,' he said. He lowered his voice. 'An' long as yer diggin' yer way past them dogs,' he said, 'yer in a position to do me a favour . . .'

'Told ya he wouldn't come,' said Neema as Fungle clambered into the Lunabird and settled into his seat in front of her.

'Had to try,' said Fungle. He glanced warily at the wood bracings supporting the ceiling. He could feel them. Up there, above the soil, snuffling, pacing, voracious, ruthless. The giblins.

'Are ya strapped in?' he called back.

'Any tighter'n I'll feel I'm snake-swallered,' said Neema.

'Right, then.' Fungle took a last look around. The small chamber was dim with the faintest mage-light. He chanted to strengthen the wards protecting the entrance to his home, to his Room of Roots, to his library and cherished belongings. His heart gave a small, heavy shudder. So much to leave behind. So many risks to take now as he began his long quest.

But no. Hadn't his mission actually begun only a few nights ago, when he'd taken a journey without distance beyond the walls of sleep?

We all begin a journey when we are born, he thought, *so I'll not feel burdened now.* He was merely continuing a voyage begun many years ago, an excursion that was its own path diverging from the twined roads of his father and mother. *Steps an' stops on the Wheel of Life,* he thought. *An' right now I'm spinnin' toward Baphomet, so best beez on me way.*

He grasped the oars and positioned them.

He glanced over his shoulder. Ka was a gnome-shaped silhouette in the dim mage-light. 'Ready?' Fungle said quietly.

'Ready,' said Neema.

Ka waved the carved pedestal leg. 'Away with ya, a'ready!'

In front of Fungle hung a rope. It dangled from the earthen ceiling, and Fungle had positioned the Lunabird directly under it so that it would be accessible when the time came. Now he steadied the Lunabird's oars and grasped the rope in his right hand.

Deep breath: *Life all around, blood a rushing river in me veins, bee buzz of magnetic currents in veins of the earth, giblins above, friends behind.* Exhale: *And I am the centre; I am centred.*

Now, he thought.

'*Now!*' he called, and pulled the rope.

The ceiling collapsed.

'*Hold!*'

The giblins halted in mid-snuffle.

The harvest moon had long ago set and left the night unlit. The wood of Fungle's island was a convention of indigo and black.

Vixen stood with the other giblins in a small clearing. The twisted shape of her wretched body showed only as a starless patch like a coal sack against the night sky. Deep within her bilious heart she felt the turning of a worm, the squirming of an ancient piece of tainted wood as it vibrated on a dark crystalline frequency to which all unearthly things nocturnal were attuned.

'*I feel them,*' she whispered.

She slathered as she sensed the growing excitement of her charges, paused in their snuffling near the ground. *Oh, my hungry ones, find them. Oh, I love this most.* And her sullen lips furled back across mottled grey gums to display a grinful of broken stained fangs.

Porcupine rose to his full bent height. His maddened eyes were so wide it was inconceivable they could remain in his head. 'There, there!' he gibbered, thrusting a twisted finger toward the ground. He cavorted happily and stamped the ground. 'There, there!' His slobber glinted starlight.

Rat put a nicked ear to the ground and closed his eyes. *Thub. Thub-thub.* But that was Porcupine dancing. 'Shut up wi' ya!' Rat snarled.

Porcupine stopped his manic jig, but continued jabbing a finger toward the ground, one hand clamped over his mouth. His lunatic eyes loomed luminous above his misshapen hand. 'Hoo hoo!' he wheezed.

Rat listened.

Told ya mumble wouldn't come.

Had to mumble. Are ya mumble mum?

Mumble mumble mum mum snake-swallered.

Rat's grin showed rotted stumps of teeth. He pointed down. 'There!' he said.

'There, there!' chortled Porcupine from behind his hand. 'Hoo hoo!'

Calloused hands firmed on axes, pikes, hammers, knives.

'Descend on them!' ordered Vixen.

The earth collapsed beneath their feet.

'Now!' called Fungle, and pulled the rope.

The wooden braces gave way where they were designed to. The chamber's ceiling folded inward and down. Earth and rock and raging giblins spilled into what was now a pit, but the Lunabird in the centre remained untouched.

Fungle urgently muttered an ancient word.

The magnetite glowed.

The Lunabird shifted.

Cursing shapes writhed among the rubble as the giblins struggled to their feet.

'Fungle . . . ?' Neema whispered as twisted clutching shapes rose ghostly round them in the faint mage-light.

'Hold tight,' was all Fungle said.

The giblins headed toward them, brandishing axes, pikes, hammers, knives.

Neema looked up from the pit. The stars looked very far away.

The Lunabird creaked and shuddered and made a prolonged cracking sound like a splintering beam – and lifted!

And stopped.

Neema peered over the side.

A giblin resembling a porcupine had hold of the left-hand wheel. He grinned up at Neema, wild eyes rolling. His hot breath made her gag.

'I'll suck yer marrow before tomorrow,' wheezed Porcupine. 'It's *sooo* good!'

Neema's mind filled with hot lead. 'Fun-gle,' she heard herself say.

The Lunabird listed to port as it struggled against the grip of the giblin.

Fungle swatted down with the port-side oarleron.

The other giblins were within reach now.

A piercing whistle sounded from within the chamber. 'Hey-hey-hey!' called a gruff voice. 'Giblins! Over 'ere, ya smelly jellies!' Ka stepped into view, waving the pedestal leg. ''Ere's yer Barfomet!'

The ancient wood writhed in Ka's grasp.

'Whew – I never saw such hidjuss creatures!' the gnome taunted. 'Ya look like ya fell from an Ugly tree an' hit every branch!'

The giblins turned toward the gnome, drawn not only by his taunts but by the inexorable pull of the dark energy emitted by the pedestal leg.

Ka stuck out his tongue, hopped up and down, and made rude noises.

Fungle swung the port-side oarleron one more time, and knocked loose Porcupine's arm.

The Lunabird righted itself and nosed eagerly into the air.

Four giblins screamed after Ka.

The fifth, who looked like a tall misshapen fox, whirled a spiked ball on a chain and loosed it toward the Lunabird. It wrapped around the tail and bit fast into the wood.

Vixen hurried to a wooden bracing protruding from the edge of the pit and hooked the free end of the chain around it. *Mine! Mine! Mine!* Vixen began hauling on the chain, pulling the Lunabird toward her like a sailor raising anchor.

Fungle glanced back and saw that they were tethered tight to the ground like a kite in a gale.

Like a kite?

He shifted the oarlerons and the Lunabird dipped and steeply banked left. Fungle kept the chain taut behind him and flew the Lunabird past the wooden brace. The chain wound halfway round it and bound the giblin fast. Fungle kept his hands firm on the oarlerons, and the frail craft pulled the chain like a dog on a leash.

Vixen freed her arms and resumed hauling in the chain, taking up the slack by winding it round the wooden brace to which she was bound.

In three pulls they were closer to the enraged giblin than Fungle ever wanted to be again (though this was not to be the case). The thrashing giblin grabbed the tail of the Lunabird where the spiked ball was embedded in the wood.

Fungle urged the Lunabird on, pulling the chain even tighter, and the giblin's scream was a hundred forks scraping a hundred china plates.

Neema shrank back in her seat. The giblin raged insensate not three feet behind her.

'Pull it out!' Fungle called, pointing at the spiked ball that anchored the Lunabird. 'Pull it out and ye'll be free!'

The giblin only pulled harder. The chain was so tight across her twisted body that her eyes bulged and her flesh strained between the links – yet she would not stop struggling.

Fungle could not believe it: the giblin would rather die holding them than be free. She was like some species of snake that, once it begins to eat, is mindlessly bound to see the entire process through – even if it's got hold of its own tail.

The Lunabird creaked ominously.

'Neema!' Fungle shouted over the giblin's ranting. 'Hold the oars!'

Neema hurriedly unharnessed herself and practically dove over Fungle to grab the oarlerons from him.

The Lunabird bobbed as Fungle hopped off.

Seeing the gnole on the ground, the giblin yanked the Lunabird's rear stabiliser. The up-angled craft wobbled. Its tail creaked, and Fungle heard something crack.

Fungle kept a respectful distance between himself and the giblin as he put a hand on the spiked iron ball biting into the Lunabird and began to tug.

The giblin went crazy: an explosion of flailing arms and frenzied groping and flying spittle. The chain bit deeply into her flesh and her eyes bulged as she strained toward Fungle. She was killing herself to get to him.

The giblin's hand clamped his. Its flesh felt like the skin of a turtle, but cold. The giblin screeched triumphantly as it pushed Fungle's palm against the sharp spikes of the steel ball.

Fungle looked into the creature's demented eyes.

The giblin grinned, showing fangs and the broken nubs of blackened teeth. '*Master!*' she called, '*O my Master!*

'– *By my blood I invoke thee!*
My heart, my hair, my eyes, my brain, my soul –
My Master's, all!'

The air grew chill. Clouds thickened high overhead.

'*By the ancient names I invoke thee, Theverat!*
Astaroth, Asmodeus, Astarte . . .'

Around them the cold air began to shimmer. Fungle struggled, but the giblin's grip had the berserk power of singleminded obsession behind it. His heart grew stony at the thought of the Presence the giblin was summoning.

Suddenly the giblin's gnarled hand contorted. Tendons stretched as her fingers curled in pain. She screamed and snatched back her hand as if burned. Fungle tugged, and the spiked ball tore loose from the wood and gouged a furrow down its length as the Lunabird shot from the pit like a flushed quail.

'Funnngle!' shouted Neema.

Fungle dove for the Lunabird's tail. The air whuffed out of him as he slammed up hard against it, but he held on.

The earth dropped away beneath him.

Fungle clamped his legs around the rear fuselage. Straddling the rickety craft he watched the dwindling form of the shrieking giblin struggling to free itself from its chain.

'Fungle?' Neema called in the calmest voice she could muster. 'Think ya could get yerself up this way? I dunno how ta fly this thing!'

Fungle inched backward toward the front of the ascending Lunabird. *Always somethin'*, he thought. When he reached the passenger seat he dropped in and turned around, then leaned out to grab the oarlerons from Neema in much the same fashion she had taken them from him.

'Climb o'er me an' strap in!' Fungle called. The rushing cold night wind chilled his face.

Neema used Fungle as a ladder to return to her seat. Fungle levelled off and headed north as Neema strapped herself back in.

The cloudy night was swirling dark and beautiful. Below them spread the valley, lush and alive. Fungle sent a silent blessing down to Ka. He spotted the distinctive shape of his island, below and behind them. *Back soon*, he promised.

But it was not to be.

'Neema!' Fungle yelled over his shoulder. 'Why d'ya suppose that giblin let go? Had me like a fly in a web.'

He glanced back just as Neema was pulling a silver needle from the hand of the little giblin-doll she'd been making when Ka had returned with Fungle.

'Thought that might come in handy,' was all Neema said.

Oh, it were a merry chase indeed! Two of 'em had fallen back so far they wasn't even sport no more, but t'other two?

Ah, t'other two!

Ka dug in a wide loop, scooping dirt like a happy duck paddling water. He broke through and emerged into a tunnel he'd just dug, then backed off, dug down just enough to hide his body, and waited.

Porcupine and Rat went screaming past.

Ka emerged into the shaft and ran back the way the giblins had just come. At his side the ancient piece of wood was hot as fevered flesh, and twisted about most disconcertingly.

'*It's like a beacon in the night to 'em, Ka,*' Fungle'd said. '*They'll follow wherever it leads.*'

And Fungle had grinned.

Hurrying along the tunnel, Ka grinned with the memory. 'Ah, this be rich!' he said. He veered into one of his older tunnels – one that headed away from Fungle's island and ran beneath the lake.

The quicker giblins' howls filled the tunnel well behind him. They were back a ways, all right. In his haste, however, Ka had forgotten about the two slow giblins, and he rounded a corner and ran smack into them.

Why have you Summoned me?

'Oh, my Master! They were here! The gnoles; they were here! We got 'em! – we had 'em! – oh, Master, I would lick your feet to cool them! The gnoles –!'

Where are they now?

'Now . . . ? Why, now they're . . . up! Up, up, up! Oh, Master, I love you, please, free me to do your will! I would give my pelt to make a blanket to keep you warm. I would –'

You have summoned me where I cannot maintain my form, yet they are not here.

'Yes . . . No! There! They're up *there*! Free me; I will find them! Bring them to you in a net, in a tangle, blooded, trussed up for your table, oh –'

I feel them. Flying.

'Yes! Flying high up in the sky, way up where the birdies fly!'

I will take them from the air. And you . . . You will be there when they hit the ground –

'Yes! When they hit, when they hit, when they hit!' She sang with insane glee.

– or I will turn you inside out.

If Ka had not been so busy congratulating himself for evading the two quick giblins, he would have realised he was right about to

stumble into the slower two, for in the cramped confines of his
tunnels in the earth their stench carried farther than any cry.

But he *had* been busy congratulating himself, so here he was:
facing two bristling slobbering bloodthirsty giblins in a deep
slick dripping tunnel with nowhere to run but back the way he
had come.

Two pairs of giblin eyes gleamed hate in the dimness ahead
of him. Their huge twisted shapes swelled as they advanced
on him. Faint phosphorescence glinted from a machete and a
Bowie knife.

Ka turned to run back the way he had come – and saw four more
blood-red giblin eyes hurrying toward him, narrowed in hate. The
faster giblins had caught up to him.

Cold water dripped onto Ka's head.

The tunnel filled with a smell that would curdle wood.

Water . . .

Wood . . .

Ka glanced around desperately. The soil of the tunnel was dense
and slick and dripping. Several wooden braces lined the sides where
he had placed them long ago as reinforcement because –

– because they were under the lake!

There came a *whick!* as something cut air immediately behind
him. Ka leapt for the side of the tunnel just as the giblin behind
him screamed and reversed the swing of his machete.

Ka skidded in the mud and hit the side of the tunnel. A
reinforcing beam was in arm's reach; he wrapped both hands
around it and yanked it free. '*Ha!*' he yelled triumphantly.

Nothing happened.

Four hulking giblins growled ahead of him in the dark, and now
there was truly nowhere to run.

Ka clutched his piece of wood.

The giblin with the machete swung.

Metal bit wood.

Water patted the giblin's head. It grew to a trickle.

The giblin looked up. He started to say something.

The tunnel gave way and the lake rushed in.

The air turned biting-cold and turbulent. It took all of Fungle's
concentration to pilot the laden Lunabird as it was buffeted about.
His hands were cramped from gripping the oarlerons, and his arms
were sore and tired. But he couldn't afford to relax for an instant,
because every time he started to, a gust of wind or an air pocket

would upset the fragile craft, as if trying to wrench the steering oars from his grasp.

The swirling clouds were dense as fungus. There was a tinge in the air that reminded him of the storm on Equinox night: a hungry, searching feeling; a sense of Presence, of *intent*.

He glanced back at Neema. She squinted into the biting wind, but had let out not the slightest peep of alarm or complaint.

The storm's fury gathered about them like a bobcat about to pounce. Neema had never been so high, moved so fast, been so tossed about! It was terrifying, and with every groan of the Lunabird's wood her heart leapt and she was convinced that the final grain of sand was falling in the hourglass of her life. But every time, the ungainly craft somehow pulled through.

Yet buried deep, Neema was surprised to discover, was a small seed that flowered and thrilled brightly every time the Lunabird surged or dropped in the air. *It's a child part of me*, she speculated, *thinkin' this is all a plaything, a page from a Howzit story.*

Or, she reconsidered, *it's a ancient dark beast that sleeps in everybody, an' eats fear and danger fer its bread an' butter.*

The child or the beast, she wondered; which is it?

The Lunabird jinked left and dropped like a stone. Neema's stomach hit the top of her skull, it felt like. Fungle struggled with the oarlerons. In the carved beak of the Lunabird's prow the magnetite crystal glowed as it fought the mounting electricity of the storm to hold onto the tangled lines of power that would lead it to Ka's.

A black shape emerged from the swirling grey clouds and flapped toward them.

Neema gasped at the winged figure limned against the clouds. She called out to Fungle, but her voice was lost in the howl of the wind.

Corpulent clouds swelled.

Lightning flared.

In the electric flash the colour of mage-light, Neema saw that the thing winging toward them was familiar; she recognised it as Molom's harbinger and envoy.

The owl.

It cut through the violent air like a knife in water, this marvellous living creature that accomplished without effort or volition what the finest spells and craft could barely maintain.

The owl glided close by the Lunabird. Fungle caught sight of it, and stared as if seeing an impossible thing.

Impossible, an owl in the air! What could be more natural?

The owl pulled ahead of the Lunabird and banked right to slowly circle away. Fungle fought to hold his course.

Lightning split the air.

In a moment the owl returned, leading the Lunabird, and banked right again. This time Fungle followed. The owl straightened, then descended until the roiling storm was a grey carpet overhead. It banked left, resuming their northward course, and Fungle followed.

Neema relaxed in her seat. The owl was leading them through the storm. It would be all right.

That was when lightning struck the Lunabird and it broke apart and fell.

Back to the Mines

Waterlogged, weary, and wambling through his muddened tunnels, Ka was slouching toward home when he felt a vibration through the sensitive soles of his digger's feet. A slight, distant *whump* as something hit the earth.

Fry me fer a fish iffin I dunno what that was, thought Ka. Exhausted as he was, he picked up his pace.

'*A fine mess y'are!*' The voice came from far away. '*An' swelp me, ya'd better be only sleepin', Fungle Foxwit, or, or –*'

Fungle slowly opened an eye, then squinted against the downpour. 'Or what?' he croaked. He hurt everywhere, especially his pride.

Upon seeing that his friend was alive and awake, Ka wiped the concerned look off his ugly mug and replaced it with one of reproach. 'Ah – I knowed it: playin' 'possum! Lookin' fer simplethy! Well, ye'll get none from me!'

Even as he said this he was helping Fungle to his feet.

All around them angry rain hissed against leaves.

Fungle patted himself, feeling for lumpens and bumpens and breakins. Plenty of the first two, none of the last, an' thank a lot of tree branches and the soft wet carpet of grass for it.

His hands stopped.

'Neema,' he said.

'Left 'er by the Lunabird while I saw to you,' said Ka. He grew sombre. 'She's hurt, Fungle.'

Immediately Fungle limped to the fractured skeleton of the Lunabird.

Neema lay propped against a piece of the fuselage. Wreckage

lay all around: the Lunabird had rained from the sky much like
the storm now pouring on their heads. Ka had apparently busied
himself with taking care of Neema before awakening Fungle, for
a rickety makeshift lean-to of fronds from the wings kept the rain
from her face, which was slack and sallow. Her left leg was splinted
with saplings bound with vines.

She was awake.

'An' ta think I'd just got to likin' flyin',' she said wryly as Fungle
approached. Pain creased her face, but she refused to let it bleed
into her tone.

'Oh-hoo, flyin's grand, it is!' agreed Ka. 'An' even the fallin'
part's a hoot an' holler. It's 'at sudden stoppin' what puts me off
me puddin'.' He chuckled.

Fungle stared down at the wet ground. Suddenly he didn't know
what to do with his hands; they felt big and heavy and stupid
hanging there useless at the end of his arms. 'Neema . . . I'm
so sorry; I feel terrible stupid about –'

'Figures you'd blame yerself, Fungle Foxwit; yer so *responsible*
fer everything!' Neema said crossly. 'Well, no one strapped me in
that seat but me. *I* broke this here leg as sure as if I jumped off
a cliff, an' I won't hear another sound about it, thank you very
much.' She looked away.

'Told ya she was sweet on you,' whispered Ka.

Fungle blushed. He found sanctuary in action: 'Er . . . best we
salvage what we can from the Lunabird, then camouflage it. We
got to get Neema outta here an' safe away. How far's yer place
from here?'

'Not a couple o' clobhops,' the gnome replied absently. He was
staring at the wreckage of the Lunabird with much the same
combination of bafflement and wonder a man might have if
he attended the launching of a spaceship made of *papiermâché*.
'Rather stop a chargin' giblin with a handfulla briars than fly in
one a these things,' he muttered, toeing a broken wooden spar to
emphasise his point.

'Speakin' a giblins,' said Fungle, 'how'd ya fare with 'em?'

Ka turned to Fungle with a tragic look. 'A sad story it is,' he
said, shaking his head. 'Killed me an' ate me, they did. Ended
up as giblin fixins just a-cause I helped a friend indulge some
nonsensicalistic loony moonin' 'bout flyin' in the sky.' He shook
his head again and clucked. 'A sad, sad story.'

'Ka.' Fungle's tone was warning.

The gnome grinned. 'Well, whadja think? It went off like a charm:

I carried yer wrigglin' stick, an' they follered like a dog on a bone. Hoo! I give 'em the slip, give 'em a bath, an' sailed on down the flue!' He beamed. 'I tells ya, it's a shame there's no witnessers; they'da wrote a epic pome.'

Fungle grinned. 'An' the pedestal leg I give you to lead 'em on?'

'Rid of it, and glad I am, too,' said Ka. 'It were like hanging onto an armful of eels. Right nightmare to carry that twisty thing, and me noggin's still fair churnin' with visions of doom an' destruction an' demons, and all terrible words what start with a "d". But this very moment that snaky piece o' wood's bobbin' merrily along a new underground current, and every giblin in the neighbourhood scurryin' after, with any luck.'

Fungle patted his friend on the back. But even while he was proud of Ka and indebted to him for misdirecting the giblins, Fungle could not help thinking about that piece of wood bobbing along in an underground current, filled with evil it had soaked up like a sponge, and he worried about what it might communicate of Baphomet should it fall into the wrong hands.

He was also conscious of the rain that sought them out, a thousand tiny spies touching them every second, each one shrieking back: *Here! Here! Here!*

They had to get under cover.

Fungle hurried to the Lunabird wreckage and removed the magnetite crystal from the beak of the prow. The stone was powerful and rare, and it wouldn't do to let it fall into the wrong hands. He bundled up his sopping books and maps and returned to Neema's side.

'Oh, Fungle, yer bootiful books,' Neema said forlornly. 'Yer maps, too!'

'We's alive, Neema, an' that's the thing,' said Fungle. 'Books an' maps're no good to nobody who ain't around to read 'em.'

He slung the roughcloth sack of waterlogged books and maps over his shoulder and smiled at her, but his smile was sad and resigned.

'Home,' said Ka. 'Towels and hot wine asides a fire ta warm hearth an' heart,' he said.

'Home,' mused Fungle, and wondered as the warm word left his lips how long it would be before he saw his home again.

Fungle and Ka supported Neema between them, and they headed north.

It rained all night.

*

In a year numbered 1934 on some human calendars, the Kentucky Mining Corporation sank shafts in a promising region of Southern Appalachian mountain country. An entire nation was hungry and poor: its people needed jobs and food, and an insatiable beast named Industry needed fuel. The Kentucky Mining Corporation had every reason to believe there were thousands of tons of bituminous coal buried beneath the rock like soft black treasure waiting to be plundered and burned to satisfy the growing maw of a nation that, for more than seventy years now, had dumped ton after ton of carbon into its unsullied air.

They plundered.

They burned.

Before the first patch of dirt could be removed, though, an entire town had to be built. Tens of thousands of trees were ripped from the earth and transformed, by a kind of unsympathetic magic, into shabby shacks and dreary dayrooms, a cheapjack community to house a labouring army, a planned ghetto meant to keep a miner down.

The shapes of the mountains themselves were forever altered.

Coal they found, but not in the hoped-for amounts. Workers died in tunnel collapses after contractors skimped on lumber costs by keeping bracing to a minimum; they breathed in silicon dust, and their bodies, stiff as the coal they so earnestly dug, were brought home on a wagon pulled by two mules and left on the front porch along with a hundred dollars for burial expenses.

Workers were cheaper to replace than mules.

Above the miners' swinging picks and sweating bodies, their sons bloodied their fingertips working as breaker boys, separating slate and rock from moving screens conveying coal torn from the land.

The land. The anguished land.

Smelters spewed poisonous lead into the topsoil where children played. Noxious runoff from blast furnaces and smelters blackened rivers and eliminated fish. Around the green hillsides, steam shovels flayed the skin of the earth in search of coal just beneath the surface.

Slowly, surely, an entire mountain's heart was hollowed by miles of honeycomb shaft. Workers died, new workers came, and coal was hewn from the body of the earth until there was no more to find.

The mine went bust. The men left.

And left behind them a wounded land. Garbage heaps combusted by themselves; shacks collapsed and rotted; tunnel bracings weakened, snapped, caved in. Elevator hoist ropes rotted; chains rusted; handpumps clotted and fused.

One day a gnome by the name of Karbolic Earthcreep was out tunnelling. He'd got his name when he was a wee gnome in the latter half of the Nineteenth Century, after Cordelia Earthcreep happened across a crate containing boxes of something called Kingston's Karbolic Kleener. What the boxes contained was soap; she used it to wash her infant son. One day she joked that, if the stuff was *Karbolic* Kleener, her baby gnome must be a Karbolic.

The name stuck.

Anyway, one day half-a-century after this christening, the kleanly named gnome was out on a leisurely day's dig when he broke into an enormous shaft. There were tunnels and side chutes and storage bins, and iron tracks with iron carts on wheels all rusted stopped. This gnome scoured the tunnels and scrounged up artyfacts: bone-dry lamps and broken helmets, rock-embedded picks like swords of legend, boots an' rings an' a thousand other useless things.

From the pattern of greedy gouges in living rock he understood that the human beans'd been after coal – though what in the world for he could not imagine – and he laughed out loud. Surely any fool coulda found the solid lake o' coal not two days' diggin' east of the easternmost shaft!

Still, despite the wooden bracings (which the gnome considered amateurish and tacky in the extreme), some of the workmanship in the tunnels were not bad at all, and the mine were actually quite cosy and luxuriant when ya got right down to it.

Ka made himself at home.

The rattle of empty beer cans was loud in the dark tunnel as Ka kicked them out of the way. They followed the rusted rails of the old coal-cart tracks, Neema sandwiched by Fungle and Ka supporting her. Fungle struggled with Neema on one side and a bulky sack of waterlogged books and scrolls on the other. Right now, he thought, I'd gladly trade all me learnin' and books for half-an-hour before a fire. An' it's freezin' down here! Only a gnome'd call this home.

He tripped on a rotted crosstie.

Neema drew a sharp breath as her weight fell momentarily on her broken leg, but she kept the pain inside. Because he was holding her, Fungle felt an echo of the white-hot jolt that stabbed up her leg.

Ka stopped moving. 'Hold on,' he said, and cupped a hand to his ear.

'What is it, Ka?' asked Fungle.

'Shhh.' Ka held that pose, brow furrowed. Ka's sense of hearing was like Fungle's sense of smell: if Fungle could smell morning breath on a mosquito a clobhop away, Ka could hear the tunnelling of worms in other countries.

Soon Fungle and Neema could hear it too: something between a roar and a hum, dim and distant, eerily echoing, growing more distinct as it neared.

Neema squinted. 'There,' she whispered, and pointed down the tunnel the way they had come.

Dim lights winked in the distance.

Fungle glanced at the rusted iron rails and remembered the night Froog had lost his leg. 'Ka,' he began nervously, 'we best –'

'It's a'right,' said Ka. 'Just wait an' see.'

They waited. They saw.

It emerged creaking and clanking from the darkness, an upright figure of metal built in the shape of a man. Its idiotic head bobbed up and down as it pumped a lever to drive a flat metal sled along the rusted rails.

It drew abreast of them, squeaking and creaking. Ka hopped on and fiddled with the metal man's back, which bent and straightened before him as if the strange figure were silently ticklish. In a moment the metal man stopped moving and the flatcar rolled to a stop.

Neema and Fungle gaped. Ka grinned and folded his arms.

'What the bloody blue –' Fungle glanced at Neema. 'Er . . . what is that thing, Ka?'

'It's me mechanical man, Fungle!' explained Ka, to no one's enlightenment. 'I calls him GizmoJo. Got 'im from Musrum the Mossman in trade for a buncha rocks all spoiled with shiny lines.' He chortled and clapped his hands. 'See here – this lever I just tripped sets off his mechanalistics, an' out he comes to this spot from wherever he be! Sometimes I'm loaded up with all sorts of good stuff, and I use him to run me around. But other times I lets him run all over the place, an' he don't never fall off the tracks, or run down neither. Well, hardly ever. Works on bat-reez, he does.'

'It's hideous,' said Neema.

Ka looked wounded. The expression was so comical both Neema and Fungle laughed despite themselves.

Fungle grinned up at the crestfallen gnome. 'C'mon, y'old

grump,' he said. 'Let's let yer whadjamacallit, yer Maniacal Can, guide us on our way.'

They lifted Neema onto the flatcar. Ka fiddled with the mechanical man's internal mechanisms again, and once more the strange construction pumped the lever that propelled the car, bowing politely at the darkness ahead of them.

They set Neema onto a big blue bag covered with patches and stitches and stuffed with little white pellets like a kind of snow that never melted. Ka hurried to a contraption made of metal pipes mounted on wheels with a little seat in the middle. He clambered onto it, grasped two handles projecting from it, put his huge feet on small blocks between the wheels, and began pedalling furiously.

'What in blazes ya doin', Ka?' demanded Fungle.

'Makin' heat an' light,' said Ka.

'On that thing?'

Ka nodded enthusiastically. 'I dunno the exacties, y'unnerstand, but the principalistics is that I pedal here, an' this contraption soaks up me labours an' pours 'em through them wires fixed to the back wheel here an' into that box there, which ya calls a *bat-ree*.' He nodded at a box on the cavern floor near the wheeled contraption. A mess of wires led to and from it, as if a drunken spider had tried to wrap it up for dinner and then called the whole thing off. 'I got a bunch of 'em, big an' small,' the gnome continued. 'Only place I know to get 'em's from Musrum the Mossman, an' he charges dear.'

Ka hopped off the contraption, already huffing and puffing. 'There! Reckon that box's taken enough outta me to help us make ourselves more at home.' He scurried to something that looked like a vase with a glass bulb on top. Ka twisted his hand near it, and sudden harsh light bleached the cavern that was Ka's main digs.

Fungle and Neema looked about.

There were boxes, and boxes with tyres, and boxes with glass fronts, and rods and curved shining shapes like silver but reflective as mirrors. There were wires and glass bulbs and metal and materials completely foreign to their experience. They didn't understand much of what they saw, but any human would have recognised vacuum tubes and doorless refrigerators, Philco and Bakelite radios and pitted chrome bumpers, hubcaps and mannequins and toilet seats. A cracked mirror on a bent brass stand reflected a dozen bedraggled wet gnoles who echoed Fungle's moves exactly. A large sheet of some kind of glossy paper, torn and tattered, was affixed to the rocky wall. Fungle could barely make out a faded depiction of a human bean with black hair holding an instrument vaguely like a mandolute. Below the picture of the man were remnants of lettering, abbreviated left and right by torn flaps bowing from the wall:

LVIS PRESLE

tarring in

IVA LAS VEGA

And everywhere Fungle looked, he saw more of the kind of flimsy metal container he had given Ka on Equinox night. Hundreds of them. Tens of hundreds! They were stacked in pyramids and cut in odd shapes to use as containers; some were unrolled flat with the tops and bottoms removed and tacked to furniture for unfathomable reasons. Standing upright near one rocky wall was an entire reconstructed skeleton of some fearocious long-dead beastie. Ka had completely wrapped the bones with unrolled metal from red-and-white containers. Fungle found them a wonder: how could someone craft so many completely identical metal cylinders, and why?

The cavern was so crammed with artifacts that it no longer seemed like a cavern at all. Fungle had never seen so many straight lines, right angles, and reflecting surfaces in one place in his entire life. It was a fairyland: scintillating, coruscating, miraculous – proof that the whole can be greater than the sum of the parts, for these parts were all junk, and not even *good* junk, really, but instead the useless rinds of human culture. Yet assembled here they had acquired a life, a charisma, all their own, each piece interdependent and connecting, leading the eye from one inexplicable artifact to the next to scale new heights in the aesthetic of . . . well, of junk! But just as you and I come long ago from ocean mud, so Ka's home had evolved from trash and into a higher order, a species beyond mere *junk*. To call it junk would be to call a diamond a piece of carbon, a baby impractical.

Fungle had scarcely taken it in before Ka scampered up to him holding two enormous towels. He handed one to Fungle and one to Neema. 'Here y'are, here y'are,' he said. 'Get that cold squishy water off, an' then we'll see to some heat.'

Fungle's towel was thin but quite well made, and it had a design on it. He held it by two corners and let the remainder drop. TAN, DON'T BURN! it read in huge brown letters. Fungle wondered what it meant.

He looked at Neema. She held her towel before her, regarding it with a bewildered expression. In bright colours it depicted a muscular human in a skintight blue-grey outfit with thin, wedge-shaped ears and narrow, oval eyes, wearing a black cloak, gloves and boots. Neema looked from the odd picture to Fungle. 'What ya make o' this, Fungle?'

Fungle smiled gently and shrugged. 'Reckon I'd make myself dry with it, Neema,' he said.

Which she commenced to doing.

Ka, meanwhile, was scurrying all about the cavern, twisting knobs and flicking switches. Plainly he was excited at entertaining guests. Just as plainly, he was not used to having them.

While Ka bustled about, muttering among peculiar lights and noises of his creation, Fungle dried himself with the huge towel, then wrapped his waterlogged books and scrolls in it and left the bundle in order to see to laying hands on Neema's hurt leg.

'Comfortable?' he asked as he squatted before her.

'As I can be,' Neema replied wryly.

He looked intently into her eyes to see what they told him about her pain. Eyes are like the rings in the trunk of a tree, like the phyllo layers of sediment laminated upon the earth across millennia. And just as a trained botanist or geologist can read those layers of wood and earth, so Fungle could read the record of wisdom and joy and pain layered by time into a person's eyes.

He gently set his curved hands over the injured length of Neema's splinted bone.

He shut his eyes and concentrated.

His fingertips sensed the echo of the beat of Neema's heart. With every drumbeat flexion her leg throbbed hotly. The break was like a beacon signalling her body's healing armies to rush to the site of a battle, a corps of cellular engines already repairing a breach. Through his fingertips, behind his closed eyelids, Fungle felt the resonance of the break like a broken strand in a tight-woven web.

He nodded slowly. From the bag he always wore around his neck because he was a shaman, he removed a small knot of curling moss. It was still fragrant and fresh, for he replaced it every morning at first light, gathered with a blessing and mixed in his spirit bag to take on the tinctures of potent healing herbs and powerful fetishes. Fungle held the clump of moss before him and spoke to it in the language of moss, a language of damp and velvet life, of sun-drinking trees and dark invigoration, summer rain and autumn dark. This single knot of moss was an emblem of growth in the world, of the gentle healing carpet of unkempt hair atop the land. Fungle spoke to the moss and the Spirit of Moss that had produced it, then laid the grey strands across Neema's broken bone, bidding the Spirit of Moss discharge the qualities of healing and growth into Neema's leg that the bone might knit quickly whole and clean so that in later life, during the long cold slumber of gnoles in winter when moss sleeps brittle beneath a frigid blanket of snow, no memory or pang of injury would trouble Neema.

He wrapped the moss in place with a strip of roughcloth from his bookbag and looked at Neema.

'Thankee, Fungle,' she said.

'Pleasure's me own,' Fungle said. He fidgeted and looked away from her.

'Can I tell you something, Fungle?'

Neema's tone made him wonder if he wanted to hear what she had to say, but he turned toward her and nodded.

'I know you think I don't show proper respect fer you,' she said, 'you bein' the valley's mage an' shaman right an' proper –'

'I've never said that,' he objected.

'Never had to. Anyways, I just wanted ya to know it's not 'cause of all that's gone 'round and 'round betwixt yer clan an' mine, or because I think yer not a good mage. It's just –' Now Neema grew uncomfortable. 'Well, I can remember when you an' little Froog useta get the wild critters to singin' away late at night – bobcats an' frogs an' wolves, when there was wolves.' She grinned. 'Remember that? The two a you'd conduct 'em, two hours past midnight, and the elders woulda shut both of ya in a cave and fed ya through a gate, except the music were so *bootiful*.'

Fungle smiled at the memory and nodded.

'An' the time there was that drought an' you tried to bring on rain, only instead ya turned ever'body's fur blue?'

Fungle stopped smiling. He blushed. Neema rushed on: 'I'm only sayin', it's hard fer me to separate them memories from who an' what you are now. You see?' She wrung her hand. 'Oh, I'm makin' a botch of this –'

'Here now!' announced Ka, setting a tall object in front of them. 'I call this me "hearth-in-a-box". Clever an' cosy, ain't it?'

It was a metal rectangle on a platform. A cord ran from the bottom to the bat-ree attached to the bicycle. The front face of the rectangle was covered by a grille; behind it, two rods glowed orange and gave off heat.

Fungle could only stare.

'Er . . . guess I were sorta *exaggeratin'* 'bout the fire an' all,' Ka said meekly. 'I mean ta say, there's *heat* an' such, an' I can get ya dry as toast, but there ain't what ya'd call chimney an' hearth hereabouts. Ya know I can't be havin' *them* around.'

Fungle nodded fatalistically. Of course: like all gnomes, Ka was afraid of fire, because burning turned a gnome to stone. Even being out in the sun too long could prove disastrous. But how much he'd been looking forward to a cheery crackling fire! In his mind his father said, *There'd be no disappointments if there weren't no expectations.*

'This'll see ya dry in no time,' promised Ka, a bit chagrined.

Doubtfully Fungle held a hand near the hearth-in-a-box. Though made of metal, the box's faces were covered with a paper designed tc look like wood. Fungle scratched it with a fingernail.

How curious. Human beans disguisin' metal to look like wood. Like as if they's ashamed of it.

Still, it was warm, though not a hundredth as cheering and homey as a fire would've been. Oddly cold, in fact, for an artifact designed to warm. Reckon I'll just set here a mite an' dry meself dry afore I set to all the work an' readin' and plannin' I have to do.

He was thinking this as he fell asleep.

Under a blue ring of mage-light Fungle pored over brittle pages gone all wavy after they had dried. The painstaking calligraphy of gnoles thousands of years dead had been salvaged to the best of Fungle's ability with unerasing spells and meticulous care. Luckily, those who had transcribed them loved books every bit as much as Fungle did himself, and they had placed charms on the fabric of the books' construction so that they would better hold the memory of the information they contained in case of just such disaster as had befallen them the night before. The beautiful illuminated words and fastidious illustrations were streaked and smudged and blurred – but still legible.

But not under the light of Ka's cavern. The glass bulbs and tubes Ka used for illumination belied that very word, for Fungle had found they *illuminated* less than they *bleached*. The harsh white lights sucked the concentration out of his eyes, blurred his vision after a few hours' close reading, and left him all headachy – the latter a phenomenon rare to Fungle's experience.

Candlelight was insufficient; the hearth-in-a-box was a poor jest. No, nothing would do like mage-light: blue-white pure, scholarly and sanctifying, and gentle on the eyeballs. So after giving up on Ka's human-bean lights, he could now hunch for hours and wander the petrified forest of resurrected words, lost in languages millennia dead and happy as a flea on a clawless dog.

Carefully he studied the ancient maps compiled by the geo-mancers among his forefathers as they had journeyed across the eastern face of Northern Americka, following magnetic patterns embedded in the land: ley lines, patterns as old as the world itself, lines of energy the gnoles called 'snake power'. Fungle listed all the information given him by Molom, and painstakingly compared it to his books of history and lore. Finally, after two days of intensive detection and paring away of possibilities, Fungle isolated the very spot that had to be the location of the Mound of the Dead. There he would find the cairn in which a voice lay locked in stone, a voice that, emancipated, would tell him the location of the crystal Baphomet.

Ka and Neema were at the other end of the cavern, endlessly staring at something Ka called a 'ghost machine'. Fungle had found the ghost machine too distracting to work near, so he had dragged a patched human-bean-bag cushion and rolled a huge wooden spool the size of a small table to this end of the cavern, and set himself up a little study.

Now he was elated with his discovery and could contain it no longer. Carefully he picked up the restored cartography scroll and carried it to Neema and Ka.

They sat before the ghost machine, staring at its flickering glass. The sight bothered Fungle a bit: their eyes were glazed and there was no shred of intelligence in their expressions. He looked from them to the ghost machine itself. The light that came from its glass was almost the colour of mage-light, but cold, flickering, and without passion. The glass swarmed with something like harsh snow, and a sound like hissing rain poured from an inset grille beside it.

'There!' said Ka, and pointed at the screen. 'I tole ya!'

'I still didn't see nothin',' said Neema.

They stared at the ghost machine as they spoke, and not at each other.

'Confounderate it!' said Ka, 'it were right there.' He flicked the glass with a sharp-fingered hand. 'Right on the glass, plain as the nose on yer . . . er, plain as day.'

'What was it, then, if it were so obvious?' Neema demanded.

Ka took umbrage that his word was being questioned. 'Why, it were a ghostie!' he replied. 'That's what this here box does! It shows ghosties! I dunno if it captures 'em fer a moment, or iffin it's some kinda window lookin' out on where they lives, but I'm tellin' ya – there, there!' His hand shook at the screen.

Fungle felt his fur prick up in a wave spreading along his shoulders and down his back, and a mortal chill stole through him like a knotted thread pulled through his heart – for on the flickering glass before him formed the pale, translucent image of a hand. It reached across the screen, picked up a pale, translucent cup, and brought it up to an ethereal face to drink.

At the same time, the hissing dimmed and a voice came from the box: '. . . ountain grown . . .'

The ghost vanished and the hissing returned.

Ka slapped his knees and jumped up and down. 'Tole ya!' he gloated. 'Tole ya, tole ya, tole ya!' He patted the top of the box gently. 'Ghost machine!' His expression changed when he realised Fungle had been standing behind them the whole time. 'Fungle!' he exclaimed gratefully. 'You saw it, din't yer?' His look was comically hopeful.

'Saw somethin',' Fungle admitted. Had Ka somehow tapped in to the human Realm of the Dead? Such places were best left undisturbed.

But Ka beamed. 'Saw somethin', ol' Fungle did! Hah!' To Neema he confided: 'Y'know, Fungle kin summon demons from the vasty deep.'

Fungle smiled knowingly. 'Why, so can you, Ka, or so can anyone.' He winked. 'Trick's gettin' 'em to come when ya call.'

Ka patted the top of the ghost machine as if it were a fireside dog. 'Sometimes this thing gets whole ghosties, like as if they was standin' in front o' you clear as you're in fronta me!'

'How do ya know they ain't?' asked Neema.

Ka's ears fell as he pondered this. 'Reckon I don't,' he conceded.

Seeing that Fungle was eager to tell them something, Neema indicated the scroll in Fungle's hands. 'Whatcha got there, Fungle?'

'Hmn?' Fungle was staring at the ghost machine. Something hypnotic about it made him feel like a bunny before a viper.

'I said, Whatcha got there, Fungle?'

'Oh!' Fungle tore his gaze from the ghost machine. 'Figure I've found the Mound of the Dead,' he said.

'Well, bully fer you.' Neema sounded only a little enthused. 'Where is it?'

''Bout three days' hike from here.'

'Three days,' said Neema. 'Hike.' She shook her head and looked down at her broken leg.

'That a map?' Ka wanted to know.

Fungle nodded. 'An old map of the north-east coast of Americka. The first gnoles to arrive here drew it, and it was copied by geomancers for generations. Me great-grandad drew this'n.'

'No foolin'?' Ka was impressed. 'Let's 'ave a look, then.'

In the flickering light of the ghost machine Fungle unrolled the ancient scroll. It would have looked a little odd to a human bean, because the ancients – who knew the earth was a sphere ages before Columbus sailed across the watery graves of their forefathers – drew their maps with the east on top, since that was the direction in which the earth spun. Always heading east, that's us.

Fungle's finger traced a broken line of mountains. 'Here's the valley,' he said. His finger moved east and a little north. 'An' here's where we are now, Ka.' He tapped an angle of mountain.

'Don't press too hard, then,' said Ka. 'Or ye'll collapse me tunnels.'

Fungle wasn't sure if his friend was joking, so he merely nodded and continued. His fingers traced the fragile surface of the map. 'Now, from here, I'll head north, across this valley, through this leg o' forest that sticks out here, 'nother valley, an' down into these foothills.' His finger came to rest. 'The Mound of the Dead is here.'

Ka took the scroll from him, frowning as he perused it. 'How recent you say this map is?'

'Ain't recent at all, Ka.'

Ka nodded. Suddenly he rolled up the scroll and handed it back to Fungle all imperious-like. 'Well,' he said summarily, 'ya can't get there from here.'

From the ghost machine came the static-laden sound of a woman's voice: '– save big during our summer clearan –'

They ignored it. 'Don't see why not,' said Fungle. 'Travel by day to avoid giblins an' worse. Valley's level an' smooth; forest's not even thick-wooded at the edge. I'll just follow the old stones that mark the ley lines –'

But Ka was shaking his huge head. 'Stones ain't there any more,' the gnome insisted. 'Even them woods is gone. Fungle, ya can study yer books an' scrolls from now 'til the sun turns into a boll weevil, but what's true in a book ain't necessarily true fer real.'

'I don't follow, Ka.'

'I'm tellin' ya that the maps've changed. Fer all the good yer map'd do ya, it may have come outta one a' yer father's Howzit nursery rhymes.'

'Just so happens I loved Wisp's Howzits,' said Neema.

Ka nodded. 'That's because they was true,' he said. 'But they wasn't real. There's a difference.'

Fungle tried not to let it bother him that they referred to his father in the past tense, as if the broadsmiling old gnole had passed from the earth years ago. But he said, 'A map's a map, Ka, an' true as the land it stands fer. An' this is a true map, drawn by –'

'– by expert gnoles, I know,' interrupted Ka. 'But it's the *land* that ain't so true no more. Human beans've changed it. Forest ain't there, marker stones gone, new freeway's runnin' through here, valley's different, no hills where hills useta be, an' new hills where God never set 'em!'

Fungle remembered Molom's words: *The very world is altered. The naked monkeys own the earth now. Throughout their history they have changed it to suit themselves, with little thought of consequences or effects. Something has made them forget the world as a shared thing.* 'How could that be?' he demanded. 'How can ya change a place so's a map won't recognise it?'

Ka shrugged. 'It's just the way they is, Fungle. Yer gonna need someone ta take ya across. That there stretch you can lay yer finger on is a great big dyin' kingdom fulla changes an' dangers no map'd warn ya 'bout. Ya need someone who knows 'em.'

'Not you, I take it,' suggested Neema.

'Oh, no no no,' agreed Ka. 'I don't venture that ways, not this ol' gnome. There's all manner a sudden combustibles there that'd take me fer granite iffin I was to get singed by one of 'em. No, no, aboveground's outta the question no matter what, an' tunnellin' that way's a frightful task 'cause of the oozlumps.'

'Oozlumps?' Fungle asked.

Ka nodded. 'Sticky slimy oozin' horrors what live beneath the Land of a Thousand Smokes an' come up outta the ground to chew a feller down past his essentials.'

Neema glanced at Fungle, who looked more speculative than worried.

'Outwittin' giblins may be easy as throwin' scraps to a dog,' Ka continued, 'but this ol' gnome just ain't equipped to deal with such as oozlumps. Fungle needs a *expert*.' He turned to face Fungle, brilliantined by the swarming aura of the ghost machine behind him. 'Ya needs to look up Musrum the Mossman at Tobacco Inn,' he said.

It was with a troubled heart that Fungle sat down a final time to study his ancient books and scrolls. Molom had said that the humans were close to discovering Baphomet themselves. It was possible they might discover it before Fungle could. And if the humans got to it before he could, then so might Theverat. Fungle was racing the clock, and he had no idea under what circumstances he might finally (if at all!) encounter Baphomet. He was supposed to summon Molom to destroy the awful stone, but what if he could not? What if he were injured, or if there simply wasn't enough time? With Theverat or humans hot on his heels, it might be impossible to perform a Summoning – especially if Theverat's campaign on the astral plane kept it as difficult to invoke Molom as it had been the last time.

Fungle needed insurance. He needed a last-resort measure should it prove impossible to summon Molom, something that would prevent Theverat or the humans from claiming the stone. And because Molom had said that destroying Baphomet was beyond Fungle's powers, Fungle knew that only one measure would suffice: the Salamander.

Away from Neema and Ka, Fungle scrupulously studied the spell that invoked the Spirit of Fire. None called forth the Salamander lightly, because the price for raising that raging entity has always been the life and soul of the summoner. Once called, the Salamander howls into the world and consumes all that exists within its burning reach, until nothing remains and it feeds upon itself, to be reborn from its own ashes the next time it is called.

Summoning the Salamander would be a desperate measure, but who knew what desperation awaited him?

Fungle committed the volatile spell to memory until he could have recited it in his sleep.

That done, the mage could see little point in staying at Ka's any longer. Neema tried to insist on coming along, which demand Fungle didn't even dignify with the obvious reply. He merely stared at her broken leg until she stopped talking. Though he was pained at her injury (no matter what she said, he still felt responsible), a part of him was relieved that the seemingly inevitable confrontation over her coming along on his quest had been rendered ludicrous. He tried to tell himself that his relief stemmed from pragmatism: now someone would remain to watch over the valley; an unnecessary burden on his journey, however well-meaning, increased their chance of detection, capture, or worse. This boon was Fungle's and Fungle's alone, placed on him by Molom, and it was wrong to ask anyone to share it with him however tempting the idea might be.

But the true reason for his relief was less prosaic. The last several days had shown him that there were more pages in Neema Cleverbread's book than the few he'd read. They had known one another for many years – since childhood (how close and far away that seemed, a frightful thought!) – yet except for festivals and gnolidays and chance cordial but awkward meetings, and especially Neema's love for his father, Wisp, the old ridiculous feud between the Foxwits and the Cleverbreads had been a veil between them. Now that he had gained glimpses of what lay behind the blunt front Neema set between herself and an admittedly harshened world, Fungle found himself, and his heart, intrigued.

And *that* was the true reason why he was relieved that she would not be going with him on his dangerous way.

Fungle left behind his books and scrolls, and charged Ka with caring for the magnetite crystal he had rescued from the Lunabird. He did not insult his friend's selfless nature by asking him to take care of Neema; he only asked him to bring her a fresh clump of blessed moss each morning for her wrapping, and asked him to try to keep her out of trouble *after* her leg had healed – meaning, of course, *Don't let her come after me, Ka!*

As he shouldered his pack and set himself to bless them and bid them well, Neema struggled to stand before him. Fungle had the good grace not to protest that she should stay off her feet. She presented him with a beautiful briar rose, a blood-red bud so tight and lush it looked as if a good squeeze would make it drip. 'For luck,' Neema said. 'An' I'm expectin' ya to give it back to me when yer done chasin' all 'round the countryside.'

Velvet perfume rose beneath him. His fingers closed around its thorn-shorn stalk. 'I'll keep it near me heart,' he said. 'An' give it up when I see ya again.'

She nodded. For a moment they looked at each other – really *looked*, in a rare unguarded way people can seldom bear – and this time it was Neema who turned away quickly.

Ka had GizmoJo, the McManical Can, cart him and Fungle back through the abandoned mineshafts. Fungle tried to ignore its blank smiling idiot face as Ka kept up an echoing patter about Tobacco Inn all the way: be careful how ya go in, Fungle. Be careful while yer there, Fungle. Be careful how ya leave, Fungle! It's a wild an' rowdy place, Fungle, an' a careless word's as good as a thrown stone to them folk. Keep yer wits an' mind yer drink, an' tell ol' Musrum that Karbolic Earthcreep sent ya. He's a tough'n to get to, an' even tougher to bargain with. He's a decent codger at his core, but his core's buried under a lot of . . . well, let's just say it's buried. Still, I've faith ye'll hold yer own. Ah, Tobacco Inn! I'm makin' meself thirsty just tellin' ya 'bout it!

– and on and on, until they stood blinking daylight on the raw mountainside. To Fungle it felt like months since he had seen the sun; Ka, of course, hung back in the dark mine entrance, well out of the light.

'Well, Fungle,' said Ka, being brave about it and all, 'ya come back to us soon, hear?' Then he was blubbering and hugging Fungle like a mother saying goodbye to her only child striking out on his own.

Fungle held him and patted him, and finally pried him away. 'Somethin' tells me ye'll be comin' to me first,' said Fungle.

Ka only looked bemused. Suddenly his expression changed. 'Well, fry me fer a fish!' he exclaimed. 'Nearly fergot.' He dashed back into the mine, then re-emerged holding a tissue-wrapped package. 'Here. This might come in handy.'

Fungle unwrapped the tissue and removed a metal object that sparkled in the sunlight. It wasn't silver, but something like it. 'What is it, Ka?' Fungle asked.

'Leverage,' replied Ka, grinning, 'in case ol' Musrum decides to get all stubborn-like on ya. Just a little trinket, nothin' to you or me, but Musrum'd give his skin fer it. I been holdin' onto it a goodly while in case I wanted something outta the bleeder, an' I can't think of a better time to use it.'

'Why, thankee muchly, Ka,' said Fungle.

'Hold on, hold on,' said Ka, waving his hand and a bit embarrassed. 'There's one more thing.' And he gave Fungle a grey, boxy object with a handstrap, a button on top, and a glass eye in the centre.

'I calls it a Light Box,' Ka explained. 'Ya press this button here, an' it makes a flash o' light that'd blind a rock. Figure it might save yer fur iffin ya use it at the right moment. Works on bat-reez, too, like me mechanical man, but be careful – it takes a while between blindin' flashes, an' it wears out pretty quick.'

Fungle turned the box in his hands. 'Well, then I'll use it in good health,' he said. 'And thank you again.'

Ka waved it off, and Fungle smiled – fondly and sadly – and patted the gnome on the shoulder once more, then touched the wishing feather on his tall cap and set a hand to the briar rose tucked in his tunic.

Then he turned away and began walking north toward a dark battalion of firs.

Not until he was several clobhops on his way did Fungle stop to wonder if the old clan feud was truly what had kept Neema in the valley after all other gnoles but him had gone, and where, in Ka's cavern hundreds of feet beneath the ground, she could've got hold of a briar rose.

7 *Tobacco Inn*

'More grog!' The drunken troll pounded the long bench table with his dented mug. 'Ain't near numb enough yet!' He stood and roared: *'More grog, I says!'*

The other trolls seated beside him snickered among themselves. One of them offhandedly reached up and yanked the yelling troll's stubby tail. He buttocked back to the rough bench with a jar that creaked wood. The drunken troll stared at his offending drinking companion with an oddly childlike expression of bafflement, but the tail-yanker continued his conversation with the pipe-puffing lumpkin beside him who could barely be seen nodding agreement as thick blue smoke eddied around his murky outline. A scaly, thick, scarred claw emerged from the wreath of smoke to lay a coin on the gaming table where the hedgehogs were being inflated. The hook-nosed croupier nodded acknowledgement and added the creature's wager to the pile favouring the larger of the two squealing hedgehogs – the smaller pile, for the larger hedgehog was the underhog, by virtue of the unfortunate creature's size.

Around the croupier, grotesque shapes dim in the swirl and curl of blue-grey pipe-smoke, horned, scaled, corrugated, scarred, and encrusted, the gathered creatures shouted, croaked, and rasped encouragement at the 'bellows fellows' who sweated away in a hissing squeezing frenzy as they pumped air into the hedgehogs.

The *sss-sss* of the competing bellows rose in pitch, and with it rose the hedgehogs' squeals. The bettors' shouts increased.

POP! The gathered gamblers were pelted by chunky wet bits as the smaller hedgehog burst.

The winners' cheers were undercut by losers' boos as they set upon the winning hedgehog with their boots. The croupier absently scooped in the smoke-wreathed creature's wager. The bellows fellows swabbed themselves dry. The bucket brigade, black dwarves one and all, sloshed away the mess. The pipe-puffing lumpkin pushed out another coin. The motion caused him to lean out of the fortress of pipe-smoke he had erected around himself, revealing a lumpy face that looked like dough rolled in pebbles and split by a vast gob filled with stalactites and stalagmites of stained and rotting fangs. His drinking companion, the troll, paid no attention, but continued to babble at his nodding, smoky frame. Somebody sang '*Pop Goes the Hedgehog!*' off-key, which brought forth a rolling thunder of guffaws. Another pair of unlucky hedgehogs were brought forth. The disgruntled, drunken troll gave up shouting for more grog in favour of pushing his way through the ten-deep clamouring boozers pressed up against the long L of the bar.

Just another night at Tobacco Inn.

It was a ghost town, a decaying clump of ramshackle shacks that had played host to hopeful hobos long ago, when an entire nation wrote itself a rubber cheque that bounced and left a country poor.

Fungle picked his way among the remnants. Kudzu, the relentless Oriental vine, had grown up around the dirt streets and wooden buildings, and the buildings had long rotted into the landscape. In places it was hard to say which was forest and which was building, for it looked like the one had been caught in the midst of transforming into the other.

Who builds such ugly homes, Fungle wondered, all stark squares and rectangles that seem so deliberately out of step with the land that holds them? They build as if to deny the very forces that reclaim their homes – time, death, rebirth – instead of making them a part of their surroundings. Even in death their works are defiant. Molom is right to fear such creatures possessing a stone as powerful as Baphomet.

He sighted the façade described to him by Ka. Once it had been a storefront, though even then it had truly been little more than a shack. Now it was a hollow corpse, skinned alive by kudzu's ever-lengthening tendrils.

But what do their works defy? thought Fungle, pursuing his line of thought. *The world of Nature, or something in themselves?*

A trampled path led through a riot of nettles and briars and around the ruins of the general store to a heavy storm door. Beneath it . . .

He shook his head and took a moment behind a tree to collect himself. Wouldn't do to just go bargin' on in. There were precautions to take first. This place was a magnet for unsavoury characters, and he was a gnole, and unsavoury characters had lately taken an interest in gnoles. So Fungle wove about himself a spell of nondescriptness. Like most of his spells, it was the result of economy and efficiency. Though he had the ability to totally change his appearance – in the mind of a beholder, if not in actuality – such a spell would defeat its purpose by calling attention to him if someone were on the lookout for magic spells. But 'simplest is bestest', and it was easier, and more practical, to surround himself with an aura much like the one guarding Neema's door that had momentarily vexed him – a spell that made him slippery to the attention, that caused the eye to slide off without pausing to collect any memorable detail. In fact, there are people who generate such spells without any formal training in magic, and it is quite likely you have met a few.

Spell completed, Fungle approached the storm door. What plans he had for after he descended down there, like Dante into Hell, were loosely formed at best. Too much was unknown. Ten per cent inspiration, forty per cent improvisation, and fifty per cent perspiration – that's what Wily Barktea had taught him about getting by in the world, and that's how it was shaping up to be.

He raised the storm door and bent to his purpose, and thick smoke engulfed him.

To hear them you'd think they were hurling insults at the bartender: 'Gutrot!' they shouted. *'Noggin knocker!'* 'Shandy!' *'Potwallop!'* 'Arf an' arf!' *'You-reeka!'* 'Scrumpy!' But no, they were calling for drinks – each to his own and every one his personal poison.

And poison it was: one in three taps was marked with a skull and crossbones, and half the barrels too.

Smoke billowed up from the patrons' mouths and nostrils like the breath of some infernal machine. The room was a tapestry of bedlam woven with a *mêlée* of voices: insults friendly and cutting, threats whispered and shouted, good cheer likewise:

''Arry! I 'aven't seen you in a dog's age! – Ey, now I think of it, 'ave a bita me moggy sammitch. Loovly stuff!'

'Bets, gennelmen, place yer bets!'

'– an' iffin I so much as smells ya round here again, I'll sew yer ears to the inside o' yer thighs so's ye'll spend the rest o' yer days starin' up at the brown moon of yer stinkhole!'

'– *so the travellin' slavesman says, "Take my life – please!"*'

'– that s'posed to scare me? I cuts me toenails with bigger blades 'an that!'

'*Scrumpy!*'

'– an' take yer bloated entrails widja!'

POP!

The drunken troll (admittedly not a very helpful description, since it applied to just about every troll in Tobacco Inn, past, present, and future) ploughed toward the bar, unmindful of complaints as he elbowed aside potwallopers either furred, scaled, skinned, scarred, muscled, or any combination of the aforesaid. He was like a bowling ball cracking through skittles. He horned his way to the bar (easy, if you've horns), burped volcanically (it disappeared without a ripple in the vocal menagerie), and pounded the counter with both huge-boned fists. He yelled something to the bartender, who either had more than two arms or moved as if he did.

'Whassat?' called the bartender, ladling chunky bits into a chipped mug.

'I SAID,' bellowed the troll, 'SLOW NIGHT, INNIT?'

The bartender (there was only one) shrugged and shoved a handful of black-flecked ice into the broken-handled mug, then shovelled it toward the eager upthrust claws clutching at him over the rusted rail.

'Whatcher poison?' the bartender hollered.

'GROG!' the troll bellowed.

'Comin' up!'

The troll's satisfied grin showed teeth arrayed like topsy-turvy tombstones in a vandalised graveyard. 'Grog!' he shouted happily, and shoved the hunchbacked dwarf on his right in a comradely fashion – comradely for trolls, that is, but it sent the dwarf cartwheeling backward into a rather nondescript little fellow who went sprawling. The troll reached down a great hand and yanked the roly-poly little character to his feet. 'SIDDOWN!' he bellowed, and pulled out the barstool next to him. 'BUY YA DRINK!'

It seemed to the troll that his new drinking buddy nodded acknowledgement. It was hard to tell. Things was kinda fuzzy, an' his gaze kept slidin' off the fella's face. Iffin it wuz a fella. 'G'devenin'!' he shouted.

His breath could have fried rocks.

'Evenin',' acknowledged the stranger. Funny tall pointy hat he was wearin'.

'Whatcher drinkin'?' the bartender demanded.

The figure muttered something.

'WHASSAT?' screamed the bartender.

'Ginger beer!' shouted the genial little gent in the funny tall hat.

POP!

The swan-song of the latest hedgehog was loud in a room gone stone quiet. Suddenly the only motion was eddying smoke ropes.

'Did oy 'ear you say,' the bartender inquired, '*ginger beer?*'

'If ya please,' agreed Fungle.

The bartender's slight brow furrowed. He kept trying to get a fix on the stranger's face, but his eyes wouldn't hold still. They kept slidin' away like an egg in a buttered pan. 'Didja bring a note from yer mum, my little lammykin?' he asked, sweet and sharky-like.

The bar erupted in laughter. The bartender smirked in self-satisfaction and squeezed lumpy brown water from his rag into a mug. 'Bilge!' he called out, and slid the mug down the counter to an eager black elf.

Next he refilled the troll's mug, holding it under a rotting, lidless barrel. Unidentifiable lumps bobbed on the thick, heady surface. The bartender yanked the spigot and muttered, 'Ginger beer!' to himself as sludgy liquid plopped into the glass. When the glass was full, the bartender turned to Fungle with a sickly sweet and nasty grin. 'Still want yer ginger beer, sonny?' he asked.

Beside Fungle, the troll stood with his mug in his catcher's-mitt hand, grinning and collecting flies. 'Awr, he don't want no ginger beer!' he shouted. 'Gi' my frien' here a pint a' Ol' Pekuliar!'

POP!

The bar grew silent once again.

'Mmph.' The bartender's bent fingers drummed the counter. Suddenly he broke into an evil grin. He clapped his hands and rubbed his palms. 'Poynta Ol' Pekuliar,' he said, 'comin' up!'

There was a mutter throughout the smoky room. Fungle heard the words *Ol' Pekuliar* being passed around as disbelievingly as a baton in a snake relay race.

The bartender dropped from view as if a trap door had opened beneath him. There came much muttering and sputtering and banging and clanging, accompanied by curses we dare not repeat here for fear the page would combust. Eventually the bartender re-emerged, holding – with the trepidation of a one-armed man clutching a rattlesnake by the tail – a hunk of dust the exact size and shape of a bottle.

He held the dustbottle high for all to see, and then, with great ceremony, drew a deep breath and gushered it out again.

A dust cloud billowed from the bottle.

A goblin standing to the stranger's right scrambled forward on tiptoe to snort up the specks that settled onto the bartop.

The drunken troll inhaled some of the particles. 'Ba-*shooo!*' he sneezed, soprano.

The bartender glared and dabbed globs from himself with his squishy rag.

'Pardon,' the troll said meekly. He swabbed his nose with a finger, which he licked.

The bartender laid the bottle-top against the corner of the bar, and with the assuredness of a lifetime of repetition, thumped it *just so* with the hardened heel of his palm.

There was a great exhalation, the fermented breath of ages. It was as if an encrypted mummy, holding its lungless breath down through the centuries as it waited for its sarcophagus lid to lift, had at last seen a sliver of daylight, and expelled the dusty accumulated wisdom of ancient unknown air carried with it into death and immortality.

The bottle-cap plopped on the beerlogged floor. A starveling dog licked eagerly at the brown circle of sludge accumulated on the cap's inside. Immediately its bones, clearly visible in its fleshless body, began to shake and rattle. Its eyes rolled wildly and it keeled over with its legs stiff in the air, a rictus grin frozen on its face.

The bartender selected a mug. He chose it with care, as if some second sight had shown him that this mug would forevermore hang in a revered place in Tobacco Inn, and that drunken creatures of every shape and size and persuasion would point to it and reminisce (and lie) about being there the night the stranger drank the pint of Old Pekuliar. No mug of mere glass or pewter would suffice to contain such heady fermentation.

This called for iron.

The patrons pressed forward, anxious not to miss an instant of the high drama being played out here in Tobacco Inn.

The bartender hefted the mug with two hands, lifted it high, and brought it down as if beheading a criminal with an Arab scimitar.

The Wagnerian boom of it hitting the scarred counter was like the slam of Vulcan's hammer.

So there it was: a clean mug – an historic occasion by itself, in this place.

With royal aplomb the bartender turned the bottle upside-down above it.

Everyone waited.

Across the globe strange insects that live for but an hour hatched from seven-year-old eggs, matured, mated, and laid eggs of their own.

In Tobacco Inn the bottle hovered above the mug.

Across the universe a star exploded, its light speeding on a ten-thousand-year journey toward the earth.

In Tobacco Inn there came a single gurgle.

In far Japan an earthquake swayed skyscrapers like undersea fronds.

In Tobacco Inn a slight brown bulge of thick liquid formed at the suspended mouth of an ancient bottle.

Strange ephemeral insects lived and died. Nova-light hurtled eleven million miles. An island nation trembled.

The first long tendril of Old Pekuliar touched the bottom of the only clean receptacle in Tobacco Inn. The engrossed patrons stared enthralled as the remainder piled on top of itself in thick brown ropes that coalesced but slowly. At last what came from the bottle was a thin brown string, then a sliver that bowed with the stale

breath of warm air running through the tavern. The barkeeper twisted his wrist and the sliver broke. He set the bottle on the bar and gripped the counter's edge.

Fungle hefted the mug. 'Well . . . cheers,' he said, then threw back his head and upended the mug.

The thick brew descended earthward like a boiled slug. Fungle kept his mouth open the while. He looked like a sideshow sword swallower, like someone eating a never-ending snake. The thick rope of Old Pekuliar slimmed to a string that thinned to a sliver, and Fungle twisted his wrist to break the strand and banged the mug on the bar.

He nodded appreciatively at the troll. 'Much obliged,' he said.

The troll could only nod, gaping like a fish out of water.

Fungle turned away from the bar. Within three steps he was drunk as a sailor's leave.

Two giblins were rolling the bones against a back wall of Tobacco Inn. One giblin looked like a porcupine and the other looked like a rat, and two more appropriate furnishings in this malodorous drunkbox could not be imagined.

There was some kinda commotion going on up at the bar, but the giblins didn't much care. Rat was into Porcupine for about a hundred years' wortha drinks, and aimed to keep at it 'til luck turned back his way, which any fool knew luck hadda do sometime or other.

Porcupine cackled and wheedled, gettin' on a feller's nerves, if ya wanta know the truth. Rat tried to ignore him as he shook the dice in his enormous spiderlike hands. The more Porcupine rode him about his bad luck, the more it drove Rat to try and reverse his fortune. He wondered if Porcupine knew that.

He blew hot foundry breath into his clenched fist for luck and rattled the dice. There was luck in this throw. He could feel it. Sometimes a fella gets a *feelin'* – can't explain it, just the notion of a certain sure thing, like when ya throw yer knife and just *know* it's gonna bite heartmeat, or when ya see the jolly step of a happy bloke an' just *know* his wallet's loaded full up. Rat felt that now: there was winning in this pass. And winning would be pretty terrific after the run he'd had these last coupla days. Walkin' coffee-pots and escaping gnoles, the ground collapsing all around 'em, and gnoles gettin' aways again, and long chases down tight tunnels, nearly drownin', and even a *gnome* gettin' the better of 'em. One more screw-up an' it'd be the Old Codger they'd hafta answer to, and nobody wanted to have to take a direct account with Him, 'cause ya tended to come away from them accounts a mite different than when ya went in. Like what'd happened to Vixen.

Rat shuddered. Best not think about what Vixen'd become. Best think about this pass of the dice, about the sure-thing feeling he had humming in his hand.

He brought back his hand to throw.

Someone bumped him and he spilled the dice.

The dice clattered on the stone floor. Two black dots stared up at Rat like black cancers in white bone.

'Snake eyes,' Porcupine sniggered.

Rat turned, teeth bared, ready to tear out the throat of whoever'd lost him his chance to even-up on Porcupine – and stopped.

'Terribly sorry,' muttered the drunken roly-poly figure who'd nudged him, then politely tipped his tall green pointy hat and staggered off.

But it wasn't this interference that set the stiff fur prickling across Rat's head, down his neck, along his shoulders, and down his back. It was a smell, a smell, a smell . . .

Gnole.

Thorn sat in the shadows near the entrance to Tobacco Inn. He sat alone, the empty space around him remarkable in this crowded place. Equally remarkable was the way everyone avoided looking at him. Their eyes resisted lingering on his leathery, spiky form; the mere act of glancing at his barbed projections seemed almost to pierce their pupils. Something about him suggested that they certainly didn't want him looking back, either, just as they wouldn't try to stare down a fevered dog with a foamy muzzle. Meeting his eye was like meeting a killer in an alley, grinning and holding your death in his hands.

Tobacco Inn never closed, and Thorn had been here since last night, the same mug in front of him. He drank from it often, yet it never seemed to empty.

He had noted the presence of the giblins when they came in to drink and gamble. Good, good, elements were converging here. It would only be a matter of time before –

– the gnole came in.

Thorn felt him coming down the steps before he actually saw him. Maybe the gnole shaman thought he was clever and subtle with his spell of nondescriptness – and doubtless to the simple drunken fools in this room he was – but Thorn knew exactly what to look for. He had been prepared. He had been sent.

The gnole passed by him unaware and headed for the bar. The giblins played dice in the corner. Thorn drained his mug and set it on the table. He grinned, and a wine-glass held by a nearby elf shattered.

With satisfied expectation Thorn leaned back in his chair to watch and wait. On the table in front of him, his mug slowly refilled itself.

Hornets warred in Fungle's head. As soon as the Ol' Pekuliar reached his stomach he felt it working on him, tingeing his blood like a teabag in water. The alcohol raced along his veins to his brain and clamped its chemical jaws on his mind like a pit bull on a windpipe.

Within three steps he was stone cold drunk. The room became warm taffy: the walls began to stretch and yaw like sickening funhouse mirrors. Support beams grew elastic, the ceiling bowed and oozed toward his feet while the stone floor reared near his snout and coalesced with the roof. Solidity became a matter of faith as around him churned a glittering sea of tobacco smoke jewelled with the merry eyes of trolls, elves, goblins and lumpkins.

One more step and he set his body to work: he sped himself up inside, and hurried up the natural metabolic processes that converted alcohol to sugar.

On his fifth step his head was clearer but he felt sleepy.

Sixth step he was hung over. His scalp was two sizes too small for his head. All sounds were unnaturally loud. It seemed he could hear his fur growing, could hear every nerve-grating creak of eyeball movement.

Seventh step, he called up reserves of adrenaline and minerals, water from fatty tissue, and complex vitamins.

Eighth step he bumped into someone. Refusing to become distracted, he muttered an apology and continued toward the back.

POP!

By the time he reached the far end of the room he was sober as a hoot owl and thirsty as a whistler eating salted crackers in the desert.

He turned his inner vision outward once more.

The bucket brigade slopped up hedgehog mess; two more hedgehogs were produced, money changed hands (and paws), threats were made, drinks were spiked, dirty deals were done and undone, pockets were picked, ornate meerschaum pipes were lit anew, mugs (of many varieties) were smashed, bones were rolled (and sometimes broken), rat-tail pies were gobbled, gravies sloshed and splashed, fur flew, tattooing needles resumed their beautiful wounding, and throats well-oiled struck up an impromptu and many-keyed arrangement of 'The Scrumpy Song':

> *It be love-a-lee stuff –*
> *Vermin likes us can't get enough.*
> *We drinks it all day,*
> *Night-time, too!*
> *Slurps it fer breakfast,*
> *And on the loo.*
> *Glugs it at dinner,*
> *Then takes it ta bed –*
> *It be bad fer the bowels,*
> *But grand fer the head!*
>
> *Scrumpy! Scrumpy!*
> *It be love-a-lee stuff!*
> *But we likes it 'cause it's cheap an' rough.*
> *Brewed from wormy apples,*
> *An' beady rats' eyes, too,*
> *Oodles o' piddle,*
> *An' meat gone blue.*
>
> *Scrumpy! Scrumpy!*
> *It be love-a-lee stuff!*
> *Vermin likes us just can't get enough!*

By the end everyone had joined in, and Tobacco Inn rang with a sound not quite music – more like a pack of castrated wolves lending their talents to a requiem mass. And scrumpy became the shout of the hour. Mugs of it were passed overhead back from the ten-deep bar like waterpails at a bucket brigade.

There's a fire to put out, a'right, thought Fungle. *And most everyone here's been quenching it for the better part of their lives. But the more they pour, the brighter it burns.*

A hand clapped on his shoulder. He turned to face a muscular goblin with tic-tac-toe scars running up and down his bulging arms. Behind him another goblin, equally muscular, picked his needle teeth with a rusty bayonet.

The first goblin grinned evilly. 'Boss wants ta see yer,' he said.

The second goblin pointed his bayonet to a curtained partition at the back of the inn.

Fungle didn't argue.

THUNK!

'Nother triple twenty, Rat thought with disgust. *Here I thought darts was me own game, an' turns out this loon's a deadeye.*

'I'm tellin' ya, it's him!' Rat insisted as Porcupine yanked the slim-beaked darts from the board. 'That mouldy ol' gnole! Smelled him, I did.'

Porcupine merely held the lacquered plucked hummingbird-body darts out to Rat. His mad red eyes were eager.

Rat was incredulous. 'You know what'll happen to us iffin he gets away?' he asked, taking the darts.

A spiky hand clamped his shoulder and spun him around. '*I* will happen to you,' said Thorn.

The deadbird darts leapt from Rat's hand and impaled themselves in the bullseye.

Through the curtained partition was a narrow corridor. The goblins led Fungle to a doorway draped by a back-lit, translucent sheet. Fungle heard odd music from the other side.

The goblin with the tic-tac-toe tattoos rapped the doorframe. 'Mmmm,' from within.

The goblin snatched aside the sheet, and thick waves of blue-grey smoke billowed into the corridor.

'Person y'asked fer, sir,' said the goblin.

'Mmm.'

The goblin hooked a thumb toward the room. 'He'll see ya now,' he said.

Fungle went in.

The air was thick and choking with smoke. Book-shelves were crammed with ledgers. Against one wall was an odd contraption of glass and metal and spinning disks and blinking lights. It looked like something Ka would put in his home, and it was where the odd music came from.

Barely legible through the haze was a sign against the far wall:

WARNING!
The Surgeon General has determined that smoking may be hazardous to your health.

Plumes the colour of ostrich feathers curled up from below this, venting from a pipe so large it looked like a piece of furniture. It sat on the wooden floor beside a writing desk on which glowed a battery-powered Coleman lantern, and so massive and ornate was the pipe that at first Fungle did not realise there was a person sitting behind it.

'I understand you are looking for me,' a voice rumbled.

Fungle saw him then: gravid, stately, pebble-eyed, and such a centred, powerful aura that he seemed like a force of nature, a presence who had always been here, and these weak structures merely grown up around him.

'Musrum the Mossman,' said Fungle.

'I know who I am,' said Musrum in a voice all upper-crust and sherried. He set down the mouthpiece of his enormous pipe. 'And if I am not mistaken, you are Fungle Foxwit, son of Wisp Foxwit and shaman of some renown. Drink? You're fond of Old Pekuliar, I believe. A drastic vice, if I may say so, old card.'

Fungle thought rapidly. What use denying who he was? 'Er, no, thankee. That is, yes, I be Fungle Foxwit, but I think one Ol' Pekuliar a lifetime's me limit.'

Musrum frowned. His thick fingers drummed the desk contemplatively. 'Larry,' he said.

The doorhanging was drawn aside and an inquiring goblin head appeared.

'Two teas,' said Musrum. He eyed Fungle appraisingly. 'Lapsang Souchong,' he specified.

The goblin nodded and withdrew.

Musrum drew on his pipe and regarded Fungle. 'Yes, I know something of who you are, Mr Foxwit; it is my job to know such things. And you are either very courageous or quite foolhardy to come here. I stand to make quite a tidy sum by handing you over to any number of reprobates who have recently made inquiries about you in my establishment, some of whom are waiting outside even as we speak.'

Fungle's pulse leapt.

'What they want you for I have no idea,' continued Musrum, 'and to tell you the truth I do not care.' He puffed his pipe. 'I am a moderne businessman. I am interested in – and derive great pleasure from – making the best possible deal for myself.' He interlaced his fingers on the desk and leaned forward. 'What do you want from me, Mr Foxwit?' he asked.

Fungle reached into his tunic and withdrew his parchment map. He hesitated a moment before unrolling it. Musrum had just inferred he would hand Fungle over to the highest bidder unless Fungle made him a better offer. Could he show Musrum his destination without being betrayed?

Well, he decided, *iffin he's to be me guide, I gots to tell him where I'm headed.* Fungle spread the map out on Musrum's desk. 'I needs a guide,' he said. 'To this hill, here.' He tapped the place that represented the Mound of the Dead.

'What an amusing fellow,' Musrum said, barely glancing at the map. 'That is a very powerful place, and you would do well to avoid it.'

'I've no choice.'

Musrum's smile was sly but humourless. 'Well,' he said, 'I operate a drinking establishment. I am not a tour guide. Unless, of course, there is substantial profit to be found.'

There was a rap on the doorframe, and the goblin named Larry entered carrying a tarnished silver tea-service. He set it on a stand beside Musrum's desk, then left, but not before giving Fungle a speculative look.

Fungle reached into his tunic again and withdrew the tissue-wrapped bundle Ka had given him before he left. He set it on top of the map before Musrum.

Musrum regarded it blankly, then looked at Fungle. 'Honey, lemon, milk?' he asked. 'I also have lump sugar for those of coarse persuasion.' He ignored the bundle and poured two cups of tea.

'Just honey, if ya please,' said Fungle.

Musrum spooned in a generous dollop of thick honey and gave Fungle his tea. Ghostly vapour rose from it. Fungle lifted it under his nose, closed his eyes, and breathed it in. 'Ah, lavender honey, if I'm not mistaken,' he said. 'Northside, probably from one o' the Greymountain swarms. Daresay I even know the hive.' He frowned. Beneath the aroma of tea and honey was something else, some unpleasant undercurrent . . .

Fungle's eyes snapped open. Musrum was looking at the map, lifting the tea to his lips, about to drink –

Fungle bolted forward and slapped the tea-cup from Musrum's hand. It knocked against Musrum's pipe and splashed against the wall, then clattered to the floor.

The goblins were in the room before the cup stopped moving. 'Everything awright, boss?' asked the one with the tic-tac-toe scars on his arms.

Musrum was staring at the wall where the tea had splashed. The wood was smoking and a faint acidic hiss could be heard as it burned.

He looked at Fungle, and Fungle nodded slowly.

'Everything's fine,' said Musrum. 'I seem to have spilled my tea.'

The goblin Larry picked up the cup and saucer. 'Pour ya another'n,' he said.

Musrum glanced at Fungle. 'That's very good of you, Larry. Why don't you pour yourself one as well.'

Larry stopped in the midst of picking up the tea-cup. 'Er . . . heh-heh . . . ya know I never touch anythin' weaker'n rotgut, boss.'

'But I insist.'

'Ah.' Larry straightened. 'Well.' He set the cup and saucer on the tea-tray, lifted the pot – and swung it at Musrum's head. Musrum ducked and the pot hit his huge pipe. Larry drew his bayonet and snapped it toward Fungle, who was already getting up from his chair. The bayonet bit into the chairback so hard the chair tipped backward. Larry never broke stride as he bolted for the doorway.

Tic-Tac was ready for him.

Goblin fights are faster than the feline eye can follow and deadly as a cyanide shake. First it seemed that Larry and Tic-Tac were extending hands to shake in greeting. Then in a twitch Tic-Tac was on the floor nursing his arm while uneven footsteps ran down the corridor.

Tic-Tac instantly regained his feet. 'Broke me favourite arm!' he said. 'Sorry, boss. Think I broke his leg, though.'

He gripped his wrist with his good hand and pulled. Even across the room Fungle could hear a sound like grating porcelain as the bone set.

'Go after him, Vinnie,' ordered Musrum. 'Get him and anyone he's with. Send Wubbish and Bludjin to guard the door.'

The goblin sped off.

'And tell Larry he's fired!' Musrum yelled after the goblin.

Fungle picked up the silver teapot and looked inside. What he saw made his nose wrinkle in disgust. To Musrum's curious glance he responded by holding out the pot so that he could see what lurked within.

In the remaining puddle of tea floated a creature the size of a fist. Long-legged, black-furred, red-eyed, barb-tailed, it looked like something between a scorpion and a spider.

Fungle shut the teapot lid.

'How did you know, dear chap?' asked Musrum.

Fungle smiled tightly. 'It's me job to know such things,' he quoted.

'I suppose you consider me in your debt.' Musrum's tone was disdainful.

'Not at all, sir,' said Fungle, and followed the line of reasoning he expected Musrum was pursuing: 'Yer tea probl'ly wouldn'a been poisoned iffin I hadn't been here.'

Musrum nodded absently. He unwrapped the tissue-covered bundle Fungle had set on top of the map. 'But it does make matters more urgent for you,' he said, removing a shiny metallic object which he held up to the light, 'since I think it highly unlikely you're going to be able to walk out the front door and skip merrily on your way, old card.' He looked away from the silver object. 'Where did you get this?' His tone was as detached as ever, but Fungle sensed eagerness underlying it. Sometimes silence speaks louder than words, and this was such an occasion: Fungle clammed up.

Musrum looked back to the object as if hypnotised. 'Nineteen-thirty-seven Rolls-Royce Silver Shadow hood ornament,' he said reverently. 'One of the only three remaining to complete my collection. Chevys, Fords, Buicks – plentiful as rocks. But the Rolls-Royce Silver Shadow? The nineteen-forty-eight Bentley R-Type? Try finding an Excalibur hood ornament on this ridiculous continent!'

Fungle had no idea what he was talking about, but he nodded agreeably.

'Very well,' Musrum acquiesced. 'How much?'

'Me friend Ka said you'd have a use for it.'

Musrum's eyes narrowed. '*Use* and *desire* are entirely separate things, my good fellow. But I assume you are referring to one Karbolic Earthcreep, gnome by birth and scavenger by trade?'

'The very same,' said Fungle. 'And yer holdin' his gift by way of introducin' yours truly.'

Fungle was astonished at the transformation that overcame Musrum. The disinterested businessman became animated and enthusiastic, and he grinned wide enough to eat a sideways banana. 'Why didn't you say so in the first place! We could have saved ourselves all this nonsense, in addition to preventing the destruction of my favourite pipe. Karbolic Earthcreep and I have been trading favours since before –' he eyed Fungle '– well,

not since before you were born, I'll wager, but for longer than
a gentleman my age cares to dwell upon. What an amusing
fellow he is. Tell me, has he figured out his television yet?' He
chuckled. 'No, of course not.' With surprising delicacy for one so
large and thick-fingered, Musrum rewrapped the silver ornament
and pocketed it. 'Nineteen-thirty-seven,' he said, shaking his head.
'When I see that gnome again, I shall have to break out the
gorgonzola, and perhaps waste a perfectly fine Warres 'Thirty-five
on him.' He sighed.

And as quickly as the friendly ease had swept across his
demeanour, it vanished. Once more Musrum the Mossman was
all business and efficiency. 'We must leave at once,' he said.
'Whoever purchased Larry's loyalty will be alerted by now. They'll
be waiting.' He waved Fungle away from the map the gnole had
begun to roll up. 'That's no good to us,' he said. 'Much of your
parchment's blank space is anything but, Mr Fungle Foxwit gnole.'
He pulled out a desk drawer and reached inside. 'Let's see,' he said.
'We'll need my Magic Fairy Liquid if we're to get past the Land
of a Thousand Smokes without becoming an oozlump lunch.' He
fumbled about in the drawer and Fungle heard a click.

'Ah,' said Musrum. 'Never leave yourself only one way out of a
place where you are likely to get in trouble.' He went to a bookcase
on the far wall and pushed the left edge.

It opened inward.

Musrum paused and looked back. 'Coming?'

Fungle shut his mouth and followed.

Thorn watched the entrance to Tobacco Inn from behind a tree, his
dark and spiky form camouflaged by thick kudzu around him.

He was furious.

The attempt to poison the gnole had failed, which hadn't
surprised Thorn because it had been a dim opportunity in the
first place, though one well worth taking. No, fury glowed in his
narrow eyes because the goblin had panicked, had run through
the bar with a limping, broken-legged gait, and gone straight to
Thorn himself, alerting the goblin's pursuers to the fact they were
allied. Gone was the opportunity to steal into the back-room while
the guards were pursuing the goblin. Gone was the chance to spirit
away the gnole and end the job neat and tidy. Gone was the chance
to impress Theverat with a task well and quickly done.

He glanced to his left, where the giblin Vixen kept watch on the
east side of Tobacco Inn in case there were other exits. He could

just see her there among the kudzu. She stared unblinking at the rundown shack, and even when flies lighted on her eyes, she did not bat a lid. A silver line of drool extended from her mouth to the green vines below. What was left of her mind was focused entirely on getting the gnole.

Theverat had left her that much.

The remaining giblins, Rat and Porcupine, watched the north and west sides. Thorn was certain there were other exits, hidden exits, but he had a feeling . . . That was why he had been sent to oversee the giblins, because Thorn often got *feelings*, and his feelings had a tendency to work out. Right now his feeling was that the front door was the one to be concerned about, so he'd posted himself at it and set the giblins around the rotted shack above Tobacco Inn with orders to come full-tilt if any of the others gave the word. They may have been crazy, but giblins were also useful, if you understood how to manage them. If you directed their raging energies efficiently, they would pursue your quarry with obsessive determination, like knife-wielding bloodhounds. Giblins were tools. These few, the scattered others converging on this place. Tools.

All good tools need is a good craftsman.

Thorn looked at the pack strap near his shoulder. Hanging from it was a tiny doll, a figure in the shape of a goblin with a broken leg. It was remarkably lifelike.

He patted the goblin doll roughly. Tiny squeals came from it.

Thorn grinned meanly, thinking about craftsmen and tools.

The gnole had to come out sometime.

'Ah, here we are.' Musrum opened a door and entered a dark room, Fungle close behind. Wubbish and Bludjin, the two goblins Musrum had summoned, remained in the narrow corridor to guard the door.

Musrum switched on a battery-powered lantern and proceeded to rummage among boxes and bins, every so often muttering, 'Hmmmm,' and 'Oh, really?' and 'Why, I'd forgot I had this.'

Fungle glanced around the room. Stacked everywhere were boxes and jars, footlockers and shelves and sheet-draped shapes. Some were labelled, some not. BUTTONS, read one label scrawled atop a wooden crate. Others were HANDLES, HUBCAPS, HARDBACKS, PAPERBACKS, KEYS, AA BATTERIES, CLOCKS (WIND-UP), CLOCKS (AUTO), MISC. BRASS, MISC. COPPER, EYEGLASS FRAMES, INFLATABLES (PATCHED), PIPES (PLUMBING), PIPES (SMOKING), HANDS (MANNEQUIN), and HEADS (VARIOUS).

Fungle thought of the labyrinth of dim and dusty corridors through which Musrum had led him to this room. Tobacco Inn, he realised, was the smallest part of Musrum's holdings. But it was the part that anchored all the others, for it was the magnet that attracted those who brought these pekuliar items and those who wanted them.

'Ah!' Musrum straightened, holding a brightly-coloured box and wearing a satisfied look. TIDE was printed on the box in large letters. Musrum went to another box marked CONTAINERS (PLASTIC – EMPTY) and retrieved a milky squeeze bottle. He unscrewed the cap, opened the box, and shook out a handful of coarse white powder, which he then sifted into the bottle.

Musrum, Fungle mused, is a kind of mage himself. But where I've herb and root and ancient ley, he has a storehouse of human-bean lore and artyfacts for his apothecary. He wondered what kind of shamans existed in the human world, what spells and remedies were handed down along the furless generations of the Land of No.

Musrum filled the plastic bottle with water from a pitcher,

screwed the cap back on, and shook it vigorously to produce a foamy white liquid. He looked at Fungle. 'Fairy Liquid,' he explained, and winked.

'What's it fer?' asked Fungle.

'Oozlumps, creatures risen from the miry deep. Flesh of tar and sump oil, blood of bilge and battery acid, blessed with life infernal by the alchemy of sun and toxic irradiation.' Musrum replied distractedly, already looking for the next item on his mental list. 'Only thing in the known universe that will stop them, and I'm the chap who has the formula.'

'Fer a price,' Fungle ventured.

'Fair value for fair measure, my good fellow. Ah, here we are.' He stood on tiptoe and retrieved a large corked clay jar from a shelf. 'Be a *mensch* and hold this for me, won't you?'

He handed the jar to Fungle, and Fungle instantly sensed the swarming electric life inside. The jar, thick clay though it was, practically vibrated in his hands.

Musrum turned away, then hesitated and turned back to Fungle again. He pointed to the grey box-like thing Fungle had tied to his pack. 'Now, there's an item you don't see often. Not in decent condition, at any rate. Where did you come by it?' He held up a hand. 'No, don't tell me: Karbolic Earthcreep.'

Fungle nodded. 'Tole me it's a Light Box,' he said.

'What an amusing fellow.' Musrum stroked his chin. 'Here, just a moment . . .' He rummaged in yet another box, and emerged with a flat rectangular package. He pressed a spot on the Light Box, and the back part of it swung out. Musrum slapped in the flat package and closed the back part of the Light Box. Fungle heard a brief mechanical whine that stopped with a click. 'There you are,' said Musrum, and patted Fungle's shoulder. 'No extra charge. The amusement I will gather from the knowledge of its existence will more than compensate me.'

Fungle was not to know what Musrum meant until much later and in a very different place indeed.

'Well,' said Musrum. 'Shall we?'

They were at the curtained partition that led to the bar proper (surely a contradiction in terms). Wubbish and Bludjin stood behind them.

'Yer sure ya don't want me givin' us a spell or two to ease us out o' here?' Fungle asked again.

'Know a good spell to prevent stings?'

Fungle smiled wryly. 'Ya won't be stung long as yer with me. That's a promise.'

Musrum nodded soberly. 'That's probably as well,' he said. 'In this place I am more comfortable with my own methods than with spells. My house, my rules, and all that. Are you ready?'

Fungle nodded.

Musrum looked back. 'Ready, lads?'

'Yup.'

'Let 'er rip, boss.'

Musrum nodded. He looked back to the crowded bustle of the bar-room and sighed. 'Shame to lose a good evening's business,' he said. 'But sandcastle builders can't quarrel with the tide.' He looked at Fungle. 'Very well, Mister Gnole. Set us on our way.' Musrum drew back the curtain.

Fungle pulled the cork from the jar, reared back, and heaved it with all his might.

POP! went the hedgehog, and bets were collected and offered again. Pipes fumed, brawls brewed, brews chugged, patrons mugged, mugs hoisted, pockets picked, insults flung, and darts flung back.

A seedy elf tattooing a dwarf hiccoughed drunkenly and lanced a lovely and anatomically correct rendering of a lumpkin heart with his dirty needle.

A drunken troll lying on the sticky wet floor beside a stiff dead grinning dog hollered for more grog.

A huddle of pipe aficionados oohed and aahed over a meerschaum carved into the shape of a rat skull from which acrid smoke vented like evil thoughts.

The bartender smashed an empty bottle into a pail and added dishwater. 'Pipe cleaner!' he called, and slid the pail down the counter to eager lumpkin hands.

A curtain parted.

A jar sailed overhead and crashed against a wall.

A cloud of enraged hornets emerged.

The bellows boys stopped their labour. All bets were off as the hedgehogs slowly deflated. The croupier ceased his constant calls. The railhuggers stifled their colourful epithets and glanced nervously over their shoulders. Pipe-smoke stilled in kippered lungs like fog in slimy caverns.

In the sudden quiet, the buzzing of hornets was like the distant roar of an approaching war machine.

Pandemonium erupted. If the bar had been chaotic before, it was a vicars' picnic compared to the trampling pushing writhing swinging crawling bashing desperate blind panicked flight toward the stairs that led up and out.

There was a splash as the bartender jumped into a barrel of rotgut.

The drunken troll hopped up from the floor and ran for the stairs, clearing his way by swinging the stiff dog like a club. 'Beeez!' he bellowed. 'Outta muh way! Um allergic ta beeez!'

The first wave of escapees up the stairs got the door open.

'On our way, then,' Musrum said calmly, and he, Fungle, and the goblins Wubbish and Bludjin stepped into the *mêlée*.

Thorn heard the commotion before he saw it. It grew like the approach of a stampeding herd – it *was* the approach of a stampeding herd. He tensed himself, ready to hurl spells and commands. He had time to think that this was odd, that there was nothing subtle or evasive about this getaway, before the storm door popped open and drunken creatures poured out like maddened ants from a flattened hill.

To his left he saw Vixen move forward with her spear. Thorn held up a hand and she stopped still as a stone. Thorn thought furiously as screaming meemies boiled from the inn and scattered into the woods, arms flapping and legs jittering like manic dancers, and screeching like banshees to boot.

An elf ran directly toward him, stopped, and batted about himself, still clutching a handful of house darts. He must have realised this, because he stopped flapping, selected a dart, took careful aim, and let fly.

The hummingbird dart bit wood near Thorn's cheek.

The elf let fly his last two darts, then began waving frantically, as if bidding farewell to the entire world, and ran screaming into the night.

Thorn glanced at the dart embedded in the tree. Impaled on the beak of the dart was the body of a hornet the size of Thorn's thumb.

A *distraction*, he realised. *They want us at the front door –*
Because they were coming up somewhere else.

He hurried across to Vixen.

Fungle saw the strange figure moving through the forest just as he emerged from the hidden exit. Around him hornets and patrons swarmed, the former stinging, the latter stung. Musrum and the two goblins kept tight to him, not daring to venture from whatever sphere of influence the mage had over things that fly, sting, and buzz.

The figure that slid through the forest like a shadow was spiky, angular, lean, lithe, tall. It moved with dangerous quiet and ease. If the forest weren't an extension of himself, if he had not spent his life with its motion and light and shadow, Fungle would never have spotted this alien and ominous silhouette.

It stopped.

Fungle had the sense of it *looking*. Searching.

Glancing at Musrum and the goblins striding away from the poor lumpy wretches shrieking and stumbling from the inn, Fungle realised that they stood out like blazes in their very calmness. 'Ahhh!' he suddenly screamed. 'Ooooh! Beeez! Stingy beeez!' He flapped his arms and danced a manic jig.

Musrum and the goblins looked at him as if he had gone stark foaming mad. Fungle scowled at them. 'Act stung!' he whispered.

They looked perplexed.

'Ah! Ooh!' Fungle cavorted in mock pain.

Musrum caught on. 'Yaaaaagh!' he bellowed. 'Waaaaagh!' He waved his arms and stamped his feet.

Fungle felt the hesitation of the figure in the woods.

'You bein' stung, boss?' asked Wubbish.

'Shut up and holler,' Musrum ordered.

'But boss,' Bludjin asked reasonably, 'how can he shut up an' holler at the same time?'

'Just do it!'

So the goblins screamed and twitched as they were stung by imaginary hornets, glancing at each other in pitiful befuddlement, while Fungle led them to the edge of the woods where they could stop their merry manic dance and hurry on their way.

Fungle felt the gaze of that ominous, alien, spiked creature as it touched on them and passed them by. In the midst of his panicked dance he glanced to the opposite side of the clearing and saw the silhouette slide like vapour to a tree – where Fungle recognised the outline of a giblin.

But now he had reached the woods. He could guide Musrum and their goblin guards through the lush greenery of his world, and out of his world and into places more familiar to Musrum. The thought ought to have filled him with foreboding, but right now all Fungle felt was relief.

He touched the wishing feather on his cap, and his hand froze as he heard a phlegmatic voice beside him:

'Eat yer marrow before tomorrow!' said Porcupine. 'Sooo good!'

The Land of a Thousand Smokes

The smell was Fungle's first indication that they were near the Land of a Thousand Smokes.

For two days Musrum and Fungle had pushed east through dense forest. Though they had spoken little, they had formed the kind of bond that comes with the shared labour of a long journey through difficult territory. Some of that territory was internal as well, and the gnole and the mysterious Mossman kept it to themselves. But they had acquired immense respect for one another – Musrum for the gnole's astounding knowledge of the forest and its ways, and Fungle for the mysterious Mossman's sure direction and encyclopaedic knowledge of humankind – the latter of which Fungle found most unsettling.

Wubbish and Bludjin were no longer with them. The goblins were fiercely loyal to Musrum, and protective – more so because one of their own, Larry, had doublecrossed them and betrayed Musrum. With a score to settle and pride to maintain, they had stayed behind to stop the giblins, or at least slow them down as much as possible.

Fungle and Musrum never saw them again.

The second night out from Tobacco Inn, Fungle sensed a thick, pungent odour of rot – not maggoty or putrid like a giblin, not the velvet damp smell of forest decay. This was the festering of materials beyond his ken. He asked Musrum what the smell was. 'Don't smell a thing, myself, dear boy. But from your colourful description, I would venture you are inhaling the unique perfume of the Land of a Thousand Smokes.'

The smell intensified as they pushed on. In the late afternoon of the third day out from Tobacco Inn, Fungle and Musrum broke from the rough terrain of rock and close-packed trees to emerge at a clearing near the base of a mountain, and Fungle saw the birds.

There were thousands of them, wheeling and gliding on the endless shimmering thermals that ovened from the sunbaked ground. Blackbirds, dirt-grey gulls, crows, pigeons – their rusted creaking filled the air as they circled and dove and squabbled like gathered scavengers patiently awaiting the death of some gargantuan beast.

Much later those hungry and imploring bird cries would haunt Fungle's forced narcotic sleep. The calls seemed always to lie at the edges of humanity, for wherever mankind was, those birds flew at the fringes, and the sound of their forlorn calls would pull like an eerie thread through the drugged tapestry of Fungle's fitful slumber.

But narcotic sleep lay in the future. Right now Fungle merely gazed up at thousands and thousands of birds, so many birds it seemed the fabric of the sky itself was a crawling, feathery canopy.

Musrum touched Fungle's shoulder and pointed behind them. The sun was on the horizon.

'Best push on,' Fungle said determinedly.

Musrum looked grim. 'It will take hours to wend through that labyrinth,' he said. 'Night's no good time to be caught out down there.' He pointed ahead of them, and that was Fungle's first true glimpse of the Land of a Thousand Smokes.

At first he thought it was a mirage, because it wavered below him like a vaporous image: low hills that rose as far as the eye could see.

But such pekuliar hills! They were symmetrical, cone-shaped and arrayed in rows as if someone long ago had planted stones and grown an orchard of hills. They were mottled and rough-edged, and flecked with colours that rarely occurred in exposed rock: bits of red, pieces of pure white, yellows, oranges, greens, all forming an enormous odd quilt of flotsam and jetsam heaped upon the earth. *Patchwork hills*, thought Fungle. The earth had never made such hills.

The wind shifted and the stench hit him.

When he smelled it, he wondered if his initial impression of the birds as patient scavengers awaiting the death of some gargantuan beast wasn't correct, after all, for it smelled as if there were an enormous corpse down there, rotting below the sun that broiled the land. But there was more here than the odour of mere decay.

Fungle's sense of smell was such that he could sniff a pine-cone and take you to the very tree that had dropped it. Few odours in nature were foreign to him. Thus in this heady mixture he identified rotting vegetables and meat readily enough, along with mouldering cloth and a damp heaviness that was wet paper. That green fuzzy odour was rotting wood, wet ashes was burnt pine – his snout sifted and sorted a thousand other familiar aromas.

But there were strange smells, too; sharp, corrosive, somehow threatening. Fungle didn't know how an odour could be unnatural, but that was exactly the word that came to mind in those first few seconds after he was aware of the stench that lifted from the hills.

It was the oddest place Fungle had ever seen or smelled – so far.

Motion distracted him as Musrum produced his bottle of Fairy Liquid and shook it. He saw Fungle watching him and smiled thinly. 'Nectar of the gods, dear boy,' he said, popping the cap over the spout. He bowed stiffly and indicated the nightmare mirage below. 'Shall we dance?'

Fungle shrugged his pack closer, touched his wishing feather, muttered a prayer to his guardian angel, and nodded.

They headed down.

After Fungle and Musrum had left Wubbish and Bludjin behind to delay, divert, or destroy the giblins, the woods had felt fine and clear. But the second day out from Tobacco Inn, Fungle had felt a Presence. That was how he thought of it: as a Presence, an entity. He felt it stalking them through the woods. It had an aura, a *glamour*, and sometimes when they stopped to rest Fungle sensed its burning gaze on him. He had never felt such hate. It strained, it churned, it burned so brightly that it seemed Fungle should be able to see it glowing nearby in the forest. It was not Theverat, for Fungle was certain he would instantly sense the invasion into his world of a being so alien and malevolent as the demon that sought him. But there was a whiff of Theverat about the Presence, something . . . allied.

Fungle knew the forest, knew the signs: the downwind stench of rotten tomatoes (an aroma entirely different from the faint but growing miasma of the Land of a Thousand Smokes to the north), the quick nervousness of deer (who were never nervous in Fungle's presence), the shrivel of a leaf that a certain type of foul creature had brushed past, the sudden silence of birds in the trees behind them to the west. They were being followed by giblins.

So there was no question of making camp and waiting for tomorrow's daylight to help them weather the labyrinth of garbage and brave its monstrous inhabitants, no question of even stopping for a brief rest.

Remembering his last sight of Bludjin and Wubbish, Fungle shook his head in a mixture of awe and incomprehension. Fungle and Musrum had shouldered their packs that first morning after the getaway from Tobacco Inn, and Fungle had blessed the two goblins – the most magic they would allow him to perform. Then Musrum had held out a hand, and Bludjin had clasped it with his own scaly claw, followed by Wubbish. They held the three-way clasp a moment, until Musrum nodded in a sombre way that somehow conveyed sorrow and gratitude and farewell. Then the clasp broke. Musrum turned away and did not look back, and he and Fungle headed out.

Just before the forest hid them from view, Fungle had looked back: Bludjin was whittling a stripped sapling into a stake while Wubbish scanned the trees with a strategist's eye. Bludjin called out some friendly insult which Wubbish matched with equal crude fondness, all without interrupting their businesslike preparations to defend employer and honour.

Remembering this, and thinking of the signs of pursuit revealed to him by the forest, Fungle shook his head sadly now as he and Musrum descended into the Land of a Thousand Smokes. Whatever had happened back there, he thought, whatever brave stand those loyal goblins had made, it hadn't been enough.

'You takin' a nap?'

Wubbish looked up from his contemplation of the dark-stained bandage around his forearm. 'Thinkin' 'bout that giblin,' he told Bludjin. 'Shoulda killed that stinkin' bleeder.'

Bludjin grinned evilly. 'Well, pretty soon now we's gonna get our chance to right a coupla wrongs, I reckon. Like it or don't.'

'Gonna eat that pop-eyed porcupine's pump an' spit out the pits,' swore Wubbish.

'Not talkin' about it, y'ain't.'

Wubbish nodded. 'Right y'are, Bludge ol' bean.' But his expression remained disgruntled.

Bludjin finished pulling back the sturdy low branch of an oak tree and used a vine fashioned into a slip knot to hold its curled tension to the trunk.

Wooden stakes adorned the branch's length.

Bludjin wrapped the free end of the vine low around the trunk of the oak tree and stretched the remainder at ankle height to a sapling ten feet away. 'Wubbish Wetmarsh,' he scolded, straightening, 'if ya don't stop yer sulkin' and lend a hand, I'm gonna carve ya up meself and toss the pieces to yer Mister Porky-pine so's he can eat 'em with mint sauce.' He approached his comrade and punched him goodnaturedly on his uninjured arm.

The blow would have powdered a bowling ball.

'Ya did better'n awright,' Bludjin continued encouragingly, 'what with him poppin' out from behind that tree, an' that gnole between you an' him, an' all. Stopped his axe an' give him what-for, an' who coulda done better, I ask you?'

Wubbish nodded. 'He *were* lopin' kinda funny when he made off, weren't he?'

'With a leg bent scary backwards?' Bludjin's grin would have sent a wolf yelping. '"Why, I should think so, old card."'

Bludjin's impression of Musrum was uncannily accurate, and Wubbish felt a little better in spite of himself. '"What an amusing fellow!"' he said, and felt resolve course through him.

'Right, then,' said Bludjin. He patted his friend's shoulder and together they resumed their preparations. Quickly, because some goblin instinct for imminent confrontation told them they'd better hurry, they looped and rigged snares, planted and camouflaged sharpened stakes, erected a heavy logfall in the crotch of an old spruce tree, and took up their positions beside three close-set pines at the edge of a clearing, where they could fight back-to-back and have one side covered.

They waited.

The woods were filled with birdsong.

'Bludge old bean,' Wubbish said conversationally, 'd'ya think we shoulda accepted that little mage's offer of a spell or two to help us along?'

Bludjin spat. 'No honour to it, and shame on ya for thinkin' it.'

Wubbish grinned sheepishly. 'Just makin' conversation, brother.'

'Can't blame ya fer that, brother,' said Bludjin.

Goblins call each other 'brother' or 'sister' because of their belief that they all descend from a common ancestor, Gob the Great, which means all goblins are related.

The forest grew quiet around them.

'Still,' continued Bludjin, 'I didn't mind receivin' his blessin's on us.'

A twig cracked as it was trod on.

'Me neither,' said Wubbish. 'He seemed a right good sort, he did.'

Two startled quail exploded from the bushes across the clearing and whirred loudly away.

The goblins drew their knives.

The forest was still.

'Nice day,' said Wubbish after a while.

'Is,' agreed Bludjin.

From across the clearing came a quick succession of sounds:

a hiss

    a frantic thrashing

        a scream.

Someone's foot had parted a low-lying vine.

'Bit humid though,' amended Wubbish as he brought his dagger to his bandage and drew the point across it. The bloodstain freshened. Wubbish dabbed his finger on it, then brought the wet tip to his forehead to paint the Wetmarsh family sigil.

Bludjin firmed his grip on the vine attached to the logfall in the tree above and behind them. ('*This'll drive some giblin into the dirt like a tenpenny nail,*' he'd told Wubbish as they'd set the trap.)

Frenzied trampling came from the forest.

'Don't embarrass me, now, Bludge,' said Wubbish.

A stench of rotten tomatoes grew around them.

'Heh! Don't *you* embarrass *me!*'

They stood back-to-back as a dozen giblins screamed into the clearing.

The terrible odour strengthened as Fungle and Musrum lowered into the odd terrain. The mountain shadow cast by the lowering sun behind them slid into the land like the knife of a wraith. In the dying light Fungle saw thin trails of black vapour curling up from many scattered pockets ahead of him. Far overhead they coalesced to bruise a sky troubled by crows. *Land of a Thousand Smokes*, he thought. *An' so it is.*

'Is it burning?' Fungle asked Musrum.

'Not burning, exactly,' replied the Mossman. 'I mean to say, it *is* burning, but there's no fire to speak of. It's always like that here, during the day. The sun cooks the ground hereabouts, I'd venture. I've seen entire hills smouldering this way, all smoke and combustion without a fire. Quite strangeful, isn't it? Strange and beautiful all in one.'

'It's awrful.'

Soon they were among the snaking columns of acrid smoke. Fungle was thankful for the watertight soles of his fine old-fashioned gnole boots, for they trod a morass of sharp, twisted metal, rusted nails upthrust through rotting boards, and a vile black liquid that took on a deceptive rainbow allure when light reflected from its slickened skin.

It was the first time Fungle had ever walked on ground that was not natural.

The lumpen hills loomed around them. This close, Fungle realised that they were not hills at all in the true sense of the word, but enormous heaps of broken artifacts. He understood little of what he saw. *Is this a human-bean burial mound?* Fungle wondered. *Their version of a Mound of the Dead?* Fungle knew that there were an awful lot of human beings. Perhaps they brought all their dead to a single, sacred place, and buried them along with objects that were important to them during their lifetime. But before an object can be included, he speculated, it must be broken so that its spirit is released from its physical housing. Then it can accompany its owner into some human version of afterlife.

If true, the explanation did little to comfort him. Human-bean bodies coffined under all these heaps? And him walking among 'em bold as ya please with night pulling down its nocuous shades?

He shivered. *But let's don't worry 'bout ghosties 'til we's sure of a haunting*, he reminded himself.

He turned to ask Musrum if he knew what the purpose of this place was – and stopped.

Musrum was not there.

Fungle found him about a hundred yards back, standing motionless. At first Fungle thought Musrum was in a trance, so intent was his gaze on something that Fungle could not see, but as Fungle neared he realised Musrum was fighting for his life.

Musrum stood inside a ring of Fairy Liquid, clutching the bottle containing the precious mixture. Outside the sudsy ring, between Musrum and Fungle, lay a thick black puddle. Fungle started to call out, but stopped when the sludgy puddle quivered like a coal-tar gelatin.

Musrum raised a warning hand to Fungle – and the black mass surged up toward the Mossman with a sickening sucking sound. Fungle got a quick impression of enormous eyes and a gaping maw as the thing shot a viscous tendril across Musrum's ring of Fairy

Liquid. Musrum squeezed his bottle and a frothy stream shot out. The effect was dramatic: the tendril dissolved, and the creature let forth an enraged bubbling bellow like an underwater scream. It withdrew again, once more becoming a thick black puddle beyond the range of Musrum's bottle.

Fungle was trying to think what sorcery would best defeat the oozlump (for that is what the creature was) when Musrum's subtle wave caught his attention.

The oozlump quivered eagerly.

Slowly Musrum drew his arm back.

An anticipatory ripple coursed along the oozlump's surface.

Musrum threw the bottle of Fairy Liquid in an underhand toss.

The oozlump surged toward Musrum.

The bottle arced over it.

Fungle raced forward and thrust out a hand.

The oozlump shot a dripping tendril toward Musrum.

Fungle caught the bottle.

The thick tendril wrapped Musrum's arm.

In two running steps Fungle was right behind the oozlump.

Musrum's free hand batted at the tendril and stuck.

Fungle squeezed the bottle. A spray of white-foamed Fairy Liquid cut across the oozlump like a sword. The oozlump released Musrum and rose screaming before Fungle. It stretched itself tall and wide, like a shroud about to envelop him. Fungle sprayed an X across it, and the creature immediately contracted. One more squirt and the oozlump dissolved into a bubbling mass of black bile.

Musrum stepped from his sudsy version of a conjurer's ring and accepted the bottle back from Fungle. 'Much obliged, dear boy,' he said calmly.

Fungle could only stare.

Vixen had gone crazy enough to have the Sight. Thorn frowned down at her, spike-elbowed arms folded, fingers tapping biceps with a chitinous sound as he pondered. 'How many?' he asked again.

'Two.' Vixen writhed upon the ground, joints straining painfully. 'Two, two, two, two!'

'Where?'

Vixen clutched her head and ripped away a clump of red-rooted fur. 'Smoke!' she grated. 'Hills! Smell! Birds! Rats! Ooz –'

'The Land of a Thousand Smokes,' interrupted the giblin named Rat. A filthy bandage wound around his head and across his right eye – the bequest of those accursed goblins. 'I been there,' he continued. 'There's all kinda –'

Thorn whirled to face him. The angry slits of his eyes were black as the heart of a man of coal.

Rat shut up.

Thorn turned back to Vixen. The insane giblin writhed and bucked upon the ground. Thorn had heard the giblins muttering that Theverat had done this to her for failing him. Well, let them whisper; it was probably true anyway, and even if it wasn't, such rumours could only help keep them in line. Carrying out a mission with a team of giblins was like walking a dozen wild dogs with half-a-dozen long leashes. Thorn could direct them, but he could not really control them. He was the lens that focused their scattered fury.

Thorn had impatiently waited until the sun dropped below the horizon for his dark abilities to come alive. These powers were still new to him; he was still discovering himself. He had some vague memory of a trifling existence before he had heard the voice of Theverat, but it seemed unimportant now. Theverat had made him something else, something different, something broader. Theverat had *increased* him. Thorn was *important* to Theverat, and all he remembered of his past life was that he had wanted more than anything to be important to somebody. Anybody.

He forced himself to ignore the half-dozen remaining giblins who watched in superstitious fascination as he squatted before Vixen, who shivered and spasmed now as if freezing to death. 'Do you see them?' he asked gently.

Vixen rose to her hands and knees, swaying idiotically to some secret music. Her rapid panting blew foam from her muzzle. Her eyes snapped open to stare wildly past Thorn. 'See them!' she screamed.

'What do you see?' Thorn snapped. He fought down the impatience in his tone. 'Tell me what you see.'

Vixen stared. 'Two. Innkeeper. Gnole. Oozlumps all around.'

Thorn smiled. 'Really? Oozlumps?'

'Past hill with bathtub, shiny chrome fender, iron bar, rubber tyre. I –' Vixen's brow furrowed. 'I *know* that hill!' Her expression grew ecstatic. 'I *take* you there! Take you to them!'

'Yes,' agreed Thorn, 'you'll take us there.'

Suddenly Vixen's face went completely blank. She sat upright. 'Someone coming,' she said. Her voice was flat and dead. Her eyes were dead as fish scales. Drool formed on her muzzle, welled, dripped in a thin glistening line to the ground. 'Coming *here*,' she said. 'Coming *now*.'

Behind Thorn the giblins muttered fearfully. A few made the warding sign of the Evil Eye.

Thorn waved them quiet. 'Someone coming here, to us?' he asked. 'Who comes here, tell me; who –'

Vixen looked directly at Thorn, eyes bright. Dark intelligence animated her face; the insanity was gone.

'Thorn,' she said mildly.

A needle of fear pricked Thorn's heart. The voice that came from Vixen's throat was not her own. In fact, Thorn recognised it. He felt his body bow down, felt his face press into the grass. Behind him he heard the giblins grovelling, abasing themselves, rending their garments, speaking in tongues.

'Master,' said Thorn.

*

Fungle could sense the oozlumps as he followed Musrum through the nightmare landscape. He felt their hunger, their eagerness, their expectation. He felt them waiting – for a blind turn into a cul-de-sac, for a fatal misstep into a living black puddle, for a slip and a tumble.

For Musrum's bottle to run dry.

Fungle and Musrum had battled sixteen of the creatures so far. Fearing the deadly stream of Fairy Liquid, they had learned to keep a respectful distance, but occasionally one of the creatures would slither close as if taunting, daring Musrum to use more of the precious fluid. And if the oozlump got close enough, Musrum really had no choice. He would give the bottle a slight squeeze, but the oozlump would stream away untouched, leaving them that much closer to an unthinkable fate.

Even apart from the oozlumps, the night was alive with horrors. Moonlight glinted from metal, shone from puddles, reflected from feral eyes of rats the size of cats and cats gone wild as tigers. Every shadow was a lurking giblin; every puddle a hungry oozlump. All around them was a Sargasso of jagged daggers of broken glass and rusted metal edges. A single fall could prove as fatal as a high dive into a pool of oozlumps.

Musrum picked his way surefootedly through the unearthly territory. Earlier Fungle had learned to his horror that Musrum had never actually crossed the Land of a Thousand Smokes, but he was intimate with its geography because he had ventured in from so many places along its perimeter. 'Really, if you come by day and well prepared, it's the most amazing potpourri, my dear fellow,' he'd said. 'Half my trade goods come from here, and the salvage I recover is invariably worth the journey's risk. If my regular customers such as Karbolic Earthcreep could bring themselves to forage here, I should have to tighten my belt and tend my own bar – a dismal fate for such a polymath as myself.'

But at the moment it was hard to reconcile such a glowing recommendation with the frightful territory they traversed, and Fungle, eager to relegate this part of his journey to bad memory, caught up with Musrum and asked him how much farther they had to go.

'A few more hours, by my reckoning,' he said. 'Before dawn, if all goes well.'

'An' how be our supply o' Fairy Liquid?' Fungle asked.

Musrum held out the bottle, milky in the waning moonlight.

'Half empty,' Fungle said grimly.

'Tut tut, my dear fellow,' said Musrum. 'I prefer to think it half full.'

'An' I prefer to think us more'n halfway across this wretched place,' added Fungle, 'which means ye've not enough fer the journey back.'

'Oh, I shan't be returning the way we've come,' said Musrum. 'Considering recent events at my drinking establishment, and those vulgar ruffians nipping at our heels, I think I shall be better served by taking the long way round.' An oozlump slithered boldly close; Musrum barely glanced at it as he held the bottle up threateningly. 'I'll head east and then south to skirt the edges of this place,' he continued. 'It will add a few days to my journey, but that will also give the local situation a chance to cool off.' His expression turned wry. 'It will also give trouble more time to remove itself from our quaint region in its eager pursuit of you, my young friend. You seem to be something of a trouble magnet.'

'I don't normally attract trouble,' Fungle said, feeling a bit defensive. 'Usually I'm quite the homebody. Cookin', cleanin', an' conjurin' is most o' what fills up me days.'

'I sometimes wonder if all of us attract an equal share of trouble in our lives,' mused Musrum. 'But it is apportioned differently for each of us. Some of us have a constant little bit of trouble all our days, while some of us weather early difficulties to navigate a calm stretch of remaining years.' He gestured with the bottle again and a looming oozlump slunk off. 'Now in your case, my dear fellow –'

'*Now!*' said a voice from the darkness ahead of them.

They came by exactly where and when Theverat had said they would. In the darkness Thorn grinned. Oh, the power of such knowledge!

He signalled the giblins to keep still and silent. Oh, you strain at the leash, my dogs of war! But not yet, not yet.

Thorn and his war party had moved swiftly through the landfill, stealing among the detritus of human existence, encountering nothing more dangerous than rats and starving dogs. With her eyes still closed and her Sight still claiming her, Vixen had led them unerringly in a broad arc that quickly overtook and intersected Fungle and Musrum's path. The giblins took up positions behind doorless refrigerators, gutted stoves, lean-to automobile hoods, heaped plastic garbage bags. Thorn kept Vixen with him, relying on her Sight to tell him when the gnole was near. He could see quite well in the dark, but Vixen could See beyond the horizon. Thorn found himself idly wondering if it might be worth losing one's sanity to acquire such a sense.

Staring at her drooling, twitching form, he decided that it would not.

He gazed up at the lopsided moon. Thorn saw a skull when he looked at the moon, and more than once he had wondered if it were the head of some dead god, an endlessly circling moon of bone staring grave-eyed at the earth.

A hand clapped his spiky shoulder. He looked away from the hollow-eyed gaze of the moon to the lunatic stare of Vixen. She lifted her hand from Thorn, curled her fingers, and raked ragged claws down her cheek. 'They come,' she said.

Thorn looked left. Nothing. No, wait – was that a shadow? Or some mass of black liquid flowing between the heaps of rubbish? Whatever it was suddenly didn't matter to Thorn (though shortly it would), because behind it came the innkeeper and the gnole. Thorn stood.

'Now!' he shouted.

The first giblin to reach them was Rat. He brandished his axe and charged toward Fungle with murder in his eye, his vengeful frenzy eclipsing stern warnings that the gnole was to be taken alive. 'This is fer me frien' Porcupine!' he screamed, and r'ared back.

Fungle was ready with a mindywarp spell, but the brave mage never got a chance to utter it, for Rat charged onto a black puddle that surged up and wrapped around him like a tar blanket. He screamed like a sould in torment and chopped at the oozlump with his axe, but the blade merely sank into the creature's body like a stick hitting tar. The oozlump flowed around the axe and down the handle to envelop the giblin completely. 'Help!' screamed Rat. 'Help!'

Soon his screams were nothing more than bubbles swelling the
surface of the oozlump that had absorbed him. But by then there
was no one left to hear them anyway.

The other giblins had their hands full as well. At the shouted
command from Thorn they had charged headlong into a ring of
oozlumps surrounding Fungle and Musrum, and now they were
fighting for their lives against opponents that literally absorbed
every blow. If punched, the oozlump flowed around the offending
arm. If hacked, the oozlump swallowed the blade. Once entangled
there was no escape; it was easier to wrestle mud than to fight an
oozlump. They stuck and flowed and absorbed and digested and
disappeared with the remnants of their prey.

Fungle and Musrum stared in horrified amazement at the giblins
trapped like flies in a black web. Their nemesis had become their
unwitting salvation.

An oozlump flowed like oil toward Musrum, and Musrum sprayed
it to dissolving jelly.

Fungle felt the Presence, the *glamour*. Frantically he looked
around.

There.

It stood by a sheet of metal in front of one of the garbage hills. In
the moonlight it was a vaguely man-shaped silhouette, but horribly
thin, with spikes at all the joints.

Fungle felt its gaze upon him, and the distance between them
became no distance at all. They were face to face, the mage gnole
and this alien creature, and in that naked fearful instant of contact
they became ancient enemies.

The creature raised a thorny hand to break a barb from its
leathery flesh. The hand drew back, and Fungle felt the power
there. He heard Musrum shout his name. The hand twitched, and
the barb cut air toward Fungle. Fungle's mind went blank.

It was the moment the oozlump beside him had been waiting for.
With Fungle distracted and Musrum busy spraying Fairy Liquid
to save himself, the beast rose up, swelling like a bilious sail, and
engulfed the gnole.

The hurled thorn bit into its viscous taffy.

Fungle felt the creature shudder around him. It released him
and slithered back, sprouting thorns that sprouted thorns from
where the hurled barb had struck, until the creature struggled in
a biting wrap of wire-strong vines.

Fungle glanced back to the hill.

The thorny creature broke off another barb.

Musrum grabbed Fungle. 'Wake up!' he suggested.

Fungle shook himself.

The thorny hand drew back to throw.

Fungle ran.

Just before he ran, however; just before the skeletal figure hurled its deadly thorn, there was a brief tableau. A last glance exchanged. A nod of acknowledgement. A single, shared thought.

Later.

7 A Knees-up

A knock on the head awoke him. He found himself lying under a spreading chestnut tree in early afternoon light. He yawned and stretched, groaning when tired muscles protested. He cracked his knuckles, more for the sound than from any need to.

What an awful dream I dreamt, he thought. *Runnin' through mounds o' indescribable rubbish, hunted after by slimy oozlumps an' loony giblins an' all manner o' beasties the good earth never give forth!*

A second chestnut bounced on his head. Fungle jerked, then grinned. 'Thankee, goodbody tree,' he said, 'but I be perfeckly awake now.' He smacked his lips and glanced around. 'An' past ready to set about me chores – it's chasin' daylight, from the shadders stretchin' east!'

The birdsong from on high sounded very like laughter.

Fungle stood, wondering at the cramping in his legs, and straightened his cap. His hand brushed the wishing feather there. He frowned.

He fumbled fingers in the folds of his tunic and withdrew a blood-red briar rose.

Neema's rose. She had given it to him – no; she had *loaned* it to him – when he'd left . . .

'When I left Ka's,' he said aloud, staring at the rose.

Still it had not bloomed, nor wilted.

Memory flooded in.

Tobacco Inn, Musrum, the hornets, goblins, giblins, the Land of a Thousand Smokes, oozlumps, the thorny silhouette and the deadly blades of itself it had hurled, the long run away from the terrible alien moonlit landscape of litter, the sad and grateful farewell to Musrum . . .

'It weren't no dream,' Fungle said resignedly. He felt the weight of his mission settle once more on his shoulders. For a brief moment there he had been carefree, not a thing in all the world more pressing than getting his chores done before daylight leaked away. How long since he had carried such weightless concerns? Days, weeks, months? His mind was too cobwebby to untangle the ravelled string of events.

A third chestnut struck his head.

'Third time's a charm,' he uttered, and looked up into the tree.

A green, faintly phosphorescent hand clutched a fourth chestnut beside an equally green face that was grinning down at him.

'Name's Conker, Conker by name an' conker by trade. Not like what invadin' armies do t'each other, y'unnerstan', but like what y'do wif a stick to a noggin' – see? *Conk!* That's me!

'Say, ain't you a gnole? Ain't seen one o'yer kind round these parts in a oak's age! Ah, we useta have some grand ol' times, we did, me an' me friends an' the gnoles. Made us enough noise t'keep the 'skeeters away!

'So how's come ya come ta be sleepin' unner one o' me own personal an' favrite trees, anywho?

'Say, now! Bless me bark if I ain't a dumb stump! Yer name wouldn't be Fungle, now, would it? Fungle Foxwit, gnole o' the Valley o' Smilin' Water? Where ya been? Why, I been lookin' fer ya a coupla days now! C'mon wif yer – we's gonna have a knees-up!'

And before Fungle could squeeze a word in vowel-wise, the tree sprite was off and sprinting.

Whose woods these were Fungle thought he knew, for as he followed Conker's faintly glowing, spiky form through the lush undergrowth toward the tree sprite's home, Conker pointed out the name (scientific, common, then familiar) and history of every plant, tree, rock, bird, and bug they passed. 'Ah, here's a *platycerium bifurcatum*, more commonly called the staghorn fern, but I calls her Moxy cuz she's got it in gobs. Pulled through summer's drought wiffout so much as a curled leaf. An' this here's a *caladium hortulanum*, a fancy-leafed caladium, also called an ace of hearts, though I dunno why. Pretty, innit? Oh, an' that rock there what looks like a big lumpkin fist? Now, that's a rather amazin' feller –'

And on and on, through deepest darkest wood primeval to Conker's well-hidden home. For the first time in memory, Fungle found his knowledge of the forest and its ways and lore matched by someone else's.

He was utterly charmed.

Fungle located Conker's perfectly camouflaged home well before they arrived there, mostly from the noise coming from it. Amid a thorough confusion of tangled catawba rhododendron was a barrow. Its mouth was filled with clusters of hair-fine tendrils. Without hesitation Conker wormed into the hole and out of sight. Fungle hesitated, listening to the music. Well, it sounded like it were *supposed* to be music, anyways. Fungle was aware that there was a fine line between artistic experimentation and outright noise. *Well, it may be a fine line*, he thought as he squeezed into the tight chamber and brushed aside beetle-husked cobwebs, *but it ain't invisible.*

He emerged into a moss-quilted womb of sleepy contentment.

The chamber was carpeted with fresh chestnut leaves and pungent with the musk of sage, lavender and sweetest fennel, and lit by fireflies pattering the walls of glass lanterns, by arrangements of phosphorescent mosses, and by Conker's own natural glow.

What the illumination illuminated were two strange creatures indeed.

One was short and squat, mottled and a bit melted-looking, with huge droopy eyes and pouty features that made him look like a sadly happy sort of fellow.

T'other was thin as a mop, smooth, and angular. His features looked caricatured, as if drawn on to his face.

The shorter one wore a mangy mandolute half again his length, and the tall one held a banged-up bandaged banjo that looked like an appendage of his own skinny body.

Both wore downcast looks as Conker berated them. 'What's the matter wif you, makin' all that racket an' leavin' me door wide open fer all to listen?' He waved around them. 'What's the good a me disguis-o-flagin' me dwellin's if the two a you broadcast where they is like a map fer people's ears?' He pointed to the short one. 'Acorn! Me own favrite an' onliest mandolute, an' wiffout permission!'

'Wee-uns only habbin fun,' muttered the short one, Acorn.

'Humans what carve their names in trees is only havin' fun, too!' Conker turned on the tall, spindly creature. 'An' Thistle! I tole you two hundred seventeen times that yer doddy plunked all the melody outta that bang-joe years afore you was sprouted, so I don't see why ya keep on torturin' it – an' us wif it!'

Thistle frowned at the abused banjo and muttered something.

'Whassat?' Conker exaggeratedly put a hand to his long, pointed ear. 'Didn't quite catch 'at,' he said.

'Joos woondrin who yer fren iss,' said Thistle.

Conker looked surprised. He glanced at Fungle as if he'd forgotten the gnole were there. He hit himself on the head, and damn if it didn't make a certain specific previously described but as-yet unheard sound, *conk!*

'An' you, Conker,' Conker berated himself. 'What kinda manners ya got, ya hostile host? The manners of a giblin wif a toothache, that's what kind, an' yer pa'd spin in his grave if he could see how ya carried on. If ya'd had a pa.' He escorted a somewhat reluctant and befuddled Fungle farther into the dim chamber. 'This here's Fungle Foxwit, lads. He's a gnole!' He said it proudly, as if he'd invented Fungle himself.

'We kin see that,' Acorn said dryly.

'Thuh one yoo been tooken aboot?' asked Thistle.

'One an' the same,' replied Conker, literally beaming.

'How is it you folks been expectin' me?' asked Fungle.

Conker, Acorn, and Thistle giggled like schoolchildren.

'You-uns kiddin'?' asked Acorn. 'The birdies been gibberin' yer name like it's stuck in their throats and they-uns tryin' to sing it loose.'

'Creekits roobin they leggins,' corroborated Thistle, 'callin' oot: "Gnooole, gnoole, Foongle thuh gnooole!"'

'An' the frogs,' Conker concurred. '"Fuuun-*gle*! Fuuun-*gle*!"' He grinned wide enough to unzip his ears. 'The wind, the trees – yer name be on the breeze!'

Thistle began beating a rhythm against his banjo, and Acorn took it up on the mandolute. Fungle stared as they cavorted to their impromptu daffy music.

'The flooowers get gnoole messageez / carried to 'em by the beez!'

'Methinks me eyes'll never see / the end o' gnole pomes writ by trees!'

The music stopped.

'Acorn,' chided Conker, still grinning to shame a dirty-minded demon, 'that were terrible.'

'Oorful,' agreed Thistle.

Acorn bowed slightly. 'Thankee, thankee,' he said modestly.

'Here here,' said Conker, pulling Fungle's pack off him, 'make yerself comfortable, take advantage of our legendary hospitality. Have a bite, have some wine –' he sniffed, and eyed Fungle up and down '– have a bath if ya've a mind.' He carelessly tossed Fungle's pack in a corner before the gnole could protest. The flap popped open and a dull grey box spilled out. Conker beat Fungle to it and turned it about in his hands. 'What'siss, then?' he asked.

'Me friend Ka called it a Light Box,' said Fungle. He grabbed for it, but Conker turned away.

'Light box?' He weighed the object. 'Don't feel so light ta me.' He squinted into the lens, held it away from himself, glanced back at Thistle and Acorn. His fingers found a button and pressed it.

White light washed the room. The box whined and stuck out a tongue of glossy paper. Conker yelped and dropped the Light Box. It landed on the button and the room lit again.

'I'm blinded!' hollered Acorn. He collided with Thistle. 'Blinded!'

Quickly Fungle snatched up the box and the two slips of paper and tucked them back into his pack before they could cause any

further mischief. Then he hurried to Acorn and made the little
creature hold still while Fungle stared into his eyes.

'Blind?' Acorn repeated
uncertainly.

'Close yer eyes,'
said Fungle.

Acorn closed his eyes. 'I can see!'
he shouted with his eyes closed.

'Whatcha see, Acorn?' asked Conker.

'Big white spots,' said Acorn. He opened his eyes. 'They's goin'
away now,' he said. He sounded a bit disappointed.

'Anyways,' Conker said to Fungle, as if nothing had happened,
'I heard yer name from a mutual friend of ours – rather a sombre
old fogey name o' Molom.'

'Molom!' Fungle couldn't have been more surprised if Conker
had sprouted antlers with little flags on the tips.

'Came to me in a dream,' continued Conker. 'Tole me ta be on
the lookout fer ya so's I could give ya a message. Ruint a good
night's sleep, too.'

Fungle's befuddlement turned to alarm. 'What's the message?'
he asked fearfully.

Conker looked embarrassed.

'He doon rememboo,' said Thistle.

'Don't remember!' Fungle sputtered. 'But, but –'

'He writ it down,' Acorn said helpfully.

Fungle reminded himself to remember his manners. *Never was a situation, son*, his father'd taught him, *made worse by the introduction o' manners*. 'Well,' Fungle asked as mildly as possible, under the circumstances, 'could I impose on ya to see yer way to tellin' me what message from Molom ya writ down fer me?'

Conker's glow dimmed.

'I'll get it,' said Acorn. He dashed to one end of the chamber and rummaged among the chestnut leaves while Conker fidgeted and shifted from foot to foot.

'Ain't much of a message,' Conker muttered. 'I mean to say, I wouldn't set much store by it, though I'd allow as how maybe it's got special significance fer yerself that I don't see.'

'A-ha!' Acorn produced a Blue Horse lined writing tablet and brought it to Fungle.

Fungle stared down at the page, on which a single word was written. He leafed through the tablet, but the remaining pages were blank. There was nothing more than the single scribble before him. Confused, he looked up at Conker.

'Broccoli?' he asked.

Conker looked sheepish. 'Well, I were sleepin'!' he defended.

'I woonce dreamed I saved all the creechoos in the foorest when I put me body in a soortain position,' declared Thistle. 'Boot next day I cooden rememboo which one.'

Fungle could only stare.

'Oh, now, look,' fretted Conker. 'I gone an' dispirited me new-frowned fiend here.' He turned to the others. 'Nothing left to do, lads, except –'

'Have a knees-up!' Thistle and Acorn harmonised (the only harmony they managed in the entire evening, in fact).

'Now, wait,' Fungle said desperately. 'Please –'

But Acorn removed the weathered mandolute and without so much as a glance tossed it to Conker, who caught it just after pitching a bodhran Acorn's way. Acorn caught the ancient drum and beat a four-count on it, and Conker joined in, plunking off-tune chords in a waltz tempo. If anything, Conker played the mandolute worse than Acorn had.

> *Knees up, silly ol' clown,*
> *Knees up, don't let 'em down!*
> *Under the table you must go,*
> *Eee – eye – eee – eye – eee – eye – oh!*

Fungle stood uncomfortably, knowing they were only trying to put him in a festive mood (the only sort a tree sprite recognises) and wanting to join in because their merrymaking was contagious, but he could not rid himself of the anxiety that had grown in him when Conker said he'd received a message for him from Molom. Yet Fungle also knew the importance of being a polite guest, so he pushed his anxiety into a special room in his mind he had long ago constructed for storing such things, and firmly shut the door.

If I catch yer bendin'
I'll saw yer legs right off,
So –
Knees up, knees up,
Gotta wake yer fleas up,
So knees up, ya silly ol' clown!

They finished more or less at the same time, and laughed together. Fungle bowed good-naturedly and gestured politely to Acorn. The little creature glanced uncertainly at Conker, who nodded brightly. Acorn shrugged out of the mandolute and handed it over.

Fungle slung the strap across his shoulder and adjusted it. He strummed a chord and winced. Acorn shrugged philosophically, and Fungle smiled gently and tuned the instrument from cacophony to concord.

Then he began to play.

At first they were too stunned to move. They merely gaped in awe while Fungle held that instrument and wrung from its battered wood and gut a music less likely than squeezing orange juice from a cow.

But they were forest sprites, after all, and the crack of doom would not sit them still for long. In no time (and with no time, either), they were clapping and cavorting and carrying on to wake a hibearnation, which as everybody knows is a country full of hibernating bears.

Fungle himself was the eye of this whirlwind of sprites. Eyes closed, he swayed gently to the rhythm of the music he made. Sometimes it seemed to Fungle that when he made music he created a place, an actual place that he visited every time he played. So he always made sure his music created a place he loved to visit. His mother, gone these many years now, had taught him to play. 'It's in the wood, Fungle lad,' she used to tell him. 'The music's in the wood, and in your life's time you'll learn the lore of wood.'

Fungle opened his eyes.

He looked down at his hands.

They were still.

The chamber was quiet.

Someone sniffed.

Fungle looked up to see Conker wiping one eye dry.

Thistle sniffled again.

'Aww, whadjer gone do that fer?' demanded Acorn. 'Jess when it were gettin' lively an' hettin' up me feet.'

Fungle blinked. 'Apologies, friend Acorn,' he said. 'I were thinkin' o' someone near an' dear to me heart, an' missin' her sorely.'

'That were byootifool,' mooned Thistle.

'An' ta make up fer it,' insisted Conker, 'ya got to play the liveliest tune any of us ever heard.'

'That's some doin', I reckon,' acknowledged Fungle. 'I accept.' And commenced to playing.

Now, Fungle knew his music had the power to make a body crazy, if he'd a mind to play in such a fashion. There were musics to do any conceivable thing: to make night-blooming flowers yearn for daylight, to bring together estranged lovers; musics for healin' and musics for hurtin', musics to make the dead tap bony toes in their quiet graves.

There were musics that were the very essence of celebration, and it was just such a distillation of revelry that Fungle's hands now conjured forth. It drove the pulse and pulsed the brain; it raced the heart and fevered the skin. It was the kind of music lemmings might play as they marathoned ecstatically toward the cliffs, a hoedown of the gods, the heartbeat of wheeling space.

It was exhilarating. It was exhausting.

Fungle paused to wipe sweat from his brow.

'More!' they clamoured. 'Oh, more!'

'A moment!' he pleaded breathlessly. His matted fur was thick with sweat, and he was conscious of being a bit downwind of himself. Being both civilised and furry, gnoles are scrupulously hygienic.

Conker brought him stream-cooled berry wine. Fungle thanked him and drank. 'Friend Conker,' he asked when he had caught his breath, 'would ya be knowin' how far distant it is to a place my people know as the Mound of the Dead?'

'Mound of the Dead?' Conker's brow knitted. 'Mound of the Dead . . .?'

'He means that hill with them funny rocks,' said Acorn.

'That place?' Conker frowned. 'Whatcher wanna go there fer?'

'Scoory place,' intoned Thistle. 'Voory scoory.'

Conker nodded agreement. 'Some sez in long-ago times them rocks is gnomes got caught out in sunlight an' turned to stone.'

Acorn grinned and clapped the tree sprite on the back. 'Ain't it just like you to believe in fairy stories?'

'Please, Conker,' said Fungle. 'It's important to me.'

'Well, it's only a couple clobhops north a here,' Conker said.

After a moment Fungle realised his mouth was hanging open. He closed it. He started to speak, hesitated, started again, said, 'I, I – that is, I, I,' stopped, and took a calming breath. 'Friend Conker, I'm thankin' ya fer yer kind hospitality and festivities – but I must go there immediately. This very instant!'

'Well . . . But . . . I . . .' Conker clapped his long green hands. ''Nother song!' he exclaimed. 'A final number, one fer the road, sumpin' ta tide us over.'

In spite of himself Fungle grinned. 'Ye'll drain me dry!' he protested.

'Ah, c'mon widja,' said Acorn.

'Sooong!' pleaded Thistle.

'Well . . . One more, then,' Fungle agreed.

They cheered. Fungle set them clapping and wove his melody around their metronome – which fell completely akilter in no time, forcing him to ignore them in order to maintain the tempo. Then he took the melody and ran with it, played it not with hand or mind but with heartbeat, with blood, with love of life and growth, with everything that made him *Fungle*.

The three sprites were bouncing off the walls. Thistle leapt furiously, as if trying to launch himself to the moon. Acorn spun like a dervish's top. Conker, especially, was driven to new heights of rapture by Fungle's music. He cavorted and kicked, cartwheeled, collided, and –

Conk!

The music stopped.

Acorn, Thistle, and Fungle stared at Conker.

Conker stood straight and still and smart as a stump. His gaze was fixed and vacant.

'Aw, now he gone an' dunnit,' observed Acorn.

'What happened?' asked Fungle

Acorn rolled his eyes. He mimed striking himself on the head.

'Coonk,' Thistle added gravely.

'He-uns gets a bit excited sometimes.'

'Well,' asked Fungle, 'is there anything we can –'

'*Fuunnngle.*' The voice was deep, resonant, ancient, the creaking timbre of bamboo in wind.

Molom's voice. It came from Conker.

'*Fungle.*' Conker raised a long thin finger to point at the gnole. '*You must hurry in your cause, brave mage. The humans, those meddlesome monkeys, are close to bringing Baphomet to light. They tear great gouts of earth asunder, and by the vastness of their demolition they are nearing the resting place of the stone. The web of being trembles with disruption as the earth around it is disturbed. If the humans find Baphomet before you do, it will be the end of them. But more grievous to me, it will be the end of you and your kind, the end of the forests, the end of this age upon the earth. They will destroy the world, or Theverat will own it. Remember your dream, good mage, and ready your most potent spells, and hasten on your way. The time is shorter than we thought.*'

'Poor gnole. Brave gnole.'

Silence.

Conker cleared his throat. 'Well,' he said in his own voice. 'Weren't that innerestin'?'

'Guess ya remembered yer dream after all,' said Acorn.

Fungle began removing the mandolute.

'No, no,' complained Conker. 'Ya didn't finish yer song!'

'You heard the voice of Molom,' said Fungle. 'I must go, or there'll be no more songs.'

'One more!' pleaded Conker. 'Just one more!'

'Sooong!' Thistle chimed in.

But Fungle realised that for the forest sprites there would always be one more song to play, one more jig to dance, one more joke to tell – until the time for songs and dances and jokes was gone for ever from the world. So he handed the mandolute to Acorn and turned away, a gnole possessed and bent on a mission. He thanked them again and continued toward the burrow entrance.

He wormed out of the cramped tunnel and headed northward on his way while the raucous cacophony resumed behind him, only to cut off abruptly at the slamming of a door.

Mathemagics

'Only a couple clobhops north,' he said – 'ha! An' a mountain's *only* a big rock, an' a ocean's *only* an ambitious puddle. An' I'm *only* a gullible gnole, an' me stride's only *so* long, an' I've *only* made ten or twenty thousand of 'em this evenin' which is now this mornin', thank you very much, an' me talkin' to meself long enough to be tellin' jokes an' laughin' at the ones I ain't heard, an' that's *only* a big ol' funny-shaped rock I see ahead o' me –'

Fungle stopped in his tracks.

The stone loomed before him like a dark door in the sky, darker than the fading night. It was tall and rectangular, regular in shape, with cut edges.

Not a troll stone. Ancient stone, hand-hewn stone, gnole-carved stone.

A menhir: a standing stone.

Fungle felt a tremble deep inside as he approached the mystic monolith with hands outstretched. But before he could touch it he was restrained by something pressing against his belly. He looked down to see a broad yellow ribbon of some glossy foreign substance painted with uniform black letters. The ribbon formed a square around the menhir, supported by stakes driven into the ground.

**ARCHAEOLOGICAL SITE DO NOT DISTURB ARCHAEO-
LOGICAL SITE DO NOT DISTURB**

Its meaning eluded him. Was it a warning not to disrupt the harmony of this sacred area, or was it an admonition of lurking danger?

Well, Fungle already knew this was a sacred site, and he sure understood the danger well enough. So the ribbon's warning was already well-heeded, far as he was concerned.

He ducked under the yellow tape.

The menhir rose imposing before him in the pre-dawn chill, backdropped by the overgrown hemisphere of a small hill. Fungle sensed the ancientness, the history, embedded within the stone. His ancestors had erected it in their southward trek across the continent after the fall of Atlantis. There were many such places on the North and South Americkan continents. Some were calendars, some memorials; the purposes of many were lost in antiquity.

The menhir . . .

Fungle frowned.

The menhir was the only naked rock in sight. The surrounding area was lush with copses of oak, verdant lichen and vines, strangling ivy and creeping kudzu, a rough rock landscape softened by a thick green carpet of fern and vine and grass and moss. Yet the menhir was bare rock. Around the standing stone's base was a space where the growth had recently been cleared away.

Humans, he realised.

Fungle thought of the ancient maps he had studied: ten menhirs set on cardinal points in a ring around a large burial mound located on a key ley line. Beneath his feet he could feel their combined energy counting off the great slow pulse of the earth that beat through a network of magnetic veins across the body of the globe. Near the southernmost menhir there should be a stone cairn containing a spirit sealed by a spell, awaiting the deciphering of commands carved on its surface to unlock its voice, the voice that would reveal the location of Baphomet.

Fungle frowned. The hill behind the menhir looked too symmetrical to be a natural hill . . . He imagined it stripped of greenery – and saw in his mind a burial mound.

Fungle had approached from the south and found this standing stone straight away, which meant this was most likely the southernmost of the ring of menhirs. And his map had indicated that the cairn containing the stone-sealed voice was located to the immediate west of the southernmost stone – which meant the cairn had to be nearby.

Fungle craned his head to regard the menhir looming before him. The stone stood impassive, like an alien god.

Fungle ducked out of the square of yellow tape, feeling oddly as if he were leaving a safeguarded space similar to the protective pentagrams in which a mage stood when conjuring potentially harmful forces.

He searched east of the menhir and found no sign of the stone cairn depicted on the ancient maps, but he did find the next menhir in the ring around the mound. Like the first, it was surrounded by the yellow tape with its printed warning. Unlike the first, however, the rock was not bare but lichen-pelted and vine-shrouded, barely distinguishable as an artifact at all. Fungle wondered how long it would be before the humans stripped the growth from it and exposed the worked stone to the sun and moon once more.

He searched to the west of the southernmost menhir and found the next menhir in the ring, still tangled in overgrowth. The humans had not discovered it – yet.

But no cairn.

In the pale of false dawn he searched to the south and north; after boxing the compass he had found an abandoned rabbit warren, a mound of fire ants, a family of badgers, a rare mushroom of

the agaric family, a foil chewing-gum wrapper, foraging possums readying for bed with dawn's approach, and a cigarette butt – but no stone cairn.

He wondered if the humans had found it.

Birds were taking up the daytime verses of the crickets' evening song.

Filthy, exhausted, and frustrated, Fungle again entered the square of yellow tape and confronted the menhir mute against the lightening sky.

There are ways to ask questions of stone. But each requires energy, and Fungle had none.

He needed sleep.

But he also needed answers.

A molten ingot spilled the horizon.

Fungle touched the menhir

and gazed out across snow-covered countryside. Distant noonday sun stole shadows; biting cold wind had flayed the trees to bone. He recognised the hillside and lines of mountain ridge as the place where he had been standing when he touched the menhir. But there was no symmetrical hill here; no menhirs rose in a guardian ring.

Fungle's winter coat was not yet full on him; the fatty layer beneath was not yet grown protectively thick, and the frigid wind cut past his fur, leeched heat from his skin, and settled into his marrow. The chill told Fungle's body it was time to hibernate, time to slow to a state deeper than sleep and lighter than death. In just a few minutes his blood thickened and his mind clouded with sleep.

But no! He'd stood in autumn, not winter! The leaves were only just feeling winter's burn; days were still thick and goldenrod in bloom. Autumn – not winter!

He fought to ignore the messages his body was sending him. He drew strength from the very earth on which he stood, for this area was a node of magnetic energy – the very reason the Mound of the Dead had been built here in the first place.

Had been built? Then where was it?

As if in answer he saw a procession heading toward him.

There were several hundred of them, dark against the white snow, bundled in rags and struggling under burdens of pack and parcel. Some shouldered palanquin poles or dragged travois sleds.

Shivering, Fungle waited while they neared.

As they came closer, Fungle felt a shock that chilled him more deeply than any winter could. The hapless, freezing creatures struggling with their burdens were gnoles!

More shocking was their cargo: supplies and portable shelters were obvious from the way they were bundled; Fungle identified these readily enough. But he stared at the palanquins, the travois sleds and stretchers. The figures on them were neither gnole nor human, but the vanished beings that had once been the master race of Atlantis: warriors, mages, scientists, priests, millennia dead, living only in ancient lore and legend – yet here they lay before Fungle's snow-lashed eyes, stragglers from a vanished continent, carried by the anguished labour of gnoles!

The stragglers stopped not far from Fungle and began making camp. Freezing, Fungle could no longer stand idle. He stepped forward, raising a hand in peace and calling out against the howling wind. 'Brothers!' he cried. 'Brother gnoles!'

They ignored him as they dug pits in the snow and erected shelters for their masters. Fungle stood watching in their midst, but they did not see him.

I'm not really here, he realised. *I feel it, but I am not really here at all.*

He watched as the gnoles lit fires and set battered pots cooking to make a thin gruel, most of which was given to their masters, who ate little of it.

Wraith-like, Fungle walked among them.

Thin, wretched and starving, the masters were wasting away despite the charms and herbs and healing vapours of their servants the gnoles, who had over time and from necessity been entrusted with the learning of their masters. On Atlantis many of the mages had been keeping themselves alive well past their time with spells and potions, and with their homeland gone, some of the magic that maintained them had drowned, too. There were also new hardships in this new land: new diseases, harsh weather, hunting beasts, unknown geography. Time was catching up with them. The masters were dying.

The gnoles were a pitiful sight to behold as well, and Fungle's heart ached to see them. To travel they were forced to fight their natural instinct to hibernate. But unlike their frailer masters they were furred against the winter and hearty from generations of hard labour. They would survive.

'We *did* survive,' Fungle said aloud. Watching his people suffering for their apathetic masters, Fungle felt angrier than he ever

had. Lies, he realised. All our lore, all our legends and histories
and genealogies, all our pride in partnership with the Atlantean
race – lies. Perhaps true once, our cherished apprenticeship under
this wise and powerful race. But that was long ago, millennia before
even this travesty played out before me by ancestors themselves
millennia dead. If that time of partnership had ever been real,
it had been before Baphomet came to light in the land and
corrupted it, twisting the Atlanteans and bending my people to
the lash. *Lies.* What he had learned when he had summoned
Molom was corroborated here: his was a young race, brought
wild from the wood and enhanced, indentured to those who had
increased them. Doggedly faithful temple wardens whose masters
would never return, and who had eventually learned to reckon with
the world on their own.

He felt heartsick.

The winter melted. Day and night-time strobed; phases stole
across the hurtling moon as stars sleeted past. Branches thickened
with colour-bled leaves, rivers flowed with melted runoff.

The sun slowed to hang molten in the springtime sky.

Fungle stood beside a menhir. Freshly hewn from living rock, the
stone sentinel stood at the periphery of a smooth granite mound.

The Mound, thought Fungle, *of the Dead* – and understood the
tragic history behind its name at last.

He saw the depleted caravan of gnoles struggling southward
down the mountain ridge, carrying and dragging the few Atlanteans who had survived the harsh Appalachian winter. Eventually
those Atlanteans were to found a civilisation in warmer climes,
a civilisation that would vanish and leave only poorly understood
remnants of itself. But that founding was many years away, and
even though Fungle knew it to be doomed, he could not help
making his blessing upon the ragged, winding line.

Remnants. And a fledgling race of gnoles left behind to preserve
a priceless body of salvaged knowledge locked away in a mountain
cavern whose location even they forgot as, over thousands of
waning generations, they settled across the thick forests of the
Southern Appalachian Mountains, a race of remnants themselves,
basking in a garden grown up around a ruin.

An odd bundle of emotions stirred inside him as he watched
until the caravan was out of sight. Finally he turned to confront
the newly erected Mound of the Dead. Without the dense layer
of tangled overgrowth it was an imposing and sobering sight.
Spell-charged menhirs stood tall around a grey granite hill carved

with protective symbols and emblems of eternity. The surrounding air seemed to crackle; the ground felt like a vibrating drumhead.

Fungle drew in a sharp breath. Without the overgrowth, he realised, the cairn would be sitting in plain sight! Quickly he searched the area around the southernmost menhir, the area that had proven so fruitless only hours before. *Hours before*, he thought wryly, *but thousands o' years hence.*

But still he could not find the cairn.

Frustrated, he confronted the southernmost menhir. Something was niggling at the back of his mind, the kind of feeling he got when he left his home and just knew he'd forgotten something he'd meant to bring along, though he couldn't think what it might be. There was something, some simple thing, that he knew would set this mystery aright.

The new-standing stone loomed before him.

'Well,' he said to it, 'ya sent me back here ta get some answers. So I reckon touchin' ya one more time can't hurt.' Fungle set his hand against the stone

and broke the yellow tape as he fell backwards in utter exhaustion.

The sun was rising. Fungle stood and blessed the breaking day, then turned away. Tired as he was, he had to continue his search for the cairn that held the location of Baphomet. But where could it be? It wasn't where the maps had shown it, on the south-east side of the mound.

He stepped away from the menhir. His shadow pointed west toward the Mound of the Dead. Something about that . . . He turned east again to face the sun.

East.

He pictured the maps he had studied to locate the cairn. There was the cairn, on the bottom-left side. South-west, right?

Wrong.

Fungle's ancestors had drawn maps with the east on top, to face the direction of the earth's rotation. *Always heading east, that's us.* He'd been assuming that the top of his map was north. Mentally he rotated his remembered map ninety degrees, one quarter of a circle, until the real north was on top. Which put the cairn . . .

North-west.

He chased his shadow 'round the mound.

*

Fungle stood on high ground. The growth on the north-west side of the Mound of the Dead was dense; the humans had not yet cleared this side. Where the cairn was indicated on his revised mental map lay a ring of oaks. Oak is a protective wood, a sacred and potent tree, and these trees were ancient and huge. The horizon was clear and hard against the early morning sky. With slow majesty the sun lifted over the rim of the earth to gild the valley. Eyes dazzled, Fungle imagined the oak ring as a crown of gold.

Next thing he knew the sun was higher in the sky, shadows were sharper, and he found himself staring blankly at a vine that had wound its way round a rock outcropping. What had he been about . . .? He scratched himself and pondered as small yellow butterflies flitted about the fields.

Oh yes: the cairn.

From his vantage point he could see a ring of oaks among the dense growth to the north-west of the Mound of the Dead. Oak is a protective wood . . . perhaps . . .

It was late afternoon and he was staring at the rock again. His muscles were cramped from standing motionless for hours.

What was I about? Oh, yes: the cairn.

He looked around from his vantage point – and stopped. Looked down. Frowned. Wasn't there . . . ? Yes, over there: a ring of oaks. How had he known?

Because he'd found it twice already.

He smiled. There was a spell of distraction around the oaks! A warding spell similar to the ones he used to guard his home and books, much like the one protecting Neema's cave home – but far more powerful.

Gnolecraft.

Hurriedly he waded through great stands of wild parsley to enter the ring of holy oaks. In thick forest now the light lay green and dusky under the canopy of leaves, and the air was dank as an ogre's pocket. No song of bird or clatter of cricket penetrated the thick gloom. Twisted trunks stood thick about, and in the murky aquatic greenness of the mystical light the mage could easily believe he had stepped into the underworld. The tension within the ring of oaks was palpable. Powerful forces had been bound here.

A single shaft of golden afternoon sunlight broke through a gap in the dense canopy and shone upon a great owl perched upon a low branch of the largest oak. Fungle recognised it as the owl that had fallen down his chimney the night of his awful dream – Molom's owl, the Elemental's eyes and ears upon the world. The gnole was about to bless the bird and give it his greetings when he felt a great presence rising all around him. It filled him with an awe that turned muscles to water and rooted his feet to the ground. He felt no fear or urge to flight, just the sense of an august presence growing nearer. *Oh, this be gnolecraft, a'right!* By now any ordinary gnome, elf, human, or even troll would've kicked their own backsides with their heels in their haste to be away from such a sensation arising in such a place.

Which of course is why Fungle held his ground.

A thick mist rose from the earth in the centre of the oak ring. Within seconds Fungle was enveloped by it, but he stood fast. In a moment he discerned a milky glow off to one side. When nothing else happened after a few more minutes, Fungle headed towards the faint light.

It brightened as he neared, lighting up a sphere of mist around it. Soon Fungle found himself standing before a glass object of complicated design, suspended in the air at gnole-head height and pulsing with light from deep within.

Fungle studied the strange and complex pattern while mist swirled dreamlike about him. Before making any move he turned the various shapes in his mind, rearranged broken curlicues and unravelled mazes, aligned corners and collapsed dovetails until he felt sure there was a shape to be made from this design before him.

Fungle reached out and touched the shining glass. It was smooth and warm. He began deftly rearranging pieces of the pattern, re-forming the puzzle along the lines he had already worked out in his imagination. It took him less than a minute, and when he was done he lowered his hands and nodded his head in satisfaction.

Before him hung a glowing glass key.

Fungle plucked the key from the air, and immediately the mist parted to show an enormous locked gate. Fungle approached it and gingerly placed the key into the lock. Fearing the fragile key might break, he turned it gently, feeling the clicking mechanism through his fingers, never forcing but maintaining a firm pressure, until he felt a slight jolt.

The lock sprang open.

The gate swung inward.

Beyond stood a tall figure, little more than a smudge of darkness against the mist. It held a lantern high. 'Come,' it ordered in a perfectly ordinary voice carried cleanly by the mist, and shuffled off.

Fungle followed the yellow lantern light of his spectral guide. They had not travelled more than a few hundred yards before the light was extinguished and Fungle found himself standing in pitch blackness with no sign of the tall figure or sense of place.

Around him pale, indirect light rose. Fungle discovered he was standing in the centre of a low, circular chamber. Seated around the perimeter, on roots grown into shapes of thrones were twelve 'oakmen' – the spirits of oak trees. The largest of the oakmen sat upon the largest throne, his head adorned with a crown of acorns. Fungle understood from the arrangement of the spirits in the room around him that he was in a twilight world, a borderland between the earth and the astral regions, and that the figures around him were manifestations representing the actual ring of protective oaks near the Mound of the Dead. From this he realised that the chief of these spirits was Wurzel, the Oak King.

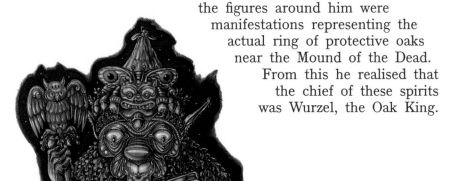

Fungle felt humbled at the complexity of the ancient mage spell that had been wrought so long ago, still potent and cunningly protective after all these centuries.

He bowed low before the ring of seated manifestations.

'Welcome, gnole,' whispered the Oak King on his throne. His voice was a rattle of windshook leaves. 'What do you seek in this hallowed place?'

Fungle thought rapidly before speaking.

> *'Wurzel, Oak King wise and old,*
> *I seek the secret that you hold:*
> *The cairn that on its stone face shows*
> *The long-lost Library of the gnoles.'*

'Who has sent you on such a quest?'

'Lord Molom.'

There was a rustle among the oakmen. 'To Molom, Lord of Trees, I also make obeisance,' whispered Wurzel. 'Do you know of his war with the Harrower in his realm?'

'The Harrower?' Fungle said slowly. 'Mighty Wurzel, do you speak of Theverat?'

'This is a holy place, mage among gnoles, and you will not speak that name here.'

Fungle bowed low. 'I ask your pardon, King of Oaks. For better or for worse, I am drawn into this conflict between Molom and . . . and the Harrower.'

'We know you are named Fungle of Foxwits,' whispered Wurzel, 'and that you are Molom's champion upon the theatre of the earth. What you seek is here stated, good mage, but we must tell you that the great Library, and the terrible thing it contains, was hidden with great effort by your first forefathers upon this land to ensure that only a true mage of power would be able to unlock the ciphers and spells that protect it. Among those many trials is one entrusted to us. We understand the importance of your quest and bestow our blessings upon it, but our pact with the first mages is ancient and binding. We may impart to you only the ciphers and not their solution.'

'I understand, good King, and I be muchly grateful for yer blessin's.'

Wurzel nodded with the patience of a life of root and growing wood. *'Six,'* he said.

Fungle started to ask if that was all, but the voice of another oakman stilled his tongue. *'Sixteen,'* said the spirit on his throne of roots.

Clockwise around the ring every other oakman spoke:

'Thirty-five.'

'Fifteen.'

'*One.*'

And Wurzel completed the ring by saying, '*Forty-nine.*'

Fungle turned a complete circle as the oakmen yielded forth the code. When they were done he repeated the numbers aloud, head buzzing: 'Six, sixteen, thirty-five, fifteen, one, forty-nine –'

He stopped. Wurzel and his court had vanished. The mist rolled back into the surrounding wood, and Fungle realised he was back in the ring of holy oaks near the Mound of the Dead. Above him the wind barged among the leaves. Fungle looked up to see all twelve of the great old oaks pulling back their inmost branches to reveal the sky. Sunlight speared the gloom in the middle of the ring. The patch of earth it illuminated began to swell, then to crumble, until rising there before Fungle stood the cairn, an ancient Atlantean marker of carved sandstone bathing in the waning light of day. Deeply graven into its surface were a sun and moon, whorls and mazes. At the base were carved angular runes in the alphabet of his forefathers. The cairn was solid but it did not look real; if there were such a thing as the ghost of a stone, this was it.

Fungle stood admiring the ingenuity of the carvings upon the cairn. A deity was etched deep in the sandstone. The sun was its head, its arms were outstretched, and it held a key in its right hand. Its body was ornamented with carved cups and concentric rings. Seated at its clawed feet was Lady Moon, with stars in attendance. From sun to moon, head to foot, ran a straight line calibrated with twenty deeply scored notches. At its base, the ancient runes spelled out a poem:

> *Twenty are the Sun's crown,*
> *The Key is to the East.*
> *South to the Moon*
> *For the Stone of the Beast.*

Fungle read the message forwards and backwards, and rearranged the letters in every combination he could think of, but beyond the words – which were general enough to be of little help – he could find no message hidden there. He fought the rising panic that threatened to possess him and subdued his fear of failure in order to wrestle with the message.

First he thought of the sequence of numbers given him by the oaks. They had to relate somehow to the carving on the cairn. Fungle sent his spirit travelling along the grooves and whorls and angles etched into rock, but found no clue there. He felt certain the answer lay not in the picture but in the letters.

Six, sixteen, thirty-five, fifteen, one, forty-nine . . .
A carved message in the ancient gnole alphabet . . .
A sequence of numbers . . .
If each number corresponded to each letter, so that 'one' was the first letter, then perhaps the numbers given him by the oakmen stood for –
Fungle grinned. He didn't even need the runes to work it out: 6–16–35–15–1–49. Match the numbers to the letters they represented, and they spelled out –
'Yanto!' he said aloud. 'Yanto, Yanto, Yanto!'
He shook his head in boggled wonder. Yanto was the Lord of Secrets, a simple sort indeed. His Summoning was one of the first a young mage learned, because everybody wants a guardian for their secrets. As a young apprentice Fungle had invoked him many times. Thinking he had made exciting new discoveries in alchemy and magic, he would bundle his spells up in one overriding spell which he entrusted to Yanto's care, for Yanto would only yield a secret up to the proper user. Yanto demanded a password which he assigned to the secret you wanted him to keep, and when next you summoned him, you had to give him the password or he would not retrieve your secrets for you.
Fungle could hardly believe it. For the ancient gnoles to use Yanto to guard the location of Baphomet was absurd. But the more he thought about it, the more appropriate it seemed. Yes, any gnole child with a rudimentary knowledge of Summonings could invoke Yanto – but who else would? What other being would know the Summoning, or even think to use it? *Simplest is bestest* – he felt like doing a little jig in the excitement of his discovery.
All right, then – Fungle would Summon Yanto from the stone. But to get the Lord of Secrets to yield the location of Baphomet to him, Fungle needed to know the password, the key, that unlocked the secret entrusted to him by gnoles a hundred centuries dead.
He studied the cairn for some clue.
The Sun with a twenty-pointed crown, the Moon and stars, the notched line, the carved whorls, the outstretched hands, the key –
Fungle began to laugh, for of course the word was *mei-nesh't* – the Atlantean word for 'key'.
Immediately Fungle recited the spell to summon Yanto:

'Yanto, Lord of Secrets,
Keeper of mysteries,
Unraveller of puzzles,

Yanto, face of concealment,
Appear before me now.

'Mei-nesh't *I use to Invoke thee, Yanto*
Mei-nesh't *to give me that entrusted you.*
Mei-nesh't, *Yanto.'*

A face appeared in the rock. The face *was* the rock, was the stone
itself made animate.

'About bloody time,' it said.

'Lord Yanto,' said Fungle.

The face frowned. 'Yeah, yeah; in the flesh, if you'll pardon the exaggeration,' said Yanto. 'Didn't catch your name,' he hinted.

Fungle touched his wishing feather and bowed. 'Fungle Foxwit gnole at yer service,' he said.

'Hmph. More like *me* at *your* service, since you did the Summoning,' Yanto said irritably. 'Gnole, huh?'

'Of the race of gnoles, Lord Yanto.'

'You better hurry, then, if you want to catch up with your group. They turned tail out of here a ways back – but not before locking me up in this cheery rock. Oh, I tell you, it's a joy doing favours for gnoles!' The stone eyes turned skyward.

'There's to be no catchin' up to 'em, Yanto,' said Fungle, 'fer they's dust ten thousand years now.'

'Ten thousand years?' Yanto looked doubtful. 'I've been stuck in this rock for ten *thousand* years?'

'More or less,' admitted Fungle.

'Well, for crying out loud, man, say the secret word so I can tell you what I know and get out of here. I left the kettle on!'

'*Mei-nesh't,*' said Fungle.

'Atlantean word, huh?' The stone face swung as if shaking its head. 'Lots of secrets, those Atlanteans. Difficult people, they are.'

'Were,' amended Fungle.

'Were? Really?' The stone eyebrows rose. 'Turn your head for ten thousand years and everything changes. Go figure.'

'*Mei-nesh't,* Yanto,' reminded Fungle.

'All right, already. Don't get your britches in a twist.' The face began to recede into the stone. 'Sit tight,' said Yanto, 'I'll be right back.'

Fungle waited. From the stone came mutterings, rummagings, exclamations. 'Let's see, now . . . *Ways to Keep a Lover Faithful.* I must have a million of these. *Spell for Keeping Lawns Trim.* You gotta be kidding me. Oh, well; I don't make 'em, I just keep 'em. *Location of the Lost Monet.* Nope. *Why Dogs Howl at the Moon.* No kidding? Well, that's pretty interesting. *Who Killed Kennedy. How the Dinosaurs Died. How They Get the Lead in Pencils.* Say, that's a good one. *Why the Whales Went Back to the Sea. What Caused the Ice Ages. What a Cashew Shell Looks Like.* You don't say? *Where the Light Goes When You Turn It Off.* Ah, here we are: *Location of Baphomet.*'

The face re-emerged in the stone. 'Listen, Fungle, I found a bunch of spells and alchemickal formulas you stuck me with when you were a kid.' The stone eyes looked downward as if reading. '*Homework Spell*,' Yanto recited. '*Transmute Lead to Steel. Change a Worm to a Butterfly. Transform Seeds into Plants. Turn an Enemy Green.* That kind of thing. Want 'em?'

Fungle felt himself blush. He knew it was ridiculous to be embarrassed about spells crafted and kept secret when he was a child, especially when he was on the verge of learning the location of Baphomet, but he couldn't help it. If Death himself reminded you of the time your pants fell off in gym class, you'd probably feel a bit sheepish even as he swung his scythe. 'You can get rid o' those,' Fungle said meekly.

'No can do, boss,' said Yanto. 'Gotta have the secret word before I can lay a finger on them.'

Of course Fungle had long forgotten any overly clever passwords he had given Yanto as a child, but he was reluctant to say so. 'Best hold on to them for now,' said Fungle.

'The Baphomet one, too?'

Fungle's pulse quickened. 'Er, no,' he said, a quaver creeping into his voice. 'You'd better tell me that one.'

'Your wish is my, *et cetera*.' Yanto looked down. 'Ready?'

Fungle nodded.

'"Twelve clobhops west across the mountains to the Valley of the Moon."' Yanto looked up. 'Pretty name,' he observed.

Fungle bit back a reply.

'"Once there, seek ye the north on west side facing the sun's morning climb. There find a great cross of pure black rock, black as coal, grained deep into the mountain's skin. 'Neath it find a hole such as fit for rabbits and badgers, and within it find harsh wards. Only the worthy shall pass them: the Warrior, the Scholar, the Wise Mage, the Honourable Seeker. If you be such, then past them you will find the cavern and all you seek."' Yanto looked up once more. 'That's it,' he said, a bit apologetically. 'Kind of vague, isn't it?'

But Fungle was shaking his head excitedly. Twelve clobhops west, across the mountains, across the Valley of the Moon? That was a day's journey from here!

'It's perfect,' he whispered.

'Terrific,' said Yanto. 'So you're happy, and if you're happy, then I'm happy, because it means –' the face pushed farther out from the stone – 'that I'm –' the true form of Yanto strained from the cairn – '*outta here!*' Yanto jumped up, arced over, and dove straight down into the earth without a ripple.

'Blessin's on ya,' Fungle murmured distractedly.

The face appeared in the ground. 'Likewise,' said Yanto, and disappeared a final time.

Fungle touched the stone cairn. His fingers trembled. *A day's journey*, he thought. *A day's journey, a nice walk, a vigorous hike.* Yanto's message orbited like a litany in Fungle's mind: *Ten clobhops west, across the mountains, across the valley, north-west side, look for the black cross on the mountain's eastern side.*

Ten clobhops west, across the mountains . . .

Fungle touched the stone cairn. His fingers trembled. *A day's journey*, he thought. *A day's journey, a nice walk, a vigorous hike.* Yanto's message orbited like a litany in Fungle's mind: *Twelve clobhops west, across the mountains, across the valley, north-west side, look for the black cross on the mountain's eastern side.*

Twelve clobhops west, across the mountains . . .

The Mound of the Dead

He wanted to set out that very moment, but night was falling and he was desperate for sleep. His body was still reacting to the cold, still sending out signals of hibernation. He had not slept since those brief hours after he and Musrum had fled the Land of a Thousand Smokes, and since then he had walked with Conker through the forest, eaten only a light meal, and hiked nearly till dawn to reach this place, been shot back twelve thousand years to a glacial winter, stood all day in one spot under the spell of an ancient ward, met with Wurzel the Oak King and deciphered the oakmen's code, summoned Yanto, and learned the location of Baphomet.

He could use a nap.

Near the top of the hill he found a small cave. The entrance was choked with weeds and vines. Fungle tore weakly at them, once nearly toppling backward down the hill as a handful of vines suddenly parted. Finally he had cleared a space large enough to admit him, and he stumbled into the cool dark of the chamber.

But even after finding shelter he could not allow himself to sleep. He forced himself to make the passes and say the ancient words that would erect a spell wall in the chamber, making it a protected bubble much like the one that guarded his bedroom at night in his underground home.

Home, he thought as mage-light began to shimmer in the chamber. *What a faraway notion.*

Reality ebbed.

Thorn regarded the overgrown mound from behind a sheltering tree. Far overhead, deadly patches of waning daylight glimmered through gaps in the canopy of leaves. So long as Thorn hugged shadows he was safe. It was not daytime he feared, but daylight.

But soon would come the enormous night.

Within the mound slept the odious gnole.

Behind the tree Thorn plotted.

Losing half his giblins to those cursed goblins had been an inconvenience. Losing the remainder to the oozlumps had been frustrating, but still not a disaster. If it had been possible, Thorn would gladly have used the oozlumps against the gnole in their stead. But the creatures could not leave the landfill, and Thorn doubted they could be controlled anyway – not enough mind in that hungry black mass.

Still, Thorn was resourceful. Being left to his own devices was for him a return to the *status quo*. It meant he was now forced to rely on the person he relied on best.

Smiling, he broke off the spiny tip from one of his elbow joints. He broke off the other, and continued snapping the tips from his spiky joints until six briar tips lay writhing in the leathery palm of his hand. Indigo blood thick as sap welled from the truncated spikes at his joints.

Well, he thought to himself, gnoles are social creatures – I imagine those dead old gnoles in their hole will welcome an addition to their crew.

The thought happily blighted his day as he approached the base of the mound, avoiding patches of faint daylight and planting the squirming thorn tips deep in loamy dark, fertilising each with a drop of his black blood.

Fungle snapped awake from a lulling dream of hibernation. To come quickly to consciousness from so deep a sleep can be like hauling a hook up from the lowest ocean floor: sometimes ancient things get snagged on it and dragged to the surface.

Fungle blinked away fading remnants of a childhood memory. He and his brother Froog had been out just before cold dawn, collecting morning dew from the petals of a night-blooming jasmine. He had recently begun serving his apprenticeship under Wily Barktea, and Froog had talked him into concocting a potion that would make his two favourite frogs fall in love with one another – the sort of thing children do when they are learning their first magic spells. Gold from lead, a homework spell, a spell to make faery light glow under the bedcovers for late-night reading, love potions – Fungle's affection for Froog, and faint guilt at being named Wily's successor when his brother had no vocation in sight as yet, eased Froog's task of talking Fungle into lending his hand at such novice spells.

Froog was leading Fungle to a special place he knew where the jasmine grew in profusion. This region of the forest was new to young Fungle, and anything new was a source of constant delight and amazement to him (as, in later life, anything old would be as well). The path Froog followed would only have been called so by a gnole; few other creatures could have perceived it at all. Fungle saw an interesting blossom, some night-glowing flower, and stepped off the path to examine it. Just a few steps, really, but a surprise can hide in any step taken anywhere. The surprise in this one showed itself when the carpet of moss gave way beneath Fungle's feet. He plunged – and was immediately caught in a tangled net of roots and vines. The moss that had covered the gopher hole tumbled in after him, landed on top of him, and hid him from the eyes of the world. He tried to uncover himself, but when he moved he felt a tearing beneath him. The roots and vines supporting him were only barely doing so. Fungle imagined how far down the hole might go, and what might lie at the bottom of it, and was terrified.

He tried to call out to his brother, but his voice would not come. His throat had closed itself so tight that only a rasping whistle would emerge. It was the only time in his life Fungle had been too frightened to speak. It lasted only a moment, and then he regained his voice and called out to Froog, who quickly found him and helped him out of the hole. Then Froog showed him that the gopher hole went down only a few more feet, and the brothers laughed about it and collected their jasmine dew, only to find out when they got home that the frogs had both laid eggs and didn't need to fall in love with each other at all. So it had been a journey of discovery in many ways.

As the shards of that memory dissolved in Fungle's mind, they left in their place an eerie resonance in reality – for when Fungle unmade his protective spell and tried to leave the chamber that had been his resting place by pushing at the growth around the entrance, his palms were pierced by many sharp thorns. The entrance was barricaded by a web of thick, thorny vines.

For an instant he felt a young Fungle's terror, seemingly trapped forever above a miles-deep hole above a monster's lair.

His palms felt hot. They began to throb. In a moment they had begun to swell. He looked at the puckers where they had been pierced by thorns.

Poison?

He summoned forth a deep awareness within himself, a body consciousness swimming like a whale in the ocean of his self. It surged upstream along his veins and into his limbs, and sensed the poison flowing towards his heart. Not enough to kill him, but easily enough to make him ill and weak.

He marshalled his body against the poison, and used the everyday magic of chemical and gland and enzyme to convert the poison into inert material that would pass through his body unnoticed. He had learned the ability as a child, for deadly poisons are as natural a part of the forest as beautiful plumage, and a gnole must learn to appreciate both.

When he was sure that he would be all right, he approached the thorny barricade once more. This time he bent to examine it but did not touch it. The thorns were nasty leathery hooks the size of his little finger, curling from green-black vines thick as his arm. Pale silver patches showed through the thick growth, and from the quality of light Fungle reckoned it was mid-evening and the waning moon had risen. The barricade of thorns had grown up around the entrance while he slept.

Fungle fetched his pack and pushed it against the briars, trying to force through the barricade, but it was too strong.

Fungle frowned. This was no natural barricade. It was spellcast; he could sense it. He wondered if the barricade was a response to his intrusion, a protective reaction on the part of the vestiges of the guardian spell imbued into the ring of menhirs.

Carefully he set his hand on a section of vine between two razor-sharp thorns. He felt it there beneath his fingertips: the reverberation of the source magic that had created the wall of thorns, like the signature of an artist.

But it was not the signature of any gnole, past or present.

Thorns . . .

Fungle thought of that spiked figure he had encountered in the Land of a Thousand Smokes, of the deadly piece of itself it had hurled, the thorn that had sprouted to cage the oozlump in a terrible thicket of thorns. Hand still lightly touching the imprisoning vine, Fungle dug deep into his senses, put his awareness into the nerve endings at his fingertips. He felt for a certain Presence, a certain *glamour*.

And found it.

Something waited for him out there in the night.

Fungle tried force. He tried spells. He tried makeshift potions from ingredients in his pack. He couldn't get out. The thorny barrier had him like a spider.

He searched for another way out.

The chamber was small and cramped, large enough for three or four gnoles at most. When Fungle had discovered it shortly before sunset he had been as tired as it is possible to be and still be moving, and had paid scant attention to it as he crawled in. At the time Fungle wouldn't have cared about sharing the place with a den of vipers; the fact that it was a shelter he could protect with a warding spell while he slept had been enough – and now the sheltering chamber had become a tomb.

A tomb . . .

A shadow blotted the moonlight showing through the barricade.

'Gnole!'

It was a horrible voice. The sound of it made Fungle think of whirling blades chopping meat.

'Gnole! Wake up in there!'

Fungle figured he knew who it was calling to him now that night was well entrenched, but also figured he had nothing to say to him just now. He continued searching for a way out of the chamber.

'All right, then – here's something that'll wake you up! I've got your goblins here, gnole! You left them behind, and now I got 'em right here, dangling on the end of my favourite spear!'

It's a burial mound, Fungle thought, trying to concentrate and ignore the terrible voice outside. A gnole burial mound. Which means the entranceway will be a small room, an antechamber. And an *ante*chamber –

– Leads to a larger chamber.

'I know you're all lonely in there, lonely and sad! So I'm sending you some company! How do you like that, gnole? A visitor!'

Fungle's lips pressed bloodless hard. Concentrate, he willed himself. There is no outside. There is only here. There is only the task at hand.

But another voice spoke inside him with the panicked desperation of a hummingbird beating against the walls of a tiny room:

O Froog I'm struck it's dark please Froog come get me I'm hanging here and it goes down down down for miles Froog help me there's big-eyed monsters with poison fangs

'Master! O my Master!
– By my blood I invoke thee!
My heart, my blood, my eyes, my brain, my soul –
My Master's, all!'

Fungle groped for a loose stone along the inner wall. But this was gnole workmanship, and even after millennia the stones were as tight-fitting as the day they had been set.

Fungle hesitated.

'By the Ancient Names I invoke thee, Theverat!'

A gnole mound'll have an antechamber leading to the burial chamber, he reasoned. But it'll be blocked off from desecrators an' thieves.

But because it's a *gnole* mound . . .

'Astaroth, Asmodeus, Astarte . . .'

. . . there should be a way to admit gnoles.

'S'boleth,' said Fungle, using the classic gnole word meaning 'open'.

Nothing happened.

The daemonic recitation continued outside.

Who would they have wanted it to open for? he thought frantically. Not for just anyone who happened to know the gnole word for 'open', or anyone who could read a map. But for someone who understood the gnoles well enough to show respect for this resting place, someone who came as a friend . . .

'S'boleth'k,' said Fungle. The 'k following *S'boleth* indicated familiar case, like the French *tu*. The way one would address a friend.

-click-

The sound came from the centre stone. Fungle hurried to it, set a hand on it – and it slid inward smoothly.

Ancient air rushed into the antechamber.

Fungle rushed out.

The dead lay all around him.

Even before he said the spell that would provide him with a ring of mage-light, Fungle felt them there. Millennia dead, their sarcophagi had rotted away and their wrappings weathered to dust. But because they had been mages a residue of their power remained, and their bones were preserved. White-picked and improbably long, bonefingers laced over boat-hull ribs, they stared hollow-eyed at infinity. They lay in a pattern, stationed at cardinal points on the compass, with east foremost because that was the primary direction for Atlanteans.

Fungle commenced to setting the most powerful protective

ward he knew around the burial chamber. Though desperate
from the knowledge that Theverat was ripping into reality as
he was Summoned outside, Fungle was also rested and confident
after finally attaining his major objective, learning the location of
Baphomet, and he wove his spell with the resources of a lifetime
of training as a shaman, drawing on his deep inner wellspring of
self. But the fly in the ointment was that he *did* know the location
of Baphomet, and Theverat would try to shred him like a cabbage
to find it.

When the spell was complete he sat under pale-blue light in the
centre of the chamber and waited. The burial chamber was circular,
and the bodies placed at cardinal compass points, still holding a
residue of magic, made the chamber a natural conjurer's circle,
a protective haven for the mage. *If I'm not safe here, I'm not safe
anywhere.*

A body's just a body, a container for the spirit, and normally
Fungle would be no more frightened by the presence of corpses
than by a jelly jar. But these containers were long and lean and alien,
and though they had been buried here a thousand generations ago,
Fungle had seen them alive and ailing only the day before. He knew
it had been an illusion, a vision – but he had *been* there; the winter
had chilled his marrow and he had felt the fear and uncertainty of
the gnole labourers losing their masters to plague in a wild and
uncertain land.

Fungle shook his head. The dead were the least of his worries
right now. He shut his eyes and sent his awareness along the
shining silver cord that connected him to the fabric of reality.
And felt the cord trembling. And felt a patch of reality ripping.
And felt Theverat forcing his way in through the tiny rent created
by the thorny creature's Summoning. And felt a shudder in the
walls of the world as Theverat was born into the night.

Unconsciously Fungle's hand touched the wishing feather on his
cap. Lowering, his hand brushed the briar rose tucked into his tunic.
Resting, his hand joined the other hand palm-up a few inches below
his navel. Mind, heart and soul: an ancient affirmation.

Rage approached his protected space.

He willed himself calm.

Rage enveloped his protective space.

He felt himself grow centred.

Rage shook stones around him.

'*Knock knock,*' said a pleasant voice.

Fungle opened his eyes in surprise.

That voice! It was not at all the kind of voice one expected from evil, the guttural deep voice of an enraged father buried in a child's memory. Not the raw, twisted, soul-searing breath of hate one expected from the mouth of the face of corruption. This voice was mirthful! It was saturated with wit and irony, brimming with deep appreciation for the fullness of life, a timbre enriched by fine wines and the soot of expensive cigars. The kind of voice you traded old jokes with in front of a fire after a fine gourmet meal.

'*Knock knock knock!*' it repeated jovially.

'Nobody home!' said Fungle.

The voice laughed richly. 'That's more like it,' it said – and Fungle's protective barrier shredded around him like a paper doll in a rainstorm.

A small fire sprang up in front of Fungle.

'There we are!' said the voice, nearby now. 'Much more cheery than that gloomy mage-light of yours, don't you agree?'

A figure sat on the opposite side of the fire.

Fungle leaned forward to get a better view, but the figure shifted. 'Now now,' it chided, 'that's not polite. There is a certain decorum to be maintained, you know.'

'Theverat,' said Fungle.

A long pause while the fire wavered between them. *It doesn't crackle*, Fungle realised. *The fire isn't making any noise.*

'An old name,' said the figure. 'And inadequate, I think. But I suppose it will have to do.' The fire flared, then dimmed. 'Fungle. Foxwit. Gnole.' Theverat's tone was fond. 'You're a terribly difficult person to call on.'

'Thankee,' said Fungle. 'I been tryin'.'

'You have indeed.' The shadow shifted and hands clapped. 'And I love a good chase as much as anyone who still has a child living inside them.'

'I bet you got a couple of 'em in there,' said Fungle.

Theverat chuckled. 'Very good! You have quite a wit, Fungle. May I call you Fungle?'

Fungle said nothing.

'Well, I understand your reticence and I'm glad to see you've kept your sense of humour after your many trials and tribulations – just as I have kept mine after centuries of fruitless searching. But all that is behind us now, yes?' And that friendly chuckle again. 'Never mind; I can see you are still mistrustful. I would be, too, in your shoes. So tell me, Fungle: what can I do to win your trust?'

'Return to yer own world and leave this one be.'

'I can't do that,' Theverat said. 'Truthfully, now – if *you* were to ask *me* how you could win my trust, and I demanded that you never tamper in my realm but remain in your own for the rest of your days, how would you respond?' he asked reasonably. 'You are a mage and a shaman, Fungle. As I was in my fleshly existence. We have that in common; we are colleagues really.'

Fungle did not want to be lulled by Theverat's way of speaking. The warm tone, the congenial manner – a transparent ploy. But Theverat's remarks were nevertheless sensible, and Fungle could not help responding to them on a conversational level. 'There's many kinds of mage in the world,' said Fungle, 'an' I don't feel colleague to 'em all.'

'Well said!' acknowledged Theverat, laughing. The longer he spoke, the more Fungle constructed an image to accompany the voice. He knew that this was what Theverat wanted, but he could not prevent it; it was automatic. The shadowman across the silent fire from him suggested just about any conceivable humanoid shape, and the voice moulded the shadow into a more concrete form for him. Fungle felt himself being seduced by Theverat's voice even as he was aware of it luring him.

The fire dimmed further and Fungle found himself looking at a silver tea-service on the stone floor beside it. If it was conjure-work, it was flawless: the silver curved and smeared the fire's light, and a breath of steam rose from the narrow S of the teapot spout. Yet no spell-word had been uttered, no gesture made. The magician in Fungle admired such handiwork even as the mage understood that this admiration was exactly what Theverat was trying to extract.

'I imagine it has been some time since you had a good cup of tea,' said Theverat. 'And a good meal.' A plate of food appeared. 'In comfortable surroundings.' The silent fire began to crackle, and Fungle saw that it was now blazing in a hearth. *His* hearth, Fungle realised, in his home! They were back in Fungle's hidden home in the middle of the lake, and he and Theverat sat in the very same chairs used by Fungle and Ka after the Equinox feast. The chairs faced the fire, and Fungle was aware of Theverat's shadowform occupying the overstuffed easy chair, though it was difficult to see because the chairs were not turned toward one another. Fungle could smell the food on the plate now in his hand, smell the beeswax and lemon oils he used to keep his wooden floors glossy. Home, oh home!

His heart ached as he set the plate down beside his chair. 'D'ya think I'm bought so easy?' he asked.

'Bought?' said the friendly voice beside him. 'I don't want to buy you, Fungle; I want to *negotiate* with you. Negotiations are always much more pleasant in pleasant surroundings. But if it will make you more comfortable –'

The silent fire glowed between them on the cold stone floor. Fungle glanced around and saw recumbent skeletons.

'Or we could talk on the beach,' continued Theverat, 'or in the desert, or the forest. Whatever makes you comfortable. Personally, I like it here as it is. Sombre, basic, death lying at our periphery. It reflects our situation well, I think.'

'*Our* situation?'

'Certainly. We are both trapped in aspic until we resolve our differences.'

'Our differences are unresolvable,' said Fungle. 'A cat an' a mouse don't sit down to tea to resolve their differences.'

'Not so long as the cat continues to remind the mouse that the cat is a cat,' agreed Theverat, 'and the mouse merely a mouse.'

'An' ya think that by puttin' me at ease in me own hole o'er cheese that I'll fergit that?' Fungle asked.

The fire flared between them. Fungle thought he saw crystalline reflections in the shadow figure's eyes before it dimmed again.

Theverat's tone lost its friendly butter. 'You have something I want,' he said evenly. 'You have some . . . *glimmer* –' the fire turned white hot '– some *puny inkling*, of what I am capable of.' The fire cooled back to orange as Theverat fought to keep his tone calm. 'I have many resources at my disposal to take what I want from you, but I believe you are strong enough to resist them long

enough for them to kill you before I could find out what I want to
know. So I am trying to learn if there is some way I can obtain what
I desire and leave us both satisfied. Otherwise –' The fire flared to
the ceiling, and took on the twisted, tortured shape of a tormented
soul aflame.

Quickly it dimmed.

Fungle smiled ruefully at the telltale flame. 'Not easy fer ya ta
be civil, is it, Mr Theverat, sir? I'll wager this is the longest set-down
ya've had since Baphomet came yer way.'

At the word *Baphomet* the fire froze. It simply stopped moving,
as if painted there between them. Fungle felt sudden violence in the
air, felt the stretching of the thin membrane containing Theverat's
rage. He looked across the frozen fire and saw the shadow literally
struggling to contain itself like a monstrous embryo struggling not
to be born. *Why, there's no more feelin' there than in a bobcat after a
rabbit*, thought Fungle. *Don't be taken in by manners an' magics and
mild mouthin's.* He pictured writhing maggots beneath the shadow.
*Th' only thing keepin' him from crushin' you like a walnut is that you
got somethin' he wants.*

An idea glimmered.

The fire resumed its silent burning. 'But why be unnecessarily
unpleasant?' Theverat continued, honey warming his tone once
more. 'You must remember not to make this a *personal* issue,
Fungle. I have no personal interest in you at all. I am perfectly content to let you go on your way and live out your days unmolested
. . . once I obtain some information I believe you have?'

'That's it?' Fungle asked, preparatory to drawing Theverat out.
'I give ya the key that unlocks the world, an' in return I get to skip
merrily along me way, thankee very muchly, Mister Gnole?'

The shadow grinned. Sensing his foot in Fungle's door, Theverat
forgot himself and let the merest sliver of his true Self show
through, so that what Fungle saw when the shadow grinned were
the jagged mountainous fangs that had closed around him in his
nightmare. The lapse was startling and frightening, but a good
reminder that what sat before Fungle was a thin container for
Theverat's fury, and not the true face of the demon at all.

'Naturally you shall receive some adequate compensation,'
Theverat was saying. 'Fair value, after all.'

'What can you give me that I don't a'ready have?' Fungle
demanded.

The shadow threw back its head and laughed. The demon's
diplomat façade cracked enough to let a hideous grating howl slip

into its mirth. 'What do you already have? A patch of land, some scruffy trees, a collection of flea-ridden animals, a leaky hut on a piddling lake! Country spells to remove warts and dazzle infants! Cooking and cleaning and fruitless studies in terrible light while your eyes gradually wither away! A life of servitude and minuscule victories over insignificant foes, followed by decrepitude and death and anonymity! And you want to know what I can give you? Oh, my gnole friend, you have seen so little of the world to ask such a question!' He howled again.

'Tell me,' urged Fungle.

The shadow reared. 'Immortality.' And stood. 'Power.' And broadened. 'Luxury.' And darkened. 'Reverence.' Slit eyes blazed. 'Joy.'

'Joy?' Fungle was surprised.

'Don't be a fool,' Theverat snapped. His voice shook stone and rattled bone. 'When someone regards you with mortal terror, and you hold their life in your hands like an egg – oh, that is joy! If you spare it you are revered! If you crush it, that is power! You speak of living, of joy. You know nothing of either! You cannot suck the marrow from life until you have power over it!'

Fungle sat, rapt, as Theverat rhapsodised. He was thoroughly hooked, completely entranced by Theverat's impassioned soliloquy. Like many good folk who think of evil as a force of nature rather than a state of mind, Fungle had always envisioned evil as mechanistic, cold, autonomic. Unfeeling. Because how could something sensitive, something able to feel *joy*, be evil?

But watching Theverat enumerate before him the wonder and delight of repugnant acts no being of conscience could live with, Fungle realised he had been wrong. A snake was mechanistic, cold, unfeeling – yet it was absurd to call a snake *evil*; a snake was the most natural thing in the world. What Fungle came to realise as Theverat waxed enthusiastic into the night, conjuring visions of spiritual might and fleshly delight, was that evil is not a force of nature at all. A wolf feeds – but unthinkingly, unfeelingly. A hurricane destroys – but without passion.

Evil, thought Fungle, *is only a passion for the Self above all else.* In Theverat's case, above life, above death, above an entire planet.

But some of what Theverat said appealed to Fungle. Feeling where his own desires were tugged by Theverat's polemic, Fungle realised that in every single case his temptation lay with his deepest passions. Offers of material splendour did nothing to seduce Fungle: servants, riches, mansions, jewels, rarest delicacies,

priceless objects – these held no appeal for him.

But revelations from alchemickal books disappeared for ages from the world! Spellcraft tight as a drum, flawless and impenetrable as a diamond! True knowledge of the mechanics of the universe, of the hidden powers and forces behind its endless wheeling! The fundament made whole, and contained in the mind! Didn't these visions tug at his heartfelt desires just the least little bit? Wasn't a fine mind's insatiable thirst for knowledge tempted at its quenching? Didn't the shaman, struggling lifelong to learn the hidden workings implicit in the everyday, feel a yearning twinge? A multitude of voices within him cried *Yes! Oh, yes, read me the poetry that binds the atoms; yes, teach me the philosophy of gravity; yes, sing me the song that ignites the stars! I swear to use this treasure only for good; I will unravel the atom only to heal, unleash gravity only to teach, kindle the starflame only to illuminate truths! Give me the tools and I will build a machinery of joy.*

What were these temptations but passion?

'Look upon the world I plan,' said Theverat, 'and tell me of passion.'

Before Fungle's eyes rose a vision of what could only be called a 'garden city'. From a rolling land lush with life rose great steel-and-glass structures, technorganic habitats at one with their environment, cities of trees and cultivated forests on the moon.

'A new world,' said Theverat. Clean machines flitted through an azure sky above garden-terraced temples of learning rising above the verdant land like future versions of ancient ruins. 'A new world order.' It was impossible to tell where 'city' ended and 'country' began. 'A new Atlantis.'

Fungle's eyes sparked with reflected light. This was the perfect, delicate balance between the compunction of Nature to grow and the desire of the hand to build.

'And who will maintain this harmony?' said Theverat. 'Who will be the fulcrum balancing this world of wood and metal, circuit and sap?'

'Me . . .' fell from Fungle's lips.

'You can be the borderland,' said Theverat, 'the living conduit connecting, combining, and controlling art and artifact, chaotic nature and ordered science. For that is what you already are, Fungle Foxwit, gnole and shaman, reader of books and unraveller of nature. Who better to play this role?'

'Who better?' murmured Fungle.

'We will build the devices that tell us *why* we build devices,' pronounced Theverat, 'the rubber mallets that tap the knees of God.' A procession of synchronised clocks arrayed in infinite ranks marched before Fungle's eyes. 'We are made of the universe, and when we uncoil it we shall be its mirror. Through us the universe will know itself. And us? We shall know the universe.'

Fungle gazed upon the technomagical utopia that lit the chamber.

It would work. Fungle knew it intuitively: the microcosm world revealed before him would work. He *saw* it working, right there in front of him. And he could be part of it. He could *create* part of it! And attain boundless knowledge tempered with compassion and wisdom. A benevolent tyranny . . . Who could resist?

With a will he looked away from the vision. *Who* would *resist?* he thought. *Who would dare? Your knowledge is not my knowledge; your truth rings different from mine. Who shall decide which is which?*

Tyranny.

'You see that my desires are nothing but well-intended,' said Theverat.

Fungle glanced around the burial chamber. *The grave of every tyrant,* thought Fungle, *contains the bones of the well-intended.*

'I can't deny it,' he said.

'It cannot be denied.' The vision brightened, enlarged. 'How can *knowledge* be denied?'

And even though he felt himself pulled away from the lure of Theverat's vision by the faint whispers of his reason and his training, Fungle was forced to acknowledge a dark seed that lived within himself, a part of his core that had, for one unrepentable, unforgettable moment, embraced this vision. At first it terrified him, for he feared that this kernel once fed would sprout a malignant tendril that divided and blossomed and germinated, consuming Fungle and transforming him into the kind of beast he saw before him.

But he was not consumed.

Then it disgusted him, because he was ashamed that such a blackness, however small, could live within him.

But he could not deny that it did.

Then it angered him, because he felt he had to rid himself of such a repugnant thing; a distillation of Theverat that dwelt somewhere deep within his being, a terrible thing that was a part of who he was.

But he could not destroy a part of his core without affecting the rest. Without changing what made him *Fungle*.

Which left only acceptance. And, understanding this, Fungle felt all temptation, all seduction, all fear of the evil within himself, abate. Just as a pearl is not the speck of dirt that forms it, Fungle perceived that he was not this terrible black kernel; it was merely a speck of dirt within the pearl of his soul.

Fungle felt a surge of inner strength. He sensed the solid foundation of history and training and emotion on which he stood. Here in this place of death, with his own extinction literally staring him in the face, Fungle felt more centred than he ever had.

The chamber grew chill as Theverat spilled forth a cornucopia of craving and obsession. The illusory fire had long since been forgotten. With each affirmation or denial of temptation, Fungle learned something about himself. Theverat had indeed transformed him, but he couldn't have imagined how. Fungle had confronted the Abyss – and embraced it. Now *he* contained *it*, and not the other way around.

Finally Fungle sensed that Theverat was growing angry, the way a salesman will grow angry after he realises that someone has let him continue his pitch with no intention of buying. Theverat had become so immersed in his mission of corrupting Fungle that he had barely maintained his man-like shape. The pleasantly mild tone was long gone, and the Mound of the Dead shook with the demon's exhortations. Visions of technomagical triumph spilled across the tomb to the asynchronous accompaniment of ticking clockworks: mile-high crystal towers and floating ocean cities, reined spirits of wind and rain driving the engines of ships traversing water and air, huge metal seeds powered by alchemickal combustion flung out among the planets, the machineries of a hungry thriving world fuelled by spells that harnessed the slow detonation of the sun itself. Ordered nature, ordered lives. A new order.

Fungle held up a hand to the pulsing black shape before him. 'Enough!' he said. 'If ya've not swayed me by now, it'll never happen.'

Theverat's ember eyes narrowed uncertainly.

'I confess ya've made me feel ashamed,' said Fungle.

'Ashamed?'

He nodded. ''Cause my holdin' back the middlin' little secret I got stored up inside has been an obstacle to yer vision,' he said. 'An' I'm the one that's holdin' up the birth of a New Atlantis.'

'You'll tell me,' said Theverat. He grinned unpleasantly.

'Seems to be a more'n fair trade to me,' said Fungle. 'But I got to admit to some embarrassment,' Fungle added before Theverat could continue, 'that I know where Baphomet is, but I don't know where what I know is.'

Theverat glared in suspicion. 'What do you mean?' he demanded.

'Well,' said Fungle, 'it's like this: we gnoles're a storytellin' lot, as you may know from olden times, an' much of our learnin' is given down in stories an' poems an' suchlike.'

'Get on with it.' Theverat was growing more menacing by the second.

'I'm tryin' to,' Fungle placated. 'See, a lot of secret messages're buried in them old stories, waitin' fer the enterprisin' fella that comes along to dig 'em up. I know exactly which *group* o' stories contain the location of Baphomet, but I ain't sure which one. My pa passed 'em on to me on his knee,' said Fungle. 'They's called "Howzit Stories". I figure between you an' me, we can find anything buried in them tales.'

'Where are they?' Theverat asked eagerly.

'They's nowhere,' said Fungle. He tapped his head. ''Cept here. I got to tell 'em to you, an' then we'll figure out the codes.'

Theverat clenched his shadow fists, and for a moment his rage made them solid and heavy with scars and claws and scales. 'Get on with it,' he whispered.

So Fungle told Theverat the story of 'Howzit the Birds Got Their Beaks'.

Then he and Theverat rummaged through every word of it like surgeons performing an autopsy, searching for clues to Baphomet's location. Eventually they decided that there were none, so Fungle told the story of 'Howzit the Humans Lost Their Fur'. For hours Fungle relayed to Theverat stories learned at his father's knee, and he thought how much old Wisp would've loved to have seen the gnole stalling the demon this way – for stalling is exactly what he was doing.

As Fungle concluded the story of 'Howzit the Flies Got Their Eyes', he felt the first stirrings of the birds outside.

As Theverat angrily concluded that there was nothing of value to him in the tale, Fungle felt the greying of false dawn.

By the time Fungle began the story of 'Howzit the Bat Got His Wings', he felt the faint quickening of his pulse that told him the sun had swelled the horizon.

Theverat rose to a terrible massive height before him. 'Enough!' the demon thundered. 'There is nothing in these stories!' Scimitar claws scored rock. 'How stupid do you think I am?'

'It's in there somewhere,' Fungle protested. 'We just have to sift through them an' –'

Theverat clenched a clawed fist around a skull and crushed it to powder. 'I will tear your mind apart,' he screamed, 'and sift through that!'

There would be no more stalling. Either the sun was up enough, or it wasn't – there was nothing else Fungle could do about it now.

Except say a word.

'*S'boleth'k!*' he shouted.

The walls moved outward. The web of thorny vines enshrouding them was no match for the weight of the massive stones and the power of the ancient gnole spells: the vines parted beneath the section of the Mound of the Dead that slid outward.

Theverat howled. He discarded his shadow façade like a snake-skin and began to transform. Fungle glimpsed a muscular ropy glistening black leathery form crossed with scars and reaching out feathered lion's claws to crush him like an egg. Fungle ran and the blow missed.

The next blow would not.

Daylight streamed in.

The burial chamber lit with morning sun. Fungle glanced back and

saw the terrible claw swing toward him

saw it lit by sunlight

saw it wither

saw Theverat scream

saw the skeletons of the ancients crumble in their broken slumber as Theverat raged against the birthing of the light that pierced him like a pike ramming him through the fabric of the world and back into his own.

Fungle turned and ran.

Theverat ranted and writhed. His shadowform exploded into primal fury, transformed into the True shape that had driven the giblin Vixen out of her mind. Paling in the sun's light, screaming like a braking train, he reached out to grab Fungle and turn the gnole toward him, to make the puny creature *see* him –

Ghostly fingers brushed Fungle's head. Fungle glanced back – but Theverat was gone. Fungle fled the Mound of the Dead with his life, his soul, and his foundation intact.

Next time they met he would not be so fortunate.

12 *A Close Encounter*

It was late afternoon when Fungle found the raccoon.

He had travelled all day without stopping, moving quickly but quietly through the forest toward his goal. But as he travelled the forest began to change. Plastic wrappers, crushed cans, cigarette butts, spent shell-casings, and dozens of other types of objects bloomed across the land like a strange type of vegetation previously unknown to Fungle. Rude runes were crudely carved into the boles of mighty oaks. Dells lush with grass had been ploughed under to expose bare earth. Huge areas where tall trees had stood, patiently joining earth and sky for centuries, were now stark and dotted with knee-high stumps. A mile-wide stretch of forest was charred barren and lifeless. Fungle walked through the incomprehensibly injured land like the dazed survivor of a terrible crash. Here, it seemed, was the Waste Land foretold in the oldest gnole legends as the fate of the earth after the Final Days of Reckoning.

Fungle was heading up a mountain slope and passing through maples sporting crisp leaves when he heard struggling, and his first thought was of the thorny figure that had shadowed him from Tobacco Inn to the Land of a Thousand Smokes to the Mound of the Dead; the Presence he had left behind with Theverat. So when he heard the thrashing Fungle faded into shadow among the dense undergrowth, all his senses keyed up, spells readied.

The smell of blood was a taste of rust.

He heard a unique warble, a despairing coo like an alarmed pigeon. Only one creature in the world made such a panicked sound and Fungle rushed to find its owner, knowing that it was in pain and fear.

What he found was terrible.

A raccoon was caught in a trap. The trap was heavy iron and sharp saw teeth like the jaws of some prehistoric creature. It had clamped around the raccoon's leg and cut it half through. The poor creature was suffering terrible agony, warbling as it attempted to force the jaws back with its clever hands, bleating in pain as its hands proved too weak and the grinning trap bit deeper. The contraption was chained to a stake driven into the ground. The raccoon was too small to pull it out, and it had attempted to bite through the metal until its gums bled.

Fungle did not stop to wonder what all this was about. The moment he saw the raccoon caught and in pain, he hurried to the creature's side. When the raccoon saw him it went mad with fear, bristling and hissing and letting loose an awful stink to ward him off. 'Brother Raccoon,' Fungle said gently but urgently, 'Ize here to help you.'

The raccoon grew still. 'Gnole?' it said doubtfully.

'Fungle Foxwit gnole,' agreed Fungle. 'Let me free you from that awful coontrapshun.'

The raccoon calmed and held still while Fungle bent to it and pried at the metal jaws. It took all his strength, but by bracing his foot against it and pulling with both hands he was able to prise the metal jaws wide enough for the raccoon to drag its mangled leg free. 'Thanking you, me,' said the raccoon, and began to hobble off.

'Wait!' called Fungle. 'Let me treat your leg!'

But the raccoon continued to limp away. 'Hunters!' it called. 'Smell them, you?'

Sure enough, beneath the warding musk of the raccoon's fear and the blood of its injuries, Fungle smelled an unpleasant, spoiled-beef aroma.

The raccoon urged Fungle to run. 'Face-eaters!' it warned.

Fungle screwed up his face in incomprehension.

'*Humans*,' the raccoon elaborated. 'Kill me, them. Kill me, skin me, cook me. You too, they'll eat.'

Fungle could not believe what he was hearing. 'Eat you!'

'Coming them!' The raccoon turned away. 'Run you!'

'Wait –' But the raccoon was gone. Fungle bit his lip. *That wound were stark serious*, he berated himself, *an' I never shoulda let him get away untreated. It could fester an' cause all kinds of –*

'Well, lookie here!' came a nasal voice from the direction the raccoon had gone. 'We got us a *ee*scapee.'

Frightened warbling.

Fungle hurried anxiously toward the sound, hugging shadows and moving silently.

''At leg hurts, now, donit? Well, hey, we'll put a lid own that *raht*
quick. Won't even need to waste me a shell, neither.'

Fungle parted the bushes to see a human being standing over
the injured raccoon and holding a shotgun. The man raised the
gun high, intending to brain the poor raccoon at his feet. His muscles
tensed to deliver the blow – but he stopped. *Somethin' ain't right here.*
His eyes narrowed. Slowly his head turned to regard the rifle held
high –

– and the butt squirmed in his hands as the barrel turned a
diamond-shaped head to face him with slit eyes, opened its fanged
mouth to spit out a forked tongue, and hissed.

'Gaaaah!' shouted the man. He threw the rattlesnake away from
him and ran, flapping his hands as if fighting off invisible bees.

Still sending snaky mindywarp pictures to the fleeing man,
Fungle stepped out from behind the tree.

'Gnole, oh, gnole!' said the raccoon. 'Thanking you, me! Saving
me you are! Owing you, me!'

Fungle smiled gently, though his insides were all a turmoil. 'Ya can pay me back by lettin' me treat that leg a yours,' he said, 'so's next time ya can run away.'

He knelt and removed his pack to remedy the mutilated leg.

Fungle descended into the Valley of the Moon by late afternoon. His mind remained a tumult of anger and fear at the implications of that iron trap. From the workmanship and evil simplicity of design, the abominable thing had the look of an item produced in large quantities, and it was built for one purpose: to bite and mangle the leg of an animal unfortunate enough to step upon it. *Any* animal; the device was indiscriminate.

How could such a thing be?

Printed metal signs had been nailed into the trees. So preoccupied was Fungle that he passed the signs and had to back up in order to read them: FREEWAY CONSTRUCTION! DANGER! BLASTING! DO NOT PROCEED BEYOND THIS POINT! RADIO-OPERATED EXPLOSIVES! TURN OFF RADIOS, CBs, WALKIE-TALKIES, ETC. DANGER!

Fungle didn't know what they meant, but he knew he didn't want them nailed to his trees. He pulled them out and propped them against the trunks. Why hadn't whoever nailed the signs into the trees thought of that? The signs were large and colourful; anyone passing would still be able to read them. What kind of person thought like this?

He blessed the trees and went on, cutting north-west across the valley.

The sun was low when he emerged into a clearing and saw Dragonback Ridge for the first time. Its jagged spines were curiously free of trees or vegetation. Chalky discolorations on the face of some of the mountains looked as if the naked rock had been gouged away by a god-wielded chisel.

One of them mountains, he thought, holds Baphomet. Baphomet, and the lost Library of the gnoles. The thought dizzied him. There's me goal, right there in front a me. Black stone cross on the eastern face, look fer a hole like a rabbit den, puzzle out the guardian spells, get in there, get Baphomet, an' summon Molom to destroy the stone. Not easy, certainly, but the end was in sight, rising like jagged teeth ahead of him, and actually seeing a mountain that he knew contained his goal made accomplishing his quest seem less fanciful, more real. *Find the stone and go on home,* sang in his mind. *Find the stone and go on home!*

If he'd not been distracted by having his destination in sight,
Fungle would have noticed that something was wrong. Something
didn't feel right in the forest. There was a silence, a tension, an
apprehension. Birds, toads, and crickets had stopped their music.
Deer stood stone-still in nervous expectation.

Fungle sensed these things on a subliminal level. But ahead of
him rose the mountain, *his* mountain, real and attainable! Why, in
three days' time he could be sitting in front of his fire with a glass
of honey wine in hand, telling his adventures to Neema and Ka!

This was his thought as the earth exploded around him.

Fungle was knocked sprawling. A pack strap broke and Fungle
came up ready to confront an assailant – but all there was to
be seen was a feathery plume of smoke. Rocks pattered down
around him.

Something's crashed! he thought.

Around him the forest erupted: quail exploded from trees; wild
dogs ran baying; a doe and a buck darted blindly; foxes ran a
terrified red streak.

The earth exploded again.

This time Fungle saw it. This blast was closer than the first, and
the earth shuddered with its detonation. Gouts of powdered rock
streamed in all directions, gilded by the lowering sun. The very air
seemed to tremble. Fungle sensed the invisible wave that bowed
the bushes and bent the branches just before it knocked him flat
on his back.

He sat up. Granite flakes pelted him. Squirrels were knocked
from trees. A raccoon chittered as it loped, fur up.

That blast had been close. If a third explosion came any
closer . . .

Battered and bruised, Fungle got up and ran.

A third blast rocked the world.

Fungle threw himself flat. The ground bucked beneath him.
Dirt and pebbled granite showered him. He popped up and ran
again, hard and blind as a wall-eyed horse. He pumped across the
clearing, dimly aware of the Dragonback Mountains fissuring the
horizon behind a falling shroud of dirt. One thought only occupied
his mind: *It's in sight, it's in sight! Find the stone and you'll go home!*
Find the stone –

The earth gave way beneath him and he fell.

His hand shot out and seized a clump of grass. It held, and
Fungle dangled at the edge of the pit that had opened beneath
him. He raised his other hand to pull himself out – and heard a

tearing sound. The grass was pulling from the soil.

He scrambled for a better grip just as the clump of grass ripped free. Fungle fell backward into darkness. Before he hit he remembered his recent nightmare of falling and being swallowed up, remembered stumbling into the gopher hole long ago and the brief eternity hanging in darkness before Froog found him. Then his head struck rock, and he remembered no more.

'I'm a-tellin' ya, Delbert, mah raffle up an' turnt into a snake shore as I'm lookin' atcha.'

Delbert spat a brown stream and hit the rock he was aiming for. 'Drunk some bad mash, more'n likely,' he said, rubbing his bristled chin with the back of a hand.

'An' that 'coon done got outta that trap,' Buford continued. 'Now how you think a 'coon got hisself loose from a wolf trap?'

'Easy,' replied Buford's brother-in-law Delbert, 'iffin it weren't never in it in the first place.' And chortled phlegmily at the notion.

'Delbert McCardle, you are a pure-dee fool! I could show ya the blood all over the trap!'

Delbert stopped walking and shouldered his shotgun. 'You show me a bloody wolf trap an' I'm s'posed to believe some mojo turnt your scattergun into a rattler?' He spat again. 'C'mon, we got work to do.'

They passed the signs that warned of dynamite blasting. Someone had pulled them out of the trees and leaned them against the trunks.

'Now that's a mite peculiar,' said Buford.

'Mebbe they're movin' 'em on to where they's blastin' next,' said Delbert. He spat again. Buford was always looking for some highfalutin' explanation for the simplest things. If you fell and sprained your wrist, it was because you hadn't thrown salt over your shoulder after a black cat crossed your path. If kinfolk died it was because you rocked an empty rocking chair, which invited ghosts. Life was a lot simpler to Delbert: you hunted, you brewed mash, you stayed up in the hills and away from roads and cars and people, and you used a shotgun loaded with nickels to discourage people from calling on you.

The recent dynamiting was a curse because dynamiting meant more roads, which meant more cars, which meant more people. The McCardles used to live at the base of these mountains, huntin' and moonshinin', with nary a soul around for twenty miles, and that was the way they liked it. They used their game for food, for tallow and soap and linings, and they drank their moonshine. Time was when a man could go a year without seeing a single human being he weren't related to.

But times change. Roadwork, construction, landfills – the McCardles had worked ever higher into the rough mountains, and if it got any more crowded round these parts, or if another winter went by as cold as last year's, they'd have to think about moving on.

Meantime, there was one good thing come of all the dynamiting: it flushed out game for miles around. Delbert and Buford had taken to venturing down the mountain on days they knew there was gonna be blasting, game bags tucked in their pants, shotguns slung at their shoulders, Buford chewin' hardtack and Delbert workin' on a wad of chaw like a greedy squirrel.

It was midmorning and blasting hadn't started yet. Delbert and Buford found a natural blind and waited.

'So what we lookin' fer today?' asked Buford. 'Squirrel, rabbit, 'possum?'

Delbert spat. Buford always wanted to talk. 'Sick a 'possum,' he said.

'Not the way LuEllen makes it, you wouldn't be. Fries it in hog fat, an' makes up a biscuit gravy I like to die for. Whatcha see?'

Delbert was squinting out past the blind. 'There's a hole in the ground out there where I don't remember one.'

'A hole?' Buford leaned his shotgun against the flat rock they were sitting on and joined his brother-in-law. 'Out yonder?' He frowned. 'That's where the ole springhouse use to sit, right there.'

'Mebbe the dynamitin' opened it up,' Delbert mused.

'Mebbe sumpin' fell in,' said Buford.

They exchanged a greedy glance.

Next thing you knew they had picked up their shotguns and were bending over the hole, peering to get a good look. Delbert and Buford both remembered the old springhouse from when they was boys. Buford's daddy done tole them to keep away 'cause it was fulla ha'ants, which only sent the boys scrambling there to see what they could see. But even when there'd been a rotting shack still covering the springhouse, anything worth taking had long been took.

'Think I see somethin',' said Buford. 'A bundle, looks like.'

Delbert squinted down. 'Mebbe this hole gone and done our huntin' for us,' he said.

'Well, let's have a look, then!'

'Could be anything fell down there,' Delbert said. ''Coon, deer, b'ar. Could be a man, even.'

Buford shook his head. 'Hain't no man. Hit's got fur.'

'All right then, Buford,' said Delbert, smiling meanly. 'You gone have a look. I'll wait rat here.'

Buford sputtered – but it *had* been his idea, after all.

Delbert accepted Buford's shotgun and watched his brother-in-law climb on down into the old springhouse. He kept the gun ready in case Buford needed it.

'I'm close up on it,' came Buford's voice. 'Hain't no man, that's fer damn sure. Hold on a second, hold on . . . Delbert! Hit's a b'ar! Hit's a b'ar cub! No – no wait . . .'

There was a long pause, and Delbert tried to hear and strained to imagine what might be a-happenin' down there.

Buford's face appeared in the hole. He was all aquiver. 'Delbert! Hit ain't no b'ar, an' it ain't no man, neither. It's somewheres inbetween.'

Delbert grew irritated. 'Now what's 'at s'posed to mean?'

'I'm tellin' ya! I never saw nothing like it.'

'It alive?'

'Yeah. Think so, anyway. Hit's bad off, though.'

They talked about what it might be. Buford was all for hauling it up and selling it to that freak show comes 'round outside Sooterville twice a year. Delbert wasn't sure it was such a great idea to be attracting all kindsa attention and questions and such. Still, it might be valuable somehow. You could always get a good price for a freakish hide or a skull; he remembered old Vic fetching a case of mash for that six-legged deer skin a while back.

Delbert and Buford agreed to haul it out and have a good look at it.

An hour later they knew they'd never seen nothing like it – that *nobody* never saw nothing like it. Buford had been right: it weren't no bear, and it weren't no man, but it was somewheres inbetween. And it was wearing *clothes*.

Maybe it'd excaped from a circus, and there was a *re*ward. Maybe all kindsa maybes. Whatever it was, the only thing for Buford and Delbert to do was build a makeshift travois sled out of their game bags and two sturdy branches, and haul this thing back home.

So Fungle entered the world of man.

Part Two

It's the truth,
Even if it didn't happen.

Revd Charles Dodgson

13 *The Land of No*

Sheriff Warren Horatius Sturgill ('Ray' to his friends, and if you called him anything else – except maybe 'Sheriff Sturgill' – you damnsure weren't no friend) parked his mud-spattered modified Dodge outside the McCardles' broken-down gate. He waited while the dust cloud that had followed him all the way up this godforsaken excuse for a road caught up to him. When the dust settled, Sheriff Sturgill looked out on a house that begged for a more precise definition of the word. The roof was corrugated tin patched with asphalt shingle, set atop a lanky stilt shack that was nothing more than a nailed-up patchwork of plywood, drywall, siding, and who knew what-all. The thing was held together by gravity and the grace of God. The windows were covered with tinfoil, except where patches had peeled away, and the sagging front porch with its missing planks smiled at him like a moron with missing teeth.

The yard – well, it complemented this fine example of Appalachian architecture to a T: littering the hillside were rusty springbeds and rotten mattresses, tyreless car bodies rusting on blocks, tin cans, just plain garbage, bottles, and a convention of flies.

Sheriff Sturgill sighed heavily. He wasn't too particular toward the McCardles, and he didn't especially like damnfool errands, and driving out to the McCardles' on a damnfool errand was not making him fired up about the rest of his day. Sturgill knew that, like nearly everybody hereabouts, Delbert McCardle kept a still, and Delbert *knew* he knew it. The understanding was that the sheriff would look the other way from home-brewing so long as it stayed home and didn't end up sold nowheres else. Like down in Brasstown, f'rinstance, where Sturgill had been elected sheriff.

But up here, away from all that, a fella had to turn a blind eye to certain goings-on if he didn't want to get woke up by buckshot a-knockin' on his front door.

Sturgill checked his thirty-ought six to be sure it was locked in its cradle, radioed in to Thelma that he'd arrived at the McCardle place, and got out of the car, which rose a good three inches as he relieved it of his weight. He slung his baton (which he'd carved with the name Friendly Reminder some years back) and gripped the butt of his nickel-plated .38 special, more out of habit than from any need of reassurance. He squinted at the house. Hard to tell if anyone was home. He poked the horn a couple of times and waited a decent interval. Nothin'. No one here but us chickens. Well, shoot.

He pushed his aviator sunglasses up his nose, patted his hat firm on his sweaty head, and headed toward the house.

This whole thing come about because Buford Chalmers – that no-account scheming poacher and Welfare cowboy – had got hisself all liquored up outside a Esco Hicks' dry-goods store where the same can of American Beauty Pork & Beans had been on sale since 1968. Esco Hicks' place was about the closest thing to a social centre in these parts, and gentlemen of like-minded economic and alcoholic persuasion such as Buford Chalmers tended to gravitate there, like flies on a road apple, to trade lies and chew the fat and generally complain about how they weren't appreciated and how the country was going to hell in a handbasket without brakes or a paddle.

Sheriff Sturgill opened the McCardles' gate and shooed away chickens too dumb to move. Sounded like music coming from inside. 'Anybody home?' he called. There was no answer. He continued toward the front porch.

So here's Buford Chalmers hoisting a couple of sheets to the wind at Esco Hicks' dry-goods, and the rest of the no-accounts are sitting on feed sacks, passing the jug and laughing at his boasts, when Buford gets all bent out of shape. 'Allrat,' says Buford, growing all sly like the weasel he is, 'you gone and laugh all you wonna. But I'm gown be a rich man come a month's time. I be a damn *meely*onair.'

This generated a pretty good haw-haw, which only got Buford more cross-eyed. He took another slug at the jug and hollered them down. Shouted loud enough to send Esco Hicks himself to the front to hear what the altercation was. Turned out Buford Chalmers was claiming he'd captured Bigfoot. 'Only it ain't a full-grown Bigfoot,' he insisted. 'More like a baby or sumpin'.'

'Little Foot,' chortled one of the boys.

Buford was getting a mean edge on. They could just go and see for themselves, he hollered. He had the thing chained up over at Delbert McCardle's place, he claimed, and they could all just up and go see it rat now, rat this second . . . for a dollar a look.

The boys'd laughed some more, and Buford hadn't taken it none too well. He'd stalked off, muttering about how next month he'd be driving by in a white Cadillac and he wouldn't spit on them if they was on far. And that woulda been the end of the story, 'cept Esco Hicks had thought the incident was peculiar enough to mention it to Ray Sturgill next time the Sheriff dropped by for his daily pickled pig's foot. Esco shooed flies from the jar and used dirty tongs to fish a pig's foot from the pink vinegar water, and he told Sheriff Sturgill the story while he wrapped the bloated fleshy snack in wax paper. So now here was Sheriff Sturgill, rapping on Delbert McCardle's front door and wondering what on earth he was about to get himself into.

That Tammy Wynette could tell LuEllen McCardle to stand by her man all she wanted to, but while her man was away she was gonna play, and that meant playing the radio.

At the stove, LuEllen left the centre cut of rabbit for when Delbert came home and threw the rest onto a hot iron skillet fussing with hog lard. The pan hissed and spat.

There wasn't but the one station to get up here in these mountains, but at least the Lord'd seen to it that it was the only one worth listening to: WCMS, yore *Country Mewzik Stay*shun! They played *real* music, real *country* music – Hank and Willie and Waylon and Loretta and Ferlin and Patsy and all, and not that rock and roll crud passed for country nowadays – Kenny Rogers and Highway 101 and all that what said it was country music but wasn't.

LuEllen flipped the chestnut pancakes on the other burner and finished the song a half tone below Tammy Wynette.

Delbert never listened to the radio, and wouldn't let her turn it on while he was around, neither. Claimed it interfered with his thinking. Hah! LuEllen wondered what his excuse was the rest of the time. So whenever he was gone she turned it on, tuned it in, and turned it *up*, honey! Sometimes she danced alone in the one-room house, remembering the time in Asheville when that good-looking business feller in the roadhouse had asked her Would she lak to daince? – and how good it'd made her feel, until Delbert went and smashed his face all up. Sometimes LuEllen just sang along with the radio, holding a hairbrush like it was a microphone and pretending she was wearing a sequinned outfit at the Grand Ole Opry in front of thousands. LuEllen coulda been a singer maybe, she knew. People always tole her she had a good voice, and they used to ask her Would you sing for us, sugah? at that little whitewashed Baptist church on Alvarado when she was a little girl. Course, she'd had all her teeth then and was willowy enough not to be embarrassed to appear in front of folks.

Tammy stopped singing and a group called Alabama started. LuEllen supposed they was good, but she couldn't sing along with them so she didn't care about them one way or the other.

She prodded the pieces of rabbit in the skillet, flipped the chestnut pancakes one more time, and slid them onto a plastic plate that had faded yellow and green flowers printed on it. 'Comin' up!' she called over her shoulder. A minute later she was slapping the greasy rabbit chunks next to the pancakes and sliding the plate in front of the Bo-whampus.

She hurried back to the stove, turned off the burners, and poured the drippings into an old coffee can filled with grease from just about every edible animal around these mountains. Then she hurried back to the Bo-whampus.

The critter was staring down at the food on the plate.

'Whatsa matter?' LuEllen asked as if talking to a finicky cat. 'You don't lak that, boy? Huh?' She jiggled the plate in front of its nose and inhaled deeply. 'Mmm-mm!' she said brightly.

The critter looked up at her. LuEllen thought its face looked sad. 'Whatsa matter, boy, huh?' she asked. 'Your hey-ud still hurtin' you?' She gently touched the bandage on the creature's head. It'd had a nasty knock, that was for sure. Out cold for two whole days, and LuEllen'd thought it was gonna die for certain. But it had woke up and turned out to be gentle as a kitten. Smart, too. It knew 'food' and 'sleep' and 'Bo-whampus' and 'no'.

Delbert called it a Martian, though LuEllen knew it weren't no space critter because it didn't have big pop eyes and skin like leather and fingers that glowed and all. And it was wearing forest-type clothes, not a shiny space-suit. But Delbert could think whatever he pleased; LuEllen was content to bathe the critter, and feed it, and tend its wounds. It was kinda cute, in a ugly sort of way. 'Juss don't you go gettin' too attached to it,' Delbert warned. ''Cause soon as that thing's up an' around, we're gonna get ourselves in the paper with it. Sell it to Doc Moon's travellin' freak show. Maybe even sell it to a mew-*zee*um or a zoo. Maybe even to tee *vee*.'

LuEllen waved the plate in front of the Bo-whampus and pictured herself on *The Tonight Show*, flirting with Johnny in her best dress. Or no – she'd get herself a *new* dress, a satin dress, and every woman on this mountain could just drop dead with envy for all she cared. Not that any of them had a TV anyways. Heck, LuEllen didn't have a TV! But you didn't have to have a TV to want to be on *The Tonight Show*. You just had to be an American.

The critter was turning its head away from the plate. 'Turn your nose up at my cookin'!' LuEllen huffed goodnaturedly. Truthfully, she was worried. The Bo-whampus was thin and weak, sickly from exposure because it'd been layin' out in the old springhouse for who knows how long, and also because the animal was just plain . . . well, *weird*. It didn't move or act like no wild animal ought to. Mostly it just sat quiet in the corner like a youngun with a case of the pouts. Delbert could talk about Martians all he wanted, but LuEllen knew a circus animal when she saw one. It was probably from China or some furrin place like that, like them pander bears they got in Washington.

She was racking her brains trying to find something it would eat: eggs, grits, table scraps, hogfeed, rabbit, 'possum stew, coffee – you name it, the critter turned it down. About the only thing that had got its attention was the first time she'd turned on the radio. It had perked up, eyes bright, nose quivering, brow furrowed, looking for all the world like it was trying to recall the name of the melody. 'That's Waylon,' she'd told the Bo-whampus, 'tellin' mommas not to let their babies grow up to be cowboys.' She'd smiled. 'But I 'spect you're pretty safe from that.' LuEllen'd taken to jawing at the critter all day long, 'cause Delbert was always off somewheres, looking for trouble or cooking up some scheme, and LuEllen tended to get lonesome.

The little critter quaked in fear whenever Delbert came home. Delbert teased it something awful. 'Whut?' he'd ask in mock surprise, shaking his shotgun at the trembling creature. 'Is it theeyis? You scairt a *theeyis*?' And he'd point it, or draw it back like a club. One time he even aimed it at the quaking critter and pulled both triggers. LuEllen remembered how the poor thing had shrieked at the double clack of the hammers, pulling on its short chain with nowhere to run. Delbert had laughed and staggered outside.

All of which accounted for why LuEllen McCardle had two completely opposite reactions when she saw Sheriff Sturgill's face peeking through a hole in the foil-covered windows. The first was

regret, because right away she knew she'd never get to buy that new
satin dress and go on *The Tonight Show*. But her second reaction
was relief, because the poor creature would never again have to
stare down a shotgun barrel and hear the awful sound of those two
hammers hitting firing pins, without an earthly clue that the gun
wasn't loaded.

'Oh, and Sheriff, this here's a bag with his clothes and things. I
warshed 'em an' mended 'em an' all. He had a little knapsack
with some cattails and mushrooms and things in it, along with
. . . with a Polaroid camera. It's all in there, everything he had
with him. We didn't take nothin', honest.
   'Well, Bo-whampus, it looks like this is so long. You gone with
the sheriff, now, an' he'll take good care a you. Don't fergit your hat,
now, and your rose. That's sure a pretty rose! You take care now!
   'Sheriff? Do you think . . .? I mean, I got so used to the little
fella bein' here, an' all. I wonder could you let me know what ends
up happenin' to him?
   'Thank you. That's very kind of you.
   'Beg pardon? Oh, I call him "Bo-whampus" after a story my
grendaddy tolt me when I was a little girl. "The Bo-whampus
gonna git you if you don't watch out!"
   'Oh, look, Bo-whampus, you get to ride in the *po*lice car! Maybe
the sheriff'll turn on the siren!
   'Hey, he's wavin' bye-bye! That looks like a wave, don't it? Maybe
he's blessin' me, like the Pope! Bye-bye, Bo-whampus! Bye-bye!'

LuEllen McCardle had told a little fib about not taking nothing from
the Bo-whampus. She'd given up the Polaroid, but not the pictures
it'd took. She kept them for herself. And even after the news cameras
and the hot lights and the microphones in her face, after the endless
questions and pilgrimages up to her nailed-together box of a home,
after Delbert's endless and fruitless schemes to profit off of the
Bo-whampus, she never said a word about them to anyone.
   Those grainy, smeared photographs – one showed, in an extreme
close-up that filled the right half of the image, half a blurry face of
a creature never seen in no zoo nor mentioned in the Bible, while
on the left half could plainly be seen two more creatures, one tall
and emaciated, the other short and squat; the second photograph a
streaked shot showing the same two creatures from a low angle, but
joined by two other creatures: a phosphorescent green thing, and.
the Bo-whampus – those impossible, priceless Polaroid shots were

among the few items LuEllen McCardle even bothered to rescue a few months after Sheriff Sturgill confiscated the Bo-whampus, when the burning of an entire mountain to the north forced the McCardles to evacuate their patchwork home. It wasn't until much later that she sold the rights to reproduce them to a fella from *Life* magazine, but she kept the originals. The money she received let her get away from Delbert and go to Nashville, where she tried but never really succeeded at being a country music singer.

 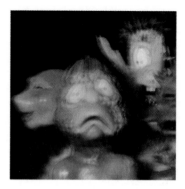

The photographs remained close by her from then on, and she counted them among her most treasured possessions – about the only things that had ever been truly *hers* and no one else's – and many years later an orderly at the Whileaway Nursing Home found them clutched atop her stilled breast.

Sheriff Sturgill frowned at his rear-view mirror. His prisoner ('prisoner' – *that* was a goodun!) stared resignedly out the window at the scenery sliding by. When the sheriff'd first seen it, shading his eyes from reflections and peering in through a hole in the foil of the McCardles' living-room window, he'd thought it was a kid wearing some kinda hippie clothes.

Then he'd seen the hairy arms and thought it was a midget. Then he'd seen it move and thought it was some kinda bear. Then he'd seen its face, and he knew he'd never seen nothing like it in his entire life – not in the army, not in Berlin, not around these mountains, not even one wild weekend in New York City when he was a youngster. This thing was something completely different. It was some kinda discovery, like the Lot Less Monster, or the Abdominal Snowman, or, or –

Bigfoot.

Remembering the story Esco Hicks had told him this morning, Sturgill grinned at the creature in the rear-view mirror. 'Hey, Little Foot,' he said. He slapped his thigh and guffawed. 'Little Foot!' he said again. It just got funnier every time he said it. He got on the horn to Thelma and told her he was coming into town, and that he'd done captured Bigfoot's little brother.

He wasn't feeling so smug when he turned onto Main Street and saw Ernie Scruggs' Land Rover parked in front of the station house, and Ernie hisself smoking a Kool on the front steps. Ernie was the only news stringer between here and Asheville (hell, he was one of the few people 'tween here and Asheville could read an' write), and his radio was always tuned to the *po*lice band.

Sturgill called hisself all kinds of idjit for being so quick to mouth off to Thelma about his Great Big Little Foot Conquest. He pulled into the station and glanced back at his prisoner. 'You just keep a low profile, y'hear?'

The critter (what was it LuEllen McCardle had called it?) didn't so much as look at him, just kept staring out the window like a kid who didn't want to go away to camp.

Sturgill was barely out of the patrol car before Scruggs was on him like a cheap suit, Sony tape recorder whirling away, Nikon camera dangling from a wide strap.

DPR Transcript #LF-83477a (general): EYES ONLY:

Q: Is it true you've captured some kinda Big Foot-type animal, Sheriff?

A: I got no comment.

Q: Is that the animal in back of the car, Sheriff?

A: No com – Ernie, you keep away from that vehicle.

Q: Jumpin' Jesus! I never saw a thing like it! Where'd you capture it, Sheriff? Are there any more of 'em?

A: No comment! Dammit, Scruggs, no pitchers, neither! I said – gimme that camera!

[Sounds of struggle]

Q: Now, Ray, you know I got a right to report the news — and, friend, that . . . <u>animal</u> in back a yore car is news! Now, whyn't you calm down some, and let me take a coupla good shots, and get out a your way so's you can go on and perform your duty. Then I'll buy you a Hot Meat Loaf Special down to Beerstecher's, and you can tell me the whole story —

A: Ain't gonna be no story. Now, I'm takin' my prisoner into the station house before Thelma gets on the phone to the Air National Guard and the <u>National Enquirer</u> and her Great Aunt Sadie and ever'one else in Creation, and you ain't gonna print nothin' 'cause there ain't nothin' to print.

Q: Now listen a minute, Ray — er, Sheriff. You ain't thought this through. When word a this critter gets out, this place is gonna be busier than a one-armed jello juggler. Now. Before all this wild and unfounded speculation can get to flyin' about, I can guarantee that the story — the <u>real</u> story, the <u>whole</u> story — gets told . . . and that credit goes where credit's due.

A: [. . .]

Q: C'mon, Sheriff, whaddaya say? Get you on the cover of the <u>Tennessee Constitution.</u> And once that breaks, who knows? Thing'll prob'ly go national. Sky's the limit. <u>Time. Newsweek.</u>

A: <u>Law Enforcement Gazette</u> . . .

Q: Shore! Why not!

A: Well . . . A coupla pitchers — and ya keep out the damn way.

Q: Y'all won't even know I'm here, Sher —

A: An' not a word to anyone, not a sound, not a peek or a pitcher, 'til I say so. Unnerstand?

Q: Fair enough. Just don't wait too long, or you'll be watching the whole story on <u>Nightline</u> like ever'body else.

Deputy Dwyer opined that the critter might have some legal status or citizenship or somesuch notions that qualified it as a person – especially if it turned out to have some smarts. Dwyer'd been taking a law course by mail for a year and a half, and he tossed around two-dollar phrases like 'diplomatic immunity' and 'minister plenipotentiary' and a bunch of other double Dutch

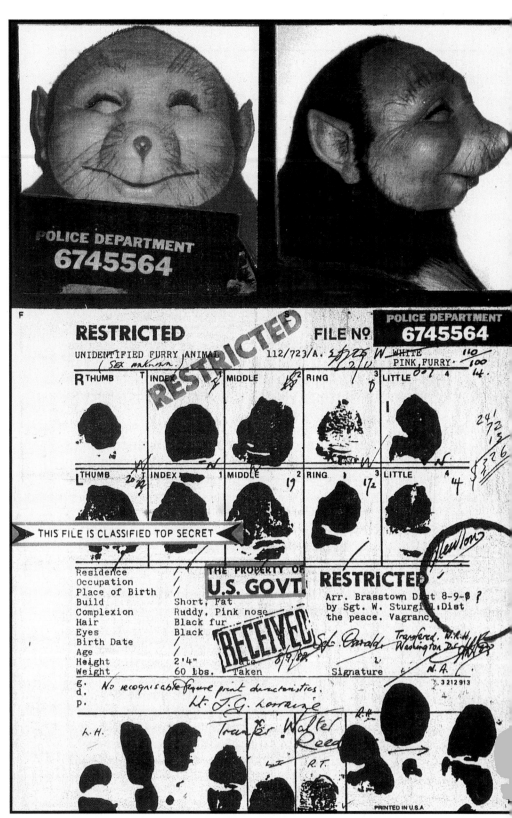

Book sheet and mugshots – Brasstown Sheriff's Department.

nobody understood, including Deputy Dwyer. It was all bull dooky, a course, but it was enough to make Sheriff Sturgill nervous about holding Little Foot without probable cause. All he needed was the ACLU crawling all over him because he hadn't known some Latin word that was deader'n dog squat. Lawmen get nervous when a situation isn't covered by the Book.

So Sturgill read his prisoner its rights according to the Miranda Decision, stored its personal possessions and wrote an itemised receipt for them, booked it on a vagrancy charge, and put it in an empty cell.

Ernie Scruggs' exclusive on the Little Foot story lasted less than an hour.

Because it was possible that the creature already belonged to somebody – a circus, a science lab, or even Walt Disney, for all he knew – Sheriff Sturgill sent the creature's mug shots and stats out over the wire. It'd get picked up locally and fed to precinct computers and matched up to missing-person descriptions (along with Wants and Warrants, which tickled Deputy Dwyer no end), and if its number came up, then bingo: another case solved, a furry critter out of Sheriff Sturgill's hair, and a feather in the cap of local law enforcement in the computer age.

Responses came back within minutes.

Big Joe Saunders rang up from the Hickton P-D: *Little late in the year for April Fools, ain't it?* Lawton McCoy called from Asheville: *You been drinkin' your DEA evidence, Ray?* Emmett Hortle phoned from Cooperville: *I got an officer who shot himself in the foot during a two-eleven at a Stop 'N' Go; a dispatcher with a stutter; a brand-new, two-hundred-thousand-dollar mobile crime unit with a thrown rod; and a K-9 out with mange. Is this supposed to be funny, Sheriff?* Sheriff Sturgill sighed and repeated the story he'd told Ernie Scruggs, who sat within sight of the cell writing down descriptions and notes for the Little Foot book he was gonna publish so he could sell it for a Movie of the Week. The Anderson County Sheriff's Department didn't even bother calling about the unusual Perfect Match and Weighted Match searches; instead they replied by faxing back a cartoon drawn by a police artist.

Little Foot's mug shots and description were out over the wire across the country. Those same information sources – not only at county and state levels of law enforcement, but also at the Bureau of Criminal Identification, Federal Bureau of Investigation, Justice Department, DEA, NSA, CIA, OSA, and a dozen other state and federal criminal investigation organisations – were monitored by the media. At the same time law-enforcement agencies were scratching their heads over Wants and Warrants requests for an unidentified three-foot-tall furry mole-like creature, the pictures were also picked up by Associated Press, United Press International, Gannett, Reuters News Services, and all the major television networks, including cable.

Phone calls were made.

By the time Sheriff Sturgill and Ernie Scruggs were sitting at a booth in Beerstecher's Bar and Grill to order the Hot Meat Loaf Special, the chain newspapers had called local Tennessee and North Carolina papers to send a reporter and a photographer to Brasstown to verify a potentially colourful dog-bites-man story. Network news executives called local affiliates to get a newsvan up to Brasstown. There were no local newspaper or television affiliates closer to Brasstown than Asheville – fifty miles away.

By the time Sturgill's meat loaf arrived, dish-antenna vans were driving down Interstate-40 to Asheville. By the time Ernie Scruggs was frowning over the cheque, trying to work out what was fifteen per cent of eleven dollars and forty-two cents, the first newsvan was pulling out of Arnie Gower's Arco station, where Arnie was kind enough to provide the reporter fellas directions to the sheriff's station on Main Street, then promptly got on the phone to his sister-in-law Thelma Whitters to find out what in tarnation was going on, since she was Brasstown's one and only dispatcher and maybe had some notion.

By the time Ernie and the sheriff returned to the station house in Ernie's beat-up Land Rover, Deputy Dwyer was having an argument with the Channel 4 Action News crew on the front steps. Sheriff Sturgill was out of the Land Rover and chugging toward the building before the car had stopped moving.

The tainted air burned his nostrils. It blew in from a grille in the ceiling that made an unpleasant grinding noise. The harsh light burned his eyes. It shone from mesh-covered tubes in the ceiling that buzzed like rattled hornets. The impure water burned his throat. The humans smelled of animal fat and curdled milk. Their breath stank of rotting meat. Their clothes, their hair, their teeth, even their furless skin exuded chemical odours.

One wall was made of iron bars.

The jail cell had a thick rubber floor. The room was cold and reeked of disinfectant that did not mask the odours of urine and bile that bespoke a history of fear and sickness. In the corner was some kind of water basin made of metal.

Echoing voices ebbed and flowed along the utilitarian corridors. He understood the tones but not the words. Machine sounds and jangling keys and metronomic footsteps and steady ticks and groaning pipes and ringing bells and ululating sirens formed an impenetrable, unignorable backdrop of noise.

His head ached.

He knelt calmly with eyes closed and turned his attention inward, toward his centre. He retained his sense of *self*, the assurance of the core that was him and no one else in the universe. But something was wrong. The core was damaged.

He could not remember who he was.

He remembered much. Training, chanting, blessing. Rituals, enchantments, spells. Cooking, cleaning, celebrating. The sounds and smells and shiftings of the forest and its connection to his soul. He was tethered to it, he knew. But the tethers were strained, and some had snapped.

His core remained strong enough to give him a sense of propriety – and, by contrast, a sense for what seemed out of place.

This place was out of place. He still knew enough of himself to know he did not belong here. Where did he belong? Where had he come from?

Warm hearth, varnished chairs, thick rugs, full larder, soft quilts, protective wood, comforting earth. Glimpses, flashes, glimmers were all he gleaned.

Where had he been going?

Crystal facets, mountain faces, demon jaws.

He shook his head.

Questions, questions. He dug deeper inward, searching for answers.

Sheriff Sturgill did a heroic job keeping the press away from Little Foot for a while. They knew there was some kind of critter locked up at the station house, but that wasn't enough story to make more than local news – what big-city newsmen snottily called 'Farm Report'. But at least there *was* a critter, and there was a mug shot, and make local news it did: the noon reports carried the story. Most stuck it at the tail-end, where the silly-season stories usually go to lighten the load of death and destruction broadcast for the preceding half-hour. America loves a happy ending, especially on the news.

The Little Foot story made good copy. Networks prodded their local affiliates for more information. Give us footage. Give us sound bites.

By three o'clock Sheriff Sturgill gave up. The station house was like a fortress under siege; from all the lights, newsvans, microphones, dish antennae, and bright-eyed fools in sports coats, you'd think they'd found Adolf Hitler making paper airplanes in his bunker.

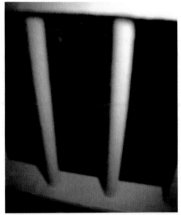

To make matters worse, Little Foot was obviously not in the best of health. He'd drink but he wouldn't eat. Mostly he either slept or he knelt in one position and didn't move. Sturgill had tried getting hold of Doc Vernor, but Brasstown's only veterinarian was off tending someone's prize heiffer or something; he hadn't returned Sturgill's increasingly anxious calls. Last call, Sturgill swore he heard a suspicious humming and a double-click like a wiretap just before he hung up. Deputy Dwyer said he was just being paranoid. Sturgill had laughed humourlessly and pointed outside, where a news helicopter was landing on Main Street.

Sturgill was forced to admit that he did not have the facilities to properly provide for his prisoner. He also did not have the facilities to deal with this media invasion of snotty city corner pokers and rock lifters, and he sure as shootin' didn't have the temperament for them. Besides which, there were just enough stills operating in the higher and less crowded elevations to make some nosy reporter wonder just what the Sheriff of Brasstown *did* do with his time.

He decided to transfer Little Foot to Asheville.

He bumped heads with Ernie Scruggs and came up with a plan to send someone out front with a phoney-baloney bundle that was supposed to be Little Foot, to act as a decoy while Sturgill slipped out back with the real Little Foot.

Deputy Dwyer put in his two cents' worth. 'Them newsboys catch you tryin' to put one over on 'em,' he drawled, 'an' they *will* crucify you.' He lit his newest Marlboro off the fading corpse of the last one. 'They ain't gonna stop you from movin' the critter, Sheriff,' he continued; 'they juss wont pitchers of it. This ain't Greta Garbo you got locked up here; it's some kinda freak.' He gestured out the barred window. 'Hell, freaks're their bread an' butter. Why would you want to keep 'em from gettin' a look at one?'

"'Cause it's *my* story!' said Ernie Scruggs.

Deputy Dwyer took a long, patient drag of his cigarette before answering. It was a James Dean kinda move, but it worked plenty good enough for Deputy Dwyer. 'Says who?' he asked, looking at Sheriff Sturgill.

Sturgill bit his lip. Dwyer was right: it looked bad if the Sheriff of Brasstown was in kahootz with the local news stringer. A law-enforcement officer was a public servant, and those boys out there would have his head on a silver platter with a side of fries if he played favourites. He shrugged helplessly at Scruggs, who looked like smoke and American flags were gonna come rolling out his ears any second now.

Deputy Dwyer leaned forward and stubbed out the cigarette. 'I'll take him down to Asheville if you want, Sheriff.'

Sturgill shook his head. 'My prisoner,' he said. He grabbed the lock-up key-ring from off its nail and headed for the cell. He paused in the hallway. 'Ernie?'

'Yeah?'

'The only words them boys outside are gonna get from me is "no" an' "comment". If I was you, I'd get to writin' my story PDQ. Understand?'

Scruggs blinked. 'Why, I appreciate that, Sheriff.'

Sturgill nodded. Then he continued down the hall, keys slapping his thigh, standard-issue boots thumping loudly toward the cell.

They escorted Little Foot out the front door.

Within minutes the creature's picture was broadcast on CNN. ABC, CBS, NBC, TBS, and Fox carried it on the evening news. Little Foot's face shone in living-rooms from Maine to Idaho to Oregon. It beamed in black and white from Sony Watchmen in Manhattan limousines; it blessed the Beautiful People cruising Beverly Hills bars.

One reporter dubbed it a 'Sasquatchette'. The epithet didn't stick. Connie Chung referred to the 'UFA' (Unidentified Furry Animal), but the acronym never caught on. Across the nation, every name from 'Harry' to 'Moleman' to 'hoax' was applied. But one name triumphed over all, and by the time plastic-wrapped morning papers slapped onto dewy lawns, Little Foot was a nationwide craze.

'Ka! Ka! Come quick! Ka?'

Karbolic Earthcreep sped along the mineshaft to his central chamber. 'What is it?' he cried. 'What? Who? Which?' He looked around anxiously. 'Neema! Oh, they've caught up to us! I knew it. Well, awright: come at me, then, ya scum! Yer not fit ta clean toilets in a troll hospital! I'll take yer an' I'll –'

'Karbolic Earthcreep, will ya please stop yer yammerin' and get over here!'

The gnome dropped his headless Teenage Mutant Ninja Turtles doll and hurried to the far end of the chamber, where Neema sat bathed in the flickering purple-white light of the ghost machine. 'What is it?' he asked. 'What's happened?'

Neema pointed at the glass. 'I've seen Fungle!' she announced.

Ka gaped. 'On there?' He glanced fearfully at the ghost machine.

'Just now!' she insisted. 'I seen his face as plain as I'm lookin' at yours!'

Ka bit his lower lip. 'Now, Neema,' he soothed, 'many's the time I've fancied a pretty gnome lady or two on me ghost machine, just because I been on me own a mite much –'

'*I saw him.*' When Neema used that tone she could make you believe down was up and a battleship was a flamingo. Believing was better than the fearful repercussions that tone implied if you disbelieved.

'A'right, Neema, ya saw Fungle,' agreed Ka. He glanced at the ghost machine, looked at the half-finished cup of tea beside Neema's big comfy chair (which had a little leg table that folded out when you leaned back; Ka had got it so she could sit with support for her broken leg, which was healing quickly but hardly mended). 'How'd he look?' the gnome asked.

'He looked . . .' Neema seemed close to tears. 'Oh, I don't know; it was only the briefest glimpse really.' She looked up at Ka, and her eyes glistened in the eerie light. 'He didn't look good, Ka. Somethin' looked . . . I don't know. Wrong.'

Ka frowned. 'Well, did you see –'

'– *approximately three feet tall, with a* zzznk!pop!pop!zzzz! *of fine black hair, a humanoid face with a mole-like snout from which* sss!pop!pop!nnnnn! *of whiskers project, powerful forepaws with opposable thumbs similar to those of a raccoon or a* pop!ffffzzz!pop! *tiny tail. The creature, commonly referred to as* zzznk!rrrr!pop! *completely dressed in a green tunic, baggy pants, and a tall, conical hat.'*

'They's talkin' 'bout Fungle,' said Neema.

'Shhh!'

'*–eriff Warren Horatius Burbill discovered Little* Fzzzok!rnrnrn! ksss!pop! *to communicate have so far proven unsuccessful. With me now is Dr Eric Dinehart, Antropology Chair at the Uni*ssss!pop! ssss!rrrr!*entific classification completely unknown, and I'm delighted that it will likely cause a furor among biologists, anthropologists, zoologists* hnnk!hnnk!tss!tss!hnnk!*ogists. Discovering such a creature alive is like, well, like finding a dinosaur in the Grand Canyon. Because of its condition and the media attention, we intend to isolate the creature* hnnn!pop!rrrrnnk!zzzzp! *damage. Thank you, Dr Dinehart. And there you have it, Dan. From Police Headquarters in Asheville, North Carolina – home of Little Foot! – this is Loran Fan*ping!snap!snap!pop!zzzzzzzzzzzzzzzzzz

'Sounds like Fungle, a'right,' admitted Ka.

'Oh, Ka, he's in trouble,' said Neema. 'We got to help him!'

Ka frowned. He looked at Neema and let his gaze travel tellingly to her splinted leg.

'That don't matter!' said Neema. 'Here, help me up!'

Ka's hand strayed to the leather bag around his neck that contained the magnetite crystal entrusted to him by Fungle, the crystal that powered the Lunabird.

He helped Neema to her feet, staring at the ghost machine the whole time. He didn't tell Neema the thought that had been in his head the moment she claimed to have seen Fungle on the screen: if Fungle was on the ghost machine, then Fungle was a ghost.

Stockbrokers numbed by numbers took cheer in the odd news of a new creature discovered in the Smoky Mountains. Homemakers anxious about the rising prices of vegetables, diapers, oil, everything, were pleasantly distracted – even excited – by the Buddha-like face of the strange animal. Businessmen shook their heads and thought, *What a world.* Lawyers, public-relations agents, licensing merchants, studio development executives, psychics, scientists, columnists, apocalypse mongers, clerics, doctors, photographers hastened to their telephones to call with offers of free representation. Unobstructed by worldly considerations, children found him merely delightful.

In Washington, the president's press secretary made a brief call to police headquarters in Asheville, North Carolina.

THE WHITE HOUSE
WASHINGTON

TO: President

FROM: Public Relations Advisory Council

CC: (See Attached)

RE: "Little Foot"

Mr. President:

With regard to the mammalian species recently discovered in the Northwestern Smoky Mountain Region and commonly referred to as "Little Foot":

Little Foot has become the largest media phenomenon in recent memory, and we have urged this Administration to quickly develop and exploit a high-profile, positive interest in and close association with the well-being of the creature, which rates highly on the Schauft/Holmen Empathy Scale.

The Asheville VA Hospital, North Carolina, where the creature is presently under medical supervision, is currently a noncontainable scenario. The hospital is overrun by media and curiosity seekers, and is poorly equipped with regard to facilities for the media and security for the creature. In addition, the hospital itself does not meet state-of-the-art standards for medical examination and care.

In the interest of maintaining advantageous public relations, it is our belief that the creature should be immediately provided with guarded transport to an intensive-care unit in a secure wing of Walter Reed Hospital in Washington, with a view toward in-depth examination of its origin and nature, and toward protecting this hitherto-unknown and potentially advantageous species from harm.

14 *ICU 2*

The airplane fought and howled every inch of its way through the sky. It was a far cry from a Lunabird. Those frail wooden craft sailed the magnetic currents that webbed the earth as naturally and effortlessly as a ship is pushed through water by the wind. But this mad beast! The bottled air within was heavy with oil residue and artificially chilled in a manner that ripped apart the atmosphere's ozone shield. The uncomfortable seats were covered with a scratchy fabric he'd never encountered. The light varied between too dim and too bright. The walls shuddered as the metal tube bucked. Fierce engines screamed like summoned demons raging the metal ship through the air, and spat behind them a vile wake that hung for ever.

Before he had been taken from the white-smelling building, a white-clad human had come into his room and stabbed his arm with a needle. He had been too shocked by the sudden and unexpected violence to stop her, and ever since then he had wavered in and out of a dreamy, fuzzy place neither sleeping nor waking where demon engines throbbed.

His mind surfaced from the ocean of disorientation.

All the airplane's window shades were pulled down, but even drugged Fungle sensed the Cities of No sliding by beneath him. He felt their directed energies, harnessed and driven along prescribed routes. He felt their metal and stone stacked and crowded and folded in on themselves. The air through which he hurtled lay heavy above the Cities of No, a thick, burning, tangible thing that could wear away the hardest stone. It was also the medium for broadcast energies that crackled his fur and confounded his sense of direction.

Fungle also felt the cities' people. He felt their directed energies harnessed and driven along prescribed routes, a hard people stacked and crowded and, like the metal and stone surrounding them, folded in on themselves. The thick burning tangible air they breathed wore them slowly away.

What cities stand hard by, he wondered, *that confound me senses so?*

He glanced at the human occupying the seat beside him. The human stared back through thick spectacles that shrank his eyes. The straightbacked man had been staring at him ever since they had boarded the metal Lunabird. There were humans at the very front of the craft as well, but no others.

Fungle wanted to make a face at the man, yell *Boo!* and waggle his fingers. But none of that. In the first place, he was aware of the metal death that nestled beneath the armpit of the man's coat. In the second place, he had promised himself he would not talk. He didn't want them to know he could speak. He wasn't sure why not, but it felt like the right thing to do for now. No talking, no magic; he would sit silent and spell-less in the face of their indignities.

The airplane howled down the night. Fungle slept, but not well.

Intensive Care Unit Number 2 at the Walter Reed Hospital was an arctic netherworld, a small, sterile, high-security wing that specialised in handling what certain governmental agencies referred to as 'sensitives'.

Little Foot was, unofficially, a sensitive.

He lay in a high, starch-sheeted bed with silver side-rails pulled up like a crib. Overhead fluorescent light puddled on the wrinkled, clear-plastic canopy surrounding him. Around the bed was an array of equipment: a cardiac monitor beeped rhythmically, oscilloscopes waved green sine trails, an Ångström respirator hissed rheumatically, IV hookups dripped glucose, urethral catheters drained, EEG pens scratched nervously. Hoses and wires and leads and needles and clips and Velcro bands formed a cat's cradle around him.

Specialists and nurses in pale-green surgical caps and masks measured ingestions, secretions and excretions; changed bottles; adjusted valves; fluffed pillows; studied earthquake tracks on EKG charts; followed the liquid green soft traces rippling across monitors.

The only human sounds among the machinery were the murmurs of diagnostic whispers and the squeak of rubber shoes on linoleum. Sometimes the humans even glanced at the small furry bundle of flesh that fed these apparatus.

Fungle floated above his body. He looked down on it sleeping there, breathing-masked, hairnetted, ensnared in wires and tubes. A white-clad, light-haired, human woman entered the room and stepped into the clear wrinkled tent that housed Fungle's sleeping self. She bent over him, slid a needle into his arm, and injected pale liquid into his veins.

Fungle felt a faint weakening in the silver cord that bound his *self* to his body. Mentally he twanged it, testing its resonance and tuning like a mandolute string. The connection seemed strong, and he decided not to worry just yet.

Bobbing near the ceiling like a spiritual balloon he wandered through the wall and into the white corridor outside his room. A very dark human being slumped on a folding chair and wearing a blue uniform and a cap and a gun nodded at two white-coated men approaching him. One of the men consulted a clipboard; both ignored the dark man's nod.

– seems to have a normal pupillary reflex, but heartbeat's fourteen bpm, blood pressure's dropped to sixty over forty, body temperature's sixty-three degrees –

– *Jesus! Is it dying, or is its metabolism just that slow?*

– All I can really find wrong with it is a mild case of malnutrition and that nasty concussion on the back of the head. Which wouldn't account for three-fourths of our findings. Of course, we don't know what's normal for this thing, but my guess is it's going into hibernation.

– *No way. What is it, some kind of bear?*

– Closer to something with a talpid ancestor, we think. An evolved mole.

They entered Fungle's room.

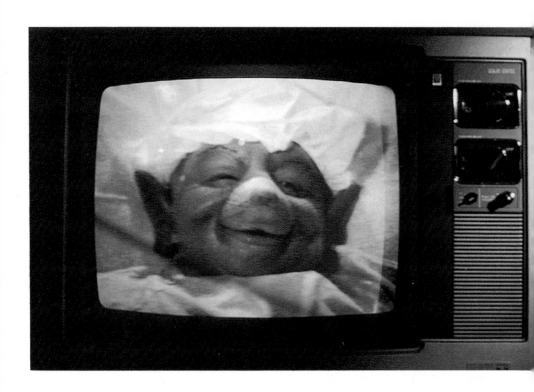

– We could cut to see if there's a layer of subcutaneous fat . . .
– Better still, go to the library and read up on hibernation. Oh, nurse, draw blood for stat; calcium and electrolytes. Tomorrow we're planning a pretty comprehensive battery of . . .
Fungle left them and continued along the hall, wandering but moored to his body like an inquisitive kite exploring this curious white place where mechanical and electrical devices orchestrated life-and-death dramas played out on stages of suffering.

'LITTLE FOOT'
GENERAL PHYSICAL EXAMINATION AND PRELIMINARY FINDINGS

OVERVIEW

Preliminary physical inspection reveals an upright, bipedal, bilaterally symmetrical, short-furred mammal possibly related to the species *talpidae*, or mole. The body is stocky, dense and muscular, with a subcutaneous layer of fatty tissue generally assumed to play a role in hibernation. The heart is four-chambered, with an average systolic/diastolic rate of 30–40 bpm active, 20 bpm sleeping, and possibly as low as 10 bpm during hibernation.

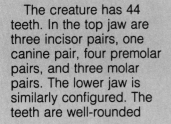

The creature has 44 teeth. In the top jaw are three incisor pairs, one canine pair, four premolar pairs, and three molar pairs. The lower jaw is similarly configured. The teeth are well-rounded

*

It took him two days to rejoin his physical self. The liquids they fed his veins made his body unresponsive to his will; the silver rope still tethered body and *self*, but Fungle was not able to hoist himself through to unite the two.

He wandered, he learned.

Eventually he grew concerned that his body would soon no longer be his to command. Every day the humans fed his veins with nutrients and drugs; every day they shaved pieces of fur, removed thin samples of flesh, examined eyes and orifices and every imaginable part of him. They put his inert body onto a wheeled slab and rolled it into various rooms, where he floated above himself and watched unimaginably powerful forces play across his body.

At first he was afraid that they were taking parts of himself to use in formulating spells against him, the way certain kinds of mage will take a clipping of hair or shaving of nail to perform sympathetic magic. He followed some of these samples to other rooms where they were bagged, numbered, weighed, placed in solution, deposited in tubes, spun, burned, and/or frozen. Finally he was comforted that no sympathetic sorcery was at work here, though he came away no less confused.

Soon the humans' testing required that Fungle be aware of his

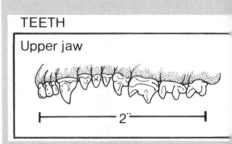

TEETH

Upper jaw

2"

and the canines are not pronounced; dental morphology and analysis of stomach contents indicate an herbivorous diet – primarily fruits, nuts, berries, and wild roots.

The alimentary canal was studied via injection of 100% stable dispersion of barium sulphate; resultant X-rays revealed a tract slightly more than twelve feet in length. The large intestine is 100% larger than the small intestine. There is no trace of cecum or appendix.

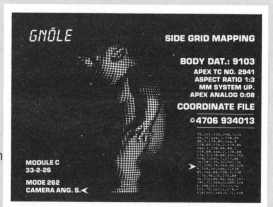

GNŌLE

SIDE GRID MAPPING

BODY DAT.: 9103
APEX TC NO. 2941
ASPECT RATIO 1:3
MM SYSTEM UP.
APEX ANALOG 0:08

COORDINATE FILE
○4706 934013

MODULE C
33-2-26

MODE 262
CAMERA ANG. S.◄

The fleshy ears are most advantageously positioned for lateral and forward hearing. The $3^{1}/_{2}$-turn cochlea gives hearing abilities of near-canine equivalence.

The elongated snout is extraordinarily sensitive, approaching (if not surpassing) that of a canine. Sensory whiskers extending up to two inches on either side of the snout seem to play a significant role. Though extensive testing in this area has not been performed, preliminary molecular partitioning indicates a possible sensitivity level of one part in three million. The overall physiognomy displays bare, pink skin over an expressive and articulate musculature.

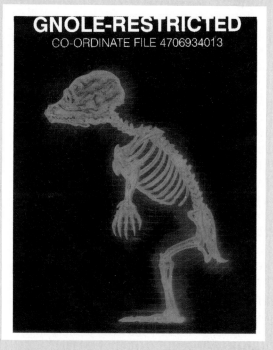

GNOLE-RESTRICTED
CO-ORDINATE FILE 4706934013

surroundings. The sleep-inducing liquids stopped flowing into his veins. The silver cord thickened. Fungle hoisted his *self* back into his self.

His eyelids twitched and opened. His first thought was that he was embedded in ice because of the distorting plastic canopy around his bed. Deformed figures clad in pale-green stood outside the canopy, regarding him intently like alien inquisitors.

Fungle went back to sleep.

The humans woke him up.

The tests continued.

Foreign smells in still rooms, faint and strong. Odd sounds from pekuliar shells fitted over his ears, slight and loud. Colour and motion near and far. He was made to stand, to sit, to crawl like an infant.

He endured. He did not know what else to do. Faint voices spoke in his head, stronger in slumber. He endured. Everpresent in his mind was the notion that there was something he was trying to do, some sense of mission to be accomplished . . . It annoyed him the way a word can cavort on the end of the tongue without emerging. He was uncertain of his origins, of who he was. He could not remember his name. He had memories – family, friends, places, names, songs, dinners, sorrows, frights – but they were isolated, they did not connect; he could not form a whole picture from their mosaic tiles.

He endured.

The shortness of leg length in proportion to overall body dimension, relatively primitively evolved foot with vestigial claws and rudimentary prehensile capacity, and pronounced curvature of the spine indicate the relatively recent evolution of upright posture – perhaps within the last half-million years, as compared to three million in the case of *homo sapiens*.

NOTABLE OBSERVATIONS

Cranial Development

While actual brain weight is unknown at present, the Little Foot cranial capacity is 1400cc. The estimated brain-weight to body-weight ratio is greater than that of *homo sapiens*. In addition, preliminary analysis of CAT scans indicates a high number of cerebral convolutions and a sophisticated morphology, both not unsimilar to that of *tursiops truncatus*, the bottle-nosed dolphin. Current theory holds that amount and architecture of brain convolutions play a key role in the attainable level of the organism's intelligence. In addition, EEG readings indicate the nearly constant presence of Alpha-type brainwaves primarily associated with

One afternoon following a debilitating regimen of tests he awoke to find dinner on a tray before him, consisting of the usual raw and cooked vegetables he found mostly tasteless, bread he found bland, water laced with chemical taints. What was different this time was a metal bowl containing a large mound of some soft, white substance. Puzzled, he touched it, and jerked back his hand in surprise when his finger encountered cold and wet. Cautiously he sniffed the finger. Milk, sugar, the inevitable chemical tinge. Not unpleasant though.

He licked his finger. Sweet.

He pulled the bowl toward him, bent his head over it, and licked. Arctic sweetness blossomed on his tongue. *Blessums!* – it was wonderful! Its smoothness soothed; its lightness delighted. The taste was vanilla with a hint of honey, but the sensation! Cold velvet holding winter's ice in summer's heat, a dessert bowl of snowballs. His rough tongue licked the bowl clean, and he sank back into his bed in quiet contentment, sticky milky drops depending from his snout whiskers. In all his days of foraging and gourmeting and enthusiastic eating, he had never tasted anything so sublime.

He wanted more.

Two days, four dozen tests, and ten bowls of ice-cream later, he sat propped up in bed, eating a dish of Peanut Butter Fudge Ripple

Comparative sketch illustrating manipulative anatomy of higher-order primates and gnole. Note fully opposable thumb situated relatively high on palm for subtle dexterity at the cost of increased leverage.

focused concentration or
deep meditation. These
Alpha waves have even
been recorded during
Theta sleep/dream states.

Hand Structure

The thumb is fully
opposable. The vestigial
nature of the claws
indicates evolution toward
grasping, throwing, and
possibly rudimentary
toolmaking abilities
such as those found
in chimpanzees. (Refer
to Videotape LF-387B.)
The left hand is callused
on the pads of the
four fingers but not the
thumb; the right hand is
callused along the outer
edge of the thumbpad.
Neuropsychological
evaluation indicates
extremely well-developed
eye-hand coordination.
Reflex response was

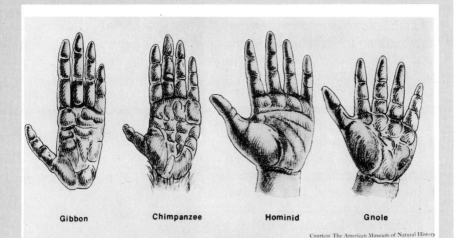

Gibbon   Chimpanzee   Hominid   Gnole

Courtesy The American Museum of Natural History

and staring at the snowy flickering on the glass of the box against the wall facing his bed. The box looked like wood but was not; the snowy image on it looked familiar. He scooped ice-cream into his mouth (yesterday he had demonstrated tool-using abilities, and now they were letting him eat with a spoon, though a fork or a knife seemed to be out of the question) and struggled to remember why the picture box seemed familiar. He associated it with someone, an old friend, an odd bumbling tunnelling fellow with a talent for saying exactly the wrong thing. But he couldn't remember the old friend's name, or the name of the machine.

A nurse entered with a cup of pills and a cup of water. He did not mind eating their pills and taking their tests so much now that they gave him snowballs (they called it *ice-cream*, a good name) whenever he pleaded with his empty bowl, which he wouldn't give back to them.

The nurse set the tray down on the nightstand. 'Watching tee vee, huh?' she asked. 'What you watching?' She held out a paper cup full of pills. Barely glancing at her, he took the cup, upended it over the ice-cream, and continued shovelling the dessert into his mouth.

'I prefer M & Ms, myself,' said the nurse, laughing. She frowned at the glass-fronted box (*tee vee*, he remembered). 'You don't want to watch *that*, do you? Here.' She picked up a flat, button-studded

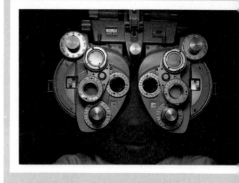

measured at .07 seconds (compared to an optimal time of .10 in *homo sapiens*). (See attached Neuropsychological Report.) (Refer to **Ophthalmological Anomalies**, below.)

Vocal Anomalies

Thus far Little Foot has communicated and reacted largely through the use of gestural/facial motions similar to those found in lower-order primates. However, examination of larynx and oesophageal morphology reveals a well-developed and articulate musculature, voluntary glottal control, and motile tongue – factors usually indicative of at least primitive vocal communication, i.e., primates, raccoons, etc.

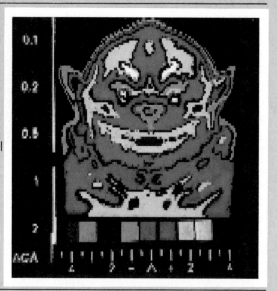

Ophthalmological Anomalies

Little Foot has two small, forward-facing eyes possessing all the structures normally associated with mammalian visual capabilities. The creature distinguishes colour. The eyelid is pronounced, with slight epicanthic folds. The eye itself is small – 3/4" in diameter – and marginally astigmatic. Physical properties (see attached Ophthalmological Addendum) indicate a myopia not unlike that rectangle from the nightstand and pointed it at the tee vee. The snow vanished and there were human beings, moving and talking right there on the box in front of him. One of the human beings was wearing a long white coat and a sympathetic expression as he placed a hand on the shoulder of a crying woman with orange hair. 'Marsha, you have to enjoy the time you've got left,' the man was saying. 'Let Brett go to Paris with that model and get on with your life. The clock is ticking.' He smiled warmly. 'Do you want some . . . coffee?'

The nurse watched the tee vee with grave concern. 'Oh, it's so sad,' she said. 'See, Marsha has an incurable brain virus, and every week she forgets who she is. She keeps thinking that her boyfriend Brett wants to run away to Paris with a high-fashion model named Saffron, but Brett died in a tragic safari accident years ago, only Marsha can't remember. And she's really married to Dr Strong there, but she doesn't remember and he doesn't tell her because it's too painful for him and she'll just forget again next week anyway.'

Fungle finished his ice-cream and held the bowl up to her. A pleasant rosy glow was beginning to spread inside him.

'More?' she asked.

He pointed to his mouth and she laughed and patted his head. 'You are so *cute!*' she said, and left with her tray.

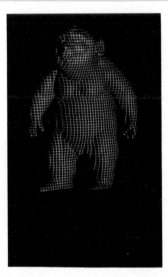

U.F.A. (cross index file 27914/E)
LF–390
Clothing
Exhibit (A) = Tunic
(B) = Pants (C) = Bag

Fabric used in these hand-made garments is a mixture of Indian Hemp (Apocynum), wild cotton and cattail fibres. The fibres were probably spun together on a stick and whorl spindle, then tightly woven on either a wide upright or backstrap loom.

The fabric is dyed green. Chemical analysis of the vegetable dye shows it contains a mixture of wormwood, nettle and elder-leaf sap, with iron ore and urine used as a 'set'.

The dyed material has been heavily impregnated with a combination of walnut oil and pine resin as a water repellant.

String twined from cedar bark and Indian Hemp, waterproofed with pine tar, has been used to stitch garments together.

String on bag handles (C) is ornately braided and the buttons of the tunic (A) finely knotted.

found in mammals of the order *talpidae*, the mole. The primitiveness of the organ suggests degeneration during the evolution of the species, possibly due to a primarily subterranean environment.

According to parameters dictated by ophthalmological measurement, Little Foot's binocular vision should be blurred beyond a range of 20", minimum, and indeterminate at a distance of 5'–10'. However, EKG, EEG, and skin-conductivity measurements taken during focal-awareness tests indicate that the creature detected minute movements from a distance of 50' or better. Further testing with targets behind soundproofed glass eliminated the possibility of vibrassic or olfactory detection, and greatly reduced the possibility of auditory detection.

How the creature is able to perceive motion and distinguish objects beyond a few feet has not yet been determined. (See attached report.)

See Appendices A-1 through S24 for A Complete List of Examinations Performed. Refer to Videolog LF, Nos. 1–392, for a visual record.

He picked up the flat box.

> **click!** *after his return to Washington the president began meeting with top White House advisors. Later, he told reporters* **click!** *I love you, dammit! But what do you care; you don't have any room in your life for* **click!** *a word from our sponsor while we're waiting for word from the president* **click!** *so let's take another look at his run! He's got the classic style of riding saddle broncs – look at that! Set-outs, reach, and lift on that rein! That's what the officials look for, and that'll get him another horse* **click!** *to help prevent leaks, Luvs have Leak Guard, a two-step system that catches and distributes* **click!** *the servicemen overseas is on a six-week rotation basis until they get their new arrivals, which are* **click!** *the latest Fall fashions for a fraction of the cost! So when you're shopping for clothes, remember* **click!** *the correct answer is 'Thomas Jefferson' for ten points! Now, Miss Honkley, would you like to spin the Big Wheel, or would you like* **click!** *the mating habits of the Thompson's gazelle are easily demonstrated by* **click!** *an eighteen-piece heavy-metal screwdriver set from Craftsman, fully warrantied* **click!** *as long as the alimony keeps coming in, a-hahahaha! But seriously, folks, it's* **click!** *a nice country music video, ain't it? And I was a-thinkin': if Kitty Wells hadda married Conway Twitty, her name'd be* **click!**

The commercials taught him more than anything else he saw on tee vee. He learned that human beings drank beer, Coke, and Pepsi, usually on the beach. They ate pizza, hamburgers, and candy in mass quantities and usually in laughing groups. They suffered from headaches, backaches, dandruff, bad breath, pimples, heartburn, foot odour, tooth decay, itchy runny sensations, stained dentures, post-nasal drip, static cling, and the heartbreak of psoriasis. They wanted close shaves, no waiting, zero to sixty in seven seconds, cost-free checking, instant relief, low-cost auto insurance, all the taste and half the calories, and to have it their way. Somehow their mating habits were tied in to all these things.

Many things puzzled him. You said 'No' to drugs, but when you were sick you took medicine. He could not figure out the difference between a drug and a medicine. Concerned groups fought to keep human sexual behaviour from television, but ninety per cent of what Fungle saw on tee vee related to human sexual behaviour. A talk show decrying television violence was sponsored by Raid

Ant and Roach Killer. Criminals were punished unless they had helped make the laws they broke. News articles on handgun control were followed by scenes from the next episode of *Nightscope*. Huge resources were expended to inform people to conserve energy and resources. Lucy and Ricky always did incomprehensibly stupid things. People paid Hallmark to express their sincerest good wishes. Candy companies did not urge eaters to brush their teeth; toothpaste companies did not urge brushers to avoid candy.

He learned how to readily identify villains and heroes, that a car was a religious object, that everyone was going to win the Lottery, that game-show contestants jumped up and down, that people driving smoke-belching cars across the grey concrete islands of the cities were environmentalists, and – most incredible of all – that the stories told on the news weren't *stories* at all.

Most of what he saw would have horrified him, had it not left him completely numb. He didn't know the Hopi Indian word *koyaanisqatsi*, which meant 'crazy life' or 'life out of balance', but after watching television he certainly would have understood its essence.

One afternoon he was trying to untangle the complex knot of relationships between somewhat unlikely characters and a human being on something called *The Muppet Show*. He was sitting in a metal-and-plastic chair, finishing his third bowl of ice-cream for the day (Peppermint Stick Bubblegum Chunk), while an orderly changed his bed linen. He clanked the spoon in the empty bowl, then held the bowl high, not looking away from Kermit the Frog arguing with Fozzie Bear. 'Ahh, that be delickshus,' he said contentedly. 'One more bowl o' that'll set me right, I think.'

He stopped.

Fozzie Bear said *Wukka-wukka-wukka*.

Slowly he turned.

The orderly was staring at him, wide-eyed, pillowcase in hand.

Calmly he lowered the bowl. *A thrown stone's gone*, his father useta say.

The orderly glanced at the muppets on the tee vee. '*¿Que? ¿Que, ¿Que?*' the stunned woman repeated.

Kermit said *Hi-ho*.

Fungle pointed at the tee vee. 'It were him,' he said. 'I didn't say nothin'.'

Pillowcase and all, the orderly ran screaming from the room.

*

Little Foot's name was *Fungle*. He was a *gnole*, Fungle the gnole. No one ever learned the name of the orderly who had held history's first spoken conversation between a human and a non-human (mostly because the orderly was a recent immigrant who insisted on anonymity), but the *Washington Post* scooped the competition in next morning's edition. By noon the networks were banging on Walter Reed's doors. Mike Wallace was buttonholing hospital personnel to ask probing questions. Ted Koppel wanted an appearance on *Nightline*. David Letterman wanted a Stupid Pet Trick, on video if he had to. Barbara Walters wanted an interview. Larry King offered to broadcast from Fungle's bedside. Carl Sagan, Desmond Morris, and Stephen Jay Gould pulled strings for an opportunity to ask some of the thousands of questions they had. All interviews were firmly declined by Walter Reed's PR director, who was mostly an extension of the White House's PR machine. The *National Enquirer* published one anyway. Greenpeace demanded that gnoles be declared an endangered species, then seemingly contradicted itself and decided that, as a United States citizen, Fungle was entitled to representation under the Constitution. Pursuing this latter logic, the American Civil Liberties Union questioned the legality of Fungle's detainment and filed a lawsuit.

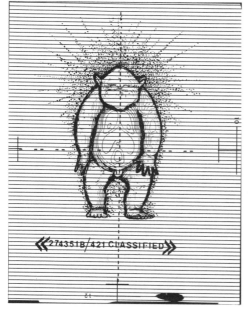
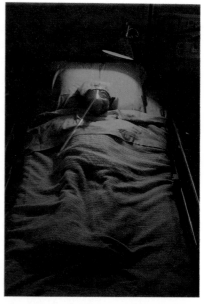

Fungle the gnole was unavailable throughout, for now he was undergoing an exhaustive battery of psychological examinations.

15 *A Star is Born*

In a world of nine-day wonders, fifteen-minute fame, and thirty-second newsbites, Fungle the gnole, Little Foot, the mountain-man mole, was a media miracle. The President of the United States was still smarting from an inconclusive military action in the Middle East; the nation itself was in a recession from its expense. The Dow-Jones was closing at record lows, oil and housing prices were at an all-time high, the national census debacle had created a shortage in federal aid to state agencies. Last winter had held the coldest national average temperatures in eighty-nine years, further depleting oil and coal resources, while the summer had lofted record highs and an attendant crime wave of unprecedented proportions.

The Fungle Bungle
Government Genetic Engineering
Experiment Gone Wrong!

WASHINGTON POST (UPI)

New York and New Jersey, he
the laws as constituti
on her

PRESIDENT SET
TO MEET GNOLE

WASHINGTON (UPI)

No. 45,598

Fungle Is A Hoax
The Work Of Hollywood Pranksters!

nnouncement formed a dra-
max to the monthslong Times
was

THE GNOLE
REALITY BEHIND THE LEGEND
OF THE GNOMES

By JOHN HOLUSHA

Special to The New York Times

DETROIT

'LITTLE FOOT'
Why Is He Kept Hidden?

By MICKEY LYONS, News Staff Writer

me Court ruled today that a dri
al to submit to a blood alc
ation

Littlefoot Loves Ice Cream
Rationed To A Quart A Day

By JACK MICHAELS, Times Staff Writer

The debate continued between proponents of global warming versus global cooling; all anyone felt sure of was that something was very wrong and pollution was a major cause. The most conspicuously thriving industry was the Hollywood fantasy mill: box-office business was brisk, and for the first time the videogame industry's profits eclipsed tinseltown's. Economists dourly pointed out that entertainment industries have traditionally thrived during national decline. Headlines and anchorpeople repeated pretty much the same message day after day – *It's not any better today!*

Enter Fungle the gnole. He didn't fix any of this; he didn't really even alleviate any of it – not at first. At first he was this year's Pet Rock, a major novelty but an irrelevant one. In fact, it was his very irrelevance to what the majority of people saw as 'the real world' or 'everyday life' that accounted for Fungle's massive popularity – for, in a world where fantasy films were drawing in the lion's share of box-office dollars, the presence of fantasy in the real world was a powerful tonic.

The very fact that so little was known about him only added fuel to the media-powered flame. This wasn't some little green man who had landed on the White House lawn with a set of warnings, plans, histories, and valuable lessons. This was a member of a race that had existed hidden alongside human beings for millennia: it was part of our world. Indeed, evolutionary scientists were theorising that it was *a part of us* – a cousin to mankind. It talked, it thought – *it ate ice-cream and watched tee vee!*

Two press releases and a few carefully selected photos emerged from Walter Reed Hospital every day. The press snatched them up and chewed them until hardly any flavour remained. Speculation was wild and rampant: the creature had fallen from a parallel universe through an interdimensional doorway into our world; flying-saucer gnoles had built a shrine to Elvis on the far side of the moon; a covert government gene-splicing project had got out of hand; toxic waste, secretly dumped by major nuclear power-plant companies, had irradiated the Appalachian countryside to produce generations of mutants; the Last Days as foretold in Revelation were upon the world, and Fungle was a harbinger of the Beast; a static 'pocket environment' had allowed gnoles to survive in isolation in the Smoky Mountain region for hundreds of thousands of years, much like the lonely and much-pursued dinosaur family trapped by climatic change in Loch Ness; gnoles had colonised the world after the destruction of Atlantis (this dead-on-the-money theory was among the most ridiculed); gnoles came from a hole in the North Pole that led down to a hollow earth; gnoles were descended from ancient astronauts who had built Stonehenge, scraped the enormous figures on the plains of Nazca, and carved the sombre faces on Easter Island; gnoles were the 'little people' that occur in the legends of nearly every human race on earth (this latter theory was almost certainly true).

Every theory, serious or cracked, encouraged the princes of commerce. Hucksters sold Fungle fashions, T-shirts, keychains, posters, coffee mugs . . . you name it. The airwaves filled with songs that ranged from cash-in silly to embarrassingly sincere. Dr Demento premiered 'Just Say Gnole', by the Gnolettes, while John Denver regained the charts with 'Mountain Brother' – a song quickly parodied as 'Smoky Mountain Guy' (to the tune of 'Rocky Mountain High') by The FunGals. Had company lawyers not advised prudence until Fungle's citizenship and legal status were determined, this popularity would have peaked with the Everest of attainable fame in America: a picture of Fungle on a McDonald's drinking glass.

Funglemania was the buzzword of the day, coined on a *Time* magazine cover devoted to both Fungle the phenomenon and Fungle the creature. *Small is Big!* ran more than one tabloid headline. Walter Reed's press secretary was forced to hire (after ensuring that salaries were at government expense) two full-time secretaries, mailroom help, and a PR assistant just to handle the volume of mail that poured in, not to mention offers for endorsements, requests to judge beauty pageants, dedicate shopping malls, attend revival meetings, and host *Saturday Night Live.* Parents brought a flood of children to Walter Reed and demanded they be allowed to see Little Foot. Pushing past the crowd that surrounded the hospital hoping for a glimpse of the creature, ignoring microphones thrust into their faces, the PR staff sorted mail, threw away nonsense, used word-processing programs to mass-mail thousands of generic personalised replies, and replied to all offers with a polite but firm 'Thanks, but no thanks.'

Life attempted a serious treatment on the origins of the gnole, but the articles were skimpy and the pictures were large. The first lucid and scholarly probings into the Fungle mystery appeared in *Omni* and *Spiritus.* Before long academics were arguing with their janitors about the gnole. Everybody had an opinion.

SPIRITUS

DREAMCREATURE
The gnole • modern Rumplestiltskin!

by Dr. Susan Mueller

An Oonark Eskimo drawing depicting a gnole in flight.

Legends about small, near-human creatures are as old as our human culture, and they conform to a persuasive traditional concept that is found in folklore the world over and widely represented in literature and art. From the Amazon to the Highlands of Scotland, from the deep forests of Germany to the Himalayas, diverse peoples have believed in the existence of strange, small humanoids covered with hair, sometimes called gnomes, goblins, the wee folk, and dwarves, often seen as guardians of the forest, charged with the safety of animals, and full of wisdom and secret lore.

The universal presence of these legends generally shares a common theme: subhuman creatures with such human traits as erect posture, speech, bipedal locomotion, manual dexterity, exceptional cunning, and magical powers—usually associated with healing and conjuration. Until now I think it's fair to state that, despite the universality of these myths, they were regarded as merely that—*myth*. But now the appearance into our modern society of the gnole must throw a shadow of doubt across færy legends: for could it possibly be that the "wee folk"—the Rumplestilskins, the hobgoblins, dwarves of Scandinavia, and gnomes— are, in fact, gnoles?

A furtive creature, small, retiring from human contact, perhaps fading from the face of the earth like the dinosaurs, yet retained in our collective ancestral memories, passed down and transcribed into the legends that abound of the secret commonwealth of gnomes, trolls, elves, and goblins.

continued, page 24

19

THE GNOLE: MISSING LINK?

By Dr. Russel Kinney

.....let us recall another mystery...that Homo Sapiens is the only surviving species of Hominidae. Isn't it mysterious, if not mystical that we should be the only survivors of the whole family, while the nearest Pongidae, boasts several surviving forms?

DMITRI BAYANOV AND IGOR BOURTSEV
in Current Anthropology   June 1976

The "missing link"—these two words resound and echo with mystery and excitement; a holy grail, a modern quest by paleontologists and anthropologists seeking in the remote sands of time a potential cousin, even brother, linking man to ape—a romance germinated by Darwin's *On the Origin of Species*, published in 1859, which theorized that man had evolved from a primate ancestor.

Darwin's theory, simply stated, was that since the reproductive powers of animals and plants potentally far outpace the available food supply, there is in nature a constant struggle for existence on the party of every living thing. Since animals vary individually, the most cleverly adapted will survive and leave offspring which will inherit and, in their turn, enhance the genetic endowment they have obtained from their ancestors. Because the struggle for life is incessant, this continual process promotes endless slow changes in bodily form as living creatures are subjected to different natural environments, different enemies, and all the vicissitudes against which life has struggled down the ages. Darwin assumed that the rise of man came from the slow, incremental gains he made through natural selection which started at least three million years ago with the first protohominids.

By the beginning of the twentieth century the ape origins of man were well established—from chimpanzee it was a quick step to Java man and then to Neanderthal and modern man. But not all anthropologists were converts to Darwinism. In 1918, F. Wood Jones, a distinguished English anatomist, expressed the heretic view that man arose from tarsioid rather than an anthropoid ancestry. The tarsier (*tarsius spectrum*), a large-eyed animal about the size of a kitten, has a brain and other characteristics which place it on a par with the lower primates. Wood Jones claimed that although present-day tarsiers are tree dwellers, this tree-living specialization has evolved from early tarsioid ancestors that walked on the ground.

Wood Jones' theories were vigorously refuted by primatologists, and even today the orthodox view persists that man is a "made-over ape," with the hominid family tree of man branching off from the primate stock below the greate ape line up into *A. africanus, H. habilis,* and *H. erectus,* and most anthropologists believe categorically that from this remarkable family *H. sapiens*, "man the wise," is the sole survivor.

Wood Jones insisted that the human line is very ancient, going back tens of millions of years to the Tertiary Period, suggesting that the ancestors of man were "small, active animals."

Now, I have this vision: Imagine that, in the dark, arboreal gloom of an ancient forest, an small shy creature hesitates, sniffing the dank air with its snout for danger signals as it watches mammoths, bisons, and the stalking sabre-toothed tiger on a sunlit plain beyond the edge of the forest. It sees man, too, hunting in packs, bringing down the bison with stone missiles, tearing flesh apart with bloody fury and gorging on the remains. The creature steals away into the dark shadows of the forest's rampant undergrowth, an outcast, erect on two feet—a gnole!

Could the gnole be of the hominid family? I believe —from the few facts on the creature made available by the Walter Reed Hospital after its untimely and tragic death, and from my own personal observations of the television transmissions from I.C.U.2—that no Pongoid (ape) can match the interrelationship between man and gnole.

HOMINID	GNOLE
Exclusively ground dwelling	Exclusively ground dwelling; large forehands suggest adapted from earth-burrowing ancestry.
Bipedal	Bipedal
Forward-facing eyes	Forward-facing eyes
Dextrous hands, opposable thumb	Dextrous hands, opposable thumb
Articulate speech	Articulate speech
Fine hair covering on body inadequate for warmth	Fine hair covering on body inadequate for warmth

Is it possible that *hominidae* beyond the Tertiary Period were two separate families, one a tree climber moving up through millions of years to become man, while its gentler brother, an earth dweller, moved into the dark habitat of the forests to evolve, unknown to man, into the gnole? The thought is cataclysmic: impious man with all his misused intelligence is faced with perhaps acknowledging another creature—possibly a close relative—that, through its own turmoil of evolution, may have acquired senses and mental powers far in excess of our own. ◫

Including the president. His advisors reminded him that he had had the gnole transferred from a backwater hospital to Walter Reed to put the creature in the limelight and form a positive association with it because tests had indicated that people empathised with the gnole – they *liked* it, naturally and right off the bat. Especially children. The hope was that an avuncular, protective public image toward the gnole would cause some of that good feeling to rub off onto the president, whose image could use a little good feeling after the Middle East fiasco. Well, events had far surpassed their hopes, and people didn't just *like* the gnole, they were demanding access to it as if Fungle were some sort of Constitutional privilege. Freedom of speech, freedom of the press, freedom to visit Fungle the gnole.

The crowd was getting a bit testy. Kids were asking beseeching questions, and their parents were getting bent out of shape that no answers seemed forthcoming. The protective image might backfire if America didn't get the ultimate talking dog and dancing bear bread-and-circus act it wanted – the show it *needed*.

Fungle had to appear on tee vee. The nation demanded it.

But who would carry the message?

White House negotiations with ABC, CBS, NBC, TBS, and Fox were like an international foreign-policy summit meeting. Closed doors, hard bargaining. 'The President of the United States does not sell television shows,' his press secretary harshly reminded those network executives attempting to outbid their competition. This wasn't the Olympics broadcast concession; this was *news*. Either the networks cooperated in delivering it to the people together (and everybody shared the wealth), or there would be no show (and nobody made nothing).

So: a two-hour extravaganza, a retrospective. An Event.

But who would conduct history's first interview with a non-human intelligence?

Closed doors and hard bargaining. Connie Chung, Barbara Walters, Dan Rather, Ted Koppel? Respectable, certainly; authoritative, without doubt. But every time anyone tried to imagine one of them interviewing something like a real live muppet, the image just didn't come off. The respectability, the authority was somehow eroded.

Carl Sagan? Stephen Jay Gould? Desmond Morris? Good scientists, great popularisers. But the ratings . . .

Letterman? Arsenio? Too trendy.

The press secretary slapped both palms on the thick-varnished table and stood. 'Gentlemen, ladies,' he said. 'We can throw names out all day and not get anywhere.' He looked around the meeting room. 'Let's try this: I'm going to describe what I think are the qualities we need in an interviewer for Fungle the gnole. What I want you to do is write down three people this description suggests

Discovery of the gnole has led to a boom in what has been termed 'archaeological hindsight', which has been wryly described as, quote, 'rarely myopic'! Representative figures and deities which were hitherto satisfactorily explained are suddenly being re-evaluated.

Mayan codex depicting Itzamna ('serpent people') and passenger fleeing 'deluge in the east'.

to you, and submit your suggestions anonymously before we break for lunch. Howard? Can you get us a shoebox, or something?'

Howard could.

'Fine. Now, as I see it, we need someone facile, someone able to work out of his depth like it's the most natural thing on earth,

Above: *Ceremonial heron plate from Mississippi basin, approx 300–100 BC.* Right: *Haniwa terracotta figure, Japan, c.300–600 AD. Evidence of post-diluvian colonisation.*

someone who can put a non-human at ease and dig deep for personal information while at the same time holding the affection of a potential audience of one billion viewers. We're looking for someone who can spot a gaffe coming, divert it, and recover quickly. Someone with history, someone with whom the audience

Above: *Pre-Columbian Aztec disk depicting goddess Coyolxauhqui. Note gnole 'familiar' amulet around her neck.*

Right: *Ipiutak (N. American) burial mask, bone carving, c. 350 BC.*

empathises every bit as much as they empathise with the gnole. Between the gnole and our interviewer there has to be chemistry, charisma and wit, as well as a deeply serious undercurrent. This person is going to be an ambassador as well as an interviewer, a host and diplomat as well as a personality. Ladies and gentlemen,

Osiris enthroned, from papyrus MS of Ani. Note kneeling figure on lower right, previously identified as 'minor dog deity'.

we're looking for someone who's an American institution unto his or her self.'

Fourteen pens scribbled on fourteen pads. Pages were torn from their adhesive bindings and placed into the ballot box. Everybody broke for lunch.

The press secretary smiled as he read the suggestions. The same

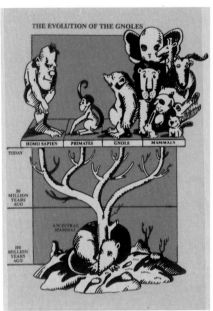

name was number one on nine of the fourteen suggestions, and occurred as number two or three on the remaining five. Apparently even the competition was forced to admit that only one person seemed to fill the bill.

When the network representatives returned from lunch and martinis, the press secretary smiled (a more official expression than his private smile) and informed them that they had all reached a decision. He told them who they had picked, and it was a sign of the winner's perfect appropriateness that even those who hadn't named him number one nodded reluctantly.

The press secretary called the president, who agreed with their decision. Both the president and his press secretary thanked each other sombrely for a job well done. The president hung up, giggled like a fool, and rubbed his hands briskly.

The press secretary gave the NBC executive a thumbs-up. The NBC executive grinned with an odd mixture of triumph and embarrassment as he picked up his cellular phone and called Hollywood, California, where he spoke at length with agents and lawyers representing Johnny Carson.

Karbolic Earthcreep was playing with his ant farm when Neema called out to him from across the cavern. Sometimes Ka watched the ants for hours, taking pleasure in their digging, their aimless efficiency. Sometimes he dropped in bits of fine, coloured glass, and over time the ant farm became an abstract mosaic of colours and pathways. He couldn't bear the thought of capriciously shaking the clear window, the way some people did, as if the ant farm were an Etch-a-Sketch drawn by living creatures for their amusement. No, life eradicated Ka's tunnels with similar capriciousness – which was why, when Neema's urgent voice cut across the cavern to him, he felt a stab of regret when he jerked, the tunnels collapsed, and ants boiled throughout their two-dimensional world.

He ran, clutching the ant farm, to where Neema pointed excitedly at the ghost machine. Ka saw nothing on the glass but snowy bits. At Neema's insistence the ghost machine was left on all the time now, which used up the bat-reez, which meant more pedalling on the bicycle that filled up the bat-reez, which meant more work for Ka since Neema's leg wasn't up to such exercise even though she seemed to stump around pretty well these days, thank you very much Mister Earthcreep, sir.

Around the easy chair and the ghost machine were piled pieces of the wrecked Lunabird. Neema had insisted they retrieve them once she was able to walk, and Ka had been unable to refuse her.

Neema could be difficult to refuse.

So now this end of the cavern looked as if some poor veterinarian, who had heard of birds but never actually seen one, were trying to put one back together. Wooden spars and struts were glued and bandaged and roped, pegged and re-notched and nailed, and in general reaffixed in any possible manner. After his griping about having to recover the smashed craft, Ka had tried to help Neema reassemble it, but Neema's own griping at his fumblesome efforts had made him leave her to her own devices. He supplied tools and bindings and replacement wood parts, and helped her hold things in place while she nailed them, and suchlike, but that was the extent of it.

She had a good bit of it put together, he had to admit. But if Ka had thought the craft was rickety before the crash, now he was as likely to fly in it as he was to sail to Tierra del Fuego in a laundry basket.

Ka held the ant farm before him like a flimsy shield. 'Whatcher screechin' 'bout now?' he demanded. 'Body can't get a moment's peace round here wiffout –'

'Fungle,' said Neema.

'Where? On the box?' He squinted at the ghost machine. A human male was drinking some kinda anaemic-looking ale on a beach while human females wearing not much at all cheered him on.

Neema nodded. 'Pitchers an' all. He's on there a lot now, Ka. I'm feared for him. He's –'

The picture fuzzed over but the sound cleared: '– *from our sponsors. Be sure to tune in Saturday, eight o'clock Eastern Standard Time, right here on this channel, as we bring you* live, *from Walter Reed Hospital in our nation's capital, history's first interview with Fungle the gnole! A two-hour worldwide special hosted by Johnny Carson. Don't miss your close encounter with Fungle the gnole!*'

'Saturday,' said Neema. 'That's two days, Ka.'

Ka looked grimly at the ghost machine. 'If them beasties've got holda him,' he said, 'there's no tellin' what mischief's up.'

'He can't carry on his mission,' said Neema. 'An' he told us there weren't much time.'

They glanced at one another. It held only a few seconds, but volumes of meaning were exchanged. Neema could see Ka thinking, *I am* not *gonna look at that loony-bird!* and Ka could see Neema thinking, *Oh, yes, you are!*

Before Neema resumed gathering Lunabird pieces to mend and reattach; before Ka sighed and resignedly removed the leather bag from around his neck, the bag that contained the magnetite crystal that powered the craft, one final thought parted their silent communion: *but there's really only one way for us to get there in time, isn't there?*

16 *Heeeeeeere's Fungle!*

They wanted him lucid for the broadcast, so they stopped filling his veins with the liquids that numbed his mind and took him away from his *self*. They limited him to a quart of ice-cream per day, any flavour he liked. Under pressure from the American Civil Liberties Union, Amnesty International, Greenpeace, the American Bar Association, People for the American Way, PEN, and – ironically – the American Society for the Prevention of Cruelty to Animals, by presidential decree a special *pro tem* passport that avoided specifying nationality was issued to Fungle Foxwit the gnole. Fungle was a citizen of the world, the president's main speech writer suggested to him, a nationless ambassador.

The president had mixed feelings about this.

Unaware of the vast whirlpool of media, political, commercial, and technical activity swirling around him, Fungle ate Ben & Jerry's Chunky Monkey ice-cream (the company had already tried to contact him about marketing a new all-natural flavour called Gnutty Gnole, or perhaps Fungleberry) and watched television. Nurses had taken to hanging out with him on duty and off; his charm was simply irresistible. They read the *TV Guide* to him, and explained the entries so that he could pick out programmes that seemed interesting. They brought him pictures to autograph for children, boyfriends, girlfriends, and pets; a baseball signed by the Yankees (who had unfortunately sweated out another mediocre season); smuggled scoops of cafeteria ice-cream; and the good wishes of the world. They told him how much their children loved him. They asked his advice for Fungle Hallowe'en costumes, for that holiday was imminent. They oohed and ahhed over the enormous flower arrangements sent by the president, Elton John, and Michael

Jackson, as well as those sent by other, lesser luminaries. It had not been long before there were more flowers and cards than Fungle's room could contain, and he had asked if they could be distributed among the patients at the hospital, young and old alike.

Even through the cloudy liquids in his veins that had fogged his brain, he could feel the fear and pain among hundreds of humans stacked like cordwood and arrayed in rows throughout the immense hive of the hospital, and the thought of easing that suffering even for a moment by giving beautiful flowers and well-wishing cards charged with the goodwill energy of children alleviated his heartache a fraction. He had also asked if he could visit the children's wing, but he had been refused. The night-shift nurses had conspired to smuggle him there anyway. They were caught gnole-handed in the halls one evening; the nurses were summarily fired and Fungle was returned to his oxygen tent *post haste*. The nurses were replaced by more taciturn medical aides with higher security clearances, but even these steel providers had eventually velveteened under Fungle's ingenuous charm and curiosity.

The doctors were another story. Where Fungle nodded at the nurses' soap-opera gossip and clucked sympathetically at poor life-affecting decisions made by the characters on daytime television, the gnole was totally unable to communicate with the straight-spined whitecoats who examined him. They chased the nurses from his room and impassively read the latest status reports on the lucite clipboard attached to his bed. They asked the nurses how he was feeling, but never Fungle himself. The only exceptions were the zoologists and animal behaviourists who tested him, and they merely cooed emptily as if he were a puppy dog.

He came to realise that they were afraid of him.

They were afraid of him because they were threatened by him.

They were threatened by him because scientists are people who live by the power of the mind, and throughout most of their history human beings have believed in the primacy of the human mind. Religious dogma and scientific doctrine held that the human mind is an entity unique in all the world, if not in all of nature itself. The mind of an ape is a clownish shadow; the mind of a dolphin is alien enough to be undemonstrable. What other mind existed by which to compare this pinnacle of evolution? None – until now.

So, it was easier for the more dogmatic among scientists and physicians to treat Fungle as an anomaly, a dancing bear – for 'the amazing thing about a dancing bear is not how well it dances, but that it dances at all.'

Clear-headed now, and with a sense of his history if not his mission gradually restored, Fungle did not try to win over these adherents to orthodoxy, these speciocentric inspectors. He could, he realised, use their blindness to his advantage.

On the television came a commercial for his interview with Johnny Carson. Nobody had bothered to actually tell Fungle he was going to be interviewed on the tee vee; lately he learned more about his status (and the difference between its depiction and reality) from the television than from any information acquired from the hospital staff. It seemed nobody took his television watching seriously. He appeared mindless and harmless watching television, no more capable of gleaning intelligence from it than those apes who are entertained by it.

Apparently humans had never watched themselves watching television.

So Fungle finished his ice-cream and beamed innocently at the nurse attending him and watched *The Tonight Show* starring Johnny Carson. He compared what he was slowly regaining of himself to what he heard about himself on the television. He also compared what he knew of human reality to what appeared on the television, and the huge gap between the two was the most informative of all.

Truth be known, Fungle delighted in television, every second of it – especially commercials. He knew that its incessant barrage was polluting his mind as surely as the humans themselves were polluting their world (*their* world – as if they had a bill of sale!). But television was like a spy that everyone knew about and so took for granted and ignored, giving it access to places in their lives and psyches they would never have given their closest loved ones.

From his bed in ICU 2 Fungle was a Lilliputian in the land of Gullivers, a Munchkin in a world of Dorothys. He looked, he listened, and he learned.

Johnny waived any fee for the Fungle broadcast but insisted that shooting take place at the familiar NBC studios in Burbank. But Walter Reed spokesmen (by now mouthpieces for government policy regarding Fungle the gnole) were adamant: the security risk was too great, and this was in no way to be construed as another episode of *The Tonight Show*, however special; other networks were carrying the show and had the right to prevent any display of network favouritism.

Two days before air time it was agreed that the interview would take place in Walter Reed's physiotherapy gymnasium, which would be converted for location shooting. Johnny, Doc, and a trimmed-down version of the band would fly from Los Angeles to Washington, D.C. The president would tape an opening salutation; the vice-president would be on hand to present Fungle with his special passport; there would be a brief documentary detailing what was known about the discovery, origins, and nature of Fungle and of gnoles in general; and then the interview would commence before a live audience.

The White House press secretary attempted to force a ten-second tape delay into the broadcast. Every network carrier threatened lawsuits for breach of First Amendment rights, claiming governmental pre-censorship. The Fungle show was *live*, it was *news*, and most important it was *live news*, and cutting a single word from it made it neither.

Further hamstringing the government, the networks then carried the tape-delay story as news. The press secretary hastily abandoned the effort to control the broadcast's outcome, however marginally.

The day of the broadcast arrived.

'Look, I dunno *how* it's s'posed to go in! I thought ya just shoved it into that thing's beak and it flew!'

They were just inside the entrance to the abandoned mine. The Lunabird faced the late afternoon like an ancient, arthritic pteranodon warming its brittle and soon-to-be-fossilised bones in the waning summer heat. Ka and Neema regarded the craft with varied expressions: Neema like a serious inventor who does not understand why her latest mousetrap has not caught a mouse, Ka like a museum spectator who has been told that the sheet of newspaper he is looking at was once a paper boat Thor Heyerdahl had sailed from Micronesia to Los Angeles to prove yet another theory.

The Lunabird's beak bit the magnetite crystal, which glittered in the late-afternoon light slanting through the tall firs. The vessel looked about as airworthy as a cow, though nowhere near as elegant.

'I don't know what else to do, Ka,' Neema confessed. 'If we don't get underway soon – well, who knows where Fungle'll end up after tonight? This is the only place we can say fer sure where an' when he'll be there.'

Ka frowned, scratched his head, rubbed his mottled jaw. He tugged the crystal from its mount in the Lunabird's beak and squinted at it in the sun. He turned the crystal upside-down and put it back in place. 'Y'think mebbe there's some magicalistic word makes it go?' Ka asked. 'Kind of a lock so's no one'll fly it who ain't supposed to?'

Neema stared at the crystal. 'It could be anything,' she fretted. 'A word, a phrase, a number. And if the crystal's in wrong, we could try 'em for ever and not know if we said the right one.'

Ka spread his hands. 'At's more yer speciality than me own,' he said. ''Bout the only magical-type words I know is *abracadabra* an' *allakazam*.'

The Lunabird began to creak.

Neema gaped at the craft, which was wavering uncertainly now as it strained against gravity. She turned her gape to Ka.

Ka gaped as well, but recovered quickly and shrugged philosophically. 'Nuffin' to it, really,' he said.

Neema set her hands on her hips. 'Well, even a blind squirrel finds an acorn sometimes,' she observed.

Ka ducked his head in chagrin.

The Lunabird slid across the dirt floor of the mine like a large balloon pushed by a vagrant breeze. Quickly Neema grabbed on to restrain it, and was pulled several feet along the floor for her efforts. Ka jumped to lend a hand, but the best both of them could do was slow the craft down. The bird-headed prow glared fiercely forward, as if determined to achieve the air despite the baggage that weighed it down.

'Make it stop!' ordered Neema.

'I dunno how I made it start!' shouted Ka.

The Lunabird was at the mouth of the mineshaft now. Ten feet farther on was a sharp dropoff.

'Well . . . climb aboard then!' said Neema.

The Lunabird nosed upward. A discouraging creaking came from the craft where Ka held the stern rudderlock in a deathgrip. Neema was already climbing into the pilot's seat.

Ka's feet dragged the ground. The Lunabird passed the dropoff, and Ka's feet dragged nothing. The gnome yelped and grabbed the edge of the passenger seat. The Lunabird tipped starboard and listed idly toward a stand of Douglas firs. Up front, Neema struggled with the oarlerons. The steering paddles resisted like oars in water as she banked left and pulled back to gain height.

They rose, but not high enough. Branches batted them as the Lunabird strained slowly through the gauntlet of trees.

Something tore loose.

Behind Neema, Ka sputtered and yelled as pine-needles stung along his backside. Whatever had torn loose caused the Lunabird to tilt to port and stay there. Neema thanked their lucky stars they were travelling so slowly – any faster and who knows what might have got torn loose from the Lunabird? Ka, f'rinstance.

Soon they were past the pines and rising above the timber line. Ka clambered aboard but did not strap himself in, for he needed to lie low in the passenger seat to hide from the deadly sunlight. The sun was on the horizon and he was probably safe, but until it was dark all around him Ka wouldn't take a chance; being turned to stone's not one of your more reversible processes. He hunched down behind and above Neema and began removing pine-needles from his clothing while cursing with admirable improvisation.

'Which way?' Neema called back.

'What?' Ka wrung a spider from his hand and the creature parachuted down.

'*Which way?*'

'Oh! Why, er, um . . . north-east!'

Neema turned back to eye the gnome suspiciously. 'You're *sure* you know where this place is?' she asked.

'Oh, wiffout a doubt,' Ka replied offhandedly. 'Got me a road atlas wif directions an' all.' He plucked a pine-needle from his patched pants.

Relieved, Neema turned forward, took note of their direction by those evening stars that always arrive early for the nightly party of luminaries, and grasped the oarlerons – then hesitated. 'Ka?' she called back uncertainly. 'Where exactly *is* your road atlas?'

'Why, it's in me cavern, Neema,' Ka replied confidently. 'Where else would I keep it?'

Shaking her head, Neema sighed.

Avoiding the view and her gaze, Ka settled back for a nap.

Hanging askew, the Lunabird ploughed on through the air.

'Okay, okay, okay – one more time. Gnole *boys*, line up here; gnole *girls*, line up *here*. Remember to look for your mark, and no talking before, during, or after we air. Your job is *atmosphere*, so circulate, look happy, make everybody feel good. Try not to scare any kids, try not to get your costume dirty or your head taken off. It's just like working at Disneyland, okay?

'All right, places everybody! Cue music! And *one* and *two* and –'

'– No no no! "Hail to the Chief" before we roll tape, no music at all while he's talking. Got it? All right.

'Can someone get that cable out of the frame? *Thank* you. Jerry, we got that acoustical tile coming in from double-u whatever it is? Well, it better get here soon; the sound in this room really bites. Sound bites, get it? Doc's gonna have a canary; it echoes like a bathroom in here.

'Okay, no . . . I thought we talked about this this morning, Eddie. I want *two* overhead spots, one on Johnny and one on the whatsits . . . I *know* it looks bare, but anything else is gonna look like we're broadcasting from a big ugly room fulla gear. This ain't a documentary, son, it's tee vee: we don't *want* it to look like what it is!

'Whassat, hon? Make-up? Hair? Christ on a rubber raft, how should *I* know? Look, they bathe him, don't they? I mean, he doesn't . . . you know . . . ? So we go *au naturel*. Look, the guy ain't selling Revlon here; just put him in that Robin Hood outfit they found him in and we'll run with it. If Johnny can handle being peed on by baby baboons from the San Diego Zoo, he can handle –

Close Encounters

by STEVEN R. BOYETT

Illustrations by Octavio Umberto

So I'm "backstage" at Walter Reed Hospital waiting to interview the biggest media sensation since the Beatles turned left at Greenland, and the first thought that comes to mind when the small furry creature enters the room is, *Great costume!* Is this what movies have done to us?

One of the everpresent guards blocks my way when I vie for a view. "No pictures," he says, and suddenly his pistol looks bigger than a moment ago. No problem: hotshot illustrator Octavio Umberto scribbles furiously while the Furred One displays an admittedly charming mixture of self-possession and unworldliness as he caroms around the room. There's a shoddy upright piano in a corner near the cheesy snacks. Seeing it, the Furry Phenom dashes to the bench and reaches up from a child's height to tickle the ivories. Great furballs of fire: this kid can *play!* But after only a few improv bars he stops and stares in frustration at his hands, which can't span greater than a fifth.

And then he's headed somewhere else, piano forgotten, before this prospective interviewer can get a line on him. His guard wears a Walkman on his belt. The seated man in the corner – who's so inconspicuously dressed that he *has* to be a Federal agent – straightens when the Gnole Wonder asks the

of the Furred Kind

guard if he can examine it.

Great Scott – that *voice!* It's sort of an Appalachian accent by way of Monty Python. This ain't no audio-animatronic!

The Walkman holds his interest only momentarily (perhaps further proof of his intelligence), and then he's off again. In the midst of getting himself . . . well, *groomed*, you'd have to call it, he catches sight of me

jotting away in my notebook. He frowns, leans forward, and points at me.

The migraine I've had all day disappears. He opens his mouth to say something, and the door opens and someone rushes in to tell him he has ten minutes before air time, everybody else out, please. Umberto throws me a worried glance and I shrug: we'll assemble this one *post facto*. The Media Mammal seems simultaneously befuddled and tickled by all the attentive hustle-bustle.

The guard – runner-up in the Saddam Hussein Mr. Congeniality Contest – ushers us firmly toward the door. In a last desperate attempt to ask *something* resembling an interview question, so that Umberto and I can justify our first-class air fare and the hotel room with the now-empty refrigerator, I holler: "Mr. Gnole – what do you think of our world?"

Without hesitation he calls back: "Oh, I don't think it's *yours* entirely." His tone, though chiding, is also friendly. As the door shuts he calls out, "An' if you'll stop drinkin' that vile brown liquid, yer headaches'll go away!"

An hour later he performs a miracle and floats Johnny Carson around a converted gymnasium. Even more miraculous, his ratings top the Super Bowl's.

Meanwhile, I've switched to decaf. ♪

'–Whassat? No, dammit: "Hail to the Chief" before we roll tape, and not a single solitary damn note while he's yapping away. Nothing! *Nada!* Zilch! *Capisce?*

'– Christ, I knew I shoulda kept my job in the mailroom. Okay: camera *two* –'

Every so often they would dip down low enough to read the freeway signs. WASHINGTON, in reflective white letters on green, followed by a number. The number kept getting smaller, so Ka figured they must be getting closer. At first they took precautions to prevent being spotted, but as time grew shorter they cared less and less. Most recently they had flown low enough to cause a traffic jam on I-95.

Despite their urgency, despite their preoccupation with not falling out of the air in the listing Lunabird, despite Ka's airsickness, Neema and Ka were overwhelmed by the sights and sounds and smells and sheer magnitude and busyness of the Land of No. The humans were *everywhere!* Who could have imagined? And not only were they everywhere, but wherever they were they announced their presence by altering the land to claim it indisputably for their own and evicting any non-human tenants – those not licensed and collared, anyway. Grass was something tamed in squared-off plots. Dwellings were differentiated by colour and little else.

Masses of beetle cars stampeded the concrete trails the way buffalo herds had once owned the Midwestern plains – but the buffalo had commingled with the land, and the automobile usurped it. In a sense the buffalo had vanished to make way for the automobile. Factories vomited smoke into the air and urinated waste into the water, mammoth infants spewing from either end. Rising heat from concrete plains trapped tainted air above the megalopolis. The smell made Ka and Neema nauseous.

From on high the Land of No was an enormous grid, as if to announce to all and sundry, *Nope! This didn't grow here! We built it!* As night fell it became hard to determine true north because the city light below bleached starlight above. Yet by night there was also something majestic about the Land of No, something timeless and ethereal. It was a glowing faeryland of motion and colour, stationary lights that contoured millions of lives, gliding lights in the air and along the ground. The Lunabird slipped among them like a spirit bird revered by a less hurried breed of humans who had lived in this very region only a few score decades ago when the land had been land and not something covering the land.

Neema and Ka wanted very much to rescue Fungle, but the farther into the Land of No they flew, the more they realised they were travelling through a realm beyond their understanding, and they were awestruck and very much afraid.

'Little Foot speaks! Stay tuned for history's most unusual interview! Thirty minutes from now!'

Fungle waited in something called 'the green room' (though it was white and not green at all). Beside him a doctor drank corrosive brown liquid from a red and white metal cylinder like those Fungle's friend Ka collected by the hundred. Fungle recalled finding such a cylinder on the day of his Equinox feast, the day that had started all of . . . what?

What was he in the midst of? What had been interrupted?

He could not remember.

He did recall that he had wanted to destroy the cylinder because it was a symbol of human encroachment on his pastoral world, but had saved it for Ka instead.

Ka . . .

Some things had come back to him. Slowly, surely. Who he was, where he was from. Names had returned: Ka, Neema, Musrum. Wisp, Froog, Peapod. A Parliament of Personages. He remembered them: their faces, merriment, sorrow, stories, departures.

But other names remained only words: Molom. Yanto. Theverat.

Baphomet.

Fungle shivered.

On a table against one white wall of the green room were cubes of cheese and slices of bread and meat speared by slivers of wood. People kept asking Fungle if he wanted anything to eat, probably just as an excuse to speak to him. He kept refusing. Fungle remembered the panicked warnings of the raccoon he had freed. *Face eaters.*

For some reason this recollection made Fungle realise that this was the longest time he had ever spent indoors. What would be happening back in his valley right now? Leaves turning sunset colours. Late afternoon naps, hammocking gently to the rhythm of the biting wind that thrilled the nerves but sent a premonition of winter along the spine. Fattening gnoles readying themselves for a long winter's –

The door opened and a man wearing spectacles appeared. 'Five minutes!'

The door closed. Outside it, Fungle sensed, stood two guards with death holstered at their hip.

The doctor glanced at Fungle. 'Nervous?' he asked nervously.

Fungle shrugged. All this busy-bee bustling may have been important to the humans, but that didn't make it important to him. And if it wasn't important to him, then what was there to be nervous about?

He sent his imagination out of the white green room, beyond the corridor with its guards holding sledgehammer death, beyond the building stacked with suffering, past the cities' directed fury, past the template geometries of greenery where every tree was a lucky tree because it was allowed to grow at all, beyond the dome of metropolitan light that bruised the sky. He arced the ballistic hummingbird of his imaginary self over the ragged mountains and into a carpeted valley, into the lush pupil in the eye of a placid lake, and beneath the ground where a dusty hearth lay cold and a larder lay rotting.

The door opened. 'Two minutes!'

Fungle had never felt so alone, so far from home.

'We interrupt our regularly scheduled programming to bring you the following special broadcast . . .'

Willaby Davis cursed the gas pump's mindless clicking. Normally he resented how quickly the numbers rolled upward, like the score on an amped-up pinball machine, but tonight the numbers weren't clacking fast enough. Tonight he was throttling the life out of the hose and impatient to get moving, because he'd forgotten to set the timer on his VCR and he was gonna be the only person in America who missed out on the broadcast –

'Er . . . beggin' yer pardon, sir.'

Davis frowned. It was a bum; you could tell by the gravelly voice trashed by roll-your-owns and cheap wine. A guy can't even pump gas anymore without getting hit up for change. He glanced around but saw no one. *Get a job*, he sent telepathically.

'Er . . . I wonder if ya might know the way to the Walter Reed Hospital?'

Davis looked up. The voice had come from behind the Supreme Unleaded pump. Accented. Not American, though. Davis grunted. *Least he speaks English.* 'Walter Reed Hospital?' Davis echoed. He squinted. Reflected in the burnished steel side of the pump he was using he saw the blurry, distorted image of the person to whom he spoke, crouched behind the next pump.

At least, he *hoped* the image was distorted.

The image moved. 'If yer in the way a knowin',' it said throatily.

'Uhhh . . . sure.' Hand still squeezing the pump, Davis leaned out for a better look. 'Stay on the 395 past the Capitol,' he said. 'I'd get off on . . . Massachusetts, and go left til I hit Scott Circle. Sixteenth Street runs smack into that; go right on Sixteenth and head north about five miles. You'll see the signs for Walter Reed; you can't miss it.' If he leaned out another six inches . . .

'Thankee, sir; much obliged.'

'You're quite welcome,' said Davis – and flinched as the figure darted away from the pump in an awkward stooped gait that revealed flashes of dwarfish proportion, mottled skin, long curved fingers, tiny black eyes, and an enormous nose.

It didn't look human.

Splashing brought him round. He was squirting gasoline on his dress shoes. He resumed cursing, slapped the cap back on the tank, shoved the hose into the pump, got into his BMW, and burned rubber.

In the sky above him wood creaked softly.

At 7:45 pm the Dancing Gnoles took their positions and performed a schmaltzy maypole dance number to the tune of 'Somewhere Over the Rainbow'. The audience ate it up, though, and after the Dancing Gnoles had bowed their short little bows they seeded themselves among the audience members in the bleachers, giving out candy and 'autographed' glossies of Fungle.

At 7:55 pm the band struck up Paul Anka's *Tonight Show* theme, and Johnny Carson walked onto the tiny stage erected in the physiotherapy gymnasium of Walter Reed Hospital. The crowd went wild. Johnny put his hands in his pockets and bowed, grinning his Boy Scout grin, then held up his well-manicured hands until the applause diminished to a drizzle. He was nattily attired in white and soft grey that showed off his deep Californian tan and bright blue eyes. Everyone in the audience was surprised how much Johnny looked like himself in person.

'Good evening,' he said with a perfect combination of smoothness and appreciation. 'Thank you. I gotta tell you, folks, I feel kind of naked up here without Ed to laugh at all my jokes . . .' the audience laughed '. . . but you see, we were a little short-handed coming out here, so Ed said he'd stop off and pick up drinks for us, and we haven't seen him since!' He waited while the laughter died down. Stage left, Doc imitated Ed's beefy guffaw. The director made a peace sign: two minutes. 'Seriously, though, I'm sure you're all aware what an historic broadcast this is, and before we air I just want to say . . .'

'Live from Walter Reed Hospital in our nation's capital, it's the Fungle the Gnole Special! Featuring history's first interview with Little Foot himself, Fungle the gnole! With your host, Johnny Carson! Special appearance by the President of the United States! And now . . . heeeeere's Johnny!'

In the green room Fungle watched the tee vee with mild interest. The picture changed from a shot of Fungle waving cheerfully from his hospital bed (a quart of Häagen Dazs cradled in one hand) to Johnny Carson performing his trademark tie adjustment in front of the cheering audience.

Fungle's interest grew keener. Something about the man intrigued him.

Johnny bowed and grinned and put his hands in his front pockets. 'No, it's not the Oscars,' he said. He indicated the minimal stage set. 'And no, the network did not cut our budget. What we have here tonight is a first, folks – for me, for television, and for the world. Tonight we're going to be talking face to face with Little Foot – Fungle the gnole.'

The applause was deafening.

'Now,' continued Johnny, enjoying himself immensely, 'if that name doesn't mean anything to you, you've probably been on vacation for the past few weeks – in the Bermuda Triangle. But in the meantime, the rest of America has been learning to Just Say Gnole.'

Another wave of cheering and applause.

Johnny slid his hand Napoleon-fashion inside a tailored lapel, grinning whitely at the joke. Fungle laughed appreciatively. 'Just say "gnole"!' he repeated. 'That be rich!'

'But in case you *have* been in the Bermuda Triangle,' Johnny continued, 'here's a little history.'

CUT TO:

FILE TAPE of a rundown shack in Northern Smoky Mountains.

JOHNNY

(*voice-over*)

This is where it all began — for
us, anyway — in a little mountain
shack outside Brasstown, Tennessee.

CUT TO:

FILE TAPE of LUELLEN MCCARDLE talking to reporter.

LUELLEN

Well, mah husband foun' him in a
ole springhouse one day? You know,
where people useta keep things cool
underground? Anyway, it was rat
before they put Delbert away fer
moonshinin'? An Bo-whampus —
that's what I calt him, Bo-whampus
— he'd fallen in an' hurt his hayd
somethin' awful, so we took care a
him 'til Sheriff Sturgill came
round —

Sheriff Sturgill appeared, looking beleaguered and just plain tired
in his office in Brasstown. Patiently, economically, like a veteran
telling an old war story, he explained how he'd learned of Little
Foot's captivity at the McCardles', how he'd 'liberated' the creature
from them, and how he'd brought him to the station for safekeeping.

'Where Ernie Scruggs,' continued Johnny's narration, 'took these
pictures . . .'

Fungle in the squad car . . . Fungle in the holding cell . . . Fungle's
mug shot, which got a sympathetic laugh from the audience . . .
Fungle bustled off to the VA hospital in Asheville . . . Interview
with doctors . . . Thronging press members crowding the hospital
. . . Sound bites from scientists . . . Boarding an airplane . . . Waving
from his hospital bed in ICU 2 at Walter Reed . . . Protests from
civil-interest and animal-rights groups . . . Fungle watching *The
Muppet Show* . . . Headlines: *Littlefoot Speaks!* And a group of
beaming schoolchildren holding an enormous banner: We♥U
FUNGLE!

Funglemaniacs.

Fungle noticed that there was no mention of the endless debilitating tests, of the mind-numbing drugs, of too little sleep or too much, of grinding physical examinations and wearisome cognitive and psychological evaluations.

The door opened once more and the man with the spectacles stuck his head in. 'Mr Gnole?' he asked. 'I need to lead you out; you're on in less than one minute.' After ten years with the Carson show, he wasn't the slightest bit fazed at speaking to Fungle. Ah, Hollywood.

Fungle got up. The doctor accompanied him. They acquired several armed guards as they walked the short length down the white corridor to the physiotherapy gym. Fungle touched his wishing cap for luck and set a hand on the briar rose tucked into his cleaned and pressed tunic – the rose given him by Neema, a rose in expectation of his return. From where? Again that sensation of having his mission right there on the tip of his tongue.

'Your cue is "Somewhere Over the Rainbow,"' said the man with the glasses. 'When the band starts playing, we'll open the door and ·you'll head straight to the empty chair next to Johnny. Okey-dokey?'

'Okey-dokey,' Fungle agreed.

The man seemed surprised, then smiled. 'It's gonna be great,' he said. 'Break a leg!'

'I should hope not!' Fungle replied, and touched his wishing cap.

The landing was less than perfect, but even gnole philosophy held that any landing you walked away from was a good one. Neema scraped a good half-inch of wood off the port side as the Lunabird slid across the top of a parking structure across the street from Walter Reed Hospital. The frail craft fetched up against the backside of a battered 1970 Chevy Nova.

Ka bailed out before they stopped moving. He hit running, vaulted over the trunk of a Volvo, and crouched behind it as if expecting an explosion. Slowly his hands appeared over the edge of the car, then the top part of his face, a gnomish Kilroy drawing. 'Well,' he said conversationally, 'that were choice.'

Neema glanced sourly from the pilot's seat. 'If ya don't like my flyin',' she said matter-of-factly, 'then next time you can take yer hand at it, Mister Earthcreep.'

'Now, Neema,' said Ka, rising and going to the embattled Lunabird to help Neema down, 'I never said that.' She took his hand and stepped onto the concrete. 'We's here, ain't we?' he finished brightly.

Neema looked around. 'We certainly is,' she said forebodingly.

The night was bright and the light was strange, pale-orange eyes on slender metal stalks like alien nightglowing plants. Multiple shadows spread, or none at all. Kamikaze moths battered glowing lamp globes. The dynamo thrum of motors, machinery, factories – of the *city* – saturated the moist oily air like the deadly purr of a godlike cat.

They approached the edge of the parking structure and looked out. They were silent a moment, scarcely breathing, then Neema said, in a small voice, 'In all my days.'

Ka nodded mutely.

The hospital was enormous and all lit up. On the city streets around the massive building traffic was at a standstill. Car horns honked. Dish-antenna vans and trucks with network logos were parked in every available space and then some; Ka recognised the omniscient eye of CBS from his ghost machine. A luminous Shell Oil sign rotated creakily on its pole. In the air beyond it a helicopter cut air like a metal hornet.

'Ka,' whispered Neema, 'oh Ka, what're we doin' here?'

Ka shook his head in fearful agreement, then stopped. He slapped the concrete riser resolutely. 'We's here ta rescue Fungle!' he said, 'an' all this –' he waved at the overwhelming bright bustle surrounding them '– don't signify.'

Neema nodded. 'You're right.' She tore her gaze from the alien vista and smiled at Ka, the true and friendly and somewhat abashed smile that sometimes peeked through her gruff exterior. She clapped a hand on his shoulder. 'And so we shall, good gnome.'

'Terrific, says I, an' ready as I'll ever be,' said Ka, feeling bolstered and all fired up. He clapped his hands and rubbed them eagerly. 'So what's our plan?'

The Fungle retrospective ended and Johnny returned, rocking back and forth with hands clasped in front of him. 'Ladies and gentlemen,' he said, and gestured with one hand, 'the President of the United States.'

The president sat at his desk in the Oval Office, the Presidential Seal like a hex sign before him, American flag behind. He smiled tiredly. 'Fellow countrymen. Fellow *humans*. Tonight marks a very special occasion for all of us. Since man first acquired the ability to wonder, we have asked whether we are alone in the universe:

if there are minds out there other than our own. We have built telescopes and written fanciful novels, and even left our footprints on the surface of the moon, because we wonder. And little did we know that, all the while we were casting our nets of curiosity outward, searching for a bottle in that lonely ocean, another mind shared this earth with us. As a character in a favourite movie of mine once said, "Sometimes you don't have to look any farther than your own back-yard."

'And now, tonight, we cross a line. A demarcation separating solitude from companionship. Because tonight, for the first time since humanity has asked that ancient question, we – as a nation, as a world, as a *species* – shall converse with an intelligence, a spirit, that is not human. We shall forever be the generation that witnessed the glad crossing of that line, the first human beings to know beyond the shadow of a doubt that we are *not* alone in our ability to wonder.

'Therefore, it is with great eagerness that I shall watch my television set tonight, along with more than a billion other human beings, and with great hope that we and the race known as gnoles may teach and learn from one another. Fungle the gnole, I bring you the greetings and hopes of America and of the world.'

The president leaned back, suddenly informal, and grinned boyishly. 'And now – I've always wanted to do this – heeeeeere's Johnny!'

Johnny was elated. The thunderous applause took nearly a full minute to die down, and Johnny rode it like a lifelong surfer. 'Well, folks,' he said ingenuously, scratching his head. 'Please welcome . . . Fungle the gnole.'

The band struck up a jazz rendition of 'Somewhere Over the Rainbow'. They were only marginally louder than the audience. The door opened and Fungle was led in by the security guards, who accompanied him to the edge of the audience and then hung back, professionally eyeing the room. Fungle strode confidently to the small stage, where Johnny stood grinning like a kid on Christmas morning. Johnny extended a hand, which Fungle shook in both of his. Both bowed, and Johnny indicated the chair to his right. The music ended just as Fungle hopped in and sat with legs crossed tailor-fashion, looking for all the world like a woodland Buddha. He squinted in the harsh light and surveyed the crowd uncertainly, then broke into a broad smile and waved.

The audience waved, hooted, clapped, stomped, and shrieked carnival shrieks. Johnny slowly shook his head like a man reviewing a pleasant dream. He glanced at Doc, who shrugged with his glittering trumpet as if to say, *Well, now I've seen it all.*

The applause ebbed. Fungle was staring straight up at the overhead boom mike. Johnny leaned forward in his chair. 'Fungle –'

The crowd went crazy. The chant was taken up: Fun-*gull!* Fun-*gull!* Fun-*gull!* Johnny leaned back in his chair. 'Well, *I'm* not gonna fight the weather,' he said.

Fungle glanced at him, startled. 'Arguin' with the weather only makes ya wetter,' he said.

The applause swelled. Johnny held his hands up. 'Folks. Folks. It's only a two-hour show!' he protested good-naturedly.

They screamed, they clapped, but finally they relented.

Johnny turned to face his unprecedented guest. 'Ahh . . . what is it I should call you?' he asked.

Fungle eyed Johnny appraisingly. There was something about this human he liked, something difficult to put his finger on. 'Why, I beez Fungle Foxwit the gnole, o' the race o' gnoles,' said Fungle. 'Foxwit's me clan fer ages gone, an' Fungle's me given name fer longer than I care to think.' His eyes twinkled.

Johnny's brow furrowed as he untangled Fungle's unusual way of speaking. 'Fungle Foxwit, then,' he ventured.

Fungle beamed and thumped himself on the chest. 'That's me,' he said.

Feeling foolish, Neema walked along the sidewalk surrounding the hospital. She felt Ka watching her from the roof of the parking structure across the street, where he had stayed behind to guard the Lunabird.

There was no way to sneak up to the hospital. This wasn't the forest; bushes to hide behind were few and far between, and of little use when it came to going in by any door. Add to that the dangerous-looking humans with their dark uniforms and wide leather belts holding shiny weapons that contained lethal potential like a slumbering nest of hornets, along with the fact that Neema's leg was splinted and she did not look passably human even in dim lighting, and one did not arrive at an equation for stealth.

She rounded a corner and saw a boxy awfulmobile with flashing red lights parked before a red sign that said EMERGENCY. There was a lot of hustle and bustle, and she felt the pain of the bleeding human being unloaded from the back of the flashing automobile on a narrow wheeled bed. This was a hospital, after all, and people were in need of healing whether or not there was a special broadcast emanating from here. Perhaps she could slip in amid the confusion of the Emergency entrance.

She was secretly glad that Ka had stayed behind to guard the Lunabird. His magnificent tunnelling talents were of little value in this land of concrete and steel, and Ka looked even less human than she did. And besides, the gnome was not the subtlest creature in the field.

She fought down panic as she approached the Emergency entrance.

She wouldn't have tried this at all if she hadn't seen the group of gnoles enter the building by the front entrance. She had been furiously stumping about the roof of the parking structure, trying to ignore the smells of gasoline and oil, thinking of a way to get into the building, locate Fungle, and get him out without landing all of them in a zoo somewhere, when Ka had called her to the edge. 'Have a lookit this,' he whispered, and pointed down to the hospital. She had been startled to see a group of half-a-dozen gnoles walk up the entranceway bold as brass, wave to the guards, and go inside like they was gonna report in sick. She had only been fooled for a moment – though it had been a shocking moment, to say the least – before she realised that these were human beings dressed up like gnoles. What on earth for? Well, it had something to do with Fungle, you could bet your tea-leaves on that.

But seeing the ersatz gnoles waltz merrily into the hospital had given her an idea, and now here she was, swallowing her heart and nodding stiffly at the guard posted by the Emergency entrance. The guard's expression did not change (his face seemed so *hard*!) as his appraising eyes tracked her. She tried not to look at the dull metal death holstered near his hand.

'Hey, you!'

She stopped. *Don't run, don't run.* She turned. The guard was on his feet. Stepping toward her. His hard shoes made a terrible sound on the concrete. He was so *tall*.

'You guys were supposed to be in there twenty minutes ago!'

'I . . .' Neema swallowed the ragball in her throat. 'The human, er, the man at the front, he wouldn't let me in, y'see, an', why, if I'm late there's to be all kinds of trouble for everybody.'

'Got your pass?' asked the guard.

'Me pass?' Neema had no idea what the human was talking about. She put her hands on her hips, unconsciously mimicking the guard. 'An' where else would I be goin' dressed up like this?' she demanded. 'To kidnap Fungle, y'think?'

'All right, all right; don't get your panties in a twist. You can go in this way, but you better hurry. I think they already started.' He shook his head. 'Me a hundred yards away from the whole mess, an' I don't get even a peek. Like selling peanuts at a ball game, ya know? Don't get to see a thing.'

Neema nodded, completely at sea. 'Thankee kindly,' she said quickly, 'I kin find me way from here.' She hurried as best she could into the Emergency entrance and out of sight.

The guard knocked back his hat and frowned. 'Method actors,' he swore, and resumed his vigil.

Johnny twirled his yellow No.2 pencil in both hands. 'Fungle, ahh . . . we know so little about you. It seems inconceivable, but your people and mine are strangers to one another, really.'

Fungle nodded sagely. 'Naturally we's strangers to each other,' he said. 'We's strangers to ourselves.'

Johnny considered this. 'Well, I guess the simplest thing is to begin at the beginning and ask where you're from.'

Fungle looked surprised. 'Why, I'm from me mum, same's ever'body weren't growed from a seed. Where be you from, Mister Carson?'

The audience laughed, and Johnny seemed faintly flustered, not sure if his leg was being pulled. 'Well, I'm from Iowa,' he chuckled, 'and I'm in a much more different world now than you are, I can tell you.'

Fungle laughed, happy that his blitheness had served its purpose and distracted from the original intent of the question. He did not want humans knowing where gnoles lived; he had no desire to fly in an airplane over his people's homes someday and look down on that same lighted grid that had greeted his arrival here. 'But if yer asking where me *people* beez from,' Fungle continued smoothly, 'we be descended from them that fled the sinkin' o' fair Atlantis.'

The crowd murmured. Carson's jaw hung. 'Atlantis?' he repeated incredulously. 'Atlantis the *continent?*'

'No more,' replied Fungle.

'But, but . . . that's just a myth!'

Fungle merely smiled a bit smugly, and reached out to take Johnny's hand. He set the man's fingers against his own shoulder and made him pinch. 'So'm I, Mr Carson,' said Fungle. 'So'm I!'

*

'Excuse me. Yo!'

Ka turned away from the edge of the parking structure. A human was waving to him. Ka glanced around for someplace to run.

The man – his hair was so long it took a moment for Ka to realise it *was* a man – indicated the Lunabird fetched up against the battered green car. 'You wanna move your carnival ride so I can get my car outta here?'

'Me carnival ride . . .? Er . . . certainly, sir,' said Ka. Trepidantly he approached the human, who wore a long grey coat with a dozen airline-pilot wings pinned down the right lapel, incredibly tight black pants, leather boots hung with silver chains, and a different silver earring in each ear. 'Sorry to've . . . inconvenienced yer,' Ka added.

'No problem,' said the man. 'I just want outta here before that circus lets out.' He indicated the hospital across the street.

Ka nodded uncertainly. Not taking his eyes off the man, he grabbed the Lunabird and tugged. Wood creaked but the craft wouldn't move. Ka tried again and it slid an inch or two, but no more. The human tossed his Daffy Duck keychain onto the hood of the beat-up Nova and gave Ka a hand. Together they lifted the Lunabird and carried it out of the way of the parked cars.

'Er . . . much obliged,' said Ka.

The man merely waved. Ka could only stare as he unlocked his car, got in, started it up, and backed out. The window slid down. 'Say,' said the long-haired man, 'don't you get hot in that thing?' He pointed at Ka.

Ka glanced down at himself, confused. Suddenly he understood: the man thought he was wearing a costume! He looked up again and grinned. 'Oh, ya gets useta it,' he said.

The driver nodded. 'Well, have a good one,' he said. He waved and drove away. Ka waved back.

Neema was afraid to think. If she thought – about where she was, what she was trying to do, what strangeness and suffering surrounded her – she might go insane. Everyone here was a *human*! They were everywhere; she felt like a mouse at a cat convention. Except that the cats treated her like a cat dressed like a mouse: they assumed she was one of the dancers dressed in a gnole costume. Twice they had even given her directions when she'd mounted up the courage to ask. One had even joked about her splint.

Now she headed down a white corridor and knew she was getting close because of the increase in security guards.

Behind her came clacking sounds. 'Make way, make way!' called a voice. Neema turned to see a gurney being pushed quickly along the corridor by a very dark human dressed in white. There was a great deal of thick hair between his nose and his upper lip; Neema stared at it.

On the gurney was a man. He held a hand against his head and moaned. Red glistened beneath his palm.

Neema hugged the wall as the gurney hurried past. Ahead of her a door opened and a group of gnoles emerged.

'Fungle!' Neema called without thinking.

They all turned to look at her.

'I have to tell you, Fungle, your English is very good, especially for someone who's only been with humans – what? Two, three weeks now?'

'Why blez ya, Mr Carson, an' thanks, but this be the language I learnt at me pa's knee, an' I've spoke it all me life.' Fungle grinned mischievously. 'But, hey, dude,' he said in perfect Malibu surf-ese, 'I've learned some bitchen stuff from MTV!'

Johnny laughed so hard he turned purple. He wiped his eyes and chuckled a few more times, then said, 'Well, do you mind if I ask how old you are?'

'What's ta mind?' asked Fungle. 'This earth's taken me body round the sun ten dozen times now, an' I'm lookin' forward to as many more.'

'Ten dozen – *a hundred and twenty?*'

Fungle nodded.

'Boy, I'd hate to light the candles on *your* cake!' Johnny shook his head in wonder. 'That's incredible,' he said.

''Tweren't nothin' at all,' Fungle said modestly.

Johnny set a hand to his forehead, astonished. 'Can you tell our audience, Fungle, what your, um, *station* is among your people? What sort of position you occupy, or . . .'

'Why, that I can, Mr Carson, an' a pleasure, too, since I've not seen its like among yerselves. Among me own people an' to the forest large I'm a mage an' shaman, skilt in the arts o' magick an' secret alchemickals, ancient formulae fer summonings, healings, sowings, an' whatever else may be of service to all an' sundry. I converse wi' spirits an' consult wi' dreams, an' consort wi' everything that lives an' breathes in me homelands.' Something about this description of himself tickled Fungle's memory, his hazy sense of a forgotten *mission*.

The room was silent. Johnny's brow knitted as he unravelled this statement. 'Am I to understand that you're a kind of . . . witch doctor?' Johnny asked slowly.

'Why, I'll doctor anyone who needs it,' said Fungle.

Everyone laughed.

'I'm still not clear,' Johnny persisted. 'Are you saying you're a magician?'

'If ya mean do I yank bunnies from bowlers ta keep kids agiggle, the answer's no,' said Fungle. 'Them's tricks and foolery. I be a mage an' shaman, wise in lore an' spells older than yer people's oldest buildings.'

The room was quiet.

'Magic fer good,' stressed Fungle, 'magic fer growth. Magic fer healin' an' buildin', an' never fer tearin' down – 'less it's ta save another thing.' This niggled at Fungle as well. The mere act of speaking about himself, about his people and beliefs, was freeing memories that related to his purpose, his mission.

Johnny appeared hesitant. 'Fungle,' he began, 'my people have always believed in science, and that –'

'Always?' inquired Fungle.

Johnny frowned. 'Well . . . for the past . . . I don't know . . . four, five hundred years?' He looked up at the bleachers. 'Help me out here, folks!'

'But ya don't believe in magic,' finished Fungle.

'Well, *some* people do,' Johnny said, a bit defensively, 'but mostly –'

'So if yer sick,' Fungle persisted, 'an' I wave some herbs over ya an' say a coupla dusty ol' words, an' ya get better – that's magic?'

Johnny considered. 'Sounds like magic to me,' he admitted.

'But iffin I push a button an' ya get better – then it's science? Even if ya don't know how that button works?'

'Uhh . . . I see your point,' Johnny conceded.

Fungle held out his clasped hands. He felt *centred* again, at last, here at this hub of attention and concentrated energy; body, mind and spirit united once more, undiluted and unsegregated by the absence of drugs. 'Yer people have fergotten 'bout buttons they ain't made theyselves, or else they don't trust 'em,' continued Fungle. His look became knowing. 'But there be many kinds o' buttons in the world, Mr Carson.'

'I don't understand, Fungle,' said Johnny.

'Buttons that fix things,' explained Fungle, 'that contain power an' healing an' qualities that put a body in touch with the earth – they's everywhere in the world. It just takes half a life o' trainin' to learn how to press 'em. Usin' a plant an' a couple o' words to mend a leg be no more "magickal" than usin' a black liquid to drive one o'yer oughtamobiles, or usin' a heavy metal from the earth to burn down a city.'

The audience murmured surprised agreement.

'Me own people be in touch with these things still, Mr Carson, but yers ain't no more.' Fungle smiled a bit sadly and tapped his forehead. 'Ya done got too smart. Ya don't trust a button ya ain't made yerself. Everythin' about ya denies that it's as much a part o' the world as a bird or a dog or a spider. Even mosta yer religions separate ya from nature at yer very roots.' He raised his arms to indicate the studio. 'Why, just look around yer!' he exclaimed. 'Yer houses, yer cars, even yer clothes, all separate the animal *man* from the animals, from the world of animals.'

'In school,' Johnny said over the muttering of the crowd, 'I was always taught that one of the most special qualities of human beings is their – is *our* – adaptability.'

This met with a small round of applause. The humans' sensitivity on this issue did not escape Fungle, and he struggled to phrase himself in a way that would not alienate his audience. 'Mr Carson, me own pa travelled through this area not two hundred years ago,' said Fungle. 'An' it were trees an' brooks, an' red-skinned humans livin' among 'em same as every other animal in the forest.' Again Fungle indicated the studio. 'What've you adapted to here?' he asked.

Johnny was silent, considering.

'Ya've fergotten the *land*,' continued Fungle. 'Somehow ya've come to believe that nature's your rival, to be defeated and controlled, tamed an' occupied. The earth's a livin' organism, a body like yer own. If ya treat your body with respect, it'll live longer. An' it's the same with the earth. Ya wipe out insects with no thought that there's more a them than there be o' you, an' ya haven't an inkling that they can live without you, but you can't live without them. Even when ya set out to explore the land, ya take yer homes with you on wheels, an' ya travel to another place where there's buildings an' televisions an' such, an' ye've no conception anymore of the awesome wonder of what it's like ta be *lost* in the world. But inside ya – all yer art, yer books an' poetry an' movin' pitchers an' tee vee – all of it screams: *I'm lost! Can ya hear me out there?* An' who's listenin'?' Fungle shook his head sadly. 'The lost,' he said, 'lost at home.'

He leaned forward in his chair, staring intently at Johnny. 'Ya know, Mr Carson, I'm hearin' meself speak now, and I'm soundin' a bit harsh. But in a very real way, I can't tell where *I* end an' the world begins. An' you useta be the same –' Fungle's gaze took in the audience, the television cameras – '*all* of ya useta be this way.' He tapped his head. 'But this got stronger.' He curled his fingers before him. 'An' these got smarter, too – in some ways smarter than yer heads. And that's the problem in a nutshell. You geezers gone all technillogical over these past few years. An' technology means progress, an' progress with you blokes is measured by improving yer creature comforts. Now these creature comforts – tee-vees, fuelish automobiles, toasters, frigiderators, jakoozees – they're all closing of yer senses, narrowing yer perception of life, of Mother Earth. And the more yer senses atrophy, so yer eyes, ears, nose, tongue, body need artzyficial inducements and pleasures – and that means more technology. Fact is, you've just about lost the plot! Why, when I sees a nourishing finger of sunlight poking through the leaves of me forest, I says a little prayer of thanks, p'raps offer a flower to the spirits who guide all things on this planet. And what does the sun represent to you folks; you worry what coat to wear or what sun tan lotion to splash all over yerselves.' He fixed Johnny with a gentle but penetrating gaze. 'But those ancient senses be still deep in there, Mr Carson. Beneath yer subways an' concrete an' cars, beneath yer clocks an' clothes an' quick meals an' howlin' jets, there's that *connection* to the world. Remember? There's an older self inside there that knows better'n all this surroundin' ya, that remembers not knowin' where the world stops and the *you* starts. Remember? Remember . . . ?'

Remember. Remember . . .

Johnny started to reply, to defend himself and his race, to explain that humans had recently become aware of the damage they had caused and were taking steps to fix it. But the words never left his brain. His blue eyes were held by the swelling black pools of Fungle's own gaze, and his mind was lulled by the accented words, *remember, remember, remember.* Johnny felt himself growing large – or, no, he felt himself plunging, sinking deep within his *self*. Past a thin forebrain layer of civilisation, past memory associations of cognition and guilt, toward that most basic nub of reptilian function: of breathe and eat and sleep, mate and fight and run. He approached this most ancient component of being, but he did not arrive there. Instead he found himself suspended in the Eden that dwells below cognition, below judgement, yet above those most autonomic functions of existence. It was an area of simple *being*, of recognition without judgement – and it was a place Johnny recognised. *Yes, oh yes, I have been here, I have lived here, it lives inside me.*

He ascended layers of his self like a bubble rising to the world. He opened his eyes.

The physiotherapy gymnasium began to fill with water. It rose from the floor as if the room itself were sinking like a ship. A deep rumble shook Johnny's bones. The audience in their bleachers did not move; the red eye of the camera did not wink; Fungle the gnole would not release his gaze. Johnny felt no panic as he watched the room fill with water and smelled the salt, smelled the ocean, smelled the primal stew of ancestral origins welling beneath him, warm as blood, wetting his clothes, releasing memories as old as memory itself.

The audience . . . *changed*. As the water rose they *elongated*; their arms consolidated with their bodies; their hands protruded and their fingers fused to become flippers. Flesh grew sleek and grey, bodies curved, jutting snouts smiled. They arced into the water.

The sky was blue enough to break your heart.

Deep within his brain Johnny felt the pull, the siren song. He did not struggle as the water rose above him, as his body grew dense and heavy and fused, as parts of his brain that once controlled hands and feet now moved flukes and flippers.

Bobbing on the surface of the sea he took a last breath from the hole in the top of his well-padded head, and was amazed at how long and deep a breath his transformed lungs could draw.

He dove.

He had a third eye. He could not see with it; it was not a *visual* eye. It sent out a high-pitched sound that returned to him the shape of his world. The shape, the flavour, the texture. Around him he sensed the undulating forms of the other dolphins. He saw and felt and heard them, all with his newfound sense, his third eye. And they called out to him as well with their third eyes, and when they called he received a picture as well as a sound, a music that was both and neither speech and sight.

He swam.

His body generated a boundary layer warmer than the water around him, a laminar flow that allowed him to slide like mercury through the sea. He waggled feet and hands but flukes and flippers responded and sent him down, coldly down below the light. The ocean bottom stretched below and before him like a contour map.

He was aware of the other dolphins' joyous swimming around him, of the frontier of the surface like a rippling mirror above him, of his connection to other dolphins like limbs of his self, of the connection between land and sea, air and water, that he represented, the way a tree connects the earth and sky. He was aware of his connection to . . . to *everything*.

He could not tell where *he* ended and the sea began.

Distant forlorn songs brought him short in the deep pressure. Eddies of his motion passed him. Huge booming sounds washed over him, sad soulful notes in a wise and ancient music. These were the million-year-old tribal lays of his cousins the whales resounding along the ocean floor for hundreds of miles, unhindered by growling engines or churning screws. Poetry, histories, the changes of currents and birth of reefs, abstract mathematical formulae, and songs that were simply and beautifully *songs* and nothing else, notes that said *I'm here! And this is what I feel!*

He swam.

Bursting with whalesong he raced for the undulating glassy frontier of the surface, rising toward the light just as he had bubbled up from ancient layers of his brain, shedding cold behind him. He plunged into the air like an Olympic diver twisting off a high platform. As he arced and spun he blew stale air hot from his lungs and breathed in cool. His broad tail passed above his head, flaunting at the heartbreak sky. Below him licked the froth of waves. As he fell toward the water again his brothers shot into the air around him, a perfect circle perfectly timed. They arced inward like broad metal blades curling into the water just as he struck. Bubbles tickled along his sleek body, glassy explorers from another world.

Johnny swam.

Among the millions watching the broadcast were the hard men, the shadow men, men to whom emotions were data and wonder a tool. They worked in shifts, they drew a cheque, they had homes and families and dogs and cats. They wore small speakers the size of earplugs and worked in innocuous buildings, in tiny and isolated booths, in darkened rooms bleached with purple light from television screens, and from there they monitored the world.

On half-a-dozen screens in half-a-dozen isolated booths, on a small stage before a live audience and the world at large, Johnny Carson writhed and gasped and bucked at the feet of the creature known as a gnole.

Half-a-dozen medium-priority buttons were pressed.
Half-a-dozen throat microphones were activated.
Half-a-dozen voices reported to half-a-dozen faceless superiors. 'I think you'd better have a look at this,' they said.

The audience gasped. Security men hurried forward, hands straying towards holsters. Fungle held his hands high, letting them know that it was all right, that Johnny was all right.

The guards hesitated. The audience murmured. Fungle remained seated, watching Johnny writhing on the floor. Camera one zoomed in on Johnny's face.

He was smiling.

After less than a minute the strange undulations subsided and Johnny's eyelids fluttered open. The smile remained. Johnny sat up, gasping, and flailed out a hand. Fungle caught it and steadied him. Johnny said 'Whoa!' and 'Oh!' and 'God!' and 'Hoo!' He let Fungle help him back into his chair, where he sat breathing heavily. His cheeks were flushed and his eyes were bright. A dolphin grin spread across his face.

His tie hung askew. For the first time in public memory, he made no move to fix it.

He looked at Fungle. Nobody would know it for several days, but what Johnny was feeling was not anger or fear of embarrassment – Johnny was feeling disappointment. For a few brief seconds he had been free. Unconstrained, unfettered, unanchored by schedules and ratings and the thousand constant, niggling worries of maintaining a celebrity life. He had swum in a euphoric dream of unrestrained liberty, had wallowed in the primal stew of humanity itself, and now he was awake. But it would be obvious later, and, indeed, for the rest of his life, that some echo of that vision had remained with him.

Right now, though, all he could do was stare at Fungle in wonder and stammer, 'That, that, that . . . that was *real*!' His brow furrowed. 'Wasn't it?'

Fungle chuckled. 'Real!' he exclaimed, and shrugged.

Johnny laughed too, as if they shared a private joke.

Still laughing Fungle closed his eyes and set his hands in his lap.

Slowly his body lifted from the chair.

The audience gasped and applauded. By now all Johnny could do was lean back and laugh at the mystery and marvel of it all. Fungle hung serene before him and all the world. 'Remember,' the gnole said again.

Johnny was still laughing when he felt a fluttering sensation in the pit of his stomach, like the drop of a high-speed elevator, and felt himself becoming oddly hollow-seeming. He looked down and saw that he was floating above his own chair.

Fungle was watching him. Later Johnny would remember the expression on his father's face the first time little Johnny wheeled his bicycle unaided. Cautious, ready to catch him should he fall, but pleased. Fungle held out a hand, and Johnny giddily accepted it. The two of them floated around the room, giggling like amateur fakirs who couldn't believe they were getting away with their tricks. Later Johnny would tell reporters that, 'It was just like those dreams where, if you hold yourself in a certain position, or remember certain words, you can fly. Except it wasn't a dream: I was awake, and *I remembered the words!*'

Fungle let go Johnny's hand and Johnny took the opportunity to cavort, slowly floating around the room, bending his elbows to flap his arms like a chicken, waving to Doc, buzzing the cameramen, barnstorming the crowd, and in general frolicking like – well, like a dolphin.

Finally he rejoined Fungle above the stage, and their hands met once more, and they lowered until they stood before their chairs and a tsunami of applause. They shook hands and bowed to one another, Fungle cherubic and Johnny looking for all the world like a child version of himself. Joyous tears glistened in his eyes.

Johnny held his hands up for silence. It was slow coming. Finally the crowd noise subsided enough for him to speak. 'Folks,' he said, beaming, 'after that, the only thing I can say is – we'll be right back!'

Half-a-dozen supervisors called the same general within thirty seconds of one another. After the first call the general expressed surprise and interest; after the sixth he merely picked up the dedicated line, said, 'I'm on it,' and hung up.

The general went to another phone. 'DPR,' he said tersely. 'Get Crucifer on the line.' The general waited, counting silently to himself: One Mississippi two Mississippi three Mississippi. *If he got to thirty and Crucifer wasn't on the phone, he was gonna start chewing some new –*

'This is Crucifer.'

'You watchin' the tee vee, Doc?'

'Your man has been kind enough to provide me with a videotape, which I have replayed. I also have a live feed. I was just on the phone

to *General Westbridge when you called.'*

'Westbridge?' The general clucked. 'Shoulda called me first, Doc.'

'I'm following procedure, general.'

'Mmph. Look, this looks like your kinda thing – you want me to send a take-home team to Walter Reed?'

'Certainly I do. But this . . . creature is a rather high-profile –'

'You let me worry about that. It's national security; you want him, he's yours. But you gotta say the word now; we got maybe . . . five minutes to get a chopper out there.'

'Thank you, general. Yes, I want him.'

The commercial break ended. A slow-motion replay of Fungle and Johnny levitating around the gymnasium rolled for five seconds, and then Johnny returned live. He had regained some of his composure but his tie remained askew. 'Folks,' he said, 'during the break Fungle complimented Doc and the band. I, uh, asked if he was a musician and he said yes. So . . .'

The camera cut to Doc and the band looking on in bemusement as Fungle strapped on a Fender Stratocaster guitar with custom double humbucking pickups and a beautiful sunset finish.

'. . . we've asked if he'd like to sit in with the boys. Doc?'

Severinsen bowed an Arabic bow to Johnny. 'Wait'll the union hears about this,' he cracked.

Fungle strummed an experimental chord, frowned, and adjusted a tuning peg. The band members, jaded musicians every one, looked on in a mixture of amusement and mild disbelief. These were men who had accompanied everyone from Etta James to Kermit the Frog; they wailed in hot jazz clubs in Burbank and along Melrose in Los Angeles. It took a lot to surprise them. And when you got right down to it music was music, and if you shut your eyes it didn't matter if the player was Bo Diddley or your grandmother, long as the sound was right.

Fungle plucked a note and pushed the whammy bar to see what would happen. The note bent down like a jet augering in and Fungle grinned devilishly. Ah, this be a fine device indeed! The strings were amazingly resilient; the action was low and responsive. Even the sliding of his fingertips along the corrugations of the wound strings was picked up and amplified over the speakers. The tuning was a bit different than he was used to, but music is a kind of mathematics and Fungle intuitively understood the relationships between the notes, the necessary harmonies between the tunings of the strings. No poet in love with nature can rightfully scorn the mathematical beauty that underscores reality.

Fungle looked at Doc and nodded. The musicians took up their instruments. Fungle snapped his fingers in a brisk four-four beat which drummer Ed Shaughnessy quickly took up as a shuffle.

Fungle nodded in satisfaction and turned to face the audience. On the beat he began to sing: 'Well, it's a-one fer the money, a-two fer the show, a-three ta get ready an' a-go cat go –'

The cheering drowned out the band as the musicians ripped into 'Blue Suede Shoes'. Johnny collapsed back into his chair with delirious delight. Fungle played straight rhythm the first two verses, then kicked out all the stops for the solo. His fingers flew along the fretboard, bent notes like pretzels, hammered thirty-second-note triplets up into the cutaway, and held to ride the feedback wail. He leaned into the whammy bar and the siren wail dive-bombed as his left hand slid down the neck. He let go the whammy bar to achieve a brain-jarring tremolo and shot into Chuck Berry's trademark upsliding chords.

The band was into it in a big way. The audience was frenzied. Johnny's jaw hung.

Fungle muted the strings and turned to face Doc while the band played on. At the beginning of the next measure he played a melodic blues lead. The band vamped as Doc picked up the melody on his trumpet at the end of the phrase and prettied it up. Fungle took it right up, at one point even putting the pick in his mouth to play a double-handed tap lead that would have made Joe Satriani burn his guitar in envy. He and Doc traded licks that could shatter wine-glasses. Then Fungle cued the band and slammed back into the straight shuffle to reprise the first verse. Even as the band slotted into the nasty bluesy stripper-beat ending Fungle steered them toward, the crowd was on its feet.

Fungle ran out toward the bleachers, Strat in front of him like a wand which he waved before the cheering audience.

Gold dust sprayed from the head of the guitar, glittering as it showered down on them.

Deep drumming cut the night. Ka looked up to see a black, insectile whirlybird shoot overhead, circle the hospital once, and descend to the helipad on the roof of Walter Reed. It had scarcely touched down before doors popped open behind its bulging wasp-like eyes and half-a-dozen humans rushed out. They wore identical sharp-cut black business suits and matching aviator sunglasses. They moved with a deadly, intent professionalism that made Ka think instantly of giblins.

The helicopter blades slowed but the engine remained running as the men entered the rectangle of light from a rooftop doorway and hurried out of sight. Ka frowned. He couldn't say for sure why the dark-suited men frightened him, but frighten him they did.

Oh, where was Neema?

Gnole costumes, chaperones, guards with guns and walkie-talkies, all clustered around Neema and badgered her with questions. *How'd you get in here* where'd you get that costume *it looks so real* do you have your security badge *could you remove your mask please?*

Neema simply could not think what to say. There were so many of them, their questions echoed in her mind. 'I, I, I . . .'

Down the hall a set of double doors burst open and a group of black-suited dark-shaded men hurried through. They pulled up short at the sight of seven gnoles standing in the hall. One of them made a move toward the breast pocket of his jacket; the barest shake of the head from another halted him.

The one who had shaken his head confronted one of the walkie-talkie-toting security guards. 'Which one's the gnole?' he demanded.

'He's still in the studio,' the guard replied. 'Who the hell are you?'

The man withdrew a black billfold and flashed a federal badge. He narrowed his eyes at the costumed dancers. As if understanding his suspicions, or perhaps out of fear, they reached up and tugged off the Post Studios rubber gnole heads to show their true selves: midgets, sweaty and damp-haired, fretful and confused.

The leader of the dark-suited men looked expectantly at Neema.

The director was signalling frantically to Johnny: Johnny had about thirty seconds to bring this interview to a close. Johnny nodded slightly and quickly joined Fungle, who was still bowing before the audience, guitar slung at his waist. He told Fungle what a unique pleasure this evening had been – for the world as well as for himself – and thanked him for an experience he would never forget.

As Fungle was replying graciously the security guards stationed near the gymnasium doors and at either end of the bleachers received a hasty message over their walkie-talkies. They moved immediately to form a cordon from the door to the edge of the audience and waited.

Johnny clutched Fungle's hand and raised it in a victory clasp, and they both bowed a final time.

The camera lights winked out.

The gymnasium doors burst open.

The black-suited men rushed in.

A black sedan escorted by four police motorcycles pulled up in front of the hospital and sat idling.

Ka slapped the concrete riser in frustration. Nearly two hours now an' not a peep, not a sight, nothin'! He couldn't wait for ever for 'em to come out, an' if they didn't come out he was gonna hafta go –

Across the street, the doors opened.

Ka's hands stilled on the concrete riser.

A group of policemen appeared, glanced around the street, nodded, and stayed close to the door. A tight knot of darkly dressed men appeared. Ka recognised them as the ones who had rushed from the helicopter on the roof.

At their centre was Fungle.

Ka started to shout, stopped, frowned, slapped the concrete, and balled his hands into fists. The rear passenger door of the sedan was opened. Fungle was ushered toward it. Ka looked around – no sign of Neema. Well, he had no choice, then, didee? He was gonna have to go by hisself and rescue ol' –

Across the street, the roof-access door opened. Three dark-shaded figures appeared and hurried out toward the helicopter idling on the pad. One kept a hand inside the breast of his coat and scanned the rooftop as the other two carried a bundle to the helicopter.

Ka frowned. He glanced down in time to see Fungle pushed into the sedan. He looked back to the roof in time to see the bundle being handed up into the helicopter.

Neema.

The sedan door closed.

The helicopter door closed.

Police motorcycle lights flashed.

Rotor blades began to cut the air.

The sedan drove off.

The helicopter tore into the night.

Ka looked from one to the other. Panicked indecision immobilised him as half-a-dozen questions fired through his brain: who were these furtive humans? Where were they taking Neema and Fungle? Why separately? Why secretly? What to do? Who to follow?

The sedan pushed through the traffic and out of sight, heading toward the Capitol Beltway.

The helicopter receded into the moist overcast night alive with light.

Ka looked out across the lights of the Land of No. Millions of lights in impeccable array out to the horizon, and every one of them a human being, somehow. Determination rose in him. He turned away from the wall, from the hospital, from the myriad lights.

Patched, taped, crazily canted, the Lunabird sat before him. Ka took a deep breath and hurried towards it.

17 *The Roach Motel*

FUNGLE HOSPITALISED FOR EXHAUSTION
Collapses After Interview

RASH OF UFO SIGHTINGS ALONG NORTH-EASTERN SEABOARD
Traffic Controllers Confirm 'Ghost' Blips on Radar

RECORD ICE-CREAM, VIDEOTAPE SALES ON DAY OF 'FUNGLE' BROADCAST
Dow Jones Closes at Record High for Month

———

FUNGLE MAGIC A 'HOLLYWOOD HOAX' PROFESSIONAL SCEPTICS CLAIM
Offer to Duplicate Interview 'Tricks'

———

FUNGLE'S CONDITION 'STABLE'
Doctors Order Rest, Privacy

———

CARSON FORMS NEW ENVIRONMENTAL CORPORATION
'Dolphin Enterprises' to Promote Public Awareness

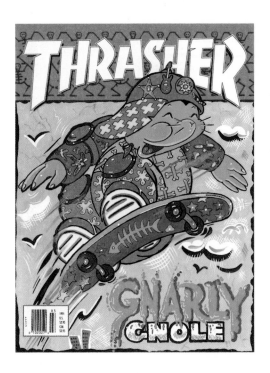

'Fungle? Can you hear me?' The gentle voice came to him from far away, from deep in a fog like a spirit calling through the astral plane. 'Fungle? We know you're awake. Monitors never lie.'

Fungle opened his eyes.

The room was white. Bright light lanced his eyes. He squinted hard, blinked, opened his eyes again. A thin, clean-cut, dark-haired man smelling of aftershave smiled gently down at him from the side of the bed. 'Good morning,' the man said. His voice was chocolate-rich. 'Or rather, good afternoon. How do you feel?'

A. TRIPLE WONDER   E. CHOCOLATE   I. BUBBLE GUM   M. SALT/PEPPER
B. SCOTCH PLAD   F. STRAWBERRY   J. ALMOND (TOASTED)   N. FUDJE RIPPLE
C. JAMACAN RUM   G. COFFEE/RUM   K. COWBOY PUNCH   O. RAINBOW
D. BUBBLE GUM   H. VANILLA   L. FATSO PLAIN   P. ROCKY ROAD

∘ FUNGLE LEVITATES ICE CREAM CONES ∘

'Thick,' said Fungle. He struggled to a sitting position.

The man chuckled. 'Thick,' he repeated. He helpfully adjusted the pillows behind Fungle. 'I cannot convey how privileged I feel in talking to you, Fungle. It's one thing to see you on the television – speaking, interacting with human beings –' he grinned '– playing the guitar. But we're used to impossible things on television. I once saw Doug Henning vanish an entire elephant, *that* fast.' He snapped his fingers. 'But here, in the flesh . . . well, as I said, I'm privileged.'

'Pleasure's me own, sir,' said Fungle, feeling a bit guilty because he felt anything but pleasured. His head ached, his muscles felt cramped. He tried to remember what had happened before he fell asleep. Fell asleep? *Had* he fallen asleep? There was the interview, the charming Mr Carson, the levitation, the music . . . And after that?

'Crucifer,' said the man. 'Doctor Crucifer.'

Fungle glanced around the room. 'An' where am I findin' meself today, Dr Crucifer?'

'Why, you've been brought here from the hospital for security reasons,' Crucifer explained. 'After your rather impressive showing the other night, we thought it might be a good idea to keep you safe.'

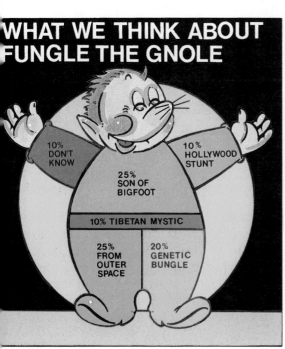

The other night? 'An' where's here?' Fungle persisted.

Dr Crucifer blinked. 'You are now a guest of the Department of Parapsychological Research,' he replied.

'Pair a sick what?'

The man smiled. 'Parapsychological,' he said. 'It refers to theoretical abilities of the mind. To foretell the future, move objects without touching them, know what lies behind walls, read a person's health or history just by touching them, heal with the laying-on of hands, know what other people are thinking.' He set a hand on Fungle's arm. 'You demonstrated parapsychological abilities on television the other night, Fungle, and we are naturally very curious about them.' The hand patted Fungle. 'And that's why you're here.'

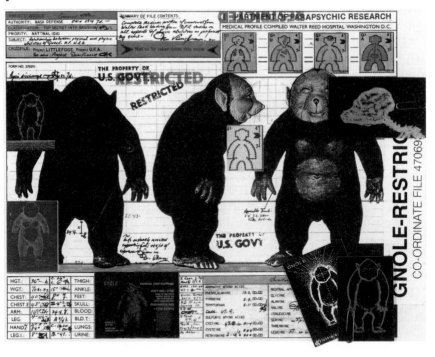

'More tests,' Fungle said bitterly.

'Now, it's not that bad,' Crucifer soothed. 'We're not going to take any of your blood, or skin, or any of that. You've been through quite enough of that. We just want to talk to you about these abilities, and perhaps get you to demonstrate some of them.' His demeanor changed. The kindliness remained in his tone, but there was a dark edge to it, an impatience, a harshness to his face.

'You know, Fungle, if we could document such powers, if we could prove beyond the shadow of a doubt that the mind is capable of even one of the things I mentioned a moment ago – why, it would create great excitement. The potential uses to which the human race could put such gifts! It would ring in a golden age, a New Order.'

Fungle lay back on the bed and shut his eyes. 'Yer underwear's blue,' he said.

Crucifer frowned. 'I beg your pardon?'

'Yer underclothes – what ya wear beneath yer pants. They's blue.'

Crucifer studied Fungle carefully. 'Why, yes,' he said measuredly. 'I believe they are blue.'

Fungle nodded and opened one eye. He was quite aware of the cat-and-mouse game going on here. 'Can I go on me way now?' His smile was wry.

Crucifer returned it. 'Well, your abilities are obviously quite developed,' he said smoothly. 'But as I said, we still have to scientifically document them –'

Fungle gestured toward the wall. 'Yer cameras documented that well an' good enough,' he said – and went back to sleep.

Crucifer hit the 'stop' button and the TV screen filled with snow. 'And that, ladies and gentlemen, is what we are dealing with here.' He turned off the TV and set the remote unit on the scarred black acrylic meeting table. Cheap wooden chairs creaked as his audience shifted. Pens scribbled on yellow legal pads. Throats were cleared.

Crucifer circled the table in the cramped room. 'It's nobody's fool,' he continued. 'It picked up the camera right away, despite the shielding. In the seventeen hours since our initial interview it has refused to provide us with even the simplest demonstration,

though it remains quite congenial. Its only demands so far have been to ask for a return of its woodland clothing. Apparently it finds the hospital garment "scratchy and aromatic".'

'What preliminary options have we considered?' a woman asked. 'Short of coercion or outright force.'

'I doubt we could force cooperation for a parapsychological demonstration,' another woman replied. 'It's his mind, after all.'

'For the moment,' amended Crucifer. He shrugged. 'But I'd rather exhaust simpler alternatives first.' He consulted a clip-board.

'Nutritional deprivation?' suggested the first woman. No one said 'starvation' around here.

Crucifer shook his head. 'Body-fat ratio indicates the gnole is in preliminary hibernation stages.' He shrugged. 'It could go months before it got hungry. We haven't got months. The media will be chewing our heels in less than a week, we estimate. File photos, videotape, and altered recordings will give us another week, but after that there'll be a demand for a public appearance. A *live* public appearance,' he amended. He shook his head. 'We need that brain of his typed, taped, and wiped within two weeks.'

An elderly man looked at Crucifer over the rims of his bifocals. 'We still going forward with the virus scenario?'

Crucifer nodded. 'That seems our most viable course,' he said. 'It has the added advantage of carrying a high sympathy quotient as well.'

'How about sleep deprivation?' offered someone else.

'I don't think it's possible,' said Crucifer. 'It seems to be able to selectively "sleep" various areas of its brain while remaining conscious. It can dream while it's awake, regardless of external stimuli.'

'Chemical dependency?'

Crucifer nodded. 'It's hard to know what is normal for the creature,' he said, 'but physical examination of the female has at least given us a comparative. We think the male has an abnormal blood-sugar level, probably due to the volume of dessert dishes it was consuming at Walter Reed.'

'He's addicted to ice-cream,' a man concluded.

'Possibly. We're using the sugar deprivation against it, but I'm not hopeful. The addiction's recent, and it's a fairly strong-willed creature. Crafty as well.'

'*Was* your underwear blue?' the first woman asked.

Crucifer coloured. His face grew harsh, but he nodded. This is a scientific inquiry, he reminded himself. 'Yes, it was,' he said evenly.

Everyone nodded thoughtfully. A few people made notes.

'What about the female?' asked the second woman. 'Shouldn't we pursue that angle? I mean, she was caught looking for him in Reed; surely there's some emotional connection. Are they mates? Can we use that?'

Crucifer nodded. 'Yes, yes; certainly we've considered this, and we'll press that button if we have to. Right now I'm opposed to it for two reasons: one, it's crude, and two, I'd prefer it didn't know we have the female just yet.'

'Our ace in the hole,' someone suggested.

'Exactly.'

The first woman chewed the end of her pen a moment, then withdrew it. 'Have we given back his clothes?' she asked.

Crucifer looked annoyed. 'Miss Patterson, I fail to see what –'

'No, I think she has a point,' interrupted the elderly man. 'We want to induce receptivity.'

Everyone nodded.

Crucifer looked contemptuously amused. 'All right,' he said, 'we'll return its clothing. Then maybe it will melt a tank tread, or tell us what's going on behind closed doors at OPEC. Perhaps if they've been well-laundered, it'll even set off a warhead at the Nevada site for us.' He snorted. 'Meantime, I suggest we cultivate a chemical dependency, then deprive it. Once it exhibits withdrawal symptoms, we'll let subsequent doses be the carrot we dangle in exchange for demonstrations of psychic phenomena.'

'I have no objection to that,' said the first woman.

Neither did anyone else. They moved to adjourn, and the designated secretary hurried out with his mini-recorder and legal pad to draw up meeting minutes to be initialled and distributed for correction and filing. Government is government, after all, no matter how covert. The elderly man offered to buy everyone lunch, which was something of a stale joke since everything was automatically dispensed in the employee cafeteria – the only place on the five floors that constituted DPR (unofficially known as the Roach Motel) where you were allowed to smoke.

They left. Crucifer hung back, shaking his head in arrogant frustration.

'Crucifer,' from the door.

He looked. It was Miss Patterson.

'The male's in the public eye,' she said. 'We have be careful how we handle it. But we'll still have the female to work with, and no one has a clue.'

Crucifer nodded. 'Shut the door on your way out,' was all he said.

Her nostrils flared, but she closed the door without comment.

Crucifer hammered the desk with both fists. He walked around the table and methodically threw each of the chairs backward to the floor. He did this impassively, without anger, simply recognising a need to vent his frustration, the way most people recognise a need to eat. He picked up the remote, turned on the TV, rewound the videotape, and replayed it. 'I don't know anything about the female's capabilities,' he whispered to the recording of Fungle lying on the hospital bed. 'But I do know about yours.'

Tuneless tones sounded outside Fungle's door as the number sequence that unlocked it was punched. A nurse entered, followed by an armed guard. Her name was Angela Mindela, and she had recently been transferred from the minimum-security children's ward. She was delighted at her current assignment, for Fungle the gnole was a huge hit with the kids in her ward and her own children at home, but she was frustrated because the little guy was a 'Q-plus' clearance subject, and that 'plus' meant there was absolutely no one Angela was allowed to talk to about him. Not even in the staff cafeteria. There were cameras and microphones *every*where in the Roach Motel, and if you didn't watch your back, you could bet your final paycheck someone else would. One of your many fringe benefits, Angela thought wryly as she pushed the dinner cart toward Fungle's bed, when you become a military nurse and decide to get ambitious.

Fungle the gnole lay on the bed, hands clasped before him. 'Dinnertime!' Angela said brightly, parking the tray beside his bed. 'And a present.'

'Present,' said Fungle unenthusiastically.

Angela nodded. You weren't technically supposed to initiate conversation with the gnole, and you were supposed to report any dialogue you did exchange, but Angela knew this room was wired like a TV studio, and anyway how were you supposed to bring someone their dinner and fluff their pillows without trading a word or two? Still, this was about as far as she dared to push regulations here at the Roach Motel.

The Roach Motel: they go in, but they don't come out.

Angela retrieved a folded bundle from below the cart. 'Surprise,' she said.

'Me clothes!' Fungle exclaimed.

'Washed, pressed, and darned,' she agreed brightly. 'No starch.'

Fungle brought them to his nose and sniffed. He lowered them resignedly. 'Smells like me gown,' he said, plucking the white cotton garment he wore.

'I'm sure it'll fade,' soothed Angela. 'And here's your hat, and here's your shoes, and I've even got your rose. Pretty rose!' she said.

Fungle stared at the briar rose. When last he had seen it, the bud had been tight as the day it had been given to him. The petals had darkened as he had travelled, turning nearly black during his time in Walter Reed. But the flower had not died. Darkened, weakened, but not died.

The flower in his hand was in full bloom. Red, lush, fragrant, alive. The same rose?

He brought it to his nose and sniffed. Yes: a trace of Neema, a whiff of the air and dirt near Ka's home, smells of his clothing and his body it had absorbed along his journey. The same rose, rejuvenated, restored.

'For luck,' she had explained. 'An' I'm expectin' ya to give it back to me when yer done chasin' all round the countryside.'

Angela Mindela set Fungle's clothing on the nightstand, smoothed the napkin over his chest, uncovered a plastic plate of steamed vegetables, and pinched Fungle's cheek. He was so *cute*!

The nurse left, the guard followed, the door locked. Aware of the camera's unblinking eye on him, Fungle controlled his heartbeat and focused his attention on eating his bland rubbery overcooked flavourless vegetables. Burning beside him on the nightstand like a ruby flame, the blooming rose cried out for his attention. Fungle willed himself not to look at it and ate robotically, thinking furiously, feeling memories awaken within him.

'*For luck,*' she had said.

She?

Neema.

'*Give it back to me when yer done chasin' round the countryside.*'

Chasing what?

Memories swam to light: ancient images; a magician finds a coffin-shaped crystal –

Theverat. Baphomet.

– a continent is destroyed. Sails of a great diaspora bow before the wind of destruction; an Americkan mountain is hollowed. A crystal is hidden among many artifacts and abandoned for millennia.

A deep, old voice, creaking like a ship at sea: *You must find the stone and summon me. I will destroy it.*

Molom.

A gravel voice, a voice of stone: *Twelve clobhops west, across the mountains, across the valley, north-west side, look for the black cross on the mountain's eastern side.*

Yanto.

Fungle fought to control his heartbeat, his breathing. They were monitoring him, they kept track of every muscle twitch and stomach groan he made. Wouldn't do to let 'em know he was all a-goggle after gettin' –

– the rose, the reborn rose! It burned beside him like a ruby laser, sang a siren song of suggestive scents and a sense of promise, unfolded within his mind soft petals of memory, of *mission*.

And with the return of knowledge of his mission came an avalanche of frustration and impatience. He had seen the mountain! His own eyes had looked upon Black Mountain on the Dragonback Ridge, the hollowed mountain that contained the ancient library of his ancestors, that held the restless, world-consuming crystal Baphomet, the stone sought by the demon Theverat to control the world. Fungle had been a few hours' walk from the end of his quest, and now here he was, locked in a white room filled with directed energies generated by alien hands, far from his goal indeed.

Only after he had eaten his dinner did he allow himself to glance at the rose. He picked it up. Held it before him.

Frowned.

Why had it opened after all this time? Out of his sight, charmed to bide its time by Neema's promise of his return –

Fungle's heart leapt as the meaning behind the re-birth of the rose bloomed in his mind. He forced his hand steady as he returned it to the nightstand and lay staring at the featureless white ceiling.

> 8:37 PM: technician on duty noted acceleration of subject's pulse rate in Room 205. Duration: 30 seconds, slowing to normal within that time. Cause unknown. Reported to DPR Special Briefing at next AM meeting.

Neema was somewhere nearby.

Late that night a different nurse entered Fungle's room. Without a word she bent before him, swabbed the crook of his elbow where a patch had been shaved, and slid in a hypodermic needle. His mind filled with the cries of gulls.

Dr Crucifer paced his office. The morning briefing had been infuriating. The gnole called Fungle would not cooperate on a PD, which was a Paranormal Demonstration. Partially it was suspicion on the creature's part; partially it was the drugs impairing its thinking. No one had any useful suggestions. Though Crucifer was certain the addictive drugs were affecting the creature, it was too soon to coerce any cooperation by withholding them. Right now the creature just sat all day in bed, sleepy-eyed and smiling like some zonked-out hippie in nature-boy clothes.

Meanwhile, psychological evaluations on the female were incon-clusive; no one could determine whether or not she had psychic abilities similar to those exhibited by her boyfriend in Room 205. If gnoles were anything like human beings, then the ability was extremely rare. No wonder the male was a shaman among his people.

Tribal shamans were nothing new to Crucifer. For years now he had investigated them, tested them, measured them, videotaped them – and caught ninety-nine per cent of them faking it.

But that other per cent . . . They could – well, they could *do* things. And most frustrating to a scientist, the things they could do were difficult to quantify in an objective manner. How do you measure mental phenomena? Intelligence itself was a mental phenomenon, and efforts to objectively measure it had proven nothing but amusing over the years. The irony annoyed Crucifer: the very organ that performed the miracles associated with thought could not prove thought even existed. Oh, you could get scratches on an EEG – but try submitting that to a research journal as evidence of a dream! Like dreams, proving the existence of parapsychological phenomena relied largely on first-hand accounts.

Crucifer was a rationalist. He religiously believed that there was a scientific explanation for everything. He believed firmly in the primacy and uniqueness of the human mind in the world – perhaps in the universe. There was simply nothing else like it: a thinking organ evolved from the basic matter of the universe itself. The human brain *was* the universe, pondering itself, casting its own eye upon itself in order to explain itself. To Crucifer, it was not only human to take things apart to learn how they worked, but failure to do so cheated the race and the universe itself.

At universities and on television he had spoken eloquently in favour of experimentation on animals in laboratories. He had also published newspaper editorials calling for the development of industrial synthetics to replace animal by-products used to manufacture slick paper, cosmetics, adhesives, and the like. Crucifer saw nothing contradictory in these two stances. His loyalty was not to causes or ideologies but to knowledge and anything that furthered it. Colleagues thought him a zealot and privately expressed concern over his amorality – for scientists are human beings, after all, and not without compassion and morality. Universities had found Crucifer to be a goal-oriented overachiever with an annoying habit of avoiding proper procedures but a delightful tendency to produce lucrative and high-profile results. Over the years his ability to gain government grants for pet projects, without compromise, had

become legendary. Fellow professors had wondered aloud what his hidden agenda was. Crucifer only smiled and clapped their backs and said that learning is its own reward, you should know that, you're a scientist, buy you another drink?

There was a hidden agenda, of course, but it was hidden only because revealing it would have made him a laughing stock, would have removed Tiberius Anton Crucifer from the rarefied company of Sagan and Bronowski and Burke and dumped him in the sideshow tent along with spoon-benders and ancient-astronaut theorists and off-kilter horror writers who claimed UFO aliens had taken them to Venus for a nightcap.

So Crucifer unflinchingly used tenure, status, and grants to edge up on his preferred research. He examined the genetic material of bees to learn how much of their behaviour was 'instinctive' and how much was communicated in ways mankind did not yet understand. He designed apparatus to measure the brain activity of captive dolphins as they communicated with ultrasonic waves and swam complex geometric patterns. Then he performed selective lobotomies on the dolphins until these abilities seemed impaired, thus isolating such functions to specific locations within the cetacean brain.

He studied information theory, probability mathematics, and statistical analysis, then surveyed lottery winners in an effort to find out if people normally thought of as 'lucky' were in fact influencing the odds in some way – through 'instinct,' genetic heritage, mental ability, or a combination of the three. His reasoning was that, mathematically, there simply should not be people who have constant good luck (or constant bad luck, either, since chronic misfortune was as improbable as a lifelong winning streak). Statistically, there ought to be a relatively predictable margin of good and bad luck for every individual.

Crucifer brought some of these lucky people to his laboratory and performed tests: reading Zenner cards, reproducing an image projected onto a wall hidden from view, sensing colours by touch, telling their dreams, interpreting Rorschach ink blots while the tester concentrated on a specific image unknown to the subject, and dozens more.

Crucifer found what he had suspected: some people are just plain lucky all the time – which meant that something more than just plain luck was operating in their lives.

With this foundation of research respectably established, Crucifer set to more detailed investigations. He joined the National

Organisation of Sceptics and became active in exposing false psychics and charlatans. Those few he could not expose he examined with secret delight for his own research. He witnessed some amazing things, but he was able to document very few of them beyond all doubt of trickery. He published none of his results, which caused some consternation among the publish-or-perish mentalities at the university.

One day Crucifer entered his cramped office to find a dark-suited man waiting for him. The man had a government ID, a firm handshake, an impressive knowledge of Crucifer's career, and an even more impressive chequebook.

Thirty minutes later Professor Crucifer stood alone in his book-crammed office staring down at a government cheque worth more than his last five grant applications combined.

Six months later he resigned his post at the university.

Two months after that the Department of Parapsychological Research opened its doors – but not to everybody. The Roach Motel was in business. Guests went in. They didn't always come out.

Crucifer sat down to review the memos in his IN basket. Most required a signature, an approval check, or filing. One item caught his eye, and he lifted the phone and punched *27.

'Pediatric.'

'Mrs Hamlin? This is Crucifer.'

'Dr Crucifer, I was just thinking about you. Did you get –'

'What is this business with . . . what's the name?' He frowned at the memo in his hand.

'Almon-Diaz. Ramón Almon-Diaz. His call curve's way down in just about every area, I think because of his medication.'

'What are we administering?'

'Five cc's methamphetamine midday, Percodan at lights-out.'

'Aptitude?'

'Well, doctor, he's a precog, and before medication he was testing out at thirty to forty per cent on the cards and the double-blind graphic perception test –'

'Yes?' Crucifer was impatient.

'Well, he was doing sixty per cent with stimulant accompaniment, but that's lowered to thirty now. Between the speed in the daytime and the downers at night, he's burning out. I'd like to take him off medication.'

Crucifer looked annoyed. 'Sixty per cent on compared to thirty per cent off? I cannot believe you are seriously asking me this, Mrs Hamlin.'

'Dr Crucifer, he's only thirteen years old! For two months now we've been injecting him with –'

'I don't care if he was found wrapped in Hebrew swaddling cloth in a basket on the Hudson river. If he's giving us thirty per cent higher with chemical assistance, then the experiment's working.' He clamped the receiver between his shoulder and his ear. 'Do you understand, Mrs Hamlin?'

A pause. 'Yes. I understand.'

Crucifer grinned as he doodled with a pencil on a legal pad. 'Good. Increase his dosage to ten cc's. I want to see if his curve goes up.'

Silence on the line.

'Mrs Hamlin?'

'Fifteen cc's.' Her voice was leaden. 'Yes, Dr Crucifer.'

Crucifer hung up without another word. Still annoyed, he scrawled a note on the memo and flicked it into the FILING basket.

He started to get up, but stopped when he saw what he had doodled on the legal pad. Eight block letters, evenly spaced, carefully drawn in a heavy hand like a schoolchild bearing down hard as he learned to write.

He settled back into his chair and stared in numb fascination at the eight letters that had changed his life when he was nine years old.

Tib Crucifer opened the door to his sister Dodi's closet as quietly as he could. Dodi was out with one of her stupid boyfriends who had a big loud car; the boyfriends liked to come revving up into the driveway and honk the horn for her to come out. Usually Dad came out instead. But tonight Dodi had managed to get out of the house and Mom and Dad were playing bridge in the living-room with some boring old friends of theirs.

Tib got the closet door open with hardly a creak. He slid the chair from Dodi's writing desk (like Dodi ever used it to write!) to the opened closet. A chair leg banged the closet door and Tib froze, straining to hear any sign that Mom or Dad had heard. They'd give him grief for sure if they caught him; he wasn't allowed in Dodi's room.

He heard laughter and the ripping sound of a Bicycle deck being shuffled. Satisfied, he slowly set one foot on the chair, gradually put his weight on it, steadily lifted himself, and set his other foot down slowly, so slowly, without a creak or a grunt or the clang of a hanger or the whisper of cloth as he brushed along Dodi's clothes hanging in front of him. He lifted a hand and stood on tiptoe, straining upward. The box he was looking for was way in back, hidden from view behind a stack of Monopoly, Twister, Mystery Date, Stratego. He slid it out from behind the stack, got off the chair, shut the closet door, and hurried back to his room as fast as he could.

On the far side of his bed, hidden from view of the door, Tib opened the box. He removed the lacquered board with its letters and odd symbols and set it on the floor. Next he removed the plastic heart-shaped thing. It had short legs with soft felt circles glued to the bottom, and a clear plastic window in the centre. In the middle of the clear plastic window was a needle that pointed down.

One night Dodi and two of her girlfriends had huddled around this thing and scared the crud out of themselves asking it questions. Tib had watched from the kitchen table, stretching a peanut butter and jelly sandwich into half-an-hour. Most of the questions were dumb: *Who's gonna ask me to the prom? Is Dodi a virgin? Will I get rich?* But then Madeleine Murray went and asked, 'Which one of us is going to die first?' and the plastic heart had arrowed straight over to Lauren Bohannon, who had sat there with tears forming in her eyes and her mouth hanging open to show her silver braces. Then Dodi had lowered her hand to the plastic heart again, and with the three girls touching it once more it had taken off like someone was driving it: 8 then 2 then 3, 8 2 3, 823, four or five times. Dodi looked at Madeleine and said *You did it*, but Madeleine only shook her head, grinning in a hideous way that said she wasn't about to admit she was scared. Dodi put the board away, and she and Madeleine talked Lauren into letting them crimp her hair.

Three weeks later, August twenty-third, a fuel truck ran a stop sign, hit a tree, and overturned onto Lauren Bohannon's car. She was killed instantly.

Dodi remembered the Ouija board's prediction and hid the game away. Tib, always that smart one, was the only one who made the numeric connection: 823. August 23; 8/23.

So now Dodi was out on a date, and Lauren was dead in the ground, and here was Tib in his room with his sister's frightening and enticing Ouija board.

He held his breath and set the planchette on the board. His heart thudded loudly. He wiped his hands on his shorts, then rested his fingers lightly on the edges of the planchette.

He closed his eyes. 'Are you out there?' he whispered self-consciously.

He waited. What was supposed to happen? Did you hear voices, or something? All he felt was nervous.

He opened his eyes and looked down.

The word *Yes* showed through the window in the middle of the planchette.

BIG FOOT   SANTA CLAUS   KUNGLE

Tib's fingers jerked from that thing like he'd just scuffed across a carpet and grabbed a doorknob. He glanced at his bedroom door. The bridge game continued in the living-room.

Tib remembered what Mr Carpenter, his science teacher, had said: 'An *experiment* is a way of proving something. If you want to prove that something works, like blending two colours to make a new colour, or that something exists, like gravity, you create an *experiment*. That way no one ever has to just take your word for it.'

Tib wiped his hands on his shorts once more and took a deep breath. *It's an experiment*, he thought, and set his fingertips on the planchette. 'Who – who are you?' he whispered.

Something lowered across his hands.

Tib's eyes grew wide. He tried to lift his hands but couldn't. The planchette began to move. It was like someone had their hands on his and was moving his hands for him – *someone he couldn't see*. He watched his hands slide the planchette toward the lower-right side of the letters.

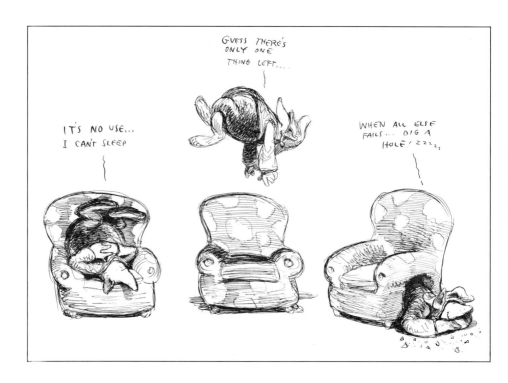

The planchette shot across the board, pausing just long enough for him to read the letter cleanly centred in the round window before hurrying (softly! softly!) to the next. Tib couldn't have spelled that fast on this board if he'd tried. Eight letters. He remembered them like they were tattooed inside his forehead. Eight letters. They didn't mean a thing to him, but he would remember them for the rest of his life. Over the years he would write them down and rearrange them and look for a mathematical or alphabetic code, but he would find nothing.

When the last letter was spelled out the pressure lifted from his hands. Any other questions he may have had, any curiosity that had consumed him, vanished. He put the board and the plastic heart into the cardboard box, then put the lid on ('*Put a lid on it,*' his dad was always telling him). He ran with the box to put it back in Dodi's room, beyond caring whether or not he made any noise. Then he went to bed and said his prayers and tried every trick he knew to get to sleep, everything he could think of to rid his mind of that awful memory of the plastic heart smoothly sliding on its felt-tipped legs, moving beneath his hands but without his control from one letter to the next.

There's an explanation, he told himself. *That's what science is all about. That's what experiments are for: explanations. Whatever happens, happens for a reason – that's science. One day I'll find out the reason why this happened.*

But not tonight.

Finally, well past his usual bedtime, he slept.

When he got up next morning the eight letters were scrawled across the dull grey face of his Etch-a-Sketch.

Crucifer started when his intercom buzzed. He glanced away from the scrawl on his legal pad and hit the TALK button. 'What?'

'Dr Hannecker on line one.'

Crucifer pressed the line. 'What?'

'You might want to come down to two-O-five. Our guest would like a word with you.'

'It asked for me?'

'By name. I'm jealous.'

Crucifer hung up without replying. Just before he left his office he glanced one more time at the eight letters he had unconsciously doodled on the legal pad.

THEVERAT

He wondered what it meant.

'Fungle! I'm delighted to see you up and about. How are your clothes? Comfortable and clean, I hope?'

Fungle merely looked at him with heavy-lidded eyes. 'What've ya done t'me?' he muttered.

'Done?' Crucifer seemed confused.

'Ya've put somethin' in me head. Some kinda fog's whaddidiz.' Fungle shut his eyes. 'There's gulls cryin' an' commercials blarin'. I kin hear th' radios an' th' lucktricals.' He pointed to the multi-plug wall socket above his headboard. 'Bizzy bizzy beez, buzzin' all th' time.'

Crucifer frowned. The gnole did not look healthy. One expected slight cognitive impairment with Librium, but the physical effects

were worrisome. The creature's face, normally a smooth pink, was blotchy and pale, edging toward grey in places. His thick fur was dulled. He looked thinner, even though he'd only been here a few days, and even though he was supposed to be in preliminary hibernation stages. Crucifer wondered if the creature had been eating. And could it really sense electrical currents in the wall wiring? 'What is it you want?' he asked.

Fungle opened one eye. 'Wanna know whaddidiz *you* wants.'

Crucifer pursed his lips as he scrutinised the alien form on the narrow bed. He nodded decisively. 'All right, Fungle.' The saccharine bedside manner left his tone. Time to negotiate. 'We are eager to conduct some experiments on you. They won't harm you in any way, except possibly to cause fatigue. These experiments may demonstrate the existence of powers we have long suspected, but which we have never been able to prove. We need you, Fungle.'

'An' after?'

Crucifer blinked. 'I beg your pardon?'

'After yer done?'

Crucifer smiled. 'Why, then you're your own man. If you'll pardon the phrase.'

Fungle nodded wearily. 'A'right.'

'All right – you mean you'll do it?'

Again Fungle nodded. Suddenly he opened his small dark eyes to look at Crucifer and gripped the man's white coat. 'But you'll take the fog outta me head,' the gnole said evenly. 'Won't yer?' The creature's grip was so firm, and its gaze so piercing, that Crucifer had a moment's doubt as to whether Fungle was feeling the effects of the medication at all.

'Certainly, certainly,' Crucifer said hastily. 'After all, we wouldn't want to hamper your abilities, now would we?'

Fungle allowed himself a small, wry smile. 'No,' he agreed, letting go the man's jacket and lying back on his bed, 'we wouldn't want ta do that.'

Dr Crucifer typed his password, RUBICON, and logged on to the computer terminal in his office. Working from his notes he entered the results of the last two days' tests onto a database program, shaking his head in wonder.

A battery of time-honoured parapsychological tests had been performed on the gnole. For two solid days now the creature had been running a psychic treadmill, and in the absence of tranquillisers, depressants, and chemical dependency, the gnole showed no signs of flagging. A deck of Zenner cards – a set of five distinctive shapes in a deck of twenty-five – had been shuffled in a Las Vegas shuffling tower. The gnole had called each off before it was turned over: 'Star. Circle. Star. Wavy line. Square. Star,' and so on.

Crucifer typed a figure: 100%.

Next, a series of related tests in which the gnole was placed in a sealed room and told to call out the image in his mind while the card dealer concentrated on the Zenner images she drew from the deck. After flawless results, Crucifer had put a fly in the ointment and slipped in random images: a picture of Mickey Mouse, magazine clippings, a page from a field guide to north-eastern birds.

Crucifer tabbed to the next category and entered the results: 100%.

Black patches had been fixed over the gnole's tiny eyes with adhesive, then a blindfold tied around them. Coloured cards were shuffled and dealt in front of the gnole, and he was asked to touch the cards and call out the colour. Only once did he pause: when he encountered a ringer Crucifer had slipped in, a baseball card picturing Kirk Gibson, former centre fielder for the Los Angeles Dodgers. Instead of calling a colour, Fungle had hesitated, blindfolded in the bright white room, and asked, 'Does yer want me ta call out *all* the colours, or just tell ya what it's a pitcher of?'

Crucifer shook his head and typed: 100%.

They gave Fungle a sketchpad and a pencil. Draw the image that comes to your mind. In the next room a doctor concentrated on photographs. For the fun of it, someone had slipped in a copy of the latest *Sports Illustrated* swimsuit issue. 'No wonder ya likes ta wear so many clothes,' commented Fungle, and commenced to drawing an uncanny likeness of the cover.

100%.

The room was cleared. Crucifer had entered with a hardback book, sat in a folding chair, opened the book at random, and commenced to reading. In the next room Fungle straightened in his schoolchild's chair and began to speak: 'The worship o' the senses has often, an' wi' much justice, been decried, men feelin' a nat'ral instinct of terror about passions an' sensationalistics what seem stronger'n theyselves, an' that they's conscious of sharin' with the less highly organised forms of existence. But it appeared ta Dorian Gray that the true nature o' the senses had never been understood, an' that they'd remained savage an' animalistical merely 'cause the world'd sought ta starve 'em into submission or ta kill 'em by pain, insteada aimin' at makin' 'em elements of a new spirituality, of which a fine instinct fer what's bootiful was ta be the dominant characteristic. As he looked back upon man movin' through history, he was haunted by a feelin' of loss. So much'd been surrendered! An' to such little purpose!' Fungle had paused. 'Couldn't agree more,' he said.

85% – an imperfect score only because of the gnole's quirky idiom.

As a control, another subject had entered the room without a book and merely sat for a while. 'No smoking,' said Fungle next door, remembering Tobacco Inn. It turned out there was a NO SMOKING sign on the wall of the subject's room.

They tested his time sense against a quartz clock: *Tell me when you think a minute has passed.*

100%.

Crucifer tabbed to the category marked TELEKINESIS and felt his heart give a kick. Fungle had slid a paperclip across a table, unbent it, and tied it into a knot – without touching it. Then he had levitated across the room. *And Crucifer had it on video, in front of qualified witnesses!* This wasn't some Vegas showman on the Carson show; this had taken place in an utterly controlled environment. For the first time, verifiably, an intelligent being had moved objects from point A to point B with the power of will alone. Mind over matter, and proof at last.

Crucifer transferred the database results to a graphic program and drew some amazing pictures. On bar-chart Fungle's line stood beside previous results like the World Trade Centre towering above a tenement. On a pie chart Fungle was a Pac Man gobbling a skinny wedge for dessert.

Dr Crucifer was more excited than he had ever been in his professional life. The creature was a gold mine! The possibilities for national defence, for national security, for the gain and comfort of humanity, were staggering. He imagined himself levitating an automobile before an awed crowd; inviting onlookers to fire at him with a gun and stopping the bullets with the force of his mind; reading the diaries of CIA chiefs; extending mental hands to the palace of a power-mad foreign dictator and confronting him in his bedroom, pushing past frail flesh with ghost hands to clutch the tyrannical heart and *squeeze*.

The intercom buzzed. Crucifer's hand shot out to thump the button. 'I said I'm not to be disturbed,' he said curtly.

'I know, doctor, I'm sorry. He said it was top priority.'

'*Who* said it was top priority?'

'A Mr Theverat. Line one.'

Crucifer grew even more annoyed and stabbed a finger toward the blinking red light of line one.

The finger stopped.

YOU CHOOSE THE CAPTION BY WOZ

'What . . . what was that name again?' he asked.

'Theverat, doctor.'

Crucifer spelled the name in his mind. Eight letters. Eight pivotal, frightening letters.

'Shall I tell him you're unavailable?'

Line one blinked beneath his finger like an alarm.

'No,' he said. 'I'll take it.'

Crucifer felt a curious mixture of indignation and fear as he pressed the button. 'This is Dr Crucifer,' he said with professional detachment.

'Howdy, Tib,' said the friendly voice. 'Long time no talk.'

Metal rasped across Crucifer's heart. He meant his tone to be demanding, but it came out pleading. 'Who is this?'

He had not been called 'Tib' since he was fifteen years old.

'Don't you remember me?' The voice sounded hurt, the tone of a favourite uncle crushed at not being recognised. 'And after all we've been through together, *doctor*.'

'Who are you?' Crucifer said – demanding, this time.

'Why, it's Theverat,' said the voice. 'That's *T*, as in *Tiberius*, *H*, as in *Hell*, *E*, as in –'

'I know how it's spelled.'

Rich laughter on the receiver. 'Of course you do.'

Crucifer tightened his grip on the receiver. 'Why are you calling me?'

'Well, I'll tell you, Tib. I'm in a bit of a fix and I need your help. I'd reward you most handsomely.'

Crucifer shut his eyes. 'I don't believe in deals with the devil.'

'I'm not the devil, Tib. I'm just an old friend who needs your help.'

'What are you, then?'

'That would be a bit difficult to explain. Especially to a scientist. You'd have to . . . *unlearn* so much.'

'How did you find me? It's been . . .' Crucifer swallowed dryly '. . . a long time.'

'Time can't diminish true friendship, I always say.' The confident laugh again, and then the tone grew intent. 'I found you because you're using magic. Not your usual card tricks and paper shufflings. *Real* magic, the *real* craft. It's like a beacon in the night to me, Tib, just calling out.'

'The gnole,' said Crucifer.

'The very creature,' agreed Theverat. 'What a reunion this is turning out to be!'

'Is this an offer I can refuse?' Crucifer felt bold even asking such a question.

'You won't want to refuse, Tib. Not when you see what I can offer you.'

'What can you offer me?'

'Ahh . . . Levitating automobiles. Stopping bullets with your mind. Stopping the hearts of foreign dictators.' The voice chuckled. 'That's just for starters.'

Crucifer was distracted by a play of light across his computer monitor. He looked to see a particoloured swirling that quickly cleared to show a succession of images: Crucifer being photographed by a swarm of photographers; a beaming Crucifer beside a beautiful redhead in a black sequinned dress; Crucifer accepting the Nobel Prize for science; accepting the Pulitzer Prize for his fifth book; *Time*'s 'Man of the Year' cover showing Crucifer's angular, stern features; Crucifer clutching a fistful of strings while generals and politicians and starlets and scientists danced beneath him.

Crucifer spoke into the phone while the mesmerising montage played across the monitor screen. 'Listen,' he said, nearly whispering. 'That computer terminal goes out the phone lines through a modem that ties into National Security Agency computers. So does this phone line. Any good hacker could have gotten into the system and –'

'You need proof,' interrupted the voice.

'I'm a scientist,' said Crucifer. It sounded like an apology.

'All right, Tib,' said Theverat – and the line went dead.

The intercom buzzed. 'Dr Crucifer?'

Numbly Crucifer pressed the button. 'Yes.' His tone was flat.

'Did you order a pizza?'

Crucifer couldn't believe his ears. 'Pizza?' he asked, as if the word were new to him.

'The guard downstairs says there's a man from Domino's with a pizza for you.'

'Tell him I'd rather spend two weeks in a Turkish prison than eat . . . Oh. Oh, yes. I *did* order a pizza. Yes. I forgot all about it. Thank you. Tell him I'll be right down.' He hung up.

Left the office.

Told his secretary to have the NSA trace Mr Theverat's call when it came through again.

Slid his clearance card into the slot to activate the elevator.

Rode down in pensive silence.

Arrived in the lobby and walked robotically to the security desk.

It looked like the lobby of a rundown hotel that hadn't been very appealing even when it was new.

A man in a tan overcoat, mirrored sunglasses, and a baseball cap waited near the desk. He held a tattered, quilted warming pouch in his leather-gloved hands.

The security guard barely glanced up at Crucifer's approach. 'Joo order a pizza, doc?'

'Yes, I did.'

The guard waved vaguely to indicate the delivery man and went back to studying the entrance monitors.

Crucifer approached the pizza-delivery man. There was something wrong with him, something *wrong* about the way the overcoat draped on his frame. Through the lobby glass behind him Crucifer saw a dented compact car with *Domino's Pizza Delivers!* stencilled on the side. A young woman sat in the passenger seat. She grinned, showing braces, and waved at him.

The delivery man removed a pizza box from the quilted warmer and gave it to Crucifer. They made a momentary tableau as Crucifer stared at the leather gloves on the delivery man's hands.

They weren't gloves.

The delivery man let go the box and reached into his overcoat. Crucifer glanced at the security guard, but the uniformed man remained slumped in front of the monitors. Crucifer looked back to the delivery man in time to hear a slight *click!* like a peapod being snapped. The delivery man withdrew his glove-leathered hand from the overcoat and set something like a black thorn on the pizza box. 'Keep the tip,' he said in a shuddering grinding awful voice, and turned away.

There was something horrible about the way he walked. As if his joints were in the wrong places and bent the wrong way. The overcoat poked in alien places.

Crucifer looked down at the leathery thorn slowly squirming like a maggot on the pizza box. He felt nauseated.

He looked up again as the pizza delivery car started up and drove away, taking with it the frightening delivery man and his passenger, Lauren Bohannon, who waved and smiled again to flash her silver braces; Lauren Bohannon, thirty-five years dead.

There was a face on his computer monitor when he returned. It wasn't a human face at all, just coloured lines forming hard geometric shapes of jewel-like eyes, a broad, narrow V of a mouth, concentric angles that might have been cheekbones or

Indian warpaint.

Shaking, pale, Crucifer set the pizza box on his desk, sat in his leather executive chair, and stared at the monitor.

The thorn writhed beside him.

The intercom buzzed.

'Dr Crucifer? Mr Theverat again, line one. NSA is tracing.'

Crucifer pressed line one and put it on the speakerphone. On the computer monitor the hardlined face smiled. 'Don't throw away the thorn,' came the distorted voice from the speaker. 'You're going to need it later.'

'For what?'

The face rushed toward him. 'All in good time,' came the cheerful voice. The eyes widened, flashed like rubies, and narrowed again. 'Don't you want to know what kind of pizza you ordered, Tib?'

Crucifer glanced at the pizza box. On top of the white cardboard the thorn squirmed like a salted slug. Careful not to touch it, Crucifer pulled the box's tabs from their slots, unbent the flap, and raised the lid.

The thorn slid onto a stack of papers on the desk.

Crucifer stared for a full five seconds at the Ouija board in the box before he screamed.

An hour later Crucifer's private fax machine hummed to life with a report from the National Security Agency:

> 15:17 EST LINE TRACE REQ T. CRUCIFER Q + CLEARANCE VERIFIED
> REPORT AS FOLLOWS: MODEM TRANSMISSION THROUGH BANK OF
> AMERICA WEST COAST REGIONAL OFFICE RELAYED FROM MUTUAL OF
> OMAHA OFFICE, LITTLE ROCK, ARKANSAS, LINKED TO MCI TERMI-
> NALS IN CLOSED-LOOP CIRCUITRY RECYCLING SIGNAL. POINT OF
> ORIGIN SHIFTS AT 30-SECOND INTERVALS ACROSS N. AMERICAN
> PHONE LINES, APPARENTLY RANDOM SOURCE-NUMBER ASSIGNMENT
> (SEE ATTACHED LIST). POINT OF ORIGIN: INDETERMINATE.

Below that someone had scrawled a note: *As far as we can figure out, this call came from everywhere and nowhere. Any ideas?*

Crucifer crumpled the fax and threw it away. He had some ideas, all right. So did Theverat.

18 *Disturbances in the Field*

A screaming came across the sky. From the south, dipping dangerously low to skim white-capped Atlantic waves, a rickety splintered Lunabird clawed bent-winged through the air. Strapped into the pilot's seat, a cursing gnome battled the frail failing craft by batting the air with battered oarlerons. 'Ya abomination over an abominable nation! Yer nuffin' but a trumped-up tree! You fly like I juggle, an' I can't juggle a single egg wiffout makin' a omelette! An' a omelette's what yer tryin' ta turn me inta, ya gravity-lovin' brick – a poor scrambled gnomelette whose only crime is tryin' to help his unfortunately deranged friends!' He wrestled with the oarlerons, hit an air pocket, and dropped twenty feet. The oarlerons momentarily became real oars as the craft bit water, then raised again. 'I'da done better ta launch meself wif a rubber band!' Ka declared. 'Poor Fungle's taken northward by hell-o-copter, an' if you was more airworthy than a plate a cheese we'd a been there an' away by now!'

Ka had conquered his airsickness days ago, mostly because anything to be sick about had long since become fishfood over the Atlantic. His stomach was empty, he was aching for a drink of water, and he'd rather drive a nitroglycerine truck in a demolition derby than spend another minute aboard this semi-aerial atrocity.

Ka was so engrossed in his struggles to hold the craft together and steer with the oarlerons that he nearly stalled and crashed when he looked up.

The Lunabird had managed to gain a respectable height. The weather was clear, but a chemical tinge tainted the air. A grey pall had dimmed the horizon.

The gnome had managed to bank the craft west, where land ought to be, and he had just levelled off when he saw it. It rose ahead of him like fairy towers from a childhood book, like an Atlantean city from Fungle's legends. Tall and jagged and crowding upward, dimmed by a grey mist of industrial pollution, busy with humanity and congress, and somehow *alive*. It was not so much a city as a monument to the *idea* of city. To Karbolic Earthcreep, collector of human artyfacts and hobbyist in things technologistical, his first view of the Manhattan skyline was like Moses' glimpse of the Promised Land, Neil Armstrong's footprint on the moon, Wile E. Coyote exploring the Acme Warehouse.

He stared. He whooped. He hollered. He was filled with a wild exuberant abandon. He completely forgot himself and his mission, his problems with the Lunabird and his fear of flying. Every fibre of his being became a sounding board for the overwhelming magnitude and potential of the city expanding slowly before him. The world's largest and ultimate artifact lay ahead, and all that had gone before was worth the revelation of this moment.

Behind him the air quaked. Ka looked back and yelled, but his voice was lost in a full-throttle four-engine roar as BiCoastal Airlines Flight 4615, an L-1011 with its landing gear lowered for its final approach to LaGuardia Airport, thundered by.

The impossibly enormous jet missed the Lunabird by perhaps a hundred feet. Onboard collision radars sounded no warnings; air-traffic controllers received no return signals from the wooden craft. No evasive action was taken. The only response was from a little boy named Eddie Parks, who clutched his Bart Simpson doll and waved solemnly at the hunched creature flying in the wooden birdie. Eddie would grow up to write books about visits from his friends the UFO aliens.

The hunched creature in the wooden birdie had more immediate problems. The backwash from the passing jet had set the Lunabird into a tailspin, and the strength of the air rushing past the downspiralling craft was too great to allow Ka to work the oarlerons.

Lunabird and gnome augered in to Jamaica Bay.

In the oddly mystical, woodsy serenity of Jamaica Bay (a piece of swamp-like faery so unimaginably unlikely this close to the model city of humanity that its existence was almost inevitable), the constant banging and splintering of wood could be heard as Karbolic Earthcreep kicked the Lunabird to pieces.

Because he knew it was important to his friend Fungle, he

salvaged the dark magnetite crystal that had powered the craft, putting it back into the leather bag he still wore around his neck.

Darkness fell.

By night, Jamaica Bay was even more mysterious. Insects performed extemporaneous concertos by still, black pools in a humid bayou.

Across the water shone a vast geometry of light. Oh, it was intimidating, and oh, it was the supreme expression of all that was meant by 'The Land of No', but oh, how appealing and eerily beautiful and unnaturally perfect it was! What a lovely monster lured with its neon call! Even across the water Ka could hear the inviting sirens singing. His vision blurred with longing, and the twinkling skyscrapers seemed to curl like beckoning fingers.

He looked out across the black water smeared with city light. Fungle was out there somewhere. Maybe Neema too.

'Well, ole gnome,' he said aloud, rubbing his hands in preparation, 'only one way ta get there from here.' He began to dig.

Dr Crucifer turned his smile on as he punched the code that admitted him to Room 205. He pushed the dinner cart ahead of him and nodded at the guard who stationed himself just inside the doorway with a hand near his taser. The guards carried firearms as well, but the high-voltage barbs, intended to stun without serious injury or death, were mandated by Crucifer at DPR. Subjects, human and otherwise, were too valuable to shoot with bullets.

Fungle floated six inches above his narrow bed, eyes closed, legs crossed in lotus position. 'Evenin', doctor,' he said without looking.

Crucifer parked the cart beside the bed. 'Dinnertime, Fungle,' he said, trying to act as if there were nothing out of the ordinary in serving a meal to a small Buddha-like creature hovering in the air. 'It's your last meal before the projection experiment tomorrow, so eat hearty.'

Fungle slowly revolved to regard Crucifer with tiny black eyes. Crucifer tried not to fidget under the penetrating gaze. Something was different about the creature. Since they'd stopped medication and it had begun meditation to prepare for tomorrow, it had acquired an unsettling aura of *otherness*. 'Didja find the things I asked after?' said Fungle.

Crucifer nodded. From beneath the dinner cart he removed a large brown paper bag. Stapled to it was a scrawled list. 'Five pure beeswax candles,' Crucifer read. 'A litre of purified water, a ball of string, a black wax pencil, five silver cups. Phials of sea salt, sulphur, mercury, lead, and copper. A box of dirt from beneath a mature oak tree. A garland of garlic. More herbs than an apothecary.' He looked up. 'And a topographic map of Manhattan. Anything else?'

Fungle shook his head. 'That's plenty,' he said.

'It's typical of Manhattan that my people had no difficulty finding any of these things.' Crucifer set the paper bag on the bed. 'I had no idea there were so many occult shops in this city.'

Fungle merely stared at him.

He knows, thought Crucifer. *Something's different, he smells it on me, he knows.*

'Do you have to fast in order to purify yourself before you can . . . can project yourself out of your body?' Crucifer asked. Despite his years of investigation into psychic phenomena, the scientist in him still tripped over phrases like 'astral projection'.

Fungle nodded. 'It's important y'unnerstand about this,' he said. 'I needs a good night's sleep tonight. Tomorrow when I makes me preparations, I can't be disturbed. I know yer people likes ta give me drugs to keep me quiet an' sleepy.'

'We discontinued that some time a –'

'When ya travel outside a this world,' said Fungle, 'yer connected to yerself by a silver cord that'll stretch f'r ever. But anythin' that weakens yer body, anythin' that makes it impure, weakens the cord. If I'm out there an' that cord breaks, I'll not make it back.' His expression became wry. 'An' that'll ruin yer experiment, now, won't it?'

'The experiment is important to us, Fungle, but we're equally as concerned for your safety.'

Fungle only gave him that unnervingly penetrating, impenetrable stare.

'I . . . need to be sure you're clear on the objectives of this experiment,' Crucifer continued. 'Can we go over it one more time?'

'Seems simple enough,' said Fungle. 'Yer gonna monitor me body here whilst I leave it an' head out across yer city to the tallest tower.'

'The World Trade Centre,' agreed Crucifer. 'There are two towers. You want the southern tower.'

'Eighty-first floor,' continued Fungle. 'Room eighty-one twenny-one. There'll be a locked door, an' a guard, an' another locked door. Behind that there's a book.'

Crucifer nodded eagerly. 'Tell us what page it's opened to,' he said. 'Tell us what it says.'

'An' after that,' finished Fungle, 'you'll let us go. Me an' Neema.'

Crucifer bit his lower lip and nodded. Fungle's knowledge that Neema was being kept just down the hall was a sore spot with Crucifer. He'd been embarrassed to learn that Fungle had known she was here almost from the beginning, had even smelled her scent on the clothing of the staff when they had come to Fungle's room after visiting the female. 'We'll transport both of you to any point on the globe you like, and we'll leave you there free as the day you arrived.'

'I didn't arrive free,' Fungle pointed out.

Crucifer coloured. 'It's just an expression,' he said. 'But rest assured that after this your future is your own to decide. We have a wealth of data on you which we will be analysing for years. We're all very excited at the prospect.'

'You an' me both,' said Fungle.

Crucifer clapped his hands. 'Well!' he said brightly. 'I'm as eager to get on with this as I'm sure you are. So let me leave you to your dinner and a good night's sleep.'

At the door Crucifer paused. 'By the way, there's a surprise for you in one of your dishes. A going-away present, if you like.' He smiled, then left.

'New York Superfudge Chunk,' Fungle muttered just before he lifted the metal dish cover.

After Crucifer had gone Fungle lowered himself to the mattress to eat his dinner. He ate mechanically, preoccupied with thoughts of the preparations he had to make, worries about the dangers of astral projection, eagerness to be reunited with Neema and away from this terrible place, a curiously eager fear at the prospect of resuming – and completing – his quest to destroy Baphomet.

While he finished his steamed and raw vegetables he thought about Dr Crucifer. Something about the man had changed. Fungle could not quite pin it down. It worried him. He did not trust Crucifer – after all, to all intents and purposes the man was Fungle's jailor – but this went beyond that. He felt sure it had to do with tomorrow's experiment.

Fungle shrugged and uncovered the last dish. Perhaps the man was merely worried and eager to get on with it. Who knew? The only thing to do was proceed with eyes open and resolve firm.

He picked up his spoon and dug into the last bowl of ice-cream he would ever eat.

Crucifer sat in his office with his arms folded tightly, staring at the computer terminal and waiting on a phone call. The memory of this afternoon's preparations – boiling the writhing thorn to attain an oily black gravy, filtering it pure, squeezing a single drop from a glass pipette onto the ice-cream dish – made him faintly queasy. There had been no smell at all, but something about the mixture filled him with disgust. *'It won't kill him,'* Theverat had insisted. *'He's no good to me dead. But it will certainly ruin his day. His metabolism will lower until he seems dead. But I can't have your well-intended medical teams rushing in there to revive him, do you understand? I need him weak; I don't want him running back to his body the moment he senses me. I need time to get in while his spirit and body are separate and find what I'm looking for.'*

'How will you do that?' Crucifer had asked.

He shuddered, remembering the gleeful malice that had coloured Theverat's reply.

'It's like peeling an onion,' the voice on the phone had answered.

At exactly four o'clock the intercom buzzed. There was a phone call for him. Crucifer had been expecting it, but he jumped anyway.

Bonk! Curses came from far beneath the ground. Ka backed away from the obstruction and gingerly fingered the knot already swelling on his head. This was the third time he had run into what he thought of as humanstone, which was smooth and regular and admirably shaped, and every bit as hard as granite. Not to mention the indignity of chipping a nail against an iron pipe he'd uncovered as he tunnelled at high speed.

So what's ta do? Back off an' change direction, or see if ya kin dig 'round it?

Well – dig a little ways, an' if ya don't reach the edge, head somewheres else.

He dug down. Down was usually safe when you ran into an object; though humans had an annoying tendency to shove things into the earth, they seldom dug very far. Seemed they wanted things out of sight more than anything else.

In a few minutes he had clawed through crumbling mortar. Slick humanstone slabs gave way to clatter down ahead of him. He had broken into an open space. It was quite dark and Ka couldn't tell what kind of mess he'd dug hisself into this time. Cautiously he widened the hole and stuck his head in to have a look-see.

Hot, stale air blew past his head. It stank of oil and ozone and hot metal. In the distance a dim green light glowed near a curved tunnel wall.

Ka eased himself into the tunnel and looked around. Once his eyes grew accustomed to the distant green light he could see fairly well. Metal rails along the floor ran toward the green light and curved out of sight. Narrow, raised walkways lined either side of the tunnel. The walls were slick with condensation and the tunnel echoed with the intermittent dripping of water leaking from a pipe.

Ka nodded his approval. 'Nice worksmanship,' he observed.

The green light changed to red. A curious cacophony rose, almost musical in its rhythm and tone. Ka bent an ear to the ground and was startled to realise that the sound was coming from the metal rails. Their iron souls were singing to him.

Distant timpani rumbled accompaniment. For a moment Ka was back in his old tunnel where he had outwitted the giblins, hearing the massive growl of the lake pouring in.

A white light grew in the distance.

The rails were keening now.

The timpani swelled to thunder and howling iron.

A hurtling metal object with blazing eyes the size of saucers blotted out the green light.

Standing on the rails, Ka turned to run from the downtown subway train.

Fungle rose with the dawn. He had not seen sunlight for weeks, but even in this windowless place unconnected from earth and sky he knew from the quickening of his pulse when another day was born.

He heard the tell-tale tone of the code that unlocked his door. Of course they had seen on their monitors that he was awake. The door opened and a guard entered and took up the customary post by the door while two orderlies cleared the room of everything: furniture, machinery, medical monitors. The hidden camera and microphone would remain in place, but Fungle wasn't concerned about them. They wouldn't record where he was going.

The orderlies set a bucket of warm water mixed with an organic cleaner, several brushes and rags, and a rag mop on the bare floor, then left. Fungle took five carefully measured breaths and emptied his mind of distractions, then knelt on the floor, picked up a brush, swabbed it in the bucket, and began the top-to-bottom cleansing of his small room.

Preparations were also under way elsewhere. Meditating on her narrow cot in Room 207, Neema sensed the zone of calm that was forming nearby. Her studies, though different from Fungle's in many respects, had attuned her to what she thought of as the Field: the ever-shifting cumulative hyper-reality formed by the emanations of living objects in an immediate area, invisible, elusive, and actual as a swift current in deep water. Neema sensed a serenity growing in the Field nearby. She had felt it before – she had even created such a bubble herself, a feeling like being outdoors in the eye of a hurricane – but she had lived near Fungle long enough to recognise the distinctive mark of his work. The mage may have been humble about his craft, but Neema knew that, despite the occasional and painful blunders he had made along his autodidactic way, Fungle's like had not been seen among gnoles since antediluvian days.

Fungle was up to something.

To find out what, Neema turned inward.

Tiny J's inna alley drinkin' Night Train fumma bottle inna crum-pled bag worn soft as yer daddy's ol' hat, when damn if this manhole cover don't start *movin'*. Juss kinda lifts on up an' shoves itself aside like the streets is breathin' too hard an' this is what's givin' way. Tiny J setsa bottle aside an' rubs his sandpaper jaw. There's alleygators s'posed to live down there, gone all white as lab mice from breedin' outta the sun, an' Tiny J's thinking about maybe re-situating this particular swiggin' address when this . . . well, this *muppet* kinda guy, only real and without someone's arm up his butt, sticks a spade-eared beady-eyed mottled-skinned head out and gives the alley the once-over.

Well, there ain't nothing to do but hit him up. 'Spare any change?' asks Tiny J.

The muppet guy sees him for the first time. He'd thought Tiny J was just another bag of garbage, but now the bag has sat up and asked him a question.

The muppet yelps and bolts down the alley.

Tiny J hugs his bottle of Night Train like the rag bear that was once his best and onlyest friend in the hole wide whirled, and loses himself to stained dreams in the drained steam of another night.

*

Two lengths of string formed a large X from corner to corner in Fungle's cell. Where they crossed Fungle hammered a small nail. He removed the string, then measured out exactly eighty-four thumbs on one of the lengths. He tied this to the nail, tied a black wax pencil to the other end, and used the nail as a pivot to draw a black wax circle on the white linoleum floor. When it was done he scanned its circumference, making certain there were no breaks, that no lint or dirt or other object crossed it. It was important that the integrity of the circle not be broken. His life was in danger should anything breach it.

Fungle marked five equidistant lines on the circle, then again used the length of string to join the lines in a star pattern which he traced to form a pentacle, the most basic symbol of the mage's art and an essential protective space from which to conjure or conduct any dealings or contacts with the other realms.

He drew a second circle around the base of the star's rays, and in the space between the rings and the star's rays he inscribed ancient magic symbols – whorls and crescents, serpentine spirals and cruciforms.

His astral fortress was complete.

Neema felt a jolt at the completion of the pentacle. Was Fungle going to conjure? Had he finally decided to seek help from one of the Elementals in the otherworld – Molom, perhaps? But surely that terrible human, Crucifer, and all the others here would stop him! They were watching; they always watched. Even now Neema felt the mindless stare of the camera eye upon her, felt it like a whirlpool draining away her soul. It was robbing her of something more than privacy, she felt sure.

What was Fungle up to?

Whatever it was, it had to do with the otherworld, with the astral planes.

Which meant there was only one sure way for her to find out.

Karbolic Earthcreep was not all that different from most first-time tourists in Manhattan: though he crept among alleys and darted from shadow to shadow and hugged obstructions wherever he could, he found it impossible to travel without constantly staring upward. The buildings rose like legends of titans, like the dwellings of vanished godly races. The sky was a ragged grey strip between their rows.

Near Little Italy he rounded a corner and saw a tall figure in a shapeless hat, sunglasses, and a filthy grey trenchcoat arguing with a man at the takeout window of Tony's World Famous.

'I'm tellin' ya,' the man behind the mesh was saying, 'I got your phone-in order, but there was nothin' about no credit cards or nothing. We don't do dat. Deliveries is cash only, take-out's cash or charge. Now, I got four meatball subs wid everything, four chips, an' four Cokes waitin' right here. I'll be mored'n happy to take ya credit card now. I'll take ya cash. Hell, I'll take a gol' watch if you got it. But I know I never took no credit-card number onna phone. Now, you wantcha order, you pay me. Uddawise, stop usin' up valu'ble oxygen.'

The trenchcoated figure banged work-gloved hands against the counter and screamed something unintelligible.

'Ya mudda!' riposted the man behind the mesh. He slammed down the window and turned away, shaking his head.

Trenchcoat clenched his fists and left the sub shop, talking to himself. Except Ka was sure he heard several voices, as if the man were arguing with himself. Out loud. And taking both sides.

Ka found this so peculiar he plumb forgot to duck back behind the wall from which he was observing. Trenchcoat spotted the gnome and stopped in his mismatched tracks. He looked down at his midsection and said something.

His midsection said something back.

Quickly he unbelted himself and opened his coat to reveal two strange creatures, one standing atop the other's shoulders. They had wild staring bloodshot eyes and pasty smooth skin. They were a hodgepodge of scavenged clothing and jewellery.

They both looked loony as a rightwise cat in a wrongwise room.

The bottom creature made a pained face, squatted, and sprang up, pushing outward to launch the creature on top toward the amazed gnome.

Ka decided now would be a good time to leave. He turned – and ran smack into another figure wearing a trenchcoat. Trenchcoat number two flew backward . . . And broke in two. And got back up. *Both* sections got back up. And came after him. And caught him. And dragged him down a storm drain.

*

Fungle blessed an earthenware jug of purified water, then poured the liquid into five silver cups which he set at each of the pentacle's five points. Beside them he placed the five pure beeswax tapers set in gold candlesticks. He used a spell to light the wicks, instead of matches or a brand. He blessed the phials of sea salt, sulphur, mercury, and various other chemicals and metals, blended their contents, and divided them into five equal shares which he placed where the star's points touched the outer circle.

Five bunches of bundled herbs, fragrant and fresh, he rested upright against each candlestick. Fresh garlic he knotted into a garland and hung around his neck.

Careful to avoid touching the black wax of the diagram, Fungle stepped into the pentacle. He had already bathed himself ritually, and sealed his bodily openings to protect himself from possession by any malicious Elemental he might encounter.

He rested on his knees with feet tucked behind him, right big toe crossing left, and held his hands palm-up on his thighs while he uttered a prayer in a drowned tongue.

By prior arrangement the fluorescent lights were turned off. Shadow waltzers wavered on the walls, brief lives led by candlelight.

Fungle closed his eyes. Breathed in. Held it. Exhaled. He had not emptied his lungs before he was fast asleep.

In the Medical Monitor Room, Miss Patterson shook her head in disbelief. 'Respiration's less than one per minute. Heartbeat . . . well, if I found a human being in that shape, I'd defib him and juice him.' She glanced back at Crucifer. 'Every time I think I'm used to what he can do, he comes up with something new.'

'Hindu fakirs have been documented in similar states of reduced metabolism. Bury them in a box for three days, no food, no water, no air, and they emerge unharmed.' Crucifer frowned at the still, kneeling form on the monitor. If Theverat had been correct, the distillate Crucifer had slipped into Fungle's ice-cream should be kicking in soon.

Theverat.

A thrill knuckled along Crucifer's spine. To use that name, to be in touch with such a . . . such a *Presence*. All his life Crucifer had felt singled out, destined for something extraordinary. And now here he was, in touch with a power that had shaped his life, well-embarked on his unique journey.

'What's the female up to, I wonder?' Miss Patterson asked.

Crucifer glanced at the monitor. The female had slid her bunk aside and chalked her own indecipherable markings on the floor. She sat crosslegged – presumably because her splint would not let her kneel. Her eyes were shut, her respiration slow.

'Was she informed of the experiment?' Crucifer asked.

Miss Patterson pursed her lips and shook her head. She pushed her glasses back up the bridge of her nose. 'She knows something's up, though. We should've tested her more thoroughly.'

'Plenty of time for that later,' said Dr Crucifer.

Fungle looked down at his sleeping form kneeling in the centre of the pentacle. Bobbing near the ceiling, he felt the bond to his physical self, watched the silver umbilicus form and strengthen and brighten between spiritual and physical states. Everything seemed satisfactory.

He thought *motion*.

He passed through the wall and into the next room. Below him, Neema sat meditating on the floor. Fungle felt a rush of joy and affection. Could it have been only weeks since he had left her back in Ka's abandoned mine? It felt like years. He thought back along the silver cord, twanging it like a guitar string to send a vibration of himself along it just to feel the blood-red blooming briar rose still tucked into his forest-green tunic. A moment only, and then he returned to hover above Neema's kneeling form.

Odd inscriptions on the floor round her. Wicce-work, looks like. Wonder what she's up ta?

He passed through her door and into the hallway where taser-armed guards sat bored on watch and orderlies rolled squeaking carts, where white unblinking daylight ruled and hidden dehuman-ised voices hailed doctors over public-address speakers.

In memory he conjured the map of Manhattan they had shown him. The towers were south. Fungle could *feel* south like a

migrating bird, in the magnetic flow of currents invisibly surrounding the surface of the earth, in the pull of the iron in his
earthbound body's blood.

He thought *up*.

His nonbody rose through the ceiling, through a dark room
where linens were stored, through ceiling again, into an air duct,
through the roof, and up into the narcotic Manhattan night.

The East River's black blood glittered. Before and around him,
above and below him, lay the discernible world. But reality was
more than the world normally discerned by the bodily senses.
Reality also lay in layers above, below, and apart from the
perceived, like an encyclopaedia drawing of human anatomy on
overlapping sheets of clear acetate: here the skin, here the muscles,
now the organs, now the bone.

Fungle moved out among the laminations of skin, muscle,
organ, and bone of reality. There was a core spark that was
Fungle and nothing else, and there was the layered reality through
which he moved – but the borderline between the two had grown
indistinct. Along the broad diffuse perimeter of his heightened
senses it was impossible to tell where he ended and the world
began. He tasted leaden radio waves and smelled the residue
of the day's heat rising from concrete plains. He bristled from
the constant pinprick shower of broadcast energies and directed
electrons, thrilled in the poetry of living auras, saw the siren song
of entropy. He tasted braying car alarms, heard flashing lights,
smelled pain and felt music on his skin.

Also out there were lone firefly sparks, islands of light that
were lost souls washed overboard by the torrent of otherworldly
travelling who had never found their way back to the world,
disembodied entities anchored to the earth who had died and not
completed the crossing, forever searching for a way home.

They frightened and saddened him.

Fungle soared like the idea of a hawk toward the twin towers
rising skyward in the distance. He reached them quickly, entered
the eightieth floor, passed into the locked room, floated past the
armed guard, slipped like a ghost through the locked door and saw
the open book on the table.

He stopped, bothered by a thought.

*They showed me a map. An' the map showed where these towers is,
but ta get me to 'em it had ta show where I started from. An' they
never woulda let me see that iffin they meant to let me an' Neema out
of there alive.*

He had attempted no escape at first because of the induced langour of the powerful drugs with which they had dulled him, then because of his realisation that Neema was also being kept at DPR. He saw now that his trust in Crucifer's promise to release them upon completion of the experiment had been naive and foolish. Froog'd always told him he was too trusting.

A'right, then. *Finish the experiment; read 'em what's writ here, get back to yer body, an' get yer body* outta *there. Yers an' Neema's both.*

He moved toward the open book on the table.

Just before he was yanked backward he felt an overpowering sense of imminence and dread wash over him, a disturbance in the Field. Then there was a tug on the tether connecting body and soul, and Fungle was pulled backward, out of the room, past the guard, out of the building, and above the night. Something was reeling him in like a kite.

He tried to send his awareness back along the cord and found the way blocked. Something was wrong with his body in the room; the connection had weakened. And suddenly he knew with horrible certainty that the imminence, the dread he had sensed, lay along the path back to his Self, blocking the way and reeling him in.

He recited a prayer intended to clear his mind, but instead he found he could not focus his concentration; his thoughts were filled with seething dark clouds.

A terrible abyss began to yawn before him in the night above the city light.

The silver cord grew dull.

'Vital functions down, Dr Crucifer.'

'Continue monitoring, Miss Patterson.'

'What do we do if he goes flatline?'

'We'll worry about that if it happens. If we revive him right now, the shock of retrieval itself might sever the connection, or cause him irreparable harm.'

'Very well, doctor.'

It was scary out there. Neema was a little boat on a large sea, and the weather was on the change. Invisible to the beholder not skating the thin ice of this particular reality, ominous storm clouds gathered. From their turbulent midst stretched a thin silver cord pure as molten moonlight.

Fungle, thought Neema, and willed herself towards it.

Fungle held firm to the silver cord and felt himself being drawn in. Soon he confronted the thing that waited along the path back to the world. It was like hauling up an anchor chain and seeing an odd discoloration in the water that swelled as you pulled, until you hauled into your little boat a snapping mindless white-eyed thing that wanted only to fill its belly with you and swim on.

It was vast. Fungle could not believe how vast it was, how reaching, how powerful. Before now he had encountered it only as a friendly voiced shape dimly perceived in the light of a fire in an ancient granite tomb. Fungle could no more have constructed a true image of Theverat from this than an aquarium fish could imagine a human being from seeing a finger thrust into the water.

This was Theverat, and he covered the sky.

'Look, if he's got vital signs, they're too weak to register on my remotes.'

'It is still possible that minimal metabolic function is a product of its out-of-body ability.'

'Dr Crucifer, his soul may be riding the elevator in the World Trade Centre, but his *body* is dying. Let me call in the med techs.'

'One minute, Miss Patterson. Sixty seconds, and then you can call them in.'

'Starting now.'

The attack came from everywhere at once. The Presence that was Theverat swallowed him like the demonic mouth from his nightmare. Theverat's awareness bore down on him, a constricting sphere of energy that sank with frightening ease past Fungle's strongest barriers of craft and will.

What little fish have I caught in my sea? The voice was omnipresent, a universe of sound more felt than heard. *Why, I believe it to be a gnole-fish! A tiny gnole-soul swimming out of his depth.*

An image bloomed: clawed hands holding a shining silver cord.

Did you ever fly a kite, gnole? I did, as a child. Oh, yes, we had kites! And oh, yes, I was once a child who flew them! And one day on a hill I ran with my red silk kite straining at its thin leash, and I stumbled. The string broke. Even now I feel the sudden slack in my hands.

Clawed hands tightened, tautened the silver cord. Fungle felt a vertiginous plummeting sensation as the connection to his drug-weakened body lessened.

And what became of that kite, little minnow, little gnole? Who could know? It may be up there still.

Fungle was given an image of island sparks forever searching in the void, anchorless and alone.

One question, gnole, and only one chance to answer. Clawed fists wrapped his lifeline and rose high. *Where.* Came together with shining slack between them. *Is.* Bunched muscles readied to fly apart and rip the cord. *Baphomet?*

Fungle readied himself. 'Well, Mr Theverat,' he sent, 'I'll tell ya.' He hoped the separation would not be painful. 'I traded it fer a dog.' If preventing the world's nightmare destiny under Theverat could be bought with his life, then so be it. 'An' then I sold the dog.'

He braced himself, marshalling every bit of will and craft and lore, knowing he could not win, but also knowing that he could not go without a fight.

Theverat invaded him.

It took longer than it should have to set up the defibrillation apparatus because Crucifer insisted the technicians respect the integrity of the pentacle, which meant they could not break any of the black wax lines. Plainly they thought this was absurd, but they could either stand around arguing or do what the man said and get to it.

The med tech squatted awkwardly beside the unconscious form still kneeling at the centre of the pentacle. 'No vitals,' she said to her partner powering up the machinery. 'How's he sitting like this if he's dead?'

'Persistent vegetative state,' suggested her partner.

'Uh-huh.' To Crucifer: 'What's he weigh?'

'Ninety-five.'

The med tech nodded. 'Don? One cc adrenaline. Ready with that defib?'

'Fired up.'

She accepted the two disks from her partner, grabbing them by their insulated handles and careful to keep the metal surfaces apart. Don lowered Fungle until he lay on his back, shaking his head at the contortions he had to undergo to prevent breaching the pentacle's integrity. His partner watched as he administered the adrenaline injection. He counted thirty on his watch, checked pupillary reflexes and respiration, and shook his head. 'You're green,' he said, unbuttoning Fungle's tunic.

A bright-red rose fell onto one of the pentacle's whorls.

Miss Patterson's voice came across the PA. 'Doctor, I think you should have a look in two-O-seven.' Crucifer hesitated a moment, looking at the hurried but not panicked med techs working on Fungle. Then he left.

The med tech glanced up at Crucifer's departing form. She shook her head and rubbed the metal disks together to dispel accumulated static charge. 'Clear!' she called. *It's like jumping a car battery*, she thought as she pressed the disks against the small creature's unbreathing chest.

*

The harsh obsessed will tightened around Fungle's core. He filled with thoughts of choking on thick blackness. His vision reddened, and the redness erupted into nightmare screaming faces with bulging eyes.

White light flooded his awareness.

He smelled the soft velvet of rose petals.

Neema? he thought.

I'm here, Fungle. You're not alone.

The faces rushed back towards him. The cosmos lit with maniacal laughter. The silver cord gave a sensation of tearing.

Fungle! Take my hand!

Neema? Neema, get out of here! Theverat –

(A faint voice shouts across an immeasurable distance: 'Clear!')

White light detonated.

The murky ocean of being grew turbulent around them.

The silver cord brightened. Strengthened.

Take my hand and I'll pull you through!

Neema, that light! Is that you?

Fungle!

Fungle reached out. There was nothing out there. He flailed, he felt himself sinking beyond recall in the churning depth that was Theverat, felt again the mounting pressures that would strip him bare, rip him body from soul. Felt the walls of his will crack like a glass dome on a muddy ocean floor, felt black rain descending. Flailed with the last moment left to him –

And connected. Out there, struggling in the fuligin ocean, desperate and alone in the small but strong boat of her soul, another minnow, tiny gnole-fish.

Neema.

They clasped, held fast, held strong. The silver cord had thickened, had brightened, and ran straight as a laser out of the yawning abyss of

Theverat struggling with a new Presence in the void, something massive and more ancient even than him. *War in heaven*, Fungle thought as Neema pulled both of them along that strengthened cord. *Could this new thing be the True shape of Molom?*

Fungle felt the gathered fury battling behind them, felt a part of it stretch toward them, felt the first inky tendrils engulf them.

('All right, one more before we try heart massage. Clear!')

Whiteout.

*

Crucifer looked at the still figure of the female in the centre of her chalked design. She was interfering somehow. He knew it.

He stepped forward. Checked her pulse, respiration, pupillary reflex.

Minimal.

He glanced back at the door. From the next room down the hall came the med tech's voice: 'Clear!' They were busy as the devil in there.

Crucifer straightened. Calmly he extended his foot and scraped the toe of his leather shoe across the diagram.

They hurtled above the streaked grid of night-time Manhattan, plummeted past layers of skin and muscle and organ toward the bone of the world, fell through roof and room and ceiling toward an empty shell of cooling flesh and stilled blood unmoving within a diagram drawn in black wax.

Fungle clutched Neema tight and hurried toward the room where her body waited. He swept into the room just as Crucifer's shoe lifted above Neema's protective circle. *No!* he sent. He dropped, holding Neema's flagging spirit to return it to its empty vessel.

He plunged.

Crucifer's shoe breached the integrity of Neema's diagram.

('Clear!')

Fungle was yanked back to the world.

Whiteout.

The EKG spiked.

'Hold on . . .'

The green line spiked again.

'Got him! We got him!'

Dr Crucifer stepped calmly into the room. 'That's great,' he said. 'Good work.'

The med tech frowned up at him.

19 *Out of the Frying Pan*

Theverat raged. He lowered part of his awareness to the latticework rivers of electrons flowing across the human city. He surged along the stream, entered the stacked grid of a particular building, flowed himself through the wired walls, directed himself into a socket and through a cord to transform into a beam of cathode rays striking phosphor dots to form an image. He was too angry to concentrate on forming a coherent image; the monitor simply seethed with chaotic light.

He felt the puny bag of organs pacing the room. It had only been hours, and the scientist – laughable word for what this human knew, *scientist* – was half out of his mind with worry and fright.

Theverat modulated the electron flow through the tiny speaker beneath in the computer's disk drive. 'Crucifer.'

The puny bag of organs stopped. Theverat felt the chill sweat in its palms and armpits, felt the blood pool in its groaning stomach. Good, good. He mustered enough control to form patches on the monitor to suggest eyes and a mouth, but let the seething colours remain.

'It wasn't my fault,' Crucifer said straight away.

The monitor flared. 'You let the female interfere.' The on-screen eyes grew hard, faceted, glinting with cruel light. 'I could destroy you with a word.'

'No – no, wait. Please, no, wait . . . What can I do?'

'Repeat the experiment. Send him swimming again in my part of the sea.'

'I don't know if he will –'

'We have the female. He will.'

'What is it you're looking for? Perhaps I –'

'Perhaps you may be reduced to a drooling mindless meatbag with a single look from me, doctor.'

'No, no, I will, I'll do what you say, please. I . . . I'll send her to you.'

'Tonight.'

'He's under heavy sedation. There's nothing I can do until tomorrow. I'm . . . I'm sorry.'

The face on the screen only glared. 'Bring him to me. Tomorrow.' The screen blurred, then cleared. Crucifer found himself staring at his own face. But it was vacant. The eyes looked on infinity. The flesh was waxy. The mouth was open. A thin line of drool inched toward an ear. 'Don't fail me,' said Theverat, and the monitor went blank.

Fungle lay in bed. Electrical hums surrounded him; dimly he felt them in the walls, through the cords, a network of slave electrons coursing the grid of the city. He tried to think. What had he been trying to think? He couldn't get a grip on it; his brain felt the way a hand feels on waking when it grasps a pencil with baby-weak fingers.

A dull grey cloud floated in his mind. Lightning flared when he tried to concentrate. Better not to try.

What time izzit? Late. Hadda be late. Hours and hours ago he'd been more awake. Tones had sounded outside his door. *Clack.* A nurse entered, followed by an armed guard. *Eight o'clock, on the dot.*

The guard had shut the door and taken up a post beside it. The nurse had smiled reassuringly at Fungle, who only stared dully.

The nurse bent before him, swabbed the crook of his elbow where a patch had been shaved, and slid in a hypodermic needle.

The nurse and guard left; the door locked; the lights dimmed. Fungle dimmed.

Now it was late. The corridors were silent. The public-address pages for doctors and nurses were few and far between. Guards sipped coffee and stared at monitor screens and magazines. Patients struggled or succumbed, but privately, quietly, quietly.

Fungle lay on his cot. On the monitor screen he seemed asleep. A little fellow with a dreaming face. No one looking at him could have guessed they were watching a battle.

Fungle felt the chemicals coursing through his veins.

Tonight a war would be waged. There were to be no more parleys, no more delays, no more concessions. The first engagement would take place on the battlefield of his self.

His breathing slowed. His eyes rolled up. Fungle fell inward.

Invaders swarmed the liquid corridors of his veins. Through chemical agents they governed and suppressed. In the capitals of organs and glands they established command posts and tyrannised the outlying provinces.

Fungle in his own body fomented rebellion. A crusade to convert the foreign usurper! Fungle rallied his armies: shock troops of epinephrine, methodical infantry divisions of chemical-altering enzymes, elite divisions of acetylcholine to attack the enemy nerve centres. We are invaded, he transmitted, on our own home front!

Riding single-celled charges reined with DNA strands, Fungle's microscopic battalions carried the fight to the tranquillising enemy. They surged along red river routes to retake beachheads zone by zone, absorbing the occupational depressants and inhibitors, converting the meddling foreign agents to inert stragglers that would be flushed from his system. He scoured and purified the nourishing systems of his body, and in a final campaign to regain control of his sovereign self he swept through the broad vessels of his brain, altering the chemicals that had dictated and subjugated it for too long now, and filling his mind with clean, white light.

Soon the day was his. Fungle had made up his mind. Now he would no longer have to sleep in it.

He marshalled his reclaimed soul to carry the campaign outward.

Howard Klumpf slouched on his swivel chair in the monitor room. In front of him were a dozen black-and-white screens with various views of high-security sections of DPR. Not much ever happened on those screens, but it was Howard's job to keep an eye on 'em – like being paid to watch the most boring goddamn TV show in the world. *Twelve* boring TV shows.

The swivel chair complained every time Howard moved. He hooked blunt thumbs with dirt-crescented nails under his wide belt and tugged to ease the pressure on his gut. All-County wrestler gone to fat, but hell – two weeks of sit-ups and he'd be back to fighting weight.

He surveyed the bank of unblinking screens. Nothing. He yawned. It was shaping up to be a five-coffee night. Terrific. Have to drink milk to keep the caffeine from turning my stomach inside-out. Coffee don't hardly touch me no more.

The lion's share of Howard Klumpf's attention was devoted to monitors eleven and twelve, which were ISW, Intensive Security Wing, better known as the Roach Motel. Right now Howard knew the Roach Motel's special guest was that little gnole guy everybody was flapping about. Howard had even seen him on the Carson show. Pretty amazing stuff, and he seemed like a nice enough little thing. No wonder they had him in here, though, with all that Vegas-magic *schtick* he could pull off. Howard had once seen David Copperfield disappear the entire Statue of Liberty on TV, which was pretty impressive – but you didn't see David Copperfield in the Roach Motel, because when the show was over, the Statue of Liberty was still there. Now, if *I* could make Johnny Carson flop around like a fish out of water, thought Howard, and float him around the room, and who knows what-all, the last thing in the world I'd do is let everybody and his brother see it on TV and not give 'em room to think it might be a trick. You do that, you end up in the Roach Motel.

Nope, thought Howard, I'd take me about a grand outta the bank and have myself a day at the dog track they'd be talking about twenty years from now – hell, a day I'd be *living* off of twenty years from now.

Howard felt kinda sorry for the little guy. Here he could be living it up at the track, or making a football go smack into a wide receiver's hands: touchdown! Beat the spread and win a zillion bucks. But instead he floats Johnny Carson around the room and ends up some kind of national security threat.

Howard shook his head, looking at the inactivity on eleven and twelve. I work not thirty feet away from some little thing that gets the cover of *Time*, and I know more about him from watching TV in my own living-room. Hell, my daughter has a poster of him! Tells the kids at school I keep him safe.

Howard felt a little surge of pride. Hmph. Well, maybe I do.

He yawned again. Better think about that second wake-up pill, bud.

He pulled open the middle drawer of his desk where the bottle of Vivarin was kept. It was a communal bottle; whoever used the last pill bought the next batch. He shook out a chalky yellow tablet and put the bottle back in the drawer. When he looked again at monitor eleven, he jumped in his chair.

Fungle's face filled the screen. His eyes were *enormous*. In fact, his eyes were getting bigger. And bigger. And bigger.

*

The man on the other end of the eye was tired. Fungle felt it. The man was tired; he would rather be home in bed, free to dream, dreaming free.

Free, Fungle thought toward him. *The eagle is free. Oh, how he flies, the eagle in the air. Curved arms feather-covered, hollow-boned and cupping the wind. For miles you could see and soar – if only you had the room. Room to fly.*

In the monitor room, Howard Klumpf watched the black-and-white images of holding cells on the screens before him slowly dissolve, until a vista of white clouds and weathered cliffs lay beyond his fingertips. Rust canyons and blue skies rose before his yearning eyes.

Howard slowly raised and lowered his arms. He could fly. He could feel it in his bones: if there was room enough, he could really fly!

But where? If he tried to fly here in the monitor room, he'd beat against the walls like a canary in a cage.

Room to fly.

An eagle flew across the panorama before him on the screens. Oh, to cross that borderland of glass that separated Howard Klumpf from an ocean of wind in which to swim for ever!

Two buttons lighted on the 'Holding Cell Release' panel of the control bank beneath the monitors: 205 and 207. No, no; he'd only *thought* the buttons showed cell numbers. What was *really* written on the two buttons was FLY and FREE.

Of course.

Howard reached out to touch the buttons and saw a beautiful strong gnarled eagle claw in place of a hand. It curled, except for a single sharp talon.

The talon jabbed twice.

FLY

FREE

The canyon vista on the monitors rushed toward him. The monitors dissolved; the frontier of glass was crossed. A desert diorama engulfed the dreary room.

Howard perched on the edge of the precipice, gathered his wings, and launched into the sky. Free to fly, flying free.

The electronic bolt clacked as it withdrew into the door-frame and Fungle smiled. Through the camera he sensed the beatific security guard in the monitor room. Fungle could feel the man soaring, feel him sensing the air through which he wheeled without budging his heavy body from the pneumatic chair.

Fungle slipped from his cell and headed toward 207.

In the monitor room, Howard Klumpf stared at the television screens for the two most exhilarating hours of his life.

No one in sight, only floor wax and harsh solvents to smell: the corridor was clear. Fungle locked the heavy door behind him and hurried along the terrible white corridor one final time. Without the cloud of drugs in his mind he could feel Neema like a fire in the night. He headed straight for the door behind which he sensed her troubled spirit.

The door was unlocked.

He pushed it open, widening a wedge of light across a narrow cot. The humped covers were tented by a slick magazine called *People* with a picture of Fungle on the cover. 'People'! How insulting to be included where you don't belong!

Fungle shut the door partway and stepped silently into the room. He approached the bed and slid aside the magazine. 'Neema?' he said softly. He touched the covers gently. 'Neema?'

'*Mmnnmh?*'

'Neema, wake up! It's me – Fungle.'

'*Fun-gle?*' She smiled sleepily. '*'S dark out there, hmm?*'

He frowned. Gently touched her shoulder. Turned her toward him. Her eyelids raised partway. Unfocused, dilated pupils beneath.

Neema was drugged.

Fungle felt his face grow hard. Ah, Neema, not you too! They've filled yer head all fulla dark clouds an' dandelion clocks. If I'd me medicine bag an' time, I could fight it off. Right, Fungle, and if ya had a heely-copter ya could fly her outta here, but ya don't.

Neema was wearing her hospital nightclothes. Fungle made a quick check of the room to see if she had anything of value she'd want him to bring along, but there was nothing.

Fungle pulled down the covers and pulled Neema to a sitting position. She felt boneless beneath his hands. 'Neema!' he whispered tightly, and pinched her ear.

'Hmm?' Her eyes opened. 'Fungle,' she murmured. 'Is you in this dream, too?'

'We's in the same nightmare together, I'm afeared,' he said. 'Now let's get ourselves out of it. C'mon.' He put her arm around him and stood.

Neema leaned heavily against him. 'When allis is over umunna make you dinner,' she slurred. 'A'right?'

'It'll be me pleasure,' said Fungle, struggling toward the door.

''Cause we's neighbours, affer all,' she continued, half mumbling, 'an' iss juss you an' me leff now, Foxwit an' Cleverbread. 'S not right us livin' so close and bein' so far aways . . .'

'Shh. Quiet now, Neema.'

'Shhh!' She smiled. 'A'right. Shhh.'

Fungle opened the door and they left.

The corridor was empty. Fungle couldn't help a gentle quick smile up at the camera, on the other side of which a heavy human in a cramped room rode thermals with happy grace. Nearly carrying Neema, Fungle hurried as best he could down the hall in full view of the cameras. He half-pulled her along the white corridor until they reached a junction. To the right was a sight that sent a burst of energy and hope racing through him: above a heavy door, a red-lettered sign marked EXIT.

'We still bein' quiet mousies?'

'Quiet as sunlight, Neema.'

She put a finger to her lips. 'Shhh!' she agreed.

He firmed his grip on Neema and started into the intersecting hallway.

Shoes squeaked on linoleum.

Fungle stopped. To the left, a shadow lengthened as someone approached. Fungle desperately looked around. The long white corridor gave no hint of sanctuary – unless they returned to Neema's cell!

He lifted Neema and ran as quickly and quietly as he could. Two doors before Neema's cell was a door marked JANITORIAL SERVICES. Instead of a number pad to lock it, there was a knob. Fungle tried it, and it turned.

Behind him the footsteps were near the intersection.

He pushed open the door and rushed into the tiny dark room.

'Fungle, what on *mmph!*' The last was Fungle clamping his hand around Neema's muzzle.

The footsteps neared.

Neema leaned heavily against him. *I gots to get her outta here*, thought Fungle. *Get her out, an' she can sleep all she wants.*

Their cramped refuge smelled of dust and decay and sharp-scented chemical cleansers: mildew, faint ammonia residue, solvents. But beneath that, from out in the hallway, a stale musk of sweat-gland fear. *Reckon weeuns is become the big prize on Wheel! Of! Fortune!* thought Fungle.

He shook his head. Would that cursed picture box haunt him for ever?

Yes.

Well, can't sit round here f'r ever waitin' on 'em to find us, he decided. 'Bout time to acquaint ourselves with the outside o' this building. He firmed his grip on Neema and yanked open the door –

– and there was a human, big as life and just as ugly.

Jerry Allesandro leaned against the laundry cart, smoking a cigarette. You weren't supposed to smoke in the Roach Motel, except for in the employee lounge, which everybody called the goldfish bowl. And the fact that it felt like being in a goldfish bowl was plenty of reason why Jerry didn't want to go there to have a cigarette. What was the point in a nice, relaxing smoke if you hadda be somewhere that made you tense to do it?

It was getting pretty hard to have a good time around here. Maybe he oughta start looking around for –

The cigarette paused *en route* to his lips.

Had he felt a draught?

He turned. Nothing there. Just the door to Janitorial Services.

Jumping at shadows, he thought to himself. Hell, this place'll make you do that. I *will* start looking for another job.

He took one last drag, let it out, waved the smoke away, and resumed pushing his laundry cart down the corridor.

Now.

Fungle opened the door and pulled Neema from the janitor's closet. The air was acrid with cigarette smoke. The building and its contents had become a catalogue of things Fungle was fleeing.

'Bye-bye now?' asked Neema.

'Yes,' said Fungle. 'Shhh.'

'Shhh!'

He pulled Neema along until they were back at the corridor junction.

Between the corridor and the door marked EXIT were twin metal doors Fungle recognised as an elevator. Struggling with Neema into the adjoining corridor toward the sanctuary of the Exit door, Fungle heard a rumble from behind the elevator doors. Above them a green 'up' arrow lit and a bell sounded. Behind them, human voices rose.

No time for niceties: Fungle yanked Neema along and bashed his shoulder against the bar across the Exit door. The door opened and they stumbled into a stairwell. Behind them, as the door hissed shut, the elevator doors opened. Looking through the narrowing slit, Fungle saw Dr Crucifer step out of the elevator. He looked pale and shaken as he headed toward the wing formerly occupied by the gnoles.

But first things first: Neema was barely conscious, and Dr Crucifer was about thirty seconds away from learning that his private little circus had pulled up stakes and left without so much as a thank-you note.

He looked around. The stairwell was stale and dim, each landing lit by a single low-watt bulb hooded by a dirty enamel shade. In here you could hear the leonine hum of power cables and the shriek of pipes, as if the building were crying out against what went on inside itself. The human beings baffled and padded the clean and professional rooms in which they conducted their business, but an area like this, stripped to its naked bone, could not mask the shrieks and groans that were echoes of human occupation.

Half-carrying Neema, Fungle headed down.

The basement was dim, humid, and thrumming with hidden machinery. Condensation bled from overhead pipes to stain the walls of narrow passageways. Why did humans feel that underground places must be kept dark and dank? The same mind that put Hell below the ground built the loud and churning drudgework machines, the exposed pipes and uncamouflaged grilles and naked lightbulbs, at the bottom of every building.

Fungle found another door without a coded lock. LAUNDRY, it read.

It was a room full of metal boxes. Some had windows like portholes. Some spun, whipping froth like huge butter-churns. Some vibrated with the force of dervishes spinning inside them. The heavy smell of starch and bleach hung in the air. *Laundry*, thought Fungle: *Don't soak it out – Shout it out!*

He jumped at a sudden motion: a bundle of laundry shot down a chute and flumped into a big-mouthed bin.

A laundry chute . . .?

Fungle considered. Were there delivery chutes as well? Some way of getting clean laundry from this room to the others? There had to be other exits!

From a bank of metal boxes against the far wall, pipes led to a large pipe that disappeared into the ceiling. Clean laundry lay on carts in folded stacks, tagged for destinations: BEHAV PSYCH, PRE O.R., WARD, FOOD SRVCS. On the wall was a sign: PLEASE LOG LAUNDRY BY DEPARTMENT FOR PROPER BILLING! Beneath that a clipboard on a nail held a pen on a string.

Fungle lowered Neema until she lay propped against a bundle of laundry. 'Take a nap?' she asked, childlike.

'Just fer now. And be quiet, remember.'

'Mousies.'

Fungle hurried to the pipes that fed the large pipe. Hot air rushed through them from the spinning machines along the wall. It probably emptied outside. But was the air too hot to endure; and if not, was there a grille or a door or some way to get in there?

He paused before the dryers. How like humans to build a loud wasteful machine to do the work the sun provided freely and effortlessly.

There didn't seem to be an easy way into the pipes. Fungle hurried to the laundry chute and stood on the metal frame of the laundry bin to peer in. No light. A hissing sound, though. Growing louder.

He jerked back just as another bundle of laundry shot from the chute and flumped into the bin. *Well, scratch climbing up there, sez me.*

Fungle desperately wanted to use a spell. He knew spells for revealing exits, spells for showing hidden spaces, spells for thousands of situations. Maybe they'd work here, maybe they wouldn't – the only way to know would be to try. But he dared not utter even the simplest one for fear of calling Theverat to him like a shark scenting blood. Here in this place of harnessed electrons and hard lines, few trees and spiritless stone, any magic at all would be a beckoning beacon.

Squeaking metal from the hall outside.

Fungle looked at Neema, asleep against a bundle of dirty laundry near the bin.

In the hallway someone chanted a rap song. Something bumped the laundry-room door. The doorknob turned. The door opened.

Jerry Allesandro pushed the canvas-lined cart full of soiled rags and towels into the laundry-room. 'Nother ton a laundry. Sheesh. How come they's a thousand loads of rags washed every week, and this building don't get no cleaner? 'Beats me,' he said out loud.

He pushed the cart to a washing machine, opened the large

front-loading lid, and released a catch on the cart. 'Don't you complain, fool,' Jerry continued. He lifted the handles and the canvas container upended, dumping laundry into the machine. 'You pullin' time-and-a-half for laundry duty in the middle of the night, Jersey Jerry.' He kicked at the canvas to knock the strays into the washer, lowered the now-empty rack, shut the washer door, and punched a red button on the front of the machine. 'You can live with that,' he finished.

Water hissed into the washer. The machine began to rumble.

Jerry sauntered to the bundled laundry on the floor and picked it up. 'Sheesh,' he muttered. 'People be washin' *bricks* or something tonight.' He stopped. Opened the washer. Dumped in the load.

Something banged against the rim of the front loader.

Jerry frowned and looked into the washer. All he saw was laundry. 'Awright,' he said. 'They want it washed, it get washed.'

He shut the door and jabbed the red button.

Hot water poured in.

Braced in the laundry chute Fungle watched in horrified frustration as the human being dumped the laundry bag containing Neema into a washer. What could he do? An irritating voice, the voice of television commercials, blared in his mind: *Really in hot water now! Cleans gnoles their whitest! Their brightest!*

He peeked down again. The human was loading another washer. The washer with Neema inside was filling with hot sudsy water. *Tide's in! Dirt's out!* Fungle dared not reveal himself. But if he didn't . . .

The human was heading toward him now. Fungle scooted back up the chute and held his breath.

Jerry stuck his head in the delivery chute. 'Last call!' he yelled – and got the hell out of the way.

Sssssss . . . flump! – and what sounded like a grunt. But no laundry bundle.

Jerry leaned into the chute again. 'Any time!' he yelled.

'Er . . . here ya goes,' called a voice.

The bundle shot out and hit Jerry square in the face. He staggered backward and the bundle hit the floor.

'Got it!' Jerry called.

'Thankee!' from above.

Jerry wheeled the bin to the next washer in line. 'You bet,' he said.

Fungle peeked out again. Jerry was at another washing machine.

Open, dump, shut, punch the red button. The drum of the washer holding Neema was lurching back and forth. *Those dirty rings!* thought Fungle. *You try soaking them out, you try scrubbing them out!* He hit himself on the head to make the commercial voices go away.

The human was heading for the door. It seemed to take forever for him to turn the knob, open the door, step out, shut it behind him.

Fungle dropped from the chute and into the bin.

Jerry came back in.

Fungle dropped like a stone.

Jerry went to the clipboard on the far wall and began writing in the laundry log. Fungle fought rising panic. Neema was going to die in there if he didn't do something soon. He could picture her in there: confused, drugged, disoriented, hot water splashing up her nose as she inhaled, filmy water stinging her eyes, white towels and stained coats winding around her like fabric eels. After all they had been through together, Neema was going to boil in that offensive contraption with Fungle not ten feet away. Ridiculous! No, he could not allow it, no matter what the consequences.

He stood up.

Jerry replaced the clipboard on the wall and left the room, never once looking his way.

Fungle vaulted from the bin and practically dove on the washing machine. He yanked the lever and threw open the door. Hot soapy water poured across him and onto the floor.

Fungle found himself face to face with a sputtering, dripping, soap-sudded, and very much awake Neema Cleverbread.

'D'ya think you could help me out a this thing, Fungle,' said Neema. 'I'm feelin' a bit . . . agitated.'

The tag on the bin of clean laundry was unremarkable; hastily-scrawled block capitals in black marker.

Fungle would remember it for the rest of his life.

He had hugged Neema close and said how good it was to see her open eyes, then told her about their escape-in-progress. Neema had nodded throughout, still a little bleary from the drugs in her system, but attentive and happy they were making their getaway. There was an edge to her gaze, though, something appraising that Fungle couldn't quite get a handle on.

'Here, Neema, look,' said Fungle. 'We'll hide under these here clean clothes. The tag says "auto room"; that must be where they keep their cars. Ford Broncos, Jeep Blazers, Dodge Aries. Rugged, tough, endurable.'

Neema looked at him strangely. 'Horrid things,' she said.

'But their cars'll be in a room leadin' out the building,' reasoned Fungle. 'We'll just stow ourselves here and get wheeled there easier an' safer than tryin' to find a way out. Maybe we can get in a car and drive ourselves out.' In his head spoke tough-sounding voices: *Feel the thrill of the road! We build excitement! Oh, what a feeling! Test-drive one today!*

'Fungle?' Neema was staring at him.

He shook himself. 'Sorry,' he muttered.

Neema nodded. She was thinking that Fungle did not look well, not well at all. The skin around his eyes was pouchy and grey. His hands kept fidgeting and his gaze continually darted as if catching motion where there was none. And the things he said! Like as if bein' human was a disease and Fungle'd been exposed to it too long. Catchin' it, he were. Best thing for him is to get out of here and get as far away as possible from this city of men. Head west and join up with the other gnoles and forget he ever saw or heard of human beings! Best for Fungle, and best for Neema, too, come to think of it.

They hid in the bin of clean laundry marked for AUTO RM 3. They piled white coats and towels on top of themselves and got as comfortable as they could. Who knew how long before they'd be delivered? It was stifling in the laundry bin, but at least the clean towels around them helped them dry quickly.

After what seemed like hours, Fungle slept. The last thing he was aware of before nodding off was Neema's hand holding his.

Motion woke him. Neema's grip tightened on his hand. Wheels rumbled below him. They were being taken from the laundry room. Escape was only minutes away!

Fungle squeezed Neema's hand in reassuring response. The human pushing above them sang tunelessly and low: 'Blue Suede

Shoes', which was back in the charts after a clip from Fungle's appearance on the Carson show had surfaced on MTV and VH-1. Voices welled and good-mornings were exchanged.

After a minute the cart stopped. A chime sounded and doors rumbled open. They pushed forward a short distance, and the doors rumbled shut. They jolted as an elevator rose, jolted again as it stopped. *Ding!* Doors opened and they were wheeled out. Fungle felt himself turning a corner, and his heartbeat quickened when he heard street-traffic sounds through an open door.

But the sounds muted as the door shut, and the cart wheeled on.

The tuneless singing broke off. 'Morning, Vinnie. Gotta make a delivery.'

'Morning, Jésus. Where's your ID badge?'

'My badge? Man, I dunno. Around. Why?'

'Gotta see it before I can let you in.'

'What? Vinnie, you gotta be kidding me. Three years I see you here, and don't say nothing when you steal doughnuts from the cafeteria for your coffee, and you wanna see my badge?'

'Not my rules, pal. Some heavy-duty stuff went down here last night. Didn't you hear?'

'Naw, man; I just got on. Gotta put away the crap the guy shoulda done on the shift before me. What kinda heavy-duty stuff?'

'Gnoles got away.'

A long whistle. 'For real? Oh Vinnie! Oh man, you guys must be really taking it from old man Crucifer.'

'Your badge, Jésus.'

'Come on, man. Look, I'm in and outta there. You think I'm smuggling, like, nuclear secrets, you can follow me. Okay? C'mon, Vinnie.'

'All I know is what I was told, Jésus. No one in or out without a badge.'

'Yeah, I know that. Look, Vinnie, they coulda put a parrot here to tell me what your orders are. But you got a brain and a gun. Okay? Don't be no parrot.'

A brief silence.

'In and out, Jésus,' Vinnie finally said.

'My man! In and out.' The cart began to move again. 'And, hey, if I see any gnoles around here, you'll be the first to know.'

Vinnie snorted. 'If they're in there, they aren't gonna be much good to nobody.'

Above them Jésus chuckled as he parked the laundry cart and left the room. The door shut behind him.

Silence.

Fungle waited. Beside him he felt Neema's tension, smelled her fear. No sounds in the room, no scent of humans.

But what he did smell was awful: excrement, urine, a metallic taint of blood. A terrible odour of formaldehyde cut through it all. Like giblins, but with a sharp chemical edge.

Fungle chanced a look.

Metal tables in the centre of the room. Gleaming metal and glass everywhere. Knives and scissors and saws on black cloth covering wheeled carts. Shelves and cabinets full of bottles and bags and jars. And in the bottles and bags and jars –

Beside him Neema stood up in the cart.

Fungle wished she were still drugged and unconscious.

'Fungle,' Neema said weakly.

'It's awright, Neema,' Fungle whispered. 'It's awright. We'll get you outta here.' He put an arm around her. 'It's awright. Come on.' He stepped from the laundry cart and turned to help her out. Behind her he read the letters on the frosted glass of the door:

Ɛ mooЯ γꙅqotuA

Neema stiffly let Fungle help her from the cart. She could not help looking at the bottles and jars and bags on tables and shelves and cabinets all around the room. Her expression was that of a child running head-on into proof that some cherished imaginary thing is not real, never was real, never could be real.

Floating in amber-coloured solution in the bottles and jars and bags were the heads and hearts and hands, brains and eyes and fetuses, of animals. Monkeys and mice and guinea pigs, dogs and cats and rats. Mouths open and eyes wide, the heads stared in drowned dismay.

The metal tables in the centre of the room had recesses and a drain. The cold tile floor had a drain in the centre.

In the far wall were two metal squares with handles. A sign on the left square read TRASH, and one on the right read INCINERATOR. A hand-lettered sign above them warned, *Please dispose in proper bin!*

Stained lab coats hung on wall pegs.

'So this is what they do,' whispered Neema. All around them floated the pieces of lives that once had been.

She turned to Fungle, and he was devastated by the horror on her face. 'Oh, Fungle, this is what they do.' All hope, all joy, all spit and fire that made her Neema Cleverbread, was gone from her voice.

And what could Fungle say? What word of comfort was there to offer, beyond an arm around her to let her know that he was there?

For the first time since he had conjured Molom and learned the task that lay before him, Fungle felt like giving up. Just sitting right here on the cold tile floor in this bright chill horrible room and waiting for the guards with their guns to find him and take him to Dr Crucifer.

To combat Theverat he had generations of lore and a lifetime of training and wisdom, a quick wit and good friends. But this? This room containing the butchery of everything he loved about the land in which he lived, denizens of the forest pickled and labelled and forgotten? What mage could fight a demon like this?

Neema had got away from him, and she walked around the room in blind dismay. Fungle reached out to her and stepped forward – and walked full into a tray of gleaming instruments. The cart tipped. For a moment it hung there, looking as if it might right itself. Fungle darted out a hand and seized the cart – but the instruments crashed to the floor.

Fungle and Neema looked at each other.

Behind the door there came a curse and a jingle of keys.

Fungle abandoned stealth. 'Go!' he shouted, and pointed to the far wall.

Neema ran for the metal squares with handles.

A key slid in the lock.

Neema reached the wall.

The door began to open.

Fungle threw the cart toward it.

Neema jerked open the right-hand square.

The cart hit the door and the door jerked back.

Neema dove into the chute.

Fungle saw the guard silhouetted by the frosted glass of the door.

The guard reached for his holster.

Fungle ran for the chute.

The studded end of the guard's taser edged past the door.

Fungle pulled open the left-hand square.

The guard ran towards him.

Fungle scrambled into the chute.

The taser touched his fur.

'Mindy-warp!' Fungle shouted desperately.

The guard triggered his taser.

Electrical energy flooded the room.

The crackling spark formed a shape.

At first it was a hallucination. Born of the fear summoned from deep within Vincent's mind by Fungle's mindy-warp, the beast was an illusion based on the guard's primal fears about protecting the autopsy room.

But magic had been used.

Mindy-warp had been uttered.

A door was opened.

Behind that door lay the demon Theverat, searching in darkness for portals, however small, that admitted a certain kind of light. And a single word had opened a tiny door; a ray of blue mage light had shone through –

– and Theverat seized it and followed it to its source, tearing past the borders of that tiny portal and ripping into the world. There the nightmare vision from the mind of the guard was made real as the electrical discharge from the taser gun took the form of a beast.

For an instant it was real.

Vincent Callienda gaped at the thing that rose before him.

Theverat rejoiced within this brief glove of crackling energy, for with a single uttered word he knew that the gnole was nearby. But even as the word that had manifested him had allowed him to use the unleashed energy of the taser to take form, so the spell and the charge faded.

The reality of the crackling glove he wore diminished.

Theverat lashed out in rage at the puny thing before him.

Fungle thrashed among ruptured bags of trash. He clawed a bag and it ripped open, pouring forth rotten garbage and a sickening stench. Fungle fought his way up toward daylight. He wallowed through bundles and clambered up boxes until he emerged at the top of a huge dumpster, blinking in the sunlight.

Sunlight! And air! When had he last seen light that was not man-made? The sun was paled by pollution haze, the air harsh with the tang of windborne chemicals – yet Fungle, filthy and reeking and exhausted, felt like a desert wanderer saved by an oasis.

He was behind the building that housed the Department of Parapsychological Research, in an alley lined with dumpsters and broken bottles and cans.

It was a wonderful sight.

Kodak Picture Spot! When every moment has to last a lifetime!

But where was Neema? She should have been here in the dumpster ahead of him.

'Neema?' he called. Not too loudly.

If she'd already crawled out, she would have waited for him.

'Neema!'

What could have happened? Where else would she be? Fungle tried to remember. The guard had opened the door. Fungle had thrown the cart. Neema had dived into the right-hand chute. The guard had come into the room with the pistol. Fungle had mindy-warped him. And had dived –

– into the *left*-hand chute.

He shut his eyes and remembered the signs on the metal squares.

Please dispose in proper bin! That was above.

TRASH That was the left side.

And the right side, where Neema escaped?

INCINERATOR

20 Wonders in Alice Land

There's a midget bum wrapped in a blanket thin and worn as an old dog's ear. He's pushing down Thirty-ninth, hooded like a Benedictine monk praying to a private Jesus, a sad scribbled page from a madman's Bible. In front of him's a Chinese Puerto Rican in a clean white T-shirt and cut-off leather gloves, amusing his friends smoking on the broken-hearted steps of a crumbling brownstone by making faces at a blind old man and his near-blind dog tugging him down the littered sidewalk. The second week of the garbage workers' strike has perfumed the streets like Black Death Paris, and last week's lottery tickets swelling in the gutters testify that everyone's only a dollar shy of being a millionaire. From offstreet balconies high above, zigzagged laundry lines hang obscure signal flags from shipwrecked buildings, warnings to unwary travellers entering the inner-city reefs where full-bellied rats stare from needle-strewn alleys with the lazy arrogance of the ruling classes.

The bum mutters and steps past a fossilised pile of dog droppings. A week-old *Times* page wraps dog-like round his shin, blown by a gust of concrete-gully wind. He palsies his leg to peel the yellowed page away, and his rustling plastic shopping bags, swelling with the lineaments of a vaguely led life, slap his hip as he ambles toward the blighted green heart of Manhattan.

Near Washington Square it's crowded as a paranoid's hit list and half as friendly. The midget bum wades upstream; autumnal grey-clad foot traffic flows around him, punch-clock rapids round a castaway rock. And who without sense would cast an eye at this stone? No one; they're fast-walking the human marathon, fretful relay racers with waylaid batons. The bum looks down at the sidewalk, a concrete backdrop now for bow-tied Florsheims below Gold Toe socks, leather Nikes capping sheer stockings.

A gaunt dreadlocked man leaning against a newspaper machine stares through the bum. His roped beard blows against the waxpaper Pepsi cup he jingles at blinkered passersby. *Change, mistuh?* Yeah, you should, buddy.

Across the street a hot-dog cart pulls up near the kerb and a man in a Yankees cap opens portals to an icy underworld stocked with canned soft drinks which the autumnal pedestrians use as passkeys for admission through doors that never stop revolving. They write their names on tape and put the tape on the cans and put the cans in refrigerators humming beside never-empty coffee machines in office kitchens. *Stan. Barbara. Shelly. Mr Jacoby.*

The sun's been shovelling the man-made overcast for three hours now. No one will see it all day long, or even notice that an entire day has passed without a glimpse of the burning ball that defines the day itself, but tonight its absence will haunt their caffeinated dreams as they lie stacked above and beside one another in tenements and brownstones and gated luxury apartments, mausoleums for the living as much as a cemetery is an apartment complex for the dead.

Guarding buildings high above the streets, stone gargoyles perch frozen in mid-scream, quarried watchmen forever calling out some forgotten silent alarm. But the ears that might have heard them have long ago turned to stone themselves.

In Central Park the bum rests with his small feet dangling from a bench tagged by aerosol Rembrandts. His shoes, the left one found in a wire garbage can twenty blocks from the right one, don't match. But then no two things about him match, so it all kind of goes together in an uncoordinated whole.

A thousand pages rustle as fearless pigeons tumble at his feet.

Across the misted emerald lawn is a lake, and in the lake an armada of ducks is bathing in the last heat of the engine summer before winging to warmer climes. The trunks of surrounding trees are carved with letters like stage greenery marked for location use. Above the irregular line of litmus trees turning colour with the season's change, the hard geometry of grey and black buildings looms like chess pieces ready to claim yet another square.

He had come here because he had seen it from on high: the only strip of green in the monochrome grey palette of the island. A heart of living wood in a body of concrete and metal, it had beckoned to him with memories of a home far removed from him – removed by distance, by circumstances, by events, and by the farthest remove of all: by the muddy sediment of recent memories. What alien distance he had come – across a geography within and without – from a life and a time where he had strung a rope hammock between sturdy trees, and there swung pendulously and read ponderously until his eyelids had leadened and he lay snoring with the book face-down on his lap like a teacher's dream of a bird, slung between trees like some strange fruit in a net basket hung in the larder of the earth itself.

He'd thought the park would remind him of home. But sitting here on this wooden bench in this man-made wood with city-grey pigeons pecking around him on this island of green in this island of grey, he felt farther from the forest than ever. He imagined himself wandering the long narrow stretch of the park, blessing every tree he encountered – for every tree here was a lucky tree to have been allowed to grow at all.

What'm I going to do about Neema? Pigeons scuttled as he kicked his feet. *I've nothing ta feed you*, he thought. *I've nothin' ta feed* me. He felt lost and alone.

But I don't have to be, he realised. *I've help I can call forth.*

He set about gathering the ingredients necessary to aid him in summoning Molom.

Tyre Iron yanked Fat J back behind the tree. His vintage World War I leather aviator's cap made him look like a pinhead. 'I do not like what we should be here, Fat J,' he said. 'The sun is out and so are we.'

'Don't blow a gasket already,' Fat J replied in his adenoidal voice. An I LIKE IKE button glinted on his leather biker's vest as he turned to face his scavenger-party partner. 'I wanna know what the story is wit' Friar Tuck over there.'

'We done took in half-a-dozen bums this week,' protested Tyre Iron. 'They never got nothing no good to none of us.'

'Don't be a nimrod,' Fat J retorted. He reached up to tug the tarnished gold ring dangling from Tyre Iron's septum. 'That honker a yours on the blink? Take a whiff. That ain't no bum.'

'CC ain't gonna like if we bring him someone else what he don't wanna see,' said Tyre Iron. He pulled thoughtfully at his nose-ring, then slid a finger under his aviator's cap to scratch at his scaly head. 'You know how he gets.'

But Fat J was peering out from behind the tree again. Beneath the black leather vest he wore a stained blue bowling shirt, and as he leaned out a section of embroidered lettering peeked out from under the left shoulder of the vest. Tyre Iron wondered what it said. He wondered what everything said. He thought maybe someone oughta teach him to read. That last time he'd brought pizza back to the shelter there'd been anchovies on it, and CC'd got all mad and pop-eyed, and yelled that any idiot coulda seen on the ticket that there was extra anchovies on this pizza. In fact –

'Holy moly,' said Fat J, derailing Tyre Iron's train of thought. 'Willya take a look at this.'

Tyre Iron leaned to peer out from the other side of the tree. St Francis among the pigeons over there had collected a buncha twigs and acorns and dirt, and now he knelt in front of the park bench and pulled back his monk-like cowl to scratch his furry head.

His furry head?

'Hey, wait a second,' said Tyre Iron. 'That ain't no bum no how no way.'

Fat J leaned back to sneer at him. 'Tyre Iron, you always cease to amaze me. Not only ain't that a bum, it ain't even a human bing.' His expression softened and he patted Tyre Iron on his thick-muscled arm. You could only have so much fun baiting Tyre Iron before you started feeling guilty about it.

Now the creature was making weird motions with its hands and chanting in a low monotone. 'Whatever it is,' said Fat J, 'it's on our turf and it's acting weird.' He grinned. 'C'mon,' he said. 'This'll be more fun than raiding milk trucks.'

Tyre Iron grew sad at the memory. 'I *miss* milk trucks,' he mooned. 'Creamy glug-glug glass, and *choklit*, too.'

'Me too, pal. Milk trucks, bread carts, rag men, Welcome Wagons, Fuller brush men.' Fat J shook his head. The earrings encrusting his ratpink ears tinkled. 'Those were the days.'

'Avon ladies,' Tyre Iron said mournfully.

Fat J frowned. 'Ah, you didn't wanna wear that stuff anyway. C'mon, putcha fangs in and let's get this show on the road.'

Tyre Iron grinned thickly. He'd forgotten about his fangs. They were cheap white plastic vampire fangs he'd found in a dumpster, but they glowed in the dark. Trash got interesting this time of year. After Hallowe'en and after Christmas were his favouritest times of all. Tyre Iron pulled the plastic fangs from the back pocket of his unevenly cut-off Levi's 501 bluejeans and put them in his mouth. He made a face at Fat J.

'Scary,' acknowledged Fat J, trying not to laugh. He slipped off his mismatched flipflops for greater stealth. 'Ready?'

Tyre Iron nodded. 'Lesh do it to it,' he said.

Fungle struggled in the canvas mailbag. It was no use. Whatever these creatures were, they were too good, too efficient. He was wrapped like a birthday present. They had obviously done this sort of thing before.

He'd been sitting on the park bench wondering what his next step should be when someone had tapped him on the shoulder. 'Eck-shkoosh me, pleesh,' someone had said. Fungle had turned to see a bulge-eyed rat-skinned short creature with a leather cap, a gold nose-ring, and a grinning mouth full of clean white fangs. He had opened his mouth to ward it off, or utter a spell, or do *some*thing, but someone behind him had stuffed a rag into his mouth and shoved a rough burlap bag over his head. In seconds his hands and feet were bound and he was stuffed with frightening efficiency into a canvas mailbag with a drawstring opening. With his mouth gagged he couldn't utter a scream for help or even the simplest spell.

The sound of his captors' shoes hurrying through the park grass changed to harder pounding on pavement. Traffic sounds rose around him, and once he heard a distant voice yell, 'Tak-*see!*' The accent was thick and the voice deep; he couldn't tell if it had been a woman or a man.

The traffic sounds faded and echoed on stone as they entered an enclosed alleyway. Fungle heard metal grating stone, then an echo of distant water splashing, like a deep well. Slung across a shoulder he bounced in time with dull gongings of shoes on iron rungs. The splashing echo rose around him as he descended. The light dimmed and the air grew moist and cool. A horrible stench rose. Bold rats screamed brazen challenges.

Soon a distant dissonant hum rose to a tortured metal screech as a midtown subway screamed past like a locomotive wrenching damned souls into hell. In the mailbag Fungle tensed, having never heard a thing like it in his life, and thought he was being left as a sacrifice to some horrific dragon that lived in caverns beneath the city.

But the monster screamed past them down the tunnel and they resumed trudging through the dank darkness. After a while Fungle heard stone grating against stone, and they passed into a passage he could tell was narrow from the flat unechoing closeness of his captors' footfalls.

They stopped. A bolt was drawn, hinges creaked. They continued walking, and Fungle brushed past a piece of cloth. If he hadn't been in the bag he would have seen that this was a heavy black curtain hanging in a narrow tunnel to cut off light from the room beyond. Two narrow ovals had been cut in the curtain about two feet from the floor and eight inches apart. Any light behind the curtain shone through these two holes. To anyone who did not know better, it seemed as if the tunnel was blocked by a rat the size of a pig.

Past the curtain he heard voices and music.

'Why, if it ain't Fat J and Tyre Iron!' called a wheedling, adenoidal voice. 'And whatta you two brought for the big game today? Anudda bum on a crutch and you might just hafta be our main event!'

'Naw, no bum,' said Tyre Iron.

'Even better,' replied Fat J.

'You hope,' muttered Tyre Iron.

'Put a cork in it,' whispered Fat J.

Fungle was deposited on the floor. He struggled, then held still when he realised the drawstring was being untied. The opening dilated around him and the bag lowered like a shed snakeskin. His grinning captors removed his gag, then stepped away.

Fungle gasped.

Crucifer stood in the shadows beneath the overpass, rubbing his hands to ward off the morning chill. Cars and buses streamed overhead, metal moths hurtling toward the magnet city, their drivers never wondering about the perpetually twilit hinterland that lurked beneath the city's bridges and overpasses. Crucifer remembered childhood fairy tales of trolls who lived beneath bridges and wondered what sort of trolls might live beneath the bridges of Manhattan. He feared he was about to find out.

Late last night, still in his office and working on his second pot of coffee, Crucifer had unlocked a drawer in his desk and removed several items: books on conjuration and magic, purchased furtively and a bit shamefacedly from several occult shops uptown. A videotape showing the astral-projection experiment in Room 205. A Ouija board.

Crucifer had studied a chapter entitled 'Communing with Spirits' in one of the books, and though his education and instincts rebelled against what he read, he followed its instructions carefully. Before long he sat naked in his office, a pentacle drawn in blue ink on his right palm, a spiral on his left, the Ouija board in front of him, an ancient Latin prayer playing in his mind.

He set his fingers on the felt-tipped planchette. 'Are you there?'

he had asked. 'Theverat?' He found it difficult to speak the name. He waited.

After a moment his computer beeped at him. He jumped in surprise and turned to look at the monitor. Two lines of words preceded the blinking green cursor:

> **REALLY, TIB. I WOULD THINK A MAN WITH YOUR EDUCATION WOULD PUT HIS FAITH IN TECHNOLOGY◄**

Feeling absurdly foolish, as if he had been caught in some adolescent ploy, Crucifer had put his clothes back on and sat before the keyboard.

> Who are you? Where are you? WHAT are you?
> **I AM THEVERAT◄**
> **NOWHERE / NOW HERE◄**
> **I'M A DEMON, TIB◄**

Crucifer had stared at the glowing letters for several minutes before he was able to summon the nerve to type again. He had many questions, and all were answered. The scientist and the – how could he say it, how could any man of reason actually use the word? – the *demon*, had conversed long into the night, and Crucifer had come to regard Theverat with something more than awe, something deeper than friendship, something close to love. Theverat understood him. Theverat knew the loneliness of a brilliant mind isolated from a world of dullards. Theverat distilled Crucifer's deepest motivations and explained them. He reassured him that there was no more natural order than that the more capable should dominate. Theverat showed him that his lifelong feelings of alienation had been for a purpose, that all wolves feel alienated from sheep. Theverat forgave him his incompetence in letting the gnole escape. They still had the female, found cowering in the incinerator shaft, and she might prove useful, if only as leverage in dealing with the male. Bait, perhaps. Theverat would cover all his bases. Theverat knew. Theverat understood, and in understanding, caused Crucifer to know and understand himself for the first time.

Theverat forgave.

He let Crucifer know that he needed eyes and ears and hands in the human world.

> **THERE ARE GREAT THINGS TO ACCOMPLISH,**

the demon had conveyed to him,

AND THERE IS MUCH WORK TO BE DONE. I NEED YOU, CRUCIFER. HELP
ME ESTABLISH THE NEW ORDER. HELP ME CREATE THE NEW ATLANTIS.
HELP ME END DISEASE, POVERTY, STARVATION, WAR, DROUGHT,
PESTILENCE – A THOUSAND OTHER PLAGUES UPON THE WORLD OF
MAN. ISN'T THAT THE PURPOSE OF SCIENCE, OF KNOWLEDGE? HELP
ME, AND KNOW THE TRUE BOUNDLESSNESS OF THE MIND UPON THE
WORLD. ◄

Crucifer had returned to his apartment in Pleasanton and slept
contentedly for the first time in years.

This morning he had entered the office to find a fax waiting
for him. It showed a hand-drawn but precise map, a clear set of
directions, and a time. There was no signature, no source-of-origin
number along the upper edge of the facsimile. But it ended with
Don't disappoint me, Tib, and what clearer signature could there
have been, really?

So here was Crucifer, miles from his office in DPR and pacing in
the shadows beneath an overpass in a part of town he wouldn't have
wanted to be in even if he'd been heavily armed in bright daylight.
Waiting.

For Theverat to appear? Crucifer didn't think so. He doubted
the

(*say it, say it!*)

. . . demon . . .

. . . could reveal himself here. Not easily, not without the
expenditure of large amounts of power, not without some wedge
of magic to open the door between the realms. Last night Crucifer
had outlined an idea for a kind of generator, a technological device
powered by magical ability, designed solely for the purpose of
serving as a conduit from Theverat's world to this one.

Theverat had been pleased.

I HAVE MANY HELPERS

he had written,

AND YOU WILL BE FIRST AMONG THEM ◄

But first, thought Crucifer, echoing Theverat's final words of the
evening, *we must retrieve the male. And for that we will use two things:
the female, and one of my . . . assistants.*

Crucifer blew warmth into his hands. He pulled back his coat-
sleeve and glanced at his watch: 9:06. Six minutes past time.
Perhaps he should –

'Crucifer.' The voice was horrible. Crucifer thought of blades chopping raw meat.

He had heard it before.

It came from behind one of the massive concrete pylons supporting the overpass. Crucifer thrust his fists into his coat pockets and stepped tentatively toward it.

A nightmare stepped into view.

Fungle was marched blindfolded down corridors echoing with the thick splashes of sludgy water beneath his feet and the feet of his dozen or so guards. From the sounds around him Fungle tried to construct an image of what the guards were doing, of where they were headed, but beyond the mere fact of their marching he drew a blank.

They had pulled off the mailbag that had bound him and removed his gag, and Fungle had sat stunned in a large stone room filled with the strangest creatures he had ever seen. At first they reminded him of giblins because of the way they dressed – scavenged human clothing, trinkets, odds and ends, obscure weaponry and implements, and a general motley feeling, though much more drab. But the resemblance ended there. These creatures were short and pale and smooth, rat-eared and thick-fingered. There was something unfinished-looking about them. Their accents were New York heavy and their manner was more surreptitious than the giblins.

There had been at least a hundred of them in the room with him.

The adenoidal voice that had called to Tyre Iron and Fat J – presumably his captors – now said, 'F' cryin' out loud! You guys rob a zoo?'

The other creatures laughed.

Fungle looked for the source of the voice. His first impression was that a pile of junk around which the creatures were gathered had somehow spoken to him. Then he realised that another one of the creatures sat in the midst of the junk, and his second impression was that this creature looked like a lunatic's description of a mad clown king on a knicknack throne.

Subsequent knowledge only served to substantiate this impression.

'Found it in the park,' said Fat J. 'It's . . . you know. Different.'

'A change of pace,' suggested the bizarre figure on the knicknack throne.

'Yeah. Variety,' said Fat J.

The mad regal frowned, and the soggy Macanudo cigar wedged into the corner of its thin-lipped frog-like mouth drooped. 'Well, it don't look nothing like that other sideshow freak you guys brought in. What is it, do ya think?'

Fungle took a deep breath. 'It's a gnole,' he said.

The room echoed with a surprised commotion. The enthroned figure waved them to silence with a flyswatter sceptre and peered out from behind what Fungle only then realised was a clown's mask held before it on a rod. The silence was briefly interrupted when he shifted on his throne and smashed an inflatable giraffe squeaky toy that protested in high-pitched baby talk.

'An' what are *you*, if you please?' Fungle asked politely.

Behind the clown's mask the pasty eyelids narrowed around bloodshot eyes. The king of these ragtag rascals – may as well call him a king, Fungle thought – hooked a heavy-ringed finger around the stogie and unstoppered his mouth. 'I'm the one askin' the questions, ace, that's what I am.' He drummed his fingers on the arm of his throne. 'And *you*,' he decided, grinning unpleasantly, 'have just become today's Main Event. Boys?'

Laughing and screeching and yapping they had blindfolded Fungle, and now here he was, being marched down these wet stinking tunnels. After a while they reached a large area formed by the intersection of several tunnels. Fungle's blindfold was removed.

Battery- and kerosene-powered lanterns and burning torches provided illumination. What they illuminated was a rickety arena formed by plywood sidings stolen from construction sites (handbills and movie posters had once covered them; now the posters shredded in the damp). Encircling three-quarters of the arena were flimsy wooden bleachers, and the strange pale creatures filled these, already cheering and stamping. The arena floor was dark with stagnant water. The unbleachered end led to a tunnel blocked by a heavy wooden door.

Fungle was led to the centre of the wet arena floor. Two guards remained holding either arm. The creatures in the bleachers began cheering wildly, and Fungle saw the huge heavy knicknack throne being carried like a palanquin by a host of straining underlings. The king was seated on it, waving with regal indifference in a motion much like someone throwing a Frisbee. After much bumping and bobbling the throne was brought to the front nearest the arena floor and set down. The creatures who had been carrying it began wringing their hands. One of them produced a mashed Hershey bar from a pocket and throttled it over its mouth to drink the muddy contents.

The king stood from his throne, yanked the squishy Macanudo from his mouth, and raised his thick-fingered, ring-encrusted hands for silence. 'My fellow metrognomes,' he said –

(*Metrognomes?* Fungle wondered.)

'– My fellow metrognomes. What time is it?'

As one the metrognomes shouted, 'It's time to play . . . *Al! Eee! Gator!*' They began stamping their feet, one-two, one-two, one-two. They jumped up and down in a curious and remarkable sequence that gave the effect of a huge wave washing around the arena. Fungle was sure the flimsy stands would collapse, but they only swayed and creaked.

The king held his palms out for silence. 'Motli!' he called.

One of Fungle's guards, a potbellied but otherwise thin metrognome wearing a black eyepatch with a blue eye drawn on it, snapped to attention. 'Yuh grace!' he replied.

The king slapped his forehead with his flyswatter sceptre. It rang lightly against the upturned pot he wore for a crown. 'We got one a our friends with the grins?'

Motli nodded eagerly. 'We sure do, Majesty!' he said. He released Fungle and went to the heavy wooden door.

'Give us a look, then!' commanded the king. 'Motli – show us what's behind door number one!'

Motley threw back the bolt and pulled a large iron ring set into a heavy iron plate. The door swung out, sending a black ripple along the arena floor. A smell like wormy gorgonzola rose from the stagnant water.

He heard splashing from the tunnel. A long low white shape emerged, growing more distinct as it neared. Soon it lay grinning on the arena floor, and Fungle could only stare in horrified disbelief.

A fourteen-foot albino alligator grinned across the arena floor – grinned at *him*, Fungle could have sworn. The creature was so pale it seemed to glow in the dim tunnel light. A broad leather muzzle bound powerful jaws lined with curving teeth. Attached to its muzzle was a leash, and holding the leash was a metrognome wrangler with one galoshed foot on the alligator's ridged back.

'Now *that's* a set a luggage!' the king shouted gleefully.

Motli grinned and bobbed his eyepatched head. 'Today's alley gator,' he said, 'is a fourteen-foot female who hasn't eaten a bite since we took her beneath the Forty-second Street pumping station the day before yesterday.' He lifted his eyepatch to leer with two perfectly functioning eyes. 'And she has an attitude with a capital A!'

More cheering from the metrognomes.

And suddenly Fungle's guard left him standing there alone in the centre of the arena, went to join the other guards standing behind a low wall in front of the bleachers, guards holding spears made of knives or broken bottles tied to broomhandles. Fungle was alone in the arena with the wrangler and the albino alligator.

The wrangler removed the alligator's muzzle and hopped back over the wall.

The alligator yawned to show a hundred teeth, then closed its wide wedge mouth with a clapboard clack. Smiled at Fungle: Howdy-doody, stay for lunch? Lazily raised itself on its short bowed legs and flowed toward Fungle, a faint ripple preceding it along the black water on the arena floor.

Fungle glanced at the metrognomes. They were cheering, making wagers, gobbling scavenged pizza crusts and stale crescents of doughnut remnants, stamping. The king on his throne leered maniacally.

The alligator was fifteen feet away now.

Fungle – well, Fungle felt no alarm, if you want to know the absolute truth. This would have been an utterly horrifying moment to just about anyone else, but putting Fungle in a pit with a wild animal was a bit like imprisoning a gourmet chef in a fully stocked kitchen. He needed no learned spells or magelore to aid him here, no devious charm or painful blasting blinding spell. The lore of the forest itself – and of mountain, of desert, of swamp, learned and loved throughout his life – that lore would see him through just fine, thankee.

So in truth it was without great drama that, within seconds of the alligator's release, Fungle was holding its snout closed with one hand and rubbing its belly with the other. Its reptile eyes rolled back, its tail swished languidly, then not at all. The alligator was asleep.

Fungle patted its pale plates a few times, then gently released the conquered dragon and stood to face the knicknack throne.

The metrognomes booed and hissed. Fungle was pelted with food and balled paper cups. A pizza box skimmed down from on high, whirled above the heads of the jilted shouting metrognomes, spun mere inches above the dank water of the arena floor, missed

Fungle, and smacked the dozing alligator square on the nose. The creature was awake and on all fours in an instant. It launched out from behind Fungle like a leathery saw-teethed missile and sped straight for the low wall. The guards thrust their spears. Without slowing the alligator snapped one into three pieces in its powerful jaws. The few remaining spears snapped against its white luggage-case hide. The alligator swarmed up and over the low wall like a bad dream, and the guards scattered as it made straight for the king, frozen wild- and wide-eyed on his thrift-store throne. For a moment their gazes met: the king's bloodshot and not a little mad, the 'gator's stony above a mouth grinning like it had caught sight of a good joke. Just the briefest pause while with their eyes they held the most primal conversation possible: *I'm going to* eat *you!* You're going to *eat* me?

Then the 'gator arrowed forward and the king pressed back onto his throne, ridiculously holding his flyswatter sceptre ready.

A brain-jarring bang and a flood of light. Fungle stood in the centre of the arena, hand high above his head. In it burned something blue-white like a little sun, but its light was somehow cold. All eyes were on it – even the alligator's. While the gaping metrognomes merely stared, the 'gator swung round, eyes shining hungrily with the reflected cold light. It clapped its great jaws several times as if giving reptilian applause, then lumbered toward Fungle, never taking its eyes from the light. What great appeal the prize lofted by Fungle held for the creature, what dazzling vision lured its ancient nature, no one ever knew. Fungle held something that drew it irresistibly, and it bellied into the stagnant water once more and glided toward him like a canoe, tail wagging like a puppy's.

Fungle lowered his hand, lowered the light, to touch the creature's head. The alligator closed its eyes and seemed to give a deep grunting sigh.

The room was silent. Fungle looked up from the contented alligator to the figure on the throne.

'Name's Corinthian Codswollop, ace, and I'm King of the Metrognomes, which is these boys here.' Many of the creatures bowed half-mockingly. King Codswollop on his throne looked smug. 'Ain't hearda us, have yuz? That's 'cause we're so good at bein' sneaky – ain't we, boys?'

'Famous for it!' declared a metrognome.

'We been around a long time,' continued Codswollop, 'livin' on the edge of the human bing world.' He grinned evilly. 'I *like* livin' on the edge, ace. There's rats and roaches and raccoons livin' between walls and under floors and raidin' garbage cans; there's coyotes and 'possums sneakin' around tryin' to beat out wild cats, and dogs scrappin' for a buncha scraps.' He thumbed his chest boastfully. 'Well, we got 'em all beat by a mile. Know why?' Codswollop grinned to show rotten teeth set in grey gums and looked around the bleachers. 'Tell 'im why, boys!'

The metrognomes each raised a finger to a temple. 'Because we're *smart!*' they responded.

'Hallelujah,' the king commented dryly. 'Now – I been kind enough to answer your questions first, seeing as how I maybe owe you a little favour, and you got your special seat there right next to my throne. So tell me who *you* are, so's my loyal subjects –' he indicated the hundred-odd (*very* odd) and truthfully somewhat pathetic band assembled in the bleachers '– can know who they're indebted to for saving their kind and generous king, which is me.'

Fungle thought it best to take the king seriously. He suspected that for the most part the metrognomes really were a band of sneak-thieves and scavengers, little more than pirates preying on what poor vessels ventured into the *terra incognita* of the city – but if they took pride in themselves he felt he should treat them accordingly. Right now he needed all the friends he could get, beggars can't be choosers, don't count the numbers on a gift calendar, Wisp always said. 'Why, I'm a gnole, yer majesty, as I said before,' he said, standing to bow graciously. 'Fungle Foxwit gnole, by name.'

'Majesty!' The eyepatched metrognome Motli was raising a hand like an eager schoolchild. 'I hearda him!' he said. 'I read about him inna *Times.*'

Codswollop frowned. His face grew alarmingly red, and objects on the knicknack throne began to rattle as he trembled with anger. 'That rag!' he shouted. 'That fishwrap? I wouldn't line a boydcage with the *Times!*' He slapped his thigh. 'The *Post*, the *Post*, and nuttin' but the *Post*, swelp me God!' He thrust a judgemental finger at Motli. 'Go up an' get me today's *Post!*'

Motli made haste. Codswollop settled back in his throne and folded his arms, all beaming friendly contentment again. 'They got no sense for the finer things,' he confided to Fungle, 'no learnin' or subtlety.' (He pronounced the 'b'.) 'If it weren't for me they'd still be a scattered bunch of half-starved orphans scrounging for breadcrusts. No headquarters, no organisation, no order.' He indicated the tunnels. 'None of this.' He shook his head and clutched his breast melodramatically. 'It's a tough burden sometimes, but what else can I do?' He shrugged it off. 'Listen, ace, that was a great trick with the 'gator. Think you could teach it to me?'

Fungle groped for a reply, and the king waved it away. 'Plenty of time for all that later,' he said. 'But I gotta tell ya, we never had nobody pull a stunt like that down here. That's gonna be harder to beat than a rubber egg.'

'Er . . . where . . . ? That is, yer majesty . . .' He indicated the heavy wooden door that once more sealed the tunnel from which the alligator had been brought.

Codswollop shrugged. 'Kids,' he said. 'They haul 'em back from Florida vacations; their parents think they're cute till they start trying to saw off Junior's fingers. Then: *foosh!* – straight downa commode. You think they die inna water? Huh-uh; they *live* inna water! So they swim along down here and munch on whatever's in front of 'em – an' believe me, brudda, a *lot* gets in front of 'em – an' they grow an' they breed. They don't never see the sun, that's why they're so white. Pretty t'rific, huh?'

Fungle could only stare.

'They can bite a tyre in half,' continued Codswollop, 'but, like you saw, you can hold their jaws shut like this.' He held thumb and forefinger a few inches apart. 'Ain't got much muscle for opening.' He grinned evilly. 'But then, they don't need to open as hard as they gotta close, know what I'm sayin'? Say, I didn't know you could put 'em to sleep by rubbin' their bellies.'

Fungle said, 'Well, er, you know . . .'

'There's crocodiles down here, too,' continued Codswollop, 'but they're so fast and mean we don't like to use 'em 'cause it's no fun. No sport in it, y'know? Alley gators may not be as fast and mean as crocs, but they're *lots* bigger.'

In a moment Motli had returned with the day's *Post* in hand. He gave it to Codswollop and bowed ungracefully.

'Papers,' said Codswollop admiringly as he slipped off the string that bound the *Post*. 'I love 'em. Always one around for whoever needs one.' He unfolded it. 'Alla news that's fit fa princes,' he said smugly. '*And* kings.' He read the headline and did a bug-eyed doubletake. 'Holy cannoli!' he said. He held out the front section for all to see. Beside a full-colour picture of Fungle's profile was a headline:

FUNGLE CRITICAL!
Doctors Hopeful, but Virus Still a Mystery

'That's you!' he said.

'It's a lie,' said Fungle.

Codswollop looked mortally stricken. 'A lie? This is the N'yok *Post!* They ain't allowed to lie!'

So Fungle explained to the metrognome king who he was and where he had come from, and how he had come to be in the city, which was the only world the metrognomes knew. Like all dyed-in-the-wool native New Yorkers, the metrognomes saw the world in terms of the City and the Rest of the World: a sort of cloudy, semi-mythical unreality through which vague forces moved, interesting but irrelevant. Fungle didn't tell him about his mission to find Baphomet – no need for that! – but he did tell about his capture and the terrible experiments conducted on him. While it seemed he had won them over, if only because they were in his debt, he still did not exactly trust the metrognomes (he'd learned a thing or two about trust in these past few weeks!). But he wanted them as allies and he needed their help, so he told the metrognome king how the humans had used Neema as a hostage and a lever against him, and about his escape. He told Codswollop about the terrible room containing parts of animals in glass jars, and that Neema was still a captive there.

'Now *there's* a story you don't hear every day,' Codswollop said. He shook his head. 'You shoulda laid low,' he confided. 'Stayed where you belonged and not stuck your head up.' He waved at the room. 'Look at us! They don't got a clue we're here, right under their big flappin' feet, and we're happy as fleas onna dog, ain't we, boys? We ain't missin' out on nuttin'! Sneak inna first-run movies, all the Chinese food and pizza you could ever wanna eat, free subway rides wherever you wanna go, yupheads in the Village you can hit up for change, whatever wardrobe you can find. Hah! An' we'll go on havin' alla this – so long's they never know we're down here. We stick our heads out, *ffft!* –' he drew a finger across his wattled throat '– the Big Nuttin'.' He shook his head sadly. 'But you! You coulda kept it quiet and hadda good thing goin'.' He shrugged and tossed the paper away carelessly. His subjects squabbled over various sections, mainly sports and the funnies.

Seeing that Codswollop was sympathetic toward him, Fungle started to frame a question – a request, actually; a huge favour. But Codswollop clapped his hands and stood. 'Well, enough a this kinda talk – Motli!'

'Yuh majesty!'

'Do we got our next contestant?'

Motli bowed and grinned. 'Ready an' waiting!' He leaned into the tunnel and snapped his fingers. 'Come on down!' he called.

A quarrelsome voice rose. Feet sloshed through the rancid water. Fungle was frantically trying to think what he could do to stop this barbaric, horrible game when he heard a voice shouting: 'Git this thing offen me an' I'll leave me knuckle prints on yer noggin!'

Three figures came into view down the tunnel.

'C'mon wif yer! I'll rip yer leg off an' make you a pogo stick!'

Soon Fungle saw that two of the figures were leading the third by ropes knotted around his bound wrists. The bound figure struggled and cursed and resisted every sloshing step of the way.

'Untie me an' I'll make ya suck this bilge water till there's more inside ya than out! *Metrognomes* – hah! *Retro*gnomes is more like it! Maybe you an' me sprang from some common ancestor, ratface, but you didn't spring far enough! Now untie me an' I'll, I'll . . . I'll . . .'

He stopped when he saw the hundred gathered metrognomes.

His eyes widened when he saw the smugly grinning alley gator.

His jaw dropped when he saw a familiar face in the crowd.

'Fungle?' he said doubtfully.

Fungle jumped to his feet. 'Ka!'

Crucifer's hands shook so badly he could barely drive. At a red light he unlocked the glove compartment and rummaged until he came up with his emergency pack of Benson & Hedges. He pushed the cigarette lighter, tore the cellophane off the pack and tossed it behind him, and tamped out a cigarette. His trembling fingers dropped it. He overturned the pack and shook several cigarettes onto the seat; he jammed one into his mouth just as the cigarette lighter clicked.

Behind him a car honked.

Crucifer glanced in the rear-view. A grey-haired woman in a business dress was giving him the finger. He looked at the traffic light and saw that it was green. He burned rubber into the intersection, brought the red-hot coil of the lighter to the cigarette, and inhaled. Stale. He didn't care.

Crucifer had not had a cigarette in over a year.

The nicotine calmed him somewhat. Now he only felt panic instead of blind raging terror.

He tried not to think about what was in the trunk.

He laughed out loud. 'Right,' he said to himself. 'And while you're at it, try not to think about a pink elephant on a highwire.' He snapped on the radio, punched a button, twisted the volume knob to the right. Thunder filled the car. It sounded like metered noise, which meant it was rock and roll. Crucifer didn't care; he beat the steering wheel in time to the thudding percussion and tried not to think.

What was in his trunk would have sent H.P. Lovecraft into a gibbering hissy fit. What was in Crucifer's trunk would turn a Chinaman's hair white.

What was in Crucifer's trunk was the Domino's pizza delivery man.

In hat and sunglasses and coat the creature had just looked *wrong*.

Without them, it was a spiked nightmare from a thousand light years away.

Crucifer blew smoke into the car and turned left toward the metal garage door set in an unassuming five-storey brick building in a decaying industrial section of the Lower West Side. He jammed the car in 'Park' and got out, reaching for his wallet. He slid his passcard into the slot and punched a code. The garage door was open by the time he was behind the wheel again.

Twenty feet beyond the entrance an elderly guard sat in his booth. Crucifer had nodded to him every morning for years. Half the time the guard didn't even look at Crucifer's ID badge, he just gave a two-fingered salute and waved him on through. They had never exchanged more than a few words.

Today, however, was the second day after the embarrassment of the male gnole's escape, and the guard meticulously scrutinised Crucifer's badge before waving him through. Yeah, right: good work, rent-a-cop. Like the gnole's gonna sneak *in* to DPR.

But you never know what might smuggle itself in, eh, Tib?

Crucifer angrily stubbed the half-smoked cigarette into the spotless ashtray. That voice, that voice! Calling him 'Tib' with easy familiarity, persuading him with confidence of the triumph of pure reason, luring him with a dangling carrot of knowledge and power, seducing him with a vision of a technocratic utopia where knowledge reigned – a New Order. But Crucifer sensed the power, the threat, that lay in the easy arrogance of that ancient tone.

Crucifer parked in his space and got out. He was halfway to the elevator, functioning on autopilot, before he remembered.

The trunk.

He turned to look at his car. It looked so innocent there, sandwiched between a Previa van and a Geo economiser. Who could've known? He pictured a police officer making him open the trunk. *Well, my goodness – how did* that *get in there?*

He took a deep breath and tasted stale tobacco. Jingled car keys in his hand. Thought briefly about not opening the trunk. About leaving that *thing* in there, walking out of DPR, booking a flight to anywhere close to Micronesia – where sooner or later, he knew, Theverat would find him.

He headed toward his car.

The key made a soft sound of acceptance as he slid it into the trunk lock. Turned it, *clack!* Lifted the lid. Stepped back.

Emaciated thorny leathery joints unfolded. The creature stepped onto the garage floor. It stared at Crucifer with great glaring yellow oval eyes. It clutched a wooden spear in one chestnut-knuckled hand. Crucifer had thought the figures dangling from the tip were fetish dolls or hex symbols – until one had squirmed.

Crucifer pulled a blanket from the trunk and shut the lid. He held the blanket out to the creature, but it only continued to stare unnervingly. Didn't it ever blink? Carefully avoiding the tips of its spines – some instinct warned him not to touch them – he draped the blanket around the broken-stickman figure and stepped back. Crucifer shook his head. 'You look about as human as a sea urchin,' he said. His smile was quick and nervous. 'No offence,' he said.

The creature's answering feral smile would have withered a plaster saint. 'None taken,' said Thorn.

'Yer tellin' me Neema's *dead?*' On the verge of tears Ka stared down at the food-stained paper plate on the cable-spool table before him. On it were a half-eaten former jelly doughnut, an upcurled wedge of old cold sausage pizza, and a handleless Far Side mug of weak black coffee made from used grounds. Around him and Fungle the stone shelter echoed with the smacking snarfing sounds of the beggar's banquet of used, semi-used, discarded, and previously inedible food being consumed in great quantities at a high rate of speed. They had puzzled over metal black-and-yellow signs reading FALLOUT SHELTER, with a bladed-circle hex symbol printed above the words. Another sign read CIVIL DEFENCE, with letters in a circle within a triangle below. Fungle wondered if they were protective markings. Throughout the stone room, great guttural belches sounded like the approach of distant Harley-Davidsons.

'I don't think so, Ka,' said Fungle, shaking his head. 'I think I'da felt it iffin she was. She was in the incinerator shaft, but I think they found her in there.'

'Rare, medium, or well-done?' asked Codswollop. The metrognomes within earshot howled with laughter. Slouching in his throne Codswollop pulled his everpresent stogie from his mouth and blew grey smoke ceilingward.

Fungle's joy at being reunited with Ka had lasted approximately one minute. Recounting their exploits after their parting at Walter Reed Hospital had taken up another ten. Then Codswollop had insisted that they all attend a feast, prepared and served by the metrognomes' slavelings, the gastrognomes. Fungle's account of Neema being left in the building that housed DPR left the gnome crestfallen.

'Whatsa matta?' Codswollop asked Ka. 'Food ain't good enough?'

Ka looked up from his plate. 'Er, no, it's . . . it's fine. I seem to've lost me appetite.'

The words had no sooner left his mouth when the hand of the diner to his left slapped onto his plate, followed immediately by the fork of the diner across from him. There was a yowl. The doughnut and pizza vanished and the fork was licked.

The metrognomes laughed.

Fungle leaned toward Ka. 'Neema's still back there, Ka,' he said. 'I can feel her. She's alive, an' we hafta get her back here with us where she belongs.' He looked away from Ka and the remnants of the 'feast' to see Codswollop watching him carefully. He seemed pretty bent for a ruler, and Fungle had no idea what he might be thinking. But the metrognomes seemed to be resourceful and adventurous enough to help him. Though they were indebted to him he was reluctant to ask them to endanger themselves on his account. He was wondering how to ask for their aid when Codswollop suddenly slapped the royal flyswatter against the worn sole of a leather shoe. 'I see you got some kinda proposition to make,' he said. He winked, and peeled away a cold sheet of cheese from a half-eaten pizza slice, balled it up, and pushed it past the stogie into his mouth. 'Come with me.'

'The goyl we can prob'ly do,' said Codswollop when Fungle had explained his needs. 'If not, ain't no shortage a dames in this city.' He held up his hands. 'Sorry. Bad joke.'

Fungle, Ka and Codswollop were in a small room with a few beat-up mismatched office chairs and a gouged conference table that tipped when leaned upon. Codswollop slouched in a creaking executive chair with his feet on the scarred table-top.

The metrognome king had led Fungle and Ka past rotting wooden shelves of olive-drab cans plainly labelled as various kinds of foods. Fungle asked why the metrognomes scavenged their food instead of eating it from the cans, and Codswollop had looked at him like he was nutsy bow-wow. 'Those are old army rations,' the king had explained. 'We gotta have *some* standards!'

'Okay,' he said now, removing his feet from the table to lean forward. 'So we'll raid the building and see what we can see, right? I can give you a better idea about gettin' away with this if you can draw me a map, gimme some idea how many of their guys are gonna be there, what kinda heat they're packin', that kinda thing. I gotta warn ya, if this guy Crucifer set you up when you went whizzin' around the universe, it means he's in kahootz with Mr Bigshot Theverat hisself. So armed guards might end up bein' the least of our worries.'

'As for gettin' you a car . . .' He shrugged. 'Depends. Whatchoo need it for?'

'Even if I can't get Neema back,' said Fungle, dreading having to use the words for fear of the bad luck they might bring, 'I still have to get to Black Mountain and try to find Baphomet before Theverat or the humans do.'

Codswollop puffed thoughtfully on his stogie. 'Black Mountain, wherezat?'

'Humans'd call it Tennessee,' said Fungle.

Codswollop shook his head. 'No can do, brudda.'

Fungle was crushed. 'Why not?'

Codswollop patted his chest. '*Metro*gnomes, that's why. Get it? *Metro*. We don't leave the city, not no how, not no way. Poysonally, I don't trust no air I can't see, an' all that clean an' fresh stuff'd prob'ly kill us.'

'But, but . . .' Fungle spread his hands in frustration. '*We'll* drive!' he said.

'You know how ta drive a car?' Codswollop snorted and began ticking off points on his fingers. 'We'd hafta get you an automatic transmission. We'd hafta find a kinda car you could work the pedals *and* see out the windshield. You'd hafta get by every hick-town speedtrap between here an' there – but why go on?' He leaned back in his chair. 'You'd prob'ly end up marryin' a telephone pole before you got ten miles down the road.'

He removed the stogie from his mouth and examined the soggy end. 'Lemme ask you somethin',' he said, not looking at Fungle.

'I'm serious, now, a'right?'

Fungle hesitated. 'All right,' he said.

'How much trouble you willing to risk for a ride down to Half-baked Mountain, or whatever?'

Fungle and Ka exchanged a glance. 'I've risked ever'thing ever' step a the way,' answered Fungle. 'Guess it'd be contrary to stop now. Why?'

Codswollop plugged his mouth with the stogie, cracked his knuckles and leaned forward, once more a leader, schemer, professional, and lover of mayhem. 'I'll call in the grimawkins,' he said. 'This is their kinda thing. Heck, they do this kinda thing on their own, for kicks. And they owe me one after that Stork Room job I helped 'em with.'

'The grimawkins?' Fungle asked.

Codswollop grinned and shook his head craftily. 'Better you should wait till you see 'em. Which oughta be as late in the game as possible. Which oughta be when they drive your boosted car up to the building for you to load your friend in an' get the hell outta Dodge.' He leaned forward and pointed the smelly moist stogie in front of Fungle's face. 'Which oughta be late tonight,' he said softly.

Crucifer emerged from his office clutching a thick bundle of papers. 'Miss Sensinella,' he said, 'I need three collated and stapled copies of this, please.'

Miss Sensinella nodded without looking at him and continued painting pink correction fluid over a government form.

'I need them immediately, Miss Sensinella,' said Crucifer.

She nodded and blew on the form to dry the fluid. With a harsh bang Crucifer set the papers to be copied on her desk and returned to his office.

Three minutes later he cracked the door to see her picking up the papers. She was making a lemony face and repeating his words as she rounded her desk and clacked down the hallway in her high-heeled shoes.

Crucifer counted thirty and bolted from the office.

Thorn was still under the blanket in the janitor's closet when Crucifer opened the door. 'Hurry,' was all Crucifer said.

There was nothing else for the two of them to do but hazard the fifty feet between the cleaning closet and Crucifer's office. It was the longest ten seconds of Crucifer's life.

Crucifer shut and locked his office door behind them. He watched

Thorn looking around the room, a creature completely impossible and real as a mugger's pistol now that he was actually here. Either there were huge gaps in the fossil record, or Crucifer was going to have to stop looking at the world through scientist-coloured glasses.

A jewelled face glowed on the computer monitor. It smiled at them. 'Welcome, gentlemen,' came the voice from the speaker grille, 'and well done. Tib meet Thorn, Thorn meet Tib.'

The creature merely stared at Crucifer with great yellow eyes in a horribly alien face. 'Thorn is a tracker,' Theverat's voice explained, 'a master hunter. And Thorn, Tib here is . . . well, I'd have to call him our human liaison while we're here in the –' Crucifer could hear the grin '– the *real* world. Our foreign correspondent, in a way.

'Gentlemen, because he is bound by a moral code as strict as it is absurd, it's predictable as rot on a log that our wayward shaman will return to rescue his lady love. So – let's make some plans, shall we?'

21 *Escape from New York*

At 12:47 a.m. Charlie Auerbach clocked out of DPR. His relief had been half-an-hour late and Charlie'd been thinking about drinking that one extra paper cup of coffee just to keep his eyes peeled, even though he knew it'd eat through his stomach and give him gas tomorrow. But his relief had finally shown. New guy, Larry something-or-other. Didn't matter. They didn't last long enough these days to get to know their names.

Charlie headed for the one-way pedestrian-traffic door that opened out onto the street. *Bad neighbourhood. Good thing I work a job that lets me have a gun, I gotta walk around an area like this. Heck*, two *guns*, he amended, remembering his taser.

He pushed open the door – and it was yanked from the other side. Charlie stumbled against a tall figure wearing a slouch hat, mirrored sunglasses and a dirty brown duster. 'Have a nice trip!' it called in a guttural voice as it awkwardly scurried past him.

Charlie reached for his taser. 'Hey, you can't go in there!' He struggled to his feet. 'Stop!' he called, and levelled the weapon at the intruder. Someone tapped him on the shoulder and he whirled with the taser trained on a similarly dressed figure standing not two feet in front of him.

'Boo,' it said mildly, and opened its coat like a flasher.

'Boo again,' said its lower half – for the figure was two dwarfish creatures, one atop the other.

Charlie squeezed the trigger. The taser barb shot out and embedded in the creature's filthy I ♥ NY T-shirt. The stored charge unloaded, and twenty thousand volts of electricity shot into the creature in one sizzling burst. Its eyes widened and it fell backwards off the shoulders of its lower half, taking the overcoat with it.

It was up again in a flash. 'Wooo-hoo! That was *great!*' It shrugged off the overcoat and slapped its partner on the back. 'Goober, you gotta try this!' It looked at Charlie with childish exuberance. 'Hey, mister, shoot Goober too, willya?'

Charlie Auerbach threw away his discharged taser and drew his .38.

Angelo Espinoza was staring at the *New York Times* crossword puzzle and chewing the end of a Bic pen like a favourite bone. Angelo considered it a victory if he could get even two of the crossword puzzle's words every day. Who ever used words like this? He never even heard 'em on *Jeopardy*, and there was some smart dudes on *Jeopardy*.

He sat in a wooden swivel chair with his feet on the duty desk, enjoying his ten minutes to himself before he had to make the rounds. He tapped his bottom teeth with the chewed end of the pen. Now this word here, eight across. It was a six-letter word he figured began with a 'z' because four down was a five-letter word for *nothing*, and since *zero* was only four letters, Angelo guessed it must be *zilch*. But the clue for eight across said *syllepsis*. Now what the hell was a syllepsis? And it started with a 'z'.

'Zeugma.'

He sat bolt upright. The word had been whispered practically in his ear. Angelo glanced around and saw nothing. He looked at the paper and frowned. Z – O – O – G – M – A, zoogma. Well, it fit . . .

He shook his head like a cat. He'd thought he'd heard voices before, calling his name. He wrote the word in the squares.

'Z – E – U – G – M – A,' came the whisper.

Angelo dropped the paper. 'Who's there?' he called. He looked at the phone on the desk. 'Jackson, was that you?' he said to the speakerphone.

A tall figure in sunglasses and a duster appeared in the doorway of the duty room. 'You order a pizza?' it asked.

'No, I didn't order no pizza. Who the hell are you? How'd you get in here?' Angelo reached for his taser.

The figure grinned and held up a flat cardboard box. 'Well, this ain't a pizza,' it said, 'so it must be for you!' It tossed a cardboard pizza box into the room and ran away.

Angelo glanced at the box. NOT A PIZZA was scrawled on the lid in red marker. 'What the hell . . . . ?' he said, and tore it open. Flash powder ignited with a *whuff!* Angelo sat blinking at violet-edged pulsings that looked like a nuclear bomb had just gone off about three inches from his face.

Professional pickpocket hands removed the taser from his belt, swapped his .38 for a different gun, and wired him to his chair.

'*Stop!*'

Angelo's head jerked right. The shout came from the west stairwell, where that old geezer, Auerbach, had headed for the foot-traffic exit after clocking out. Blinking rapidly, still blinded by the flash, Angelo tried to stand but couldn't. He reached for his taser but it wasn't there. He reached for his pistol and it was. It felt oddly light in his hand, but he had other things to think about right now. Like when he'd be able to see again.

From the west stairwell a shot rang out.

In Autopsy Room 3 Crucifer frowned down at the furry body on the table before him. He checked its vital signs and found them faint but acceptable. The anaesthetic held her firmly in its grip.

Theverat had said he was certain the male would return to rescue the female. Crucifer wasn't sure what sort of 'rescue' the demon was expecting – Fungle swinging in on a rope like Errol Flynn, maybe – but Theverat was confident.

Crucifer was decreasingly so: in his office a thorny yellow-eyed monstrosity with a voodoo stick, whom Crucifer himself had smuggled into a slush-funded scientific research establishment in the trunk of his Oldsmobile, was chatting it up with a demon on his office computer. Crucifer was into some weird stuff, but this hardly constituted your basic working day.

He moved the female's right arm out from the body and selected a fatty patch behind the pectoral and near the armpit. He picked up a straight razor from the instrument tray beside him and shaved a small area until only smooth pale skin showed.

'A tracker', Theverat had called Thorn, the monster in his office. 'A master hunter'. Whereas Theverat had implied that Crucifer was useful only so long as the demon remained in the human world. The good doctor was only just now realising that he had signed on with a power capable of using people like a master chess player, moving this pawn *here* so that, thirty moves or thirty years down the line, it would be useful *there*, at just the right moment. Crucifer had been moved then, he was being moved now. He felt it; the aura of Theverat's strategy was all around him, it seemed. And just as a pawn doesn't have to see the rest of the board to be useful, Crucifer suspected that there was more happening here, on levels above and below, and neither above nor below but just plain *other*, than he could imagine. Theverat was waiting for the gnole to return, and would probably let him get away, so that he could track him –

('*A tracker, a master hunter . . .*')

– to whatever both of them were trying to find.

Crucifer had read his Goethe and his Marlowe; he intended that his end of this particular bargain would not take that particular plummet. He was a bit of a chess player himself, and – at least on the board of his own earthly experience – he would play Theverat the same way he had played university deans and tenure committees, grant reviewers and presidential administrations: by convincing him that he, Crucifer, was indispensable.

And the best way to insure that, thought Crucifer as he put down the razor and picked up a scalpel, *is to buy some insurance.*

He paused a moment, looking at the female's face. *Funny, about the benign physiognomy,* he thought. *Like a dolphin or a Samoyed. That's why people respond sympathetically toward the things. Even unconscious, they've got a built-in smile.*

He cut.

'Goober! Goober, speak to me, Goober!' The metrognome stopped shaking the body of his friend and looked up at the stupefied face of Charlie Auerbach, who clutched his smoking snub-nosed .38 like a life-preserver. 'Aw, now look whatchoo gone and done!' the creature cried.

The metrognome released his fallen friend and stood. He spread his arms wide. 'Go ahead! Shoot me!' He began circling to the left.

'Don't move!' ordered Charlie, voice breaking.

'Or else what? You'll shoot me? That's what I *want*, ya pinhead!' He clutched his chest dramatically. 'I don't wanna live in a world without Goober! He was like a brudda to me! I knew him since we was *this* high!' The metrognome set a hand at human knee level. 'We use to sneak inna the hospital nurseries and crawl inna incubators and scare hell outta nurses fah laughs! And you went an' shot him! Well, shoot *me*! I don't wanna live without Goober!'

'Why, Milton!'

Charlie Auerbach whirled at the voice behind him.

'I'm touched,' continued Goober. 'I'm *really* touched.' He stepped toward the guard with his arms held out to hug Milton the metrognome.

'Stop or I'll shoot!' warned an increasingly confused Charlie Auerbach.

Goober stopped. 'With what?' he asked mildly, and waggled the .38.

Charlie looked in astonishment at his empty hand. 'What – How – You –'

Goober *tsked* and held the door open. 'Run away,' he suggested. He pulled back the hammer on the pistol to reinforce the notion that running away was a good idea.

Charlie looked from one creature to the other. 'I never signed on for *this*,' he said, and ran out into the night.

Goober looked at Milton tenderly. 'Milt,' he said. 'Didja really miss me, pal?'

Milton frowned. 'Not as much azzat pinhead did! What a crummy shot!'

'You *didn't* miss me?'

'Shuddup and call the others in 'fore I pop ya one.'

When he heard the scurrying noises, Alan Dills leaned away from the elevator bank to look down the hall. He didn't see anything. You heard stuff all night long around this place; it gave Dills the chilly-willies. He smiled, remembering the phrase. That was what Brina had called being scared when she was a little girl: the chilly-willies. And between the weird animals locked away, the disgusting things in jars in autopsy rooms, the crazy doped-up kids in the paediatric ward, unfathomable security rules like tonight's sudden rescheduling so that only half the normal number of guards were on duty, and the Big Moby Weirdo himself, Dr Crucifer, the Department of Parapsychological Research was Chilly-Willie Central.

Dills frowned. He'd heard something down the hall, he was sure of it. Squeaking.

A rat ran across his shoe. It was the *size* of his shoe. Dills screamed and hopped on one foot, shaking the other as if it were on fire.

Something tugged the cuff of his pants. He looked down to see a second rat climbing his leg. Black ball-bearing eyes stared up at him, naked grey whipcord tail snaked across his shoelaces. '*Gaaah!*' he shrieked, and switched to hopping on the other leg to shake the creature off.

'Evening, officah,' said a voice. 'Say – izzat a rat on your pants, or are you just happy to see me?'

An overcoated figure stood in the hallway. 'Get it off!' Dills screamed. 'Get it off, get it off!'

'My pleasure.' The figure came forward. It removed its sun-glasses to show bloodshot eyes in pasty skin. It grinned unpleasantly and set two more fat squeaking rats on Dill's shoulders.

Dills flapped his arms and ran screaming in the other direction.

The overcoated creature shook its head. 'Naytcha luvuh,' he said. He looked down at his midsection. 'You get 'em?'

'I got 'em I did so yep.' Two arms snaked out from beneath the overcoat. One hand held a snub-nosed .38, the other a boxy taser.

'T'rific.' The metrognome pulled a walkie-talkie from a pocket, shrugged off the overcoat, and hopped off his lightfingered partner. 'Fat J an' Tyre Iron here,' he told the walkie-talkie. 'Come on in; the water's fine!'

Codswollop lowered the walkie-talkie and grinned at Fungle, Ka and the other metrognomes. 'First floor's ours,' he said. 'Time to crash the party, boys.'

Karbolic Earthcreep peered around a corner. Empty hall – now 'r never. He motioned behind him and the metrognome called Plumber dashed down the hall, clutching a black Adidas gym bag. Ka and Plumber had parted company from Fungle, Codswollop and their cortege of metrognomes just after entering the building. His mission was to help Plumber find the internal and external alarm and phone lines and cut them.

Plumber opened a stairwell door. 'Dis way!' he hissed. Ka hurried after him and they began trotting down the concrete steps. 'Lotta times allat gobbidge izinna garage,' said Plumber. Ka found the metrognome's accent so thick it was nearly incomprehensible, and there was usually a time lag while Ka unravelled what Plumber had just said. Plumber thought the same of Ka's speech.

Searching the garage area, Plumber shook his head disdainfully. 'Lookit dese cahs, Ka,' he said. 'Ya gotcha Oldsmobile, ya gotcha Mitsubishi van, ya gotcha Mazda RX7 – we could boost any a dese. Whadda we tradin' favours wid da grimawkins for?'

'Grimawkins?' asked Ka.

Plumber snorted. 'Better you shouldn't know,' he said.

Five minutes later Ka was staring at a huge mass of coloured wires in a grey metal box set into the wall of the garage. 'What's all these fer, then?' he asked.

'Who knows?' replied Plumber, pulling a set of wire cutters from his gym bag.

*

'Stop or I shoot!' Angelo Espinoza stood in a solid firing stance, legs a yard apart, knees bent, left hand supporting right holding the pistol. He was conscious of his pants trying to fall down around him; they had ripped when he'd freed himself from the chair.

Sighting the gun wasn't easy, since Angelo's vision still pulsed with violet light from the flash bomb. But he could make out the four figures in front of him well enough to see that they were short, non-human shapes running toward the elevator. Anyway, they didn't have to know that Angelo could barely see; he figured that *they* could see just fine, and that what they saw was a ticked-off security guard holding a gun on them.

They halted.

They turned.

They raised their hands.

'Oh, *offi*cah,' came an adenoidal voice, 'puh*leez* don't shoot!'

They laughed.

Another voice: 'Yer majesty, what're you doin'? He's got a gun!'

'A gun! Bwah-hah-hah!' One of the figures brought its hands to its large head and waggled fingers at Angelo. It leaned forward, stuck out its tongue, and made a wet blubbery noise. '*There's* ya gun! C'mon, Fungle,' it said, 'we got a date. Less go, boys!'

'Are ya daft?' demanded Fungle. 'I've seen what them things can do –'

'You better listen to him,' Angelo interrupted. 'I'll use this if I have to.'

'Heavens.' Codswollop grabbed Fungle and tugged him down the hall, flanked by two of his subjects. 'You may fire when ready, Gridley!' he called back over his shoulder.

'Stop!' Angelo shouted a final time, and pulled the trigger.

There was a soft click as the barrel unfolded and a red flag unfurled.

 it said.

'Whadda you mean, we can't go up inna elevator? You moron!'

'Boss, no one told us you needed a card and a pass code to get upstairs!' protested Fat J. He pointed at Fungle with the commandeered taser. '*He* shoulda said sumpin'.'

Codswollop glared. 'Careful where you point that thing,' he said.

'Oh, it's okay, boss,' said Goober. 'They feel *cooool.*'

Codswollop turned on him. 'Goober,' he said, punctuating with his stogie, 'if your brains was dynamite you couldn't blow your nose.' He sighed. 'Go get the card from that poor *schlub* with the fun gun we left back there. He's prob'ly still bangin' aroun' like a bird inna box.'

'How 'bout the numbah?' asked Fat J.

Codswollop frowned. 'No time to force it outta him. Ace?'

Fungle shrugged. 'I'm sorry. I didn't know they used 'em. I could prob'ly trick it out, but it'd take some time.'

'Time we ain't got. Faster to let my boys handle it.' Codswollop smiled philosophically. 'Only thing you can count on in a operation like this,' he said, 'is that nothin' goes accordin' to plan.'

That was when the elevator went *ding!* and the doors clattered open.

Miss Patterson followed the zigzagging light as it jumped from number to number, right to left, toward L. It seemed to take for ever. This whole night – this whole *week* – had been the longest of her life. What a nightmare. The gnoles nearly killed in some stupid farfetched experiment of Crucifer's; the male escaped to God knows where. Oh, there was an alert out; the Boys in Black were out in force, scouring Manhattan to find him, you could bet your bottom tax dollar on that! But he was gone, and what a waste of valuable research.

Still, there was a wealth of data on him to be evaluated. In his brief time at DPR, Fungle had been a gold mine – even more frustrating because he had been the crack in the door leading to a psychic room whose existence they had long suspected. But there was still the female to test for equivalent abilities. They could take their time with her; no one in the world knew DPR had her. Except for the male, of course . . .

Miss Patterson sighed. If it weren't for all that hard data, she'd give notice and go back to supervising grad programmes at Duke. Crucifer had always been a little scary to her, a little too obsessive and intense; but now he was flakier than a bowl of Raisin Bran. He'd added a bolt lock to his office door; he took all his meals there, absolutely no visits without prior arrangement. He wasn't sleeping or shaving, and Miss Patterson wondered if he was even bathing. He was like a man possessed.

The number 2 lighted. Miss Patterson tightened her grip on her leather valise and readied her car keys, liking that she always had the door key ready by the time she got to her parking space, glad to be leaving this place once again.

Ding! Heaviness in her knees as the elevator stopped. The doors rumbled open. Four metrognomes and a gnole rushed in.

'Floor, please!' Codswollop grinned.

Fat J reached out and pushed them all.

Codswollop's grin disappeared. 'Oh, t'riffic, you imbezzle. Now we gotta stop on every floor.'

'Shop on every floor?' Tyre Iron brightened. 'I *love* to shop!'

'This ain't Macy's, mushbrain.' Codswollop stared at the ceiling. '*This* I'm king of?' he asked the gods.

The elevator doors closed.

Miss Patterson screamed, but Tyre Iron's hand around her mouth took all the artistry out of it.

Codswollop flicked ashes from his cigar and loomed under Miss Patterson. His grin was a shuddersome sight. 'Nice lady,' he said with ominous soothingness, 'where'd we find Neema the gnole?'

'Mmmnn mmm *MMMM* NN MMmmm!'

Codswollop sighed. 'Tyre Iron,' he said.

'Yeah, boss?'

The metrognome king mimed removing a hand from his mouth.

'Oh. Oh, yeah!' Tyre Iron took his hand off Miss Patterson's mouth.

Miss Patterson screamed something all vowels.

Ding! The elevator stopped on the second floor. They braced themselves as the doors opened.

Nobody there.

The doors shut.

They continued up.

'Glad this ain't the Chrysler Buildin',' said Milton.

Ding! They stopped on three. The doors opened. Whistling a Phil Collins song, Jerry Allesandro pushed a laundry cart halfway into the elevator. Fungle recognised him from the laundry room on the night of his escape from DPR.

Jerry stopped.

Miss Patterson and a casting call for a *Gremlins* movie stared back at him.

The elevator doors hit the laundry cart and opened again.

'Goin' up?' asked Codswollop.

'Uhh,' said Jerry. 'I'll take the stairs.' He did, too – three at a time.

'Cart,' said Codswollop.

They made room and Fungle pulled the laundry cart into the elevator. The doors closed.

Codswollop hit the red STOP button and faced Miss Patterson. The metrognome king was having hisself a terrific time. Some kinds of fish are born to swim in hot water.

Codswollop rifled through Miss Patterson's leather valise and then her purse before he found her magnetic-strip passcard. He held it up and grinned.

(*'Don't leave home without it!'* came a voice in Fungle's mind. He willed it to shut up.)

'Tell us the passcode,' Codswollop told Miss Patterson, 'or we'll come redecorate your apartment – *our* way.'

The streets were quiet outside the rundown building that housed DPR. Though the city itself never slept, it had sections that were like starved grey cells in an ageing brain, dead zones where nothing would awaken again. DPR was located in such a section. Traffic signals changed, sodium-vapour 'crime lights' glowed a washed-out amber; to the north, the paired white cells of headlights streamed along the distant artery of the George Washington Bridge. Pale thin figures, human castaways living on the orts and rinds of the city, lurked among shadows with needles and knives.

An engine roared in the distance. Tyres squealed. Headlights lit an alleyway and dispersed illicit clusters of fringe-dwelling humans. A white Lincoln Continental shot into an intersection, slewed around a corner, and accelerated, fishtailing before righting itself. A reek of burned rubber filled the air.

A tinted power window whined down and a cloud of cigarette smoke billowed out. A muscular, spike-braceleted arm tossed a full can of Rolling Rock beer like a grenade. The Lincoln screeched to a halt. The can arced ahead of the Lincoln to explode foamy white across a metal sign that read KEEP OUR CITY CLEAN!

'Yo, Skat! Anudda bullseye!'

'Keep 'em comin' Freddy!'

'Oh, man! That was *evil*, Skat! Eee-vill!'

'Trade seats! Ali up next!'

'Sorry, boys, we're almost there.'

The Lincoln shot through the seemingly deserted streets.

'Leff! No, right! You passed it, Freddy!'

The Lincoln jinked right toward the curb. Brake lights flashed as the rear end screamed past the front. Laughter from the driver's seat. 'They don't make 'em like dis in Japan!'

'*De*troit iron!'

'You *know* dat, Skat.'

'Rolling stock!'

'Absolooly, Skat.'

'Mean machines! Steals on wheels! Motah-city madness!'

'Shut up, Skat.'

The Lincoln leaned into a hard right and accelerated. It passed poor unarmed Charlie Auerbach trying to flag it down from the sidewalk.

'What's *his* problem?'

The driver's window slid down. 'Hey, man! Steal y'*own* damn' car!'

'Hey, Ali, Ali! Whyntcha give our frien' a liddle R an' R?'

'Comin' up, Skat!' Ali lobbed a Rolling Rock grenade.

The Lincoln slammed to a halt. Three heads turned to look out the back windshield. The ballistic beer can arced down and exploded on the sidewalk a few feet from the guard.

'Aw, he cheated! He *moved!*'

'Chicke-e-en!'

'Let's go back an' skin him.'

'You don' wanna skin nobody, Ali. We got a deadline to meet. It was a good toss, okay?'

'Well . . . a'right, Skat.'

'Good man.'

The Lincoln roared to life. Three blocks later Skat and Ali yelled '*Here!*' and Freddy stood on the brake. The big car drew a doughnut on the street and fetched up against the opposite curb.

Silence.

Pshhhh! 'Anybody wanna nudda beeyah?'

Lock your doors, hide your wallets, send your daughters out of town. The grimawkins have arrived.

The bright white hallways were unexpectedly silent, even for this late hour. It made Fungle suspicious. 'I don't like it, not one bit,' he told Codswollop. 'They mighta known I'd be back fer Neema. I feel like we's walkin' into a trap.'

They hurried down the hallway checking names and numbers on the doors. 'Could be,' said Codswollop. 'But look, it's about fifteen in the morning', an' this place ain't exactly Times Square.'

'I don't understand,' said Fungle.

Codswollop shrugged. 'What's to guard?' he asked. 'Everybody who don't woyk here's doped up an' locked in. From what you tole me this place is fah people to move paper clips and read a buncha playin' cards, not to build newkewlar missiles. Half-a-dozen guys with guns is more than enough to guard the joint.'

'But Neema –'

'Boss!' Ahead of them Fat J stood by a door. Fungle and Codswollop hurried to it.

AUTOPSY ROOM 3

Fungle's heart gave a little kick. Codswollop looked at him with raised eyebrows: *this* is where the woman had said Neema was?

Fungle nodded fearfully.

Codswollop slid Miss Patterson's card in the slot and punched the code. As promised, the metrognome king had let the woman go – straight to a cleaning closet, bound and gagged. When they got away from here he'd leave a note telling where she was.

The light on the card plate turned green. There was a soft click. Codswollop opened the door, and he and Fungle went inside.

Alan Dills pounded on the door. 'We're being invaded!' he shouted. 'There's . . . there's some kinda animals loose in here, Dr Crucifer. You gotta evacuate the building, or call for help, or something!'

On Miss Sensinella's desk the intercom clicked on. 'Who's out there?' came Crucifer's voice.

'It's Dills, Alan Dills. Security.'

'You don't sound very secure, Mr Dills.'

'None of us is, doc. Ya gotta get outta here! The phone lines're dead, the alarm don't work –'

'*Doesn't* work, Mr Dills,' the intercom corrected. 'The alarm *doesn't* work.'

Dills could only stare.

'Did you know that I left strict orders not to be disturbed?'

'But, but . . . this is an emergency!'

'I'm aware of our situation, Mr Dills, but a few escaped animals running around the facility are hardly an emergency and hardly my concern. I'm sure you can handle a bunch of wild bunny rabbits with admirable panache.'

'No, doc, it ain't like that. There was . . . I can't explain it. But they . . . An' *rats*, hundreds of rats! And they . . . Doc, I'm tellin' ya, we're being raided!'

The intercom sighed. From the door came a prolonged rattle as locks were unlocked. A bolt was drawn. The door opened and Crucifer emerged. He hurriedly shut the door behind him.

Dills stared. The notoriously immaculate Crucifer looked like he hadn't slept in a week. His thinning hair looked like it'd been parted with a firecracker, and a patch on either temple had gone *white*. His trademark white Van Heusen shirt was foodstained, wrinkled and smelly. His tie was unknotted and dangling lopsidedly. His skin was sickly pale. And his *eyes* – they were red-rimmed and intense, bloodshot and unwavering. But more than that, they had the thousand-yard-stare of hardcore 'Nam veterans Dills had known. Eyes imprinted by horror until nothing registered there anymore. Lizard eyes.

Crucifer was holding a Rubik's Cube. The scientist's hands obsessively twisted the colour sections without him looking at it. 'Here I am, Mr Dills,' Crucifer said wearily. 'What would you like me to do?'

'Do?' Dills couldn't take his eyes off the shifting sections of the Rubik's Cube. 'I'd like you to *leave*, doc! I can't call out for help; I can't sound no alarm, and we're being invaded by muppets from hell!'

Crucifer nodded thoughtfully. 'I'm sure you'll figure something out,' he said distractedly. 'Here.' He tossed the Rubik's Cube to Dills. The guard caught it and stared.

All the colours were in place. Crucifer had never even glanced at it, and every square matched up perfectly.

He looked up at the soft snick of a door being closed. Dr Crucifer had returned to his office.

Fat J held the taser and guarded the door that read AUTOPSY ROOM 3. Down the hall, Tyre Iron ran behind the laundry cart, then dove in and wheeled spinning along the tile floor. Every time the cart stopped, Tyre Iron would drop off a wound-up toy robot or battery-powered police car with flashing lights, or a yipping plush poodle dog. In no time the hallway echoed with whining motors and tinny sirens and monotonous yips and maniacal robot laughter.

Tyre Iron popped up from the laundry cart. A towel draped on top of his head so that he looked like a sheik. The metrognome grinned and set a toy Godzilla on the floor. It spat sparks as it stomped an invisible miniature Tokyo.

Fat J shook his head. Some people never grew up. He leaned his ear against the door, but he couldn't make out what was happening inside.

*

Inside.

Where Neema lay unconscious.

Fungle hurried to her. She was alive, he felt that right away. But something wasn't right. Something had been done to her. He patted her cheeks and shook her and called her name, but she wouldn't awaken.

'Yowza,' said Codswollop, staring at Neema's body on the slab. He looked at Fungle. 'You sure about this?'

Fungle didn't return his gaze. Against the wall were two metal plates with handles. TRASH. INCINERATOR. He remembered the ordeal of their escape, the guard firing his taser, the long frightening slide down the filthy metal chute into the dumpster. Animals and parts of animals floated in cloudy solutions in jars on shelves around the chilly room. Fungle thought of the Parliament of Personages, the delegation of forest dwellers sent to ask their mage to plead the animals' case with the humans. *Is this to be yer fate, then?* he wondered.

'I'm only sure I hafta get her outta here,' he told Codswollop. 'I'm gonna have to go in an' bring her back out.'

'Whatta you talkin' about?' asked Codswollop. 'We *are* in.'

Fungle touched Neema's forehead. 'In,' he said. He looked up at Codswollop. 'Could ya put yer lungburner out, please?' he asked.

Codswollop frowned. He pulled the cigar from his mouth and stared at it. 'Ain't been without one a these since the Cuban Missile Crisis.' He scratched his head. Finally he sighed and tossed it into the INCINERATOR bin. 'Cause cancer anyway,' he said.

Fungle took a deep breath and got to work. He set a hand on Neema's neck and found her pulse. He closed his eyes and slowed his breathing, concentrating on Neema's faint heartbeat. Within ten breaths his respiration matched Neema's. Another five, and their hearts beat as one.

Neema's body was an untenanted house. Fungle came knocking.

Ka was lost. He'd become separated from Plumber after the two of them had been chased by a guard who seemed to be having trouble with his vision, from the way he stumbled and ran into corners. Ka had shot down an intersecting hallway; the guard had raced past in pursuit of Plumber. Ka hoped the metrognome had escaped.

Right now Ka was wandering around on the third floor. There weren't many humans around here at this late hour: nurses, cleaning crew, a few guards. But these were all in a bother and running everywhichway like a stomped anthill, which Ka guessed was a pretty apt analogy.

He hurried down the hallway with an eye on the door signs and an ear out for humans.

He skidded to a halt.

ANIMAL STORES. Now what could that mean? Stuff ya could buy fer animals, maybe?

The door was locked. Ka set an ear against it. Barks, mewls, chatters.

The gnome frowned. A place ta *store* animals maybe?

He tapped the door lightly. Wood. Well now.

He cracked his knuckles and commenced to digging.

Codswollop stared at Fungle bending over Neema. The mage hadn't moved a muscle in the last five minutes. He wasn't even sure he was *breathing*. He looked from his inert form to Neema's. *What a pair*, he thought. He reached for his cigar and his fingers encountered nothing. Aargh. The raid he could handle. Guards and guns and evil demons he could deal with. But no cigar?

He clamped his jaw and sat against the wall and waited. Ten minutes, he'd said. He glanced at one of the four Rolex watches he wore. All right. Five minutes left.

The bum with the greasy squirt bottle and muddy rag had technique. That's how you get by in a cold hard world, son: *technique*. So he straightened his threadbare coat around him and rubbed his bristle jaw free of anything that might be loitering there, and he walked right up to the white Lincoln Continental with squirt bottle and rag held high. 'Cleana winsheel,' he said 'Fi'ty cents, cleana winsheel?'

The dark-tinted window slid down and the bum found himself facing three muscular, slit-eyed, mohawked, nose-ringed, leather-clad, cat-like creatures, all smoking Camel cigarettes and holding several pounds' worth of sharp things in each skull-ringed fist. The driver, Skat, grinned to reveal needle teeth. '*You* give *us* fifty cents,' he said in a heavy Jersey accent, 'or we'll clean *your* slate!'

The grimawkins laughed until blood came from their eyes. They asked the bum if he was hungry, and his hunger overcame his fear long enough for him to nod yes. They asked if he wanted a beer and he lit up and nodded more eagerly. The grimawkins gave him a bag of stale Whitecastle burgers and a six-pack of Rolling Rock

beer. Then they made him eat every one of the burgers and drink
the entire six-pack before they let him run off into the night to be
violently ill.

Ten minutes later the white Lincoln was still bouncing on its
shocks as they literally howled with laughter.

Bright headlights rushed down the street toward them.

'Whoozat?' demanded Freddy.

'Dunno,' said Ali.

'Lights're too high up ta be cops,' observed Skat.

'Goin' awful fast,' said Freddy.

'Comin' awful close,' said Ali.

'He ain't gonna stop – *abandon ship!*'

They tumbled out of the Lincoln and scrambled for the curb as a
brand-new cherry-red four-door Dodge Ram shooting toward them
at seventy-five slammed its brakes. Smoking rubber poured from
all four wheelwells as two lengthening black lines stretched toward
the parked car. The high-mounted truck could not possibly stop
before slamming the luxury car, and the grimawkins watched in

horror as it slowed, sslllloooowed, s l o w e d – and kissed the Lincoln's bumper like a teenager's first date.

The three grimawkins traded affronted glances.

Cloying burned rubber filled the air.

'Let's kill 'em,' voted Skat.

They advanced on the truck.

The Ram's doors popped open and headbanger speedmetal by Motorhead pounded at bone-powdering volume into the night. Three dog-like figures jumped out of the truck. One of them ran immediately for the nearest wheelwell and began snorting up the grey smoke from the burned tyres. The second made for the nearest fire hydrant. The third hopped on the hood of the Lincoln and stood grinning like a thief (which he was) with his hands on his hips. 'Why if it ain't the Katz bruddas!' he exclaimed. 'Ali, Freddy, an' Skat! Whadda youse doin' down here? Ain't it past ya bedtime?'

'The Rova boys!' said Skat. 'Red, Range, an' Roller! I didn't recognise youze widdout handcuffs on.' Freddy and Ali snickered. 'Whadda *you* guys doin' here?' Skat continued.

Roller shrugged. 'Cudswallow ast us ta boost him a cah.' He indicated the Ram. 'So here we ah!'

Skat made a face at the ticking smoking high-rider Ram. 'You call that a cah?' He pointed at the Lincoln. 'Now *dat's* a cah! Ol' King Dingaling ast us da same fayvuh.'

'No kiddin'? Well, he mus' be coverin' alliz bases, huh?' Roller hopped off the Lincoln, and the Rova boys and the Katz brothers began exchanging the complex and time-consuming series of handshakes all grimawkins undertake whenever they meet.

'So how'd you boys end up with the overgrown jeep here?' asked Freddy Katz when the handshakes were completed.

Range Rova shrugged. 'Hot-wyud it. Howzaboutchoo?'

Skat chuckled. 'Ali here put on a red vest an' a bow-tie an' waited outside a fancy rest-a-raunt. The real valet disappears ta pok somebuddy's cah, right? So Ali moves in real smooth, y'know, stands out front, holds his hand out, "G'devenin', sir an' lady," gets their keys – boom: a bran' new Lincoln Continental.'

'Atsa pimpmobile, boys,' said Red. The Rovas laughed like asthmatic donkeys.

'Hey hey hey,' warned Freddy. 'Atsa automotive experience ya talkin' about.'

'It's evil!' corroborated his brother Ali.

'So whadda we do now?' asked Roller Rova. 'Wait an' let 'em pick the cah they want?'

'They got some kinda job goin' down in there,' said Skat Katz. 'I don't think they're gonna wanna be makin' no vee-hiculah decisions if they come stormin' out widda pahty behind 'em, know whaddi mean?' He shrugged. 'They're headin' south and they need a driver's all I know.'

'South?' asked Range.

Skat nodded. 'Way south,' he added.

Range hooked blunt thumbs to either side of the steel Harley buckle of his wide leather belt. 'Y'all mean thuh *South* south?' he drawled. 'Greeyits an' collart greens an' red-eye gravy, mayun?'

'Pretty sure,' said Skat.

All six grimawkins looked at the huge red four-wheel-drive Ram.

'Dat Lincoln's a Tennessee trooper's dreamboat,' suggested Range.

Skat nodded reluctantly. 'Yeah, yuh right, Range,' he decided. He looked at Freddy and Ali. 'Boys? Load up da Tonka truck.'

'Neema?'

Fungle stands before the charmed doorway to Neema's cave home. He knocks and calls her name again: *'Neema?'*

No answer.

Fungle pushes on the door. It opens silently inward. Fungle steps into the cool dark of Neema's house. Instead of the ransacked mayhem he found when Neema had been abducted by giblins, the living-room is tidy and immaculate. The comfy sofa and its stuffing are in place; shelves are neatly arranged with bric-a-brac, spice racks in the kitchen ordered. But the room feels sterile; there is no sense of the warm spirit of its owner that infuses a home. The curtains are drawn and the room is dim.

'Neema?' Fungle opens the curtains. Sunlight butters the room, only partially obstructed by the intaglio of vines camouflaging the home from outside scrutiny.

Fungle leaves the living-room.

The bedroom is strangely bare, probably nothing like the place where Neema actually sleeps. There is only bare rock and a bare bed. On top of it is Neema, fast asleep.

Feeling like a gnome prince in an old fairytale, Fungle approaches the bed. He tiptoes, though he is not sure why, since his intention is to wake her. For a moment only he hesitates: sleeping there before him, Neema's face is untroubled and angelic, the carefree slumber of a child, and Fungle cannot help but feel that it is no favour to awaken her.

But Neema is not really sleeping safely within the confines of her cave home. She lies on a slab in a cold room containing parts of animals in fluid-filled bottles, and to leave her to peaceful slumber is to abandon her to the creatures that can fill such bottles.

Something pricks his chest. He reaches in his tunic and pulls forth a rose. The bud is tight as a fist. Fungle brings the rose to his nose and breathes deep. It is fresh and fragrant as the day it was given.

On the bed, Neema inhales deeply in time with him.

Fungle lowers the rose to Neema. She breathes in, and Fungle can smell the velvet scent.

The rosebud unfolds soft petals.

Neema's eyelids open.

'Fungle?' She looks around. *'We're – I'm home? Was it all a dream, then?'*

It breaks his heart to shake his head no. **'We're inside yer head, Neema. Yer drugged under, an' I come ta bring ya back.'**

Neema stretches and yawns. *'Oh.'* She smiles sleepily. *'A'right.'*

'We hafta hurry,' says Fungle.

Neema nods groggy acquiescence and Fungle helps her out of bed. She leans heavily against him as they walk to the living-room and toward the front door.

The room grows dim. Something blocks the light coming in through the vine-laced window. Fungle feels a Presence.

Theverat.

'Master.' Thorn radiated hate throughout Crucifer's office.

The constructed image on the monitor regarded Thorn fondly. 'I know what you're thinking, my wolfhound, but you can't go after him. Not now, not yet. I need him. I need his knowledge.' The image grinned.

'The gnome, then. Or the female.'

Crucifer's heart gave a little kick.

Theverat considered. 'All right.' He nodded slowly. 'Yes, all right. The female or the gnome, then – and any of those other ridiculous creatures you care to deal with. But not the mage. Not our little Fungle. We need him to show us the way to the buried treasure, yes? And I need you, my tracker, my wolfhound, to follow him.'

Thorn snatched up his spear and made for the door.

'Thorn.'

The nightmare stickman looked back impatiently at the monitor.

'Don't disappoint me,' said Theverat.

Thorn nodded. He glared at Crucifer staring from a corner of the room, then left the office.

Crucifer had said little since bringing Thorn to DPR. He had watched the creature's dealings with Theverat with the increasing suspicion that he had gotten in over his head. His ace in the hole with the female might just have disappeared out the door with Thorn and his horror-show spear.

'What are you thinking, Tib?'

Crucifer started at Theverat's voice. 'Nnn? Oh, just – you know. Off in the ozone somewhere.'

Theverat smiled. Crucifer had the feeling Theverat knew every damned thing he was thinking. 'Well, doctor,' said Theverat. 'I'd stay and chat, but it seems my presence is required elsewhere. In that ozone you were wandering. Someone's gone a-calling, and it seems they're cutting through my yard. But Tib?'

Crucifer looked questioning.

'We'll talk again later,' said Theverat.

They are an island in a storm. It rises suddenly, a black nebula in the Otherworld, extends probing tendrils, surrounds the house with glacial hunger.

'*'M goin' back ta bed,*' murmurs Neema.

'**No! Neema, listen ta me! We're inside yer mind; that's what this house is. It's like a dream, y'unnerstand? Yer house is like a dream deep inside yer mind. Theverat's outside the house because he's outside yer body, outside the world. He's on the astral plane.**'

'*Mmm-hmm.*'

'**All ya gotta do ta wake up is ta step outside yer door. He can't get to ya; it's just a lotta sound an' fury. If you'll just walk right out yer front door you'll wake up, an' you'll be in the world and Theverat won't be able to reach ya. Will ya do that fer me, Neema? Will ya walk outside yer house?**'

Neema nods.

Fungle leads her to the front door and opens it.

Without lies the sullen churning ocean of Theverat.

Neema wakes a bit more when she sees it.

'**It's all right, Neema! He can't hurt you, not if you don't hesitate. Walk out the door and take another step an' you'll be awake.**'

Neema steps into the doorway. A turgid red-lit maw swirls before her. She glances back uncertainly.

Fungle nods.

Neema steps into the maw –

– and woke up on the slab in Autopsy Room 3.

'Yeesh!' said a voice across the room. 'I thought you was lost luggage, doll.'

Neema tried to sit up, but something prevented her. Fungle's hand was against her neck. The mage stood over her, eyes closed, barely breathing.

Another figure entered her field of vision: pasty, bulge-eyed, blubbery-lipped, rat-eared.

'Who – who are you?' asked Neema.

Codswollop grinned to show stubby stained teeth. 'Corinthian Codswollop, King a the Metrognomes, at ya service.'

Fungle collapsed.

'Gnome.'

Skipping merrily along after freeing a room full of bunnies, rats, monkeys, dogs, and cats, Ka stopped stone cold statue still at the sickening sound of the voice in the hallway. Slowly he turned.

Thorn stood facing him, holding his spear. As Ka watched, the creature snapped off the tip of an elbow spine and cocked back its arm to let fly.

Ka ran.

A section of wall exploded where he'd been standing.

Thorn blinked at the settling plaster powdered by the spine's impact. He heard the gnome pounding down the hallway. He did not pursue. He knew where the gnome would head.

Returning Neema to the conscious world is one thing. Returning himself is another. Neema had to travel only a razor's edge of unreality before returning to the world. But Fungle has to cross the void between souls, and though only inches separate him and Neema in the physical world, the astral distance between Neema's spirit and his own is an immeasurable space into which much can fit.

Theverat, for instance.

Fungle is going to have to step off the threshold of Neema's allegorical home as well – but Fungle's route to his own corporeal home is through the woods where hungry wolves lurk. He will have to hope he can cross the short but dangerous space and pull himself along the silver cord of his being before Theverat can get hold of him.

He stands in the doorway confronting the churning maw. Braces himself. Jumps.

Fungle's heart stopped.

'Fungle?' Neema whispered.

'He ain't moved a muscle.'

Codswollop helped Neema to her feet and the two of them leaned over the slab. Fungle's body was stiff. No respiration, no pulse, no pupillary reflex.

Neema bit her lip. 'There's no bonding,' she said.

'Say what?'

She shook her head and tried to think clearly. 'No bonding, no link. The cord to his body's been severed, an' there's nothin' . . . nothin' left in his body to recognise the return of his spirit.'

'What can we do?'

'We've got ta get somethin' happenin' inside him. His body's got ta send a signal to his spirit. Like . . . a recognition code.'

'Neema.' Codswollop's tone was gentle. 'There ain't gonna *be* no signals.'

'No!' Neema pounded both fists on Fungle's chest. 'All we need's a heartbeat,' she insisted. 'A breath, a flow of blood in his veins.'

Codswollop frowned. 'You mean like his battery's dead?' he asked. 'Like he needs a jump start?'

'I guess so,' said Neema, who had no idea what that meant. She bent to Fungle and pushed on his chest, trying to get his heart to pump. *Just once, Fungle*, she thought. *Just a signal, a lantern hung out by yer body ta see ya home.*

Codswollop watched her for a moment, drumming his fingers on the edge of the slab. Suddenly he turned away and opened the door.

Fat J whipped around. 'Boss!' yelped the metrognome. 'Some heavy stuff goin' down aroun' here.' Behind him toy poodles yipped and little police cars whined. 'There wuz a t'rific explosion a minute ago, an' –'

'Ya shock-box charged?' Codswollop interrupted, indicating Fat J's commandeered taser.

'You bet.'

'Good.' Codswollop yanked Fat J into the room, where Neema was alternately pounding on Fungle's chest and pinching his nostrils to breathe into his pale mouth.

'Whatchoo want, boss?' asked Fat J.

Codswollop hurried to Neema and pulled her away from Fungle's body. She clawed at him, intent on getting Fungle back, but Codswollop blocked her swipe and stayed between her and Fungle.

Codswollop looked at Fat J and pointed at the slab. 'Shoot him,' he said.

'Heeeeelp!' Ka screamed down the hallway toward Autopsy Room 3.

Wind-up toys littered the floor. A laundry cart fetched up against the wall and sent liberated lab bunnies hopping away.

A metrognome popped up from the cart's dirty linens. 'Whereza fire, brudda?' asked Tyre Iron.

'Right behind me!' answered Ka. 'It's a nightmare! It's got thorns an' it throws 'em an' they blows up whatever they touches!'

Tyre Iron brightened. 'No kiddin'?' He vaulted from the cart and landed on a beleaguered Godzilla toy that spat a defiant death rattle of sparks and moved no more. Tyre Iron pointed at something on the far wall. 'Y'know how ta fight fire, dontcha?'

Ka looked where the metrognome was pointing and grinned.

Walking casually, in no particular hurry, Thorn rounded the corner toward Autopsy Room 3.

He stopped. The gnome was standing in the hall, and behind him was one of those laughable city thugs, the metrognomes. The gnome was holding some kind of enormous brass-headed snakeskin that ribboned back to where the metrognome stood ready to turn a red-painted valve beside a glass pane set in the wall.

'Now!' shouted Ka.

Tyre Iron began twisting the valve.

The fire hose swelled with water racing toward the nozzle.

Thorn snapped a spiny tip from the blade of his hip.

Ka looked backward in alarm because no water seemed forthcoming.

A hump shot along the length of hose like a python regurgitating a rabbit.

Thorn raised his arm to throw.

Tyre Iron opened the valve all the way.

The hose spat once, burped, and went limp.

Thorn threw the leathery squirming spine tip.

A powerful jet of water knocked Ka backward to the floor and deflected the hurled spine tip upward. The high-pressured stream plastered Thorn against the wall just as the spine tip hit the ceiling. There was a terrific explosion, and charred and broken ceiling panels and imploding fluorescent tubes crashed down on top of Thorn.

The hose squirmed from Ka's grip and began beating itself senseless around the hallway.

Fungle's body bucked as if having a *grand mal* epileptic seizure. Neema and Codswollop held him down to prevent him falling from the slab. In a few seconds it was over, and Fungle lay still again.

'Fungle?' asked Neema. She looked up fearfully at Codswollop. 'I don't think it wa–'

Fungle drew in a sudden ragged deep wheezing breath. The room was a momentary tableau: Neema, Codswollop and Fat J staring in hopeful fearful fascination at the arched straining immobile form on the slab.

Then Fungle began to choke. His face turned ghastly red and his fingers curled and clutched air as he let forth great hacking coughs. They helped him to a sitting position and pounded his back. Eventually the coughs subsided and Fungle's eyes fluttered open.

He looked at Neema. 'Nee–' he said, and coughed violently again.

Fat J handed him a Dixie cup of water and Fungle drank it in one gulp. 'Thankee,' he said.

'Fungle,' Neema said simply, and there was a world of love and gratification and fulfilment in the single word.

'How ya feel, ace?' asked Codswollop.

Fungle lay back on the slab and shut his eyes. 'Stiff,' he croaked.

'Not surprised,' remarked the metrognome king. 'Two minutes ago ya was one.'

Fungle opened his eyes to look at Neema. 'Took ya from yer happy home once more, I'm feared,' he said apologetically.

Neema blushed. There was no need for words. The intimate spaces of *self* they had just shared went beyond mere language.

'Jus' don't you watch no more tee vee, Fungle Foxwit,' she said, breaking the awkward moment. '"*Cleaner, brighter, new an' improved!*"' She rolled her eyes. 'It near drove me mad!'

Their gaze broke as something slammed into the door. Fat J opened it and was knocked flat by a blast of water from a fire hose thrashing in the hall.

Ka leaned his head in the doorway. 'Sorry!' he said. He withdrew, then shot back into sight. '*Fungle!*' he screamed, just before the rampaging fire hose smacked him on the head and knocked him clean out.

Codswollop regarded the unconscious gnome on the floor. 'Ama-
teurs,' he scorned, and sighed. He checked to be sure Ka was all
right (he was – though a knot was already forming on the gnome's
hard head), then turned to Neema and Fungle. 'Hate to spoil the
homecomin', you two, but if we don' get outta here quick, they're
gonna start chargin' us rent.'

Thorn lay beneath the rubble of piping and ceiling panels. He tried
to lift the debris, but one arm wasn't working properly. In fact,
he was not sure it was there at all. A toy police car kept banging
against his hip as if it wanted to give him a ticket for obstruction
of justice.

Thorn strained with his good arm against the rubble and felt a
soft tearing deep within his chest. He wondered if he were dying.

Down the hall he could see the doorway into which the gnome
had run. Several metrognomes guarded it. The gnoles were in that
room as well. Thorn could feel them. He could hurl one of his
lethal spine tips right now and obliterate the lot of them, but that
was not what Theverat wanted. Theverat wanted them alive.

He needed another solution. Quickly, because he was fading.

He struggled to get his good arm down to his hip so that he
could break off one of his deadly thorns. A fleshy pop sounded
deep within his shoulder as he forced his arm. No matter. He
got a leathery hand around a spine and wrenched it. It snapped
cleanly, and Thorn felt the odd thrill of its detachment.

He spoke an ancient word to prime the thorn as it squirmed in
his grip. He pulled back his arm to throw. Near his hand, the toy
police car whined angrily. Were its lights fading, was it running
down, or was he?

With the last of his strength he tossed the spine.

Codswollop opened the door and jumped back as battery-powered
and wind-up toys poured in. Yipping poodles and stalking Godzillas,
sparking motorcycles and black-and-white patrol cars jumped or
walked or rolled into the autopsy room.

Codswollop found this highly amusing until the bottles all around
them burst. They shattered simultaneously, and the room filled
with the reek of formaldehyde as their grisly contents splashed
onto tables and counters and the tiled floor.

The toys moved among them.

It was Fungle who felt the magic at work. Still slightly dazed from
his ordeal, he had just been helped from the floor by Neema when

Codswollop admitted the noisy toys, and he watched in befuddled fascination now as they banged and splashed among the foul mess of shattered glass and animal remains.

The mechanical devices and the animal parts were fusing. Gears and fur and wheels and eyes, motors and teeth and springs and claws, accreting to form a single creature, a mechanical animal. A *mechanimal*.

'Run,' suggested Fungle.

They ran.

The ringing of the telephone nearly gave Crucifer a heart attack. Theverat had disappeared from the computer monitor, and a moment ago there had been a dull explosion from somewhere in the building that he'd felt through his feet.

His hand reached for the phone. Line two was lit. He punched the button.

'It seems Thorn has become waylaid,' Theverat said without preamble. 'Trapped in some wreckage. Guess who gets to rescue him, Tib?'

Crucifer swallowed. 'What . . . what did you need him for?' He sensed the swelling impatient fury on the other end of the line, an electronic signal across wires and through computer banks that led everywhere and nowhere, a mounting explosion of rage that he was being questioned. 'Because,' Crucifer rushed on, playing his trump card, making himself indispensable, 'I can track them. I . . . I guarantee it. I can follow them wherever they go.'

A beep from the computer. The jewelled face had returned. 'Tell me more,' said Theverat.

The grimawkins had just loaded the last of the pizza, Doritos, Cheez Whiz, Rolling Rock beer, M-80 firecrackers, and stacks of cassette tapes into the Ram when the front doors of the building that housed DPR burst open and a gaggle of metrognomes sprinted toward them. Among them were two gnoles and a gnome. The gnome was out like a welcome mat and being carried between two metrognomes.

Ka was handed up to the grimawkins, who set him like a grocery bag in the back of the Ram. 'You be careful wid him,' warned Codswollop. Between the autopsy room and here he had managed to locate another stogie, and it stuck out of the side of his mouth and wrote a cursive smoky message to the late-night air.

The grimawkins began piling into the truck.

Fungle and Neema stood before Codswollop. 'I – *we* – can't thank you enough, yer majesty,' said Fungle. He looked out over the assembled metrognomes. 'All of you,' he added gratefully.

Codswollop beamed. 'True,' he said.

Suddenly Neema leaned forward and gave Codswollop a back-breaking hug and a quick kiss. Then, blushing violently, she turned away and allowed the grimawkins to hoist her into the truck.

Codswollop stared up with his mouth open and a hand against his cheek, still moist from her kiss, as the Ram's doors shut and the engine roared to life. He shook his head like an emerging swimmer and rapped a fist against the passenger door. 'Hey!'

The window rolled down. The fierce grimawkins stared down at the metrognome king.

'Get 'em down South,' said Codswollop. 'Wherever they tell ya to go. Don't end up in jail, don't end up married to no telephone pole, an' don' do nuttin' stoopid.'

The designated driver, Skat Katz, grew solemn and shook his head earnestly. 'Oh, dontchoo worry 'bout a thing, King Cowswallow,' he said. 'Youse can count on us. Right, boys!'

'Right!' The grimawkins howled with laughter.

Codswollop nodded. 'This makes us even, boys. An' don't fahget to buckle up fah safety.'

The window rolled up and dampered their mirth. Skat ground a pound of meat forcing the truck into gear, the engine raced, and the red Dodge Ram leapt forward – and stalled.

The metrognomes' laughter drowned out the catcalls of the grimawkins.

Something crashed behind them.

Heads turned.

The mechanimal was tearing through the entrance to DPR. It had to tear through because it was larger than the doorway.

'Think that's our cue, boys,' said Codswollop.

Skat Katz tried to start the truck again. The mechanimal took a door off its hinges and began forcing itself through the jamb.

Codswollop turned to Motli. 'Keys in that Lincoln?' he asked, gesturing with his cigar.

Motli hurried to the Lincoln, bent to the tinted driver's window, and lifted his eyepatch. He straightened and nodded his head.

The mechanimal was out of the building now. Pale orange streetlight gleamed on metallic components, glistened on wet animal parts.

'Then pile on in, boys!' shouted Codswollop.

The mechanimal was lifting the door it had torn from its hinges. At least eleven metrognomes threw themselves into the Lincoln Continental. Motli held the door open for Codswollop, who maintained his decorum whilst he strode purposefully toward the car and slid behind the driver's seat.

He turned the key.

The mechanimal threw the door.

The Lincoln started.

The Ram started.

Brake lights flashed, the Ram ground into gear, the Lincoln lurched forward, and the hurled door slammed into the street where the Lincoln had been.

The Ram headed north. Codswollop saw Fungle in the back seat, waving one last time. Codswollop blew the horn and hung a right that brought the big car up on two wheels.

The mechanimal juggernauted up the avenue in pursuit of the Ram.

'Wish 'em luck, boys,' said Codswollop. By the time they reached the subways for the journey to the abandoned civil defence shelter they called home, Codswollop was cheerfully whistling 'New York, New York'.

'What *is* that thing?'

'It's a mess!'

'Maybe, but right now it's *our* mess!'

'It's gainin' on us, Skat!'

'Ya gotta be kiddin' me – I'm doin' seventy!'

Fungle and Neema held tight as the Dodge Ram screamed down the avenue. Ka was still unconscious, but the grimawkins had thoughtfully handcuffed him to his seatbelt.

'Penn Central!' shouted Red Rova.

'Hope that thing packed a lunch!' said Skat, and cut the wheel. The Ram smashed a barricade and hurtled through the rail-yard.

'Still on us!'

Slavering jaws, spinning gears, and clutching claws filled the back windshield.

'Hold on!' Skat grinned and forced the truck onto the railroad tracks.

A metal cyclops grew before them.

'Train!' yelled Ali Katz.

'No foolin',' muttered Skat. He held the Dodge steady on the tracks. Ahead lay a massive locomotive in the service yard. The multi-faced mechanimal filled his rearview mirror.

'Allow me to introduce youse,' said Skat, and swerved.

Mechanimal met locomotive. Locomotive met mechanimal. They became inseparable.

The grimawkins were still laughing about it as, without paying the toll, they sped into the Lincoln Tunnel and got the Dodge out of hell.

Crucifer pressed a button on the flat metal box and a red dot winked on the backlighted gridded circular screen. 'There they are,' he said.

'You're certain?' asked Theverat.

Crucifer quelled his nervousness. Not only was he anxious at the thought of disappointing Theverat, but disquieting things were afoot. Theverat's screen image on the monitor kept blurring with snow, as if the demon were having trouble maintaining his connection to the world. He appeared distracted and unenthused, listless like a man too long without sleep. Even his threats seemed halfhearted. Something had happened there in the Otherworld, Crucifer suspected, but he had no idea what. 'I implanted the transmitter myself,' he told Theverat. 'It's good for a fifty-mile radius and a month's continuous operation. They may notice it, but they won't be able to do anything about it. Not without surgery, anyway.' He showed the box to the crystalline face on the computer monitor. 'Right now they're heading north on Eleventh at seventy miles per hour. My guess is they're making for the Lincoln Tunnel.'

Theverat nodded. 'Good. Very good, Tib. My investment in you, my *faith* in you, has been well ventured.'

Crucifer felt relief flood him. This was like playing baseball with a lit bomb; you whacked it away and felt so very *alive* . . .

'Tell me, Tib,' Crucifer said conversationally, 'that *box* of yours, that wonderful *device*. Since it's doing the tracking, we really don't need you for anything, do we?'

Crucifer felt the walls stretching away from him. The ceiling seemed to be ascending. 'But, but, you said –'

'I said you'd be first among my helpers,' said Theverat. The jewelled face smiled. 'And so you shall.'

Shuffling movement behind him. Crucifer turned. The first thing he saw was the horror-show spear. The last thing he saw was its owner, drawing it back to throw.

22 *Highway to Hell*

'*Yeeee-haw!*' *Blamblamblam!*

Neema jerked awake as Red Rova dropped back into the Ram's shotgun seat clutching a splintered baseball bat. 'How manyzat?' Red shouted above the radio.

Beside him Ali grinned. 'Eleven.'

'Dey juss don' make mailboxes like dey useta!' yelled Skat, driving at seventy-five and not looking at the road.

Crammed beside Fungle in the Ram's back seat along with three grimawkins, Neema slept and Ka clutched whatever he could while staring aghast as the bright red truck chewed up the miles like a shark at meat. The grimawkins had not slowed since entering the Lincoln Tunnel fifty miles ago. They had already switched drivers once because all of the grimawkins wanted a turn, but they refused to slow down – much less pull over – to make the switch. The grimawkins did not drive the Ram so much as aim it.

Ka had awakened in Jersey City. Beside him Neema slept deeply, the first true rest she'd had since her initial escape from DPR. Fungle had sat beside her staring at the streetlights and concrete landscape blurring past. Seeing Ka awake, the gnole had set a hand on his friend's arm. 'Welcome back,' he'd said. 'Are ya a'right?'

'I'm fine, Fungle.' Ka had patted the hand holding his arm. 'Answer the phone, willya?'

Seeing that his friend was all right but shaken and putting on a brave front, Fungle had nodded and looked away, needing some time alone with himself. As they rocketed westward on I-78, Fungle took stock and realised that he himself was far from a'right. Ignoring the grimawkins' constant shouting and the deafening music coming from front and back speakers, Fungle sensed that it would be days before he was even close to normal. He had not been eating well; chemical residues from processed human foods and drugs still littered his veins; psychic residue from watching the tee vee littered his mind; he had endured the strenuous labour of full astral travel twice in as many days, and he'd had to be brought back to life because of the damage inflicted on him by what he had come to think of as a War in Heaven. He shivered with the sort of marrow-deep cold that comes from a winter's drenching not even a roaring fire can warm. His body and mind were in shock from his brutal recovery into the world. In a way, Fungle had been reborn.

Back to life.

He shook his head with the wonder of it. *Back to life.* He looked at Neema sleeping beside him and remembered her peaceful slumber in the tidy house of her *self,* remembered being a part of her for some dreamlike short while. Remembered seeing the world through her eyes, sharing the comfort of the home of her mind like a favourite blanket on a stormy night. That fire – *her* fire – will always glow within me, he thought.

In a meditative state, trying to clear himself of the distraction of recent drama in order to ready himself for the challenge ahead, Fungle sensed but did not react to the westering wasteland of tenements heaped and fossilised and sagging past the fishbelly grey of the East River.

Now they were at the western edge of New Jersey, and the I-78 connector was still under construction. The grimawkins had argued directions for a while until they agreed to take surface streets across the Delaware River to US 22 in Pennsylvania. This provided them with the opportunity to burn off some excess energy and bash mailboxes, which was the sound that had just awakened Neema.

She blinked in confusion. 'Where 'm I?' she muttered. 'Who. . .?'

Ka held up an AAA road atlas. ''Cordin' ta this, yer near somethin' called Allentown.'

Neema frowned. She seemed relieved, then worried again. 'Ah, an' I'd hoped it were all a bad dream I just had.'

Fungle put an arm around her. 'There, there,' he said. 'All's right now, thanks be ta you. You an' Ka here.'

Neema blushed but did not move from Fungle's embrace.

Fungle asked to see Ka's road atlas and stared in horror at its depiction of the United States. Ka'd been right, way back when: the humans had changed near everything. Varicose veins covered east to west, north to south. The maps of Fungle's ancestors were useless in the face of such upheaval.

Blam! '*Yeee-haw!*'

'What're they doin'?' asked Neema, indicating the grimawkin Skat waving his baseball bat and yelling out the window.

'It's some kinda game,' replied Ka. 'Only I ain't figured out the rules yet.'

'I ain't sure there be any,' said Fungle. He shut the road atlas. 'Eh, Neema, I – that is . . . Well, I gone an' lost that bootiful rose ya give me back at Ka's when I left on me way.' He looked everywhere but at her.

Neema chuckled. 'That's all right, Fungle. Ya were s'posed ta give it back when we met again, if ye'll remember.' She patted his hand. 'Well, I got you back instead.' She grew serious. 'Fungle? Can I ask you something?'

Fungle nodded.

'Do you remember?' asked Neema. 'Out *there*, I mean?'

'I'll never fergit it.'

'Nor me,' said Neema. 'But that first time – that was Theverat around you, wasn't it? That's what yer up against?'

Again Fungle nodded.

'I hadn't realised, Fungle,' Neema said gravely. 'He's so . . . so . . .'

Fungle nodded once more.

The radio scanned across thundering power-chord rock and roll and Red jabbed a skull-ringed finger to keep it there. Ka put his fingers in his ears. Neema and Fungle huddled closer.

'That first time, Fungle,' said Neema. 'Somethin' come after us. It was – it was *everything*. Alien and old, an' diff'rent than Theverat somehow.'

'It weren't Theverat, Neema.'

'What was it then?'

'I don't know.'

Every time the singer screeched out, 'Dirty deeds,' the grimawkins yelled back, '*Done dirt cheap!*' It was 6.20 am and they were heading south-west at eighty miles per hour on I-81 just north of the Pennsylvania-Maryland border.

They had just robbed a McDonald's.

Fungle had been listening to his stomach groan and wondering what to do about it when Roller Rova stood on the brakes. The truck screeched like a stuck pig and left a hundred-yard skid mark. Everybody pitched forward. Naturally none of the grimawkins were wearing seatbelts. Empty pizza boxes, chip wrappers, Rolling Rock beer cans, cigarette packs, grimawkins, gnoles, and a wide-eyed gnome shot toward the front of the truck.

They slewed to a halt.

Freddy Katz opened a hungover eye. 'Who? What? Which? How?' he said, sitting up in alarm.

Roller pointed triumphantly at the lighted golden arches ahead of them. *'Cheesebuggas!'* he shouted.

Those grimawkins not already awake woke up.

Roller pulled into the McDonald's drive-through lane and rolled down the tinted window. The speaker grille crackled: 'Good-morning-welcome-to-McDonald's-may-I-take-your-order?'

The grimawkins all shouted at once.

'I'm-sorry-sir-I-didn't-get-that.'

Freddy waved the others to silence. 'That's ten quahtah-poundahs, one widdout cheese, two wid no onions; t'irteen loj fries; eight Big Macs; six loj Cokes; t'ree Happy Meals; ten cheesebuggas; four Mug McIffins; anna biggest Chicken McMaggot box you got.' Freddy frowned. 'You don't got no cigarettes 'r Rollin' Rock beer, do yaz?' He glanced back at Fungle, Neema, and Ka. 'Oh, yeah: t'ree dinnah salads an' three cupsa wattah.'

The grimawkins laughed.

The speaker repeated the order. 'Would-you-like-any-dessert-with-that?'

'Yeah, gimme, uh . . . twenny-four a them hot apple pie things.'

'Your-total's-sixty-eight-twenty-three-thank-you-drive-through-please.'

Roller rolled up the window and drove through. He pulled up to the window and waited with the engine idling high while the tape deck roared ostensible music by a band called Nuclear Lunchbox that seemed designed to make people beat their heads against cinder-block walls.

The McDonald's server worriedly eyed the ominous idling Ram while kitchen help scrambled to fill the massive order. He could see that the truck was crammed full, but not what it was crammed full of. Finally the order was ready and he pushed boxes and bags to the service window, opened it, and rapped on the black-tinted driver's window of the Ram. 'Sir? Sixty-eight twenty-three, please.'

The window slid down and the McDonald's server found himself staring at a brutish dog-like creature wearing a pirate bandanna, a Marlon Brando leather biker jacket, a lot of indeterminate but unpleasant-looking metal, and an expression of gleeful menace.

'You take travellah's cheques?' the creature asked in a smoker's voice with a distinct Bronx accent, pulling the huge carton of food and drink from the stunned server's hands. ''Cause we ain't from aroun' heeyah.' He handed the server a stink bomb and pulled the pin.

Now the food was gone and the Ram bulged with the grimawkins' explosive belches. The grimawkins prided themselves on their burps and cheered each other on. Apparently Range Rova was the undisputed grimawkin belch champion. He had not yet expressed his gastronomic appreciation of McDonald's cuisine, however, and the other grimawkins were waiting with a kind of anxious awe to witness this epicurean epic.

The grimawkins' guests – *hostages* was too harsh a word, though perhaps *captive audience* was not inappropriate – picked at their salads and drank only a little of their water. They were all faintly nauseated, not only by the grimawkins, but by the waxpaper flavour of the water, the chemical taint of the insecticides flavouring the food, and the cloying stinging odour of burning petroleum and carbon monoxide fumes coming from the truck as it raced southward.

At Hagerstown they got off the Interstate and pulled into a Shell station. Skat Katz (driving again) waited until a station-wagon pulled up to a Super Unleaded pump, then parked beside it on the other side of the pump island. The station-wagon driver, an old man in a John Deere cap and a flannel shirt half-tucked into his work pants, ambled toward the cashier, rubbing his hands in the cold morning air. Ali Katz and Range Rova hopped out of the Ram. Range put on a hat and sunglasses and skipped to the station to steal cigarettes while Ali grabbed the Super Unleaded nozzle, thrust it into the truck's gas tank, and was pumping away by the time the station-wagon driver returned.

'Excuse me, young fella,' the old man drawled, 'but I b'lieve y'all're usin' mah pump.'

Ali kept his back to the old man and shook his head. 'You're next,' he grumbled, and continued filling up the tank.

Fungle could stand it no more. The smell of gasoline was making him sick, and the noxious fumes spewed by the truck as it growled down the highway made it hard to concentrate – and right now he needed to concentrate. He yanked the leather bag holding the Lunabird's magnetite crystal from around Ka's neck, opened the door, and hopped to the pavement. He knocked Ali's hand from the pump and pulled the nozzle from the Ram.

'Whaddaya think yah doin'!' yelled Ali.

Fungle said nothing. He went to the front of the truck and tried to figure out how to open the hood.

Ka leaned past Neema and rolled down the window. 'There's a latch,' he called out to Fungle.

The old man stared. 'Well, if that don't beat all,' he said softly.

Ali caught Skat's eye and made a gesture that meant, *You want me to stop him?* Skat frowned and subtly held up a hand: *Wait.*

Fungle found the latch and popped the hood. He climbed onto the bumper and stared down into the steaming pinging labyrinth of machinery that muscled the truck along the road. He didn't really understand the mechanisms, but he could sense the energy stored in the battery. He knew the machines needed the electricity to begin working, and after that they burned the noxious liquid. So: no electricity, no burning.

He unhooked the battery cables.

Now, lessee . . . Just substitutin' the crystal fer the batt'ry weren't no good; it'd only start the machines that burnt the liquid again. He hadda get the crystal to run the machines direct.

'Ka, c'm'ere a moment, if ya would,' he called.

A few seconds later Ka and Fungle were huddled over the engine as Ka pointed to parts. 'It's all based on spinnin', Fungle,' said Ka. 'Allat energy's ta make th' in-djinn turn fast so's it can spin a long rod what connects ta two other rods to spin the wheels.'

Two minutes later Fungle had fastened the magnetite to the engine fan and created a simple spell that would cause the crystal to convert the energies of the earth's magnetic field into angular momentum – in short, the crystal would spin.

By the time he was done the old man had complained to the gas-station manager, who came out in a work shirt with *Bob* embroidered above the left breast pocket. He strode authoritatively up to Fungle. 'Man here says you took his . . . say – don't ah know you?' He snapped his fingers. 'Yeah! You were on tee vee!' He looked around for lights and cameras. 'You guys makin' a movie?' he asked.

'Movie?' asked a voice behind them. Bob the manager turned to see Range Rova grinning innocently with huge carnivore teeth and clutching cartons of commandeered cigarettes. Suddenly the ferocious belch that had been building since they'd eaten the McDonald's 'food' (for lack of a better word) erupted. It knocked Bob the manager on his keister and rattled the pump nozzles in their holsters.

Bob and the old man stared at the rest of the grimawkins, who were leaning out the truck's windows to cheer the epic burp as Fungle, Ka, and Range hopped back into the truck.

Skat connected the two wires that hot-wired the ignition. Nothing happened. He whipped around to face Fungle. 'Whaddidjoo do?' he bellowed.

'Fixed it so's it'd work without witherin' everythin' around it,' Fungle replied.

'*Fixed* it! It won't start!'

'It will if ya tells it to.'

Skat glared. Without saying a word, he eloquently conveyed to Fungle that the grimawkins were all primed and dangerous as a grenade with a glass pin. 'I just tell it to go?' he mocked.

Fungle nodded.

Skat fumed. He turned to face the steering wheel. 'Truck,' he said. He glanced at the other grimawkins as if daring them to laugh. 'Truck . . . go.'

Nothing happened.

'You gots to ask it nicely,' said Fungle, hiding his amusement.

Skat screwed his face and held up his fists. He emitted a strained sound: '*Ooooooh.*' Eight distinct pops filled the truck's cabin as his knuckles cracked.

'Skat nevah asked nuttin' nice inniz life,' explained Ali Katz.

Fungle shrugged. 'Then the truck won't go.'

Skat took a deep breath. He took two. 'Truck,' said Skat, fighting to remain calm. '*Please* go.'

The silence was deafening.

Skat pummelled the dash. 'Dat's it!' he said, and turned to Fungle. 'I'm gonna *murderlate* ya! I'm gonna *pounderise* ya! Nobody but nobody makes a chump outta me! I'm gonna –'

'We's goin',' said Fungle.

'Whassat?'

'We's goin',' Fungle repeated.

Skat looked around, and it was true. The truck was slowly rolling forward. The bemused grimawkin raised his scar-knuckled hands to the wheel like a creature in a dream and steered the truck toward the road. They glided out of the Shell station and accelerated in eerie silence up the ramp and back onto the Interstate.

Still fuming, Skat looked at Ali. 'Tape!' he barked.

Ali reached into a pocket and pulled out a purple velvet Rémy Martin drawstring bag held shut by a yellow cord. He opened it and he produced a plastic tape-cassette box which he swung open with reverence. Delicately he lifted out the cassette and pushed it into the player.

Tape hiss. Fungle readied himself for a monstrous wall of sound.

Springtime violins dawned at the opening strains of Beethoven's Sixth, the 'Pastorale'. 'Ahhh,' sighed Skat. 'It ain't Megadeth, but it's still nice.' He relaxed in his seat, driving with one hand and conducting with the other.

They shot through Maryland and West Virginia in forty-five minutes. Now that the oughtamobile's fumes had been taken care of, Fungle was concentrating on trying to breathe without choking on the disgusting lethal vapours emitted by the grimawkins' cigarettes. Of all the inexplicable human habits, smoking confounded Fungle the most. How a thinking creature could derive any pleasure inhaling carcinogens from a burning weed was beyond him. More than once, during his incarceration in the Land of No, he had seen the yellowed teeth and smelled the ashy breath of habitual smokers, and he had sensed the corruption erupting throughout their lungs like spider eggs hatching in living flesh.

Neema and Ka had opened up the windows on either side of the truck to get some air and Fungle had just worked up the nerve to ask the grimawkins to put out their cigarettes when the psychic scream tore into his mind.

– fungle help oh fungle we please it's got us fungle there's –

Fungle fell back against the seat. He was dimly aware of Neema and Ka asking if he was all right. He began to tremble. He felt faint.

– fungle please we're so scared and there's nowhere to go it's out there can you hear me fungle can you h–

Silence. The voice cut off in mid-word.

Froog's voice.

Fungle closed his eyes and trembled from the fear and violence and panic of it, and remembered a childhood time trapped in a deathly black gopher hole calling out to his brother, *oh froog I'm stuck it's dark please froog come get me I'm hanging here and it goes down down down for miles froog help me.*

He sat up. 'I'm a'right,' he said. He clasped Ka's and Neema's hands. 'I'm a'right,' he repeated.

'Fungle, what happened?' asked Neema.

'Just . . . just tired, Neema. Tired's all.' He hated to lie, especially when he knew that, after the heartfilling closeness he and Neema had shared, she would forevermore know when he was lying. But he did not want to burden his friends with this. Not now, not with the task at hand.

The cry had come across a continent. Fungle glanced out the right-side windows of the silently speeding truck, aware of the worried gazes of Neema and Ka beside him. Among the hills morning shadows pointed westward from the rising sun.

West.

Fungle remembered the bittersweet parting after the celebration of going-away when Froog, Wisp, Peapod, and Quince had piled into their Lunabird and flown west. West, toward Mount Shasta and the gnoles in exile. West, in search of a small patch of uncorrupted land beside another ocean. West.

Fungle's eyes misted with tears.

Oh, Froog, me brother. Wisp, Peapod, Quince – I'm so sorry. Whatever's wrong, I can't abandon me quest now. If I leave me course ta help ya now, it'll only be so's you can live in a wretched future under the lash of Theverat. I hafta stop him. I'm so sorry, an' I send ya my strongest prayers that ya can hold out 'til I can come to ya – but I can't abandon the path I'm on.

The truck hurtled on into the Appalachians.

Their progress slowed dramatically as Highway I-85 wound south along the mountains that hemmed their path. The land was an autumnal procession of ochre and dun, rusted leaves of chrome yellow and burnt sienna. Neema and Ka hung their heads out the windows like dogs to feel the sharp clean air of early November. Even Fungle, upset and preoccupied as he was, rejoiced in the familiar smells of loam and moss and leaf, air that with every breath reminded him he was alive. The air of home.

They were half-an-hour south of Staunton, Virginia when Fungle asked the grimawkins to pull off the interstate. Ali, the current driver, reluctantly complied. Fungle sensed the creatures' rest-lessness now that they were away from the city and the constant opportunities for trouble it afforded. Had they not owed King Codswollop a favour, they would no doubt have turned back long ago.

Ali pulled onto the narrow shoulder. He sneered at the dashboard and said, 'Please stop, truck.' The slight vibration – the only sign that the truck was in operation – ceased. 'Ya pieca a gobbage,' Ali added.

The truck shuddered once and was still.

'Pit stop!' called Ali. 'Sprinkle ya boots, boys!'

'What're we stopped fer, Fungle?' asked Ka.

'Gots ta take care o' some biznizz,' said Fungle, opening the door.

'Mmm.' Ka pursed his lips. 'Prob'ly a good idea fer me too.' He followed Fungle out of the truck.

Within a few yards of the freeway the woods ate up light and sound. Ka hurried behind a tree. Fungle walked on, feeling himself reawaken with every step. The woods invigorated his cells and nerves; he drank them up like a fish returning to water after too deadly long a stay on land.

Soon he found a powerful old oak. Beneath its shade he gathered moss, mushrooms, the rotting jelly scraped from beneath a fallen log, quartz-veined granite, the tight buds of night-blooming flowers, other things. He laid them beneath the oak and set to work.

Not long after the abrupt and tragic events that led to Fungle's becoming the shaman and mage of his clan – of, indeed, the entire valley – one of the first signs that he had the potential to become something more than any gnole mage had been for generations, a potential not seen on the earth since the time of his ancestors' first footprints on the eastern shores of Americka, was his invention of what he called 'metaspells'. Metaspells were such simple things that Fungle was amazed no one had thought of them earlier. But the *concept* of metaspells was difficult to convey, and perhaps this accounted for it.

A metaspell was simply a spell that recorded other spells. Fungle activated the metaspell and assigned it a gesture and a magic word by which to 'replay' it later on. Then he went about creating whatever spell it was he wanted recorded, and the metaspell stored all the energy produced by the motions, offerings, chants, burning of herbs, and the like, of the spell itself. After that, whenever Fungle wanted to invoke the spell, instead of repeating the motions and chants and what-have-you involved in the spell's creation, he merely used the magic word and gesture that invoked the metaspell, and the metaspell unleashed all the stored energy of the spell it had recorded.

For instance, one of the dozens of metaspells filed away in Fungle's memory was for keeping a dry space around him while it was raining. Fungle liked rain and liked being wet, but some duties such as spellcasting in the out-of-doors required dry ground.

The actual spell that kept the rain away from his person was time-consuming for such a simple result. But once saved as a metaspell, Fungle could invoke the spell with merely a word and a gesture.

Metaspells saved a lot of time.

Right now, Fungle thought that saving time might just prove crucial, at a pivotal moment, to save himself. To save his friends. To save his world.

So in the dense forest a few yards and a thousand years away from the interstate, Fungle began a metaspell. Once he was certain that the metaspell was accurately storing his gestures and words and offerings, Fungle began the long and dangerous spell that was the Summoning of the Salamander. He had memorised it from his waterlogged books in Ka's cavern home as a last-resort measure after Molom had given him his mission; he had rehearsed it many times since – in Ka's cavern, in the shack of the first humans who had captured him, in his hospital bed at Walter Reed Hospital. The more he had practised it, the more he had realised that the very nature of the emergency he would need it for would call for speed – but the Summoning of the Salamander was not a quick and easy spell.

Thirty minutes later, shaking with tension and fatigue, Fungle spoke the final word of the Summoning and made the last pass in the air. He broke sticks and spoke a simple spell to ignite them. The flame served as a beacon to the Salamander and a lever by which to gain entry into the world.

The Salamander was the Spirit of Flame. It was was fire and the essence of fire; it would indiscriminately consume all that lay before it, laying waste to forest and town alike. The Salamander could reduce whole mountains to ash and less than ash, and once it had gained entry into the world, it could not be stopped until its fury was spent.

Fungle's spell did not summon the Salamander at this moment because the invocation's energy was directed into the metaspell. Careful lest the least slip of the tongue unleash the metaspell's pent-up energy, Fungle caused the metaspell to stop recording.

Then he punched his right fist into his left palm and spoke an ancient word: '*Daësh'te!*' Now, whenever Fungle made that gesture and spoke that word, the Salamander would come.

Weary and apprehensive, Fungle trudged back. A light rain was falling by the time he reached the interstate, where a furious Ka paced the side of the road, waiting for him.

The truck was gone.

*

'Just havin' some yucks!' yelled Range Rova.

Wet and cold, Fungle and Ka sat in the back seat and dried themselves with dirty clothes.

'Hardly what I'd call "yucks",' Neema said tightly.

They were just past Roanoke. Fungle remembered that this was also the Algonquin Indian name of an island where there'd once been a settlement, long ago when European humans were first invading North Americka. It had disappeared suddenly and without a trace. No one ever knew how the settlers could have vanished so quickly and thoroughly, with no signs of struggle or hasty abandon. No one knew what fate eventually befell them – no one, that is, but the gnoles.

It turned out that the grimawkins had left Fungle and Ka because a Virginia State Trooper had pulled over to find out why the truck was pulled over. The grimawkins had led the trooper a merry chase down mountain roads at stock-car speeds. The grimawkins benefitted from the Ram's four-wheel drive and offroad design, and from Fungle's magnetite-crystal engine, which seemed to have no upper limit to its RPM.

'So what happened to the policeman, then?' asked Fungle.

Skat Katz grinned and put on a trooper hat. For the first time Fungle noticed the grimawkin was wearing a shiny badge on his leather jacket, and a pair of nickel-plated handcuffs dangling from his wide leather belt. 'Bedda you don' know,' the grimawkin said.

They rolled on.

Tennessee.

In the end it was Fungle's nose that told him he was near his destination. Every aroma is as unique as a thumbprint, and Fungle remembered all of them. Trace odours of vegetation, air, decay, water, animal life and local diet, recently torn skin of the earth – all added up to a unique combination that gave Fungle's nose a sense of place as recognisable as vision, but in his case a thousand times keener.

They had turned off I-85 and headed southeast on I-40. The road was high; the afternoon was chilly and misty from the midday rain as the silent Ram wound through the Great Smoky Mountains and the Cherokee National Forest. Many of the roads were closed from November through April, and there was little traffic.

Fungle sat bolt upright in his seat. His nostrils flared. His nose wrinkled. He breathed deeply.

'Stop!' he shouted.

They skidded sickeningly on the wet mountain road. Neema saw themselves tumbling down an embankment, saw the truck smashing itself flat as an ironing board, saw their broken bodies forever trapped in this metal coffin. The right rear wheel edged off an embankment and spun in the air before the other three gained traction and the truck lurched back onto the road.

They stopped.

Misty silence surrounded them.

'I don' see no McDonald's,' Roller said doubtfully.

Ali sniffed the air. 'Yeesh!' he said. 'What's that stink?'

'Fresh air,' Skat said miserably.

Fungle held up a hand for quiet. He took another deep breath.

Faint traces of cordite from roadwork blasting: chalky smell of powdered rock; raccoon families particular to the region, living on distinctive local nuts, berries, and human garbage; gunpowder tinge from shotgun blasts; distinctive variation of quail.

They were less than three miles from where Fungle had fallen into the abandoned springhouse that had gobbled him up and spat him farther into the Land of No than any gnole had ever been or would ever want to be again.

And just before falling into the springhouse, Fungle had first laid eyes on his destination.

As Neema, Ka, and the grimawkins looked on, Fungle stared out the windows of the truck and felt his heart race.

He couldn't see it. The heavy mist obscured the broad valley that opened onto the sawtoothed peaks of the Dragonback Ridge. He couldn't see it, but he knew it was out there. He could feel it, waiting out there in the mist, holding Baphomet within its stone vaults like malignant cells in a diseased heart.

He looked at Neema and Ka. Their faces were expectant, worried. 'We's here,' said Fungle.

'Terrific,' said Ka. 'Wunnerful. I couldn't be happier. Where's here?'

Fungle opened the door. He stepped out of the truck for the last time. He looked out into the mist where he knew his goal rose like a fang, only a few hours' walk away. 'Black Mountain,' he replied.

23 *Parting*

Cold rain bit down sharp winter teeth. Fungle, Neema, and Ka slogged through the murky forest without speaking, each alone tree's foliage, black-and-orange butterflies beat lazy Hallowe'en wet carpet of sorrel and spruce needles squished beneath their feet. Runnels flowed down granite outcroppings and patchwork autumn leaves; copperheads hid under rocks and squirrels huddled within their arboreal homes. Beneath the dense leaky umbrella of a spruce tree's foliage, black-and-orange butterflies beat lazy Hallowe'en wings while nervous sneak-thief shrews watched nibbling in the shadows.

The three travellers had all been surprised when the grimawkins had been sorry to see them go. After all the noise and chaos of their wild drive, the bashing crashing speeding careening pedal-to-the-metal into-the-red spike-the-meter twist-the-knob-off bedlam that was the grimawkins' natural habitat, Skat Katz had removed his Virginia State Trooper's hat and blubbered like a baby while hugging each of them goodbye. 'You guys're the greatest,' he had sobbed.

His brothers Ali and Freddy had nodded solemnly. 'No one's ever put up wid us this long,' agreed Ali.

'No one who lived troo it, anyways,' added Freddy.

Skat removed his massive ruby-eyed skull ring and pressed it into Fungle's hand. 'I wan' you to have dis,' he said, and snuffled.

The Rova boys fidgeted and looked embarrassed.

'Katz, we gotta get movin',' said Red.

Skat whirled on him and seemed to grow suddenly larger. 'You wanna wake up inna Alabama prison?' he growled, wiping his nose with a finger. Red lifted an eyebrow and shrugged in a what-can-you-do? gesture. Skat sniffed like a draining sink and turned back to his former passengers. 'Okay, we're outta here,' he said. 'But you guys're pals, real solid good true pals, an' if ya ever need anybody's head busted widda bat, we'll do it fuh nuttin'. Won't we, boys?'

Freddy and Ali agreed that it would be their pleasure to bust anybody's head with a bat for nothing. Fungle conjured a ludicrous image of the grimawkins swinging baseball bats at Theverat, but all he said was an earnest thankee. He granted them the magnetite crystal as a gift. In truth he was reluctant to part with the rare object, but the grimawkins had grown enamoured of the limitless speed it gave them, even if it was quiet and non-polluting, and they had given Fungle a ride to near his destination, after all.

The grimawkins piled into the Ram. Skat yanked Roller out of the driver's seat and threw him in back. He clapped hs hands and rubbed them eagerly. 'Truck,' he said, 'puh-*leez* go!'

The Ram rode silently onto the interstate. 'Or I'll brutilate yuz!' Skat finished as he turned the truck around to head north-east. His laughter could be heard well after the truck had sped into the mist like the wraith of a wrecked automobile.

But the road was far behind Fungle now and he trudged along with his dearest friends through hissing overgrowth like a primeval figure stalking prey. Which, in a way, he was.

Ka would not stop muttering how much he hated rain. Gnomes are rarely in the open air for very long, much less exposed to sun or rain for any length of time. To a creature that lives beneath the ground, the idea of thousands of wet somethings falling from the sky to land on your body is utterly repulsive.

After his harrowing layover in the Land of No (which already felt long ago and far away at the same time, it had begun to seem like a brief lurid nightmare summoned after too many sweetcakes), Fungle had never felt more aware of being a creature belonging to the forest. The greendark world of nettles and thistles, fickle coloured leaves, poisonous snakes and beautiful old webs, mushrooms on rotting logs and jewelled husks of beetles, calligraphic snails and dirt-cleaning worms, gold-filigreed sunsets and fog-lifting dawns – these were a part of him; he was a part of them. In the Land of No, when Fungle had realised that he used tools and manipulated his environment and invented ways to make life easier for himself every bit as much as humans did, he had been curious and confused about the difference in attitude between gnole and human toward the land in which each lived (the *same* land, when all's said and done, and wasn't that the most fantastic notion of all? – as if 'country' and 'city' were natural opposites and opponents, rather than possible cohabitants). But now he knew what the crucial difference was: Fungle felt connected to the world, and it seemed that humans did not. In fact, when humans thought of 'the world', they tended to picture the world of humans and not the *world* at all – though the difference between the two was growing tragically less noticeable as humans made the world their own.

Fungle's ruminations were interrupted when Ka suddenly stopped grumbling and grabbed the gnoles' arms. The gnome's sensitive ears were standing straight up and he was frowning. The three stood silent and still while Ka concentrated.

Suddenly he looked skyward. 'Hide!' he said, and dove straight down.

Well, if there's anything gnoles are good at, it's hiding. Fungle and Neema melted into the wet greenery while Ka wormed into the mulch and covered himself.

The air above the trees began to shudder moments before the trees themselves began to tremble. Branches beat in a sudden swift gale.

A helicopter shot overhead. Bulge-eyed and waspish black, it thudded south-west and out of sight.

The shuddering faded. Rain hissed into the forest.

'Wait,' came a subterranean voice.

The wait was not long. The *thack-thack* of the helicopter rotors rose from the south-west, and in a moment the metal insect shook the trees for another flyby. It circled near where Fungle, Neema and Ka were hiding, then hovered as if making up its metal mind before nosing down and gliding off across the sky once more.

Fungle and Neema came out from behind their respective trees and helped Ka out of the ground.

'Lookin' fer us, ya suppose?' asked Fungle.

'You was hauled away from Fungle's hospital in one o' them contraptions, Neema,' said Ka. 'Looked just like that one. There was men dressed all in black poured outta it like mad hornets from a nest.'

Neema nodded. 'Them men be the hollowest things I ever saw that had a brain.' She shivered in the cold November rain. 'A peek inside their heads was like leavin' yer hearth to walk barefoot in the snow.'

'Well, they ain't found us yet,' said Fungle. 'An' night-time's comin'. Best we push on.'

*

Crucifer tapped the helicopter pilot on the shoulder and pointed down. In his palm the tracking unit displayed a reading on the signal strength of the transmitter embedded in the female gnole. The signal was strong. The gnoles were close by.

Crucifer had said not a single word the entire flight. He merely hunched forward with elbows on knees and stared unblinking at the transmitter screen as it showed his quarry creeping down I–75. The Boys in Black had respected Crucifer's introspection and left him alone. They were merely messengers and gophers and moles, obsessive perfectionistic professionals with no curiosity about their mission. One privileged Republican senator from a previous administration had fondly referred to them as 'mailmen': 'They don't read the letters, they just deliver the package.' Crucifer was today's package, and that was enough.

And now they had arrived. Now the metal box showed that the gnoles – or at least the female – were close beneath them. Crucifer closed his eyes and tried to feel them, to track them not with technology but with instinct, sense them making their way through the dense undergrowth, parting fronds, mashing grass, trampling telltale twigs.

The pilot, mantis-headed in his helmet, nodded at Crucifer's gestured directions. The helicopter descended.

Crucifer examined his .45 semi-automatic pistol, liberated from one of the security guards at DPR. The angular metal felt alien in his hands, but he liked it. A good device. Impersonal, perhaps, but effective.

The pilot looked back. 'We're down!' he called back.

Crucifer nodded. One of the Boys in Black popped the door and looked questioningly at him. Crucifer motioned him aside and jumped out onto the wet grass. The agent who had opened the door noticed that Crucifer didn't hunch low when he exited, the way almost everybody did when near the intimidating rotor.

Crucifer stepped away from the grey blur of overhead blades. The waning day was cold and the sky lidded with thick overcast that hid the sun. Wet grass rippled away from the mammoth fan of the helicopter rotor. He looked at the tracking device in his hand. Close. Still close by.

He looked up at a call. The federal agent was in the doorway of the helicopter, hands cupping his mouth. 'Are we waiting?' he shouted, 'or going with you?'

Crucifer stared a moment. He shook his head slowly no and pointed skyward: *Go.*

The agent started to ask if there was a rendezvous time and place, but Crucifer had already turned away and was running towards the trees in a curious bent stride, tracking device in one hand, .45 in the other.

The agent shrugged. 'Ain't no pay phones out here if you wanna call for help, doc,' he muttered.

But of course nobody heard him.

He sealed the door and signalled the pilot to take them up.

Crucifer descended into thickening mist pooling in Hangman's Gorge. He glanced at the tracking device once more, then covered its red light with his thumb. They had to be nearby; according to the tracker he was within stone-throwing distance. And in broad unwooded daylight he might have been able to see them, but the eddying mist obscured anything more than fifty feet away. He concentrated on hearing and smell. He stalked silently down the thickly wooded hillside.

He heard the crack of a twig.

The gnoles would not have been so careless. They could slide through the forest quiet as scarves of cloud across the moon.

He raised the pistol and advanced toward the sound. In a few minutes he saw them further down the slope: three short figures, two gnole, one not. There was no wind to carry their scent to him, but that also meant they would not smell him either. Which was good, good, because Crucifer knew he smelled nothing like he looked, oh no.

He crept closer to the three figures made milky by fog.

The male, he thought, we only need the male. *I need him now as much as Theverat does. The others . . . The others don't matter. The others are forfeit.*

He raised the gun. *Which one was the male?* Closed an eye. *On the far right's not a gnole at all.* Sighted down the barrel through the notched sight. *On the left's the bigger gnole, and wearing forest clothes.* Steadied right hand with left. *The gnole in the middle's wearing hospital clothes.* Adjusted his aim. *This ought to spur him on his way.* Slithered index finger around the trigger and tightened. *Hurry before you lose them to the mist.*

Fired.

The fog carried the *crack!* across the gorge. Fungle, Neema and Ka whipped around.

'Bless me!' said Neema.

Fungle looked up the rise to see a human, misted in the distance, lowering a pistol. 'Run!' he cried.

But Neema had fallen. Fungle bent down to help her up. Neema was clutching a rose. How like her to produce another rose in the midst of calamity!

But no. The flower glistened wet on her hand and fur. Not a rose? One of the deep red petals swelled and flowed down the back of her hand. 'Neema?' he asked. This was no time to joke. There was a human being not a stone's throw away, holding a . . . holding a . . .

Fungle looked up at the human.

It was Crucifer, Crucifer pointing at Ka

no

Crucifer raising a

aiming a

gun

'Fungle?' Ka asked fearfully.

Suddenly looking down from high above he saw Ka staring in horror at Crucifer. The man staring blankly back. Squeezes the trigger of his gun. Nothing happens. Crucifer frowns. Looks at the pistol. Neema lying still beside Fungle. Ka paralysed with shock. Crucifer figuring out the action on the semi-automatic pistol, pulling it back. Thick fog carries the sound clearly, a quick series of oiled clicks. Raises his hand clenching metal.

From on high Fungle sees himself step in front of Ka. Calm, almost, deliberate. The second shot tears into his left side just as he hears the dull crack. Sledgehammer impact brought him back. He didn't feel it. He didn't feel anything. Ka was shouting. What was Ka shouting? It didn't matter. Nothing mattered now. He felt sleepy.

In the time between the second and third shots Fungle glanced at Neema. Her eyes were closed and she was smiling. Quickly he bent to touch her. He shut his eyes. He extended his *self*.

Neema.

Leaving . . .

Gone.

Fungle saw himself look up at the thick grey sky. He saw himself ball healing hands into furious fists. He saw himself grow large with welling rage. He saw himself raise his arms, open one hand, and prepare to punch a fist into a hand and shout a word that would bring fire and the essence of fire blazing into the world to destroy everything: Crucifer, Ka, land, self. What did it matter now?

He hurried back to himself.

The third bullet tore a tunnel in the air a foot from Ka's head.

Hands relax. Looks down at Neema. So empty there unmoving. Body blurs and wavers with his tears. Thin sound escapes his lips. Becomes a wail of lamentation. Drowned song, world's last whale, *Don't leave me out here, don't leave me in the deep alone, don't leave me, don't leave!* Gorge fills with grief, land sows with sorrow, listening hearts swell with furious impotence.

Crows shriek from the trees. Enraged crows rising in thousands, a black-winged storm that lowers toward Crucifer.

Crucifer looks up at the sky – and begins to *change*. Face grows gaunt and dark, lips thin and pull back to show lengthening teeth like a mad dog. Leathery spikes pierce his clothing from within, as if he is being run through by invisible pikemen. His joints wither to skeletal thinness, his head elongates, his eyes enlarge and grow lantern yellow.

Not Crucifer.

Thorn.

Looking up at the murder of crows shrieking down Thorn raises the pistol and fires in vain. Talons clutch his shredded clothes, his barbs, his leathery skin. He tears them away. For every crow he wrenches loose, two take its place. He screams guttural defiance and beats himself with his fists, a seething mass of black feathers, a Crow Spirit from Native American legend.

He begins to run.

The crows begin to peck.

Rain again.

Ka knelt sobbing by Neema's side. 'Bring her back,' he whispered.

Across him Fungle stroked Neema's damp fur and shook his head.

'Bring her back, Fungle,' said Ka. Hope grew in his tone, blossomed on his face. 'You can do it! Ya done it before!'

Fungle leaned across their fallen friend and set a firm hand on Ka's shoulder. 'She's gone, Ka.'

Ka began to cry again. He knocked Fungle's hand away. 'Ya won't even try!' he said.

Fungle looked at the body between them. He thought of a thousand things to say. He fought the rage and grief that welled to bursting from his very core. He looked away to Ka racked with sobs. He touched the gnome's shoulder again and his free hand traced a circle in the air. He took hold of Ka's hand and closed his eyes and began to chant in a low voice.

They lifted from themselves.

It was dangerous to travel the astral realms and leave their unprotected bodies behind. But Fungle did not intend for them to go very far, or for very long, and he had something to show Ka that would mean more to him than any words of sympathy or grief. It was because he loved Ka, and because he loved Neema, that he took the risk.

They rose until the mist lay below them like softest flannel. Island mountain-tops cast dim shadows across the grey-white layer, lengthening wedges in the glowering sun.

The laminations of reality hurtled past them like layers of sediment. The lights of Elemental spirits, lost souls, alien thoughts, otherworldly energies, glowed around them. Fungle sensed Ka's sad uncertain spirit beside him, and he held it tight and pushed a little farther.

Layers parted around them. They hung in the void beyond the real. Below lay the physical, the living, the realm-dwellers, the icy alien continent forms of Theverat and Molom and Elemental spirits older than the world.

'*Fungle? Where –*'

'**Wait.**'

They floated in the void.

Soon there was light. A thin gold line unimaginably far away, extending for ever in either direction to form an infinite horizon.

White-hot sparks streamed like tadpoles toward the burnished band of light.

Fungle searched among the sparks and found what he was seeking. He held tight to the simple core of lights that was Ka. '**There,**' he directed.

Shining white untainted, vital and alive and containing every portion of *self* as a seed contains the tree, nova-burning, it flew toward the infinite horizon.

'*Oh, an' it's beautiful, Fungle,*' thought Ka. '*What is it?*'

'**It's Neema, Ka.**'

'*Neema! Oh –*' And a flood of feelings: joy and sorrow, love and loss. Neema's sly grin as she lifted a cloth from a hot breadpan, and steam rising into the winter air. Her warm laughter at one of Wisp's Howzit stories before the hearth. Warm understanding of her harsh nature as a mask over her vulnerability. Panic at her capture by giblins; relief at her freedom. Cherished amusement at her friendly harangues of Fungle as they limped through the sky in the Lunabird. *'Neema, oh let's bring her back, Fungle!'*

'Remember that you love her, Ka, and that nothing living ever dies.'

He sent a final blessing to the departing spark and gently returned himself and his friend to the sad wet earth.

Fungle opened his eyes. Ka knelt across from him. The gnome was smiling gently while the rain diluted tears coursing down his mottled face. 'Ka,' Fungle whispered. 'We hafta hurry. There may be others. They may've heard the shot.'

Ka opened his eyes. 'Neema?' he asked, confused.

Fungle shook his head.

The gnome looked down at the body between them.

Lightning flared violet-white. Dark clouds spilled over the gorge.

'Neema,' said Ka, and trembled with renewed crying.

'No, Ka.' The gnome's gaze followed Fungle's finger. 'Neema,' said Fungle, and swept his arm across the sky.

They buried her beneath an old oak tree.

'Oak,' Fungle explained, 'the wood o' protection.' He picked a humble posy of rosehips, some nettles, mushrooms, an acorn. As he knelt at Neema's side and wove the posy into a wreath all ivy-bound, animals began to appear from the forest. They stood a respectful distance away with heads bowed low: a family of deer, sober tree sprites, wild rabbits with ears slicked back and pelts quivering in the cold rain, a sombre goblin, sad-eyed foxes. Dozens of forest denizens stood silent while Fungle completed the wreath and laid it on Neema's breast. He stood, and Ka stepped forward and spoke a childhood prayer to Ordaphe, King of Gnomes and Goblins and Ruler of the Underworld, to take the body of their friend and hold her safe among the stones and earth and minerals.

The trees moved their branches to shut the rain from their own roots. Frogs and crickets withheld their songs, and but for the patter of the rain on the leaves the forest was silent. The tree sprites brought forward an empty upturned cup, their traditional symbol of mourning, then stepped away. The goblin broke his dagger as a token of respect and offering of peace. Squirrels brought gifts of stored acorns. One by one the forest creatures gave a token of their sorrow that another gnole had passed from the world.

Fungle blessed Neema's body. He held one hand high to the sky and the other low to the ground.

The grass parted beneath Neema and the earth fissured outward. Neema's body slowly lowered into the soil as if sinking into some thick liquid. Once below the surface the earth closed over her and the grass sewed up the wound to hide her resting place for ever.

Fungle bent to kiss the ground. *Until I join you in that good night,* he thought. He planted deep a single acorn and blessed the oak tree and asked it to watch over Neema's grave so long as its leaves and branches brought together earth and sky. 'Above an' below,' he finished, 'all goes back from whence it came.'

The forest creatures retreated to their cold damp homes, and that night many of the old and wise among them told stories to their young and unknowing of the days when gnoles had been more abundant in the pristine land.

Fungle wiped tears from his cheeks and turned to his friend Ka. 'Let's finish it,' he said.

24 The Opera Invisible

The land began to change. First came false clearings dotted with hundreds of raw stumps where elderly trees had been felled. Next were scarred patches of upturned earth muddled by rain where the stumps of felled trees had been chain-pulled from the ground. Fresh wet earth pushed up against the lowered curved blades of flaking yellow bulldozers dripping from their oiled bones like fossilising monsters that had levelled the land. Squares of smoothed ground had been staked out and sectioned off by lengths of string; along one plot concrete foundation had been poured. An access road had been torn through the forest, leading back to some country road that met the freeway.

So this is how it starts, thought Fungle. He pictured New York, its teeming stacked energies and buildings and lives, and was shocked at the idea that the Manhattan Island of three hundred years ago might not have looked much different than the forest from which he had just emerged. Could that possibly be? Could they have turned this into that? So that to journey from forest to human city was also to travel in time? It was hard to believe.

But the answer lay around him in flaking metal bones and ruptured earth.

Their worked metal poisons everything it touches. It took that island and it's takin' this land. It'll take mine someday. It took Froog's leg an' it took Froog's wife Bedina. An' now their metal's taken Neema, oh, Neema –

He fought the wave of sorrow that threatened to engulf him.

With perfect irony the rain had stopped after Neema's death, and now the sky was clear as a bell tone. Stars shone hard and bright. *Suns*, thought Fungle. *The humans said that stars're suns like ours, but far far away. They's flyin' apart one from t'other, they said, silent an' swift as dandelion seeds on the wind.*

He picked out the North Star shining brighter than the rest and thought of another bright light streaming away from him. *But you're past them now, ain't ya, Neema? Past the stars an' beyond the night.*

An ingot of the moon swelled above a mountain's sharp crease to the east. Fungle and Ka trudged up the mountainside, burdened by more than could be seen. In the valleys below glowed islands of light from campfires, small towns, cars crossing the land that had been altered to accommodate them. It looked like a poor reflection of the sky.

And you stars above and lights below, thought Fungle. *Do ya fly apart in space and tuck yerselves abed in firelit rooms while this unseen opera plays out on this bruised land? Do ya burn yerselves to warm some little creatures readin' drowsy by electric light while their whirlin' planets face away from ya, abed an' burnin' while the fate of a world's decided here on a wounded mountainside? Can ya slumber wi'out some small fidget as the web of reality's hardfought so close by? How can this be? How many hundred other invisible dramas play about yer lives this chill November night, how many unimagined ways must the world be saved to keep yer slumber undisturbed on future nights, an' to preserve yer waking slumber, too?*

An' saved fer what?

Fer metal.

Has Neema died fer this, then? Fer metal?

But along another path lies the reign of Theverat, glimpsed in nightmare long ago by a sleeping gnole safe in his hideyhole. An' this gnole has surfaced from his safe retreat and fights not for the triumph of metal but to save somethin' he loves, to prevent that nightmare's birth into his cherished world.

And that is what Neema died for.

Fungle stopped. His side was throbbing where the hot lead of Thorn's bullet had pierced. The wound was bloody but not immediately dangerous; Ka had helped him staunch the flow and apply a makeshift bandage.

The moon cleared the eastern mountains to bathe the rocky slope in mercury. Not far ahead was a darker patch of stone on the slope above them. Fungle remembered Yanto's words: *Twelve clobhops west across the mountains to the Valley of the Moon. Once there seek ye the north on west side facing the sun's morning climb. There find a great cross of pure black rock, black as coal, grained deep into*

*the mountain's skin. 'Neath it find a hole such as fit for rabbits
and badgers, and within it find harsh wards. Only the worthy shall
pass them: the Warrior, the Scholar, the Wise Mage, the Honourable
Seeker. If you be such, then past them you will find the cavern and
all you seek.'*

Possibly the dark patch on the mountainside had been in the
form of a cross at one time. But the rock had been gouged by
blasting, and a dark cruciform was only barely discernible. Cordite
smell lingered in the air despite the day-long rain. Granite rubble
dotted the slope where it had come to rest after blowing free of the
mountain's living rock. Molom had been right: the humans were
close, frighteningly close, to finding Baphomet themselves. A few
more days of blasting and the hidden caverns would be brought
to light.

But Fungle had beat them to it.

He felt no jubilation, no exhilaration now that the end of his quest
was truly before him. Only an empty ache in his heart, a yearning
to complete his mission and be done with it. The goal had been
in sight once before, a few months and another life ago, and had
been lost to him. As Neema now was lost to him. Standing here on
mountain stone with hollow heart, Fungle felt like a mechanism
geared toward some goal, with no more eagerness or anticipation
than a clock unwinding slowly toward an alarm.

'Find a hole such as fit for rabbits and badgers . . .'

Fungle told Ka they were looking for a small hollow like a gopher
hole or rabbit warren. It had to be nearby, beneath the erstwhile
cross of coal, though it might have been covered or even collapsed
by the blasting. Ka dropped to the ground and set an ear to the
earth. He pounded his fist a few times, waited, moved a few feet up
the slope. Pounded again, waited, moved left. Pounded. Frowned.

Ka stood and counted three paces downslope and four right,
stopping where splintered rock and small boulders had tumbled
down the mountainside and fetched up against a bush. Ka thumped
a small boulder, straightened, and pointed down at it. 'Here,'
he said.

'Shh.' Fungle set a hand on Ka's arm. They fell still.

'Seemed I heard somethin',' whispered Fungle. 'A breath, a
footfall. We's follered, I think.'

'Whatsit matter now,' muttered Ka.

'Ka.' Fungle turned to him. 'Wouldja have her die fer nothin'
then?'

Ka shook his head. 'No. No, I'm terrible sorry, Fungle. It just slipped out, is all.'

Fungle nodded. 'Well, follered or not, we have to get inside.' He put a shoulder to the boulder and Ka bent to help. Straining they rolled the boulder aside. Beneath it, just as Yanto had predicted and Ka had determined, was a hole not much larger than Fungle's head. Ka bent an ear to it.

Fungle looked out along the ridge. The mountains broke through the moonlit fog like tiny islands in a mystic sea. He strained for some sound, some indication of movement, but there was nothing. Still he felt a pressing need to get into the tunnel. 'Ka,' he urged.

'Shhh.' Ka made a clacking sound into the hole, like the single tick of a huge clock, and analysed the echo the way a dolphin reads its sonar message. He looked back up at Fungle. 'Not very big. Roots grown in the way. Collapsed not far in, but it's soft ground. Oughta be able to dig past it.'

'Glad ta hear it – now get in there!'

Ka dove and plugged the hole with his round body.

Fungle put a foot on Ka's backside and pushed. The gnome slipped into the hole, and Fungle followed him.

Fungle coughed from the dirt and dust kicked up in the cramped passageway by Ka's frantic digging ahead of him. As the gnome had said, the tunnel was choked with latticeworks of roots and partially collapsed from time and recent blasting. There was little Fungle could do except force himself through the tight tunnel while Ka scooped earth to clear a way. This was the gnome's field of expertise, and any effort Fungle made to help would only hinder their progress. But it was frustrating nonetheless. The tunnel squeezed him all around; he felt he was being born. Perhaps in a way he was. The bullet wound stitched his side every time he drew breath. Ahead of him dirt flew back from Ka's rapid, molelike hands. Behind him he was vulnerable and exposed, and if anything pursued him here, there was little he could do about it now.

Or was there? Certainly there were better uses he could put himself to than watching Ka's backside squirm like a rat in a pipe. For instance, there was that opening behind them. There was not a lot of grass high up here on the mountainside, but there was some. Fungle uttered a simple spell that made the grass around the opening grow rapidly over it. It wasn't the dense thatch he would have liked, but it would hide the hole from view for a while. Next he gave his blessings to the rocks of the mountainside and asked whatever loose stones might be perched precariously if they would see fit to come tumbling down at the disturbance of any footfall upon the slope.

'*That*'s better!' Ka called ahead of him. The gnome's words echoed back: *Better! etter! et!* From the reverberation, Fungle knew that Ka had broken through. Wincing from the pain in his wounded side every time he pushed forward into long-abandoned cobwebs, Fungle hurried to catch up with Ka.

The chamber should have been dark as any cave, but the floor glowed with a pale-blue radiance like marshlight. The walls were raw mountain rock, but the gently sloping floor was smooth and glassy.

Ka stood near where the tunnel widened and gaped up at a hundred thousand bats hanging from the ceiling like black icicles. Gnomes and bats are old familiars, inhabiting caves as both creatures do, but Ka had never seen so many in one place.

He looked down when Fungle emerged from the tight passageway and helped the gnole to his feet. 'Well, here we are, then,' said Ka with no evident irony. 'The lost treasure hoard o' yer furfathers!'

Fungle shook his head. 'There's long to go yet, I'm afeared. Yanto said that within the mountain we'd find "harsh wards" that only the worthy can pass.'

'I bet I could find some harsh words fer him too,' retorted Ka. Fungle could not help but smile at his friend's way of dealing with fear.

The gnome glanced around the faintly glowing chamber. 'Well, 'less these bats're some kinda special guardian bats, there ain't no harsh wards 'round here. Ain't no way out, neither, 'cept how we came in.'

Fungle knew better than to reach such conclusions quickly. He stepped forward down the glassy incline and immediately slipped and fell – with a splash! Ka caught him as he began to slide forward, and helped him back up. 'Why – it's fulla water!' said Fungle. He bent and waved his hand. The ripples that spread across the floor were an eerie sight. 'It's so clear it don't even look like it's here. Freezin' cold too.' He frowned and stuck a finger in the water. To Ka it looked like Fungle's finger had become severed and was hanging by a string; the water was so clear that the only sign Fungle's finger was in it was the diffraction of light at its surface. 'There's a current,' said Fungle. 'Strong, too.'

'Current?' Ka's brow furrowed. 'But there's no way out.'

Fungle plucked the wishing feather from his cap. It had served him well and he did not like to part with it, but now it might serve him better. He tossed the feather away, and it pendulumed down until it landed on the invisible water. It looked as if it were suspended in air a few inches above the inclined floor.

Fungle and Ka watched as the feather slowly turned and edged toward the far end of the chamber. It picked up speed along the way, until by the time it neared the far wall it was going along at a good clip.

Then it disappeared.

'Vanished!' exclaimed Ka.

'No,' said Fungle. 'Sucked down. I saw it at the last moment: snatched down by a strong current.' He tapped his chin speculatively.

Ka recognised the expression on Fungle's face and felt as if he would cry. 'Current?' said Ka, who hated water.

'It's a way out, Ka.'

Ka sniffed. 'A way outta life, ya mean. There's no tellin' where that thing empties out, Fungle. Might just dump us out a geyser in Chiner, fer all we know.'

But Fungle shook his head. 'This chamber was *built*, Ka. An' the mages what built it meant fer gnoles to be able to regain the treasure when they finally returned. If that's the only way farther in, then I'm sure it ain't gonna kill us.'

Ka remained doubtful. 'Well, if yer wrong I ain't gonna be able to say I told ya so.'

'Ya gots ta have faith, Ka.' Fungle smiled wryly, and more than a little sadly. 'Maybe that's what it's a test of. So –'

Rather than deliberate with Ka another moment, Fungle sat in the freezing clear water and pushed himself down the glassy slope. At first he merely floated. Then he felt gentle ghost fingers urging him toward the far wall. Quickly the fingers became more insistent, until the wall was hurtling toward him, and he just had time to wonder if perhaps he hadn't been a little hasty before he was yanked downward. He got in half a breath of air before he was submerged, and hoped it would be enough.

It was – barely. Fungle shot like a fish down an obsidian-smooth chute small enough to prevent his being injured by knocking against it in the current. There was no obstruction, no handhold; the slide propelled him through the icy water without a scrape. He tumbled and bumped against the side, not realising how quickly he was moving until his fingers slid along the slick walls. He opened his eyes but the tunnel was black. His chest began to burn and pinprick novas began to detonate in his vision. His wounded side throbbed in water so cold the backs of his eyes ached.

The chute's incline decreased until it was horizontal. The current slowed. Red roman candles were blossoming in his oxygen-starved brain by the time he spilled from the chute. He tumbled across the hard ground as water roared loud in his ears. He breathed out stale air and took in a great strained breath while rolling out of the path of the water pouring from the chute.

He came to rest against a wall.

Across the chamber, the great gout of water that had propelled him here spat from the grinning mouth of a kneeling manticore carved in stone.

It was gnolecraft without a doubt.

A huge pool filling half the room lay at the feet of the manticore. A pale rosy glow illuminated a quartz-veined chamber with high-vaulted ceilings. On the wall opposite the manticore was the carved image of an Atlantean mage. She sat crosslegged with one hand held palm-out in a gesture of peace. Beside the carving, above the low arch on the dry side of the chamber, was a panel carved with Atlantean runes.

Fungle had just caught his breath when the manticore regurgitated a gnome like a cat coughing up a furball. Ka hit water and slid all the way across the room, screaming wet bloody murder all the way. 'I *hate* it! It's fer makin' tea an' washin' clothes, and nuffin' more!' He clambered out of the rectangular pool and shook himself like a dog. He sighted Fungle sitting against the wall and stopped. 'Fungle!' he shouted. 'There must be easier ways ta drown yerself.'

'Glad ya dropped in, Ka,' Fungle called dryly.

'Mmph. As if ya left me much cherce.' He sneezed. 'Pardon. Besides,' he continued, 'I hadda come. I heard rocks fallin' behind me, an' the weight of a footfall in the earth. Someone's found the tunnel.' He glanced around the chamber. 'Are we there yet?'

'*Seeker: beyond find the ways of the Warrior, the Scholar, the Shaman, the Honourable Seeker,*' Fungle translated the runes on the panel beside the carving of the Atlantean mage. '*Be these, and pass.*'

'Well, that leaves me out,' said Ka. 'Nuffin' there about gnomes.' He sat against the wall. 'I'll wait here fer ya.'

Fungle nodded. 'That beez best, I thinks. It's my journey from here on, an' my tests. You wait here, and I'll be back fer ya.'

'You better,' said Ka. ''Cause iffin you never come back, I'll, I'll – I'll never *speak* to ya again!'

Fungle smiled gently but Ka would not meet his gaze.

Fungle turned to regard the carving.

Warrior, Scholar, an' Shaman be the traditional Three Paths, the Principal Ways of Being, he thought. He frowned. *But the Honourable Seeker?* And shrugged.

The roseate light began to pulse softly. Fungle realised the rhythm was in time with the beating of his heart.

The room was aware of him.

Fungle ruffled his fur to shake off cold water as best he could. 'I'm off then, Ka,' he said firmly. 'Guard the fort!'

'Mmph.' Ka's teeth chattered. 'Least they coulda done was left towels.'

Fungle passed through the low arch and out of the room of running water.

WARRIOR

Except for ornately carved pylons in each corner, the room was featureless. It was not very large, about the size of Fungle's comfortable living-room. The pulsing light revealed a smaller version of the mage carved on the near wall. This time her hand was held in a fist and her expression was stern, an image of strength, and perhaps of warning.

Fungle translated the runes carved beneath her:

> *'The brave one holds his ground and looks ahead,*
> *Never behind.'*

Was it tellin' him not to go back?

Well, it certainly seemed ta be tellin' him to go on.

But . . . there wasn't a door.

There weren't no way outta the first room, either, he reminded himself.

Fungle walked toward the opposite wall. He stopped halfway across the room. Had he seen something in the corner of his eye? Slowly he turned his head to either side. Nothing. Blank walls, carved pillars. He looked down.

He stood just beyond a pentacle etched in the stone floor. Shadows shifted across its deep relief as the light continued to pulse.

He frowned. A pentacle . . .

The brave one holds his ground . . .

Cautiously he backed up two steps until he was in the protective circle. Again something blurred past the left side of his vision. He turned his head toward it and moved forward with painstaking slowness.

A grinning demon head floated before him.

Fungle jerked back, startled. The head disappeared.

He leaned forward again and the demon head grinned in mid-air.

A deep stone rumbling high above and behind him: it grew louder, like a flood headed his way. Fungle began to turn toward it – and stopped.

> *The brave one holds his ground and looks ahead,*
> *Never behind.*

Ka screamed from the other room as the ceiling collapsed. Fungle stared at the demon head. A single massive stone block landed with a force that jarred the ground. Fungle flinched but did not look away. The wind of the stone's impact pushed his back; granite splinters stung him. Fungle held his ground and looked ahead – looked *at the head.*

Something moved in his peripheral vision. He checked the urge to see what it was. It swung toward him, and he saw that it was a multi-bladed pendulum on a long iron rod arcing toward him. Dull rose light glimmered on its steel edges. It could not possibly miss him.

He held his ground and looked at the demon head, narrowing his eyes at its malicious grin.

The pendulum blade cut toward him. It hissed past his ear, and a cold metal edge kissed his shoulder. Fungle let out a breath – then held as still as he had ever held in his life.

The pendulum swung back on its return arc.

There was a gentle tug on his tunic sleeve, and just the barest sound: *tinnng!*

The demon head was enjoying itself immensely.

Beneath Fungle's feet came a great grinding of subterranean gears. He did not look down.

The floor dropped around him.

It dropped with a great machine roar. Fungle did not go with it. His ears popped as air was sucked from the chamber. He leaned hard against the wind that rushed in to replace it. He kept staring at the grinning demon head.

The grinding ceased. The room – now a huge cavern – was quiet.

Fungle stood atop a slender stone chimney exactly the size of the pentacle.

The demon nodded and disappeared. The chimney rumbled beneath his feet, then began to lower.

Karbolic Earthcreep stared at the heap of granite rubble that would have squashed Fungle like a ripe tomato if he hadn't been in the pentacle. Ka stood just inside the arch that led from the room of the spitting manticore to the room of the Warrior, the test of courage.

His way was blocked by a single piece of granite, heavy as most buildings, sitting snug against the archway. Impact cracks radiated across the floor.

The roar of water rushing from the manticore's mouth filled the room. Ka called Fungle's name for the sixth time, but it was no use.

Well – maybe Fungle was right: maybe it'd be best fer all concerned iffin he waited here an' guarded the entrance while Fungle went about savin' the world. He turned his back on the blocked archway and folded his arms, puffing himself large like a harem guard.

A figure shot from the manticore's mouth and splashed into the pool. Ka did not wait to see who or what it was. He followed the first instincts of generations of gnomes and began to dig.

SCHOLAR

The pentacle settled flush against the floor with a click. The light was now a steady violet. An archway stood directly ahead. Above it the carved Atlantean mage held fingertips to her forehead. Fungle read aloud what was writ on the lintel of the archway:

> *The days of the year are found in here.*
> *Autumn presses on.'*

Within the dark archway pale-violet light glowed to life. Fungle bowed to the image of the mage and passed through.

He stood within a calendar. The room was circular, the ceiling domed. On panels radiating from a central rayed image of the sun on high were carved the days of the year. Fungle pondered a moment, repeating the runic epigraph in his mind, before he strode directly to the square that represented the autumnal Equinox. Fitting, he thought, remembering last Equinox feast and the absent guests, a few months and another life ago, that had set in motion the machinery that had brought him here.

Autumn presses on.

He pressed the square representing the autumnal equinox.

The stone sky receded. Fungle descended farther into the mountain.

Karbolic Earthcreep tunnelled as if he had a subway to build and a deadline to meet. He felt himself passing below creepy magework and stonework and all kinda oddkins that made his flesh crawl. The earth down here was warm, small comfort after the chill water that had nearly stopped his heart in its bloomin' tracks.

Underground, Ka was like a shark in water: his senses were acute, registering the faintest shiftings and vibrations in and on the earth. Sometimes Ka swore he could feel the steady inexorable westward crawl of the continental plate, and who's to say he couldn't? His dreams were filled with rumblings and tectonic driftings, replete with discoveries of the fossil bones of improbable beasty fish.

Right now the entire mountain rang like church bells as stones shifted and floors moved and who knew what-all infernal machineries awoke. Ka had no idea what any of it meant, and he wasn't overly curious to find out. The sounds, the very *flavours* of the doings in the earth, were apocalyptic somehow.

He gleaned some small satisfaction from the fact that he had sealed his tunnel behind him after leaving the room of the spitting manticore, and that the only other exit was blocked by a stone big and heavy as a battleship.

He dug.

Thorn studied the runes carved beneath the image of the mage, and wondered what they said. A spell, perhaps, a puzzle, a clue to removing the fallen stone that blocked the archway leading from the room of the spitting manticore?

He had no idea.

If Thorn had been a walking horror earlier, now he was the wreckage of a nightmare. The rubble from the blasted ceiling at DPR had left him with a useless arm bent in the wrong places. The storm of enraged crows had left him scarred, torn and tattered. One great lantern-yellow eye had been pierced by a revenant beak and lay now in wet strings across his rent cheek. He had survived the murder of crows only by stumbling backwards into a shallow cold steam, and not coming up again until the talons had relaxed and the enraged wingbeats stilled. The pain was intense, but it did not hamper him. The pain was good; the pain was a way of knowing he was alive, so very alive. Bent and broken, but driven by new needs recently born within him, he had followed the signal from the tracking device to a patch of new-grown grass over freshly turned earth beneath a large oak. Understanding what it was, he had abandoned the device and brought to bear his formidable tracking skills to find the path taken by the gnole and the gnome. Their haste diminished their stealth; the overturned rock on the mountainside was like a planted banner to Thorn.

And now here he was, spat from the mouth of a stone manticore like a piece of bad meat, staring at an ancient indecipherable carving beside an archway blocked by a block of stone the size of a house.

His mastery of the hunt could not help him here. He could go no further alone. Which left only one recourse.

The antediluvian words were foreign to the raw voice that croaked from his tortured throat. The hand passes were excruciating; some required both arms, and a deep fleshy grating ratcheted in the shoulder of his wasted arm. He ignored it.

Already a column of air was darkening before him. The temperature plummeted; the last words of the Summoning were uttered in a breath all fog.

Now Thorn spoke the final words of the Summoning:

> *'I adjure thee here, Theverat*
> *Unto the earth*
> *To work your will upon me.'*

There remained one final gesture: left hand cupping right fist, both hands driven toward the breast. A symbolic stabbing of the heart.

Thorn bowed his head. Clenched right hand. Strained against the pain and cupped left hand over right fist. And did not move.

SHAMAN

The carving of the Atlantean mage floated crosslegged above elegant runes, hands palm-up on her thighs, middle fingers touching thumbs. Her eyes were shut.

> *'The final lesson completes the Shaman's circle –*
> *Through the labyrinth, the simplest path.'*

Beside her was a door. It was typical Atlantean craft: a single, simple slab of granite perfectly counterbalanced so that a slight push would open it.

Fungle had already pushed. It did not open.

He rubbed his hands on his thighs. *First Warrior*, he thought, *an' a test of courage. Then Scholar, an' a test of knowledge. Now Shaman, which means a test of magic.*

Nothing was more natural over the years than for a shaman to have acquired – or invented – any number of spells for opening things. Locked doors, tight-lipped lovers, volatile packages, stuck jar lids. Fungle knew that his ability was being tested here. He spent a few moments composing himself, then confidently uttered the most effective opening spell he knew.

Nothing happened.

He repeated it again for good measure, but there was no result. Fungle had not really expected it to work – such a test of magical ability would hardly be predictable or easy – but it would have been equally foolish not to try.

Fungle sat before the door in a meditative position, unwittingly reflecting the carving of the Atlantean mage that had been meditating for more than a hundred centuries.

He breathed: in through the nose and out through the mouth. He remembered one of the earliest lessons of his youth: *You don't eat with your nose; don't breathe with your mouth!* One by one he took his mental preoccupations and distractions and sealed them in imaginary boxes which he placed in a room in his mind reserved for such things. Grief for Neema. Worry for Ka. Anxiety about his family after the terrible psychic call for help he'd received from his brother Froog. Awe at the work of his ancestors. Anticipation of his quest's completion. Fear of the forces that followed him. Dread of his own failure. Soon his mind was clear and he meditated in a pure void of being, floating several inches above the stone floor.

Openings . . .

Perhaps a spell to destroy the stone door? Wasn't that a kind of opening?

He opened his eyes and gave it a try. He asked for the aid and blessing of the Lords of Stone, then waved his right hand above his head and extended it palm-out toward the adamant door. A ball of blue-white mage light glided from his hand to the granite slab, touched it, and was absorbed without a tremor.

Fungle stared at the non-results for a moment. Then he shut his eyes and breathed again.

A few minutes later he opened his eyes once more. He had decided that what was called for was an impressive improvisation, an on-the-spot display of his handiwork. He called forth thund'rous energies and furious spirits; he blended them with the Spirit of Water (which everyone knows is stone's natural enemy, given time enough to act) and placed a time-acceleration spell upon the mixture so that, when unleashed on a small spot on the stone door, a hundred thousand years would pass in an eyeblink and the Spirit of Water would wear the stone away. The bundle of spells and furies was like a powerful spring forced into a tiny box. Fungle readied the box of his spell, aimed it at the recalcitrant door, and fired.

Nothing happened.

Fungle considered the single word and gesture of the metaspell that would summon the Salamander, but he knew that it was inappropriate, proof of his frustration more than of his wisdom.

Wisdom . . .

He rubbed his chin slowly, deep in thought. The Three Paths that represented the Principal Ways of Being were not meant to be taken literally. The designations of Warrior, Scholar, and Shaman represented paths individuals have traditionally taken on the road to enlightenment, and not necessarily the professions themselves. The tests so far had not been designed to specifically test a warrior or a scholar, but the *qualities* they represented. The first courage, the second knowledge.

And now the Shaman was being tested, and what the Shaman represented was not magic, but wisdom.

Fungle thought of the nature of the previous two tests. The first had been difficult, but not as difficult as it would have proven for a true warrior. To stand motionless with little more than faith that you were in the only small protected space while violence and destruction raged all about you – to *not* act – that was the most difficult test of all for a warrior. To have the courage not to act.

The second test had been easy for Fungle because he did think of himself as a scholar. The test required knowledge, and there was no tricking knowledge: one had it or one did not. In fact, in both cases the tests could not be tricked. You either had the qualities that enabled you to pass, or you did not.

And now here he was, Fungle Foxwit gnole, mage and shaman, facing the test of his own Path and a stubborn stone door, and failing both.

He looked at the meditating mage carved on the wall. *The final lesson completes the Shaman's circle/Through the labyrinth, the simplest path.*

And the test was linked not to magic but to wisdom.

The simplest path through the labyrinth . . .

He clapped his hands and laughed – his first true laughter in what seemed like years. *Of course!* he thought. *What a wunnerful test!*

He realised that a part of his mind had been trying to tell him all along: remembering his earliest lessons on breathing, pointing out that a test of magical ability would be neither predictable nor easy.

Fungle could not help but delight in the elegant simplicity of what had to be the solution. For what did a wise shaman learn but that the most powerful spells, the most basic truths, the most practical solutions, were elegant and simple. *Simplest is bestest:* the first thing old Wily Barktea had taught him! An unwise mage would attempt to demonstrate the breadth and depth of his training. And Fungle knew that such a mage would never step beyond that door.

Fungle stood and held a palm out to the door.

He uttered a single, ancient word that meant, simply, 'open'.

The door swung inward.

THE HONOURABLE SEEKER

Fungle was in a small dark room. As his eyes adjusted there slowly rose to prominence the faintly glowing lines of the Atlantean mage ahead of him. Now she knelt with a serene expression on her carved face, hands forming a circle just below her navel. She knelt within the glowing outline of a door. Not a real door, but a carving of a door. Faint runes glowed beneath her:

> *'The true path lies within.'*

The Warrior, the Scholar, the Shaman. The first three had a long and venerable tradition behind them – the Three Paths, the Principal Ways of Being – which, along with the carved epigraphs, gave him clues to their resolution. But now the Honourable Seeker. Fungle puzzled over it. There was no lore to aid him here.

Was there?

He reread the epigraph, but found it unhelpful. He assumed it meant that the true path to the lost treasure and library of the gnoles lay within the carving of the door, and that whatever solution was meant to be arrived at would somehow open it.

He conjured a small ring of gentle mage light and was examining the carved lines of the door when he was startled by a voice behind him.

'Fungle!'

Fungle spun round. It was Ka. 'Izzat how yer findin' yer way through here?' the gnome said with a characteristic good-humoured smirk. 'Feelin' fer cracks in the walls?'

Fungle had never been so glad to see anybody in his life. 'Ka!' he exclaimed. He rushed toward his friend and they embraced. Ka's skin was clammy from the soaking. Fungle realised he was freezing cold as well, but his brain had been so preoccupied it had not allowed his body to register it. He pounded Ka's back and cried. 'Oh Ka, I was so afeared I'd lost ya fer good back there when the stone fell!'

'Humph.' Ka sniffed. 'Take more'n a little rock ta slow me down. Listen, Fungle, I found somethin' quite innerestin' you might oughta know about –'

Fungle indicated the carving of the serene Atlantean mage. 'I hafta get past this last test,' he told Ka. His brow knitted. 'An' how did *you* get past them others?'

'Dug under 'em,' Ka said proudly. 'How else?'

Fungle clapped his hand on his friend's shoulder. *The best-laid plans of mice an' gnoles*, he thought, *are undermined by gnomes.*

'Fungle, listen, I gots ta tell ya,' insisted Ka. 'Ya don't need ta figger out no more a these things.' The gnome grinned. 'I founda crate a dynamite them human beans been usin' ta carve away this mountain. All we gotta do is stick some sticks against whatever's in our way, light 'em, an' run like giblins.' He clapped his hands. '*Boom!* We's in!'

But Fungle was shaking his head. 'We can't do it, Ka.'

'Sure we can! There's enougha this stuff to carve the Moon into a statue a yer mum! All we gots ta do is –'

'Ka. Listen to me. I know yer tryin' ta help, an' it might even work. But there's a right way to do this, an' that's to pass the tests.'

Ka looked utterly confused. 'But all ya wants to do is get to the cavern an' find Baphomet,' he maintained. 'What difference does it make how ya do it?'

'It makes a difference,' said Fungle. 'I'm not sure how, but it does.'

Ka's expression fell. 'Ya won't blast yer way in?' he asked glumly. 'Yer gonna do it the hard way?'

'If that's the right way, yes. I'm sorry, Ka.'

But inexplicably Ka grinned from ear to ear. 'Attaboy, Fungle!' he said – and melted into the floor without a sound.

'Ka!' Fungle darted forward, alarmed.

Alarm changed to confusion.

Confusion to suspicion.

Suspicion became understanding.

Fungle turned toward the carving. *The true path lies within.* Not within a door or a wall or a spell or a gimmick. He looked at the Atlantean mage's hands forming a circle beneath her navel. The path to truth lay *within*. The Honourable Seeker: a test of the seeker's honour. A different test for every seeker – not a puzzle, not a riddle, not an obstacle to overcome. A true test, and one that could not be solved or even influenced, because the seeker did not even know he was being tested! His own test had been a vision of Ka, urging him to go against what was in his heart.

And at last Fungle understood the true wisdom of the Ancients: they cared about a warrior's strength and a scholar's knowledge and a mage's wisdom – yet a dishonourable warrior, scholar, or mage might pass these tests. But without honour they would not be worthy. So: this final test.

Motion caught his eye: the carved mage raised a hand and gave her blessing to Fungle, and with great joy and gravity Fungle returned the benediction.

Golden light saturated him as the walls fell away, and he cried out with the painful wonder of what he saw.

Thorn held clenched right fist in cupped left hand as if clutching an invisible dagger pointed at his heart. He was shouting at a light-absorbing shaft that reached up to the roof.

'Master!' he grated. 'Master! I know you can hear me! There's only one gesture left to complete the Summoning!'

The black column trembled.

'I will bring you into the world, Master – but I want something first!'

The sides of the column bulged. Thorn could sense the demon straining to penetrate the barrier separating his world from this one. Ripples coruscated along the sides of the column; the very air vibrated with its trembling.

From everywhere in the room there came a voice: '*Sssssspeak.*'

'We are near the cavern, Master!' shouted Thorn. 'I will complete the Summoning and you can enter. But I want something first. I *need* something.'

'Whhhhhat?'

Thorn hesitated. He craned the ruin of his face up at the quaking tower before him. 'Make me . . . Master, make me as I was . . . before. Before you found me.'

Pale-violet sparks flashed within the column. '*Sssssummon.*'

Thorn flinched. He breathed deep and tensed himself for the final gesture that would summon Theverat, and plunged his clutching hands towards his chest in obeisance.

The column exploded into thousands of black fragments. They rained down upon the room, and where each splinter hit it transformed into a snapping thrashing smouldering slug-like creature. The room of the spitting manticore boiled with them.

Thorn cowered as Theverat tore through the membrane of the real. This was no kindly image intended to persuade a gnole by conjured firelight within a tomb, no face on a computer screen, voice on a phone, blur on a paper. All pretence was stripped away now; the true form was revealed. Theverat boiled with faces, and lost souls screamed from the ever-shifting lamps of his eyes. He writhed with life dripping from his frame to burn acid slobber into the treasures of the gnoles. Raven wings fluttered from him; viper fangs curved below goat eyes. Glistening tendrils sprouted sharp-clawed hands that glittered with eyes across their surface. Ropey tendrils snaked from a shark-gash mouth. The stone floor burned beneath splayed feet. Theverat was no one thing at any one time; he writhed with malevolent life, erupted with lesions of horrified faces; a thousand parasitic creatures lived on his flesh.

Thorn sank to his knees.

A hundred fanged mouths smiled. '*As you were?*' the demon thundered. '*As you were? All right, my tracker, my bloodhound – you have led me to them, and I may release you. Back to what you were when I found you. And you. Were. Nothing.*'

Thorn gasped. His one eye bulged and he tugged at his chest. The symbolic dagger had become a real one. Thorn gaped like a fish. His mouth worked as he tried to say something, but his eye glazed and he fell to one side. His hands fell from the foot-long handle of the obsidian dagger projecting from his chest.

The black dagger grew spike-jointed arms and pushed itself out of Thorn's body. Its point bulged, opened piercing blue eyes, and snapped needle-teethed jaws at the still form on the floor before screaming in delighted victory and scurrying off to join its cousins in the cavern.

Theverat turned to the fallen stone that blocked his way.

Crystal and silver and gold filigreed the wall. Jade vases lined

the cavernous space. Fine pink dust of powdered stone covered
all surfaces. Locks of pure gold clasped leaden chests on stands
carved of wood from trees that no longer grew on the face of
the earth. Tiny figurines of alpaca, ocean-coloured brooches of
turquoise, pearls the size of fists and diamonds the size of pearls.
Gold breastplates embossed with alligators and herons, ceremonial
knives, silver crowns, ritual cups adorned with jewel-eyed pumas.
Fired clay pots brightly painted with rotund tattooed women held
incense. Death masks of shell and jade and black marble stared
hollow-eyed at quartz-crystal balls and garnet wands. Eyes of lapis
lazuli gazed unblinking from painted gold sarcophagi gleaming like
the shells of beetles in the coral-coloured light emanating from the
walls. A gleaming two-handed broadsword twice Fungle's height
was thrust into the rock floor. Its pommel was carved in the shape
of a goat's head; it cast a cruciform shadow across a tiny uranium
casket bound tight with silver twine.

Rack after rack held wax-plugged glass phials containing helle-
bore, quicksilver, belladonna, wolfbane, toadstool, camphor, drag-
onbile, powdered alicorn, nightshade, and a pure distillation of
every prime element of the periodic table from helium to plu-
tonium.

Everywhere Fungle looked he saw marvels; palanquins of
precious metals and painted sails, ships' figureheads of creatures
now mythical but once not, silk mage cloaks and fire-hardened
crucibles, enormous mirrors and lenses ground to microscopic
perfection for use by astronomers, a fifty-foot-tall propeller for
a ship of unimaginable size (and when Fungle saw the rudder he
realised the propeller was for an *air*ship!).

Along an entire acres-square wall were books and scrolls of
leather and vellum and parchment, paper and papyrus and clay
– every lost work of alchemy and magic, science and religion,
philosophy and politics, mathematics and poetry. The incinerated
Library of Alexandria, resurrected like a phoenix from its ashes,
would have fit into a corner. An entire army could spend years
merely cataloguing the contents of this vast cavern, much less
putting them to any use.

On the floor was a pentacle of inlaid jewels and precious metals
fitted with a craftsmanship long vanished from the earth. It was
perfection, and Fungle knew that the shaman who worked his craft
within this diagram would be a protected mage indeed.

Fungle was in awe. This was the realisation of his lifelong dream,
the ultimate adventure of every gnole child for five hundred

generations: to find the lost treasure hoard of the gnoles!

If only Neema were here to see this with me. The thought tempered his joy.

Fungle gazed at the towering racks of books and scrolls receding into the misty distance. Millions of them! The lost library, found! And he had seen the builders of this place! He had touched a menhir at the Mound of the Dead and with his own eyes had a vision of those poor doomed souls struggling across an alien and harsh land. He had *seen* them, heard them, felt their anguish. They had already built this place when he had that vision.

The earth had been long robbed of such beings as made this place and the wonders it contained. Fungle was overwhelmed with awe and a peculiar pride that his ancestors had built such a marvel as this, but he also felt a yearning sadness because those ancestors were long gone and his people could not now match such accomplishments. *We stand on the back of a whale,* he thought, *and fish for minnows.* He felt small and ineffectual.

Fungle had no idea how long he stood there marvelling. It could easily have been a lifetime. Eventually, though, even the mäelstrom of emotions that dizzied him gave way to the more immediate needs of his mission:

Baphomet.

Fungle had thought that the stone would be easy to find. He imagined that an object which had destroyed a continent, and which was sought after by powerful Elementals, would emit some kind of terrible energy easily noticed by someone with his shamanic sensibilities. Throughout his long journey he had pictured the crystal as radiating deadly black light.

But no such radiation could be perceived. No disturbance rippled the laminations above or below the real; no filaments of malevolent energy tingled through him.

He was going to have to search for it. To ransack a cavern the size of a hundred cathedrals stuffed with the treasure of a thousand museums. It could take years!

He might never find it.

Well, now, hold on with yer, he thought. *Comin' this fur an' givin' up, ya may as well never have left yer cosy fireside, Fungle! Try usin' yer noggin'.*

All right, then. Let's get comfortable. 'Come-for-the-table,' as Wisp useta say, if he didn't say 'comfort-able'.

He lay on a bus-sized bolt of raw silk and stared at the sky-high ceiling, trying to think. It was hard to imagine that an object as powerful as Baphomet didn't give off some kind of emanation, Fungle reasoned. But if it could be detected, then the likes of Theverat woulda found it quite a bit easier than it had turned out ta be fer him – an' he's had a lot longer'n I have. Likewise Molom: if the Elemental could've found it hisself, he wouldna needed me.

But the ancient mages hadn't wanted Baphomet easily found and fallin' into the wrong hands – so they had shielded it.

What would prevent such strong emanations from getting out? Dense metal might do it. Gold and silver were too light. Lead, perhaps. Ya'd want the heaviest, most dense metal available, which'd be –

Uranium.

He sat up.

The cruciform shadow of the goat-pommelled sword thrust into the rock floor fell across the small metal casket bound with silver twine.

Fungle touched the casket with trembling fingers.

That rarest and most powerful of alchemist's metals. Yes. Fungle could sense its atomic decay to lead beneath his fingertips: uranium. The heavy metal was normally toxic, for it emitted lethal radiations that destroyed the marrow. But such emanations could be shielded – by a charmed silver twine, for instance.

He picked it up.

It was astonishingly heavy for such a small thing.

It seemed to grow cold in his hand.

He thought it . . . *shifted.*

A sharp pain knifed up his left arm to stab his pounding heart. Black explosions blurred his vision. Bone fingers raked his lungs. Malignant cells bred in his blood. Arthritic pain shot through his joints. His head ached intensely like a lever prying out his eyes. His wounded side burned and his nose began to bleed.

He did not need to open the casket to know what it contained.

No time to waste, then: clutching the heavy casket, Fungle hurried to the perfectly made pentacle he had seen earlier. No work by his own hand could equal it; he would summon Molom from there.

Within the protective design he set down the silver-bound casket and began the spell to invoke Molom. He cursed himself for not thinking to create a metaspell to summon the Lord of Trees, but he'd had so little time, and what time there'd been had been so heavily burdened! '*You can make a thousand other histories with "shoulda-beens",*' Wisp had always said.

The air grew hot as Fungle began to speak:

> *'Molom, Molom, Father of Trees,*
> *Watchman of the Wind,*
> *Mouth of the Wind,*
> *Open thee mine eyes*
> *That I may see thee, Molom,*
> *Proceed here from thy hidden retreat.'*

Fungle looked up at a peculiar smell of burning. A patch of cavern wall glowed red-hot and began to drip. In seconds a pool of magma flowed inward from a hole in the wall.

A figure stepped into view, silhouetted by the dying light of the cooling stone. 'Fungle!' it called, and waved. 'Oh, thank heavens I'm not too late! Molom sent me back – there's been a terrible mistake!'

Neema.

25 *The Crucible of Reason*

Fungle stared as Neema approached. Blood a-boil, leaden taste in his mouth, forehead tight and aching – in such close proximity, the stone was affecting him even through the densest of metals.

His heart surged at the sight of Neema. She stopped a dozen feet away. 'There's been a mistake,' she repeated. 'You're not to summon Molom at all! It was a trap, a dreadful trap.'

Fungle stared at her. 'Where were we last time I was in yer home?' he asked.

Neema grew puzzled. 'I don't understand, Fungle.'

Fungle shut his eyes and forced back tears. 'No,' he said. 'No, ya don't.' He opened his eyes again – and turned his back on Neema.

'*Rise up, BAALEMOLOM
BAALEMOLOM, rise up!*'

'No, Fungle!' came Neema's voice behind him. 'It's a trap! Give me the stone!'

Neema stood facing Fungle outside the pentacle. Fungle tried to ignore her and concentrate on the spell as he made passes in the air to continue the Summoning, but it was impossible. True or not, the image of Neema stood before him. 'Give me the stone, Fungle!' she pleaded.

Fungle did not move.

Neema's voice roughened. '*Give it to me!*'

Fungle slowly shook his head: no.

Neema shredded. Theverat shot from her like a fist through a paper puppet. The demon rose to a towering height in the cavern and the floor shook with his rage. A ball of light appeared in his talon, and he hurled it at Fungle. The fireball hit the pentacle and detonated. Fungle covered his eyes from the hot white light that flared and dimmed.

A crater lay in the stone floor, rays of molten rock radiating from the impact. The pentacle remained intact, and within it Fungle and the cask holding Baphomet. But the impact had knocked Fungle off his feet and he lay choking in the heat-charged air. The pentacle of the ancient gnole mages was powerful indeed, but Fungle felt sure that, though the pentacle might survive several such assaults, he would not.

The demon was smiling down at him. '*Be reasonable, Fungle,*' he said, voice booming along the enormous cavern. '*I will use Baphomet only for the good of mankind.*'

'I am not a man!' shouted Fungle, and raised his hands:

> '*Thee I invoke: Spirit of Sunset,*
> *Angel of Wind, Ancient One,*
> *Thee I invoke.*'

The last word of the Summoning rang out in the cavern. Fungle waited.

Nothing.

Theverat laughed. '*And where is your Molom now?*' He lifted an enormous wheelless metal vehicle shaped like a teardrop. '*He is a spirit, a vapour, a bothersome gas!*' The vehicle buckled under its own weight as the demon raised it high. '*This is solid!*' shouted Theverat, and hurled the gargantuan conveyance.

Fungle knew he could not escape the deadly arc of the descending vehicle. He prepared to shout the word and perform the gesture that would uncoil the metaspell that summoned the Salamander. Everything would be incinerated: the cavern, Theverat, the treasure of his ancestors – and Baphomet.

Fungle dropped the casket and raised his arms as if to ward off the descending behemoth of metal. The single word – *Daësh'te!* – was poised on Fungle's tongue when he hesitated.

The enormous vehicle hung in mid-air.

Theverat was looking at it too. The demon looked from the suspended tonnage to Fungle.

Fungle couldn't help shrugging: *Wasn't me!*

The hovering metal crumpled like onionskin and imploded with a loud grinding sound. It re-formed into the shape of an enormous shining owl, and then the owl contracted to a luminescent sphere floating high in the cavern. From the sphere came a creaking deep voice: **'You will not harm this child of my forest.'**

'Molom!' shouted Fungle.

'Good gnole. Brave gnole. I am come. Give to me the stone that I may send it to the void.'

'*No!*' The shriek came from Theverat. He was close to Fungle now, and the gnole winced as the demon lifted a thirty-clawed hand.

Light flashed and the clawed hand turned to stone and crumbled to sand. Theverat howled. **'You are no match for me, Theverat,'** said Molom. The kindly voice directed itself to Fungle. **'The stone, good mage.'**

Fungle lifted the casket toward the translucent orb. A thin beam of pure white light shot out from the sphere, and Fungle felt it tugging the casket from his hands.

The light broke off as Theverat stepped in front of it. The beam turned red and the cavern filled with the stench of burning flesh. '*Give it to me!*' he screamed. Parasites abandoned his body from the pain of the light-beam burning into his back. '*I will usher in the New Atlantis! The humans are ready for it; this time will be –*'

'The humans are ready for nothing,' said Molom.

Theverat held a hand up to the beam. It burned the flesh of his palm. '*I will build a better world!*' he screamed.

'Better for who, demon? For humans? For the world of metal and machines?'

'*They are my clay!*' he insisted. He turned to Fungle. '*Give me the stone!*'

'The world is their clay.' The beam lancing down on Theverat grew brighter. The cavern floor shook as the demon fell to his knees. He struggled beneath the light.

'The stone, Fungle,' said Molom. Another beam of white light lanced out from the orb high overhead.

Fungle felt the gentle pressure of it drawing the casket upward. He would never be sure why he hesitated – perhaps because of the note of hunger in Molom's tone, perhaps because of the revulsion with which Molom uttered the word 'humans'. Perhaps it was Theverat's notion of the 'New Atlantis'. Whatever it was, Fungle firmed his grip on the casket and resisted the pull of the light. 'You'll destroy it as you said?' he asked.

'*Destroy it! He will destroy the humans with it, you fool!*'

The pressure of the light beam strengthened. **'Let go, Fungle,'** said Molom.

Fungle fretted. He glanced at Theverat's hideous form writhing on the cavern floor like a tortured god. Why should he allow the demon's words to plant a seed of doubt within his mind? Still – *'True rings true no matter what bell rings it,'* Wisp used to say.

'Molom,' Fungle said slowly. 'Will you use Baphomet to destroy the humans?'

'Of all creatures in my forest, little mage, I would think that you more than any would want the world rid of humans.'

Fungle hesitated. 'Great Molom – I do not want the world rid of *anything.'*

'They have taken your Neema, your home. My forest. They have raked beauty from the Garden, and now they strip its life as well.'

Theverat managed to struggle out from beneath the searing light. Now the demon stood and held a horn-knuckled fist up to the sphere. *'A jet plane's no more unnatural than a flower basket!'* he shouted. *'They're taking what lies in nature and natural law and using their brains and hands to build and cure and know! They're no less natural than one of your precious oak trees!'*

A pearl of light dropped from the radiant ball. It touched Theverat, and the demon was knocked violently back into ancient bookshelves that crumbled to dust as he landed upon them.

Fungle felt dazed. 'You want Baphomet so you can destroy the humans,' he said incredulously. He could not believe how betrayed he felt. This was not a friend going back on his word, this was an Elemental who had deceived him! It was like a violation of natural law, like the sun not rising one morning. 'You never meant to destroy it at all.' He looked numbly at the heavy casket in his hands.

'I will make the world as once it was,' said Molom. **'I will restore the Garden.'**

'The humans were part of the Garden!' shouted Fungle.

'They have built refineries where it used to be,' countered Molom.

'Fungle.' Theverat was rising from the ruins of the ancient books. *'He is stronger than me. Give me the stone and we will defeat him.'*

Fungle did not know what to do. To learn that Molom had a hidden agenda for Baphomet was the deepest betrayal of his life. He had been used. Yet he felt the tug of more than the beam of Molom's light; he felt the tug of Molom's reasoning. There was no denying that the world was not the Garden it had once been, and that the humans were largely to blame. Fungle resented their intrusions and their speciocentricity. They had turned his people into gypsies and killed his friends and wounded his land. If he could not live with them in peace, he did not want to live with them at all. How then must Molom, the Father of Trees and Voice of the Wind, more than any other Elemental the Spirit of the Land itself, loathe them?

Theverat, on the other hand, would use Baphomet to create an iron technocracy. Not a Garden, but a Utopia of Machines. Give complete domination to the humans, he argued, and they will fix whatever's wrong. Their ingenuity was limitless: if they ran out of trees, they would *manufacture* trees. And Theverat would preside over this boundless unstoppable society.

'You sent me my dream,' Fungle said suddenly.

'I sent you my vision of a world under Theverat,' replied Molom.

'*He sent you lies!*' said Theverat.

'Will the two of you fight, then?' asked Fungle, disgusted. 'Will ya hurl bolts an' match spells an' destroy all the hoarded artifacts an' knowledge of a land long vanished, so that one of ya may possess this miserable hunk o' rock, an' in so doing possess the world?'

'*In a New York minute!*' Theverat shouted defiantly.

'You are favoured by me among the forest creatures, brave Fungle,' said Molom, **'and were I to destroy Theverat now you would surely be harmed. But if that is what I must do before I may possess Baphomet, then I must. Avoid this agony and give it to me. I need not harm even Theverat, if that is your wish, for once I receive the artifact he is less than a caterpillar upon me.'**

'*I* found *that* artifact!' said Theverat. '*I used it to govern a continent!*'

'You used it to destroy a land and end an age.'

Fungle sat crosslegged in the centre of the pentacle and rested the casket in his lap. A strange calm fell on him. 'Do either of ya know the story o' the passenger pigeon?' he asked.

'This is not a time for stories,' said Molom.

'This be a perfect time fer this one,' replied Fungle. 'The passenger pigeon, y'see, was a pesky feller. He flew in flocks millions strong. *Millions.* He'd foul the land with his droppin's till it were unliveable, an' then he'd fly off somewheres else an' do it again.'

'*Fascinating,*' said Theverat. '*Now give me my stone.*'

'Them birds was alive up until 'bout a hundred years ago,' Fungle persisted. 'Me pa useta tell me how they'd black out the sky fer days when they swarmed. But the humans couldn't tolereat 'em, y'see. Millions o' birds foulin' ever'thing in sight?' He shook his head.

'Who could live with that? So they come after 'em with guns, an' fer years they blasted away, an' before ya knew it, ever' last one o' them birds was gone from the face of the earth.'

'**Then you understand my sorrow,**' said Molom. '**Give me Baphomet, and no species will be driven to extinction again.**'

'*Except for humans,*' added Theverat.

But Fungle was shaking his head. '*You* are the humans,' he said, pointing to Molom, 'an' the humans are yer passenger pigeons. An' Baphomet's yer gun.' He turned to Theverat. 'An' *you* want ta give the gun to the pigeons.' He shrugged. 'Yer both right, an' yer both wrong. An' I'm sittin' here holdin' the gun in a protected little bubble, no way in 'r out.'

'**You must choose,**' said Molom.

'I a'ready have,' said Fungle – and before the ancient and powerful adversaries he extended his arms to either side, right hand balled into a fist and left hand cupped to receive it.

He brought both hands together with a loud slap.

'*Daësh'te!*' he shouted.

The metaspell uncoiled and the Salamander burned into the world.

A bright pinprick appeared in the air before him. It was the colour of the sun. Sharp shadows fled its ignition. It swelled and sent out rays until it looked like a dandelion seed made of pure coherent light.

It grew hotter.

The air around it began to burn.

Superheated air rose toward the roof of the cavern. A hot summer wind swept Fungle's face.

The air caught fire.

The entire world became kindling: statues and maps and gold palanquins, crystal vases and delicate shells, even the stone walls of the cavern itself. Within the pentacle Fungle watched. The mage's circle would only protect him for a few moments against such mindless fury, but Fungle had known that and accepted it when he called forth the Salamander. His life was a small price to prevent either Molom or Theverat from possessing Baphomet. He would die, they would *all* die, and the stone would be destroyed, and the world would keep on spinning as it always had.

Having made the decision not to choose, Fungle could accept his fate. He felt at peace with himself as he watched the cavern burn around him. A tall statue of a slender Atlantean priestess cut from a single quartz cracked and splintered and shattered to fine powder that melted to run like water. Gold filigree palanquins that had once propelled themselves with a magnetite crystal, much like a Lunabird, were as butter. Sealed glass bins of brittle parchment maps, nearly as ancient as some of the lands they depicted, combusted. A labyrinth of tall wine-racks holding the world's oldest vintages bubbled and boiled. A chambered nautilus the size of a building burst into fragments. Mammoth teardrop conveyances cried into the stone. The salvaged efforts of an entire race turned to slag before the Salamander's onslaught. Art and artifact, mage-lore and scientific device, delicate statues of men and women of peace and terrible tonnage of weaponry – all were as one in the insensate nova-heat of the Salamander.

Fungle felt his face blistering as he watched Theverat struggle against a foe that allowed no resistance. The demon swatted with enormous leathery fists, swung ridged tail and beat the air with great bat wings, but it only fanned the flames higher.

He burned.

Gold and glass and silver and lead and iron flowed in molten rivers. The air was so hot Fungle could scarcely breathe it in. He panted in painful gasps.

Above him the luminescent ball that was Molom grew brighter as it sent out shafts of searing light to strike at the Salamander. But heat was the Salamander's only friend in the world, and Molom's greatest efforts only fuelled the voracious conflagration. In the end, the Elemental tried to open a portal and flee back into his world, but he was too late. The melting rock of the cavern ceiling poured red-hot upon him and sealed the Elemental for ever within a prison of stone.

Across the cavern a container of gas exploded. The fireball swelled like a flower and raced across the enormous vault. The overpressure wave of its detonation knocked Fungle flat. The obliterating heat would follow in moments.

Fungle clutched the casket containing Baphomet and braced himself.

The floor rumbled beneath him as if something were burrowing up from the depths of hell.

A moment of pain's all, he thought.

A wave of burning air washed over him. *Oh Froog me brother I'm so sorry I couldn't come to help ya.* The stench of singed fur filled his scorched lungs. His clothes were aflame. *Neema be there for me*, he prayed.

The earth opened up beside him.

A long-clawed cone-fingered hand shot out from it and seized him.

The fireball rushed across the scalding floor.

For an instant Fungle glimpsed the true form of the Salamander, a vision of claws and feathers and yellow slit eyes all painted in flame, and he caught a flash of the creature's glee as it spent its fury upon the mountain. Then he was yanked into the hole and dragged into the cool shelter of the earth.

26 *Flame and Healing*

All night long Ka watched the mountain burn. Spotter helicopters from the National Forestry Service were circling the area within the first hour, until the intense heat impaired their ability to fly and they retreated. News helicopters arrived soon afterward, flew perilously close to shoot their footage, and left. Sluggish C-130 Hercules cargo planes from the Knoxville division of the Air National Guard dumped a few loads of flame-retardant chemicals before their pilots realised they were doing little more than spitting on a bonfire and banked their empty planes back to base.

Ka tied knots in long stems of grass and felt the heat of the mountain's death against his skin. He tried to see how many knots he could tie in one length of grass before it broke. His record was only eight; he had never been a delicate craftsman, and the patch of flesh below his thumb that had turned to stone when the Salamander's fiery tongue licked across it did not help any.

He ran a finger across the stony patch and shook his head. Coulda been worse. Coulda been *much* worse.

Beside him lay a pitiful bundle of scorched rags and fur. Periodically Ka set down a knotty blade of grass and checked on the blackened bundle, but he came away no more informed than before.

By one in the morning the Hercules cargo planes returned. They circled the mountain like bloated mosquitoes and disgorged their loads downwind of its base to keep the flame from spreading. They sewed in and out of dark smoke seething with orange light, dropped cargo, and winged back to base.

Toward dawn the bundle beside Ka stirred and sat up, shedding knotted stems of grass. Beady black eyes blinked in a blistered face glistening with pus.

'Fungle?' said Ka.

Fungle stared at the burning mountain in the distance. He looked at Ka blankly. 'Didjoo bring the marshmallows?' he asked, and passed out.

Sunrise lit the land no brighter than a full moon. But moonlight was pure and cleansing, and this was grey and ominous. Ka was reluctant to move Fungle, but now that he knew his friend was alive, he was aware that he would need plenty of water. Gently he lifted the poor bundle that smelled of burnt fur and grilled meat, and he carried it to a cold-running stream that cut through the valley floor. He bathed Fungle's burns and changed the dressing on the bullet wound in his side. He made him drink when he awoke. Burns are the most painful wounds, and Ka knew that Fungle was destined for weeks and possibly months of intense pain.

When he felt sure Fungle was able to travel a bit he pushed deeper into the forest. He stayed with him for seven days, leaving his side only to fetch water, herbs, and roots to prepare healing salves under Fungle's direction.

One day Ka returned with a handful of thick sappy leaves and found Fungle sitting against a tree and staring intently at a blood-red crystal shaped like a coffin. He watched for a few minutes but Fungle never moved a muscle. Finally Ka cleared his throat and stomped noisily among the dead leaves of mid-November. Fungle started at his approach and hurried the crystal back into its casket.

'Izzat what all the fuss's about?' Ka asked, setting the dripping leaves before Fungle. 'A hunka rock?' He snorted. 'I coulda dug up ten just like it, only brighter an' bigger.'

'Not like this one, Ka.'

'Mmph. What's so special about it, then?'

'First of all I'm not so sure it's a rock at all. It's crystal, but there's wires inside thin as hairs. I think it's a crystal, an' then I think it's a machine. Sometimes I think it's alive.'

'Might as well be a cabbage fer all you know,' said Ka, and would speak no more about it.

Fungle's burns were completely healed within a few days after Ka saw him handling the stone. Ka could not believe it. Fungle were a great mage and a fair healer, but Ka doubted he coulda healed hisself all pink-skinned and full-furred in less than a month's time. He wanted to say something about it but he was afraid to. He concentrated instead on nursing Fungle back to health so they could leave this terrible place and return home.

When Fungle was ready to travel, however, it became evident that he would not be returning with Ka. He had told the gnome about the terrible mental cry for help he had received from brother Froog, and now he intended to venture into the unknown west to find him and his family. 'Ya've risked ever'thing ten times over a'ready, Ka,' he said. 'Ya've got a home waitin' fer ya an' a land to help watch out over. My mission here's over, thanks ta you an' Neema. I'll not lose my last close friend chasin' across the width of Americka.' He looked out toward the blackened area on the horizon. 'That's the problem with adventures, I think,' he mused. 'Any worth havin're bound ta get outta hand, an' any worth riskin' yer life fer are bound ta get serious afore it's all over.' He grinned wryly. 'Kinda takes the fun outta adventurin', don't it?'

'But, Fungle, if ya need my help –'

'I'll know right where ta find ya,' Fungle finished. 'Go back to our valley, Ka. If ya want ta do somethin' fer me . . .' He looked away.

'What is it, Fungle? You kin tell me; I'll do it.'

Fungle blinked rapidly. 'I know ya will, Ka.' His smile was forlorn. He looked at the gleaming stream as he said, 'I want ya ta go to Neema's house an' collect her things. Keep 'em safe in yer own deep home. Light a candle 'neath the willow tree she loved so much, an' send her a prayer.'

Ka was crying now too. 'I will, Fungle. I will.'

Fungle nodded. Suddenly he knelt to the stream and splashed his face with cold water. 'It's not so bad, Ka,' he said, wiping his face dry against a furry arm. 'We won, after all. Even after we was betrayed, we won.'

Ka was not persuaded. 'Neema gone; yer furfathers' treasure hoard melted to a piddle; you burnt to a crispy critter.' The gnome shook his head. ''Nother victory like that'll kill us, Fungle.'

Fungle laughed. 'That's my Ka,' he said. 'Always one ta see that every silver lining's obscured by clouds.' He clapped his friend on the back.

The truth was that Fungle really did want Ka's help, but the burden he now carried was more than anyone could rightfully be expected to share.

Finally Fungle wrapped the heavy casket in a black plastic garbage bag Ka had found for him, and they removed all traces of their meagre camp and readied themselves for the sorrow of parting.

Ka looked out across the valley to the distant charred patch where once a mountain had stood. 'It's a mess, ain't it?' he said. 'A mess an' a shame.'

Fungle stood watching with him several minutes before he answered. 'It'll heal in time, Ka,' the mage said. He blessed his friend and set a hand on the gnome's chest above his heart. 'It'll heal, in time.'

EPILOGUE: *Westbound*

JOHNNY CARSON MEETS WITH DALAI LAMA
Discusses Opening 'World Spiritual Academy'

VOLCANIC ERUPTION IN TENNESSEE?
Spy Satellites Measure Flash
'of Nuclear Magnitude' as Entire Mountain Explodes

FUNGLE DIES AT WALTER REED
Ailing Gnole Succumbs After Battling Unknown Virus
President Declares Day of Mourning.

The Southern Pacific Californian sobbed into the switching station. A hot iron smell filled the air. The train flexed muscles and hugged the rail with preening lion indifference whilst freight cars were unhitched and new ones attached. The train slept while power was cut as passenger, café, and sleeper cars were added almost as an afterthought.

Up ahead, on the station platform, husbands waited impatiently while wives drawled long goodbyes. At their feet like loyal dogs were battered suitcases and brand-new valises; in their sweating hands were tickets soon to be punched for points west: Nashville, Fort Smith, Oklahoma City, Amarillo, Albuquerque, Flagstaff, Los Angeles.

The final car was locked down. The switching foreman signalled the station master and the engineer released the brake and powered up the massive engine.

Steel wheels ground iron rails. The sleepy locomotive eased toward the station.

No one saw the small figure run from the cover of the forest on the other side of the tracks. No one saw it match speeds with the slow-moving train, grab a hand-rail, and swing itself aboard. No one saw the sigil it inscribed in the air before the handle of a refrigerator car, or heard the click of it unlocking.

Marbled carcasses swayed on hooks as the train rocked along the tracks. The walls were coated with a layer of fine frost. The cold did not bother him, it only made him sleepy. Hibernation time was upon him, yet there was far to go before he could let that little death claim him.

Fungle sat crosslegged in the centre of the car, humming and gently undulating with the arrhythmic rocking motion of the train. He thought of the train dancing on the rigid path laid out before it as the struggle of a strong-willed creature against fate.

In the late afternoon he emerged from his deep meditations. He opened the flap of the worn canvas rucksack patched with duct tape he had found one night while foraging outside a KOA campground. From the rucksack he withdrew an object wrapped in rags, surprisingly heavy for something so small. Fungle unbundled it until before him lay a casket of uranium bound with a charmed silver cord. He spoke a secret word and the Gordian knot untied itself; he unwound the silver cord and set it aside. With the charmed cord removed the metal became toxic again. Its lethal radiation sought his marrow. Fungle would have to be sparing and judicious in his removals of the protective silver cord, for frequent exposure would sicken him.

He removed the casket lid.

Strange lights glittered along the stone's dark facets. And deeper: faint flickers and bright collisions. Fungle thought of trapped souls.

He upended the casket and the crystal dropped into his hand.

Immediately it grew warm as flesh. Deep within the stone energies began to play along near-invisible filaments. The force of Fungle's being coursed along a circuit to fuel whatever micro-mechanisms lay within.

Something stirred within the crystal. Its translucence grew turbulent, as if some restless sea creature rolled over deep within its blood-red ocean.

Fungle sensed that it wanted something from him.

A question, a task, a display.

He kept his mind clear. He would not handle the stone unless he had meditated for hours beforehand so that his mind would not transmit anything to it. No desires, no questions, no needs, no images. Whatever he gave, Baphomet would take. And amplify. And make real.

There had been a night a week ago when, heartsick and homesick, Fungle had gazed upon the naked face of the stone without properly emptying himself first. He had lain in a makeshift hammock in the sturdy middle branches of a tree near the banks of the Tennessee River. He had removed the stone for a last look before sleeping, because he was certain the stone was changing. Subtly, gradually, but changing nonetheless: evolving, or perhaps metamorphosing, into something else. Fungle told himself he was not being seduced by Baphomet, that it was necessary for the safety of himself and his world that he be aware of whatever happened to the stone, inside or out. But he was not reassured, because every night before bed he burned with curiosity to glimpse the stone and register what changes had taken place within its crystalline world. And this particular night his thoughts had been sadly filled with memories of home and friends, family and feasts. He had shut his eyes dreamily, Baphomet held loosely in his hand.

Suddenly he had bolted awake.

Instead of coming to suspended between the branches of a tree, Fungle found himself inhaling the aroma of fresh-baked bread. He straightened up from the oven with a hot pan clutched between two thickly padded mitts and hurried with it to the counter before it grew too hot to hold. As he set it upon the counter he glanced toward the living-room and smiled, for there before the friendly fire dancing shadows across the accumulated articles of a lifetime's learning and deep contentment, Wisp sat in Fungle's favourite overstuffed easy chair and told stories of the old days before the You're-a-peons found North Americka. When Froog smiled, his seamed face crinkled like thick paper crumpled and smoothed again. He held one arm around Quince and the other around Peapod, and the children's eyes were bright as they heard stories of giant three-toed sloths and sabre-toothed tigers in the southlands. Ka sat on the floor hugging his knees, staring into the hearth and letting the wavering flame become a burning stage upon which were enacted the old lost adventures Wisp related.

In the other easy chair, across from Wisp, a figure sat in shadow. In the kitchen Fungle frowned. Sauces simmered in decorated pots upon the stove. Fungle stared at the silhouette before the fire and nodded in time to the lullaby rhythm of Wisp's story. The silhouette leaned out of shadow and turned to face him.

Neema.

Fungle saw her as if from across a vast distance, as if they were separated by oceans and eons and not a span of twenty feet.

She smiled at him.

From the stove came an odour of burning. Fungle ignored it. He was paralysed. Neema nodded knowingly and turned away from him to settle slowly into the chair once more and bask in the glow of the fire and the good company.

The burning smell grew acrid around Fungle, and still he did not look away. His gaze bore into the back of the easy chair.

It ain't Neema, he thought. *This can't be me home an' those can't be me family an' friends, an* that can't be Neema, *because – because . . .*

Because Neema was dead. He had seen her shot down by Thorn's bullet, had held her and felt the life leave her body, had returned her to the womb of the earth.

His eyes had begun to mist from smoke that filled the kitchen. His vision blurred and he began to cough. He rubbed his eyes and lowered his hands –

– to find himself sitting in a hammock in a burning tree.

Fungle had quickly tossed the unshielded Baphomet into his pack along with the metal casket, then untied one end of the hammock and used the length of dirty sheeting to swing out past the blaze consuming the base of the tree. He had charred the seat of his britches and come to light out of harm's way, and watched the flame eat the tree down to blackened bone.

The image had reminded him of Old Man Tree in his own valley, and remembering Old Man Tree had made him think of Molom.

The burning tree began to move. It extended clutching twig-fingered hands toward him. '*The stone!*' it called. '*Give me the stone, and I will save the world from Man!*'

Fungle had reached into his pack with panicked hands and fumbled Baphomet back into its casket. He replaced the heavy lid and bound it over with the silver twine, then spoke the word that knotted it.

When he looked up at the tree again, it was as it had been: the burning skeleton of an oak tree.

In the distance the downbending song of a lone train had cut the night.

*

Fungle concentrated on breathing and blanking his mind as he held the red crystal before him in the frigid air of the freight car. Clacking crossties beat a ceaseless tattoo, a drumsong ceremony for railway passage. It was easy to believe that the train created the world as it went.

But such thoughts – *any* thoughts – were dangerous with the crystal revealed. Fungle had examined the stone long enough. Time to put it away.

He found himself reluctant to, and that very reluctance frightened him enough that he knew he *had* to put the stone away. He fitted it into the uranium casket and covered it with the lid, bound it with the silver cord and spoke a secret word, then wrapped it in its dirty rags and put it back into the worn rucksack.

Baphomet, Fungle had realised, was a thought amplifier. It took what you were thinking and made it real. The stone itself was not evil; Molom had either lied to Fungle about that as well, or else the Elemental had not understood the nature of the artifact. Baphomet was no more evil than a knife. The evil lay in its use, not in the object itself. But just as a knife lent itself wonderfully to peel an apple or carve beautiful art in wood or cut the living heart from a creature, so Baphomet was the perfect instrument for certain uses. Making, unmaking. Powering a world. Destroying a continent.

A knife in unskilled hands cannot sculpt beauty no matter how strong the desire in the mind of the wielder. Baphomet as a lens that focused untrained thought was equally useless. It was as good or evil, as creative or destructive, as the mind that used it. There was a method, a technique, a way of thinking, that allowed one to effectively wield Baphomet.

Fungle was afraid that he was slowly learning it. Worse: he was afraid that Baphomet was adapting itself to be easier for him to use.

He was afraid of its power. This was no juggernaut, no rampaging berserker that required only aiming and triggering to lay waste to whatever the wielder chose. This was a more insidious power, one too subtle for most. Fungle imagined that Baphomet could have gathered dust for generations on the mantelpiece of the average human's home before any trace of its ability became known. But to the mind aware of its potential . . .

He shivered. Sides of beef leaned in macabre unison as the train rounded a bend.

The night of the burning tree had been real. Not an effective illusion, not an image conjured before him. *Real.* Neema was dead, but she had been there. He could have pinched her as surely as he could now slap his own thigh. *That* was the power and the seduction and the danger of Baphomet: that it had filled the lonely ache of his grief merely because he had missed all that he loved most, that it had made what Fungle most longed for as real as the frost on the walls of this refrigerator car.

And I'm now custodian o' this thing, Fungle thought. *P'raps Ka's savin' me from the Salamander were a bit hasty.* Better to've destroyed this thing than for it to continue to exist in the world, because there would always be a battle over its uses. The selfish, the altruistic, the greedy, the naive, those with vested interests, the zealots, the well-meaning ignorant – all would have a use for Baphomet, and all would gladly pay the price of the world-that-is to realise the world as each thought it should be.

Fungle did not want this burden. It was the weight of every conceivable world, and these past few months he had shouldered enough cargo to last a lifetime. He did not think it fair that gnoles should be the caretakers of the fate of the earth; he did not think himself wise enough to judge who should have the fulcrum by which the world may be levered.

But who else should possess it? The humans? Hardly – they were still in their adolescence as a race; they warred over land and its issue; they bombed places of worship over arguments about ghosts. Molom had been right about one thing: the humans were as likely to use Baphomet to destroy themselves from good intentions as from greed.

The Elementals, then? And who among them was wise enough to cast with this stone? Molom's own hidden agenda had been proof enough of the entrenched inflexibility of the Elementals' admittedly well-intentioned views.

Return Baphomet to the earth, then, and seal it from discovery?

Nonsense. This whole enterprise had come about because the stone had been hidden. Baphomet had been found in the Atlantean earth by Theverat. If a thing can be hidden, it can be found.

Destroy it, then.

But to do so was as much a judgement as any decision to use the stone. Fungle had tried to destroy Baphomet when the choice had been that or allowing it to fall into the hands of two fanatics. But, except for Ka, no one now living knew he had the stone, and the truth was that Baphomet was a tool with such enormous potential for good that Fungle was reluctant to eradicate it from the world when there was a chance, however small, that it might one day be wielded to improve the world.

Fungle was afraid to trust such notions, for Molom and Theverat, in their own ways, had thought the same thing.

Fungle had briefly considered the idea of his race as the stone's wielders rather than as its caretakers. But he had been forced to face some harsh facts about his people: his was a declining race, living in the shadow of past achievement. They possessed neither the wisdom nor the ability to use Baphomet well. No, the truth was that gnoles were not the earth's movers and shakers but its natural caretakers. That was what they did best, and that was what Fungle, as a gnole, should continue to do.

Fungle did not reach this decision easily. Angels and devils wrestled on his shoulders and robbed him of sleep each night on the westbound train. Fungle could avoid the terrible burden of safeguarding Baphomet from the world – and the world from Baphomet – only if he saw no future hope for the stone's use.

And that is where the humans came into the picture. They were in their adolescence, true – but what is an adolescent but a potential adult? The same race that had nearly destroyed Fungle had also delighted in his discovery. The same race that fouled its own nest like the passenger pigeon had also taken to the air – and not in collaboration with the earth, but in spite of it. They had *forced* their way into the air, and however ugly the method, there was no denying the achievement.

The very pride that let the humans segregate themselves from the earth also sent them learning about it in leaps and bounds. They *knew* more about the world than Fungle's people could ever hope to. Most adolescents feel set apart from their surroundings – unknowing, unknown, demanding notice, and arrogantly claiming social and geographical territories adults are wise enough to let them stake out, knowing that one day they will, it is hoped, learn perspective.

In a way, humans represented the same potential for good or evil as Baphomet itself. Theverat had not been far off the mark in his claim that humanity could use the stone to usher in the New Atlantis; certainly all the ingredients were there. But Theverat's vision of this Utopia was quite different from Fungle's, and Fungle guessed that the demon had been at least a thousand years premature as well. It was ironic that it had been Molom, the Lord of Trees, who had tried to obtain the stone to destroy the humans, because the potential role of humans on the earth was not so different from that of trees: trees could appear as obstacles to some, but to Fungle they were bridges connecting earth and sky. Humans could also appear as obstacles – and for the next several hundred years, at least, they would continue to do so – but one day they might become bridges connecting Science and the Garden.

Was it worth the risk, then, to hold on to Baphomet for what might be a hundred generations or more, against the hope that someday an accord might be reached between humanity and the world, that one day that race might be wise enough to justify bringing the stone to light?

If bringing the stone to light could bring the world to light, then yes, it was worth the risk. Fungle would make no more judgement than that.

An' so I'm become a new Fungle, he thought. *Fungle Foxwit gnole, mage an' shaman, an' the first Steward of the Stone. Someday I'll take on an apprentice to hand down the teachin's of me books an' me lessons from Wily Barktea an' the wisdom of me father an' those before him, an' into that heady mixture must come a new an' more soberin' ingredient: Baphomet. An' my apprentice'll take on an apprentice, an' so it'll continue, until in the judgement of some Steward untold generations hence, the stone may be delivered to those who can wield it wisely.*

Fungle looked around the frigid car. The marbled sides of beef swung vertical as the train pulled out of the curve. *There's an awful lotta track between here an' there,* he thought.

He vowed to keep Baphomet hidden away, and to avoid using the crystal in his attempts to find and safeguard his family endangered somewhere in the unknown regions of the western coast of North Americka, no matter how much he might be tempted or how much danger he might find himself in.

Fungle felt the sunrise in the quickening of his pulse. He had spent the entire night wrestling with his dilemma. The clattering of the train was lulling him to sleep. *An' p'raps the train that brings me nearer ya's the very one that took yer leg, brother Froog. Who's to say what strange connections're made along our lifelong journeys?*

Fungle yawned and stretched. Enough philosophisin' fer one day. Time fer bed.

He lay with his head on the bundled pillow of a rucksack containing the pivot around which turned the fate of his world. Sleep was a long time coming as the wilful train fled the dawn.